ABOUT TIME

THE UNAUTHORIZED GUIDE TO
DOCTOR WHO

1963–1966

SEASONS 1 TO 3

TAT WOOD & LAWRENCE MILES

Also available from Mad Norwegian Press...

THE ABOUT TIME SERIES
by Lawrence Miles and Tat Wood

About Time 1: The Unauthorized Guide to Doctor Who (Seasons 1 to 3)
About Time 2: The Unauthorized Guide to Doctor Who (Seasons 4 to 6, upcoming)
About Time 3: The Unauthorized Guide to Doctor Who (Seasons 7 to 11)
About Time 4: The Unauthorized Guide to Doctor Who (Seasons 12 to 17)
About Time 5: The Unauthorized Guide to Doctor Who (Seasons 18 to 21)
About Time 6: The Unauthorized Guide to Doctor Who (Seasons 22 to 26,
the TV Movie; upcoming)

DOCTOR WHO REFERENCE GUIDES
*AHistory: An Unauthorized History
of the Doctor Who Universe* by Lance Parkin

I, Who: The Unauthorized Guides to Doctor Who Novels and Audios
three-volume series by Lars Pearson

FACTION PARADOX NOVELS
Stand-alone novel series based on characters and concepts
created by Lawrence Miles

Faction Paradox: The Book of the War [#0] by Lawrence Miles, et. al.
Faction Paradox: This Town Will Never Let Us Go [#1] by Lawrence Miles
Faction Paradox: Of the City of the Saved... [#2] by Philip Purser-Hallard
Faction Paradox: Warlords of Utopia [#3] by Lance Parkin
Faction Paradox: Warring States [#4] by Mags L. Halliday
Faction Paradox: Erasing Sherlock [#5] by Kelly Hale (upcoming)
Dead Romance by Lawrence Miles, contains rare back-up stories

OTHER SCI-FI REFERENCE GUIDES
Redeemed: The Unauthorized Guide to Angel (upcoming)
by Lars Pearson and Christa Dickson

Dusted: The Unauthorized Guide to Buffy the Vampire Slayer
by Lawrence Miles, Lars Pearson and Christa Dickson

Copyright © 2006 Mad Norwegian Press (www.madnorwegian.com)
Cover art by Jim Calafiore.
Cover colors by Richard Martinez of ArtThug Studios (www.artthug.com)
Jacket & interior design by Christa Dickson (www.christadickson.com)

ISBN: 0-9759446-0-6
Printed in Illinois. First Edition: January 2006.

table of contents

how does this book work ?

About Time prides itself on being the most comprehensive, wide-ranging and at times almost *shockingly* detailed handbook to *Doctor Who* that you might ever conceivably need, so great pains have been taken to make sure there's a place for everything and everything's in its place. Here are the "rules"...

Every *Doctor Who* story gets its own entry, and every entry is divided up into four major sections. The first, which includes the headings **Which One is This?**, **Firsts and Lasts** and **X Things to Notice**, is designed to provide an overview of the story for newcomers to the series (and we hope and trust there's more of you, considering what happened in 2005) or relatively "lightweight" fans who aren't too clued-up on a particular era of the programme's history. We might like to *pretend* that all *Doctor Who* viewers know all parts of the series equally well, but there are an awful lot of people who - for example - know the '70s episodes by heart and don't have a clue about the '60s. This section also acts as an overall Spotters' Guide to the series, pointing out most of the memorable bits.

After that comes the **Continuity** section, which is where you'll find all the pedantic detail. Here there are notes on the Doctor (personality, props and cryptic mentions of his past), the supporting cast, the TARDIS and any major Time Lords who might happen to wander into the story. Following these are the **Non-Humans** and **Planet Notes** sections, which can best be described as "high geekery"... we're old enough to remember the *Doctor Who Monster Book*, but not too old to want a more grown-up version of our own, so expect full-length monster profiles. Next comes **History**, which includes all available data about the time in which the story's supposed to be set.

Of crucial importance: note that throughout the **Continuity** section, *everything* you read is "true" - i.e. based on what's said or seen on-screen - except for sentences in square brackets [like this], where we cross-reference the data to other stories and make some suggestions as to how all of this is supposed to fit together. You can trust us absolutely on the non-bracketed material, but the bracketed sentences are often just speculation.

The only exception to this rule is the **Additional Sources** heading, which features any off-screen information from novelisations, writer interviews, etc that might shed light on the way the story's supposed to work. (Another thing to notice here: anything written in single inverted commas - 'like this' - is a word-for-word quote from the script, whereas anything in double-quote marks "like this" isn't.)

The third major section is **Analysis**. It opens with **Where Does This Come From?**, and this may need explaining. For years there's been a tendency in fandom to assume that *Doctor Who* was an "escapist" series which very rarely tackled anything particularly topical, but with hindsight this is bunk. Throughout its history, the programme reflected, reacted to and sometimes openly *discussed* the trends and talking-points of the era, although it isn't always immediately obvious to the modern eye. (Everybody knows that "The Sun Makers" was supposed to be satirical, but how many people got the subtext of "Destiny of the Daleks"?). It's our job here to put each story into the context of the time in which it was made, to explain *why* the production team thought it might have been a good idea.

Up next is **Things That Don't Make Sense**, basically a run-down of the glitches and logical flaws in the story, some of them merely curious and some entirely ridiculous. Unlike a lot of TV guidebooks, here we don't dwell on minor details like shaky camera angles and actors treading on each others' cues - at least unless they're *chronically* noticeable - since these are trivial even by our standards. We're much more concerned with whacking great story loopholes or particularly grotesque breaches of the laws of physics.

Analysis ends with **Critique**; though no consensus will ever be found on *any* story, we've not only tried to provide a balanced (or at least not-too-irrational) view but also attempted to judge each story by its own standards, *not just* the standards of the post-CGI generation.

The last of the four sections is **The Facts**, which covers ordinary, straightforward details like cast lists, viewing figures and - where applicable - the episodes of the story which are currently missing from the BBC archives. We've also provided a run-down of the story's cliffhangers, since a lot of *Doctor Who* fans grew up thinking of the cliffhangers as the programme's defining points.

The Lore is an addendum to the Facts section, which covers the off-screen anecdotes and factettes attached to the story. The word "Lore" seems fitting, since long-term fans will already know much of this material, but it needs to be included here (a) for new initiates and (b) because this *is* supposed to be a one-stop guide to the history of *Doctor Who*.

A lot of "issues" relating to the series are so big that they need forums all to themselves, which is why most story entries are followed by mini-essays. Here we've tried to answer all the questions that seem to demand answers, although the logic of these essays changes from case to case. Some of them are actually trying to find *definitive* answers, unravelling what's said in the TV stories and making sense of what the programme-makers had in mind. Some have more to do with the real world than the *Doctor Who* universe, and aim to explain why certain things about the series were so important at the time. Some are purely speculative, some delve into scientific theory and some are just whims, but they're *good* whims and they all seem to have a place here. Occasionally we've included footnotes on the names and events we've cited, for those who aren't old enough or British enough to follow all the references.

We should also mention the idea of "canon" here. Anybody who knows *Doctor Who* well, who's been exposed to the TV series, the novels, the comic-strips, the audio adventures and the trading-cards you used to get with Sky Ray ice-lollies, will know that there's always been some doubt about how much of *Doctor Who* counts as "real", as if the TV stories are in some way less made-up than the books or the short stories. We'll discuss this in shattering detail later on, but for now it's enough to say that *About Time* has its own specific rules about what's canonical and what isn't. In this book, we accept everything that's shown in the TV series to be the "truth" about the *Doctor Who* universe (although obviously we have to gloss over the parts where the actors fluff their lines). Those non-TV stories which have made a serious attempt to become part of the canon, from Virgin Publishing's New Adventures to the recent audio adventures from Big Finish, aren't considered to be 100% "true" but do count as supporting evidence. Here they're treated as what historians call "secondary sources", not definitive enough to make us change our whole view of the way the *Doctor Who* universe works but helpful pointers if we're trying to solve any particularly fiddly continuity problems.

It's worth remembering that unlike (say) the stories written for the old *Dalek* annuals, the early Virgin novels were an honest attempt to carry on the *Doctor Who* tradition in the absence of the TV series, so it seems fair to use them to fill the gaps in the programme's folklore even if they're not exactly - so to speak - "fact".

In Volume I, there are a couple of extra features that don't appear in later volumes. Since the first twenty-five *Doctor Who* stories don't have "definitive" overall titles, The Facts includes an AKA section, listing any alternative titles that the story might have picked up over the years. But more noticeably, we've included a section on **The Plot** of certain stories from the 1960s. Generally we've avoided plot summaries in *About Time* (on the grounds that most readers won't have any use for them), but the truth is that even long-time *Doctor Who* fans aren't always familiar with the storylines of episodes which no longer exist on video. As a rule of thumb, we've only included plot summaries for stories that are at least 50% missing from the archive.

There's a kind of logic here, just as there's a kind of logic to everything in this book. There's so much to *Doctor Who*, so much material to cover and so many ways to approach it, that there's a risk of our methods irritating our audience even if all the information's in the right places. So we need to be consistent, and we hope we have been. As a result, we're confident that this is as solid a reference guide / critical study / monster book as you'll ever find. In the end, we hope you'll agree that the only realistic criticism is: "Haven't you told us *too* much here?"

And once we're finished, we can watch the *new* series and start the game all over again.

1.1: "An Unearthly Child"

(Serial A, Four Episodes, 23rd November - 14th December 1963.)

Which One is This? Clearly, it's the first one ever. A police box is found mysteriously humming to itself in a junkyard, a schoolgirl bewilders her teachers by talking about a 'fifth dimension', and a cranky old man begins a long-term career insulting the intelligence of human beings. Then there are three episodes of messing around with cavemen, and nothing will be the same again.

Firsts and Lasts There are enough "firsts" to sink a battleship, obviously, and many of them will be mentioned in the accompanying essay (**Where Did All This Come From?**). But in terms of what we get on-screen, here we have - in order of appearance - the debut of *that* title sequence, the debut of *that* music, and shortly thereafter the debuts of the TARDIS, Barbara Wright, Ian Chesterton, Susan Foreman, the Doctor, the roundels in the console-room and the never-bettered hexagonal TARDIS console. Within mere episodes, someone's doing the 'Doctor who?' line (in this case it's the Doctor himself); the Doctor's already using the word 'companions' (although here it's not a generic term for anyone who happens to be a passenger on the Ship, and it won't be for a long, long time); and William Hartnell's already fluffing his lines.

The very first words said in the series, spoken by Barbara: 'Wait here please, Susan, I won't be long'. The very first piece of unconvincing acting from an extra: the schoolboy who enunciates the words 'ha ha ha… ha ha ha ha ha… ha… ha' when required to laugh at Susan for not knowing about pounds, shillings and pence.

Since it's a well-known cliché that *Doctor Who* storylines largely involve people getting captured and escaping, it's worth noting the structure of the "plot" here, at least after the TARDIS leaves present-day Earth at the end of the first episode. Episode two: the Doctor and company get captured. Episode three: the Doctor and company escape. Episode four: the Doctor and company get captured, then escape. And that's about it, because as we're about to see, this really is supposed to be

Season 1 Cast/Crew

- William Hartnell (the Doctor)
- William Russell (Ian Chesterton)
- Jacqueline Hill (Barbara Wright)
- Carole Ann Ford (Susan)

- Verity Lambert (Producer)
- David Whitaker (Script Editor)

a story about the characters.

And, it's the last time that we see the Doctor smoking.

Four Things to Notice About "An Unearthly Child"…

1. If you've seen any *Doctor Who* before this - and we're guessing that you have - then it'll seem very odd indeed. It's obvious that strapping young schoolteacher Ian Chesterton is the hero, and that the Doctor is an old ratbag who's there to drop the humans into awkward situations. Even leaving aside the one controversial scene in which it looks as if the Doctor's about to kill a wounded caveman (inevitably, we'll come back to this later), he isn't the moral crusader we recognise from later years but instead comes off as an autocratic, paternalistic curmudgeon. At various points during the first year, fans and commentators have found key moments where the Doctor magically becomes the creature we all know, but as early as "The Daleks" (1.2) the programme-makers are trying to find ways to make him more affable.

Thus, it's hard to miss the tussle for supremacy between Ian and the Doctor, and some suspect this may also have been happening off-screen. Hartnell was clearly the star, and paid as such. But as we'll see, Ian's position within the programme's format had been developed and refined long before anyone came up with the character of the Doctor. So in episode three we see Ian and the Doctor locking horns just like cave-rivals Kal and Za, and then in episode four, both Za and the audience are astonished to hear Ian deny that he's the leader of the TARDIS "tribe".

2. Even by the standards of early-'60s BBC drama, the direction of this story is peculiar. One scene lasts a shade under eleven minutes, and the Doctor's unconscious for much of it. Two key

Where Did *All* of This Come From?

For the purposes of this essay and much of the rest of this book, the world came into existence in January 1960.

The BBC had existed since 1922 in some form, and television began on 2nd of November, 1936 (although Nazi Germany had been broadcasting a limited service for a year before that). Commercial television started in 1955, two years after the Queen's Coronation had inspired millions to buy sets. All of this led to what's usually termed the "duopoly", as tram companies, music-hall owners and caterers set up local commercial franchises but tried to look responsible and established, while the BBC tried to look youthful and relevant. The government was beginning to wonder whether having something publicly-owned but not state-controlled was such a good idea. They got a committee of the Great and Good, such as boxer Freddie Mills and writer / actress Joyce Grenfell, to sit in judgement on the future of Broadcasting.

While they deliberated, Hugh Carleton Greene - brother of novelist Graham Greene, and scion of the Greene King brewery chain (see 19.2, "Four to Doomsday") - became Director-General of the BBC. Rather than wait for the committee to decide its fate, Greene came out fighting. In January 1960, within days of starting work, he used his contacts (he was a journalist first and foremost) to investigate flaws in the companies holding ITV franchises. Under Greene, the BBC in general and television in particular was more confident than ever before. In fact, it was downright bellicose. As it turned out, the committee was favourable, and one of the suggestions was that if the BBC were to try to take on ITV at popular mainstream programming, then it should get a separate channel for less orthodox, minority, "public service" television.

Michael Barry, who'd been head of the Drama Department since 1950, left in September 1961 partly because of the shift in emphasis from plays to serials. The following January would see the start of the first outright "soap" on BBC TV, *Compact*, and the radical new cop-show *Z Cars* (see the essay after 2.1, "Planet of Giants"). In the six months since April 1961, when Stuart Hood had taken over as Controller of BBC TV Programmes, Greene's policy of undercutting the ITV companies without surrendering quality had been followed with such zeal that it had started to make many old Corporation hands nervous. Not half as nervous as they got in January 1963, when

their biggest rival was poached from ABC for £2,000 more per year than his new boss, but that's yet to come. This is the context, and a lot of what will be said in this volume will only make sense with that in mind.

Now, let's step back and start at the beginning.

May 1960 sees the head of the BBC Script Department set up a body to look into new subjects. It's called the Survey Group, he's called Donald Wilson, and in spring 1962 the Group is asked to investigate the dramatic possibilities of science fiction.

This is thought to be very BBC-ish material, because although monsters and spaceships are popular on the big screen (and *Quatermass* worked when viewer expectations were lower), it's the more speculative, social-commentary form of SF that they're interested in exploiting. Kingsley Amis - in his book *New Maps of Hell* - has made it seem that anything not satirical is inferior, but that the satirical SF of *Galaxy* magazine and the various anthologies edited by Brian Aldiss is the only relevant fiction of the age. Alice Frick and John Braybon, of the Survey Group, submit a three-page proposal that's critical of efforts to make SF work on television and queries whether the printed form is suitable for mass audiences. BBC thinking, in the main, is that original ideas should be televisual first and SF second. The conclusion of this first report is simple: SF can be done well on television, but only for literate adults who can mull over the implications of what they're seeing. Mainstream audiences and children need visual "clues", which are risky because they look silly unless done better than is affordable.

But within weeks, over on the London weekend station ABC, the massively successful drama strand *Armchair Theatre* did exactly what Frick said was impossible. The series has been making one play in four "experimental", including a play about stranded astronauts. (Hilariously, the critic of *The Times* dismisses the play in question - *The Man Out There* - as far-fetched. A month or so later, Yuri Gagarin goes into space.) Now it makes an adaptation of John Wyndham's *Dumb Martian* as the pilot for an SF adaptation series, *Out of This World*. This is overtly modelled on *The Twilight Zone*, with a dinner-suited Boris Karloff introducing every story just like Rod Serling.

The same company is also scoring a big critical and commercial hit with *The Avengers*, a series

continued on page 9...

scenes are directed so as to avoid the viewers seeing something, first the attack of a wild animal on Za (the first "Monster POV" shot in the programme's history... once lightweight video cameras turn up in the '70s, this will become a standard part of the series' repertoire), and later the discovery of the body of the Old Mother (so they didn't have to pay anyone to be a non-speaking corpse).

Other unusual elements include the "flashbacks" to Susan's odd behaviour in class - a standard of television before the recording of programmes on videotape, but even by this time a little old-fashioned - and the chases. These look worryingly like actors jogging at minimal speeds while stage-hands hit them with branches. However, with all this stageyness afoot, the extraordinary effects scenes make even more of an impression; as with the theme music, the most important thing to remember is that the era of "psychedelia" isn't officially supposed to have started yet.

3. But perhaps the most obvious thing to say here - at least, obvious to anyone who grew up before the 1980s - is that this series has obviously been assembled as a *family* programme. The idea of family broadcasting pretty much disintegrated in the '80s, by which point television had been carved up according to audience demographics and "lifestyles" (see **What Difference Does a Day Make?** under 19.1, "Castrovalva", for the way that Saturday Night TV went from being the cultural heart of the nation to a near-guaranteed ratings-loser), but here the programme goes for the widest-possible spread of viewers by presenting us with characters from three generations.

Comparison with the first episode of the 2005 series says it all. The 2005 series desperately wants to resurrect the Saturday Night time-slot, yet it still shows us the *Doctor Who* world from a teenager's point of view and asks the grown-up audience to tolerate it. In "An Unearthly Child", the grumpy old Doctor almost comes across as an identification figure for grumpy old granddads, while the lesser authority-figures of Ian and Barbara mirror the parents in the audience who were *also* trying to give instructions to semi-comprehensible adolescents. It's been a long, long time since anybody on British TV tried to claim that schoolteachers can be heroic people living action-packed lives.

4. It was the first story to be broadcast, and *already* people were complaining about the fact that everyone in the history of time and space speaks BBC English. Only at the very last minute was it decided that the "Gums" (as the tribespeople are called in the script) should talk at all. The cast were a little confused by this too. Mercifully, they refrain from the embarrassing mime that's usually employed by actors playing cavemen, but instead enunciate lines like: 'I remember how the meat and the fire joined together...'

The Continuity

The Doctor To outward apparances he's a man in late middle-age, but whose manner and bearing all say "old". He has longer hair than was normal for 1963, and the overall appearance of a scholar from the turn of the twentieth century. He appears to need protection from the chill and damp of a British autumn, and wears a college scarf as well as a cape, wing-collar shirt and astrakhan hat [which we won't see again until the end of this volume]. He also wears a ring with a large ruby set into it [this will become important later, apparently, and see **What Makes the TARDIS Work?** under 1.3, "The Edge of Destruction".]. Susan Foreman, who always refers to him as 'grandfather' here, has let it be known that he's a doctor. Yet he doesn't respond to the name "Doctor Foreman". Nor does he refer to himself as "the Doctor" here. He's listed as Susan's guardian in the Coal Hill School records, but he doesn't appear to be using a pseudonym of any kind.

On meeting the Doctor in the junkyard where the Foreman "family" supposedly lives, Ian and Barbara immediately discover that he's an awkward, irritable individual who clearly values his privacy and wants them to leave him alone. Right from the start, he acts as if he's a higher form of life than the locals, consistently underrating their intelligence and refusing to accept that they might possibly understand anything worth understanding. He's prepared to fight to stop Ian barging into the TARDIS, and the immediate impression - backed up by the schoolteachers' belief that he's keeping Susan prisoner - is that he isn't a stranger to violence.

The Doctor's character is unpredictable throughout the events that follow. He's snappish and overbearing when his Ship is overrun by nosy teachers, but his mood lightens as soon as he

Where Did *All* of This Come From?

...continued from page 7

which has transformed itself from just-another-crime-show to *almost* the series you're thinking of, but at this stage it's still made in a TV studio and shot as-if-live. (If you get a chance, look at a few of the Honor Blackman episodes to get a feel for what could be done this way, and thus how much more ambitious *Doctor Who* was.) The Prime Mover of this little empire is Sydney Newman, 'a Canadian who looked like a Mexican', whose deal with ABC is £8,500, a free mortgage and a Jaguar; presumably the car, not the cat, but in his case we can't assume too much. Through a series of Byzantine secret meetings and lunches, the BBC somehow manages to poach him for rather less, although more than most BBC senior staff. And Newman likes SF.

He joins in January 1963, at the same time that a former journalist on *Tonight* - Donald Baverstock, source of the aforementioned "Mexican" comment - becomes head of what's now called BBC1. It's been renamed because the government has agreed on the creation of a BBC2, for the "less orthodox" programmes, and it's clear that the Drama Department will need rethinking and more money. The money comes almost immediately, so Newman sets about revolutionising everything.

Alice Frick's final report is less than complementary about *Out of This World*, especially the robots and monsters. Instead, from a suggestion by Aldiss, the Survey Group looks into the idea behind Poul Anderson's book *The Guardians of Time* and suggests a "*Z Cars* of Science Fiction". Individual stories within an overall framework, with strong characterisation and no Bug-Eyed Monsters. See 3.1, "Galaxy Four", for what else follows Frick's memo. By this time, Baverstock has realised that there's a need for a family-friendly adventure programme on Saturdays at around six o'clock.

When we think about a family-friendly SF series, two possibilities already exist in the early 1960s. One is the puppets-and-explosions style of Gerry Anderson, although in this era only *Fireball XL5* conforms to what we think of as "classic" Anderson. The other is *Pathfinders*. In this we have a family jetting off to other planets, the kids getting into scrapes and explaining basic science to the viewers, plus a stowaway nasty scientist (George Colouris; he's Arbitan in 1.5, "The Keys of Marinus") and a "proper" scientist (Gerald Flood;

he's the King, sort of, in 20.6, "The King's Demons"). It looks smug, didactic and frightfully BBC, but it was made by... Sydney Newman at ABC. Newman, unsurprisingly, advocates a similar format for whatever new show the BBC puts on after *Juke Box Jury*.

Frick's notes are refined by C. E. Webber, her colleague. "Bunny" Webber (no, we don't know why either) issues a ruthlessly functional character breakdown of what kind of protagonists will work for the anticipated audience, ruling out children as young viewers don't take to them, and recommending a thirty-year-old man and a slightly younger woman as principals. There should also be an older man, whose advice is sought, and an HQ combining hi-tech gubbins with Victoriana. Newman wants a young girl to make mistakes and be "kooky". (Or, more accurately, "Kooky". As in the character from US cop show *77 Sunset Strip*, with jive-talk and an off-beat style that had made a big impact with teenagers and - shortly thereafter - advertisers.) He also wants the older man to be almost the antagonist, a law unto himself. We hesitate to use the words "pot" and "kettle" here. Wilson's idea of a time machine that can go forwards, backwards and sideways in time appeals to Newman, and a story proposal in which the crewmembers are shrunk to one inch in height and left in a lab seems like the ideal starting-point. Newman puts one other recommendation verbally: the old man is a fugitive from the future.

Now things accelerate. Newman's regime has put the idea of a production-team-per-series into place, instead of the usual BBC practice of producer / directors using any staff needed on the day. The new programme has a team including Rex Tucker, a staff director who's now made acting producer (and who may have proposed the title *Doctor Who*), and a budget and studio allocation: £2,300 per episode, and Studio D at Lime Grove. Bunny Webber's still involved, making notes on the technicalities and the characters. Biddy, the girl, is fifteeen years old and speaks slang but not dialect. Lola McGovern is 24 and timid. Cliff is 27 and athletic. Dr Who is 650 and an amnesiac. Lola and Cliff are schoolteachers, while Dr Who has an invisible time machine that needs repair, but they can't get the spares in the present or the past. One of the party has to stay behind in the machine to make sure they get back to 1963 at the end of each adventure.

continued on page 11...

arrives in caveman country, and he becomes more interested in looking around than in shouting at people. Though he seems to find Ian a constant irritation, at one stage he tells the others - Barbara in particular - that he's 'desperately sorry' for endangering them. And he insists on calling Barbara 'Miss Wright'. [There's a suggestion that he's prepared to be much nicer to women than men, and certainly it's hard to imagine him treating a grandson with the affection he obviously demonstrates towards Susan. As has already been noted, the struggle against Ian is a struggle for dominance which doesn't appear wholly practical. It's worth remembering that although the Doctor rarely demonstrates any interest in mating-rituals (and although it's often assumed that there's no sex where he comes from), he'll insist on playing the alpha male throughout his career.]

He's prepared to act irrationally when Ian gets his back up, but can nonetheless be sly and intelligent in a crisis, predicting the behaviour of the cavemen with an ease that suggests a good understanding of human nature. Most of the time he just doesn't seem to care what other people think of him.

• *Background.* The Doctor describes himself and Susan as 'wanderers in the fourth dimension' and 'exiles', cut off from their own planet without friends or protection. He believes that one day 'we shall get back'. He claims the children of his civilisation would be insulted at being compared to Ian [indicating that Susan isn't considered a child].

School documents give the address of the Foreman household as 76, Totter's Lane [so presumably the five months that Susan has spent in London have seen the junkyard used as a base, although this doesn't necessarily mean the TARDIS was there all the time]. The junkyard has the words "I. M. Foreman" and "Scrap Merchant" on the gates, but there's no indication as to Foreman's identity or any clue as to how the Doctor ended up with this property. The Doctor is of the opinion that he and Susan can't possibly stay on Earth once they're found to be not-of-this-world, and he indicates that it wasn't his wish to stay in one place for so long. He states that he doesn't enjoy the twentieth century, and he considers Susan's insistence on going to school as 'ridiculous'. [More on the Doctor's agenda in this period is revealed in 25.1, "Remembrance of the Daleks". Natch.]

The Doctor obviously knows a fair amount about human history already. Susan states that before now, the TARDIS has disguised itself as an ionic column and a sedan chair. [The ionic column may be a "standard" shape for TARDIS architecture. See 18.7, "Logopolis".] Interestingly, the Doctor's half-expecting the police to turn up at the junkyard [he may have been stealing materials for the TARDIS, as theft is certainly in character for him], and he obviously feels free to help himself to the items in the yard.

• *Ethics.* When Ian and Barbara force their way onto the TARDIS, the Doctor wastes no time in shutting them in and electrifying the console, stating that he and Susan will have to leave if the teachers are released from the Ship. Yet he also seems to consider holding the teachers on board permanently in order to allow Susan to remain. [Presumably a bluff, and apparently a way of convincing Susan to get off this planet, as he has no wish to hang around on Earth any longer. See **Additional Sources** for why his motives here seem so fuzzy.] He eventually "abducts" Ian and Barbara by accident rather than design, as Susan leaps on him while he's flicking switches on the console and causes the Ship to take off.

The big issue, of course, is that at one stage - when Za is wounded, and slowing the party down - the Doctor picks up a nasty-looking rock and quietly moves towards the caveman with a grim "do-what-must-be-done" look on his face. The implication is that he's thinking of doing Za in, although he claims he was just going to get the caveman to draw a map. [This might conceivably be true, although it's odd (a) because he's spent the proceeding moments telling everyone that Za is a liability, and (b) because this would require the caveman to conceptualise in a way that doesn't seem possible, judging by the rest of the story. Also, the Doctor's bluster when Ian catches him with the rock suggests someone who's improvising an excuse. Alternatively, if you want to ret-con this, he might be telling the truth but not used to having his authority challenged.]

When the Doctor doesn't get his own way, his petulance verges on childishness, even in a crisis. But significantly, he's the one who insists that the cave-folk should be judged by their own standards rather those of "modern" society. His solutions to problems depend on precisely this faculty, in that he tries seeing the world through the cave-people's eyes [which might indicate that he

Where Did *All* of This Come From?

...continued from page 9

Close… but not quite. Newman hates the "invisible machine" gimmick. Henceforth it's a ship with an identifiable shape. By 15th of May, this is a police box that's bigger-on-the-inside-than-on-the-outside. Wilson (now Head of Serials), Newman and Webber have all signed the document, but incoming writer Anthony Coburn is the one who suggests the police box. Baverstock's impressed. They now have two months before filming starts in July. In early June, Tucker asks his friend Hugh David if he'd like to be the Doctor. David has just been in a long-running series, *Knight Errant*, and wants to try directing instead (see 4.4, "The Highlanders"; 5.6, "Fury from the Deep"; and indirectly 4.5, "The Underwater Menace"). Because of the technical oddities, Mervyn Pinfield has been hired as associate producer, as his series *The Monsters* is deemed to have solved various previously-intractable problems. Newman wants Don Taylor to be producer. Taylor will go on to have a distinguished career in drama, but still kicks himself for saying no to Newman.

The next person Newman asks is one of his ABC subordinates, Verity Lambert.

You may have heard an urban myth about an actor dying on live TV and everyone covering it up. It's no myth, and it was Lambert who fixed it. (It was called *Underground*, TX 28/11/58, and it starred Peter Bowles and Warren Mitchell. The late Gareth Jones also appeared, to begin with at least. It was about people stuck on a tube-train after an explosion.) Sydney Newman takes notice of things like this. Lambert's forthright, direct approach - or, as Newman put it, 'piss and vinegar' - is to make a lot of BBC executives eat their words; even so, she's described in the press handouts as a "27-year-old girl". At this point in time a producer is more or less left alone unless something goes horribly wrong, so from now on *Doctor Who* is her responsibility, almost completely.

Now, disaster strikes, and being the BBC it's all down to paperwork. Lime Grove Studio D is really the runt of the litter. It's pokey, it's badly-lit, it has no back-projection facilities and it's upstairs. The lift for props isn't big enough for the usual *Dixon of Dock Green* police box prop, so a slightly smaller one will have to be built. All the electrical equipment has to be stored in the studio itself, and in summer it's an oven even with the lights off. And it's not big enough for the giant-scale sets required for the debut story. Every other suitable studio has been earmarked. The simple fact is that the only completed script, "The Giants", can't physically be made with the resources allocated. Coburn's caveman script, originally to have been Story Two, is made the debut.

Lambert asks Terence Dudley if he wants to help, and is given a dusty answer (see 18.2, "Meglos", for the first of his eventual contributions to the series). Newman has roped in former colleague John Lucarotti to rewrite his old Marco Polo script as a possible third story, and incoming Story Editor David Whitaker - pulling in a few favours - has got Terry Nation a gig writing a space story. But with the dispute over whether they can use the newly-built, bigger, better-resourced studios at Television Centre running on, no-one knows what's logistically possible, so no finalised scripts or lists of sets and props are available. This close to the intended start-date, these delays can't be accommodated.

Coburn's script for the first story is coming along, though, and the characters have new names. Whitaker takes advantage of Coburn's changes and defuses the potential prurience by making "Sue" the Doctor's granddaughter, thus opening a different can of worms altogether. Newman is still keen for the series to be didactic and based in facts. Whitaker has decided that the cavemen will have to be able to speak intelligible English. Coburn has said that Suzanne (another near-miss… the girl was also going to be called "Mandy" at one stage) is royalty, Whitaker that the Doctor should be played like the Wizard of Oz.

Meanwhile, Lucino Visconti's film *The Leopard (Il Gattopardo)* has opened in London, and Lambert notices that one short, middle-aged English actor is holding her attention despite the lavish sets, Claudia Cardinale's chest and Burt Lancaster. Leslie French is her idea of the Doctor. French thinks otherwise. Cyril Cusack (Whitaker's idea) and Geoffrey Bayldon (he's the astrologer Organon in 17.3, "The Creature from the Pit", and much later voiced the Doctor in Big Finish's *Unbound* series) also decline. Rex Tucker has sort-of-left by now, and his casting suggestions for the female leads are dumped.

On the plus side, Coburn's thought of a catchy acronym for the Ship. Pinfield's been in touch with Bernard Lodge about a title sequence using howlround; point a camera at its own monitor, set up a feedback loop with a torch or a match flaring, then mix in other images from a rostrum camera. It's

continued on page 13...

was thinking of butchering Za, since killing the weak is a standard part of life with the Gums, as Hur points out in the same episode]. He also values hope in the face of fear, though when the travellers are imprisoned for the first time, he sits around complaining until the more dynamic Ian spurs him into action. While Ian seems surprised when the Doctor has a good idea, the Doctor's surprised that Ian offers to help. He almost instinctively bargains for Ian's life at one point, when Ian has shown next to no respect or concern for him.

At this point in time, the Doctor appears to have absolutely no interest at all in protecting the established order of history. He has no qualms about trying to get Ian and Barbara back to Earth [even though there must be a risk of them telling everyone about the possibility of time travel; again, compare with **Additional Sources**], or about changing the destiny of the cave-folk by giving them fire. Indeed, he's initially happy to give them whatever they want, as long as it helps him get back to the Ship.

• *Inventory*. The Doctor has a satchel filled with assorted notebooks and equipment, including a Geiger counter, a meerschaum pipe and a box of matches. One of the notebooks contains the 'key-codes' for the machines on the TARDIS. Any amount of this material may or may not be lost during events here. [The fate of the notebook with the TARDIS codes is particularly important. If it's left on prehistoric Earth, then the failure of the Doctor to steer the TARDIS in future stories may be a consequence of this loss. On the other hand, the codes would seem to be for machines on the TARDIS *other* than the main console and navigational systems. Besides which, Susan clutches the notebooks to herself in such a way as to suggest that she's about to pop them into her pocket, though we can't be sure one way or another.]

The Supporting Cast

• *Ian*. Ian Chesterton is a science teacher at Coal Hill School [apparently specialising in physics, but biology homework is listed on his blackboard and his experiment with inactive chemicals suggests that he takes O Level chemistry… he also seems to teach maths to the same class]. He's somewhere between 28 and 35, but for someone of this age at this time, he's surprisingly knowledgeable about pop trivia. He can drive a car, and is already on first-name terms with his colleague Barbara.

On entering the TARDIS, Ian does the predictable 'it's impossible!' routine for some time before accepting the evidence of his eyes and ears, and tries to argue against the Doctor's claims rationally instead of assuming that it's obviously ridiculous. Upon being transported to the land of the cave-people, he's obviously interested but too concerned for the well-being of the womenfolk to enjoy himself, and he demonstrates an angry resolve to survive the trip rather than fear or confusion. He's already starting to look like an old-fashioned hero, the voice of conventional British values as opposed to the Doctor's wider outlook. It surprises nobody to discover that he doesn't think females should be left to do the hard work.

Oddly for a science teacher, Ian doesn't carry matches. Not only can he light a fire the traditional way, but he has enough common sense to advocate that Za's whole tribe should know how to do it.

• *Barbara*. In contrast to Ian's pragmatism, history teacher Barbara Wright appears to have premonitions that interfering with Susan's life might not be wise. She's apparently as old as Ian, unmarried [unusual for a woman her age in that era], and more inclined to consider the consequences of what the Doctor and Susan tell her. [Which may be part of her teacher training, to ask questions rather simply to deny the possibility of what's happening.] That said, she initially denies the reality of the TARDIS interior upon seeing it, rather hysterically claiming that it's a 'game' despite the evidence to the contrary. Whereas Ian does all the manly things like facing off against wild animals, Barbara tends to end up with all the typical "mature woman" tasks, so it's difficult to describe her without using phrases like "feminine intuition".

Unlike Ian's studious efforts to be down wit da kids, Barbara dresses older than her real age, with sensible shoes, a tweed pencil-skirt, a cardigan and Jackie Kennedy hair. At this stage, her jewellery is fairly demure as well. [This might seem trivial, but in later stories her bangles and knitwear will prove integral to the plot/s. As we'll end up saying time and time again in these volumes, it's vital to remember that this was never designed to be "an SF show", certainly not in the modern *Star Trek* sense. The programme's priorities are, from day one, altogether more domestic and "mumsy".] Back home, Barbara lives in a flat. [Ian speculates that the flat must be full of stray

Where Did *All* of This Come From?

...continued from page 11

been done before, notably in the opera *Amahl and the Night Visitors*, and a large amount of test-film exists for Lodge to show to Lambert (the first five seconds of the original *Doctor Who* titles are Ben Palmer's *Amahl* work... but we'll go into more detail under 4.7, "The Macra Terror"). And after a few false trails, they've got Ron Grainer to write a

theme and Delia Derbyshire at the BBC Radiophonic Workshop to make it out of odds and ends (see **How Important is the Music?** under 9.3, "The Sea Devils").

By the end of July, they have the cast, the set-up and the "trademarks". They can now make the series we all know today. Except that they didn't, to start with…

cats and dogs. Let's hope not, as she won't be getting back to it until 1965.]

• *Susan.* The girl calling herself Susan Forman is believed to be fifteen, and never denies this. Her English is slightly too precise, despite diligently using the right "period" argot. It seems as if she's enrolled at a local school as part of her cover-story, like a foreign agent or a fugitive, rather than to learn anything. Nonetheless, she honestly seems to have loved her five months there. Her enthusiasm for popular beat combo John Smith and the Common Men is unfeigned, but it's as an authentic detail; she's a tourist, excited about the possibility of visiting other times and places, so she appears shocked and horrified when she realises that other times and places aren't always pleasant. She's certainly more at home in technological societies than in "uncivilised" ones. [In this story - as in many others - it's running through jungles and dealing with unreasoning people that reduce Susan to a gibbering wreck, not getting caught up in vast machine-like spaces as with Barbara.]

Actually, Susan seems quite highly-strung and sensitive, very nearly bursting into tears when her teacher and classmates can't understand what she's talking about [so obviously she's the one who's going to end up having the most advanced telepathic powers]. She's also the one who senses when they're being watched. There are times when it doesn't look as if she really understands how serious the situation is, cheerfully playing around with bones and fire when she's condemned to death in the Cave of Skulls, and inadvertently giving Ian an idea as to how to scare the cavemen. [Or at least, that's how it's played. As scripted, however, she puts the skull on top of the flaming torch after someone suggests finding a way of frightening the natives. On paper it looks as if Susan is the one with the clever, creative idea, yet in the finished episode she looks as if she's just messing about, and Ian steps in and takes the credit for the scheme. In an episode that's at least

in part about the generation gap - see **Where Does This Come From?** - "the kids" are already being given a raw deal...]

Susan flips through a book on the French Revolution and comments 'that's not right', implying that she's been there [see also 1.8, "The Reign of Terror"]; she knows that Britain will have decimal currency one day, and forgets that it hasn't switched from imperial 'yet'; she's far more advanced in chemistry than a girl of her years should be; and she believes that Ian's fairly simple three-dimensional problem can't be solved without adding two extra dimensions, the fourth being time and the fifth being 'space', weirdly. Aside from all this freakishly precocious knowledge, Susan has evidently learned either Balinese dancing or tai chi, though she's never learned to make fire. She borrows a book that looks as if it's about 400 pages long, and promises that she'll have finished it by the following morning. [See "City of Death" (17.2) and "Rose" (X1.1) for more speed-reading from the Doctor's people. Still, it's not impossible for a bright fifteen-year-old to read a book in one evening.] Her homework's been suffering lately, leading her teachers to wonder if something's wrong at home. [If so, then we never find out what. Maybe the Hand of Omega's been keeping her up.]

Susan speaks of being born in another time and on another world, unsurprisingly. The Doctor refers to her as his granddaughter, just as she refers to him as her grandfather. She never calls him "Doctor", but he does call her "Susan" [given his contempt for '60s human customs in this story, this may imply that "Susan" is something like her real name, and not just one she's adopted as part of her '60s cover]. No other family is alluded to.

[The mystery of Susan is one that has long obsessed fan-fiction authors, most of whom claim that the link between her and the Doctor isn't a straightforward biological one. The most notable / notorious "pro-level" fan-fiction explanations can be found in Eric Saward's contribution to the twentieth anniversary *Radio Times* special (if you haven't read it, you've missed nothing), and Marc Platt's novel *Lungbarrow* (more about this startling work under 13.5, "The Brain of Morbius").]

The affection between the Doctor and Susan is quite obvious, with Susan respecting his authority and displaying obvious guilt when she makes him angry. Although she claims that she'd rather leave her grandfather than leave the twentieth century, it looks as if she's just bluffing to get her own way, and she doesn't seem to know what to do when the Doctor calls that bluff.

The TARDIS This may come as a shock, but the Doctor and Susan live in a time / space machine that's bigger on the inside than it is on the outside. It's currently disguised as a police box in order to blend in with its surroundings, although on being discovered by Ian and Barbara it's rather incongruously parked in the junkyard at 76 Totter's Lane, London. It can be heard, and felt, humming with power.

While the Ship - and both the Doctor and Susan do *call* it a Ship - is in this form, its arrival is accompanied by the lantern flashing in synch with the grinding of the engines. This sound is heard from within the console room when the Ship leaves the 1960s, and again when the vehicle departs from the land of the cave-people. [Note: for the first two years, the Doctor's home / vessel is generally referred to as 'TARDIS' or 'the Ship', only routinely gaining a definite article when it emerges that there's more than one of them in service. However, contrary to what books like this one usually say, Susan refers to it as *the* TARDIS the very first time the name is spoken on-screen.]

At this stage, the TARDIS' dematerialisation is neither explained nor described by anyone on board. When the TARDIS leaves modern-day Earth, the scanner in the console room shows buildings getting further and further away as if the Ship's literally taking off; yet when the Ship leaves the prehistoric landscape, it's simply seen to vanish. There are also luminous fractal-patterns on the screen during "flight". [The same as those seen in the title sequence, so not for the last time, the credits sequence seems to suggest the space-time vortex. See also 9.1, "Day of the Daleks"; 13.5, "The Brain of Morbius"; 14.3, "The Deadly Assassin"; 17.6, "Shada"; and 19.1, "Castrovalva".] On this occasion, the stress of take-off knocks

those on board unconscious, which could be because Susan grapples the Doctor while he's adjusting the settings on the console [but see 22.4, "The Two Doctors", for another possible explanation].

The console room is the only interior part of the Ship seen here [but isn't named as such, yet]. It's a white, spacious area with recessed circles [later termed "roundels"] set into the walls, apparently providing some of the lighting. The doors are the same height as the walls, about fifteen feet, and are hinged in a zig-zag. From the outside, nothing's visible through the police box doors except darkness, but from within it looks as though the doors lead directly out of the Ship [with no darkened "atrium" area between console room and police box, as there is in later stories]. An interior door is suggested, though not seen.

The console room is approximately thirty feet on each side, and surrounds a hexagonal central console on a hexagonal metal plate [the plate reappears in 1.3, "The Edge of Destruction", but comes and goes after that], above which is a hexagonal ceiling-mounted unit. [Rarely seen hereafter; 2.8, "The Chase", is the last occasion on record. Even when the ceiling rig isn't seen, the lighting is masked as if it were still there.] At the console's centre is a cylindrical, transparent piston, filled with electrical wiring and lights. This column rises and falls when the machinery is in use, and occasionally rotates when the scanner is in operation.

The scanner is a TV monitor arrangement, approximately ten feet from floor level, and is directly opposite the doors. Its "eye" is somewhere high up on the exterior. [Later stories will suggest that it's mounted inside the lantern, but this raises the problem of where it goes when the Ship disguises itself as a boulder or an elephant's howdah, as suggested in "The Time Meddler" (2.9).] On the console, taking the scanner as twelve o'clock and the doors as six o'clock... the main take-off controls are at about eight o'clock, and at three o'clock is the door switch. This panel, and perhaps the whole console, can be electrified with a control near the take-off levers in order to ward off nosy teachers. Above this are the radiation monitors, which seem a little sluggish in giving readouts. The exterior atmosphere can be monitored on the same part of the console.

Also found inside this striking domicile are several antique chairs, an old clock [usually

This product is not authorized by the BBC. Doctor Who and TARDIS are trademarks of the BBC.

described as Ormolu but probably not], a spinette or harpsichord, and what appears to be a church lectern standing in for a hat-stand. Strangely, by the time the crew gets back to the Ship at the end of the adventure, the console room has slightly rearranged itself; the architecture has shifted, it's gained an interior door, and the radiation counter has moved across the console. There's 'lots' of anti-septic on board.

Susan states that she made up the name TARDIS, an acronym for Time and Relative Dimension in Space. [That's "Dimension" singular. From about the end of Season Two, "dimensions" becomes the norm. Susan's claim to have made the name up herself seems odd with hindsight, as all the Doctor's people use and understand the term in later stories. *Lungbarrow* gets around this hitch by claiming that Susan was born on ye olde Ancient Gallifrey, and was around when TARDISes were new, but readers can no doubt think up their own slightly mad explanations.] The implication here is that the vessel is unique, and the Doctor's clearly attached to it.

Most significantly, the TARDIS begins to act erratically as soon as it leaves Earth. Though it's supposed to assume an inconspicuous disguise, from now on it's stuck in the shape of a mid-twentieth-century British police box, and the Doctor appears more disturbed than one might expect after this apparently slight breakdown. On top of that, from this point the navigation never quite works properly, though it's not 100% clear whether the Ship could be steered properly *before* it arrived in 1963. At one point the Doctor indicates the console and says 'I do wish this wouldn't keep letting me down'. ["Logopolis" hints that these are symptoms of a fundamental systemic failure rather than two separate faults, whereas "Attack of the Cybermen" (22.1) sees the Doctor able to steer perfectly well even though the 'chameleon circuit' - as it's later called - is wilfully perverse.] On arriving in the prehistoric wilderness, the 'yearometer' claims that this is year zero, and the Doctor believes it's not working. But see **History**.

One 'filament' of the Ship is faulty even before leaving Earth, and the Doctor is returning with a replacement when Ian and Barbara run into him in the junkyard. The Doctor describes the replacement as 'an amateur job' [suggesting that he got someone else to make it]. It isn't replaced before the Ship takes off [which may, feasibly, be part of what triggers the breakdown]. The Doctor claims that he can't take Ian and Barbara back to their own time, as the Ship isn't operating properly, 'or rather, the code is still a secret'. [Compare this with the Third Doctor's exile on Earth in Seasons Seven, Eight and Nine, when he can't remember the 'dematerialisation codes' to make the dematerialisation circuit work. The 'key-codes' in his notebooks may be his attempts to overcome this problem. With hindsight, there's a strong impression that he's stolen this TARDIS, and doesn't have the cosmic PIN number that'll let him use it properly.]

Feed the Ship with the right data at the start of the journey and a destination can be fixed, yet the Doctor has no data at his disposal. Susan believes that the TARDIS *can* be navigated, as long as it doesn't have to take off in a hurry... [This comes up again in the next story, but obviously turns out to be untrue.]

History

• *Dating*. No date is given for the prehistoric antics in the land of the cave-people. [The assumption is made that this is Earth, but nothing in this or any subsequent story confirms it. The planet is certainly Earth-like, although for all we know it's Mondas (4.2, "The Tenth Planet", and it'd be ironic if it turned out that Ian's advice to Za - 'remember, Kal is not stronger than the whole tribe' - was that thing that got the natives interested in the idea of a collectivised society and ultimately led to the creation of the Cybermen).

[Assuming that it *is* Earth, and that the Ship has travelled in time and not in space... the second version of the script was entitled "100 000 BC", but this is clearly wrong, as the people we see aren't Neanderthal. The human remains we see in the cave are manifestly *Homo sapiens*, suggesting a date not much earlier than 40,000 BC. This date also coincides with one of the periods when cave-lions and macaques are known to have lived in the London area. The last ice age, 10,000 years back, altered the course of the Thames; prior to this, semi-permanent tribes regularly inhabited the area around Ilford and Beckton. The earliest known use of fire predates modern humans, and happened a shade over 250,000 years ago. The details here seem contradictory, though. The wild animal that attacks Za and the skin worn by the children playing by the fire suggest a tropical, savannah setting, yet the strong hint that an ice age is coming militates against this. There were seventeen ice ages in the Pleistocene epoch, with interglacial periods about ten to fifteen millennia long (so the current warmer weather may be an anomaly, and see 5.3, "The Ice Warriors").

[One other possibility should be mentioned: that the TARDIS has moved into the future, not the past. It's certainly possible, given the way the *Doctor Who* version of history seems to work, that a future catastrophe causes humanity to revert to a more primitive state. The Doctor *does* believe the Ship has gone back in time, but then, the TARDIS instruments are faulty. If the Doctor and Susan's society exists in our future - as the writers seemed to believe in 1963, given the reference to the forty-ninth century in the pilot episode - then the yearometer reading of 'zero' might indicate that this is the Doctor's "present". Then again, if the members of the Tribe of Gum really *are* supposed to have lived 102,000 years ago, then that *might* be the Doctor's "present". Or it might just be a glitch.]

The cave-people seen here are a curious mixture of matriarchy and patrilineal inheritance. Za, the current leader, is the son of 'the Great Firemaker' [possibly "Gum" himself]. As the alpha male, he's given authority and "ownership" of Hur, the daughter of elder tribesman Horg. Kal, a member of another tribe which supposedly died in the 'last cold' [though they may just have expelled Kal, as we know he's capable of lying], has joined these people only recently and presents himself as another alpha male. In many ways, then, this is classic baboon-style male-dominance politics. Yet the Old Mother seems to be the arbiter of succession, not Horg, and her insight into what's happening seems accurate [perhaps a psychic ability, as would be almost traditional in stories like this]. Horg was once a leader of men himself, yet like Kal, his people died during the cold.

Leadership and fire are seen to be interrelated, so Za isn't considered an adequate leader until he can make fire, but the Old Mother remembers that there were leaders before fire and believes this newfangled invention will destroy the tribe. She thus makes an alliance with Kal, at least until he murders her and attempts to blame Za for the deed. Once Ian has introduced the tribe to logic and democracy, Za isn't that grateful, as his own position depends on having the monopoly on fire-making "technology".

The natives are religious, and wouldn't do anything to upset the sun, which they revere as 'Orb'. They're superstitious enough to be spooked by burning skulls, and sacrifice is performed on the Stone of Blood. The tribe believes that Orb has sent the Doctor's party specifically to be killed. Za speaks of trapping bears and tigers, there are the skulls of things with antlers lying around, and the tribe has access to leopardskin. They have no concept of compassion, killing the weak. Za believes the travellers to come from 'the other side of the mountains', though Hur is cynical that anybody lives there.

Meanwhile, in 1963... John Smith and the Common Men have, according to Susan, 'gone from nineteen to two'. [For more on the dating of the first episode, see "Remembrance of the Daleks".]

Additional Sources As we'll see in the accompanying essay, the BBC decided to make a pilot episode, which is *almost* the same as "An Unearthly Child" but with a few notable differences. Some of these are technical, such as the layout of the console room set, which includes a blow-up photo of a vacuum valve as well as an even larger section of the packaging material that's used as a wall. And the outside of the Ship makes a high-pitched whining noise, not a reassuring hum.

The main technical difference, however, is the inability of the stage-hands to get the doors to shut properly. The last scene needed to be remounted to avoid the noise and distractingly obstinate behaviour of the doors, as they banged against the wall and opened themselves behind the cast's backs. A few smaller problems were also ironed out for the finished version, such as William Russell knocking a shop-window dummy over into the path of the camera that was meant to glide ominously towards the police box. There are various fluffs in the pilot, some awkward camerawork, and the book Barbara gives Susan doesn't have a bright dust-cover with "The French Revolution" conveniently printed on it in bold face.

But the most important changes are in the script. Susan states explicitly that she was born in the forty-ninth century, while the Doctor claims that the people of his world had turned unlimited space travel into 'a game for children' before humans invented the wheel. Earlier, Susan does less Balinese dancing and instead makes a Rorschach-esque inkblot pattern, scribbles a hexagon around it and then looks up anxiously as if she's given something away. (Sydney Newman vetoed this scene specifically, amongst many more general changes he wanted. It was replaced by Susan spotting a mistake in the French Revolution book, with the same music.) The Doctor is abrupt, dictatorial and - Newman's word - not 'cute' enough. He hardly bothers to persuade Ian and Barbara that he's right, but talks to Susan as if the schoolteachers aren't there.

Perhaps most importantly of all, the Doctor's motive for imprisoning Ian and Barbara is different, and prefigures much of the later series. In the finished version he simply doesn't want to be bothered by the other human beings they'd inevitably bring to the TARDIS. Yet in the pilot, he explains to Susan that history could be catastrophically altered if the teachers are allowed to tell the world about the Ship. The fact that this was hastily re-written between versions may explain why the Doctor's plans for his captives seem so vague in the broadcast episode.

Smaller changes include the lessons on the blackboard (in the screened version it's chemistry on one board and history prep on the other, in the pilot we see that Barbara has explained how shillings work to the entire class) and the fact that John Smith and the Common Men are clearly getting a lot of airplay; *twice* we hear their song issuing from the TARDIS when Susan opens the doors. Inside the TARDIS, Susan wears a more overtly "futuristic" metal-effect tank-top over what looks like a one-piece costume. The Doctor's attire is less Edwardian, with a dark tie in a Windsor knot and a regular collar on his shirt. The main difference that a casual viewer would spot, though, is the TARDIS take-off sound effect. In the pilot, this begins as a sequence of loud bleeps in irregular pitch-intervals. The bleeps get faster and the more familiar wheezing, groaning sound (© Terrance Dicks, every single Target novelisation he wrote) is introduced sporadically. As with the theme music in this version, a sound like thunder or a gunshot is also heard.

On top of this, David Whitaker's novel *Doctor Who in an Exciting Adventure with the Daleks* (published 1964, and yes, it was really called that until it was reprinted in the '70s) offers an alternative introduction to the characters. In this, Ian is late for a job interview because he has to report a car crash, and at the nearest police box he finds an old git with inextinguishable matches who stops him from making the call. Many of the features we've

long assumed to be TARDIS standards are mentioned here and here alone, like an automatic clothing-repair device and a hot-oil shower which heals bruises and cuts in moments. In this account, Ian thinks Susan fancies him - horribly inappropriate, considering that the "schoolteacher" version of Ian was still regularly appearing on television when the book was first published - and is rather put out that Alydon the Thal is so chummy with Barbara.

At around the same time, the big-screen version of the "origin" story (*Doctor Who and the Daleks*, also penned by Whitaker and starring Peter Cushing) re-introduced Ian as Barbara's boyfriend. In this version, Barbara is Dr Who's elder granddaughter, and they live in a nice little cottage with a time machine at the bottom of the garden. The other granddaughter, Susan Who, is about seven years old and reads heavy textbooks while Dr Who reads *The Eagle*. We'll discuss the two '60s feature films further under "The Dalek Invasion of Earth" (2.2), and *The Eagle* under "The Rescue" (2.3)...

The Analysis

Where Does This Come From? The whole format - with police box, Adventures in Time and Space, and so on - is the subject of the accompanying essay, but the specifics of this story are worth a book in themselves. Let's start in '60s Britain.

One of the things which many younger or overseas readers may fail to spot is that the children at Coal Hill School aren't wearing uniforms of any kind. Coal Hill looks like a Comprehensive, a new kind of secondary school intended to bridge the gulf between vocational and purely academic education styles. (Strictly speaking these didn't come into being until the summer of 1964, when Harold Wilson's Labour government got in. This being the case, we're looking at a superior Secondary Modern or a very lax Grammar School.) Likewise, Ian and Barbara are clearly supposed to represent the newer type of teacher, coming to the profession from different backgrounds. Ian in particular has experience from other fields, including military experience, as we'll see in later stories. A recurring theme in the '60s episodes is the suspicion of clever children, accompanied by some incomprehension on the part of their elders. Teenagers in 1955 were expected to be miniature citizens, trainee adults. From 1956 onwards, the teenager as a separate identity and subculture was a distinct menace.

We'll look at the way this manifested itself in the series later on, but here we need only mention one popular book which crystallised the fears of many parents: John Wyndham's *The Midwich Cuckoos*, famously filmed as *Village of the Damned* (1960), in whose shadow all other "creepy child" horror movies exist. In this, all women of child-bearing age in the village of Midwich fall pregnant after a mysterious cloud sends everyone there to sleep. All the resulting children are blond, super-intelligent and telepathically conjoined, and anyone who resists them is somehow coerced into self-mutilation or suicide. A generation of parents who found they didn't understand their children identified with this idea. There was a survey of teenagers carried out in 1961, entitled *Generation X* (yes, fifteen years before Billy Idol), which revealed that - golly! - teenagers had sex and liked popping pills. After World War Two, the idea of the future being "just the past, but better" didn't really hold water.

The war babies found that their parents were having second families; even the Queen did it. Anyone trying to study for exams with a baby in the house would naturally go out more. They were all turning sixteen between 1956 and 1962, and were trying out their own music, fashions and amusements. And the immediate post-War "boom" in childbirths meant that all these weird teenage activities were now big business. Even the BBC, previously somewhat patrician, had cottoned on to the fact that there was a sizeable section of the public in need of its own forms of entertainment (commercial television had been wary, not wanting to scare off advertisers at a time when there was no official teenage "demographic"). *Doctor Who* was partially a response to this, but it's significant that in the first story, we're encouraged to empathise with the adult authority figures as they try to unravel the mystery of Susan.

It has to be said: the opening half-episode is a lot like a well-meaning TV play about a domestic tragedy, with teachers following a girl home and finding out that she's living in squalor / a sweatshop / an arranged marriage / a family with no parents and six younger children… but the familiarity of the directing style is mainly to make what's said and seen seem more arresting. It's interesting, also, to compare it to the direction of the prehistoric sequences. While episode one seems specifically designed to look as close-to-

home as possible, to look as "contemporary" as any *Doctor Who* story until "The War Machines" (3.10), the sequences in the jungle and the wilderness come across as an attempt at something far more dynamic.

Much of later *Doctor Who* will look distinctly "stagey", often deliberately so, as if the programme-makers are trying to do Shakespeare with monsters rather than an SF movie on a BBC budget (although this agenda changes somewhat in the 1980s). But however much the limitations of budget and studio setting thwart the production, however over-written the scenes may be, and however ludicrous the chases may look, in episodes two, three and four there is a conscious effort being made to give the story a rare sense of movement and urgency. This isn't surprising, given that Waris Hussein was part of a new generation of director that wanted to make television look less like televised theatre. The overall impression is that Ian and Barbara have been abducted from TV "reality" and dumped in the middle of something rough-edged and threatening. There's rapid cutting, there's a fight sequence in which we're asked to watch the reactions of all the characters on the periphery as well as the burly cavemen, there's even a brief tiger's-eye view of its prey. All of these things are trying to establish Gumland as a three-dimensional space, not a two-dimensional stage-set.

Back to London, and back to Susan. She's clearly intended to seem foreign here. Her comment in the pilot, 'I like the English fog, it's mysterious', is - maybe unwittingly - a near-verbatim quotation of a line by Guillaume Apollinaire (one of many French artists and writers of the late nineteenth century who approved of the mystery and possibilities afforded by a London pea-souper). Foreigners in London were occasionally the subjects of suspicion, but usually perceived as romantic exiles or exotic enigmas. In the wake of James Bond, this was the era of "Spymania", when known Russian agents were feted in society rather than shunned. Susan's dress-sense may be a little on the odd side, but it's odd in a chic, continental sort of way. Even her sort-of-martial-arts skills say "well-travelled" instead of "alien". The efforts of foreign visitors to assimilate were perhaps amusing, yet they were also seen as touching and flattering. The Doctor and Susan aren't from Earth, but they don't seem out of place in the capital.

The idea of exile is mentioned in the original

notes, possibly hinting that they're aristocrats on the run. The Romanovs are an obvious parallel, and so are the refugees of the French Revolution, which perhaps isn't accidental given Susan's familiarity with the era. But Prospero and Miranda from *The Tempest* work rather well, too. And a more cogent precursor for the Doctor's behaviour in this story is another French exile: Captain Nemo. (Yes, all right, he wasn't actually French but his creator was.)

"Nemo" is Latin for "Nobody", which makes the title *Doctor Who* sound like a deliberate reference. In the 1955 Disney film version of *20,000 Leagues Under the Sea* - the one with which most people are familiar - James Mason plays Nemo as an explorer first and a political dissident at best fifth. His ambition is mainly to see the world without being seen. His ship, the *Nautilus*, is - like the TARDIS console room - at once domestic and imposing. Moreover, the visual spectacle of the *Nautilus* is one which combines advanced technology with Victoriana. Most crucially, Nemo tells the audience-identification figure Ned Land that Ned's friends can't leave the ship because they'll tell the world, turning the *Nautilus* into a spectacle and potentially a weapon. In the sequel *The Mysterious Island*, Nemo is revealed to be fighting the British Empire and slavery, seeking a utopia. He's motivated by revenge, but believes that tolerance and technology can make humanity better.

We'll soon see that some of the people creating *Doctor Who* thought along similar lines, as far as the Doctor's motivation was concerned. There was, prior to the Disney film, a version of *20,000 Leagues* made for television in Canada. It was produced by Sydney Newman, and he's near-as-dammit the creator of *Doctor Who*. Mind, if you want to consider the origins of "Who" as a name and aren't convinced by Nemo / Nobody, then bear in mind that this wasn't long after the release of *Dr No* in 1962. Another scientific genius with a hi-tech world of his own. Like we said, Spymania.

Some commentators have seen the caveman story as a retread of William Golding's novel *The Inheritors*, an account of how the Neanderthals were out-evolved. There are certainly similarities in the make-up of the tribe, and in some of the conjectural prehistoric names. But Za's angst at meeting a new "tribe" with superior technology could equally come from Edgar Rice Burroughs' *The People That Time Forgot*. Really, though, the roots of the "messing around with cavemen" parts of the story seem a lot less literary; these people

have more in common with Hollywood's idea of primitive Earth than Golding's. The title "100,000 BC" is the giveaway, because at heart this is just a slightly more sensible version of *One Million BC* - not *One Million Years BC*, the remake with Racquel Welch - with marginally less contempt for (pre)historical research, i.e. it's still not very accurate but at least there are no dinosaurs. *One Million BC* is also about the trouble that's caused when an exiled member of tribe X gets involved with tribe Y, although Kal's a lot more antagonistic than Victor Mature ever was. Still, the decision to let the Gums talk was made late in the day, so maybe the programme-makers originally had more serious things in mind.

And the main thrust of this story is a lot closer to home. Fire represents all technology, all knowledge. It confers power, and is monopolised by someone hoping to use technology as a political resource. In the Britain of 1963, this was a hot topic, in part because of the ongoing concern over nuclear weapons (at this point it's only been a year since the Cuban crisis, remember). If it seems like a stretch to connect grunty cavemen with anything atomic, then bear in mind that by this point the two had already been linked in the public consciousness. The population of the Western World might not have been aware of *all* the consequences of a nuclear war, but most had a sneaking suspicion that if somebody dropped The Bomb then we'd all go back to wearing animal-skins. Newspaper cartoonists had picked up on it. Half a decade before *Planet of the Apes*, the then-recent movie *Teenage Caveman* was perhaps the most eloquent-yet-stupid expression of this, a film in which the half-naked primitive Robert Vaughn discovers that his seemingly prehistoric world is actually Earth after World War Three (this low-budget classic would be shamelessly ripped off by *Doctor Who* for 23.1, "The Mysterious Planet").

Seen in this light, the world of "An Unearthly Child" doesn't look like a serious attempt to depict the world of our ancestors - given that it's the start of a series which was meant to be educational, a shockingly small amount of research seems to have been done - as much as it's depicting a fundamental "anyworld" which could be past, future or anything else, where basic human lessons have to be learned. This goes a great deal beyond nuclear weapons - in this period, *all* uses of science for the good of the public were made the subject of debates, speeches and earnest editorials. Ian suggests that everyone in the tribe should learn to make fire, and introduces the concept of consensus, and these aren't unrelated. Science teachers were recruited in large numbers to train a new generation with the skills to give Britain a role on the global stage; for the consequences of this, see Volume III, particularly Season Seven. It's always made clear that Ian's background is less academic than "hands-on".

Unbelievably, we've come this far without mentioning H. G. Wells. This is partly because it's almost too obvious, although we'll be talking about him a lot more when we get to the *next* story. But all time-travel fiction in the "scientific" age - which is to say, all time-travel fiction that involves an actual device - owes a debt to *The Time Machine*, "An Unearthly Child" more than most. For the time being, we'll skip over the fact that the TARDIS is as much a "magic cabinet" as much as it is a scientific instrument, because it's Wells on the inside even if it's C. S. Lewis on the outside. Even by the 1960s, time-travel in literary SF was becoming an "institutional" thing, a form of technology that was possessed by futuristic law-enforcement agencies rather than something within the reach of amateur inventors. But *Doctor Who* smacks of the amateur, and as we'll see over and over again in these volumes, a love of the amateur and a distrust of the professional is one of the defining factors of the British psyche. Wells' time-traveller built his time machine in his own back garden. The Doctor keeps *his* in a junkyard (although the '60s movie version obviously gets back to source by turning Doctor Who into an eccentric inventor… you didn't need to be told that). And we're left in no doubt here that the TARDIS was at least in part the Doctor's own work.

The figure of the lone inventor has, since the industrial revolution, been as important to British culture as the lone frontiersman has been to the Americans. After World War Two, it was more important than ever (we'll see why under 2.1, "Planet of Giants"). Perhaps more than any other factor, this has to be remembered if you're going to make sense of the country in which *Doctor Who* grew up: the series was developed by a generation which had seen the decline and fall of the British Empire, but still had aspirations to do things nobody else could do. We should remember H. G. Wells' own statement, that 'the whole of the universe is not too small for Englishmen'. Wells was no triumphal imperialist, yet he still believed in an innate ingenuity and sense of civilisation in the British character, regardless of the excesses of empire in his own time. Following World War Two, and with the rise of a younger generation that saw Britain as a parochial, unglamorous little country and couldn't understand why their parents still called it "Great", this sort of philosophy seemed positively charming. With Britain no longer having any *actual* imperial power, the image of the Victorian gentleman-traveller or gentleman-inventor embodied a "nice" version of the nation's past glory.

Hartnell's Doctor will later describe himself as a citizen of the universe, and a gentleman to boot. That *is*, at least in part, code for "I'm British and it's great". If the country had genuinely been a world-dominating force, then this would have been wholly nauseating, but it's a kind of fiction; a sense of want for a mythical Britain where people would rather have tea with foreigners than shoot at them. The nation's achievements in this period were scientific or cultural, not military or territorial. The Doctor's grumpiness in "An Unearthly Child" masks it a little, but this ideal is still visible in his character. And once they're dragged away from contemporary London, the straight-laced English schoolteachers with the sensible haircuts quickly find a way of adapting to a hostile universe without oppressing the natives, much. Ian, particularly, is always on hand to balance the Doctor's "judge them by their own standards" approach with solidly "good" Home Counties values. But it *is* a balance, and neither of them has the upper hand here.

One last thing to note. A theme tune by Ron Grainer, based around a syncopated-but-odd riff; an opening scene in a junkyard; a grumpy old man with a trendy younger relative who wants to sample London's new opportunities… and this is only a year after the hit sitcom *Steptoe and Son* had gurned its way onto our screens.

Things That Don't Make Sense They've followed a fifteen-year-old girl into a junkyard, and then they hear this stentorian, phlegmy old man's cough. And Barbara asks: 'Is that her?' Does Susan have a record of smoking behind the gym? This comes mere moments after Ian reacts to a humming police box with the rather startling exclamation '*it's alive!*', as if it's more likely to be a man in a police box costume than a police box with some kind of machinery inside it.

Nor does the Doctor's way of dealing with human beings do him a lot of credit, as he essentially spends several minutes explaining that the TARDIS is a time machine before announcing that the teachers can't be allowed to leave as they now know that it's a time machine. Given his ability to smooth-talk the cavemen later on, couldn't he at least have *tried* something like "yes, myself and my granddaughter are travelling carnival people with a box of illusions, now sod off"? And why does he shout 'get back to the Ship, child!' as the TARDIS takes off, when they're both standing in the console room at the time? [One answer is that Hartnell was meant to say "seat" rather than "Ship", because at this stage the TARDIS take-off is still seen as being akin to a rocket launch. It won't last.]

Susan's spent five months in London, wearing fashionable clothes, listening to hit records on a state-of-the-art transistor radio and picking up the vernacular, but has no idea about pounds, shillings and pence. Either she obtained all of these items (and her entire food supply) from the TARDIS stores, and never bothered even glancing at the coins from the Ship's magic currency-vending machine that let her use the buses and get into clubs, or she wasn't there for the youth culture so much as for the overwhelming need to be ridiculed by fifteen-year-olds. Surely the TARDIS database has a time-travellers' tourist guide, a *Rough Guide to Merseybeat Era London*? That's another thing: with a fully-functional time machine, they go to grotty old East London and not Liverpool? Or Greenwich Village, where her beatnik girl pose wouldn't stand out so much?

Emerging into a bright prehistoric landscape, the Doctor completely fails to notice the bloke standing right in front of him who's casting an enormous scary shadow and holding a big club. Aside from the Y-fronts revealed during the fight between Kal and Za (q.v. the vegetable-monster deaths in 23.3, "Terror of the Vervoids"), and Hur's animal-skin bra top (3s/6d from Cavegirl at C&A), the most noticeable anachronism is that people living on meat and berries have decaying teeth and - sorry to get personal - cellulite.

We've got to mention it somewhere… precisely *why* does the lamp on top of the police box flash when it's taking off or landing? If the Ship's disguised as a motorbike, then do the indicators flash as well? If it's disguised as a sedan chair, then do the people carrying it feel the need to lift their hats up and down as it dematerialises?

Critique Counting "Tomb of the Cybermen" (5.1) and "Spearhead from Space" (7.1), there have now been five attempts to introduce *Doctor Who* to the viewing public. In most cases, there's been a distinct split between telling an adventure story and setting up the ground-rules, and conventional wisdom claims this is the most extreme. A whole episode is given over to introducing the series, and then there's three episodes of running around and escaping, as everyone knows.

Everyone's wrong. The full extent of the programme's potential is impossible to set up in twenty-five minutes, because at this point the programme-makers didn't know it themselves. What this story shows is that even with a twenty-five minute exposition sequence, the adventures the travellers have when they arrive are at the core of this programme, not how they got there. Yes, in context the first episode really is shockingly good; yes, it's *odd* in a way that nothing on Earth has been since; and yes, the other three parts feel hopelessly slow compared to *Doctor Who* as we later come to know it. But anyone who treats the caveman story as an optional extra is missing the point.

This is a story about making four people who barely know one another learn to trust each other, and turning tribespeople who are at each other's throats into a solid, united clan. An obvious comparison can be made with "Rose" (X1.1), in which the relationship of the protagonist to the Doctor forms the main thrust of the plot, and then the details of his lifestyle are revealed bit-by-bit as the story unfolds somewhere in the background. (We could also mention that scene where, shortly after kissing Grace, the McGann Doctor delivers what may be the most egregious info-dump speech in television history.) "An Unearthly Child" is different. It isn't just setting up the *Doctor Who* we know it now, but all the things it could have been, including the originally-envisaged series where Ian is the hero.

What we have here is a four-part adventure story that uses up a quarter of its screen-time before it really gets started. In this story, fire, hope, loyalty and the concept of murder are shown as human knowledge in all its glory and potential for evil. Possession of the secret imbues certain individuals with power over others. It's hard to avoid seeing this as a nuclear parable, especially with "The Daleks" waiting to start. Now that we know that everyone in the cosmos speaks English unless otherwise stated, the Gums don't seem as weird as they did at the time.

The title of episode one places the emphasis on Susan, and rightly so. Even when the Doctor has made his presence felt, Carole Ann Ford is the dominant figure in the first episode. She's never allowed to be this good again. In the last episode she even gets a moment of macabre humour, which might have been a trait worth investigating, but she reverts to screaming from now on. However, let's not forget that this tale sees all *four* leads terrified of the situation, something else we won't really see again ('fear makes companions of all of us…'). It's a moment of genuine feeling, which the derring-do of "The Daleks" - and just about everything afterwards - makes somehow out-of-place.

We've already mentioned that this was supposed to be a "family" event, but it's hard to overestimate the difference this makes. Once the series settles down and decides that it's categorically an adventure show, it becomes a programme about *doing* rather than *being*, and from that point on it's bound to favour the boys. All the usual arguments about whether *Doctor Who* features "strong female characters" are irrelevant, next to the simple fact that the time-travelling family unit we see here lets you see things from everybody's point of view, regardless of gender or generation. After the original TARDIS crew breaks up in Season Two, and it becomes a series about the Doctor and his assistants, this will disappear; the supporting cast will become wholly functional, big-C Companions rather than characters, and we'll no longer be asked to consider how other people might actually *feel* about things. But, again, we'll come back to this later.

Until everyone knows what *Doctor Who* is going to be like, they have to muddle through with half-decent scripts and convincing acting. Enjoy it while it lasts.

The Facts

Written by Anthony Coburn, though C. E. Webber is usually credited with "additional material". Directed by Waris Hussein. Ratings: 4.4 million, 5.9 million, 6.9 million, 6.4 million. Due to the exceptional circumstances (a partial powercut, and the whole assassination-of-Kennedy business), episode one was repeated just before the scheduled broadcast of episode two, getting a much healthier 6.0 million viewers. Episode three

followed the edition of *Juke Box Jury* in which the four panellists were the Beatles, which explains the ratings spike. The 1981 repeat, on BBC 2, got 4.6 million viewers for the opening episode.

Supporting Cast   Derek Newark (Za), Alethea Charlton (Hur), Eileen Way (Old Mother), Jeremy Young (Kal), Howard Lang (Horg).

AKA…   Here's where the fun starts. No *Doctor Who* story before "The Savages" (3.9) has an on-screen title, although each individual *episode* does. This means that fandom has yet to agree on what the "proper" names for things are. We'll go into this in detail later on (**What Are These Stories Really Called?** under 3.2, "Mission to the Unknown"), but the first story is particularly problematic. Though "An Unearthly Child" is unquestionably the name of the opening episode, and the name that virtually everyone uses in "everyday" fanspeak, its author called it "The Tribe of Gum" (a title that's still occasionally used to describe episodes two to four, and was used when the script was published in book form in 1988) and one draft went by the name of "100,000 BC" (which is, as we've already said, historically cockeyed).

Episode Titles   "An Unearthly Child"; "The Cave of Skulls"; "The Forest of Fear"; "The Firemaker".

Working Titles   "Nothing at the End of the Lane" (for the first draft of the first episode). Episode three was originally to have been called "The Cave of Skulls", episode two "The Fire Maker" and episode four "The Dawn of Knowledge".

Cliffhangers   The police box from Totters' Lane has - inconceivably - arrived in the middle of a wilderness, and *something* is casting a looming shadow over it; imprisoned in the Cave of Skulls, Ian points out that the skulls in question have been split wide open; Kal and his followers block the way back to the TARDIS as the travellers make their escape.

The lead-in to the next story: the travellers depart the Ship, not noticing that the TARDIS' radiation meter is now indicating "danger".

The Lore

N.B. Here we'll restrict ourselves to the making of the four finished episodes, and refer the reader to the accompanying essay for everything leading up to it…

• The designated director for this story, Rex Tucker, had booked a holiday in Majorca which clashed with the rearranged recording dates (in those days a holiday in Spain had to be planned like a space mission). The reasons for the various delays are many and varied, but here's a quick summary: everyone hated the first draft script. Waris Hussein had been hired to direct the planned second story, "The Masters of Luxor", and the obvious solution was to swap directors. By the time Tucker finally left for his holidays, he was committed to directing an adaptation of Flaubert's *Madame Bovary*. It was generally agreed that this was more his style, but he did return to *Doctor Who* for 3.8, "The Gunfighters".

• The regular characters had to be cast quickly. Tucker considered several people for the female leads, including Anneke Wills (see 3.10, "The War Machines") and Phyllida Law (see 3.5, "The Massacre"), but Verity Lambert began from scratch. Barbara - or "Lola", at this stage - was easy, as Alvin Rakoff was an old friend and Lambert met his wife Jacqueline Hill at parties. Carole Ann Ford had been given a reasonably large role in the universally-loathed film version of *Day of the Triffids*; Hussein saw her on a studio monitor, and brought her to Lambert's attention. Despite appearances, Ford was 23 and had a young child.

• Ian was easier still. William Russell had been the star of *Sir Lancelot*, one of those historical adventure series that clogged up the schedules after *The Adventures of Robin Hood* started riding through the glen. He was Oxford-educated, and had changed from his birth-name "Russell Enoch" at the suggestion of Norman Wisdom[1]. (Since the second run was made in collaboration with NBC, *Sir Lancelot* was the first British-made TV series filmed in colour, and was thus in almost perpetual syndication even though it had been made in 1956. The company that made it went through various name-changes, but we'll simplify by using "ITC", the one by which most people identify Lew Grade's organisation. It'll be mentioned a lot in this volume.)

• As far as the pre-publicity and wages were concerned, the star of the series was the Doctor. Quite whose idea it was to approach veteran com-edy actor and - in recent years - screen "heavy" William Hartnell is unclear. He'd begun as Billy Hartnell, in pre-War quickies like *Midnight at Madam Tussauds* and *I'm an Explosive!* (for an odd coincidence involving that title, see 24.1, "Time and the Rani"). Post-War, he managed to hold his own on screen opposite Richard Attenborough's blistering performance in *Brighton Rock,* and as a result became known for "hard man" roles. In 1958 he starred in the very first *Carry On* film, as the eponymous *Sergeant*, on the back of his most famous TV role up to that point: Sergeant-Major Bullimore in *The Army Game*. He'd also gain acclaim as the callous trainer in *This Sporting Life*, but again, it was a bitter-old-man kind of role. It was the typecasting that followed this which led to Hartnell even considering a children's show, so Lambert and Hussein met him at his home and persuaded him.

• Hussein's lack of confidence in his ability to use film well led to his assistant, Douglas Camfield, being asked to handle whole scenes during the second pre-filming session at Ealing Studios. The first cliffhanger, and the shot of the spears flying through the dematerialising TARDIS (achieved with relatively simple optical printing), were shot on the 19th of September; not quite the first thing filmed, as a week earlier a test session for the howlround sequences was shot. See **How Did They Do Those Titles?** under 4.7, "The Macra Terror"… and it's definitely "howlround", not "howaround" as you may read elsewhere. The jungle chases and the big fight sequence were shot on the 9th of October, but only just. The sets and props arrived late the day before, because the BBC couldn't muster a van-driver. Camfield hired the fight-arranger for *Z Cars*, Derek Ware, to choreograph the final tussle (Ware ended up doubling for one of the cavemen) and had him sit in on the editing. During the edit, Hussein and Lambert had a heated row about whether a squelching sound should accompany a shot of the rock hitting Kal's head.

• Hussein asked actors auditioning to play cavemen to remove their shirts in order to prove they were sufficiently hirsute. A story has done the rounds that one background performer quit rather than remove her false eyelashes, possibly the same one whose agent had told her she'd be modelling furs, but it's on record that Margot Maxine stormed out rather than have her teeth blackened. Moreover, the sand brought into the studio was infested with fleas, which took residence in the furs worn by the cast. Another "hitcher" was a lizard hiding in the tropical plants that had been hired for the forest set. Ford adopted him, and kept him as a pet for many years.

• Eileen Way, cast as the Old Mother, has played both a witch in the BBC's *Macbeth* (1980) and - on stage - Lady Macbeth. The Old Mother combines elements of both characters. She'd just appeared on the big screen in the Kirk Douglas costume romp *The Vikings*, as yet another conniving matriarch, and later she'd return to *Doctor Who* as Madame Karela (17.3, "The Creature from the Pit") as well as appearing in the film version of "The Dalek Invasion of Earth" (2.2).

• The pilot episode was shot at Lime Grove Studio D on the 27th of September, after a week's rehearsal. The technical problems with the TARDIS set were the main worry. This set had been designed almost nonchalantly (according to Hussein) by Peter Brachaki, and had originally included various impractical features. Even the stripped-down version, using a photo-blow-up of the packaging material which had formed the production model's walls (and lacking the perspex columns which were supposed to light up or turn black according to the Ship's location, or something), cost a sizeable chunk of the budget. This cost was defrayed over the remainder of the first year.

• Barry Newbery took over design duties for the remainder, and most subsequent "historical" stories. He made the cave walls from a new material, usually called "Jablite" in guide-books like this (unless they spell it "Jabolite", which is wrong); basically, expanded polystyrene. Making grubby walls was easy, but gluing it together using the standard adhesive wasn't. Once the right glue was found, it proved useful for adding texture to surfaces, especially when gently scorched. However, the substances were potentially highly inflammable and toxic, so Newbery's team had a steep learning-curve. When the decision was made to remount the first episode, it emerged that the TARDIS set was the only one that had been retained, so Newbery - filling in at short notice, as Brachaki was hospitalised (and Lambert had asked for him to be replaced in any case) - had to remake the school and junkyard from notes.

• The record Susan listens to on her radio while bopping so oddly is a piece of stock music, "Three Guitars, Mood Two" by the Arthur Nelson Group. It's almost exactly the sort of instrumental that The

Shadows (Cliff Richard's former backing band, not the monsters from *Babylon 5*) had in the charts at any given time between 1958 and 1965. Curiously, Ian Chesterton was originally to have been called "Cliff". Incidentally, "Three Guitars, Mood Two" also popped up in the first episode of *Z Cars* (see the essay under 2.1, "Planet of Giants").

• "John Smith" was at one stage called Olly Typhoon, and before that Fred Grubb. As "Sue" said in the original script: 'Grubb, dub […] …oh, Mr Chesterton, he teaches me to… throb!' You see why there were so many rewrites.

• Susan's hairdo, which doesn't seem at all strange now, was the trial run for the Vidal Sassoon "asymmetric" look; the BBC asked him to come up with something just slightly ahead of fashion. (An attempt to do the same for Tegan failed abysmally. See 20.1, "Arc of Infinity".)

• The fight with the (unseen) tiger / leopard / whatever-it-is was pre-recorded on VT a day before "The Forest of Fear" was committed to tape. This was, as we will see, fairly uncommon for stories of this era.

• By 1963 standards, *Doctor Who* was launched with a publicity blitz. A trailer was broadcast a week beforehand; there was a radio ad narrated by Hartnell, as himself rather than the Doctor; and the *Radio Times* ran a sizeable feature on the programme (it was actually intended to be the cover feature, but in the end the return of comedy star Kenneth Horne to BBC radio was given priority).

• The ITV stations had got wind of the coming threat, and scheduled a scientific thriller series called *Emerald Soup* against the new BBC offering. It lasted for six weeks, after which you may notice a sharp rise in viewing figures for *Doctor Who*. *Emerald Soup* was about a bunch of children whose scientific parent-figures develop a revolutionary new "atomic" process, and are thus menaced by crooks who want the secret for themselves. This is interesting, partly because it gives you some idea of what people expected *Doctor Who* to be like, partly because it sounds like exactly the kind of story you'd find in the *Eagle* (again, see the essay under "The Rescue" for the *Eagle's* influence on *Doctor Who*), and partly because of the way these children were portrayed in the programme. The makers of *Emerald Soup* were concerned that traditional English child-heroes were much too prim and proper, so the series' writer took his inspiration from wilderness-loving

Australian kids, and had them larking about in caves for much of the story. Australians, caves… it all seems terribly familiar.

• Oh yes, and President Kennedy was assassinated the day before the first episode of *Doctor Who* was broadcast. This *didn't* cause transmission of "An Unearthly Child" to be delayed, as a generation of fans once believed, but it was a bit of a distraction and unquestionably dented the ratings. (Later than night, *That Was the Week That Was* featured a lament to Kennedy in which singer Millicent Martin cried a single, incredibly-well-timed tear halfway through the performance. This clip is constantly being hauled out of the archives for documentaries about seminal '60s television, so the 23rd of November, 1963 was obviously a good night for BBC TV. On the other side, *The Avengers* were taking on "The Medicine Men", a not-unwatchable episode by Malcolm Hulke. Of whom you'll hear a lot more later.)

1.2: "The Daleks"

(Serial B, Seven Episodes, 21st December 1963 - 1st February 1964.)

Which One is This? On a planet with a petrified jungle, in a city of inhuman angles and surprisingly smooth floors, *something* with a sucker for an arm threatens Barbara Wright and brings the TARDIS travellers into contact with their first alien culture. For the second time, nothing will ever be the same again.

Firsts and Lasts Yes, all right. It's the first appearance of the Daleks, the Thals, the planet Skaro, Terry Nation's name on the credits, the word 'extermination' (but *not* 'exterminate', yet) and the "classic" extermination effect (all done with over-exposures, no bones visible). However, it's also the first time we see the fault locator - that handy piece of TARDIS lore - and its close rival the food machine. It's the first time we hear of the magical properties of mercury and static electricity, while both the music and the sound of the doors opening in the Dalek city will be turning up a lot in future stories. The Doctor dons his rather beaten-up Panama hat for the first time; he likes to wear this in deserts, usually in Terry Nation stories.

We're also privy to the first time the Doctor gets Ian's name wrong. And Ian, as it happens, becomes the first TARDIS traveller to suggest the "let's split up in the middle of a hostile alien environment and meet back here later" strategy.

Unfortunately, it's also the first time we can see the shadow cast by the boom mic, and the first really notable "Billy Fluffs" turn up here (see **Things to Notice**). It's the first story for which Daphne Dare does the costumes, and she'll be doing it for the rest of this book. We could make a long list of *Doctor Who* conventions that come into play at this point (an alien planet occupied by both English-speaking humanoids and "others"; a monster who turns up at the end of the first episode; supporting characters who heroically sacrifice themselves for the good of the party; a doomsday countdown that's halted with mere seconds left on the clock; an obsession with Nazism and machine-people; corridors; and many, many more), and a lot of the "standards" here are specific to Terry Nation - including the platitudes about cowardice, the daring lift-shaft escapes and the "living city" with an all-important antenna on the roof (q.v. 11.3, "Death to the Daleks"). But more significantly, it's the first time the set designer has to create an entire alien world in Studio D at Lime Grove.

Some things, however, aren't typical at all. For the only time in the programme's history, there's a light breeze blowing on a studio-bound alien planet. After this, the wind machine is only brought in when there's a raging storm required. Another curious feature: when a desperate Susan thinks back to what Ian told her earlier, we hear Ian's voice as if in "flashback", a technique we won't be seeing much of in this series (although there's something similar in 1.4, "Marco Polo", when Susan hears a sandstorm shouting her name and we're allowed to share the experience).

And whether you see it as business-as-usual or not, this is the first obvious example of women being treated incredibly badly in *Doctor Who*, with the script making it clear that Only-Speaking-Female-Thal Dyoni isn't capable of holding any political opinions of her own. She even underlines this by pointing out how much weaker the female time-travellers are than the males. Some of this material really does defy belief. (That said, see **Just How Chauvinistic is *Doctor Who*?** under 9.5, "The Time Monster".)

Plus… Ian makes sure that the lead character is routinely known as 'the Doctor', treating it as his normal title after Barbara's throwaway use of it in the last story. This is likely to stick.

Seven Things to Notice About "The Daleks"...

1. Ah, "Billy Fluffs". Given the complexities of making this programme - under conditions which partially resemble live TV, and partially resemble a very complicated play - the real surprise is how rarely any mis-delivered lines occur, let alone how rarely they damage the story. Yet, we have to say, Hartnell has a rare knack of making his messed-up dialogue amusing. The ripest examples turn up in the second year of his stint, but here we have the particularly noticeable: 'It's possible that they may have been anti-radiation gloves. Drugs. I can't be certain'. On screen it's both funny and *entirely in character* (thus, strangely, heightening the tension rather than dispelling it... this won't be the case later on.)

2. If the cast seems distracted in the first two episodes, then it's hardly surprising. Episode one is a remake. They shot "The Dead Planet" on the 5th of November, but it needed to be redone (see **The Lore**). The second episode, "The Survivors", was being recorded as the news broke that John Kennedy had been shot. The third episode was taped a week later, and notice the discrepancy in Hartnell's wigs. On the 6th of December, a remount of the first episode was recorded, amid growing uncertainty as to whether the series would last three months. The final two episodes were made after the word-of-mouth buzz surrounding the Daleks had made the papers, and many critics have noted a perceptible increase in the cast's enthusiasm.

3. The unexpected bonus from this odd rescheduling is that there was a second chance to make the model city. For all the jokes about *Doctor Who* using Fairy Liquid bottles in its effects work, the home of the Daleks isn't at all bad and at least *looks* like a city. In later episodes the camera zooms in on specific parts of it, as if we're supposed to recognise where in the city the subsequent scene is going to be taking place. The inlay shot of the TARDIS crew looking across the plain to the city is good even today, and marred only by the use of joke-shop binocular goggles when the Doctor and Susan want a closer look. (Presumably the TARDIS also has a stock of X-Ray Specs, Sea Monkeys and Charles Atlas bodybuilding courses.)

4. One of Sydney Newman's imperatives to the whole Drama Department was 'use television'. This story does exactly that. Not only are cameras integral to the plot in a way that we won't see again until the end of Season Two, but the Dalek control room has built-in monitors relaying other parts of the set, or howlround patterns like the title sequence. And compared to other stories of this period, the use of inserted stock footage and photos is assured and audacious. Even the presence of the camera telling us the story is factored in, as Jacqueline Hill puts her hand on the lens as if oblivious to its presence. The camera in this story is more mobile and fluid than in almost any other TV drama of the time, as though the operators and the Dalek performers were in competition. And then it hits you: the Daleks are BBC cameras as a child would see them. How do they kill people? By over-exposing them...

5. But aside from the Daleks' physical appearance, the real key to this story's immediate impact wasn't the set design, nor the acting, and certainly not the originality of the script. It was the music. Tristram Carey's soundtrack looks forward to '70s "ambient" albums (some tracks are almost indistinguishable from Brian Eno's *Music for Airports*) and back to '50s *musique concrète*[2], but it doesn't belong in any one time. For the average viewer in 1963-64, Skaro is an environment where odd things might happen with no warning, simply because there's never been anything like this coming from the speakers of their tellies before. It isn't quite recognisably melodic, but it isn't just sound effects and neither is it negligible aural "wallpaper". In this soundscape, any event - even somebody assailing Babs with a sink-plunger - is automatically five times more unpredictable and thus scary. The score has been re-used more than any other incidental music in the programme's history, in stories like "The Rescue" (2.3) and "The Ark" (3.6), as well as Christopher Barry's other Dalek story "The Power of the Daleks" (4.3).

6. The Daleks themselves are rather more eloquent than they later become. They describe the Thals as being 'disgustingly mutated', and say things like 'a few questions will remove the mystery'. They even speak of 'our Dalek forefathers', which rather suggests that they inherit their travel-machine shells as family heirlooms.

7. Such is the production team's faith in the power of photographic blow-ups that the ranks of the Daleks are swollen with life-size cardboard facsimiles. The scenes with these blow-ups are shot from angles which make it inconceivable that *any* halfway competent director would let episode seven go to air, if they were honestly intended to

Who *Really* Created the Daleks?

Well, everyone knows the answer to this one: Davros. Even though a completely different "origin" story is to be found in the *Dalek Pocketbook and Space Travellers' Guide* (which differs only slightly from the version of Dalek history described in the *TV 21* comic-strip in 1965), since "Genesis of the Daleks" (12.4) the Skaroine horde has had a single, definitive creator. Yarvelling - an engineer who survived the holocaust on Skaro, and developed protection for the mutants - is replaced in "Genesis" by Davros, who foresaw the mutation and deliberately accelerated it. Whereas Yarvelling traveled the universe to collect the Flidor Gold and Silcronium needed to construct the casings, Davros sat in his bunker and proclaimed there was no life in the seven galaxies.

Of course, many people would say that the Daleks were created by Terry Nation. It says so in the credits of all the Dalek stories written by other people, except "The Power of the Daleks" (4.3) and "The Evil of the Daleks" (4.9), where the production-teams forgot and a BBC announcer had to point it out instead. Indeed, if you play *Trivial Pursuit*, you may be under the impression that Nation created *Doctor Who*. All scripts using the Daleks had to be cleared by Nation, and his agent Roger Hancock zealously preserved all rights and merchandising revenue. And this has long been seen as a little unfair, as all Nation did was write a sketchy three-line description of a metal box and a grating voice, with a throwaway mention of the Georgian State Dancers. In the eyes of most fans, the real creative genius was the set designer, Raymond P. Cusick.

When the BBC hierarchy announced a new, regular family space adventure, the Visual Effects Department voiced grave concerns. Not to put too fine a point on it, they refused to touch *Doctor Who*. To commit themselves to something like this would require them to either not do anything else or do slapdash work. So the decision was made to assign all special effects in the series to the same unit that made the sets and props. Thus the Dalek city and the occupants were integrated visually, and Nation's one-sentence description became part of Cusick's overall strategy to remove right-angles from all the worlds he created. Cusick's starting-point was that an occupant had to operate the prop, and that this would be best done on wheels, sitting down. Everything else - manipulation, shooting and vision - was based around this. The idea that the Daleks pick up static electricity from the floor was a late addition, and was Mervyn Pinfield's contribution (see also 2.1, "Planet of Giants", where once again the end of the story was suggested by what was possible).

The *real* genius of the Dalek design is this: it's the greatest of all predators. Predation is, almost by definition, the scariest thing a living being can imagine. In any children's fiction, the biggest predator is the best villain, which is why the tyrannosaurus rex is every boy's favourite dinosaur and why could-have-been Dalek designer Ridley Scott made sure that the monster in *Alien* looked like a combination of as many cannibalistic, man-eating entities as possible (including giant spiders, World War One German soldiers and a certain part of the female anatomy).

The Dalek is less visceral, but in effect it's a predator for an industrial society. It's every machine that might possibly hurt children, and key to this is the fact that *it doesn't have a proper face*. Both Nation and Cusick wanted to avoid it looking like a man in a suit, yet this is only half the story. The Dalek's head-piece and eye-stalk make clear that this is a self-willed thing, that it's a kind of mechanised, technological life-form, but at the same time - and in a way no other screen monster has been able to match - it has no hint of an expression, nothing to link it to humanity or suggest that it's anything but a threat. Even Cybermen have features. Give a Dalek *two* eye-stalks, and it becomes altogether too familiar.

"Genius" is probably the word. If the creature seems vaguely ludicrous *now*, then it's only because we've had four decades of jokes about stairs, but try coming across one unexpectedly (difficult, we admit, although it has been done) and see how big a start you get. It simultaneously hits a primal human nerve, and reminds you of every time you've felt a bit anxious about the mechanism on the back of a dustcart. Yet, despite this stroke of greatness, as a BBC staff member Ray Cusick wasn't allowed the same copyright privileges as a freelance writer such as Nation. Eventually Cusick's basic fee was augmented with an *ex gratia* payment of £100 and a gold *Blue Peter* badge. The BBC still owns the rights to the Dalek design, even as the Terry Nation estate owns the name and the "concept".

All very well, say Nation's advocates, but the basic idea of a world ravaged by atomic war lead-

continued on page 29...

fool the viewers. So either director Richard Martin wanted to imply that the Daleks take photos of their wives into work with them, or he was a hamfisted hack whose mind was on something else. Watch "The Web Planet" (2.5) and "The Chase" (2.8) before making up your mind.

The Continuity

The Doctor No longer being quite so snide and aggressive to Ian, but has instead taken to being generally irritating, calling the man "Chesterfield" or "Chesterman". [We *assume* this is deliberate, but in "The Massacre" (3.5) he can't get Ian's name right even when he's talking to himself.] Physically, he tolerates radiation less well than the others. [See "The Mutants" (9.4), "Planet of the Spiders" (11.5), "The Android Invasion" (13.4) and "Destiny of the Daleks" (17.1) to see how his radiation immunity varies over time. Here, the subtext is that he's particularly vulnerable because he's an old man.] He finds that the gulf between Susan's age and his own can make communication difficult.

The Doctor's vain enough to believe that if he leads the Thals against the Daleks, then the mind will triumph and they're bound to succeed. He's obviously proud of his ability to sabotage Dalek surveillance technology with simple objects and a basic knowledge of physics. He claims - dubiously - that he never gives advice, but his philosophy is 'always search for truth', and he states that his own truth is in the stars.

Tending to the sick Doctor, Ian speaks of him having a 'pulse', singular. [More on the Doctor's number of hearts in Volume II.]

• *Background*. The Doctor has apparently never been to Skaro before, but he recognises the effect of a neutron bomb on vegetation. It's not entirely clear whether he recognises the Daleks on hearing their name, but he certainly doesn't seem to know much about their history. [Obviously the script was written in the belief that the Daleks never left their homeworld, and the author assumed - like everyone else - that the Doctor had never heard of them. However, given their huge impact on cosmic history, it seems odd that he has no idea of their existence. Yet there's no scene in which the Doctor says "Daleks, what are they?", so it is feasible that he may have been told of them in passing. His expression on hearing the word "Dalek" might be interpreted as horror, and compare with the

Monk's reaction in 3.4, "The Daleks' Master Plan".]

Here the Doctor claims that he was a pioneer once, 'amongst my own people'. [Since the previous story implied he had a part in building the TARDIS, this might have been intended to hint that he was one of the first of his kind to explore space and time. Later stories seem to deny this.] He says he's too old for that sort of thing now, and too far from home, but he envies the Thals' chance to rebuild a world of their own.

• *Ethics*. Very murky, although he's still determined to get his own way, even if it means resorting to childish behaviour. When Ian and Barbara insist on leaving Skaro, he's prepared to sabotage the Ship in order to explore the interesting-looking city there, his main priorities being a keenness to learn and an obsessive need to protect Susan. At first he's prepared to leave Barbara to her fate in the city, as long as he and his granddaughter get back to the TARDIS.

In fact, the Doctor seems to go through something of a conversion here. At first he's content to leave the Thals to their fate, but when captured by the Daleks and told of their plan to irradiate the planet, he angrily complains that it's 'murder'. Once the Daleks are defeated, he instinctively goes to check the reactors to make sure there's no leakage, apparently not out of pure self-interest. Indeed, at this point he sounds less than interested in getting the Ship working again, and later he even analyses the local soil for the Thals' benefit. Again, there's no hint that he sees it as his duty to protect history, and at one point - before, it seems, he realises quite how awful they are - he even offers the Daleks the secrets of the TARDIS in exchange for his life and that of Susan. [We'll never see this happen again. Considering everything we learn later, he may be bluffing.]

• *Inventory*. Aside from his hat, the only addition to the Doctor's wardrobe is a pair of spectacles [he becomes short-sighted again when he's older / younger, in 19.1, "Castrovalva"]. He carries binocular goggles [apparently auto-focusing], a walking-stick and a torch, but not much else. [But the torch isn't just *any* torch. It's evidently self-recharging, and about five times as powerful as anything commercially available, on top of which it may well be the same prop used to represent the original sonic screwdriver in "Fury from the Deep" (5.6).]

Who *Really* Created the Daleks?

...continued from page 27

ing the survivors to encase themselves in metal was all Nation's work. Well... not exactly. Remember the rapacious agent, Roger Hancock? His brother was Tony Hancock, the comedian for whom Nation wrote. Tony Hancock dominated British comedy in the 1950s, making decisions that defied the "rules" of radio, and later television. If you go from this essay to look at the one under "The Reign of Terror" (1.8), then you'll get some idea of how influential *Hancock's Half Hour* was.

When Hancock left the BBC, and his writers Ray Galton and Alan Simpson (creators of *Steptoe and Son,* which we've already mentioned), it was as much to do with his ambition to be taken seriously as a thinker and auteur as because of all the cash he was offered. One series he proposed was a bleak comedy history of the world from the cavemen to the apocalypse. He called it *From Plip to Plop,* and in the final episode the last survivors of a nuclear war took refuge in dustbins and evolved into mutants who ate radiation. Hancock's reaction at the Daleks' success was similar to that of

Cusick: peeved amusement, with a bit of admiration for Nation's gall. (It has to be said, though... as a 1950s self-styled intellectual, Hancock was bound to have seen Samuel Beckett's play *Endgame,* in which the last four residents of the world while away their hours in futile power-games. Two of them live in dustbins.)

If we look at the first storyline submitted by Nation, then it's obvious that a lot of the ideas he'd later use are already there, but also that David Whitaker stood over him and insisted on a lot of rewrites. Whitaker was responsible for much of what became Dalek lore, and also wrote the comic strip for *TV 21* (see also 3.2, "Mission to the Unknown" and 25.1, "Remembrance of the Daleks"). While the scarred, desperate technocrats seen in the Daleks' debut were the result of an accidental collaboration between Ray Cusick, Samuel Beckett, the Georgian State Dancers and Tony Hancock, the concept of the Daleks as galaxy-dominating forces of darkness was Whitaker's work. With, it has to be said, some creative input from Adolf Hitler.

The Supporting Cast

• *Ian.* He's started flirting with Barbara [he'll stop doing this properly after a while]. Even when paralysed by the Dalek ray, he believes it's his manly duty to go to the Ship and retrieve the phial of drugs that's been left there. Here Ian again acts as moral arbiter, reminding the Thals of their past as warriors and urging them into making a stand against the attempt to wipe them out; however, like the Doctor, he only does this when he needs something from the Dalek city. At first he can't bring himself to risk the Thals' lives for his comparatively selfish ends, nor disrupt a society's whole way of life even when it's faced with extinction, but Barbara brings him round.

• *Barbara.* Does all the first-aid duties. Characteristically, she's perfectly happy to go on hair-raisingly dangerous missions in caves with unseen swamp-monsters and precipitous drops. But put her in a well-lit uninhabited city, and she's near-hysterical in ten minutes. She's clearly tempted by Thal attempts to chat her up, and kisses Ganatus goodbye in a way that makes her look as if she's trying to reign herself in. [This is Barbara as potential romantic lead, an idea that's never really developed in the series until younger, less matriarchal companions become the norm.] She

persuades Ian to enlist the Thals to save Susan, herself and the Doctor, apparently having less sympathy with their pacifism. [Neither Ian nor Barbara is entirely consistent here. Some lines of dialogue may have been exchanged.]

• *Susan.* Doesn't argue when Ian says that only the Doctor can operate the TARDIS. Here Susan does her "everyone treats me like a child" routine when nobody believes her story about being groped by something in the jungle, but before long she's cowed and apologising. She apparently trusts the Thals purely because she fancies one of their number, Alydon [something the novelisation makes abundantly clear], but occasionally laughs at the Daleks. Even the thought of people living inside the machine-casings makes her giggle. Once again, wildernesses scare her far more than cities, even machine-like cities full of robot-monsters and surveillance cameras. She's terrified by the prospect of journeying through the wilderness alone, yet when trying to escape the Dalek city, she excitedly helps Ian with the deactivated Dalek casing as if she's a *Blue Peter* presenter.

Susan seems to have a partial immunity to radiation that the Doctor lacks. Even *she's* appalled that the Doctor could play such a dangerous trick as removing the fluid link from the TARDIS.

[Since she generally does what her grandfather says, she doesn't always admit how petty he can be sometimes.] She instinctively wants to help the Thals when they're in trouble, in contrast to the Doctor's 'they're no concern of ours' stance.

The TARDIS   Although the metal plate under the console has temporarily vanished, the main changes are permanent ones. The console room has gained a side-wall covered with banks of computers. This is the fault locator, and it's separated from the rest of the room by a perspex screen. When in operation, the device makes a distinctive noise like an early computer, and there's a constant paper read-out like a seismograph or lie-detector. Once this system has run its diagnostic, the readout lists the malfunctioning component; the fluid link is listed as "K7". An armillary sphere can be seen in the background of the console role [but not the harpsichord / spinette, this time]. When there's a tapping noise from outside, the Doctor responds as if it's the scanner "camera" that's being tapped on. Like everything else in the universe, the TARDIS controls are labelled in English.

The biggest development is that the console room is no longer the whole of the TARDIS interior. Through a door there's a corridor, with living quarters leading off it. It appears that this area includes some kind of wardrobe, with clothes in Ian's size. It definitely includes the food machine. The contraption, the size of a large fridge, has dials on the front denoting numbers and letters; from a school exercise book, the Doctor is able to enter the combinations to create any taste. The machine then delivers a rectangular plate bearing a pale lump, like a white Mars bar, which tastes of whatever was requested. Water comes separately, in transparent plastic bulbs like the ones astronauts used. There's a drug on board that does wonders for headaches, and facilities for running chemical tests.

The fluid link is a small cylinder, partially filled with mercury and located inside the pedestal of the console. Without it the Ship can't go anywhere. The mercury can be refilled if it leaks, but the Ship has no stock of mercury as it's never been necessary. There are spare components on board, yet no replacement link, although the Doctor indicates that the link itself isn't particularly important as long as mercury's available. He removes the link after the Ship begins to take off,

and this stops it dead, causing some shaking. The Doctor speaks of the 'power take-up' rising normally on take-off.

The door to the TARDIS has a complex lock, and it's not just a question of turning the key. There are 21 holes inside it, according to Susan; selecting the wrong one will melt the insides. Also, the whole lock can be removed from the door [it happens in 1.7, "The Sensorites"]. Susan has her own key, on a silver chain, but she doesn't seem to recover it after using it to sabotage a Dalek security device. [If she'd had the key in 1.4, "Marco Polo", then the story would have been a lot shorter.] The Doctor claims he can always make another key [which he does in "Marco Polo"].

The Doctor is confident that if he stays on Skaro and takes accurate readings of the stars to fix their location, then the Ship's navigational systems can be recalibrated and all will be right. [Yet there's no pressure to leave Skaro at the end of the story, and the navigational systems still aren't working after this. The Doctor would, as ever, seem to be talking big.] Susan claims there's a meter connected to a 'great big bank of computers' which records their journeys, and which can take over the running of the Ship and navigate successfully, given adequate data. According to Susan, it isn't that the Doctor doesn't know how to operate the Ship, it's just that he's 'forgetful' [has he forgotten the all-important 'secret' code, mentioned in the last story?].

Here Susan adds a Thal cloak to the TARDIS wardrobe, while Barbara takes some Thal fabric, apparently planning on making a dress out of it. The Doctor takes some specimens, in test-tubes, as his own sort of souvenir.

The Non-Humans

• *The Daleks.* Completism demands a full description, so…

The machine-creatures which occupy the city on the planet Skaro are roughly conical in shape, five feet tall and with a hemispherical "helmet" at the top. Set into this dome are two lights, one on each side, which light up in synch with every syllable they speak. [We'll gloss over the question of how this works, when their words are presumably being translated into English for our benefit. After all, we don't ask why the Thals' lips move in synch to *their* words.] At the front of the dome is the eye-stalk, a rod with five discs halfway along its length and a bulbous end-piece. An iris in the end-piece dilates or contracts like the pupil of a human eye [we won't see this facility in full use again for another forty-two years]. The eye-stalk is attached to the dome by a simple pivot, but the dome rotates 360 degrees, giving a Dalek the potential for all-round vision with only immediate proximity to the base being a blind spot.

Immediately beneath the dome is a mesh grille, covered by what looks like ventilator plates, and beneath that is the reflective metal "collar" on which is mounted the front unit. This unit contains the universal ball-joints for the gun-arm and the telescopic sucker-arm. On the end, usually, is a rubberised cup; this is used to manipulate the Daleks' various devices, and can also be used to hold pieces of very solid-looking paper. Some Daleks can be seen sporting a cutting-tool instead, capable of slicing through the city's doors. The gun is a squat tube with lateral metallic strips, and small flanges emerge in a rapid in-and-out motion when used. Though the weapon can clearly be aimed, there's no visible beam [Daleks don't fire actual rays until 12.4, "Genesis of the Daleks"], and it's possible that one shot can take out several targets. Victims are surrounded by a blaze of light and usually killed, although the rarely-used "paralyse" option causes Ian Chesterton to lose the use of his legs for some hours. Dalek weaponry is capable of blowing up other Daleks.

Under the "collar" are six vertical panels, each with four hemispherical nodes in a line, down to the rubbery-looking skirt at the base. Daleks can move in any direction, and often with great speed and grace. Nonetheless, their culture seems somewhat stunted. Trapped in their sterile, near-functional city, they display little concept of individuality and have an obvious dislike for anything that isn't Dalek-shaped. They're capable of disgust, and express this by wanting to exterminate the Thals, seemingly afraid of anything unlike themselves. When one of the Daleks is manhandled, it starts screeching 'keep away from me' as if it's terrified of having its personal space invaded.

[These aren't the militant, galaxy-conquering Daleks we know from later stories, but a small and clearly terrified faction which desperately wants to get out of its imprisoning city. Working out Dalek history is a nightmare for a later entry, though with hindsight these *do* look like the Daleks who got left behind when the others went off to invade places, and who've since become a less mechanised group. This would explain their occasional

moments of near-poetry. Their interest in the Thal anti-radiation treatment, and the self-disgust implicit in their talk of what the Thals must look like after so long outside, might indicate that deep down these Daleks have a desire to be humanoid again. This is the exact opposite of the more recent Daleks we've seen.]

When the Daleks move, there's a smell like dodgems at a fairground, and if a Dalek is rolled onto a piece of non-conductive material, then it immediately shuts down. It doesn't re-activate when it's rolled off the material, at least not when the lid's open. It turns out that these Daleks run on static electricity, drawing power from the floor and "streets" of their city, and they don't currently have any way of leaving it. In part, this is because they believe the outside world to be too highly-irradiated. The Dalek mutant itself - the machine's occupant - is imputed to be hideous and gelatinous, but only a blackened, scaly, claw-like hand is ever seen. The mutant is small enough to be wrapped up in a cape, and looks distinctly weak once it's removed [the one we see is possibly dying, though the "solo" mutant in "Resurrection of the Daleks" (21.4) crawls around for ages without ill effects].

The metallic, grating voice is apparently a function of the machine, as humans also talk like that when they occupy one, but the staccato monotone in which they routinely speak is evidently the organic Dalek's own doing. They don't all speak at the same speed or at the same pitch.

The inner Dalek sees the world on a screen inside its casing, and when things are seen from a Dalek's point of view, everything looks perfectly normal. [So its visual apparatus isn't wired directly to the brain, and there are no computer-symbols all over its field of vision, as there are in certain Dalek stories made after *The Terminator*. Again, this suggests a more primitive form of machine than those we see later.] The casing is full of controls, and it takes Ian a while to figure out how to use them once he's inside one. Other Daleks can't tell when somebody's hiding inside a casing. The city floor can be magnetised, halting the movement of escaping prisoners "dressed" as Daleks, and the upper levels have windows [potentially a bad move, tactically speaking, so they still have *some* aesthetic needs].

The Daleks know the Thals have somehow survived the radiation outside the city, but don't know what the Thals look like. In the last two-hundred days, the radiation count outside the city has fallen by nearly half [the implication is that the Daleks are somehow responsible for this], but they can't yet leave. During events here, they discover that they've become conditioned to radiation and need it to survive, while the Thal anti-radiation treatment makes them lose control of their functions and then die. Thus, they have to irradiate the planet afresh in order to escape captivity and re-build the outside world. [The radiation-hunger is never addressed in any subsequent Dalek story. This is yet more evidence that the Daleks we see here are "drones", left behind when the main force left Skaro, and who've evolved to need radiation more than most others.]

They don't have any neutron bombs, and it'll take them twenty-three days to make one of a sufficient size, so instead they plan to bombard the atmosphere with radiation from their nuclear reactors. For some reason, this takes a couple of days of preparation and requires a dramatic countdown from one-hundred. In the city are pieces of measuring apparatus which look decidedly Earth-like, involving ink and ticker-tape print-outs; rangerscopes, laserscopes, vibrascopes and videoscopes, which can track Susan as far as the jungle but no further; and a sonic chamber, which appears to have a medical purpose. They also claim to have the capability to grow vegetables in artificial sunlight. The Daleks in the city are apparently controlled by a 'council' [the same sort of structure seen in "Planet of the Daleks" (10.4), but presumably applied here on a much smaller scale].

Like the Thals, it appears that Daleks can read English, even writing "danger" on a piece of paper and sticking it to the radiation meter in their city. [We might conclude that this is being translated for our benefit, but see the connection between Thals and humans under **Planet Notes**.] However, their lifts have the floor numbers in binary rather than Arabic numerals, and their computer programmes are pieces of sort-of-paper covered in what look like multi-coloured squares [the script describes one of them as a "printed circuit"]. They don't know the word "TARDIS", don't seem to comprehend laughter and only have a sketchy idea of individual naming, yet they recognise Susan as a 'child' [later Daleks will use terms like 'small human'] and recognise Barbara as a 'she'. They're capable of beginning statements with 'I feel…', and offer to 'help' each other.

There's breathable air in the seemingly-airtight subterranean city, and the Daleks have 'oxygen distributors'. [Suggesting they breathe oxygen. Later Daleks will be able to move underwater and fly through space without difficulty.] When one of the consoles in the Dalek control room is blown up, the power supply to the city wastes away, leaving all the Daleks immobile and apparently dead. Air and lighting are still functional [and obviously the doors still work, as nobody seems to have any trouble getting out].

When a Dalek dies from power-loss, the eye-stalk points vertically up in an amusing fashion [this won't always be the case in future, sadly].

Planet Notes

• *Skaro.* The twelfth planet in its solar system. Centuries ago there was a neutronic war that created petrified jungles, turned all vegetable matter white and ashen, and killed the animal life on the surface. This life included a spiny, metallic, dog-sized reptile - the Magnadon - which may have attracted other metal life-forms as prey. According to the Doctor, the Magnadon corpse discovered in the petrified jungle seems to be made up of discrete elements, bound together by internal magnetism. Underwater beings mutated, but endured in the gaseous swamps near the lakes. One of these creatures generates its own whirlpools, one is a maggoty thing that takes an interest in Barbara's feet, while another resembles a giant starfish with eyes and is capable of inflating itself to stalk prey. It's unclear whether the thing which grabs Elyon belongs to any of these, or is another occupant of the same glowing, chemically-polluted lake.

On a plain beyond the edge of the jungle, backed by the mountains, lies a white city of spires and audacious arches. This is merely the surface, as the bulk of the metropolis lies miles below ground. On the other side of the city wall, there are mountains, a swamp and the aforementioned lake; the city gets its water from here. It is, of course, the city of the Daleks. As well as the inevitable Dalek control room, equipped with all manner of monitoring equipment and [we're sorry, but it's impossible to suspend disbelief here] decorated with life-sized images of more Daleks, there are miles of corridors, plenty of lift-shafts and various chambers that can be used as cells. These cells contain furnishings for humanoids, and the Daleks have no trouble summoning up food that human prisoners can consume. Other prison areas contain wall-mounted manacles, in the right places for human arms and legs.

The Dalek version of Skaroine history: over five-hundred years ago, there were two races on the planet, the Daleks and the Thals. After the neutronic war, 'our Dalek forefathers' retired into the city, protected by their machines. Most of the Thals perished in the war, and the Dalek city was originally a kind of bomb-shelter. [If the Dalek city was originally a shelter, then was it the Kaled bunker seen in "Genesis of the Daleks"? "Destiny of the Daleks" (17.1) seems to suggest otherwise, but see the essay under that story.]

The Thal version of Skaroine history: the Daleks were teachers and philosophers, yet the Thals speak of them as old enemies [there's little doubt that the two sides fought *each other* in the war, though this is never actually said]. The Thals were a race of warriors, implying that they were the ones who started the conflict. [Note 'race' rather than 'species', indicating that Daleks and Thals may have been different racial groups of the same species. Mind you, in this series 'race' is frequently used wrongly.]

Most of the early Thals - depicted as men with armour and swords in the historical record - died in the one-day neutron war and the rest mutated. But the mutation came full circle, leaving the Thals as pretty as they are today. It took 'hundreds of years', according to the Doctor, who also states that in the case of the Daleks the mutation hasn't completed the circle. Why, the Doctor doesn't know. [As in many other Terry Nation scripts, races seem to have a "genetic destiny" regardless of their environment.] The forebears of the Dalek mutants, the 'original' Daleks, were called Dals in those days.

The blond-haired Thals are now a race so traumatised by the neutronic war that they've become almost incapable of imagining violence. Today's Thal is tall, muscular and pacifistic, and carries a decent supply of anti-radiation drugs [implying that the Thals regularly use these drugs themselves, though that's never explicitly said here]. Even the token speaking female, Dyoni, insists on being blonde and cute. [As with the Thals in "Planet of the Daleks" and "Genesis of the Daleks", the female-male ratio is about seven to one, so we might be assuming a great deal about their reproductive system if we think they're *exactly* like humans.]

The remnants of the Thals' former technology haven't been totally abandoned, and their possessions include neatly-manufactured metal boxes and glass phials. They use electric torches, recharged from the dead Magnadon creatures found in the forests. More importantly, they've kept their historical records on what look like chunky tape-spools, and have a map of several solar systems - as far as their 'regiscopes' could see - printed on a series of hexagonal plates. The Doctor estimates that the records must go back half a million years. [However long the Skaroan year may be... as Skaro is the twelfth planet from its primary, this could be centuries in terrestrial terms. Yet everything else here seems to have been translated for our benefit, so they may be using our time-scale. Also, 'half a million years' is the Doctor's estimate after a brief glance at the spools, and he's given to wild exaggeration. See **History**, and consider the complete rot he says about Dalek history the *next* time he meets them.] Some of the hexagonal plates bear child-like pictures of Thal history, and it's from these that the Doctor pieces together Skaro's past.

[Here it should also be pointed out that the history of the Thals may not be wholly true. Obviously this is very different compared to the history of Skaro given in "Genesis of the Daleks", in which the Daleks are borne out of a thousand-year war which *began* with nuclear-age weapons. If we want to try to reconcile these two histories, then it's easy to see the version given here as a distortion of the facts. After lasting for centuries, the Kaled / Thal war suddenly ended in a single day, when the Kaled city was destroyed by 'distronic' weaponry. It's not difficult to believe that later generations, living on an already-radiation-scarred planet, might have contracted this into a memory of a one-day neutron war. It's worth noting that according to the version of history given here, the war was primarily the Thals' fault; considering their peace-loving nature, this may be a guilt reaction, and much of the history may put the blame on them rather than the Kaleds.

[And note that no Dalek ever uses the word "Dal". Feasibly the Thals might have turned their former enemies into mirror-images of themselves, referring to them as "Dals" instead of "Kaleds" and getting the Kaleds' intentions completely wrong. The Thal belief, that they became mutated but then mutated back, could well be a twisted recollection of the alliance between Thals and Mutos which seems to have taken place by the end of "Genesis". However, if this is the case then presumably there were petrified jungles on Skaro even at the time of "Genesis", though all we see there is quarry-like wasteland. For more, see **What's the Dalek Timeline?** under "The Chase" (2.8).]

On encountering dark-haired strangers, the Thals unthinkingly offer help. The Daleks' xenophobia is incomprehensible to them, as is Ian's suggestion of resistance, at least until he threatens to kidnap a passive Thal female and Alydon unexpectedly discovers the ability to punch him in the face. Not only can the TARDIS crew's first alien friends seemingly communicate in English, they can read letters written to them in the same language, even with Susan's wonky handwriting. More curiously still, Ganatus talks to Barbara about 'one of the customs of your planet… ladies first'. [There are no signs of interplanetary travel anywhere else in this story, and "Planet of the Daleks" - which takes place *after* this - sees the Thals exploring space for the first time. Then again, the TARDIS crewmembers have been hanging around with the Thals for a while when the 'ladies first' comment is made, so Ian may have mentioned it before Ganatus tries to impress Barbara with his knowledge of her culture.]

There's enough radiation on Skaro to make humans very, very sick in a matter of hours, but luckily Thal drugs are effective on the time travellers. After the war, the Thals who survived cultivated small plots of land, and that's how they've survived ever since. But they've had to be careful, as the crops are always in danger. There's a great rain every four or five years, and the present one is overdue, so the 'whole Thal race' has been forced to leave its plateau and go in search of food. The Thals speak of leaving the plateau 'four years ago', although confusingly Susan says that the rain is two years overdue. There's lightning and thunder, but no downpour. The Thals' intention is to make some sort of treaty with the Daleks, even though they have no idea what the Daleks' philosophy is.

With the Daleks defeated, the Thals intend to use the technology in the city to grow food. The Doctor believes the soil isn't as barren as it looks, and that even this generation of Thals might live to hear the birds sing again.

History

• *Dating*. Hugely debatable. ["Planet of the Daleks" is set in 2540 and has the Thals describe the events of "The Daleks" as taking place 'gener-

ations' ago, indicating some centuries at least as the Doctor's existence has passed into myth. So it can't realistically be any later than 2300. In "The Dalek Invasion of Earth" (2.2), the Doctor makes the extravagant and not-remotely-true claim that "The Daleks" took place 'millions of years' in the future - again, something utterly contradicted by later events - although at the very least, the tenuous implication is that "The Daleks" occurs after "The Dalek Invasion of Earth". But honestly, almost any date between the 1960s and 2300 would fit. It can't be *too* close to Ian and Barbara's native time, however, since in "The Edge of Destruction" (1.3), the Doctor describes the travellers' last adventure as taking place in 'the future', hence his reason for using the fast return switch.

[And here it's worth mentioning that one of Terry Nation's synopses for "The Daleks" sets a date of "the twenty-third century", which gels perfectly with his later script for "Planet of the Daleks". Though this date is by no means canonical, it works at least as well as any other. Since there's a *Doctor Who* tradition of setting stories exactly x-hundred years after the year in which they were written, for now this volume will fatuously suggest that 2263 would suit "The Daleks" nicely.]

The Analysis

Where Does This Come From?   You'd have to be blind and stupid not to notice the Post-Nuclear Holocaust cliché-counter rising as fast as the radiation meter on the TARDIS, but there's an unexpected influence on this story: J. R. R. Tolkien.

When David Whitaker commissioned the script, he pointed out that it seemed like a chapter in a much longer story about a whole world, rather than a planet made up to tell one tale and make one point. This isn't something Tolkien invented, but in the publicity surrounding *The Lord of the Rings* in the 1950s, it was a feature mentioned by a lot of critics. Tolkien himself noted it in the many interviews he gave before it all got too much for him, and Nation echoes Tolkien on many points in his own publicity material.

On-screen, the biggest hint of Tolkien is the Lake of Mutations, and its obvious similarity to the scene in *The Lord of the Rings* in which an unseen tentacled monstrosity lies waiting in a lake near the gates of Moria; like the Daleks, the forces of darkness use the local wildlife to guard the entrance to their citadel. But a bigger clue is the much-derided 1965 cash-in, *The Dalek Pocketbook and Space Travellers' Guide*. In amongst all the maps of Skaro - containing a Sea of Rust, an Ocean of Ooze and a continent called "Darren" - is a glossary of the Dalek language, and a chronicle of the world's history which Nation claims to have found and translated. Not even *Dan Dare*, a more overt and frequently-cited source for this story, went overboard on this level of background. (The glossary is particularly significant here. Part of the reason for the apparent "depth" of Tolkien's world is that he invented the Elvish language first and *then* came up with a story that might involve it, although it's hard to imagine Nation writing "The Daleks" as an excuse to use the word "rangerscope".) And in the '60s, *The Lord of the Rings* was also read as a nuclear parable in certain quarters, despite Tolkien's protests to the contrary.

We've mentioned *Dan Dare*, and much of what we could say about the influence of this very English sort of comic-strip on *Doctor Who* will be explored under "The Rescue" (2.3). But in the case of "The Daleks", it's high time we mentioned its Yankee forerunner, *Flash Gordon*. Saturday-Morning Serials are an obvious influence on the twenty-five-minutes-and-cliffhangers format of *Doctor Who*, especially when Terry Nation's involved. For all his seriousness of intent here, scratch any Nation story and you'll find either a *Flash Gordon* or a Rider Haggard squirming under the surface. Nobody else would give his episodes adventure-functional titles like "The Escape", "The Ambush" and "The Expedition". And as we'll see when we get to "The Keys of Marinus" (1.5), Nation had a fascination with all things American. The shiny future-cities of the US adventure serials were just bigger versions of New York, at least to people who didn't actually *live* in New York, and here we have a post-War British writer giving us a city that's a gleaming metropolis on top and a bomb shelter underneath.

It's also worth considering the original comic-strip incarnation of *Flash Gordon*, in which the ideal environment for a lurid outer-space adventure isn't a black-and-white set made from recycled props - like the '30s movie version - but a gaudy, misshapen jungle. Directly or indirectly, this is where the surface of Skaro seems to come from. There's at least as much from comic-strips in this story as there is from any other kind of pulp adventure, though it's not as clear as it should be simply because it's shot in monochrome. Cartoon space-jungles, as depicted by Alex Raymond (best known for his *Flash Gordon* work) and later Frank Hampson (he created *Dan Dare*), are supposed to be the colour of forbidden fruit. But this is a black-and-white story, so Skaro's vegetation has to be 'white and ashen'. You only have to look at the colour-era remake, "Planet of the Daleks", to get some idea of the kind of jungle Nation would rather be playing with (natives wearing purple animal-furs, for pity's sake... although how much of this is the writers' work, and how much the director's, is open to question).

A slightly more highbrow influence here is that of the Victorian Utopianists. As the nineteenth century ended, there was an explosion of moral and political tracts that liked to disguise themselves as visions of the future. In the red corner was H. G. Wells, with his tendency to stretch aspects of society (imperialism, social stratification, over-specialisation...) over geological timescales and planetary distances.

In the, erm, other red corner was George Bernard Shaw. While Wells' influence on the Daleks is so obvious as to be almost funny - we'll come back to it in a moment - overtones of Shaw are to be found in the Thals, especially their rather arch dialogue and in the rhetorical nature of the story. Anyone who's sat through all five hours of Shaw's *Man and Superman* will recognise not only the City of Millennius from "The Keys of Marinus", but also the overall tone of the Dalek-Thal version of the future. One might also point out that when Wells tried to steal a march on Shaw, in the film *Things to Come*, he depicted a gleaming tomorrow-world built on the ruins of a ghastly scientific war. Any doubt that Shaw was an influence on Nation is dispelled by "The Chase" (2.8), when Ian quotes *The Doctor's Dilemma*.

One thing that pre-War utopias embrace - and which post-War stories would find questionable - is eugenics. Once present-day humanity is viewed as a work-in-progress, not an end in itself, the idea inevitably arises that mankind's future development can be shaped. It might be rough on individuals, but in the long-term and looking at the big picture, the sacrifice is necessary. Today we tend to associate eugenics with Nazism, which isn't wholly unfair but which misses the point. The Holocaust had very little to do with evolution and a lot to do with banal, self-serving tribal politics, yet in Nazism there is an expression of the need to shape human destiny. Hitler didn't arise out of nowhere, but was part of an entire approach to the idea of destiny, humanity and social engineering which had been coming for half a century. Stalinism, fascism, the BBC and the Empire State Building were all manifestations of an idea of the Public Good, to be served by science in the interests of the People, not individual egos. (Is it a stretch to see the Dalek casing as a Volkswagen Beetle with a gun?)

And the Daleks are blatantly Germans. A once-noble race who went mad and destroyed everything, driven by xenophobia, rampant futurism and a military-industrial complex out of control... they even have a Bauhaus-style city, shot like a '30s expressionist movie. Just to make the metaphor more compelling, the Thals are Teutonic and live in the woods. In the earliest versions of the storyline, their names were Germanic before becoming more epically Grecian, and they're the very model of the Nietzschean philosopher-athlete ideal. Antodus is ashamed of his failings, and his brother covers for his apparent "cowardice" in a manner not a million miles away from *All Quiet on the Western Front*. Even the Thals' request for an aid treaty is suggestive, in light of when the Marshall Plan and the Berlin air-lift were still in the public consciousness.

"The Daleks" not only sees the beginning of *Doctor Who*'s obsession with Nazis (for more on which, see **Is This Really About the Blitz?** under 2.2, "The Dalek Invasion of Earth"), but also the start of its obsession with surveillance technology. There's an obvious link between the philosophy of the "great" twentieth-century dictators and the need to keep the masses under constant observation, even if that means getting the population to spy on itself. The Daleks, like all good totalitarians, fill their city with cameras but know virtually nothing about the outside world. By the time of "Genesis of the Daleks", the symbol of the fascist-substitutes has become an enormous eye. Meanwhile, the "moral" provided by Temmosus is that you shouldn't fight the inevitable but you *should* question how inevitable your fate really is ('surprising how often apparent defeat can be turned to victory'), which is a typical piece of stiff-upper-lipness from the British generation that had been surprised to come out of World War Two in one piece.

And as if to prove how tough and manly this stance can be, Ian's advice to the Thals to 'make them respect you' makes him sound like a mouthpiece for every hot-blooded Westerner raised during the Cold War. That's the voice of Kennedy you can hear, or possibly an older Churchill, warning the world about how the Iron Curtain has fallen across Europe. Western leaders liked to use this take-the-fight-to-them tone to stir up public feeling about the advance of the Red Menace, even though memories of World War Two were still powerful and most people wanted to avoid another conflict above all else. Ian's haranguing of the Thals in episode five - when Alydon speaks of the horrors of their past, and Ian insists they can't let the Daleks find a way of leaving their city and attacking - isn't *just* about good-versus-evil (and compare the Thals with the peacenik Dulcians in 6.1, "The Dominators"). Ian even does the "they're after your women!" routine with Dyoni, and Dyoni is suitably impressed by the hunky way that Alydon smacks him in the mouth. Naturally, it's morally sound for the Thals to attack the city, as it turns out that the Daleks are planning to trigger a neutron bomb and kill everybody.

The Daleks themselves may be fascists rather than commies, but the language being used here is a post-War language. This is the rhetoric of people who no longer believe that "appeasement" is an option.

Well, we've already mentioned Wells, so we might as well state the obvious. If all twentieth-century time-travel stories exist in the shadow of *The Time Machine*, then all twentieth-century "alien monster" stories exist in the shadow of *The War of the Worlds*, this one particularly. Wells' Martians are unimaginably hideous octopoid creatures that live in metal tank-bodies and fire death-rays. But this is the early '60s, so George Pal's movie version is still a technical benchmark for screen SF. It's inconceivable that those working on "The Daleks" didn't think of it at some point. Compare, especially, the final shot of the movie (in which one slimy hand of a dying Martian is seen extending from the hatch of an alien vessel) to the slightly more subdued shot of the Dalek mutant extending a claw from under a cloak.

In fact, the film's influence will stay with the Daleks for the rest of their history; Pal's version of a Martian probe is virtually identical to the Exxilon root in Nation's "Death to the Daleks" (11.3), and the movie death-ray kills human beings in such a way that their skeletons become visible as they're knocked off their feet, a standard of Dalek stories from 1988 onwards. Just to rub it in, the Thals here look as if they've walked straight out of Pal's other messing-about with Wells, the 1960 film version of *The Time Machine*.

But beyond all the obvious imagery, it's worth reminding ourselves that this was only the second story broadcast, and that no clear idea yet existed of what would routinely happen in this programme. So while we may see it as "typical", the original viewers had no idea whether the regular cast could survive in this hostile world, and didn't even know whether the Doctor would side with his fellow-scientists, the Daleks. The metaphor of scientists-as-disembodied-brains will crop up repeatedly in the programme from now on (explicitly in Nation's next script, "The Keys of Marinus"), and this has often been part of a cluster of similar ideas about such people being heartless and self-centred. The Doctor begins the story by putting his own interests first, and is constantly self-congratulatory when demonstrating his technical prowess.

Throughout the 1950s, British culture had been increasingly polarised between "arts" and "sciences", despite an attempt every so often to endow a sense of national ownership in exploration, discovery and the "New Elizabethan" overall world-view (see the essay under "The Rescue" for more about this). Gadgets, domestic appliances and prestige were one thing, but the people who provided these wonders were still a breed apart. Sydney Newman's directive that the Doctor should be more clearly denoted as an empirical engineer rather than an aloof theorist is usually thought to have amounted to just one line of dialogue in "The Aztecs" (1.6), but this kind of thinking is in fact at the heart of the programme. He's mysterious because he's after some indefinable goal (and is thus a philosopher / scientist), but he's heroic because he gets involved and puts his skills to recognisable use in the service of others (an engineer).

One more thing to note: it's 1963, and we're in the age of the space-race. The effect of this on *Doctor Who* will make itself clear over time, but it's especially worth noting the way it affects Terry Nation's view of the TARDIS. David Whitaker seems to have primarily seen the Ship as an object of mystery, something very nearly alive (q.v. the next story, and consider also Ian's immediate reaction to the humming police box in "An Unearthly Child"), and from the 1970s onwards it's taken as read that the TARDIS is in some way a mystical artefact. That isn't the case here. At this point, the first few human beings are being sent into space,

and the public is used to the idea that space travel is a hazardous business, and that one faulty component could doom the astro- or cosmonaut at the controls.

It may seem bizarre *now* that a hyper-dimensional object like the TARDIS could be put out of action by a little thing like a leaky fluid link, yet this is the way everybody expected space-rockets to work, and in Nation's view the TARDIS is little more than a jumped-up space-rocket. Compare this with the astonishingly primitive version of the Ship he gives us in both "Death to the Daleks" and "Planet of the Daleks", and consider that this is the story which also shows us the Ship's supply of concentrated space-food, not to mention the astronaut-style space-cups. Once the TARDIS has been established as something more remarkable, a story in which a minor supply shortage jeopardises the crew would seem downright weird (and, indeed, it does… see 22.2, "Vengeance on Varos").

Since we've mentioned the space-food, we may as well point out that the scene in which Ian gets a mouthful of concentrated bacon and eggs is surprisingly similar to the four-course-meal-chewing-gum scene in *Charlie and the Chocolate Factory*. Which Roald Dahl would have been writing at about the time this was broadcast. Not that we're suggesting a causal link or anything.

Things That Don't Make Sense We'll start with the same question that puzzles the Doctor's companion in "The Curse of the Fatal Death" (see the appendix in Volume VI, if you really want to): why does the Dalek city, designed and built specifically for Daleks on the understanding that the Thals have either been wiped out or mutated beyond recognition, have a prison cell with furnishings? And if they haven't seen a living Thal for five centuries, then why do they have guns with "paralyse" settings? [One whimsical suggestion is that they mean to kill Ian rather than paralysing him, unaware that he's rifled the TARDIS wardrobe and found the Cardigan of Rassilon… given the following year's celebration of knitwear (2.7, "The Space Museum" and 2.8, "The Chase"), this isn't as far-fetched as it might seem.] They also use devices that spew out ticker-tape, which must be incredibly messy and awkward for people with no fingers.

Another recurring Dalek concern: if the mutant inside is so small, then why is there room in the casing for a human being? [Later Daleks, e.g. the ones on Christopher Eccleston's watch, fill up the spaces inside with useful gadgets like anti-gravity devices, force-fields and DNA-splicing mechanisms.]

Ian, disguised as a Dalek, bluffs a Dalek guard by telling it that 'the council' wants to question the prisoners. How he's found out that the Daleks answer to a council is a mystery; for all he knows, the city could be run by a Dalek Mayor. Then the Daleks magnetise the floor to stop him escaping, as if they've installed this feature of the city just in case Daleks have to be routinely frozen on the spot for any reason. Indeed, mobility's obviously an issue for them. They're desperate to leave their city, but can't because - they believe - the radiation level is too high. Even assuming that these Daleks have lost the technology to get off the planet, or to build robots capable of scouting out the terrain and learning how the Thals have managed to survive (because somehow they've detected the Thals' existence without knowing what Thals look like)… if they've got the ability to somehow reduce radiation in the vicinity of the city, as episode two suggests, then are they *really* not smart enough to build radiation-proof vehicles and start setting up other homes elsewhere on Skaro? Are they, more importantly, really such rubbish scientists that they haven't *noticed* they're dependent on radiation until now? They're certainly sloppy enough to hand out the anti-radiation drugs to large numbers of their own kind without proper testing.

Despite all the CCTV inside the city, Dalek surveillance beyond city limits is restricted to a series of still photographs, as if they haven't perfected outside broadcast cameras yet. The Daleks' letter to the Thals, when read by Temmosus, sounds oddly different to what the Daleks dictated to Susan [she's a bad secretary]. When desperately trying to warn the Thals that they're walking into an ambush, Ian politely waits for the Thal leader to finish speaking before shouting 'it's a trap'… and just to be even *more* English about it, afterwards he says 'sorry I was late' to a Thal who's just seen large numbers of his people wiped out right in front of their eyes. The Thalettes are dressed suspiciously like Playboy Bunnies and, like the males, don't let impending starvation or genocide stand between them and a trip to the hairdressers (that the males all act like ladies' hairdressers anyway need not detain us). Almost everyone pronounces "antenna" as if it's in the plural.

Why does Antodus volunteer for the Mission of

Death, and why is he selected, given that everyone knows he's afraid of the dark and that they'll be going through caves? And as has already been noted, the Thals don't seem to know how long they've been travelling. Since they apparently don't know about space travel, it's also weird that they leave anti-radiation drugs for the travellers. Even if Alydon saw the TARDIS pop out of nowhere, surely they *must* assume that the TARDIS crewmembers are locals, and have drugs of their own? [It's a ritual greeting.] And if the Thals have only recently arrived in these parts, then why don't they make the obvious assumption that Susan and company are Dals?

How to wipe out the entire Dalek race on Skaro: push one Dalek into one control panel in one room of the city. Considering that the Daleks seen here aren't averse to bumping into things, it's a miracle they've survived *this* long. Afterwards the Doctor believes that Alydon might live to hear birds on Skaro again, as if the wildlife's going to rapidly evolve out of nothing now that the evil Daleks are defeated.

More Billy Fluffs: 'I do hope your effects outside the Ship haven't affected you too much', 'we'll send the big bag lift down for you', and best of all 'I'd like to run a few chests on those'. He gets extra marks for 'sedi-solified', just because it sounds like it *might* be a real pseudo-scientific term.

And how could Ian or Barbara be fooled by the Doctor ducking down behind the console, yanking something out and then calmly announcing that the fluid link's up the spout?

Critique   It's hard to be objective. So much of what we now think of as the show's formula starts here, and so much of what we get will be done less well later. So this story almost exists outside orthodox *Doctor Who*. But…

…what strikes the casual viewer now is how self-confident it all is. There's never any doubt that the filmed inserts, the inlay work and the Daleks will all come off. So much hinges on these details that any flaw would have undone everything. The scripts seem to be planned with no capacity for covering bad effects. "Show, don't tell" is film-scripting lore, but in 1960s TV it's usually a recipe for disaster. Nation had unbelievable luck.

Not just luck, though. Director Christopher Barry's willingness to try effects and techniques would later result in embarrassments like "The Mutants" (9.4), but here he made sure that the visuals would be effective. Note, though, that the most impressive effect (the "wall blistering under Dalek weapons" one) is in an episode directed by Richard Martin. We won't see him get away with quite so much again. Nation put a lot of energy into getting these scripts done quickly, and when you compare this with the perfunctory nature of his later efforts, one conclusion is obvious: his instincts were usually sharper than his imagination. When he has time to do it more thoroughly, he comes up with "The Chase", and his work in the '70s is full of sharp, of-the-moment ideas that end up turning to mulch on the screen. (In "Death to the Daleks", he spots the Von Daniken trend before everybody else but ends up telling a '60s-style space-police-and-Daleks story anyway. In his post-apocalypse series *Survivors*, he latches on to the insecurities of the age but turns them into a very dull programme. "The Keys of Marinus" is a classic example of Nation getting complacent. When he sees what the directors and designers were able to achieve with "The Daleks", he concludes that they can do anything.)

Virtually every scene has something visually interesting in it. The first-ever shot of the Daleks, pulling back from the horrified faces of the TARDIS crewmembers to show them surrounded by incomprehensible *things*, is a work of modern art in itself. One element of particular note to modern viewers is that the use of surveillance cameras and subjective point-of-view shots makes the television-ness of it all look years ahead of its time; it's media-savvy before the term was coined. The Doctor even speaks of knocking out the Daleks' 'television waves'. The script which this story sort-of-replaced, "The Masters of Luxor" - see **The Lore** - also has a fascination with visual technology, hinting that it may have been the script editor's pet obsession rather than the writer's.

This in mind, it's worth re-considering David Whitaker's own scripts for the series. "The Evil of the Daleks" (4.9) essentially has the Daleks set up their own game show, while "The Enemy of the World" (5.4) gives us a whole plot that rests on surveillance and the power of TV to create false worlds. Whitaker may have been more aware of the "architecture" of the visual media than he's usually given credit for.

But this is what makes "The Daleks" watchable today. Skaro isn't just a lot of sets and character actors, but a light-and-soundscape, a series of connections between images, noises and alien spaces. Yes, the cornball storyline is merely adequate, in places the dialogue is truly excruciating and episode six is padding beyond all sense and reason, but really the script's just a pretext for the work of Ray Cusick (see **The Lore**), Brian Hodgson (handling special sounds) and Tristram Cary (handling the incidental music). It's not just that the Daleks never went away. Forty years on, people can still remember being dragged off to their natural habitat the *first* time.

The Facts

Written by Terry Nation. Directed by Christopher Barry (episodes one, two, four and five) and Richard Martin (episodes three, six and seven). Ratings: 6.9 million, 6.4 million, 8.9 million, 9.9 million, 9.9 million, 10.4 million, 10.4 million. See how this series catches on.

Supporting Cast John Lee (Alydon), Alan Wheatley (Temmosus), Virgina Wetherell (Dyoni), Philip Bond (Ganatus), Marcus Hammond (Antodus), Jonathon Crane (Kristas), Gerald Curtis (Elyon); Peter Hawkins, David Graham (Dalek Voices).

AKA... As we'll see later, the 1973 *Radio Times* special on *Doctor Who* - the first publication to even *attempt* to give "proper" names to the early adventures - listed all the stories before "The Savages" (3.9) according to the name of the first episode. The first *book* to name all the stories, the second edition of *The Making of Doctor Who*, didn't take the same tack. Except in this case. It plumped for "The Dead Planet", and as a result, the spawn of the 1970s grew up thinking that was the "real" title. They were a little startled, then, when '80s volumes on *Doctor Who* decided that "The Daleks" was the better option.

However, the production documents of 1963 referred to it as "The Mutants", a name that was never likely to catch on after 1972 for obvious reasons, but which still turns up on rare occasion. It's been suggested that it was meant to be called "Beyond the Sun", but this title also seems to have been used in at least one draft of Malcolm Hulke's abortive story "The Hidden Planet", so the two may have become confused. See also the next story...

Episode Titles   "The Dead Planet", "The Survivors", "The Escape", "The Ambush", "The Expedition", "The Ordeal", "The Rescue" (this last one becomes ever-so-slightly confusing, from Season Two onwards).

Cliffhangers   Trapped in the metallic city, Barbara cowers from something that extends a sucker-like sensor in her direction; Susan, exhausted and terrified, stands at the open doors of the TARDIS and prepares to step back out into the storm-lit jungle; after our heroes remove a Dalek mutant from its casing, a claw-like hand emerges from the cloak in which they wrapped it; on the verge of going back to the TARDIS and leaving the planet, Ian realises that the fluid link is still in the city; Elyon (Fall Thal #1) is pulled into the whirlpool at the Lake of Mutations, with a horrible scream; Antodus (Fall Thal #2) drops into an abyss in the cavern, the rope pulling Ian down after him.

The lead-in to the next story: there's an explosion in the TARDIS console room, and the Ship is plunged into darkness.

The Lore

• Anthony Coburn, who'd written the final choice for the debut story (see the essay under 1.1, "An Unearthly Child"), was commissioned to write the second story as well. This yarn - entitled either "The Robots" or "The Masters of Luxor" - began with the TARDIS leaving prehistoric Earth to land near a futuristic building on a mountainside, and featured "perfect" robots outwitting their creators and absorbing human life-force. David Whitaker kept trying, as late as November 1964, to get this script into useable shape. (Titan books published the script in 1992, so you can judge for yourself whether it could have worked, but its insistence on bringing Christianity into things may have been a problem.) The fault locator is a legacy of this script. With the dispute over the financing of the TARDIS set rumbling on and Donald Baverstock threatening to pull the plug on the series before the first episode aired, the decision was made to move "The Robots" to the fourth slot, still to be directed by Rex Tucker.

• Meanwhile, Whitaker got in touch with his agents. This was a collective, Associated London Scripts, whose "star" writers were comedians Spike Milligan and Eric Sykes. One of Whitaker's colleagues there, Dennis Spooner, recommended Terry Nation. Nation had adapted stories by Clifford Simak and Philip K. Dick for ITV's *Out of This World* anthology series (if you've just read the essay after "An Unearthly Child" then this will seem particularly incestuous), and Nation was in the middle of being fired by Tony Hancock, after a disastrous live tour following the lukewarm reception of the ATV *Hancock* series. Nation had been asked to write for that series by... Dennis Spooner.

• Nation's original concept was that the war between the Dals and the Thals had been started by a third party, outsiders from another world. The attempts by these off-worlders to send a peace envoy stirred up further trouble, as each side thought the other was launching a missile. No sooner had the commission come than Sykes offered Nation work on a comedy special to be broadcast from an Anglo-Swedish cruise liner, and as Nation found this brief more interesting, he banged out his *Doctor Who* scripts one per day for a week in August. Thus they were ready, and in fairly close to broadcastable shape, long before "The Robots" and "A Journey to Cathay" (see 1.4, "Marco Polo"). Due to the decision by Lambert to make this a seven-part story, the deadline of thirteen episodes for a possible "exit strategy" led to Whitaker commissioning himself to write a two-part story. Hence 1.3, "The Edge of Destruction".

• Jack Kine, head of Visual Effects, had decided that the timetable and budget of *Doctor Who* wouldn't allow his team to provide satisfactory work. He recommended various external contractors, so Lambert decided that the set designer should conceive the various items and tender out their construction. The firm Shawcraft Models, of Uxbridge, was contacted. They'd go on to do a lot of work for the first five years of the series.

The original designer allocated to the story, one Ridley Scott, left a week before to go to Granada Television in Manchester and train in directing. Scott was one of the people with whom the new designer, Ray Cusick, discussed the Dalek design when the brief was given to him; like Nation, Pinfield and Lambert, Cusick wanted to avoid any hint that it was a man in a suit. (Fifteen years later, Scott had the same problem with *Alien*.) A desultory phone conversation with Nation raised the point that the Georgian State Dancers moved as if they were on wheels. From this Cusick developed the "pepper-pot" look, although he's always stressed that the design wasn't actually inspired by kitchenware.

• Shawcraft's first attempt at the model city was small and seemed a bit… '50s. Photos make it look like something knocked up on *Blue Peter* (to be fair, 1950s plastic bottles were designed to appear space-age, so anything else attempting this "futurism" would inevitably end up resembling a pile of detergent containers). The revised version, made possible by the remount of the first episode, was more to Cusick's liking.

• The episode had to be made again because the signal of the production gallery's messages to the floor staff had been "induced" onto the recorded soundtrack. The remount only required the cost of hiring the four regulars for an extra week; most of the other costs were saved, as they reused the sets and props, and the staff were on contract anyway. This meant all sorts of financial juggling, even when the series was reprieved by Baverstock, and various complications arose whenever one of the four principals took a week off.

By this point they'd had to remake *two* episodes (see "An Unearthly Child"), so by the time "The Daleks" was in the can, the original thirteen-week contracts were up and all renegotiations were complicated by a BBC policy about spending in any given fiscal year. It was all horribly complicated, and was only really resolved with "Mission to the Unknown" (3.2), Lambert's swan-song as producer.

• Although Jacqueline Hill had let it be known through her agent that a film offer had come up, and that she might be leaving in January, this seems to have been a negotiating position. The extra week of production on this story made it unlikely that Hill could leave the series in time to start the movie. Out of loyalty, she avoided burdening Verity Lambert with all of this, and contacted Donald Wilson. He used the threat as a bargaining chip, and Baverstock agreed to extend the series to twenty-six weeks on the same budget. However, a fresh problem was to come from an unlikely source…

• … Sydney Newman took one look at the script and blew his top. The Daleks were, in his view, the very thing he'd expressly demanded should never be in this series: Bug-Eyed Monsters. Lambert countered vigorously that the Daleks were primarily characters and a state of mind, not BEMs per se. Meanwhile incoming director Richard Martin, whose background was in avant-garde and fantasy directing, thought Lambert was being too conservative in her approach. Once the story was broadcast, Newman decided that Lambert was cannier than he was, and stepped back until the crisis at the end of the third year (see 3.7, "The Celestial Toymaker" et seq). On the other hand, Martin and Lambert would clash repeatedly over the next eighteen months.

• When asked how he came up with the name "Dalek", Terry Nation blah blah blah telephone directory blah blah blah "Dal" to "Lek" blah blah blah but in fact no 'phone directory in the world blah blah blah those letters.

• Alydon's ghostly hand, in the first episode, is actually that of floor manager Michael Ferguson. He's also the one holding the Dalek arm at the end of episode one, and operating the Dalek mutant at the end of episode three (see 3.10, "The War Machines", for what he did next). He was picked because he had an Equity card.

• A number of techniques were investigated for the Dalek voice-effect. The Post Office had an electronic character-reading device which synthesised a voice, and some prototype vocoders. The former sounded great, but needed ages to program and was impractical for studio work with actors. In order to cut out post-synching, the Daleks had to speak in real-time to the actors playing humans. But in a radio serial a few months earlier, Brian Hodgson of the BBC Radiophonic Workshop had used reconfigured ex-Post Office equipment to break a human voice into 30 pulses per second. The Ring Modulator, as it was called, was reused to achieve the Dalek sound.

• Actors Peter Hawkins and David Graham supplied the voices. Hawkins was also responsible for the voices of Bill and Ben the Flowerpot Men, and Captain Pugwash, and Daddy Woodentop, and Sir Prancalot, and Bleep and Booster… basically, he *was* BBC children's TV in the 1960s. David Graham did voice-work for Gerry Anderson shows, and his finest hour was as Parker from *Thunderbirds*. See "The Gunfighters" (3.8) and "City of Death" (17.2) for his two on-screen appearances in *Doctor Who*.

• Christopher Barry had worked with Tristram Cary before, on *No Cloak, No Dagger*. Carey had done conventional film scores, for *The Ladykillers* among others (that's the good one with Alec Guinness and Peter Sellers, not the Tom Hanks insult to common sense), and had experimented with atonal electronics. The challenge of combining the two was appealing and, as only one person was needed, he'd be cheap.

• William Russell claims that nobody was terribly impressed when the Dalek props were unveiled. However, once the operators had demonstrated what happened when they moved, everyone wanted a go at "driving" one. Hartnell immediately realised that children would enjoy seeing this sort of thing. Any doubts within the BBC were dispelled when Controller of Programmes Huw Weldon announced that his son Wynn and daughter Sian had spent the weekend with waste-paper baskets on their heads, exterminating people. We'll be hearing more about this family (see 3.4, "The Daleks' Master Plan")…

1.3: "The Edge of Destruction"

(Serial C, Two Episodes, 8th - 15th February 1964.)

Which One is This? Two episodes of nothing but TARDIS, with no monsters, no external threat and no apparent logic. But it *does* have the regular cast acting quite irregularly, losing their memories, trying to kill one another, running with scissors and pointing at things in terror.

Firsts and Lasts Most obviously, it's the first and only *Doctor Who* story which involves no characters except the regular cast and no sets except TARDIS interiors (well, at least until the end, and the cliffhanger into the next story). But it's also the first sight of the sleeping arrangements on the Ship, the first time the Doctor namedrops anyone famous from history and the first story to use stock music throughout. And, joy, oh rapture unconfined; it's the debut of Barbara's "battle-dress" of big jumper, capri-pants and court shoes. (This isn't just us being facetious. The production team called it that, and Ian says so on screen in 2.8, "The Chase".)

More crucially, it's the first time we have any indication that the TARDIS is intelligent, aware and possibly even a bit psychic. Meanwhile, for the first example of *truly* shocking over-acting in the series, you might want to watch William Russell falling over and going '*uuuuhhhhh*' at the start of episode two. This is apparently "fainting".

Two Things to Notice About "The Edge of Destruction"…
1. As you might expect, this is the cheapest-

ever *Doctor Who* story. But that wasn't the original objective. The basic premise was that after a story set in the past and a story set in the future, the programme should try one "sideways" in time, preferably a two-parter to make up the thirteen episodes the series had been granted at the time of writing (see **The Lore**). In short, this was potentially the end of the series, and they wanted to make a suitably inventive exit. So all four of the regulars go way out of character, and three of them return to normal - we only count "three", because they craftily re-configure the Doctor's personality right under our noses. Each of the four travellers contributes to the solving of the problem according to their character notes, but it's the Doctor who actually learns something, not only about the human "stowaways" but about the TARDIS as well…

2. Susan, in her psychic distress, screams something about the Ship being haunted by 'shadows'. Unfortunately, this alerts the viewer to the twin facts that (a) the boom mike is very obviously casting a shadow at the time, and (b) William Russell and Jacqueline Hill end up standing between a spotlight and the wall of the TARDIS set a few moments later. As this happens at a point in the story when everybody's under the impression that something has infiltrated the TARDIS, anyone unaware of the *real* plot might think this is a tremendously clever creepy effect.

The Continuity

The Doctor Again, Ian examines him while he's unconscious, and speaks of his 'heart' being all right. Faced with what he believes to be certain death, the Doctor is dignified and prepared to accept his fate, even lying to the womenfolk about how long they've got left in order to spare their feelings. Unlike Susan, he doesn't know where all the TARDIS controls are on the console, and needs his glasses to find the fast return switch.

• *Background.* For some reason, the Doctor got an Ulster cloak from Gilbert and Sullivan, and it's much too big for him. [He only says that he 'acquired it' from them, not that they gave it to him voluntarily. Perhaps the entire TARDIS wardrobe is the result of his career as a celebrity stalker. Gilbert and Sullivan worked together between 1871 and 1900, so this is the first of many, many indications that the Doctor's spent time hanging around Victorian Britain.] Prior to spending time on Earth in 1963, the Doctor and Susan visited the planet Quinnis in 'the Fourth Universe' [see 4.9, "The Evil of the Daleks", for further discussion of this strange terminology]. Susan says Quinnis is where they very nearly lost the TARDIS, four or five journeys back.

Another detail worthy of note is that as the Doctor regains consciousness, he mutters: 'I can't take you back, Susan. I can't.'

• *Ethics*. Even with none of the TARDIS crewmembers acting in a way that's entirely sane, the Doctor refrains from killing directly. He threatens to put Ian and Barbara off the Ship instead, without knowing what's outside or whether it's possible for human beings to survive there. His paranoid belief that someone's trying to sabotage his Ship doesn't seem to be *entirely* the result of unusual stress. The Doctor's position of moral autonomy [as demonstrated in the first story of this series] is restated here: 'One man's law is another man's crime.'

The Supporting Cast

• *Ian*. Wears boxer shorts. By now, he's evidently been shown how to operate the bed-switches on board the TARDIS.

• *Barbara*. She's already fairly familiar with the console layout. She speaks of 'going to bed' on the TARDIS as if she's used to it by now, and as if she already has a room marked out as her quarters.

• *Susan*. Has changed her clothes. [The only definite sign that any time has passed since leaving Skaro, as the others are in the same clothing they've had since the latter part of "The Daleks", though Barbara's still clutching her Thal fabric when the crisis begins.] Susan's the one most affected by events here, viciously stabbing a sofa with a pair of scissors. [And apparently thinking of Ian as she does it. Considering the telepathic gift she reveals in 1.7, "The Sensorites", it's not surprising that she's the hardest-hit by all of this.]

The TARDIS The Doctor describes his Ship as having a built-in defence mechanism, but claims it can't think. Later he admits that it *can*, though as a machine thinks, not as a human being. He seems to be learning things about this vessel which he's never considered before [our first hint that he wasn't the prime mover behind its construction]. Its "mind" obviously isn't very logical, as the Doctor's reason can't spot the clues it provides, but Barbara's intuition can.

The TARDIS' power source is referred to as the 'heart' of the Ship. The column at the centre of the console is directly over it, and if even a fraction of this power were to break free, then everything else would be annihilated. The column only moves when the power is 'on', and the Doctor believes it's impossible for it to move otherwise. When it rises, it 'proves the extent of the power-thrust'. The column holds the power down, as the energy wants to escape [there's a hint here that the power-source itself is conscious], but it'd take a 'magnetic' force as strong as an entire solar system to let it get out. When this looks likely, the Doctor speaks of them having five minutes to survive [as if it's a known problem for TARDISes].

The metallic plate beneath the console has returned, as has the ceiling-mounted hexagonal unit. Here there's also the first clear sighting of the drum-like lighting units suspended from the ceiling behind the scanner monitor [their precise function is unknown, but see "The Moonbase" (4.6) for a popular theory]. The scanner is mounted on a frame, which is on castors. [Both this and the "drums" were present in the last story, but only partially visible.] When things go wrong, the Doctor speaks of being worried about the 'main unit'. Ian mentions the 'control column' as if it's a phrase he's picked up off the Doctor.

On the console, near the scanner controls, is the fast return switch. It's easy to spot this switch, as it's marked "fast return" in marker pen [this may be a recent modification by the Doctor, but for Heaven's sake...]. After leaving Skaro, in 'the future', the Doctor used this switch to try to get back to Earth in the twentieth century rather than setting co-ordinates. [So contrary to later fan-lore, such as the novel *The Witch Hunters*, it *doesn't* cause the Ship to return to previous destinations - which would let the Doctor get Ian and Barbara back home in no time at all - but simply to hurtle the Ship backwards through time at great "speed".] The crisis on the TARDIS is caused by the switch becoming stuck in the down position, so the Ship is tumbling backwards towards the start of a new solar system. This 'strong force', as the atoms rush towards each other and fuse to create matter, is enough to destroy the Ship. [Feasibly it might be the gravitational forces involved which put the vessel at risk, though the Doctor doesn't put it that way. See **How Indestructible is the TARDIS?** under 21.3, "Frontios".]

In refusing to let the Ship be destroyed, the Ship's defence mechanism arranges most of the curious events here in an attempt to warn the crew of the problem. It starts with an explosive flash in the console room, which causes the lights to dim and knocks everybody out. When the passengers recover, they briefly suffer from partial amnesia, and for some time behave in an unusually paranoid and erratic way. [Conventional fan-wisdom is that the Ship is somehow making them behave oddly, but this may not be the intention of the script. Much of it could be stress and paranoia rather than telepathic manhandling.] At first, the fault locator reveals no problem - as the fast return switch isn't *faulty*, just stuck - but odd things keep happening. The food machine malfunctions. The doors keep opening and closing. Images and sounds are relayed by the scanner which have nothing to do with what's outside: England [the countryside, implying that the TARDIS may have been there at some stage], then Quinnis, then a sequence pulling away from a planet and revealing a galaxy. Then the clock in the console room melts, along with Ian and Barbara's wristwatches.

It seems that most of these things form a message, telling the crew that time's running out. As the end grows near there's a 'danger signal', apparently from the locator, which sounds like a very loud and annoying klaxon [something rather more distinguished is in operation by 18.7, "Logopolis"]. When a component fails on the Ship, a bulb lights up on the fault locator, but now the *whole* of it lights up. From this the Doctor knows the Ship's on the point of disintegration. Though the part of the console where the fast return switch is located is safe, anyone touching the other panels receives what feels like a blow to the back of the neck. All of this ends, and normal lighting returns, when the Doctor repairs the spring in the switch.

When the Ship's systems offer images via the scanner, the Doctor mentions the memory-bank that records their journeys. The photographs are accompanied by sounds: the English countryside has birdsong, and Quinnius has space-jungle noise. [The development of a solar system is accompanied by spooky music, so possibly the Ship has a music library. See 6.2, "The Mind Robber", for a similar incident.] When in flight, the doors shouldn't open [see 2.1, "Planet of Giants", for one unfortunate consequence of this], but when they open spontaneously it's to a blank white void [see also "The Mind Robber"; 18.5, "Warriors' Gate"; 16.1, "The Ribos Operation"; 5.4, "The Enemy of the World"].

Near the food machine is a leather settee and a low, circular coffee-table. Behind these, in a room with a window which has been darkened, is a bedroom. Two - possibly three - sinusoidal beds fold down from the wall at the touch of a switch. There's a small dresser nearby, with a first-aid kit; in this are medicated bandages, the darkened bands of which fade as the ointment is taken up by the patient, and some long-bladed sewing-scissors. At one point the Doctor deals with Ian and Barbara by slipping a sleeping drug into their tea.

The Doctor describes a 'rather extensive wardrobe' on board, with nice, snug clothing for missions on cold planets. Working from the console, the Doctor can't even tell when the TARDIS has landed on Earth.

Planet Notes

• *Quinnis, in the Fourth Universe*. Judging by the photo on the TARDIS scanner, it's an overgrown sort of world with tall and unpredictably-shaped trees. The noises of Quinnis make it sound like a typical jungle planet, with the usual animal and bird screeching.

The Analysis

Where Does This Come From? If you think it looks a bit stagey, then you're right. The obvious precedents for this story are mostly plays. From the point-of-view of characters trying to figure out who they are and what they're doing there, we can cite Luigi Pirandello. His *Six Characters in Search of an Author* made an enormous impact on a generation of playwrights. Even if you've never seen it, you've seen things influenced by it; this is a form of drama that isn't about an "actual" place or time but about the process of drama itself, where the stage is nothing *but* a stage, the characters know they're characters, and the theatre is a venue for exploring the limits of the theatre. The TARDIS, being set apart from the normal span of space and time, is theoretically the ideal setting for this sort of messing-about.

Another theatrical role-model is J. B. Priestley. For a while, just after World War Two and his Sunday evening radio talks (which were avidly listened-to in bomb shelters), Priestley was the most famous writer in Britain. What a lot of his fans might not have realised was that he was heavily influenced by odd theories about time, notably the ideas of J. W. Dunne and Henri Bergson.

What Makes the TARDIS Work?

Well, for a start, we're not going to say "The Eye of Harmony". According to "The Deadly Assassin" (14.3), this mysterious force is to be found on the Doctor's homeworld and lies at the heart of all time-travelling power, which may or may not mean that TARDISes literally "tap" it whenever they go anywhere. According to the TV Movie (27.0), every TARDIS has an Eye of its own. According to fan-lore (and, all right, the novelisation of the TV Movie), that means the one on the TARDIS is just a conduit for the big Eye back home.

Maybe it is, maybe it isn't. The exact location of the fuel supply isn't the issue. And if we're talking about TARDIS-power, then it seems inescapably true that we're talking about two separate power-sources anyway. One runs the Ship's systems, life-support, fault locator and so on, while the other sends the Ship through time and space. The former can be tapped, occasionally, for powering other things (as we see in 3.1, "Galaxy Four"). We're not really very interested in this, and it could be a peat-fired turbine for all we care; after all, if you've got the resources of the whole of universal history at your disposal then it's not as if you're going to run out of peat.

More interesting is the time-travel facility, Eye-of-Harmony-related or not. In "The Edge of Destruction" it's strongly hinted that there's a power-source under the console which is somehow alive, attracted to large gravitational fields and capable of destroying the Ship if set free. And intriguingly, it gets more and more dangerous as the travellers go further and faster back in time. In "Castrovalva" (19.1) a nearly-identical scenario shows us something called 'the time-force', which is like mega-gravity, from the field of the Big Bang. "The Wheel in Space" (5.7) hints that somehow mercury is important in all of this, not just as a means of making intermittent connections but because of its curious magical properties. (We'll explore the strange world of Whitaker Science under "The Wheel in Space", but it's not for the faint-hearted or the scientifically-literate.)

Let's assume, for the moment, that the power in question is that wonderful stuff known as artron energy ("The Deadly Assassin" again, and 19.2, "Four to Doomsday"). A quick glance at the possible odd effects of this - **What *is* the Blinovich Limitation Effect?** under 20.3, "Mawdryn Undead" - would seem to suggest that it's a by-product of "collapsing" waves of probability. If you're up to speed on quantum physics, then you should know what's coming next. If not, then it's too complicated and weird to explain in detail here.

Just accept for a moment that particles below atom-scale aren't really "particles" but areas of probability, tendencies towards particle-ness, until someone actively looks for them. Once a conscious observer examines the scene, a particle distils itself from the possibility of being somewhere-around-here to being wherever the observer happens to be looking. Well, we said it was weird. So what happens to all that potential for there to be particles? In mainstream quantum theory, the energy of that area is made into mass as the particle resolves. The process is called "collapsing" a wave.

Now, this would seem to fit the bill. As you go further back in time, there's obviously going to be more potential, with more things yet to definitely happen or exist. If the TARDIS has a sort of accumulator battery to soak up artron energy from travelling forwards in time (as things go from possible to actual) and expend it in going backwards, then there'd seem to be a pattern. A logical consequence of this is that the TARDIS can only gain power where there are conscious beings, and it *does* have a remarkable talent for picking out the inhabited planets in the universe. Even given that there seems to be a greater proportion of occupied worlds in the *Doctor Who* cosmos than one might expect, it's notable that - for example - the Ship only ends up straying near Pluto once there are people present (15.4, "The Sun Makers").

And there's another interesting piece of evidence to back this up. The Ship's systems may all run off a different power-source, yet the one part of the "routine" operation of the Ship that's got more to do with the drive than with the lights, the food machine, etc is the door control. After all, this is the interface between dimensions. So we can see that the doors opening in "The Edge of Destruction", or indeed "Planet of Giants" (2.1), is significant. And on two separate occasions, the Doctor is able to bypass a problem with the doors by using his ring (2.5, "The Web Planet" and 3.4, "The Daleks' Master Plan"). What's so special about this ring? We're never told, but very shortly after he transforms into a new man (4.3, "The Power of the Daleks") he discards the ring, after treasuring it as if his life depended upon it.

"Mawdryn Undead" seems to imply that regeneration and time-travel both require large

continued on page 47...

45

Dunne's book *An Experiment with Time* held that linear, chronometer time was a misleading abstraction, and that time flows in different ways for different people at different locations (we'll return to this for 2.7, "The Space Museum"). Meanwhile, Bergson maintained that interior time was more significant than the consensus time of clocks and calendars. Marcel Proust and Virginia Woolf were both influenced by what they thought he was saying.

In the 1930s, Priestley wrote three plays exploring the impact of these ideas on ordinary families. Well, ordinary by theatrical 1930s British standards. *Dangerous Corner* features two different sets of consequences of nearly identical events, and if you've seen *Sliding Doors* then you know the bonehead version; *I Have Been Here Before* investigates *déjà vu*; the most famous of these is *Time and the Conways*. Then, in 1945, he delivered his killer blow. In *An Inspector Calls*, a wealthy family's various connections to the death of a working-class factory-girl are investigated by someone who seems to have an unusual degree of inside knowledge… *before* the girl's suicide is discovered. As we'll see, Whitaker believes time to be more complex, more *proactive* than later story-editors do. For him, time isn't a direction but a force (see **Can You Rewrite History, Even One Line?** under 1.6, "The Aztecs"). If we look at this story from that point of view, then the inference is clear. Internal time - which is where the TARDIS is located - is an attitude, an aspect of consciousness. Thus, memory and clocks can both be affected.

As a self-contained story, this seems to have been devised at least partly to set a puzzle for four generic characters. In this regard we're in the realm of existentialism, again, and Jean Paul Sartre's play *Huis Clos*. (Fortunately "The Edge of Destruction" doesn't go quite as far as the play. Look it up if you don't know it already.) This was not, in early '60s Britain, an obscure source or an elite cultural reference. In an era when four or five plays were broadcast every week, and theatre-going was common, people *knew* about plays. After all, it had been the theatre that set the agenda in the late 1950s. Much of BBC drama was founded on a theatrical tradition. Even those who didn't get out much knew about the plays from the press coverage, and from the way the writers all wound up working for *Armchair Theatre*.

Beyond the stage, there's a strong influence from literary SF here, and for the first time we see

the programme deliberately trying to subvert expectations of the sort of things that happen in science fiction. Much of the plot consists of one whopping great red herring, as Susan sets us up to believe that an alien force has infiltrated the TARDIS and is hiding 'in one of us'. Possession is nine-tenths of SF cliché, and the idea of formless monsters either taking hold of or impersonating humans had long been a standard (we might as well mention John W. Campbell's *Who Goes There?*, just because it'll be an influence on so many later *Doctor Who* stories, directly or otherwise). Here, the audience is half-expected to know this, and to be surprised when the truth turns out to be something else entirely; something which Whitaker obviously felt was a lot more subtle (see the **Critique**).

The fig-leaf of "teach the kids about planetary formation", when we see the sequence on the TARDIS scanner, is particularly perfunctory. However, the graphics closely resemble the "Rite of Spring" sequence from Disney's *Fantasia*, a film with a very BBC-like remit of giving the kids high culture with a sugar-coating of entertainment.

Things That Don't Make Sense We keep coming back to this, but let's start with the obvious: the clock and wristwatches melt. Why do no other functions relying on one-way, linear, entropic processes seem to be affected? We see people eating and drinking, just to give an example. The Doctor's bandage is a timepiece of sorts, so why does his head not explode? Melting chronometers, or at least their faces, is rather specific; any power that can distinguish between these and other mechanisms ought to be able to fix itself. As a method of warning the passengers, what we see here is like setting cryptic crossword puzzles with the answers "the building is on fire" and "run for it". And wiping the memories of the people you're relying on to stop you exploding isn't just "alien", it's downright perverse. [Although the TARDIS has some sort of consciousness, it isn't *intelligent* in the normal sense. Its actions here may be instinctual, grasping at the minds of the passengers in order to get them to act, but not really knowing how those minds work. If this is the case, then the melting clocks may be a result of the Ship probing the humans' unconscious and finding an all-purpose symbol for "time".]

Why does Barbara, who presumably has a limited knowledge of things like TARDIS defences,

What Makes the TARDIS Work?

...continued from page 45

amounts of artron energy. The Doctor's ring would therefore seem to represent some kind of back-up supply, to be used as and when he needs to jump-start the TARDIS or regenerate (as we'll see in Volume II, his first transformation is more complicated and apparently more dangerous than all the others). The other part of the Ship which interacts with the outside world is the scanner, and that's got some odd features too. Its 'collection-field' is said to furnish the Matrix with data (23.1, "The Mysterious Planet"), so the images shown are more than just TV feed from the lamp on top of the police box. They'd appear to be selected from local consciousnesses, where present (see 19.4, "The Visitation", for a noteworthy example).

In pondering all this, a curious thought arises. As discussed under "Planet of Evil" (13.2, **What Does Anti-Matter Do?**), there was once a theory that anti-matter was regular matter running backwards through time. Nobody takes that seriously any more, but what if the direction in which a TARDIS travels affects its relationship with the exterior cosmos? In short, does it attract when it goes backwards and repel when it goes forwards? If so, then by hurtling backwards in "The Edge of Destruction" it may be forcing matter to coalesce, thus creating a solar system. Possibly *the* solar system. And then the Doctor lectures Barbara on changing history in "The Aztecs"…? Honestly.

In "The Edge of Destruction", the Doctor talks about the attraction of the nascent solar system as a 'strong force'. If we get all quantum about it, then there *is* a thing known as the Strong Force, but it only really works inside atoms. There's also a Weak Force, which works over longer distances. The Strong force is repulsive, the Weak force attractive. If travelling backwards in time switches these around, then things could get very odd indeed. In fact, what's the opposite of going from probable to actual? Going from less likely to more likely, i.e. entropy. Artron energy could be some kind of anti-entropy (see **What Do The Guardians Do?** under 16.1, "The Ribos Operation", for why this might be important). Or then again, it could be something altogether weirder, which would be fun.

---

assure Susan that it's not possible for an alien force to have got into the Ship? Why does she then change her mind about it a few minutes later, and make the suggestion as if it's her own idea? How does the Doctor make tea without any water, given that the water comes from the (broken) food machine? Does the TARDIS have separate tea-making facilities? Because it's certainly a very quick cuppa.

Some spectacular Billy Fluffs: 'Don't under-weight… underestimate me!'; 'you rather suspected that I was upset to some mischief'; and of course 'we're on the brink of disgust… of destruction'. (Entertainingly, Ian has to respond with the line: 'Why did you say that?')

Critique There are stories more pointless. There are stories more tedious. What there *isn't* is a story that seems more obviously there to do a job, to fill time before the programme-makers know what's going to happen to this series. There's the spark of a comprehensible (if fairly straightforward) idea, of an alien intelligence which has infiltrated the Ship and is now hiding in one of the crew, but that's misdirection. So the question is: what was David Whitaker *thinking*?

There *is* a good answer to this, and it becomes clear if you compare the way Terry Nation treats the TARDIS in the previous story with the way Whitaker treats it here. From the very first shot of the very first episode, the TARDIS is parked on an uncomfortable line between being a scientific arte-fact and being a magic cabinet. For all Sydney Newman's talk of the programme being rooted in "facts", the door of the police box might as well lead to Narnia, and it's a contradiction that the series never really resolves. In "The Daleks", the Ship is a space-rocket. Not here. It's ironic that this story had the formative title of "Inside the Spaceship", because its main agenda is to try to explain that it isn't one. Whitaker, the man who later informs us that you can build a time machine out of mirrors and static electricity (see 4.9, "The Evil of the Daleks"), likes the symbols of quasi-mystical Victoriana a lot more than he likes any-thing remotely rational. Here we're being present-ed with the TARDIS not as a vehicle that can take the characters from A to B, but as a space where magical things can happen in itself.

We have to say "magical", really. For all our talk of existentialism and twentieth-century theatre, to most viewers this will just look like a world where Vaguely Mystical Things are going on. For these two episodes, this vessel is supposed to look *haunted*. "An Unearthly Child" (1.1, if you still needed to be told that) set out to startle viewers with their first sight of the TARDIS interior, and the aim here is to stop it becoming functional, to make it clear that within these walls the unexpected can still take place. If this looks odd, it's because it's part of a strand that'll be all but abandoned after "Planet of Giants" (2.1), in which nothing is convenient or taken for granted. Even the characters' home base can turn out to have extra dimensions. We won't see this in the series again until "Logopolis" (18.7).

And more than that, it turns out that the TARDIS is intelligent. Virtually everybody who watches the story now misses the importance of this. The ending seems risible because we're looking at the wrong thing; the twist isn't "d'oh, the fast return switch was stuck", the twist is that *the Ship has been communicating*. For anyone who grew up in the '70s, the idea that the TARDIS might be conscious is as natural and as normal a part of things as free school milk, yet here it's a surprise. The whole point of the story is that we're supposed to wonder whether the party responsible for the crisis is one of the crew or an alien force. We're not supposed to notice that the Ship itself is a suspect. Forty years on, it doesn't just look like a suspect but the *only* suspect. We're still a decade away from 'telepathic circuits'.

Contrary to what most critiques of this story claim, it isn't really about the characters at all, but if you *do* pay attention to what the regulars are saying then it just sounds weird. On more than one occasion in the first episode, it's as if the camera's about to execute a whip-pan across the console room and reveal Rod Serling saying 'portrait of four characters in search of some answers…'. The comparison is pointedly in *The Twilight Zone*'s favour. Whitaker seems almost to be writing a morality play about paranoia, using the TARDIS crewmembers to represent different points of view, but it doesn't work because they have the same names and actors as people we've seen in the surprise hit series *Doctor Who*. Ian and Barbara are the reliable baseline against which we measure the worlds and times we visit in the TARDIS. To have them go out of character would be worth trying if the Ship were a safe, familiar setting, but the whole point of this story is that it isn't.

The truth is that even when we've re-set our brains to run on 1963 time, even when we're ignoring the characterisation and looking at this

as an example of a brand of *Doctor Who* that never developed, the story *still* blows it. We get a Ship that becomes a "secret place" again, and then… in the last five minutes, it turns out that the whole crisis has happened because there's a sticky button on the console. Nothing is supposed to be predictable, nothing is supposed to be convenient, yet the problem is made and unmade with the flip of a switch. As a result, the entire story looks like a technical fault. We now return you to normal service.

The Facts

Written by David Whitaker. Directed by Richard Martin (episode one), Frank Cox (episode two). Ratings: 10.4 million, 9.9 million.

AKA… "Inside the Spaceship" or "In the Spaceship". As with the previous story, it's occasionally been called "Beyond the Sun", apparently due to confusion with Malcolm Hulke's abortive story about a doppelganger-planet (see **The Lore**). *Doctor Who Weekly* described it that way as early as issue #3, which misled an awful lot of people.

Episode Titles "The Edge of Destruction", "The Brink of Disaster".

Cliffhangers While creeping around in the control room, the Doctor's suddenly attacked, and a pair of hands moves to strangle him.

The lead-in to the next story: in the snow outside the TARDIS, Susan calls out to the others, having found a footprint which appears to have been made by a giant.

The Lore

• At the time this story was commissioned, the programme's long-term future was in the balance. It was known that if the plug were to be pulled, then it'd happen after thirteen broadcast episodes, so a two-parter was needed. The uncertainty over the series was partially resolved between the commissioning and recording of "The Edge of Destruction", but at this stage it was only given another thirteen weeks. A seven-part story and a six-part story (either Coburn's "Robots" / "The Masters of Luxor" or something by Malcolm Hulke) were on the blocks, but still there was a two-week gap before the director's joining date for "Marco Polo".

• Richard Martin had been engaged to work on the series very early on, during Rex Tucker's fifteen minutes as producer. Before the first episode of *Doctor Who* had been broadcast, during rehearsals for "The Cave of Skulls", Martin prepared some notes on what he thought the TARDIS operating principles might be. Newman succinctly noted these as "nuts". One of them was the suggestion that the TARDIS interior is an effort of will, and that a leap of faith is needed to experience it as anything other than a police box. It's tempting to suggest that much of the first episode of "The Edge of Destruction" conforms to Martin's vision, but the script was David Whitaker's and was faithfully adhered to by Martin and Frank Cox, who directed episode two. The schedule for this story also, at various points, had Mervyn Pinfield and Paddy Russell down as director.

• It was during rehearsals that the most famous unbroadcast Billy Fluff occurred; a line about the fault locator became 'check the fornicator, my child'. It was probably deliberate. The cast seem not to have understood a word of the script, and while Hill claims to have enjoyed all the cathartic yelling, Hartnell resented his long speeches.

• As has already been mentioned, the front-runner for Story E was Malcolm Hulke's proposal about a hidden planet beyond the sun where things weren't quite right. (Fandom has been arguing for years about this non-existent story's non-existent title. Episode two was to have been called "The Year of the Lame Dog", so why not call it that?) It was logical that Hulke would be asked to contribute, as his pseudo-science episodes of *The Avengers* had worked with audiences, if not always with the stars of the series. While Newman was in charge, *Doctor Who* had Hulke's name on it. But Whitaker demanded substantial revisions at short notice in April 1964, and Hulke bailed. Precisely why Whitaker thought a script that had been all-but-abandoned in February was back on the blocks by April is unclear, as is the reason for its postponement. Since the plot hinged on Barbara being the doppelganger of the planet's Matriarch, and since "The Aztecs" was panning out to be a story about Barbara being mistaken for a goddess, it may have been thought unwise to run two such stories back-to-back. However, with "sideways" stories still being contemplated, Hulke's idea wasn't too far from the programme's formula… yet.

• Robert Gould, meanwhile, had proposed a six-part story in which plants were in control of people. He was politely told that it was a bit too close to *The Day of the Triffids*, so he persevered with "The Miniscules". See "The Keys of Marinus" (1.5) for what happened next, and "Planet of Giants" for another reason that Gould was less than entirely pleased by what they went and did without him…

1.4: "Marco Polo"

(Serial D, Seven Episodes, 22nd February - 4th April 1964.)

Which One is This? Once again, the title spells out this story's Unique Selling Point, but this is also the one with the Cave of Five-Hundred Eyes (which scared the willies out of a generation that now half-remembers it being in an outer-space story).

Firsts and Lasts Given that all the business with the cavemen in "An Unearthly Child" seemed to be set in a vaguely prehistoric "anytime", this is really the first story of a breed which later fans will come to know as "the historical". It's certainly the first time our heroes are seen to encounter a Famous Person from History. Two, in fact; Marco Polo is fairly close to the way we imagine him (although a bit more British than expected), but Mighty Kublai Khan is a real surprise.

Another soon-to-be-familiar feature of stories in this era is that William Hartnell takes a week off and vanishes from most of episode two, requiring the other characters to talk at length about how the Doctor is sulking in his tent and won't talk to anyone.

The story also introduces something we'll see a lot in this first year but not so much later on - the one-story companion, in this case Ping-Cho. On top of that, it's the first story to use a genuine, no-kidding villain rather than an out-and-out monster - namely the warlord Tegana. It's also the first "adventure" (presuming the previous story doesn't count as one) in which the TARDIS becomes a meaningful presence in the plot rather than just the thing the characters have to get back to.

It's also the first appearance of Tutte Lemkow, the Hartnell era's all-purpose dodgy foreigner of choice, and episode seven sees the first of the programme's many climactic sword-fights.

A novelty here: it's the first time that real-world

ABOUT TIME 1963-1966

narcotics are mentioned in the series, as Ping-Cho's fairy-tale in episode three is blatantly and unashamedly about hashish. It isn't going to happen very often after this (see 14.6, "The Talons of Weng-Chiang" and... that's about it).

Seven Things to Notice About "Marco Polo"...

1. For reasons we won't go into just yet, this story doesn't exist in the BBC's archives. A decent audio recording exists, as well as a few production photos, some off-air stills of episode six and the odd publicity shot here and there, but it was only recently that director Waris Hussein popped into his attic and found his own collection of telesnaps. (Taking photos of a 405-line screen showing fifty half-frames per second is specialised work. Professional photographer John Cura was hired to provide stills-from-screen of actors who might want a portfolio, but not this early on in the series' run.) With a bit of Photoshop chicanery, some of the production shots - those available before Waris' find, that is - have been turned into a slideshow-style "reconstruction" video[3]; ironically, this makes it the only colour Hartnell story. From this, we discover that Barbara's "Velma out of *Scooby-Doo*" jumper is a disappointingly girly pink.

2. Almost uniquely, this story has a voice-over narrator. Marco's journal is read aloud, by Mark Eden, as a rostrum camera pans across a map of Cathay. This is turned into a plot-point in the second episode, when Tegana contrasts it to sword-practice, and later when Ping-Cho finds the TARDIS key secreted in the one thing Marco never leaves: the book we see him write. Aside from giving us a measure of how much time elapses (episode two takes more than ten days), we're given a means to differentiate between what he says and what he thinks. Thus, on its own terms, this story is about Marco Polo - i.e. the Doctor is one of the obstacles he faces - rather than simply being a *Doctor Who* story with Marco Polo in it. Which means that Marco, and not Ian, gets to do the sword-fight.

3. The *Radio Times* listing for episode three claimed that "the Doctor outwits the Gobi Desert". While this is more or less true, it raises expectations that this is going to be a different kind of story altogether. For the most part, the presence of 1960s British observers (and their time machine) is the only fantasy element in a dramatised-documentary format that was to become one of the two basic set-ups of Hartnell-era *Doctor Who*. Most noticeably, the bulk of this episode is involved in paedogogy. We get a quick physics primer about condensation, a philological footnote on the roots of the word "assassins", a fairy-story told in dance and mime, a tutorial on the use of quartz in sculpture and a tourist guide to Huang Chu's thousand temples.

4. At the time this was made, the main thing that made it stand out from all other Chinese-set stories (and those set in Japan, which were seen by Hollywood and ITV as pretty much the same thing) was the absence of "me velly solly" comedy accents. We refer the reader to Marlon Brando in *The Teahouse of the August Moon* (1956) for an especially pungent example.

We must note, however, that some of the actors are having a go at "authenticity" while some are just playing the part in their usual voices. Even this isn't as bad a flaw as it could have been, as the most obvious instances are those scenes where a multi-racial mix is part of the story. (It's like later stories set in France that give non-Parisian characters "Mummerset"[4] British yokel vowels. See 1.8, "The Reign of Terror" and 3.5, "The Massacre".) In this case, they were doing so well, making realistic, multi-cultural, well-motivated characters with no stereotyping, no condescension and no schoolboy jokes with people's names... and then they go and add a character called "Wang-Lo".

5. Susan's a beat-girl again this week, and says things like 'crazy', 'way out' and 'dig'. Her explanations to Ping-Cho are almost - but not quite - as patronising as grown-ups solemnly telling us that, for the youth of the nation, "bad" means "good" these days. One scene in episode five has the girls laughing at the 'with-it' goldfish.

6. Anyone encountering this story for the first time will be at a slight disadvantage in following the storyline about Ping-Cho. This girl is betrothed to an old man she hasn't met, and fascinated by the excitingly big world of her older companions. There's a Mongol warlord on her case, too, and lots of argy-bargy in a caravanserai. In the wake of *Crouching Tiger, Hidden Dragon,* it'd be reasonable to expect her to confront Barbara in a kick-boxing duel, then face the Doctor in a sword-fight up a tree before a torrid bath-scene with Tegana rounds off her day. Instead, we get Tutte Lemkow (as Kuiju) and an incontinent monkey.

7. One memorable non-speaking role is that of

Whom Did They Meet at the Roof of the World?

Peruse *A Description of the World* by Marco Polo (actually mainly the work of arch-fibber Rusticello of Pisa, with whom Marco shared a cell), and you'll find no mention of blue boxes. Neither is there anything about a Great Wall, something you'd expect a Venetian to notice; he mentions a boundary in the Caucasus, which he hasn't personally seen. And in seventeen years at the Chinese court, no-one offers him a cup of tea.

We can't be sure that Marco didn't write about all these things. There are so many corrupted versions of the original forty-page book, and the earliest extant edition is from 1351, long after he died. However, most historians now conclude - reluctantly, because it's a great read nevertheless - that Marco probably never got further than Karakoram. Everything after that is either Rusticello's retelling of an old story, or based on tales from other merchants. The truth would seem to be that history's most famous traveller didn't really go to that many places.

In the days when Marco Polo was a solid historical figure to be found at the court of Mighty Kublai Khan, we could make-believe that the Doctor's adventure in Cathay was real. But if he never went there, then precisely who was it accompanying the TARDIS crew across the Singing Sands and thwarting the dastardly Tegana every twenty-five minutes? Even if he gave a false name to Barbara (and by some fluke made up a name identical to the most famous Italian-in-China never to have been), we still have to account for a European serving the Emperor and somehow vanishing from all the documentation. The imperial oligarchy - the most rigorously-trained and punctilious bureaucracy the world has ever known, which invented paper specifically to document everything in triplicate - failed to record any Italian merchant rising in the ranks.

The Khan had met several Europeans. In 1245, a Franciscan called Giovanni di Piano Carpini was sent by the Pope. Carpini was over sixty and fat, and his translator was worse than useless, but he went from Lyon to Karakorum as part of Innocent IV's cunning plan to stop Europe falling to the Mongols. Carpini's mission was to convert Genghis Khan's sons, one of whom was Kublai Khan's dad. Eight years later, the King of France sent another Franciscan, Guillaume de Roubrouck. And Innocent sent another mission, under a prat called Anselm, which was a disaster.

But the presence of all these Westerners is recorded, as is that of many Muslim travellers. Intriguingly, Marco Polo's account uses Persian names, omits any reference to pork (the staple of Chinese food), and claims that Messer Marco supervised the use of Persian military hardware in the siege of Siang-Yang-Fu, which hints at a Muslim source for his stories. There's no mention of the Chinese practice of foot-binding, either, which is something a Muslim almost certainly wouldn't have discussed and a European almost certainly would.

Around 1280, Brother John of Monte Corvino

continued on page 53...

Kublai Khan's Spittoon-Holder. He's a little fella, and judging by the stills seems to undertake his duties with a quiet stoicism, though it's unclear whether he got an on-screen credit. In the estimable Andrew Pixley's archives in *Doctor Who Magazine* he's cited as "Spittoon-Holder to Kublai Khan - Harry Dillon". If we could prove that this made it to the screen, then it'd qualify as the single greatest credit ever, beating the one from "The Web Planet" ("Insect Movement - Roslyn de Winter").

The Continuity

The Plot The TARDIS suffers *another* technical fault after landing at the Roof of the World, on the thirteenth-century route to Cathay / China, and the travellers have to ask a bunch of hairy Mongols for help in order to avoid freezing to death. Lo and behold, it turns out that they're part of the caravan of Marco Polo, who's on his way to the court of Kublai Khan to ask for permission to return to his native Venice. Reasoning that the TARDIS would make an extra-special gift for the Khan, Messer Marco confiscates the Doctor's key, then drags him and the others on an epic journey to the court. This isn't an easy voyage, not simply because the route takes them through the Gobi Desert but because Tegana - a Mongol warlord accompanying Marco, supposedly as a peace envoy from the Khan's rival Noghai - is actually doing everything he can to sabotage the mission. Marco isn't very sharp at spotting this, even after Tegana depletes the water supply and menaces the Doctor's party at every opportunity.

After stopovers at various way-stations, a visit

to the Cave of Five-Hundred Eyes and an apparent bandit attack, the group reaches the summer palace at Shang-Tu, where the Mighty Kublai Khan is revealed to be less mighty (and yet a lot more amiable) than anyone was expecting. With Noghai's army approaching, the court decamps to Peking, and there the Doctor tries to win back the TARDIS in a game of backgammon. He fails, and blows the chance to win the island of Sumatra as well, but it's shortly after this that Tegana makes an attempt on the Khan's life. Warned of the plot by the travellers, Marco steps in and prevents the assassination with some nifty sword-play, after which Tegana throws himself on his own blade. In the confusion, a repentant Marco gives the Doctor his TARDIS key back, letting the travellers escape as Marco himself gets permission to go home.

The Doctor Still getting Ian's name wrong, and his idea of researching the terrain is to shamelessly ask people where he is and what year he's in. The Doctor suffers from terrible back-pain, and consequently resents all the horse-riding. Astonishingly, he sleeps through a sandstorm, after sulking so badly about the loss of his TARDIS that he won't even talk to Susan. Once again he can't see too well without his glasses, and he's the most susceptible to 'mountain sickness' due to the altitude.

The Doctor is a formidable backgammon fiend, beating Kublai Khan in all but one game, although he never says what he was going to do with his potential winnings of 35 elephants, 4,000 white stallions, 25 tigers, the sacred tooth of Buddha and all the commerce from Burma for one year.

• *Background.* Susan speaks of seeing the metal seas of Venus [in the '70s, Venusians will be a standard part of the Doctor's anecdotal repertoire]. The Doctor's medical knowledge is insufficient to cure the Great Khan's gout or his own aches, and for the first time he denies being a physician. He claims he's never met Kublai Khan's grandfather, Genghis Khan. [See also the TV Movie (27.0) and "Rose" (X1.1)[5].]

• *Ethics.* In a crisis, facing a bandit raid, he seriously proposes that everyone - Tegana, Marco and all - should leave in the TARDIS and go anywhere else. [That he knows almost as much as Barbara about Marco Polo's place in history makes this all the more remarkable. The Doctor may believe he can navigate the Ship at least a *little*, as he doesn't seem to be proposing to haul them off to other planets.]

• *Inventory.* While travelling, he's able to repair the 2LO circuit from the Ship, with only the facilities of a caravanserai and what he has on his person. He also manufactures a spare key, using the TARDIS' resources. This, and his original - on its black satin ribbon, as always - are surrendered to Marco, and it's not clear whether he gets both of them back. As a consolation prize for losing the backgammon game, Kublai Khan gives him a piece of the newfangled paper currency.

The Supporting Cast

• *Ian.* At some point he's been taught unarmed combat. [The most likely explanation is that he was trained during his National Service. This would also account for his knowledge of bamboo's explosive reaction to fire, if he was posted to Burma or the Philippines. See 2.5, "The Web Planet", for supporting evidence.]

• *Barbara.* As a history teacher, Barbara is well-informed about Marco Polo's travels, and keeps almost giving things away. On the whole she's enjoying all of this, but she's understandably freaked out when the bandits play dice to decide who's going to kill her.

• *Susan.* Has had many homes, although she's never seen a moonlit night [on Earth?]. She's 'in her sixteenth year' [she says this so readily that it's obviously true], and is horrified at the idea of anyone her age marrying, even voluntarily [see also "The Aztecs" (1.6) and, ultimately, "The Dalek Invasion of Earth" (2.2)]. Her desire to leave in the Ship is balanced by her need to stop travelling once they know 'all the mysteries of the skies'. She's prepared to respect Ping-Cho's vow not to reveal where the TARDIS key has been hidden, even though it means being stranded.

Susan gets edgy when she's stuck on thirteenth-century Earth for a few days, but she digs that crazy Gobi Desert. When puzzled about historical figures, Susan instinctively asks Barbara for answers, and by now she's started saying "Barbara" instead of "Miss Wright".

The TARDIS After landing, one whole circuit of the Ship burns out [presumably as a consequence of 1.3, "The Edge of Destruction"]. This means that the lighting doesn't work, nor does the water supply or the heating. In the Gobi Desert, the air condenses on the interior walls overnight, resulting in cupfuls of marginally potable water. [This effect on the Ship's insides would seem to contra-

Whom Did They Meet at the Roof of the World?

...continued from page 51

claimed to have baptised six-thousand people in the church he'd built in Peking. In the eleven years before he wrote to his order and requested more books, he also claimed to have taught Greek, Latin and musical notation to 150 boys, sending them off to teach others in turn. Maybe one of these boys grew up to be the fake "Marco" our heroes meet. Again, that he identifies himself to Barbara and Ian as "Marco Polo" from Venice is a baffling thing to make up, but it *has* to be false. Note that when Barbara asks him if he is who she thinks he is, he never bothers asking her where she's heard of him, as if the name's already become an all-purpose cover-story by this point.

In 1368, a resurgence of Chinese nationalism finally closed off all contact with outside traders for almost five centuries. There's no indication of any attempt to rewrite history, as had happened when the Chin dynasty had begun and the original Great Wall had been constructed, and if "our" Marco had been Tipp-Ex'd out of the record then why not all those other westerners? Was a time-traveller responsible for purging the histories? Again and again, there's the nagging sense that there's something not quite *normal* about the man we see beavering away at his journal for these seven episodes, this wandering imperson-ator who accepts the idea of time-travel within seconds and believes the TARDIS to be a flying car-avan with no evidence but Ian's word.

One westerner who was reputed to have been in Cathay before the thirteenth century was Prester John. He's now largely believed to have been fictitious, a Frenchman (some versions say English) who traded with the East about a century earlier. Marco mentions him in passing on a num-ber of occasions. Now, if someone not-quite-natu-ral with pale skin and blue eyes had been in the region for over a hundred years - and wanted to avoid nosy people like the Doctor asking too many questions - then he might feasibly have claimed to be Marco Polo. If Marco never got as far as Peking, then the impostor could have spent an entire career posing as the Venetian, knowing that any traces he left behind would be covered by the real Marco's fiction...

dict practically every other story, with the notable exception of 10.4, "Planet of the Daleks". The technical fault may have something to do with it.]

The faulty circuit is called the 2LO [this was the call-sign for the precursor to BBC Radio, so peo-ple old enough to have been listening circa 1920 would have known the number]. It's a black box, the size and shape of a paperback book, with dials on the front. It takes days to repair this, but it only seems to take the Doctor a night to fashion a new TARDIS key.

The whole Ship isn't so heavy that Marco's men can't drag it. There's some form of altimeter on the console, which indicates height above sea-level. The Doctor is sure he's succeeded in bringing Ian and Barabra back home, as he directed the TARDIS towards Earth [although 1.8, "The Reign of Terror", suggests that he hasn't been trying to hit the target *that* hard]. The TARDIS gets another wardrobe boost here, as the travellers leave the scene with their Chinese duds.

History

• *Dating.* According to Marco, the TARDIS arrives on the Plain of Pamir in Central Asia in 1289 AD. [This is near the approximate edge of the Hindu Kush, more-or-less modern Afghanistan. Kublai reigned from 1256 until his death in 1294, and his approximate age in 1289 was 75, yet the description in Polo's book is of a vigorous man still fathering children by his many concubines. Although the account includes detailed and colourful descriptions of most of the places we see in the story, in 1289 Polo's move-ments would have been further east, possibly - *if* we read his version as truthful and accurate - returning from Vietnam. But for now let's concen-trate on what we see here...]

Now in his late thirties, Marco Polo desperately wants to go back to Venice. He used to live there with his father and his uncle, and came to Cathay in 1271, the journey to Peking taking three-and-a-half years. On his 25th birthday in 1277 [his-torically it should be 1279], he was given an appointment in the Khan's service, and has been travelling ever since. He once transported an entire army from Cathay to India. Two years ago, Marco asked permission to go home but the Khan refused, so he now wants to give the TARDIS to his mighty employer as a means of currying favour. He doesn't dispute that the Ship is a flying caravan, even without seeing what's inside it.

Polo is depicted as an intelligent and open-minded traveller who, like the Doctor, doesn't judge strangers by appearances; at the Khan's court in Peking, he's seen Buddhist monks levitating cups of wine [see 5.2, "The Abominable Snowmen"], so all things are possible except time-travel [even so, he picks up on the concept suspiciously quickly]. Ultimately he comes to believe in the Ship's full capabilities, but states that people in Europe wouldn't believe half of what he's seen in Cathay [i.e. this is why there's no mention of the Doctor in his book].

Mighty Kublai Khan, meanwhile, is revealed to be a little old man with gout. He's wise, and capable of administering the greatest empire the world had ever seen, but lives in fear of his wife. Tegana, the Mongol warlord who's travelling with Marco, is a special emissary sent to the Khan from the court of Noghai. The conflict between Noghai and the Khan is supposedly over as Noghai has sued for peace, so officially Tegana is going to Peking to discuss armistice terms. In truth, Noghai's army is fast approaching Peking, and Tegana plans to kill the Khan before his master gets there. He also hopes to get hold of the TARDIS so that Noghai's 'sorcerers' can figure out how it works. Though Tegana dies here, the army isn't dealt with. [Noghai, the Ukrainian Tartar leader, is now generally assumed to have been defeated in late 1299. The name "Tegana" appears once in Polo's account, in a list of minor Mongol warriors. It's unlikely that "our" Tegana is the same one.]

Twenty years earlier, the Mongol conqueror Hulagu wiped out many of the murderous Hashashin sect at Tun-Huang. In the Cave of Five-Hundred Eyes, once the Hashashin hideout, 250 scary images of the Hashashins are painted on the walls. Marco and Ping-Cho both believe that the Hashashins - whose name is ostensibly the source of the English word "assassins", as Ian insists on pointing out - were so-called because of their use of the drug hashish. [This has long been a fashionable theory, especially with hippies, but it's historically questionable. There's no reliable evidence linking the Hashashins with hashish, although funnily enough some scholars have suggested that the confusion only began with Polo's book. It's not even certain that "Hashashins" and "assassins" are connected, however confidently Ian says it.]

The crusaders were in the Holy Land twenty-five years earlier [we'll come back to this for 2.6, "The Crusade"].

The Analysis

Where Does This Come From? Well, evidently, the main source is the book compiled from the various versions of what Marco Polo said while he was in prison in Genoa. The Penguin translation, which diligently annotated the differences between these, came out in 1958. Prior to this, the most widely-read English account was Moule and Pelliot (1938). This would fit writer John Lucarotti's claim to have been fascinated by the subject as a schoolboy. (Not that a new translation would have been absolutely necessary. Even so, this was an especially potent subject at a time when the British were running Burma, and a new, comprehensive version was the kind of thing that a twelve-year-old might have got for Christmas in the days before PlayStations.) Lucarotti later adapted the story for radio whilst living in Canada in the 1950s, and spun fifteen episodes of material out of it.

At a more fundamental level, though... the roots of this story lie in Sydney Newman wanting to get his choice of writers onto the series, and the original plan to do stories set in the past which were instructive. Newman's influence over the series is going to wane from this point, but the stories generically known as "The Hartnell Historicals" are the closest we get to his original ambition for the programme. Lucarotti was a veteran of *The Avengers*, and it's significant that he left Toronto and the Canadian Broadcasting Corporation so soon after Newman came to Britain and ABC. Lucarotti was living in Majorca when the scripts for this were written. As well as Canada and the US, he'd also lived in Mexico (see 1.6, "The Aztecs"), so Marco's wanderlust and Susan's ambivalence about "home" could equally be the author speaking.

But when it comes to British TV companies turning historical events into exciting adventures, we have to bite the bullet and talk about ITC again. Whilst the first few ITC examples were based on folklore and chosen more for their ability to include picturesque British / European locations (by which we mean castles) into something banal enough to palm off on a global market (by which we mean America), eventually the quality improved. They hired historical advisors and decent fight-arrangers. Marco Polo would have been an ideal production for them, if enough Chinese actors had been available in the

Shepperton area. Indeed, the script for this story is of a similar quality to the last great ITC tights-opera, *Sir Francis Drake* (the story-editor of which, Ian Stuart Black, will be mentioned again later in this book).

Things That Don't Make Sense   Time for historical pedantry. Leaving aside the contradictions with Marco Polo's own account, and bearing in mind what we'll say under **Whom Did They Meet at the Roof of the World?**... some of the words and names are translated, and some aren't. Khan-Balik, or Cambalu, is never used - they anachronistically call it "Peking" throughout - but "Cathay" is the preferred term for China, and Marco even corrects Barbara on the subject. They all speak whichever language Ping-Cho speaks (and why is someone from Samarkand given a Chinese name, anyway?), but she has to ask what 'dig' and 'crazy' mean. In fact, even if Marco's book is only half-accurate, Ping-Cho ought to be a Muslim.

How obviously evil does Tegana have to get before Marco takes the hint? He could be twirling his moustache, laughing like Valentine Dyall and wearing a big neon sign saying I AM THE VILLAIN in Mandarin and Italian, and Marco would still need proof. Tegana is so desperate to be bad that he'll deviously poison the water supply and arrange an ambush for the caravan when it turns back, rather than - oh, say - just killing everyone in the middle of the Gobi Desert and leaving no witnesses. He also suggests that driving a stake through the Doctor's heart is the best way of killing this 'magician', anticipating nineteenth-century vampire fiction six-hundred years early.

Critique   Imagine how frustrating this is; the audios, the telesnaps, the memories of cast and viewers all tell us that this was a gem, but we can't see it. What we know about it is that the plot hangs together as an adventure, but also as a means of showing us a world unlike any we'd seen before. Most of what we're told is true, and almost all of it was *thought* to be true when they made it, but it's a more interesting and exotic world than Marinus or Skaro. Marco's description of Buddhist monks levitating objects, the hallucinatory Singing Sands and the story of the Hashashins are far more fantastic than anything Terry Nation ever gave us. Even the desert is radiophonic.

Where it really scores is in the performances, or rather, the way the performances are supposed to

fit together. In a series about travel and visiting alien cultures, you'd expect Marco Polo to be a patron saint, as Sherlock Holmes is for the mid-'70s version of the series. But he and the Doctor clash from the start. Marco is authoritarian, sceptical and irritable (like the Doctor), but heroic, practical and a born leader (like Ian). In theory this ought to have made the usual lead actors redundant, yet instead it allows Hartnell, Russell, Eden and Nesbitt to play against one another in a variety of combinations. Similarly, Ping-Cho gives Susan some long-delayed depth. Even supposedly throwaway comic-relief stooges like Kuiju and Wang-Lo get more to do and have more dignity than the characters played by the same actors in "The Crusade". Yes, even with the monkey and the silly names.

Along the way, the story does things that would never be done in the same way again, but are inescapably *Doctor Who* anyway. A modern eye would find much of it painfully slow, yet that's only because it's working to a different agenda than the one we're used to. Ping-Cho's story in mime is exactly what the programme was supposed to be about; entertaining, educational, visual and - above all - something you wouldn't see anywhere else. Maybe it's just hindsight, but even its overly-didactic tone seems charming rather than annoying ('you know, it's rather surprising to find the daughter of a high government official working as a servant in Marco Polo's caravan'). For once we have a sense of three months and thousands of miles actually meaning something to the characters, not least to Ian, who wears the same shirt for the next seven episodes after this story ends.

The Facts

Written by John Lucarotti. Directed by Waris Hussein (except episode four, directed by John Crockett). Ratings: 9.4 million, 9.4 million, 9.4 million, 9.9 million, 9.4 million, 8.4 million, 10.4 million.

No episodes exist in the BBC archive.

Supporting Cast   Mark Eden (Marco Polo), Derren Nesbitt (Tegana), Zienia Merton (Ping-Cho), Martin Miller (Kublai Khan), Jimmy Gardner (Chenchu), Charles Wade (Malik), Philip Voss (Acomat), Tutte Lemkow (Kuiju), Paul Carson (Ling-Tau), Gabor Baraker (Wang-Lo), Peter Lawrence (Vizier), Claire Davenport (Empress).

AKA... "A Journey to Cathay", although nobody's ever really called it anything but "Marco Polo".

Episode Titles "The Roof of the World", "The Singing Sands", "Five Hundred Eyes", "The Wall of Lies", "Rider from Shang-Tu", "Mighty Kublai Khan", "Assassin at Peking". (The end credits of episode two announced "Next Week: The Cave of Five Hundred Eyes", according to many sources.)

Cliffhangers While the Doctor hysterically admits that he has no idea how to retrieve the TARDIS key, Tegana instructs one of his Mongol minions to begin the sabotage against Marco's caravan; in the desert, Tegana pours away Marco's water supply and gloats; Susan screams, as the eyes of one of the images move in the Cave of Five-Hundred Eyes; Ian finds that the sentry is dead, and Tegana has already arranged an attack; Tegana holds Susan at knifepoint as she tries to escape back to the TARDIS; Tegana, who's doing a *lot* of villainy around here, finally draws his sword and challenges Ian to attack him.

The Lore

• Although it was the first two Dalek stories that finally made it to the big screen, this was the first *Doctor Who* story to be considered for cinematic treatment. Amazingly, the Disney company made the first approach.

• John Crockett, who stood in on episode four for Waris Hussein at short notice when the director fell ill, was a misfit within the BBC. He'd helped set up the Compass Theatre Company in 1944, and was a painter, dancer and occasional actor. His 1950 production of Marlowe's *Doctor Faustus* is still cited as one of the best. He was available as he was preparing for his own story, "The Aztecs" (1.6), and his immediate reaction to being given an episode of *Doctor Who* was to consider other possible historical subjects. The list he sent David Whitaker included some obvious choices, but also some unlikely ones; the fact that the next few seasons contain six of these (Romans, Richard the Lionheart, Elizabeth I, Viking raids, Cornish smugglers, Bonnie Prince Charlie) is worth noting.

• Tutte Lemkow's character, Kuiji, is named after a place mentioned in Polo's book. The director had the idea of giving him a monkey, to make him "exotic". (As if an eyepatch and being played

by Tutte Lemkow weren't enough. Incidentally, Lemkow is in *Raiders of the Lost Ark*, wherein Vic Tablian plays a dodgy Arab with a monkey and an eyepatch...) Unfortunately, the monkey kept up a constant stream of urine throughout recording, which remains Derren Nesbitt's main memory of the story.

• The idea of Mighty Kublai Khan as a hen-pecked husband was devised by the director of Lucarotti's CBC version of the story. Claire Davenport, here playing the Empress, would later appear at the court of Jabba the Hutt in *Return of the Jedi*. She's listed on the end credits as "Fat Dancer". ('Gee, mom, you were in *Star Wars*? What as?' 'Er...')

• By an odd set of coincidences, Mark Eden (Marco), Derren Nesbitt (Tegana) and Martin Miller (Mighty Kublai Khan) all appeared in one episode of *The Prisoner*, "It's Your Funeral". Nesbitt went on to become a household name in the swish cop-show *Special Branch*, but in 1964 was a recognisably familiar face, often playing escaped convicts or Nazi officers. In the first run of *Sir Lancelot* he'd played a different character in each of all but two episodes, so at the time it was a real surprise to see him on set with William Russell and not having a sword-fight. Eden had been around a bit too, and by virtue of playing Marco got himself onto the cover of the *Radio Times*, to the ire of Russell and his agent.

• The original music was again by Tristram Carey, but a total contrast to his previous score for "The Daleks". The Eddie Walker Ensemble, who'd also participate in his soundtrack for "The Daleks' Master Plan" (3.4), played it on conventional instruments. The drums for the fight at the end were played by Charles Botterill, whose percussion would be all the "new" music for "The Time Meddler" (2.9). Carey was also responsible for some electronic sounds, making the voices of the Singing Sands. Stock music was used to add flavour to some of the scenes at way-stations.

• At this point Terry Nation was putting together his next *Doctor Who* script, set during the Indian Mutiny. As Waris Hussein was the Indian of the group, Nation asked him for any useful details to make the script seem less rushed and better-thought-out. We'll never know what the result would have been, as Malcolm Hulke's story about a tenth planet (the one that probably wasn't called "Beyond the Sun", but was about a planet beyond the sun) fell through again, and Nation was asked to come up with another space-romp at short notice. How well he did, you'll see in the next story…

1.5: "The Keys of Marinus"

(Serial E. Six Episodes, 11th April - 16th May 1964.)

Which One is This?   *Voord of the Rings*. It's the "quest" story, with tons of memorable images that the children of the 1960s still vaguely recall: soldiers coming to life after being entombed in ice, slug-like brains in glass cases, acid seas leaving a punctured rubber suit with no occupant and commandos in alien frogman gear creeping around a deserted palace.

Firsts and Lasts   As the first "space" story to be screened after the success of "The Daleks", *and* Terry Nation's follow-up story, expectations were high that lightning would strike twice. This is therefore the first story with a monster to be hyped as "the successor to the Daleks", and was the first time that the monster in question - the Voord/s - failed to set the world alight. (Bear in mind that at this stage, the production team doesn't know the series will feature recurring monsters, so the return of the Daleks themselves isn't inevitable *just* yet.)

It's the first time we see real squeegee-bottle-style vehicles (the Voord submarines), the first time a solo soprano voice is used to represent icy wastes (see also 5.3, "The Ice Warriors") and the first time a villain's identity is kept secret by focusing on his black-gloved hand instead of his face (at the end of episode four). We see the debut of some more favourite Nation obsessions here: magic travel-bracelets, nasty aliens who brainwash humans to use as slave labour in work-gangs, plants that are more like animals and a character with a name that sounds a bit like "Tarrant". It's not unique to Nation, but we also have the first *Doctor Who* planet with a ridiculously appropriate name; the first thing we find out about this world is that it has interesting and unusual oceans, so obviously it turns out to be called "Marinus". Though there's an argument that "Skaro" is supposed to suggest a "scarred" planet, this is the first time it's really blatant, and from hereon in we'll be hearing about places called things like "Aridius" and "Desperus".

It's tempting to say that this is the first "quest" story, involving a hunt for all the titular Keys of Marinus, but to be honest it's the *only* "quest" story. In later years, this sort of thing will be done with what are now called "story arcs" rather than with individual episodes within one plot. (Q.v. the whole of Season Sixteen. Although to be honest, in the early Hartnell stories - which lack overall story titles, and which weren't advertised in the *Radio Times* as having a set length of "x episodes" - individual stories are often story arcs in themselves, and nobody watching was ever sure where one adventure would end and the next one begin.) More importantly, and underlining the fact that so much of this is Saturday Morning Serial adventure-fodder… it's the first time that a *Doctor Who* title involves the words "of Death". In fact, *two* of the episodes here do it, "The Sea of Death" and "Sentence of Death". The "of" style of naming has been around ever since the first story ("The Forest of Fear"), but this is where it becomes a series standard.

Six Things to Notice About "The Keys of Marinus"…

1. This story's main baddies are the Voord. Or Voords. The script doesn't seem sure about the plural, but we're unanimous on one thing: the Daleks they ain't. While stair-climbing seems more practical for these rubber-clad malefactors, they're still rather clumsy. The commando raid in the first episode suggests that they were trained by Norman Wisdom[6]. If there's a hidden death-trap to stumble into, then they'll find it, usually in the most slapstick way imaginable. In the final episode, one notoriously trips on his own flippers (it's actor Peter Stenson, who also plays the Voord who stabs himself in the back in episode one, the Judge whose beard won't stay on in episode five and one of the knights in episode four… he later wrote about playing the Clumsy Voord in a rubber fetish magazine).

2. But in charge of the villainy is Yartek, Leader of the Alien Voord. This styling of his name has become hallowed among fans after *The Making of Doctor Who* and the *Radio Times* tenth anniversary special made the story seem a lot more fun than it really was. He only turns up in the last few minutes of the final episode, but is dispatched in such an obvious "The End… or is it?" manner that his return was inevitable. (His return in the *Doctor Who* annuals, anyway.) Whereas the Daleks have been finally, definitively destroyed on-screen at least three times and *still* keep coming back, we've

yet to see a TV adventure in which the first episode ends with 'Yartek, Leader of the Alien Voord... but I thought you were dead!' (Still, Russell T. Davies has an obvious fascination for stupid names from the '60s - see 2.5, "The Web Planet" - so let's not lose all hope for this yet.)

3. Because "The Daleks" ended up looking and sounding roughly 300% better than it had any right to, here Terry Nation seems to believe that anything he comes up with can be realised on-screen and make a big splash. On the plus side, we get a planet which is considerably more than a few corridors and people in tinfoil bikinis. On the minus side, it means that whereas the designers had a seven-parter budget to create Skaro, here they have to make a new world every episode. Ray Cusick and director John Gorrie *almost* get away with it, but odd little touches of bathos emerge, such as the rather 1960s plumbing in the ice-chamber and the rather obviously human hands of the moving statue.

4. The exotic names that gave "The Daleks" so much of its texture are a distant memory now. As we've already seen, the planet with the big acid seas is called "Marinus"; the city with the sleep-inducing brains is "Morphoton" (and yet nobody takes the hint); the city of highly-advanced culture is called "Millenius"; and the hard-working arbitrator is called "Arbitan" (we assume that this is a name rather than a title, but if it isn't a hereditary job then his parents had remarkable foresight). David Whitaker seems to have decided that Nation knew what he was doing, and just left him unattended for six episodes.

5. In some ways it's a fully-realised, detailed and diverse alien planet. With wolves, chickens, pomegranates and grapes, it might be anywhere on Earth, but the brain-creatures, killer plants and defrosted soldiers are as surprising to people who've spent their lives here as they are to the TARDIS crew. Nobody in any one area of Marinus knows about the others, except that the Millenians have vaguely heard of Arbitan. The net effect is that this world seems to be a theme-park for people wanting to have an adventure, and when they've completed each task they're immediately relocated to the next "zone". These days this sort of plotting is commonplace for computer games (and Hollywood movies as a consequence), but in 1964, it must have seemed like a crazed patchwork of Rider Haggard and *Flash Gordon*.

To modern audiences the oddest thing about

this is that the Voord aren't chasing the heroes, and there doesn't seem to be much of a time-limit to this quest. Whereas "Marco Polo" lasted seven weeks for us, and a dozen or more weeks for Ian and Barbara, this lasts six weeks for us and three days for them. Despite being about a rather frantic search for vital micro-keys, this is even more languidly-paced.

6. Like virtually every other *Doctor Who* story in this era, "The Keys of Marinus" has to find a way of incapacitating the TARDIS, to solve the old "why don't they just leave?" problem. Unfortunately, in order to tell a story that spans several continents, Nation also has to invent 'travel-dials' to flip the travellers from place to place. Which gives him exactly the same problem all over again, and means that he has to keep finding methods of separating our heroes from their bracelets. Spot 'em as they turn up.

The Continuity

The Doctor Over the course of events here, we witness the Doctor move from comically absent-minded to a razor-keen brain capable of acting as Ian's advocate in an alien legal system. Given the chance to ask for anything he desires, his first choice is a laboratory [difficult to credit for any later version of the Doctor]. He's rather impressed by Arbitan's travel-dials.

• *Background.* He's met Pyrrho, founder of scepticism. [So he's visited the third century AD, and probably Rome. This makes sense when one considers the Renaissance scholars he'll later claim to have known, who would have read versions of the texts of Pyrrho's circle.] But he's never seen an acid sea before.

• *Ethics.* By now he's genuinely concerned for Ian's well-being. Coerced into helping Arbitan recover the Keys of Marinus - which will allow the Conscience to remove free will from the planet, for a supposedly "good" purpose - the Doctor does so, but afterwards gives a lecture on why everything they've just done was actually a bad idea. Even though he's blackmailed into going on the mission, he still agrees to hunt down the Keys rather than (for example) taking on Arbitan and finding a way of releasing the TARDIS.

Contrary to his prior claim about never giving advice, he's happy to chip in and tell the people of Marinus how to run their societies. Having informed the guardians of Millenius about scepticism, he specifically takes Sabetha to one side to tell her that it's wrong for man to be controlled by machines, as only human beings can preserve justice. He says goodbye to her with a 'bless you, my child'.

The Supporting Cast

• *Ian.* More resistant to cold than Barbara, even though he's wearing a silk robe from China and she's got her nice pink jumper. [In fact, he seems to have been wearing the same trousers for six months non-stop.] Before the brains of Morphoton start hypnotising him, *he's* the one asking what the price-tag will be for getting one's heart's desire. Interestingly, we don't find out what his is. [In any later story, this would be unthinkable; we'd see the wishes of the companions, but *not* the Doctor, so we can tell who's still supposed to be the lead hero here.] He's prepared to leave the nasty trapper Vasor to the mercy of the ice soldiers, at least when he thinks he'll be gone by the time the soldiers arrive at Vasor's hut, yet he looks shocked when Vasor's killed in front of his eyes.

• *Barbara.* Knows about Central American Indians and their architecture [see 1.6, "The Aztecs"]. Once again, dressmaking seems to be her forte. She's the one who points out that Earth standards aren't appropriate in alien cultures, something which is usually the Doctor's job, although she does say it when someone's offering her nice clothes for no logical reason. Unlike Susan, she often resents Ian coddling her and feels the need to rebel.

Her reaction to teleportation is panic and vertigo, while all the others find it quite bracing. Not for the last time, she seems to like putting on bracelets, bangles and snakey pieces of jewellery.

• *Susan.* She's in the jungle less for than five seconds before freaking out, a record even for her. She also starts blubbing even when Ian stops her paddling in acid in the nick of time. She's evidently learned to make fire recently [since 1.1, "An Unearthly Child"].

The TARDIS
The scanner is in black-and-white, as the colour model is 'temporarily *hors de combat*', according to the Doctor. He also speaks of a fault in the 'time mechanism', which requires advanced equipment to repair. [Here he finally seems to be admitting that his failure to steer the Ship is a mechanical one, rather than just due to a lack of data.]

This week's souvenir: the final Key of Marinus, which Ian decides to give to the Doctor after the Conscience blows up.

The Non-Humans

• *The Voord.* Look very much like web-footed human beings in black frogman outfits, though there's no way of telling what their faces are like, apart from a vague impression of flickering eyes behind the mask. The suits are acid-proof, but not impossible to tear. The only really "alien" feature on this clothing is the antenna, attached to the wedge-shaped helmet and suggestive of an evil Teletubby. Led by the curiously antenna-less Yartek, the Voord's goal is to seize the Conscience of Marinus, and thus control the planet. They assaulted the island where the Conscience is kept many years ago, but now they've decided to try again, arriving in one-man submarines that look like glass torpedoes.

Each Voord is equipped with a dagger, and what might be either a discoid torch or a ray-gun, carried on the belt. One inhabitant of Marinus believes that Barbara might be a Voord, even though she doesn't resemble their 'race', while Arbitan refers to one of them as a 'man'. [This hints that they're humanoid under the outfits, so "Voord" may have been the name of a political faction before they cut themselves off from the rest of Marinus and became a race in themselves. In an early draft of the script, the Voord are explicitly described as inhabitants of Marinus who've been processed to be immune to the Conscience, and that's still the impression given by Arbitan's story here. Despite the name given to them in *The Making of Doctor Who*, they're never called "alien".]

According to Arbitan's story, Yartek was the first man to find a way of overcoming the influence of the Conscience, 1,300 years ago; see **Planet Notes.** He refers to his troops as 'my creatures'. [Which would make sense if Yartek started re-processing other people. Does he beam propaganda directly into their heads, via the antennae?] Although "Voord" is used as the plural of "Voord", Arbitan says "Voords" when speaking of the early days of Yartek's campaign. They're capable of speech, and Yartek seems particularly alert, quickly picking up on the fact that Sabetha and Altos are in love. He even attempts to fake some compassionate concern, although it backfires on him horribly. He's apparently killed in the destruction of the Conscience… *or is he?* [Yes.]

Planet Notes

• *Marinus*. A planet with more than one kind of terrain, which makes a change. Despite having at least one sea of acid, strong enough to melt human / Voord tissue, remarkably Earth-like life has developed there. The TARDIS arrives on an island with a glass beach, with an impressive flat-topped pyramid at its centre. This is home to Arbitan, the keeper of the Conscience of Marinus. The Conscience is a large, transparent dodecahedron full of electronics. The technology of the planet reached its peak two thousand years ago, culminating in this Conscience; at first it was a mechanised judge and jury that never made mistakes, but the people improved on it until finally it gained the ability to 'radiate' its power over the planet and control the minds of men [and, presumably, women]. Evil was eliminated. Robbery, fear, hate and violence were unknown, and Arbitan believes that this made the planet unique in the universe [the first hint that Marinus is, or was, part of an interplanetary culture].

For seven centuries, Marinus prospered, until Yartek found a means of overpowering the machine. [Unless he did this by sheer accident, we can assume that the power of the Conscience wasn't total, as it should have removed Yartek's will to find a way. People around here are extraordinarily long-lived. Arbitan says 'we' when he's speaking of those who built the machine, so he may be over two thousand years old himself.] Yartek and his Voord followers began to rob and cheat, but the people were unable to fight back. Arbitan's people hoped to improve the machine to stop the Voord, so instead of destroying it or allowing it to fall into Voord hands, they removed the five 'micro-circuits' or 'micro-keys'. Arbitan kept one of these, while the other four were supposedly put in places of safety across the planet. [This was evidently some time ago, as people elsewhere on Marinus have fully-equipped police and judiciary forces by now, which wouldn't have been needed while the Conscience was in operation.] Only Arbitan knows where the micro-keys are. It's indicated that the sea of acid is a deliberate protective barrier [devised by Arbitan, and if so then other seas on the planet may be rather less dangerous].

Now it's time to recover the Keys of Marinus, as Arbitan has perfected the machine and made it irresistible. But over the years, all his friends and followers have gone and never returned; last year he sent his daughter Sabetha to find the Keys, but she never came back. Despite doing this for "good" reasons, Arbitan is willing to blackmail the TARDIS crew into going on the mission, throwing up a force-barrier around the Ship from inside the pyramid. He gives them travel-dials, bracelets which can automatically transport them to the next "zone" where a Key is to be found. It's implied that he himself developed these bracelets, and he claims that the principle is similar to that of the TARDIS, though only through space and not time. [Here, as in many of the early tales, the Doctor is thought to be an engineer / pioneer who built the TARDIS on sound-if-highly-advanced scientific principles. There's no hint that the TARDIS is the product of an ancient and quasi-mystical super-race. He and Arbitan are very nearly two of a kind; see **Where Does This Come From?** for another connection between them.]

Ultimately, Arbitan dies at Yartek's hand, and the Conscience destroys itself with a huge bang when a fake Key is inserted into it. But before then, we get to see some of Marinus' other hotspots…

- The City of Morphoton. It *appears* to be an elegant castle, where servants offer the travellers their hearts' desires, including rich food and lots of things to play with. In fact it's all an illusion, created by disembodied brains in bell-jars with snail-like eyes on stalks [described in the design notes as "Morpho Brains", though this term is never used in the dialogue]. They wish to use their 'mesmeron' to seduce and then subdue the travellers, hence the web of hallucinations; the brains created this city, and need slave labour to carry out their plans. The castle is actually a grubby, cheap-looking place, where the posh clothes are really rags and the expensive silverware is really tin. Servants re-enforce the illusion by putting 'somno-discs' on the sleeping travellers' foreheads, and Barbara's knocked out with flashing lights and alarming noises when she gets suspicious. She starts to see through the illusion when she recovers [something of a misfired strategy on the brains' part]. It's unclear whether the grapes, pomegranates, truffles and chicken mentioned here are native to Marinus, or figments of the travellers' imagination.

Sabetha and Arbitan's courier Altos have been in Morphoton for some time. Sabetha has Key #2, which was given to her by the brains as it was the thing she desired most. [Surely, Arbitan wouldn't have left the Key in possession of the brains? The most likely explanation is that more civilised people used to live here, and the brains stole the Key when they took over.] The brains die when Barbara starts smashing their jars, releasing all the slaves from the mesmerisation and starting a revolution which burns the city. [We, of course, never see any of this city beyond the castle.]

- The screaming jungle, so named because the plants sometimes make maddening screeching noises. They start as soon as Susan arrives, but stop when her friends turn up [this might be a result of her mildly telepathic nature, or alternatively they might just be winding her up]. In a half-ruined building in this jungle lives the half-mad biologist Darrius [though he's only named in the credits], who knows Arbitan and looks after Key #3 - at least, until the foliage strangles him. In his home there are jars marked with symbols for odd-sounding chemical formulae like "DE^{3}O^2" [unless this shorthand is being translated into almost-Earth-type scientific terminology for our benefit, this might indicate that the people here came from our planet originally].

It seems that Darrius' research increased nature's 'tempo of destruction' with a chemical growth accelerator, so the plants are determined to overrun everything as quickly as possible, the creepers eventually trying to kill the travellers. The ruins in the jungle are in the Malayan style, and they look fairly ancient [though the 'tempo of destruction' might be responsible for this]. There are moving, booby-trapped statues, and one - with mobile and surprisingly human-looking arms - is adorned with a false Key made by Darrius. Ian has no problem reading Darrius' diary.

- The mountain regions. Blizzard-bound and inhabited by wolves, here there's a series of ice-caves, where a unit of frozen soldiers guard Key #4. The soldiers wear chain-mail, quilted tabards and cylindrical helmets like Medieval Teutonic knights [people like this are often found hanging around special keys; see 16.1, "The Ribos Operation"], and they carry swords. The Key is in the middle of a block of ice, surrounded by pipes for easy defrosting, though the soldiers wake up at the same time. They're not very communicative, but they do scream when they fall into crevasses. Also found in this rugged landscape is a lusty trapper, who lives in a hut and whose business is animal furs. [It's possible that Marinus has been terraformed and stocked with Earth animals. This

might explain the unnatural acid seas, anyway.] The trapper considers the frozen men to be 'demons'. The nearest village is three miles away.

- Finally, there's the shiny city of Millenius, full of people who wear Grecian-style robes and talk as if they think they're terribly enlightened. The legal system of the city is well-established, though murder is said to be rare and carries the death penalty. The three tribunal judges wear robes and head-dresses like Greek Orthodox priests, while the 'guardians' wear Gestapo-style uniforms. Their approach is one of guilty-until-proven-innocent, and they use psychometry in the same way that twentieth-century police use fingerprinting, having the science to detect the characteristics of those who come into contact with solid objects. They don't, however, seem to know what fingerprints are. Despite the futuristic look of the city, they use hardback books to store data rather than computers; they have telephones; and they measure time in zeniths. There's a glass factory in a desert somewhere nearby, and anyone who disturbs court proceedings can be sent there for a year without trial. The symbols on the court walls look a bit Swastika-like.

Key #5 has traditionally been kept in a maximum security vault in Millenius. Eprim, Arbitan's second courier, is murdered by the corrupt Prosecutor who wants to take the Key for its cash value. The vault can't be entered by anyone without a full 'property check', while the police use a 'heat-reflector search' and an 'orza-ray scanner' to look for the missing artefact. The people of Millenius remember Arbitan as a wise traveller [and apparently know nothing about the Conscience, though they must have noticed a period in their history when they woke up one morning and found the crime rate reduced to zero], yet the Key is known to be valuable as there are only five like it in the 'universe'. The Elders have a sworn duty to protect it, yet don't mind giving it up to Arbitan's agents. The mace found in the vault is said to be a weapon used in primitive, savage times, but right now a ray-gun of some kind is the assassin's weapon of choice. Arbitan's travel-dials, on the other hand, are weird and unbelievable to the people of Millenius.

These people's classical demeanour may be common on Marinus, as Altos is also rather regal and dignified, even when wearing a short toga in a blizzard. Sabetha's "do you know who I am?" routine in front of Yartek would seem to suggest that she sees herself as the daughter of a powerful and respected man, in spite of Arbitan's isolation. After the big bang on the island, Sabetha and Altos look set to return to Millenius, to carry on Arbitan's work of preserving justice but without the disturbing mind-control elements.

The Analysis

Where Does This Come From? The most noticeable element of this story, and a lot of others that Terry Nation churned out over the years, is jungle warfare. 'When the whispering starts it's death, I tell you, *death*!'

We're in full B-Movie mode here. Nation will henceforth use jungles as the main arena for Dalek action, and in stories like "Planet of the Daleks" (10.4) the script only has the promiscuous use of the adjective "space" to distinguish it from a World War Two flick starring Dana Andrews. Not that the Cold War influence from Nation's first story has completely left the scene. Remember, this is a time when all viewers over the age of twenty have seen the end of both Hitler *and* Stalin, so in Britain any epic-scale parable about human society isn't likely to focus on "fascism" or "communism" but on free will in general. And after six episodes of derring-do, the moral here is that anything which seeks to control free will is innately wrong, however beneficial the results.

When the series tackles this issue again in the '70s (8.2, "The Mind of Evil"), the focus is on the way thought-control might affect criminal behaviour, and perhaps the actions of individual soldiers. But it's too early for Vietnam now, and here the Conscience represents something bigger, a force that can remove freedom of purpose from a whole society in one go. We're still in an age when people think of social engineering in grandiose terms, when a single mind is seen to be able to steer human destiny, always for ill even if there are positive side-effects. Everyone knew that Hitler at least made the trains run on time, and that a Stalin or a Chairman Mao was capable of imposing mechanised "order" on a society from the top down. Mao's "Cultural Revolution" was just a couple of years away. For those who believed the myth of a virile and super-efficient Soviet Union, or of a powerful and aggressive new China after the debacle of the Korean War, this sort of thing was a genuine concern.

As ever, no discussion of a Nation script is complete without a nod to American adventure serials

and British pulp adventure stories. In the third episode of "The Keys of Marinus", we get *Tarzan*-style ruins in the jungle, but incidents in other episodes have a '30s serial feel too. In fact, the whole structure of the story - each episode a new continent, in much the same way that *Flash Gordon* offered a new part of Ming's empire every week or two - is familiar. It looks plotless and meandering now, but let's not forget that at this stage even non-space-age stories like "Marco Polo" (1.4) are prone to take the same tack.

Then there's *The Lord of the Rings*, again. We've already seen its influence on "The Daleks" (1.2), but the "quest" motif is particularly Frodo Baggins; the scattering of the Keys, to Marinus' various cultures, makes you wonder if three went to the Elves and seven went to the Dwarves. Of course, it's possible that the same impulse for cultural self-improvement on Nation's part - the one that led to his watching the Georgian State Dancers - also led to his getting into Wagner, which is where Tolkien lifted these ideas from in the first place. On a similarly mythic note, it's not too much of a stretch to spot items from Homer's *Odyssey*. Screaming Jungle, meet the Sirens; for "Morpho Brains" read "Lotus Eaters"; Frozen Warriors and Killer Statues, didn't we meet you in the Palace of Alkinoos? The speed with which this story was written makes this entirely understandable, if not inevitable.

And there's one other noticeable influence here from an older tradition than *Dan Dare*. When we were talking about "An Unearthly Child", we mentioned that the Doctor and Susan were perhaps a little suggestive of Prospero and Miranda in *The Tempest*. If it's sort-of-true there, then it's inescapable here. Arbitan is a lone "magician" on a mysterious island, making bizarre elemental discoveries in the company of nobody but (until recently) his daughter and his astrally-projecting couriers. Despite the fetish-wear, this makes Yartek an outer-space Caliban, the resentful monster who's bound to the magician's will but eventually breaks free. SF versions of *The Tempest* weren't new even in 1963, but episodes one and six are closer to the source than most. In Shakespeare's version, Prospero's main concern is that his daughter will run off with an unsuitable boyfriend; weirdly, here it's not Arbitan who asks whether Altos will make a fit husband but Yartek-disguised-as-Arbitan. It's the only time in *Doctor Who* that a monster expresses concern about the supporting cast's marriage prospects.

Let's move on to Millenius. As a first desperate attempt to do a detective story in *Doctor Who*, we inevitably get the Doctor saying 'elementary' like Sherlock and refusing to reveal the true killer to his companions until the right dramatic moment, while stupid criminals are tricked into giving themselves away. But the setting's more interesting. Aydan's death - in a crowded room, as he's being escorted away under arrest - is rather tactlessly like the shooting of Lee Harvey Oswald by Jack Ruby. "Tactlessly" because this was less than four months after it happened. Actually, there's a lot of contemporary America in the Millenius section of the story. The glamour of the US of A, and of New York in particular, is a big feature of many Nation scripts. Before cheap transatlantic travel, those who'd seen newsreel and movie footage of the thrusting, gleaming skyscrapers saw this as a vision of how the future should look. This was doubly true after World War Two, when London was full of rubble but New York had survived unscathed (note that it's "Millenius", suggesting a brave new era). For all the ray-guns and psychometrics, the citizens make 'phone calls and live in apartments.

Another topical reference is the look of the judges: the Greek Cypriot movement for independence (from either the British or the Turks… it's a long story) was led by an Archimandrite, Archbishop Makarios. He was frequently in the news in the late 1950s, and his beard and mitre were easily caricatured.

Things That Don't Make Sense   Even given that he's apparently such a wise and impressive figure, Arbitan has done an implausibly good job of convincing people to guard his Keys. Key #4 is frozen along with the ice-soldiers, suggesting that they were put there specifically for the task of looking after it. [Maybe they get paid time-and-a-half. Terrance Dicks' *K9 and Other Mechanical Creatures* (1979) confidently asserts that the soldiers are actually robots, which would explain a lot, but there's no evidence for it here.]

It might also have been a good idea if Arbitan had left all the Keys with reasonably friendly and accessible cultures, rather than cities threatened by disembodied brains or associates who live near screaming jungles. He acts as if he's too old to retrieve the Keys himself, but this wouldn't have been a problem if he'd made sure that they all ended up in the hands of people who know his face, thus removing the need for perilous adventuring. Some of them have obviously fallen into the wrong hands over the years, although that is exactly what he was trying to avoid by scattering them.

And why do the travel-dials land the party in such arbitrary and often inconvenient places? Ian pops into the vault where Key #5 is kept, which is handy, but why deposit the adventurers in a frozen wasteland rather than the cave where Key #4 is actually to be found? And did the Doctor arrive in the same part of Millenius as Ian (in which case, why didn't he just take the Key)? Or somewhere else entirely (in which case, why does Ian arrive in the vault)? Where did the others turn up, since they were with Ian when he left the scene of the *last* Key? And why has Eprin, Arbitan's doomed courier, been hanging around in Millenius for so long without trying to nick the Key before now? In fact, he didn't even need to steal it, as the Elders have no problem handing it over to anyone with Arbitan's authority.

It takes about twenty seconds for Ian, Susan and the Doctor to follow Barbara to the City of Morphoton. In that time, she has a nasty accident with the travel-dial (and recovers from it), takes the bracelet off and leaves it on the floor (for no reason), is shown to a decadent chaise longue, gets pampered by the servants, is offered a choice of materials for her robe and has an unseen meeting with their "host" in the City. Do the other three travellers get lost in transit, or does Barbara just *imagine* that all this has happened? Similarly, the trapper claims that Sabetha's been in the mountains since the previous day, even though Ian and Barbara seem to leave the screaming jungle no more than a couple of hours after she does. We could pretend that there's some kind of relativistic time-dilation effect going on, but really, it looks more like the writer is routinely assuming that "time passes" after each episode. You could probably get away with that sort of thing, in the days before video…

When the Doctor splits the party into two teams for rapid Key-recovery, he puts Susan in the other team to himself, which is contrary to every protective instinct we've ever seen him demonstrate. Ian's decision in the jungle, to send Sabetha on to the next destination and tell the others that the Key they've found is a fake, doesn't make any sense either. Wouldn't it be better for Sabetha to help him find the real one? What possible advantage is there in keeping the others that well-informed? There's also some confusion about the numbering of the Keys, with the Doctor believing that he's skipping *two* jumps ahead by going to Millenius, rather than three. Anyone would think this was being made up week-by-week.

Although the snowflakes in the icy wasteland come down rather gently, there seems to be a fairly stiff breeze blowing on the mountain. The trapper's a thieving rapist who doesn't mind killing people off for profit, but he doesn't think of dealing with Ian while the travellers are unconscious, instead preferring to resort to the old give-him-a-bag-full-of-meat-and-hope-the-wolves-chase-him ploy. We also have to assume that his claim to have killed wolves with his bare hands is bluster, given that he doesn't put up a fight against Ian and looks scared of skinny Altos. Plus, Ian knows the trapper's name, apparently without being told it. Unless Barbara's mentioned it to him off-camera, but it's a strange thing to talk about in the middle of a blizzard.

The "sea of death" is supposedly a barrier against attack, as if it's inconceivable that anyone might try approaching with submarines. Or, say, aircraft. [Then again, we never see anything fly on this planet. The only bird we're shown is a chicken, so if the people of Marinus have never even considered the possibility of movement through the air, then they won't have tried to build aeroplanes.]

When Yartek disguises himself in Arbitan's robe, Ian cleverly realises that it's not Arbitan because of inconsistencies in the Voord's story. Neither he nor Susan notice the much more obvious clue, that Arbitan's head seems to have extended to three times its previous size. And this is *after* the TARDIS tribe cheerfully strolls back into the pyramid, having already been warned that the Voord might have taken charge by the time they return. Did all the empty submarines on the beach not give them a clue that a takeover was imminent? Once the Voord are found to be in control, Ian mumbles something about being afraid that this would happen, but it's a bit late by then.

Nor it is explained who switches off the forcefield around the TARDIS, as Arbitan dies immediately after the Doctor and company leave, and Yartek hardly has a motive to do it [unless his troops have been trying to blow the lock?]. Stranger yet… finding the TARDIS unguarded on their return, the Doctor still intends to give Arbitan the final Key rather than just running off.

Minutes later, he announces that the Conscience was a menace and that Marinus is better off without it.

The real villain behind the "Millenius Job" is the city's Prosecutor, who later creeps into the local police station to steal a crucial piece of evidence. To do this, he disguises himself with a sinister black hood (why, since he's surely got good reasons to be there?) but doesn't bother to take off his Prosecutor's uniform. Then there's Terry Nation's latest attempt at Big Science. Nature has a tempo of destruction, right? Plants overrun old buildings, right? So if you speed up the tempo, then plants try to strangle people, right? Not unless entropy's got a wilful grudge against human beings, no.

Billy Fluffs: 'If you'd been wearing your shoes you could have lent her hers', and the self-contradictory 'I can't improve at this very moment… I can't prove, at this very moment'. In episode one he comes within a hair's breadth of saying 'I don't stink', but sadly pulls out of it just in time. We might also mention the Doctor's reaction when asked if the sea might be frozen: 'No, impossible in this temperature. Besides, it's too warm.'

Critique   And suddenly, Sydney Newman's refusal to use BEMs makes absolute sense…

At stake is the whole essence of the programme. We now understand the series to be "about" aliens, scary moments, cliffhangers, mind-blowing concepts and the Doctor's relationship with his human chums. The programme's Founding Fathers saw it differently. The Founding Mother had the casting vote, and circumstances (and Lambert's populist instinct, often spot-on in giving people what they didn't know they were going to want) pushed the show from the classroom to the sixpenny stalls. Saturday Morning Serials replaced literary adaptations as the role-model.

Watching this story in isolation, it looks like edited highlights of a dozen or so other *Doctor Who* stories where they got this sort of thing right, but watching it in sequence - especially with "Marco Polo" on audio - it jars. Even the sense of urgency is missing. Why should we care if the TARDIS crew get the Keys, when the reason they're searching is to get back to the TARDIS, which is in a death-trap anyway? There isn't even anyone chasing them, and the "prize" is to enable someone to take over everybody else's minds. Meanwhile, Susan does nothing but blub.

On its own terms, though… there's a lot that would have entertained an uncritical kid in 1964, and the rest can, on occasion, be endearingly stupid. Some of the ineptitude is engaging, like the arms of the statue. (We've seen this defended as a homage to Jean Cocteau. To prove that this sort of thing could work in *Doctor Who*, see 14.3, "Pyramids of Mars"; 18.5, "Warriors' Gate"; and 20.7, "The Five Doctors".) Some of it, like the ice-soldiers milling about on the ledge as if they're extras from *Monty Python and the Holy Grail*, gets points for effort as we can at least see what they were getting at. Some of it, like the Evil Brains of Morphoton, still works given that it's *Doctor Who* and that someone had to invent the clichés. The Voord, however, remain pathologically hopeless.

The trouble is that the thing for which "The Keys of Marinus" deserves credit is also the thing that kills it stone dead. After this, we'll be seeing a lot of alien planets that are just a handful of similar-looking sets and some filming in a quarry. This story is something else entirely. Yet even apart from the budgetary problems, the epic scale means that it never stands a chance of being interesting. With "The Daleks", Nation gave the BBC a fairly banal setting, but one in which the Corporation's world-builders had the chance to expand, experiment and create something pleasingly alien. Here he gives them *half a dozen* fairly banal settings, and no room to manoeuvre. Not many interesting things really happened on Skaro either; it didn't matter, because of the spooky city and the radiophonic jungle. But this doesn't look like *those* bits, it looks like the bits where the Thals prance around in caves while the audience waits for the action to move back to the Daleks. Only it lasts for six episodes.

The Facts

Written by Terry Nation. Directed by John Gorrie. Ratings: 9.9 million, 9.4 million, 9.9 million, 10.4 million, 7.9 million, 6.9 million.

Supporting Cast Robin Phillips (Altos), Katherina Scholfield (Sabetha), George Coulouris (Arbitan), Stephen Dartnell (Yartek), Fiona Walker (Kala), Martin Cort (Aydan), Donald Pickering (Eyesen), Francis de Wolff (Vasor), Henley Thomas (Tarron), Michael Allaby (Larn), Raf de la Torre (Senior Judge), Alan James (First Judge), Peter Stenson (Second Judge), Heron Carvic (Voice of Morpho).

Episode Titles "The Sea of Death", "The Velvet Web", "The Screaming Jungle", "The Snows of Terror", "Sentence of Death", "The Keys of Marinus". (Yes, this time the "accepted" title is the name of the episode at the *end* of the story.)

Cliffhangers The Doctor, Ian and Susan find Barbara's travel-dial, AND THERE'S BLOOD ON IT (the drama of this is somewhat less overstated in the recap at the start of the next episode); the screaming jungle starts screaming at Susan, who collapses to her knees like a wuss; in the middle of a blizzard, Ian tells Barbara that if they don't find shelter then they don't stand a chance; arriving in the museum of Millenius, Ian is knocked unconscious, allowing an unseen figure to steal the Key and frame him; still in Millenius, Barbara receives a 'phone call from a (typically) terrified Susan, saying that her kidnappers are going to kill her.

The Lore

• This story was a desperate, last-minute, rapidly-written (no, really) replacement for the Malcolm Hulke "Hidden Planet" idea. Terry Nation was busy researching the eighth story for this season, a historical piece about the Indian Mutiny of 1857. He was hard at work on a first draft when he was told to make a start on a space adventure story, pronto. (Well, that's the official version. Not even a draft script has ever been displayed in public, which is odd for a writer whose effects have been researched so diligently.) Because the scripts for "The Daleks" had been submitted in such a rush, Nation had a reputation for promptness and creative solutions to problems. By the end of this volume, the irony of this will become apparent…

• On reading the scripts, director John Gorrie was less than entirely enthusiastic. The usual account has him with his head in his hands, groaning. He'd only recently trained with the BBC as a director, and would have preferred a "straight" drama, or - if lumbered with *Doctor Who* - a historical story. Lambert specifically asked for him, after his work on the glossy magazine soap *Compact*. He was a theatre director before this, and had trained Katherine Schofield (Sabetha). The cast all seemed to like him, but Cusick noted his lack of interest. The making of episode three was affected by scenery troubles, which the Head of Design blamed on the script's late arrival.

• As we've already mentioned, Robert Gould had been asked to have another crack at his "Miniscules" story, and his new idea was a world where plants were in control of people. Lambert wanted some assurances that it wouldn't be a retread of *Day of the Triffids* (for obvious copyright reasons, and because she was negotiating for John Wyndham to write her a script). Eventually, Gould was thanked and let down gently. Imagine how pleased he and his lawyer were when they got wind of Nation's "Screaming Jungle" episode. David Whitaker defended the script on the grounds that it was a variation on the "House That Jack Built" idea from episode one, but set out-doors and in a jungle so as to make a better con-trast with the following episode. Don't imagine for a moment that this is the last we'll hear about that "Miniscules" thing, either…

• As most of you should know, George Colouris (Arbitan) was a member of Orson Welles' Mercury Theatre company, and played Mr Thatcher in *Citizen Kane*. He'd also been in the various *Pathfinders* yarns as the vaguely sinister Harcourt Brown.

• According to an early draft of episode one, the reason the TARDIS was in Totter's Lane in 1963 was that the Doctor was trying to pinch colour TV technology from the BBC. Like that would take five months.

• There's now a work of gay pornographic liter-ature called *The Velvet Web* (the same title as episode two). It was published by Virgin in 1997, penned by a well-known *Doctor Who* novelist under a pseudonym, and sadly features no brains in jars.

1.6: "The Aztecs"

(Serial F. Four Episodes, 23rd May - 13th June 1964.)

Which One is This? "Doctor In Love". Barbara becomes a goddess but refuses to steal a man's heart, Susan is engaged to a hunk but would rather stick needles in her eyes (or thorns through her tongue, anyway), while the Doctor makes a mug of cocoa and isn't exactly upset about being betrothed. Ian escapes romantic entanglement, but he's busy knocking people out with his mighty thumb. Other than that, it's mainly about Aztecs.

Firsts and Lasts It's the first time that the various heated debates in the production office about whether the TARDIS crew can / should change history have plot consequences. This means that, unusually, the story starts off by being built around a conflict between members of the TARDIS crew rather than a conflict with the vil-lains. It's also the first time the programme-mak-ers are allowed into BBC Television Centre to shoot a story, so they've finally got the potential to do zooms and wide-angles (but they don't, much).

More noticeably, it's the first time Ian gets to have a big punch-up with the villainous heavy in the last episode.

Four Things to Notice About "The Aztecs"…

1. At a time when the programme isn't yet about "the Doctor and sidekicks", this is categori-cally Barbara's story, in a way that none of her other appearances ever are. The entire plot revolves around her decisions and other people's reactions to them. She even gets a chance to pull a knife on a high priest. Her three colleagues have things to do as well: Ian is sent off to fight people, while Susan is sent to school, allowing a two-week holiday for Carole Ann Ford and lots of speeches showing off how much research everyone has done. And uniquely for the TV series, the Doctor gets engaged. Although he's ostensibly desperate to get the TARDIS back, he doesn't seem all that reluctant to stay, either. He appears downright melancholy at story's end, and his farewell to his fianceé, Cameca, is apparently more painful than the one he eventually gives to his own grand-daughter (2.2, "The Dalek Invasion of Earth").

2. In stark contrast to other stories this year, where the studio's so small that they can't show too much of the set, this story's middle episodes see sets designed for Lime Grove D suddenly being moved to twice-as-large TVC3. And they *still* have to do tight shots, in case they accidental-ly reveal too much. Designer Barry Newbury's other problems included the lack of any detailed reference materials and the loss of half the garden set in transit, but the thing to look out for is the 2D backdrop. On video it looked all right, sort of, but DVD and digital jiggery-pokery don't do it any favours. However, the detail in the rest of the set rewards close attention, if you can draw your eyes away from the extraordinary hats.

3. John Ringham's performance as the thor-

Can You Rewrite History, Even One Line?

Over the years, the series has presented us with a set of irreconcilable views of time-travel. One week we may be hard-line determinists, the next we may be stoic existentialists, and the week after that we may be quantum-mystical monadists. One story assumes History-with-a-capital-H to be a living, intelligent force, the way Hegel said it was (we'll explain all of this in a bit), while the following adventure depicts history as a set of contingencies and accidents.

We'll be presenting one possible model in **How Does Time Work?** under "Day of the Daleks" (9.1), but even *that* isn't waterproof. To sum it up here: the only people immune to causality are the Doctor's people. Every other sentient being has consciousness, though not true "free will". The presence of free will alone can rewrite history, and those who fly TARDISes are the only ones who have it, at least as far as we know. This accounts for a number of seeming anomalies. And yet, the Doctor is terrified that his human associates will somehow wreck the timelines. Three times in the first year, even leaving aside the unscreened pilot episode, the Doctor admonishes the crew for attempting to change events. If history - or History - is running on pre-determined lines, then what possible effect could Barbara have? You could argue that as a traveller under the Doctor's protection, she counts as an extension of the Doctor's free will; you could even argue that it's the presence of a TARDIS which makes the difference, not the presence of its pilot. But this still leaves occasional oddities, like the potential ruined Earth that Sarah sees in "Pyramids of Mars" (13.3).

More importantly, why is Earth's history sacrosanct, and not Skaro's or Traken's? An obvious answer would be that the people doing the intervening might never be born if their own world's history is amended, but this doesn't wash. If the history of Vortis were to be altered, for example, then the great fire of Rome wouldn't have happened. (No, think about it. Even though the TARDIS goes to Vortis *after* the fire, Rome is founded by people who are descended from Vicki's boyfriend's cousin in 3.3, "The Myth Makers". No Menoptera, no Doctor, therefore no Trojan Horse.) People crossing time and space make every world's history equally contingent.

Moreover, the future of Earth - with respect to the human time-travellers - is up for grabs. By the time we get to "The Moonbase" (4.6), it's every time-traveller's moral imperative to fight evil, even if 2070 is ancient history for Vicki or Steven. Ian

and Barbara remember meeting people from the twenty-eighth century (1.7, "The Sensorites"), so they can be confident that the Dalek conquest isn't permanent (2.2, "The Dalek Invasion of Earth"). Yet any action they take is apparently improvised, not following a "plan" like the death of Robespierre or the rise of Napoleon (1.8, "The Reign of Terror"). If they'd left in the TARDIS in the 2160s, allowing the Earth to be either destroyed or turned into a Dalek spaceship, then somehow they wouldn't be committing as big a crime as if they'd prevented Barrass and Bonaparte meeting in a pub one night.

When a viewer asked about this in the early days, script editor David Whitaker wrote:

"The basis of time travelling is that all things that happen are fixed and unalterable, otherwise of course the whole structure of existence would be thrown into unutterable confusion and the purpose of life itself would be destroyed. Doctor Who is an observer. What we are concerned with is that history, like justice, is not only done but can be seen to be done."

Whitaker's comment about "the purpose of life itself" is striking. Not only does he seem to have an idea of what that purpose is, he's confident that there is one at all. Aside from anything else, it's interesting that the characters in Whitaker's own scripts who act as if they've figured out the Meaning of Existence are all mad or evil. But the tone of his reply might hint that, once again, free will is the issue here. In this case, the Doctor isn't free to interfere because it'd destroy the freedom of everyone else in creation. History can't be changed, not because we don't have free will but because free will has to mean something in the long-term. Note, especially, how Whitaker instinctively links history with a need for justice. Justice is meaningless in a predetermined universe. His script for "The Evil of the Daleks" (4.9) makes it clear that a free choice between good and evil is one of the basics of humanity.

Shortly before the French Revolution, German philosopher Hegel (from whom most of the Enlightenment values that *Doctor Who* champions can be said to start) suggested that there was a course of History - "Destiny", if you will - but that certain individuals have the power to divert it. This power he designated "charisma", from the Greek *kharis*, meaning "grace". The modern meaning of the word is a bit diluted, when applied to movie

continued on page 69...

oughly villainous and sacrifice-obsessed Tlotoxl… yes, you occasionally expect him to offer his kingdom for a horse, but how *else* could anyone play a character like this? With all the odd names needing careful diction, and all the pressures of near-enough live TV, anything halfway casual would have been so wrong as to seem ridiculous. After all, a man who makes a living carving people's hearts out isn't a part you can method act, at least not without facing arrest. What's really entertaining, though, is that Ringham will go on to appear in "Colony in Space" (8.4) as the weedy eco-friendly colonist leader who looks as if he wouldn't threaten a lentil. After watching "The Aztecs", it's like getting Brian Blessed to play a librarian. (And see also 4.1, "The Smugglers".)

4. But the most important thing to notice about Tlotoxl is this: as the *villain*, his main motive is to prove that Yetaxa / Barbara is a fraud and a false goddess. And of course, he's right. We're being asked to cheer people who are preying on the beliefs of others, and even by the standards of our own culture, Tlotoxol never does anything really bad until he gets desperate in the last episode. He's in favour of human sacrifice, but the sacrifices *want* to die for honour, and in the same episode even the Doctor supports their right to. (Besides, how many acquaintances of the Doctor have sacrificed themselves for what they believed to be a greater good?)

In any other tale, a sceptical mind like Tlotoxol's might make him the hero, and only the hunchback and the permanent leer would raise "trust" issues. Autloc, who's supposed to be the 'reasonable' and 'civilised' Aztec here, actually just believes everything Barbara tells him without asking for evidence. Yet astonishingly, after pretending his companion's a goddess and seducing a charming, intelligent Aztec lady in order to get his TARDIS back, in episode three the Doctor grandly announces 'I serve the truth!' as if it's the credo of the whole series.

The Continuity

The Doctor Claims to be a scientist *and* an engineer. He admires the architecture - 'the Aztecs, they knew how to build' - and he tells Cameca, as he tells most people, that he's not a medical doctor. Yet, less than three minutes later, he's finding the precise cactus needed to drug someone in a fight. He knows a great deal about Aztec culture, though not the marital significance of cocoa beans, and tries to stop Susan witnessing a human sacrifice.

• *Ethics*. After the Doctor inadvertently becomes engaged to Cameca, it's difficult to tell whether he's stringing her along or seriously thinking about staying put. As has already been noted, he seems distinctly unhappy when he has to part with her. But more importantly, he singles her out for attention the first time he sees her, as if he actually fancies the woman.

For the first time, the defence of history is an ethical concern for the Doctor. His outrage at Barbara's plan to alter time is genuine, and he's adamant that such a thing isn't to be attempted. His claim is 'you can't rewrite history, not one line', stating that he knows such a thing is impossible [he sounds as if he's speaking from bitter experience]. He later reassures Barbara that even if she hasn't saved the Aztecs, she's saved one man, and he honestly seems to believe that this is the best kind of victory. [This will be a major part of the Doctor's outlook in years to come.] Indeed, he's happy to interfere in the small details of Aztec life, and there's no suggestion that they might have big consequences.

• *Inventory*. He's still packing that torch.

The Supporting Cast

• *Ian*. It's already been established that he's good at unarmed combat, but now we see the full extent of this. He not only willingly accepts his duty as a warrior, but confidently takes on Ixta - his rival to command - several times. In their first encounter, Ian uses a thumb between the shoulder-blades to knock his opponent unconscious.

• *Barbara*. It's obvious that her detailed knowledge of this culture is a result of lengthy study, and she states that the Aztecs were one of her specialities. [This would seem to indicate that she was a historian who took a post-graduate teaching diploma, rather than someone who went from school into teacher-training college. B.Ed students rarely get to specialise to this extent even today, and in the late 1950s it was frowned upon.] Still, the use of sacrifice revolts her. She has no qualms about passing herself off as a reincarnation of the High Priest Yetaxa; actually she seems to enjoy it, and positively relishes the idea of changing history for the Aztecs' good.

• *Susan*. Once again, the prospect of forced marriage horrifies her, but this time it's her own

Can You Rewrite History, Even One Line?

...continued from page 67

stars and recording artists, unless Cher really *can* turn back time. We might tentatively suggest that, aside from his own kind, people the Doctor "recruits" to travel with him possess it (maybe the TARDIS recognises it… see **Who Decides What Makes a Companion?** under 21.5, "Planet of Fire"). Alternatively, perhaps it's a side-effect of good old artron energy, and you get charisma just by virtue of travelling on a TARDIS. So certain time-travelling monsters might have it, too.

Whatever the mechanics, this Force of Destiny makes sure that certain key events happen willy-nilly, and guarantees that time isn't changed by annoying little butterfly-effect things like treading on the wrong small mammal in the Cretaceous era. This is certainly the logic at work in "The Aztecs", where the Doctor worries about Barbara trying to alter an entire civilisation while posing as a goddess… but has no objection to her changing *Autloc's* destiny, and never considers the possibility that Autloc himself might alter civilisation. The little man doesn't count. These days, we instinctively sense that small actions taken by one individual can catastrophically change the world, but the idea of history being shaped by "big" people was bound to be popular in the wake of Churchill, Hitler, Stalin et al. As the discussion at the end of "The Reign of Terror" makes clear, at this stage in his career the Doctor believes that Robespierre would always have met the same nasty end, no matter what the TARDIS crew did. Whitaker's prologue to the novelisation *Doctor Who and the Crusaders* tells you who wrote that scene.

An earlier German philosopher, Liebniz, had conjectured that individual consciousness was "along for the ride" but had no say in what happened in the universe. If you flip a light-switch, then it was always scheduled that the light would come on at that point. But God has a plan which requires the essences of things ("monads", which Liebniz sometimes used to mean "souls" and sometimes what we'd call "atoms") to be there playing their parts as witnesses, though not causally affecting one another. God's tried all the other ways that events could go, and has opted for this one.

The logical extension of this would be for one person's preordained role in the world - *scripted* role might be a better term - to occur regardless of what the world does, and therefore changing all of history is impossible. Barbara might have created a world in which Cortes never destroyed the Aztecs, but she'd be that world's only occupant. Something of this kind appears to befall the Doctor/s in "The Two Doctors" (22.4), when the Second Doctor is transformed into an Androgum. The Sixth Doctor is affected, even though we never saw the Doctors in-between sprout orange bushy eyebrows, and Peri wasn't eaten by a peckish Fifth Doctor when they first met. Her personal timeline isn't affected, but the Doctor's is, at least until it gets changed back.

Whitaker's successor as script editor, Dennis Spooner, quickly sets about undoing the theory that was spliced into the conclusion of his "Reign of Terror" script. We get three successive stories exploring the idea of altering history. "The Chase" (2.8) begins with the Doctor being exactly the kind of observer Whitaker described, even using a glorified TV set to tune in to Shakespeare and the Beatles. By the end of the story, the Daleks have caused one of the great unsolved mysteries by landing on the *Mary Celeste*. "The Space Museum" (2.7) hinges on the idea of alternative paths, and ends with the Doctor being freed from "inevitable" history by the companions overthrowing a military occupation. Time, we're told, has dimensions of its own. And, contrary to the notion that the Doctor's people alone can do it, he's asleep in a fridge when the key events take place.

History is no longer a place you visit, a landscape or a theme park, it's a process. In case this seems like a late reversal, consider how the presence of Vicki changes the dynamic of the series. She's the first future-human on board the TARDIS. She thinks of Ian, Barbara, John, Paul, George, Ringo and all of us at home in the same way that we think of Elizabeth I. By the same token, 1066 isn't something confined to textbooks, but a year with real people in it… and the Battle of Hastings could have gone either way (2.9, "The Time Meddler"). Nobody at the time thought of the Normans as unavoidably destined to rule, after all. The TARDIS crew shift from being observers to protectors of history.

Therefore, there's a *preferred* sequence of events, but not a pre-ordained one. The timestream, like any other stream, likes to follow a channel but can suffer a change of course if you put a big enough boulder in the way. The theological implications of a micro-managed causality are soft-pedalled, and after the Doctor's people are

continued on page 71...

impending nuptials to the doomed Perfect Victim which cause friction. Unsurprisingly, she's said to be more capable than the other girls in the Aztecs' seminary, and to know things only the priests should know. [When Cortes arrived in Mexico, the Aztecs were expecting a pale-faced man with a black beard, and accepted him as a prophesied envoy of the gods. Given her maltreatment here, it's tempting to think that Susan is the one who told them to wait for him, just to get back at them.]

The TARDIS No technical faults this time. One indicator, on the console panel closest to the doors, informs the Doctor when the Ship has landed; another, on the panel to the left of this, indicates that the Ship is still in motion after it arrives on a spaceship [the lead-in to the next story]. The Doctor acts as if this is a mystery [he's never landed on a spaceship before, odd considering how often he's going to be doing it from now on]. The TARDIS wardrobe gets another "period costume" boost here, as the travellers take their Aztec togs with them when they leave.

History
• *Dating.* Obviously sometime before the arrival of Cortes, who turns up in 1520 according to Barbara. [Actually, he arrived in the spring of 1519 and destroyed Aztec society within two years]. Barbara believes the tomb is from the 'early period', circa 1430, and the body within looks like it's been there awhile. The warrior Ixta, who's still fairly young, is the son of the man who built the tomb. [This would suggest a date around 1460-80. Lucarotti's novelisation gives a date of 1507, which is feasible if Barbara's estimate is a bit off.]

The Aztecs, as they're depicted here, are able to predict rainstorms and solar eclipses. A single male, a Perfect Sacrifice, has his heart cut out during one such eclipse. The Aztecs have many gods [although the actors are spared the burden of having to say "Quetzalcoatl" or "Huitzilpochtili", and only the weather-god Tlaloc is named directly]. Barbara, taken to be a reincarnation of the High Priest Yetaxa, is accepted as a 'god' or 'spirit' by the current High Priest of Knowledge [see **Things That Don't Make Sense**] but not the High Priest of Sacrifice. [The logic of human sacrifice, as it's presented here, is at odds with known history. Current thinking is that the offering of a young

warrior was a "sacrifice" in the truest sense, surrendering something the culture urgently needed as a recompense for the gods providing the things it needed most of all. Here, it's assumed that sacrificed individuals think they're either going to become gods themselves or messengers of the gods.]

The Analysis

Where Does This Come From? There's a school of thought that this was the BBC's way of cashing in on the hit National Theatre Company play *The Royal Hunt of the Sun.* In fact the dates don't quite work out, as the play was first performed in mid-February 1964 at the Chichester Festival, and the suggestion to make a Mexico-based story was put to Lucarotti during filming of "Marco Polo". The latest possible date for Whitaker and Lucarotti to have had this conversation is the 17th of February, which is cutting it a bit fine. The press coverage of the play's preview might have been uppermost in their minds, but neither of them would have seen it performed. (Contrary to what's sometimes said, Lucarotti was in Britain this time around, and spent whole days in the production office writing the scripts in March.)

Nevertheless, Peter Shaffer's play about the Conquistadors made something of a splash, not least because of the costumes and music. According to Shaffer, the outfits used up almost the whole supply of available Chinese pheasant-feathers in Britain at the time, and the new colour supplements in the Sunday newspapers took advantage of the colourful trappings for their photo-spreads. The music for the play also caught the mood; Marc Wilkinson's score was exotic, in the days when pan-pipes weren't too New Agey to be taken seriously. It became standard-issue "South America" music, even in "Four to Doomsday" (19.2). Richard Rodney Bennett's score for "The Aztecs" is more conventional, but in a similar vein. Later on, Mexico City became the place to be, as the Olympics and the World Cup came in rapid succession (see 4.5, "The Underwater Menace"). Lucarotti had lived there before, and knew the Aztecs and their world well. The subject was even being taught in schools, as the memoirs of one of the Conquistadors were published in a Penguin paperback edition in 1959.

The other point to make is that the theme of

Can You Rewrite History, Even One Line?

...continued from page 69

written into the format this isn't an issue. Yet, as we see in "Pyramids of Mars", it's still a murky area. A literal interpretation of the scene in the alternative 1980 would suggest that the arrival of a TARDIS makes history "soften", only to become "fixed" once the Ship leaves. Obviously, the presence of two or more time-travellers makes this more complex; see the essays under "The Mark of the Rani" (22.3) and "Mawdryn Undead" (20.3) for more. If this "soft" idea works, then what precisely happens in "The Space Museum" or "Inferno" (7.4)? These seem to involve disengagement from 'coterminous time' (to quote "the Two Doctors"), and a crossing-over to another "fixed" timeline, rather than rendering the normal timeline contingent and malleable. Both involve malfunctions with the console.

(Note that this "soft" idea is subtly different from another popular theory: that in its natural state, history isn't fixed at all, and only the presence of a TARDIS makes it inevitable. Or at least, inevitable unless someone does something truly catastrophic at an earlier point in time. While the "soft" option

implies that the Doctor is putting time at risk just by travelling, *this* version implies that every definite event in history is his responsibility. It also explains why the Doctor can't actively change his own past, and it's a notion that was included by Virgin Publishing in the guidelines for the '90s novels. On-screen, the Doctor suggests something perilously similar in X1.13, "The Parting of the Ways". Russell T. Davies once wrote for the Virgin line, of course…)

We should also note that the Doctor's fear of changing history in "The Aztecs" seems to be prompted by a painful, personal memory rather than by mere theorising. When he's finally apprehended by his own kind (6.7, "The War Games"), he's arraigned for interfering in the affairs of other races, not for altering history per se. We now know that the Doctor was on the run from people capable of detecting alterations in the timelines, so the assumption has been - since 1969, anyway - that his low profile in the early stories was simply an attempt to evade their gaze. "Silver Nemesis" (25.3) opens up the possibility that there may have been something more dubious behind the Doctor's travels involving his own people's history…

---

this story is exactly the sort of thing David Whitaker wanted to explore. The Aztecs, for all their barbarity, had a culture which survived in marginal circumstances and produced extraordinary advances. By what right does anyone from our culture sit in judgement? We'll see this theme re-examined in later stories this year, and others Whitaker wrote (even so, Tlotoxl is clearly made out to be "wrong" while Autloc is explicitly said to be reasonable, civilised and an exception to the norm for Aztec society, so the script's still being quite English about this). Moreover, as we'll see in "The Reign of Terror" (1.8), Whitaker's attitude to the immutability of Earth's history is at odds with that of his successors. See also **Can You Rewrite History, Even One Line?**.

Things That Don't Make Sense Everyone's a bit over-dressed for Mexico, aren't they?

But as far as plot-logic goes, and overlooking the historical niggles, there's only one major flaw. The story begins with everyone accepting Barbara as a reincarnation of a priest. Then, in the space of one line - spoken by Susan, but never contradicted for the remaining three-and-two-thirds episodes - Yetaxa is a 'god', and the whole empha-

sis is on Tlotoxl trying to prove that Barbara's mortal. It's true that the dead are occasionally re-classified as deities in "primitive" cultures, but the suddenness of it is hard to swallow.

A side-effect of this is that Autloc recognises the bracelet from the tomb. If Yetaxa died within living memory, as we're led to believe, then Autloc - who's no spring chicken - would have known him. The only other way he could recognise the bracelet would be if he'd been in the tomb himself, which is impossible, unless the entire story is based on a false premise. So instead of asking questions about Aztec culture, why not ask about Yetaxa's favourite colour or his wife's name?

If we're going to be pedantic, then we might also point out the massive coincidence that sees the Doctor zero in on the one woman in the Aztec old people's home who had a relationship with the architect of the temple he's trying to get into, while Ian becomes a sworn enemy of the architect's son on the same day. Still, it *is* TV.

Critique When this was released on grubby old videotape, everyone loved it. Now it's on reconditioned DVD, and suddenly it looks as if it's been shot on VT instead of some ancient and exotic type of film-stock. The people who felt that watching this was like watching a movie filmed in Mexico circa 1500 AD now realise it was done at Lime Grove in 1964. Not everyone is pleased. However, it stops the casual viewer from having to "make allowances". What you see is what you got. It's now revealed as an efficient script, as we always knew it was, but also a very slick production. Hartnell is never better, and the rest play up to his standard. Just in case the children watching need a monster, there's Tlotoxl. Most of the violence is suggested, but two people fall to their deaths and there are three good fights.

If it has a fault at all - and remembering that the educational info-dumps are considered normal practice at this point, not flaws by the series' own standards - it's that it plays things a little too safe. The villains are effective enough to get boos and hisses from the kids, and have half-decent reasons for what they're up to, but they're never really allowed to be characters. Perhaps that's inevitable; by the time "The Aztecs" was written, the series had established itself as a hit, and everyone involved was starting to get a grip on The Kind of Things This Programme Does. Leering villains were all part of the package, and with hindsight the end result looks like what we might recognise as a *Doctor Who* story, in a way that none of the previous five did. Terry Nation's last effort may have permanently bound the series to monsters and escapes, yet it lacks the near-Shakespearean plotting that becomes part of the programme's standard repertoire here.

The only thing that looks odd, now, is the Cameca subplot. Is the Doctor human after all, or simply manipulating a vulnerable old woman? Either interpretation doesn't fit with the Doctor we all know, but in itself, the story makes it work. Everyone involved is playing it straight, which makes it amusing as well as touching. It also helps to turn the Aztecs into people, not props in a TV story but a genuine culture. Which is, after all, the point.

The Facts

Written by John Lucarotti. Directed by John Crockett. Ratings: 7.4 million, 7.4 million, 7.9 million, 7.4 million. Down on "The Edge of Destruction" (1.3)... soon, everyone will be wondering whether they should bring the Daleks back.

Supporting Cast Keith Pyott (Autloc), John Ringham (Tlotoxl), Ian Cullen (Ixta), Margot van der Burgh (Cameca), Walter Randall (Tonila), Tom Booth (First Victim), André Boulay (Perfect Victim).

Episode Titles "The Temple of Evil", "The Warriors of Death", "The Bride of Sacrifice", "The Day of Darkness". (See? Two weeks after "The Keys of Marinus", we get another "of Death" already.)

Cliffhangers Tlotoxl looks into the camera to announce that Yetaxa is a false goddess, and that he shall destroy her; when Ian is defeated in combat, Tlotoxl tells Barbara that if she's Yetaxa then she should be able to save his life; Ian is trapped inside the temple's secret tunnel as the water-level rises.

The lead-in to the next story: the TARDIS console indicates that although the Ship has landed, it's still moving (weirdly it's Barbara, not the Doctor, who points out that they might have landed inside something).

The Lore

• The Doctor's claim to be an engineer, as well a theoretical scientist, was probably inserted after Sydney Newman sent a memo requesting that the status of engineering should be given a boost by the programme. How far Newman's suggestion was responsible for other scenes, such as the Doctor's detailed knowledge of molybdenum's properties in "The Sensorites" (1.7), is uncertain. Newman's very earliest comments, however, poured scorn on the "philosophical arty-science" type of hero that Bunny Webber wanted.

• The filmed sequences for episodes two and three were shot during the making of "The Keys of Marinus", episode five. Carole Ann Ford, Keith Pyott, Andre Boulay and Walter Randall did the seminary scenes; Billy Cornelius and David Anderson, supervised by Derek Ware, did the stunt fight at the end; Tom Booth jumped to his death (well, pretended to) for the end of episode one; and someone got his feet wet as Ian for the end of episode three. This was all done at Ealing, and Barry Newbery requested that the sets be kept. Which is just as well, as when the VT production moved to TVC from Lime Grove, part of the garden set was destroyed.

• The music for this story is by Richard Rodney Bennett. He has an Oscar for Best Score to his name, for *Murder on the Orient Express*, and is just about the most distinguished composer to have worked on the series. (Humphrey Searle - 3.3, "The Myth Makers" - is his main rival.)

• John Crockett didn't work on the series again, and eventually left the BBC. In the end he went to live in a monastery, and is buried there.

1.7: "The Sensorites"

(Serial G. 6 Episodes, 20th June - 1st August 1964.)

Which One is This?

'Get up ev'ry morning, plate feet and grey head,
Certain that every mind can be read.
Whoaahhh-hoaahhh, we're Sensorites.'

Firsts and Lasts If the previous story was the first history-based adventure to begin taking the form of what we might now call a "proper" *Doctor Who* story, then this is the first SF-tinged story to do the same. "The Daleks" was primarily a weird audio-visual exercise, and "The Keys of Marinus" was a patchwork thing that with hindsight looks almost improvised, but "The Sensorites" has what we tend to think of as a conventional *Doctor Who* plot in a conventional *Doctor Who* setting. Significantly, it's the first story to be commissioned from a new writer who's seen the programme in both its forms (contracts were signed just as "The Daleks" was ending on BBC1), and thus the first story to take the programme's remit as read.

So it's worth noticing that it's the first time the Doctor, rather than Ian or Barbara, is the instigator of much of the action. In fact, it's the first time the Doctor saves a planet not simply to get his Ship back but because it's the right thing to do. As the first "typical" *Doctor Who* story, it's interesting that for the first time the clichés of the series are commented on by the regulars, especially Ian's mention of how often they split up and get captured. Expanding the range of the programme's standard set-ups slightly, it's the first time the TARDIS lands inside a spaceship, and we see the spaceship leave from the outside (suggesting that the TARDIS is hovering in space).

The struggle between the nice and nasty Sensorite politicians is our first sight of a factional dispute between non-humans, and we'll hear their arguments from the mouths of endless other aliens in the years to come (7.2, "Doctor Who and the Silurians", is the story that immediately comes to mind... even the "plague" subplots look similar). Until now we've been told that different cultures have different ways of seeing things, but now we're told that even telepathic aliens are Just Like Us, prone to bickering, plotting and senseless behaviour. From a modern viewpoint, it's also notable that it's the first time a character who's befriended the TARDIS crew - Carol - is threatened at the end of an episode as if the viewers care about her as much as they care about Susan or Barbara.

And, turning up surprisingly early in the series' run, it's the first time an alien speaks of 'the one they call the Doctor'.

Six Things to Notice About "The Sensorites"...

1. So let's reiterate: this is quite possibly the most important *Doctor Who* story of all. The key scene comes in episode four, and most people miss it. Ian is cured of his illness; the nature of the "plague" has been discovered; and the Doctor has done everything the First Elder requested of him. And yet, the Doctor decides to go and investigate the water supply. He isn't doing it out of idle curiosity, and he's aware that it might be dangerous, but he elects to go into a hazardous place and save a planet *because he's good*. It's at this precise point that *Doctor Who* as we understand it comes into existence.

2. It's Barbara's turn to get a fortnight off. While the others are down on the planet, she's in orbit with Captain Maitland, probably the most boring astronaut ever. (Given the human muzak that NASA have sent into space, this is quite the achievement.) There seems to be nothing to do on this ship, although she *does* get a tan while she's in orbit, so either there's a sunbed or something's wrong with the radiation shielding. No wonder she zooms down to Sense-Sphere at the first opportunity, and seems almost happy that someone's trying to kill the humans.

3. When the Sensorite City Administrator's lackey swears loyalty to his boss near the end of episode three, he has to deliver the line 'command me' immediately after the Administrator speaks of someone strong and manly taking over the Sensorite Nation. In itself, there's something worryingly fetishistic about it, but the line's delivered in such a way as to suggest that he's going to follow it with the words '...big boy'. If it were in a programme made today, *nobody* would be able to

ABOUT TIME 1963-1966

watch it without assuming there was a deliberate kinky subtext, or at the very least thinking of Smithers and Mr Burns. To make it worse, the Administrator starts the scene by talking about them being 'bound hand and foot' by the humans.

4. Oh, all right. If you didn't know, or had no idea why it mattered: the City Administrator is played by Peter Glaze. He was a short, tubby, bespectacled comic actor best known for children's series *Crackerjack*[7]. We don't stand a chance of explaining this show's success, as we don't entirely understand it ourselves, but Glaze is ideally cast. Or rather, he's brilliantly mis-cast. His screen persona, developed as a straight-man to pre-War funsters "The Crazy Gang", was of a pompous little prig being ridiculed by the tall thin joker. This makes his portrayal of the xenophobic, self-important Sensorite into a very recognisable British character, an extraterrestrial *Daily Mail* reader... possibly not what the script intended.

5. It's the only story to revolve around bottled spring water. The idea of yuppies on other planets is vaguely absurd now, so imagine how it must have seemed in 1964. This is the fourth story this year to make a big deal about drinking water, and indeed, every story up until now has mentioned water supplies at some point. Here it's not only vital that Barbara and Susan walk past a tank with "WATER" written on it in big letters, but that Ian is too thirsty to wait for pure spring water and drinks from the city's contaminated supply instead. After the success of the latter half of "The Daleks", it was perhaps inevitable that a story would crop up involving dark caves with aqueducts, and using the presence of a monster in the cave as a cliffhanger. However, this monster is not all it seems...

6. At the risk of giving it away, the villains of this story are the Sense-Sphere's first human explorers, who've spent ten years in the caves there. They all have Robinson Crusoe beards and raggedy uniforms, and still maintain rigid military discipline after being driven utterly mad by the telepathic natives' attempts at friendship. Mercifully, no pith-helmets, big pink snakes or "trip" sequences are needed to make the point (q.v. 19.3, "Kinda").

The Continuity

The Doctor Even *he* speaks of having a heart, singular. He knows enough medicine to identify the poison in the water supply *and* tell everyone the remedy, as well as coming up with a quick first-aid treatment for Ian. He can fly a spaceship almost unassisted. Being defied by Susan sets off his most spectacular huff yet. When Ian echoes the Doctor's own statement about not being able to navigate the TARDIS properly, the Doctor takes offence and abruptly decides to kick the humans off at the next port of call.

• *Background.* At some point he and Susan left the TARDIS in the Tower of London, and deliberately got into a quarrel with Henry VIII in order to get back to it. Henry threw a parson's nose at him, and he threw it back, something he describes as taking place 'long before' Ian and Barbara came along. The Doctor and Susan have also visited the planet Esto, while the fashion arbiter Beau Brummell [see also 21.7, "the Twin Dilemma"] claimed that the Doctor looked good in a cloak. [He lied.]

Susan describes their home planet as being quite like Earth, but with a burnt orange sky [see 15.6, "The Invasion of Time"] and trees with silver leaves. When Susan speaks of going home, the Doctor - uniquely - indicates that they can't go there purely because they can't steer the TARDIS. [Obviously not true.]

• *Ethics.* He's reached the stage where he's keen on meddling in other people's business, as long as he can deny doing it. As has already been noted, this is the first time the Doctor is seen to be actively interfering in a planet's affairs when not forced to. He's not fond of weapons, but politely accepts a stun-gun from the First Elder.

• *Inventory.* He evidently carries a fountain pen with a copperplate nib, judging by the letter he writes. [Other stories - e.g. 2.3, "The Rescue" - hint that this may not be the Doctor's handwriting at all, as it's too legible.] He wears his glasses when flying a spaceship. His little pen-torch has obviously been recharged; any brighter, and the map he reads with it would start to smoulder.

The Supporting Cast

• *Ian.* Shows remarkable powers of recovery after being poisoned, leading the Doctor's rescue and taking on the human "warriors". In fact, now that the Doctor's taking the active role, Ian comes across as a lot more aggressive [he's still hyper after the fight at the end of the last story]. More impressive still is his ability to read spectrographic analyses of planetary masses, not something

How Telepathic is He?

In the novelisation of "The Nightmare Fair" (see Volume VI), Peri asks the Doctor if he might be a bit telepathic. He replies: 'You either are or you aren't. I aren't.' Then adds: 'At least, not much.'

This is a pretty fair summary. There are stories where the Doctor gets the chance to read minds, as in "Kinda" (19.3). There are stories where he projects, or allows his thoughts to be read, as in "The Pirate Planet" (16.2). He and his people frequently hook themselves up to telepathic technology, even if the 'reflex link' in the Doctor's brain has been cauterised (15.2, "The Invisible Enemy").

But for every one of these, there's an example of the Doctor being a non-entity, psychically speaking. The telepathic "primitives" on Uxarieus (8.4, "Colony in Space") can't detect the Doctor's thoughts, or else he'd never be able to fool the guards with his useless conjuring act. In the same story, the Guardian of the Doomsday Weapon doesn't seem to detect the Doctor or the Master's presence on the planet until they're in the room with him. True, the Doctor's people can shield their minds; "The Brain of Morbius" (13.5) finally comes out and admits it, after years of hi-jinks with mind probes from "The Space Museum" (2.7) onwards. But there's an anomaly or two even here.

We know that the Doctor and the Master are both formidable hypnotists. As presented in most of these cases, hypnosis is a matter of mental projection. A mind powerful enough to overwhelm another might not be receptive to weaker impulses. If we take the usual analogy of radio-waves, then the Doctor's ability to withstand onslaughts from beings like the Great Intelligence (5.2, "The Abominable Snowmen") would weigh against him being a natural telepath. Indeed, being receptive to mental impulses would seem to make you more vulnerable to mind-control or scanning by others. That's if we take the radio idea as read.

Anyone familiar with pseudo-science of the early 1970s will have another possible "explanation" of this ability. A combination of half-digested quantum physics, Jungian psychology and decaf Buddhism led to a sort of orthodoxy. Basically, we're all part of the same nature, and consciousness makes particles behave in odd ways and relay that behaviour to their anti-particles (see **How Do You Transmit Matter?** under 17.4, "Nightmare of Eden" and **How Does Evil Work?** under 8.2, "The Mind of Evil"). Therefore, dreams allow access to the Collective Unconscious; beings with high mental ability can teleport and time-travel; and all conscious beings have the potential to make objects levitate, although most never do (11.5, "Planet of the Spiders", is a compendium of all this *Tomorrow People* twaddle). Hence, only the Doctor's ego gets between him and the true understanding of all things.

If this weren't the case, then the amount of suffering he routinely encounters would leave him traumatised, and totally incapable of killing. Maybe it does; he practices Aikido, a form of martial art which - putting it crudely - works by making the aggressor empathise with the victim. (Well, terrestrial Aikido does, so if Venusian Aikido doesn't then he ought to call it something else. See 10.5, "The Green Death", for an example.) Killing seems to upset him as an activity, as well as a necessity. Even the Sixth Doctor has these scruples, but note that the seemingly-innocent Fifth Doctor is actually more steeped in blood and less adept at psi-functions than the others. He never hypnotises anyone who isn't already under another influence.

In 26.3, "The Curse of Fenric", we see psychic phenomena of a different kind. The belief of any individual can create a mental barrier against the Haemovores. Ace and the Doctor are equally

continued on page 77...

---

that a secondary school teacher would routinely have done.

[This is as good a time as any to mention that the spin-off novels, picking up the hint from Ian Stuart Black's novelisation of "The War Machines" (3.10), describe an older Ian taking the things he learned on his TARDIS travels into 1960s British technology. On his return, he becomes - so to speak - a pioneer among his own people. While this is an appealing conceit, there are obvious absurdities, especially with the idea that in the space of one year Ian can go from unemployed ex-secondary-modern teacher to noted engineer and friend of Sir Charles Summers. But on the other hand, he clearly has more experience than his teaching job ever required. Perhaps the Doctor's refusals to explain things don't usually mean that the thing is too complex to understand, but that it's simple enough for a human to copy.]

• *Barbara.* At the start of events here, it must have been a while since the TARDIS landed on the spaceship as Barbara says she's 'got over' the Aztec business. She obviously has a strong mind with clear thoughts, using the Sensorites' thought-transference device without difficulty.

• *Susan.* Now carrying a TARDIS key on a chain, and doing the locking-up duties. Her mental powers are, even untrained, evidently more potent than those of the Doctor or the Sensorites. [Assuming she *is* the same race as the Doctor, it's worth noting that she's a genuine teenager, whereas he's a mature male. In human culture, psychic powers are often linked with adolescence, especially in girls.] On the Sense-Sphere she can receive clear telepathic messages without any apparatus, and reply unassisted. The Doctor surmises that she has a gift in that direction, which she might want to develop once they get home.

Susan can quote Robert Louis Stevenson, and has reverted to her know-it-all stance regarding science lessons, wandering off just as Ian warms up for a lecture. She can give injections, and is instructed to use artificial respiration if Ian deteriorates [so the Doctor thinks she's good at first aid]. Not for the first time, she admits that she'd like to belong somewhere. Despite her recent sobbing and screaming, she calmly acquiesces when the Sensorites take her to their planet as a "hostage". [They may be reassuring her telepathically, but even so, hi-tech environments once again don't seem to hold any fear for her.]

Here she's more defiant of the Doctor than ever before. The Doctor claims they've never argued until now [blatantly a lie], and he's angry at the Sensorites for causing a fight, but Barbara believes Susan to be growing up. Indeed, Barbara insists she's not a child any more, and the Sensorites can read the misery in her mind. [She's obviously being set up for her departure in 2.2, "The Dalek Invasion of Earth".]

The TARDIS The Doctor admits that the Ship is 'an aimless thing'. The lock can be removed from the door intact, without any ill effects [this is mentioned in 1.2, "The Daleks"], and it comes out when the Sensorites try to burn it open. This removes the opening mechanism, and breaking down the door - though theoretically possible, judging by the Doctor's reaction to the idea - would disrupt the field of dimensions [see 2.1, "Planet of Giants"; 2.9, "The Time Meddler"; 5.7, "The Wheel in Space"].

The scanner's covered in static when the TARDIS arrives on the spaceship, something

which the Doctor agrees could be caused by an unsuppressed motor or a magnetic field. [As if it were just a normal sort of TV, and compare with 1.5, "The Keys of Marinus". The scanner has become altogether more complex by the next story, so does the Doctor fix it up at the same time that he re-installs the lock?] From the console, the Doctor can check the temperature outside as well as the air.

When Maitland's ship departs, the travellers watch it on the scanner. [As the story began with them landing inside the Ship, they may be hovering in space, or the TARDIS may have been brought down to the Sense-Sphere.] This week's boost to the TARDIS wardrobe: a snug black cloak from the Sensorites.

The Non-Humans
• *Sensorites.* The Sensorites are, broadly speaking, humanoid. They look almost identical to one another, with bald, bulbous heads, and beak-like mouths hidden behind wisps of what's presumably hair. Their eyes are black and featureless, and they don't have eyelids, while their feet seem to be disc-shaped. Their hearts are in the centre of their chests. All Sensorites that we see wear identical tunics in what looks like grey lycra, but there's a rigid caste system, with elders, warriors and a 'lower caste' to whom the human visitors aren't allowed to speak. Although no apparent females are seen, the Second Elder is persuaded to co-operate with the City Administrator's plans when threats are made against his 'family group'. Sensorites are acutely sensitive to sound, always speaking in whispers, and they're terrified of darkness. The pupils of their eyes contract in the dark, strangely [see **Things That Don't Make Sense**].

When Susan and Barbara think hard at two of them, the Sensorites clutch their heads in agony, though Susan herself collapses soon afterwards. It appears that although their powers of telepathy are formidable, they aren't naturally able to use thought-transference to communicate, and thus rely on thought-relay technology. Their mind-amplification devices resemble stethoscopes, with a disc that's applied to the forehead. These devices are usually only used to send messages, and there's no hint of the technology being able to probe the subconscious or detect lies, although they *can* be used to stun other Sensorites. Anyone can receive a telepathic message without such a device, but nobody except Susan can send one.

How Telepathic is He?

...**continued from page 75**

effective at this, more or less. By this stage we've had any amount of double-talk about the way degenerate matter releases energy on 'psychic frequencies' ("The Pirate Planet", again) and how even human psychic power is enough to reanimate Azal (8.5, "The Daemons"). Ordinarily, it seems, the Doctor's mind is no more "powerful" as a transmitter or receiver than anyone else's. But it *is* qualitatively different in what's transmitted or received, and better-trained. It would also appear, to take the metaphor from "The Sensorites", that the Doctor's mental 'eyelids' are more solid. Yet, from other stories later on, this is open to question. Intriguingly, it's the original Doctor who's most able to resist mental assault (see 20.7, "The Five Doctors", for a very clear comparison), suggesting

that the process of regeneration is one that opens him up mentally.

Finally, it's worth mentioning that according to "The Two Doctors" (22.4), human minds - unlike those of more developed beings - are hard to read because they're so 'flabby'. Possibly it's this that gives the Doctor his distinctive telepathic status, of being able to resist attacks but not particularly empathise. His mind is stuffed with hundreds of years of nonsense, more "human" even than our own, so no inherent telepathic ability is required. In "The Invasion of Time" (15.6), he can hold off the psychic advances of the Vardans simply *because* he's so easily distracted, while the sharp-minded Borusa wouldn't be able to last for a minute. This is far more in keeping with the Doctor's character than, say, the idea that he's got godlike mind-powers.

The Sensorites have been using their powers to put a human spaceship out of action, keeping the crew into a death-like state of paralysis as well as somehow controlling the craft itself. Fear makes this psionic attack easier, and in some cases individuals can be driven mad by it, though the Sensorites are capable of curing this with a machine that involves an elaborate helmet [the first of many hairdressing-salon-type mind-machines in the series]. Those suffering this madness are said to be 'open' and capable of sensing other minds, but under the influence of the machine the mind is 'closed'. The Sensorites won't let the human ship leave that area of space, yet they refrain from killing the crew and keep them fed. They even designate an area on their planet where the humans can live, rather than letting the outsiders tell Earth about the presence of molybdenum on their world.

The Sensorites believe themselves to have a culture based on trust. Optimistic Sensorites feel that this is a perfect society in which everyone is content and secret plotting is impossible. They're wrong, of course. Though all of the Sensorites here believe in a fixed order, and apparently don't have names, there are different agendas in their ranks. The First Elder wants peace, while the City Administrator has a xenophobic fear of the humans and is prepared to take any steps to sabotage the outsiders' plans. And it seems that Sensorites aren't great at telling each other apart, especially at a distance. When one of the astronauts points out to the Administrator that she

can't identify Sensorites without their marks of office, the Administrator looks stunned, and says: 'I had never thought of that.' Soon after, he begins impersonating the Second Elder by wearing the Elder's sash.

[This is just about conceivable. If an alien from a particularly aggressive military culture arrived on Earth, and saw - to pick an obvious example - that Gordon Brown wanted to be Prime Minister, then he might reasonably ask why Brown doesn't just slaughter his boss. The answer is that human beings have consciences, yet in human society there are individuals who don't. If we think of this "criminal" mentality among humans as a kind of revelation (i.e. sociopaths have realised something the rest of us *refuse* to realise, that murder is really very easy and convenient), then the "criminal" mentality among Sensorites isn't that different (i.e. bad Sensorites have realised something the rest of them refuse to realise, that Sensorite society is unworkable without their marks of office). For a society with such a rigid caste system, changing sashes around is normally unthinkable.]

But yes, it's the marks of office that let the humans tell these creatures apart. The First Elder, elected thanks to his great brain, wears two sashes across his chest; the Second Elder, appointed by the First, wears one sash; and the City Administrator has a dark collar around his neck. The scientists / medics wear a chest-design combining an alembic (one of those conical test-tubes) with the asclepion associated with medicine on Earth (the sword-and-snake symbol). The warriors, if that isn't an exaggeration, have three black armbands on each arm and answer to a Senior Warrior. Their hand-rays are rather art-nouveau silver loops, which can generate heat or paralyse living beings for about an hour. The Elders also have access to a 'disintegrator', a large and complex beam-weapon that targets individual body-parts.

Sensorites have spacecraft, reaching at least as far as orbit of their world, but don't have the technology to cross the universe [no warp-drive, then]. The rather nippy 'machines' which transport them through space make a high-pitched whining noise, and look roughly pod-like when glimpsed at long range. Sensorites can, it seem, survive in the vacuum of space with no obvious equipment. They indicate that they've been visited by destructive aliens more than once before, even apart from the nasty humans who've started putting belladonna in their water supply. This year, three in every ten Sensorites have died from the poisoning. Last year it was two in ten. [This apparently means that 20% of the population died, rather than that 20% of those who were poisoned died from it. This is truly devastating.]

Like everyone else in the universe, the Sensorites seem to write in English, use Arabic numerals and measure distances in yards [though their version of "feet" may be different, for obvious reasons]. And like a surprising number of cultures, they evidently use felt-tip pens [see 1.2, "The Daleks" and 1.3, "The Edge of Destruction"].

Planet Notes

• *The Sense-Sphere.* The world of the Sensorites is apparently arid, with a major settlement near the desert and the Yellow Mountains. The City Administrator speaks of a 'Sensorite Nation'. [This implies that Sensorites only live in one part of the planet, and everything we see here suggests that this city is the *only* city.] There are ten districts in the city, and the elders have a palace which the First Elder thinks of as his own. The architecture is predictably futuristic and shiny, based on curves and asymmetric arches, some of the openings looking out onto the mountains or onto gardens of plants. The building is defended by electro-thermal couples, capable of tracing visitors by the heat of their bodies.

A pure spring is located in the Yellow Mountains, discovered by the First Elder himself, and from it comes the sparkling mineral water that the elders favour. But pure springs are unusual, so most water is filtered and piped into the city through the aqueduct under the city. [When the Doctor suggests that *all* the Sensorites should drink water from the spring until a cure is found for the poison, the First Elder agrees, again suggesting there really aren't many Sensorites in the world.]

Since the planet has unusually high concentrations of the valuable element molybdenum, there are understandable fears of a human takeover, while the humans describe the world as having a 'slightly bigger land-mass than usual' [an odd assertion, given that most planets don't have water… possibly it has a large land-mass for an *inhabited* planet]. It's unclear whether the belladonna used by the mad humans is native to the Sense-Sphere, but the Sensorites *do* have a juicy fruit that tastes like a peach. Before discovering the truth about the humans in the aqueduct, they believe there are 'monsters' down there, so they're obviously not very inquisitive.

The First Elder claims that the 'frequencies' over the Sense-Sphere are numerous, and that Susan can tap into the 'major' ones, while the Senior Scientist claims that it's only the Sense-Sphere's ultra-high frequencies which allow her to use thought-transference unaided. At the end of events here, the mad humans are taken back to Earth on Captain Maitland's ship; the treacherous former City Administrator is exiled to the 'outer wastes'; and there's obviously peace between human and Sensorite. [If this is the twenty-eighth century, as we're led to believe, then the Sensorites may be in for trouble. Other stories indicate that this is a period of aggressive imperialism on Earth, even if Maitland's crew are "nice", so humans may try to strip-mine the planet after all. In fact, the novel *Original Sin* takes place in 2975, and mentions the Sense-Sphere having capitulated to Earth a few years prior in the "Wars of Acquisition".]

• *Esto.* According to Susan, the plants there use thought-transference. Stand between two of them and they start screeching, as they can sense another mind breaking their transmission.

History

• *Dating.* The crew of the spaceship 'come from' the twenty-eighth century. [This might indicate that they've been travelling a while, perhaps in suspended animation, and that it's later than the twenty-eighth century now. But see later.]

Human spaceflight technology is sufficiently advanced to allow them to use robustly-built ships with lots of corridors, more like cruisers than submarines. [The flight-deck is standardised, and the controls are predictable. We know this from two things: the Doctor's been there less than five minutes before he starts operating the controls, and an almost identical flight-deck is found on a ship that crashed three hundred years earlier in 2.3, "The Rescue".]

The ship that's now in orbit of the Sense-Sphere is part of a space fleet, and has a crew of three. The fleet sends vessels out to unexplored planets, but they don't seem to be crewed by specialists in first contact etiquette. Tellingly, one of them is a minerologist. [Again, see 19.3, "Kinda". Here we see Ian pull a service flash from a uniform that reads INEER, and many have taken this to be the name of the space fleet, but the flash is damaged at one end and is clearly just meant to be the end of the word ENGINEER. What makes this more confusing is that Hartnell fluffs his lines, again, and claims that it reads I-N-N-E-R when we can plainly see that it doesn't.]

The ship isn't the first one to come here. Ten years ago, five humans landed on the Sense-Sphere. The Sensorites welcomed them, but the humans' minds were closed to these approaches. Then the five quarrelled, some of them apparently driven mad by experiments with the Sensorites' thought-transference devices. Two of them disobeyed the commander and took off in their ship, which exploded as a result of the commander's sabotage. The survivors of this mission have been lurking in the aqueduct of the Sense-Sphere, poisoning the water, and the Sensorites no longer trust humans as they've noticed that their sickness only started with the explosion in the sky. The commander believes that as he and his men have fought the 'war' against the Sensorites, any 'treasure-trove' is theirs rather than Earth's.

People in the twenty-eighth century think that astronauts from the twenty-first century might plausibly still be around [either through cryogenic suspension or travel at relativistic speeds]. Back at home, the place that used to be London is now part of Central City, which takes up the lower half of England. It hasn't been London for four hundred years, and nobody knows what Big Ben is. Space-travellers still carry family snapshots [photos, it seems, not holograms or recordings], and on Earth they still have thick juicy steaks. Inside the spaceship, odds and ends sit on shelves instead of being neatly contained in cabinets, including hand-held heart resuscitators and electromagnetic cutting tools. The astronauts have non-winding watches, recharged by the movement of the wrist.

Astronauts John and Carol plan to marry on their return. [The voyage back must take less than a lifetime, then. They speak as if it's the same century for them as it is on Earth, so despite the "old-fashioned" design of the ship, this doesn't seem to be some pre-spacewarp vessel that started its journey centuries ago. The vessel may well be old, but if so then it's probably because it was built to last, as the economics of space exploration evidently involve a need to show a return on each voyage.]

Humans don't seem to be well-versed in countering psychic assault. [In 5.7, "The Wheel in Space", twenty-first century astronauts have Silenski capsules to prevent mental interference. It's possible that the Sensorites are using an altogether different form of psionics, as the rest of their technology seems well below twenty-eighth-century human standards. Alternatively, Silenski capsules may simply not have proved useful on these sorts of missions, and been abandoned in favour of other technologies.]

The Analysis

Where Does This Come From? Ah yes, 'thought-transference'. It was inevitable that this would become part of the series' standard repertoire, and indeed, part of the standard repertoire of *all* SF on the small screen.

Telepathy is the ideal "prop" for TV drama, and TV is the ideal medium for stories about telepathy. In part this is because the very idea of "broadcasting" leads into to the notion of broadcasting thought (SF typically stretches technology into the realm of metaphor, so the line between characters' thoughts being transmitted to *us* and to other characters gets blurred), but in part it's because the technology of television *production* also lends itself to the concept. The BBC, particularly, was in the business of drama rather than spectacle. It was in the nature of any BBC SF series that the story wouldn't focus on the spaceships, but on tight close-ups of actors looking angst-ridden in uncomfortable, alien situations. In that kind of environment, the optimum "science-fiction" event isn't going to be something big, physical and expensive, but something that allows the character's thoughts to be put on the screen or channelled through the speaker.

In the '70s, things will become even more blatant, and telepathy will be everywhere on TV; cheap colour video effects will make it easy to suggest freaky internal states of mind. As we'll hint in Volume III, the boom in psychedelic imagery in the late '60s - now romantically thought of as being a result of mind-expanding drugs - was at least as much to do with the rise of colour television, plus a new understanding of what was possible on it. So a whole generation will grow up believing that howlround is a natural symptom of mental stress. You might want to try "The Green Death" (10.5) or "Planet of the Spiders" (11.5) for some choice examples of all-too-visible mental phenomena, but things get off to a start here with the Sensorites' telepathic connection to Susan. This being '60s Doctor Who, the angst-ridden close-ups aren't accompanied by anything visual but with radiophonics. Noise is presented as being the correct medium in which to suggest mental shock. Even the Sensorites retreat from it.

(You may notice that there are hints of telepathy even in non-SF, non-fantasy TV. The standard technique of having a character "remember" someone's words by dubbing those words onto the soundtrack - as happens to Susan in 1.2, "The Daleks" - turns the process of thought into something external, something very nearly psychic, and it's notable that "serious" drama is more willing to flirt with the possibility of telepathy than with any other supernatural phenomena. On television, it seems very nearly normal. One more point to note here: if it's inevitable that telepathy will be a key feature of a fairly low-budget and experimental SF series, then it's just as inevitable that it won't be a key feature of a big-budget spectacular. In '60s and '70s television, "thought-transference" is an idea to be played with, a subject for discussion in itself. In the 2005 series of Doctor Who, with an army of CGI and animatronic monsters cluttering up the screen, it's just a convenient way for the Nestene Consciousness to animate hordes of Autons.)

Alice Frick's memo, as mentioned in the essay under "An Unearhtly Child" (1.1), suggests that the BBC was thinking about telepathy as the theme for a whole series. In "The Sensorites" we see a society of telepaths, but unlike many of the stories Frick examined - such as, most obviously,

Alfred Bester's The Demolished Man - crime is not only possible but unstoppable, as nobody on the planet has ever thought of doing it before.

This is the era in which everyone was getting excited about "psychic" experiments, and rumours that the Soviets had almost cracked some sort of mind-reading technology. In a period when so much had been discovered or invented, nobody was going to dismiss the idea outright, and universities suddenly got funding to investigate it. Here the natural telepath is the teenage girl, which is part of a much older tradition of adolescent females having supernatural powers (Victorian culture, especially, saw connections between a girl's hormonal yearnings and the ability to contact spirits... see X1.3, "The Unquiet Dead", for a story that takes this for granted without even having to investigate the reasoning behind it), and which also ties in with more modern scary-child-telepath stories like The Midwich Cuckoos.

We've only just had a story set in China, but that was about Mongol rule. Now we get all the clichés of the inscrutable Orient disguised as an alien culture. "I can't tell them apart", check. Run by wise old men, yep. Caste system and exams to find out who does what, uh-huh. Suspicious of foreigners, present and correct. Even the foot-binding mysteriously left out of Marco Polo's account is alluded to, and the Doctor chastises Susan for mocking the Sensorites' inability to run. This city is clearly a Forbidden City, although a little less swish than Mighty Kublai Khan's pad three stories ago. Worth mentioning too that although the rigid Sensorite doctrine is obviously modelled on the pre-revolutionary version of China, by this point the country had been communist for a decade and a half, and was presenting itself to the world as a place where everyone was content and self-interest was unthinkable. This is exactly the way the "optimistic" Sensorite in episode five describes his planet, and Carol's claim that 'some people always want more than others' is a typical Western assessment of why communism can't work. As even the Sensorite seems to notice.

While all of this is a pleasant change from the usual run of alien cultures that are obviously meant to be Imperial Japan in drag, the first two episodes have an oddly familiar ring to them if looked at in this light. Yangtse Incident (starring William Hartnell and Richard Todd... he's in "Kinda") involves a British warship stranded in

China during the 1949 revolution, subjected to propaganda messages and sporadic fire. A more overt source is Peter R. Newman's own experience, both as a pilot in World War Two and in military intelligence. His earlier play for BBC TV was about Burma. The final episode of "The Sensorites" has very British officers going mad as a result of their refusal to crack under pressure, if that isn't too paradoxical. There are many documented instances of this in the South East Asia campaigns, not least Hiroo Onada, the Japanese pilot who refused to believe that the War was over and continued to repel anyone who came near "his" island. He held out until 1979, by which time he'd entered folklore.

Another element we'll just mention here is the post-War feeling, at least among those who *didn't* see international communism as a serious threat to world order, that commercial imperialism was as bad as military conquest. Encountering other cultures should be about what we can bring, not what they have that we want. In early '60s Britain this meant India, Africa and - still painful a century on - China.

Ray Cusick's sets once again avoid the obvious. This time, the spaceship was designed to look as different as possible to the Mercury capsules and glorified B-52 bombers in most big-budget American space movies. We might also note that Carol speaks of the spaceship as hurtling towards the planet at 'Mach-4', at a time when the concept of supersonic flight was still exciting and - yes - space-age. (In Britain, at least, there wasn't always a clear dividing line between aircraft and spacecraft. See **How Believable is the British Space Programme?** under 7.3, "The Ambassadors of Death".) The architecture of the Sense-Sphere was loosely based on the Sagrada Familia cathedral, Antonio Gaudi's gloriously bizarre work-in-progress in Barcelona.

Things That Don't Make Sense As the Sensorites arrive on the spaceship, the director decides to linger on them for as long as possible in order to build up the tension. And he starts with a close-up of their feet. Their *feet*. Have you *seen* their feet?

Sensorites are afraid of the darkness, and when the light falls below a certain level their eyes contract, cutting out yet more light. One need not be Darwin to see a flaw there. Also, it's a particularly weak set-up for an alien species; analysing their weakness, the Doctor concludes that *these people*

can't see when it's dark. Really. What a coup. Similarly, sound affects them physically, but they communicate through speech even with telepathy devices as widespread as mobile 'phones.

When the Doctor and company find the Earth-people being held prisoner by the Sensorites aboard the spaceship, the astronauts tell them to get away while they still can rather than saying "for God's sake, help us" or even "can you send a message to Earth, please?". For the first time in the series, sound travels through space, with the shrill noise of the Sensorite space-pods clearly audible inside the ship [unless it's all part of a devious psychic attack]. And that's another thing: the Sensorites aren't shy about travelling, and there are regular space-launches from their city. Yet it's apparently the only settlement on their planet. Do they not breed easily? Is this *really* the only part of the Sense-Sphere that's fit for habitation? [This may be one of those calamity-devastated planets that's had its population reduced to a bare minimum, but if so, we never hear about it.]

Hilariously, the Doctor wonders why the disease doesn't affect the Sensorite elders mere moments after being told that the elders don't drink from the usual water supply, *and* while Ian's choking himself half to death on contaminated water. The Sensorites themselves checked the water supply for poisons, but found nothing because they took water samples from the wrong part of the city, which in itself might be considered sloppy work. But evidently, Sensorite medical science is so crap that they can't even spot the presence of an alien poison in the bodies of the plague victims. Do they not have autopsies?

Military science isn't up to much, either. The City Administrator talks of the 'disintegrator' as if it's an all-purpose super-weapon capable of massive damage, but actually it has to target the individual body-parts of the visiting humans, so a revolver with five bullets in it would do just as well. Nevertheless, the villains treat the weapon's firing-pin like an irreplaceable sacred artefact. And Ian seems to know an awful lot about Sensorite weaponry, immediately identifying the technical fault in the hand-ray given to him by the "bad" Sensorite faction.

During the "science montage" in episode four, the Doctor has a checklist of the city's ten districts, and writes the results of the water-tests next to each one. This checklist simply reads "District One", "District Two", "District Three", and so on. The writing is calligraphy so neat and regular that it can't possibly be in the Doctor's own hand, nor that of the Sensorites. So apart from the question of why such a handsome checklist is needed during the rush to cure the poisoned Ian, somewhere on the Sense-Sphere there's obviously a DeskJet printer that's got a "human joined-up" font. In the same episode, the Doctor asks Susan whether she can really hear the Sensorites' minds talking, as if she hasn't been doing it since episode two.

So... where does the belladonna come from? Either it's issued to Earth astronauts for some ungodly reason or - against all odds - it's the one species of terrestrial plant-life which originated on another planet, despite being a close relative of the tomato. And what knocks the Doctor unconscious and shreds his clothes, at the start of episode five? It can't be the mad humans, who later welcome him as an envoy from Earth, and who don't have claws anyway. Are there *really* monsters down there, after all?

At the start of the story, a Sensorite sneaks onto the flight-deck of the spaceship while nobody's looking and cuts the TARDIS lock out. There's no clue as to when it arrived, and there's no indication of it leaving, since the sound of the Sensorite space-machines doesn't start until two more of them turn up. Which means there's a Sensorite lurking around on the vessel all the way through the story, something which nobody mentions or worries about. Is it still there when the ship heads off home?

While we're on the subject of the ship... what exactly does John do to the doors, that can't be undone by anyone else and requires them to use 'electromagnetic' cutting equipment? He waves his hand rather vaguely at the light-sensor, like the Queen Mother. Later he demonstrates to Ian and Barbara how to lock the doors, and it's the same gesture, which is what Susan's been doing to open them. And why does it take Susan so long to figure out how to do this, when the light-beam system (and the sound they make, funnily enough) is identical to that of the doors on Skaro?

Billy Fluffs: 'I rather fancy that settled that little bit of solution', and the description of the astronauts' watches as 'the non-winding time'. But most satisfying of all is the fluff of this week's education supplement. 'Now, let me see. Iron melts at 1,539 degrees centigrade, and molybdenum melts at 2,622 degrees centigrade. So, you know... that's... er... give you some idea.'

A Sensorite Fluff (apart from the stuff they've

got on their faces): 'I heard them over... over... talking.' Obviously, they have Porky Pig on this planet.

Critique Opinion is divided over this: the common reaction is "why?", but the correct answer is "aww... bless". There's so much about this story that's endearing, interesting and occasionally scary. There's also a lot that's awkward, unfeasible and silly. But fortunately, it's silly in ways that only *Doctor Who* can be, so it's worth having.

Let's start with the plus points. The story revolves around xenophobia and the Sensorites are the scared bigots for most of the time - but they've got good reasons to be worried. Once again we're shown as much as we're told, and what we hear comes from two very different sources, so it's as much about character as exposition. The Sensorites themselves are fantastic, from the shoulders up. They're less fantastic when we're allowed to see that they're short fat men in velour suits, although they can be endearing even when they're a bit pathetic. It's hard not to go "ahhhhh" when they retreat from the darkness on board the spaceship, and the "When Sensorites Attack" moment in episode five - which ends with the supposedly tragic death of the Second Elder - is inadvertently the funniest thing this season. Charmingly, even the humans in the story can see the creatures' shortcomings, not in a self-referential "these are terrible costumes" sort of way but in a "this is a bit weird" sort of way instead.

But they have to say some breathtakingly stupid things. For all of Cusick's attempts to build an interesting, curvilinear city, the culture of this world is too flat to let you believe in the backdrops. It doesn't matter that the Daleks don't have names and proper linguistic skills, because they're pure evil, but if this is supposed to be a fully-functional society then you need something a damn sight more convincing than a one-city state where people are called things like "Senior Warrior" and nobody has any form of fashion sense. The humans aren't that much better, and Maitland is played by the worst actor in the series up to this point; no wonder William Russell tries to hit him in the face with a spectrographic analysis. Making the bathos complete is the music. Norman Kay's score is almost identical to those of "An Unearthly Child" or "The Keys of Marinus", except for a brassy "da-da-da-da-daaaaah!" which accompanies absolutely anything happening at all, no matter how trivial.

But look! Susan gets to do something. This is one story where all four regulars and the guest-companion get equal emphasis. Susan's almost the spooky girl from Coal Hill School again, though now she's capable of resisting her grandfather. Even Barbara gets plenty of work, and is properly written out and back in, rather than making a token pre-filmed appearance as per normal. Ironically, in a script where everyone goes back to their character-notes, we begin with a scene about how much they've all changed after everything they've been through. They haven't; it's the Doctor who's been rewritten, and now he comes into the spotlight as never before.

The real crime of "The Sensorites" is that parts of it worked so well, they did it again. And again. Coming to it after later *Doctor Who*, so much of it seems routine and ordinary, but if you watch the first season in order - and especially if you get to it fairly quickly after "The Keys of Marinus" - then it all starts to make sense.

The Facts

Written by Peter R. Newman. Directed by Mervyn Pinfield (episodes one to four) and Frank Cox (episodes five and six). Ratings: 7.9 million, 6.9 million, 7.4 million, 5.5 million, 6.9 million, 6.9 million.

Supporting Cast Stephen Dartnell (John), Ilona Rodgers (Carol), Lorne Cossette (Maitland), Ken Tyllsen (First Sensorite), Joe Greig (Second Sensorite), Peter Glaze (the City Administrator; credited as Third Sensorite) Eric Francis (First Elder), Bartlett Mullins (Second Elder), John Bailey (Commander), Martyn Huntley (First Human), Giles Phibbs (Second Human), Ken Tyllsen (First Scientist), Joe Greig (Second Scientist), Joe Greig (Warrior).

Episode Titles "Strangers in Space", "The Unwilling Warriors", "Hidden Danger", "A Race Against Death", "Kidnap", "A Desperate Venture".

Cliffhangers The fluffy face of a Sensorite appears at the window of the spaceship; Susan calmly agrees to leave the ship with the two Sensorite warriors, saying that everyone will be killed if she doesn't; Ian collapses in the Sensorite palace, and the First Elder announces that the fallen human is dying of the disease; down in the darkness of the aqueduct tunnel, something roars at the Doctor; the Sensorite formerly known as the City Administrator sneaks up on Carol and kidnaps her. (The episode is called "Kidnap", so really, the audience should have seen this coming.)

The lead-in to the next story: in a huff, the Doctor informs Ian and Barbara that they can get off the TARDIS at the very next stop they come to.

The Lore

• Sport stopped play. There was a two-week gap between episodes two and three, as it was Wimbledon fortnight, and episode three was late even when it *was* shown; England was playing Australia, and in those days you needed more than Peter Glaze in a Babygro to justify cutting away from an Ashes test. (We won, by the way.)

• Mervyn Pinfield's role as "associate producer" was mainly a question of him supervising the technical aspects of such a complex show. He was well-qualified to do this, as a member of the Langham Group - a team of directors based in the Langham Hotel, opposite Broadcasting House - charged with the task of finding new ways to make drama on-screen. Early TV drama had been, essentially, cameras pointed at plays. The lenses couldn't be changed without cutting to another camera, so the motion was static even compared to theatre. The Langham Group had been influenced by German expressionist plays and silent films, and sought to suggest locations and emotions through a more codified set of visual cues. They were responsible for a lot of "arty" sets that consisted of black backdrops with white objects in front of them, and extreme close-ups of parts of faces.

• But Sydney Newman wanted rid of all that. The new generation of TV directors - Derek Martinus, Waris Hussein and the like - thought of Pinfield as representing everything they'd been brought to the BBC to sweep away, right down to his habit of wearing suits and ties in the studio. (Remember this when we talk about how hot Lime Grove got in summer.) Pinfield got things done on time and on budget, though, so he was given "The Sensorites" to play with.

• His biggest claim to fame, however, was what he called the "Piniprompter". Everyone else calls it an "autocue", and his estate gets a commission on every one sold.

• Peter R. Newman was mainly a radio writer with one well-received TV play, *Yesterday's Enemy*, under his belt. Even historian Andrew Pixley seems uncertain of what became of him after "The Sensorites", so we thought we'd try to settle the matter. A trip to Chingford failed to uncover any gossip from his old school, St Egbert's (it closed in 1970, but the Old Boys' association has a couple of authors on its books), while even the playwrights' inventory has no photo and no details not already mentioned in *Doctor Who Magazine*. To save you the bother, here it all is: he didn't get anything else on telly, although there was a near-miss with future *Doctor Who* producer John Wiles; he was diagnosed with depression; and he was apparently dead by 1970.

1.8: "The Reign of Terror"

(Serial H. Six Episodes, 8th August - 12th September 1964.)

Which One is This? The most inevitable historical of them all. The aftermath of the French Revolution: Robespierre, Madame Guillotine and special surprise guest N*p*l**n B*n*p*rt*.

Firsts and Lasts This is, believe it or not, the first time any location filming is done for the series. To everyone's relief, it's the last story to have any connection to Lime Grove, at least in this volume. It's the first script by Dennis Spooner, who's going to bring a whole new dynamic to the series in the next year or so, and for the first time we have an on-screen caption telling us what the setting is (it's Paris, folks). And it's the first full-on romantic interlude for Barbara, but amazingly Ian isn't involved…

It's also the last story to be broadcast before 1964's six-week break. Thus, for our purposes, it's the end of a continuous run (barring the unexpected gap in 1.7, "The Sensorites") which the BBC would have called "Series One" but we've ended up calling "Season One"[8].

Six Things to Notice About "The Reign of Terror"…

1. It's a Dennis Spooner script, so everyone starts talking like Abbott and Costello ('you don't say'… that's *the Doctor* talking!), except the ones handing out amazingly obvious exposition ('that is why we are here, Jean; a crowded street and a successful rescue never mix') or those with obvious regional accents. Chief amongst these is the jailer, who's straight out of a pre-War comedy.

"Hilariously", he's drunk and two-faced, the way that amusing working-class characters in pre-War films were allowed to be. As Spooner's from the East End of London, he decided to write this bloke wi' a Yorkshire accent, 'appen. (If another writer had written the same character as a Cockney, then Spooner would probably have complained about the stereotype. The director might not have been aware of the nuances of regional accents in British TV, so we'll credit Spooner's script for all the accent-related oddities in this tale.)

2. But the role of Mr Exposition in this story - although it's chiefly confined to the material missing from the archive - goes to Citizen Robespierre, and boy, does he ever exposit! Yes Sir! (Sorry, it's catching.) Not only does he provide all the information about what year he's living in and what's just about to happen, he also gives us statistics on how many people have died recently and the reasons he killed Danton, a person unknown to anyone unfamiliar with this period. Admittedly Robespierre *was* a tedious bureaucrat, and probably liked reeling off lists of facts even more than people in fandom do, but this is pushing it.

3. Considering that this is fast becoming The Monster Programme, it's a story that expects younger viewers to accept an awful lot of supporting characters who don't have hugely overstated costumes or distinctive make-up (remember, the last historical was so full of leopardskin that the Aztecs might as *well* have been aliens). There are nearly a dozen spies, politicians and counter-revolutionaries manoeuvring their way through the plot, many of them working as double agents, planning elaborate conspiracies or destined to die just when you think they're going to be important. In fact the first three episodes seem rather slow, simply because the script's taking its time to set up all the background, and it only gets exciting when we start to realise who's doing what (and why) in episodes four and five. Sadly, episodes four and five are the ones that are missing from the archive.

4. The Doctor is apprehended as a tax-dodger and put on a work-party. His scheme to get out of it has a fairy-tale ingenuity to it, and is played entirely for laughs. At last, Hartnell gets to do the kind of thing he went into acting to do, and the result is straight out of Chaplin or Keaton. The scene ends with a piece of gallows humour on the Doctor's part; the programme-makers make sure

'60s *Doctor Who*: How Was It Made?

In British television production, the big divisions are as follows: before and after colour, before and after 625-line transmission, before and after *Hancock's Half Hour*.

Colour is easy to explain, and the consequences of this shift need not detain us (for our purposes, they're mainly limited to CSO, odd costume decisions and a feeling in the BBC that maybe tired old *Doctor Who* still had a place in the Saturday schedules; see Volume III). 625-line transmission is a bit more technical, but essentially… all TV signals are sent in horizontal lines. There used to be 405 lines per frame, but in order to be ready for colour, the British transmission system reconfigured it to UHF transmission and 625 lines per frame. This was one of the things that BBC2 was set up to develop and refine before the mass-market BBC1 and ITV switched over (see 5.2, "The Abominable Snowmen", for a look at the effect of all this on *Doctor Who*). One consequence of the sharper picture was that set design needed a rethink and a budget-hike. Another was that less intense lighting was required, which had obvious costume consequences and allowed longer recording sessions. The heat of a 405-line studio could be torturous.

Now, one of the things we've been careful to stress so far is that contrary to popular belief, *Doctor Who* never went out live. We've even overstepped the mark a little by referring to the "filming" of episodes. (Only 7.1, "Spearhead from Space", was entirely made on film. Well, unless you count the Paul McGann movie. The twenty-first century series is made on frame-removed VT, the so-called "film-look" technique mentioned in the essay after 12.3, "The Sontaran Experiment".) In November 1958, the BBC had forked out for an Ampex video recording system, the first in the world. It could record whole programmes, yet the tape couldn't be edited the same way as film.

Or so they thought. The recording had an electrical pulse that had to be continuously maintained. Physically cutting the tape would disrupt this. A method was eventually found (by accident) to cut the tape safely, although as late as 1963, the ITV companies didn't officially acknowledge that this was possible. The person whose serendipity changed everything was Duncan Wood, producer of *Hancock's Half Hour*. Suddenly the number of shots per half-hour increased. Up until that time, a pair of cameras was needed for each scene - out of five or six in a studio - while the others were put in position for the next scene. Once video editing became practical, almost all the cameras could be used in the same scene, and then moved between scenes.

Prior to this, much of the craft of TV drama was in finding natural-seeming ways to cover these transitions. Many scenes carried on for a few moments after the principals had left, to allow a change of jacket and a swift sprint across the studio. One of the hallmarks of the new style of TV drama ushered in by *Z Cars* was that in many cases the "link" scene was cut (see the essay after 2.1, "Planet of Giants", for more on *Z Cars*). *Doctor Who* often has these "lscenes" scripted, but they're not always necessary; see, for example, the prosecutor Tarron marvelling at the disappearance of the travellers halfway through the last part of "The Keys of Marinus" (1.5).

For reaction shots - such a big part of the success of *Hancock*, and later *Steptoe and Son*, from the same stable - one camera could be reserved for each principal. This allowed a BBC sitcom to be as pacy as *Bilko* or *Lucy*, while retaining the intensity and intimacy of live performance. Up until then, only two options had been available: point a camera at a stage-like performance, or make a movie for television and edit it conventionally. *Doctor Who* is an example of one of the many compromises between these options that the BBC invented.

The complex of studios at Lime Grove had been built as film studios in 1913, and converting them for television had been a godsend after the original BBC TV headquarters at Alexandra Palace. There were several studios, and a row of terraced houses had been turned into offices nearby. This provided a nucleus for some of the trademark "new" television of the early 1960s, whilst the purpose-built Television Centre was for the mainstream shows (ones with live audiences) and the prestige projects (requiring much bigger sets). All studios were booked long in advance, and in the case of *Doctor Who* one day a week - usually Friday - was reserved for recording up to 75 minutes of footage.

For the first year this was almost exclusively done in Studio D at Lime Grove, which was hot, cramped and badly-resourced, but more practical than any other Lime Grove studio as it was big and square (Studio G had greater floor space but was long and thin). The cameras installed there were CPS Emitrons, equipped with four lenses on a

continued on page 87...

we can hear the overseer snoring in a "funny" way, but he'll probably be executed for letting his prisoners go.

5. Ian and Barbara go undercover as a landlord and barmaid. Two things stand out here. One is that Babs adopts a Mummerset accent to pass herself off as Breton. The other is that they seem so comfortable doing this, it's hard to imagine them going back to teaching. And Susan's gone a bit weird again. This time, she gets horribly miserable and defeatist as soon as they're put in a perfectly ordinary prison cell. She even scuppers Barbara's promising escape plan, by whinging about the cold and screaming at the rats. Imagine if she had to go down a real sewer (2.2, "The Dalek Invasion of Earth")...

6. Who is the mysterious Man of Destiny that Robespierre's Deputy, Paul Barrass, has arranged to meet at the Sinking Ship Inn? It can't be Napoleon, can it? That'd be like meeting Marco Polo at the court of Kublai Khan in 1289, or finding fully-developed *Homo sapiens* larking around in 100,000 BC. Anyway, we thought he'd be shorter.

The Continuity

The Doctor Won't waste time on goodbyes to Ian and Barbara when he thinks he's finally got them home. However, Ian is able to ask him out to the pub for a quick jar. Ian also suggests that until now, the Doctor hasn't really been *trying* to get them back to the 1960s. [If this is his first real effort, then eighteenth-century Paris isn't all that bad a result. Closer than Skaro, anyway.]

Given a parchment and writing implements, the Doctor has no trouble forging documents to fool agents of the Revolution. Here, more than ever, he sees history as a force rather than a string of mere events [see the essay after 1.6, "The Aztecs"].

• *Background.* The French Revolution is his favourite part of Earth's history, and he's remarkably quick to exploit the bureaucracy of the Terror. [This isn't his first visit. See also Susan's reaction to the book in "An Unearthly Child" (1.1), and the other unseen trip to France - a few years earlier than this one - mentioned in "The Ark in Space" (12.2). The New Adventures make the claim that Revolutionary Paris was the first place the Doctor visited after stealing the TARDIS and leaving his homeworld, and this makes sense;

given the conservatism amongst his own people, revolution must have seemed extraordinary to him.]

• *Ethics.* Under duress, he resorts to a brutal ploy to get out of the chain-gang, and ultimately hits the overseer over the head with a heavy implement. More seriously, his confrontation with Robespierre - in the guise of a District Commissioner - would seem to reveal the Doctor's politics more clearly than ever before. Even though he's attempting to play a role and secure the release of his friends, he can't resist outspoken criticisms of the regime.

The Supporting Cast

• *Ian.* Half-believing themselves to be back on Earth in their own time, Ian and Barbara are obviously a little reluctant to leave. Ian's once again knocked unconscious here [as far as we can work out, that's four times in ten days, counting the cactus spine and the atropine in the last two stories].

• *Barbara.* Has had a holiday in Somerset. In a spectacular outburst against Ian, she expresses a belief that the ideals of the Revolution - however much they've been suborned - were admirable. [Part of this may be because she fancies Leon Colbert, the apparent good guy who turns out to be a "mole" for the Revolution.]

• *Susan.* Looks as if she's had a haircut, even though nobody's changed their clothes since the last adventure. Separated from the Doctor, she suddenly becomes fatalistic, and doesn't have much enthusiasm for escape plans. She drinks brandy with no complaint and usually has an enormous appetite. Rats horrify her so much that she jumps on furnishings to avoid them.

The TARDIS The scanner can be focused on things further than the eye can see, through trees and around corners. [Compare with 18.3, "Full Circle".] The Doctor believes he can now navigate the Ship without difficulty, even though he doesn't actually know where on Earth the TARDIS lands, and he's two centuries out to boot.

History

• *Dating.* It's July 1794, and the TARDIS has landed about fifteen kilometres north of Paris.

Terror is the order of the day. Bands of ill-mannered, ill-trained Revolutionaries are stalking the land, shooting down royalists and hauling prisoners off to the guillotine. English agents are operat-

'60s *Doctor Who*: How Was It Made?

...continued from page 85

rotating drum called the "turret", so to change lenses for close-ups or long shots required the director to cut away to a different camera for a few seconds. Instead of a zoom facility, the cameras had to physically approach the actor, occasionally running into something on the floor and jolting. Just look at the bit in the pilot episode where Ian discovers the TARDIS. For these reasons, camera rehearsal took up most of the Friday sessions.

Actual *film* filming was, as we've said, possible. In 1955, the BBC had bought Ealing Studios, where the celebrated late '40s / early '50s comedies had been made (*The Ladykillers*, *The Lavender Hill Mob*, *Passport to Pimlico*, *Kind Hearts and Coronets*, to name just a few). If a scene needed a larger set, or tighter editing, or filming in advance to cover an actor's holiday or a link between scenes, then it was done there. Usually, this would be the first part of a given *Doctor Who* story to be made. Fight scenes, in particular, would be more effective if done with a more mobile camera and edited like a movie or a commercial. Similarly, location work would be made well in advance of the electrical studio work. All pre-filmed inserts would be run in the studio as the video recording was made, and often timed to allow for costume changes or alterations to the set.

Thus it was frequently the case that an actor rehearsing a story for recording that Friday would take half a day off to pre-film something for the following story, often with little idea what the context would be. The often-told anecdote of Deborah Watling running down a Welsh hillside while making "The Abominable Snowmen", and not realising that the guest star would be her father, Jack Watling, until they met during the take is just a bit more plausible with this in mind.

So a director, a designer and a writer were all assigned to an available slot. With a budget of £2,300 per episode, and an expectation that overspending in one episode (usually the first, usually for sets and costumes) would be recouped in later ones (so a seven-parter could go for broke), options were limited. A simple decision to have a few non-speaking extras might be the difference between using a specially-commissioned score or using stock music. The story editor's job involved deciding how much filmed material was possible, and when in each episode it should be deployed. Music and what was then still called "special sound" would be commissioned well in advance.

You'll notice that rather than having a specific piece of music for each scene, there'd be four or five "generic" pieces composed for each story. One for "spooky" bits, one for "action" scenes, one for "moody" moments, and so on.

Rehearsals were usually in a nearby hall, rented by the day. For the bulk of the Hartnell era, it was the Drill Hall on Walmer Road (for the uninitiated, a Drill Hall is where the local Territorial Army reservists would train in the evening, and during the day it'd be let out to TV companies). The other regular venue, another Drill Hall on Uxbridge Road, had a sandwich man with a runny nose who made terrible coffee. At least, according to Hartnell. The star would find other excuses for tantrums as the years progressed, but facilities at these venues were rudimentary. The sets would be ready for a studio day, but the layout would be known in advance. Gaffer-tape would be laid on the floor to show where the walls and major furnishings of the set would be, and Monday, Tuesday and Wednesday would be given over to learning lines and moves. Typically, Hartnell would have the whole script memorised before Monday morning's session and be reluctant to incorporate new lines or scenes, or to shift the emphasis from what he'd decided to what a director wanted.

Of course, this is assuming that the finalised script - and not the draft version used by the designers - was ready by Monday morning. Frequently it would arrive by taxi after a couple of hours of everyone sitting around a table. One writer in particular was a frequent culprit... not naming any names, but he created *Blake's 7*. The Monday read-through, just reading lines off the page, was used by the director to figure out timings, by the producer to catch anything that shouldn't have been there and by the story editor to make sure things were working properly.

Wednesday afternoons seem to have been the prime day for pre-filming. Costume fittings tended to be early on Tuesdays. Thursday was the nearest thing to a day off that anyone had, as this would officially be the day when everyone committed their lines and moves to memory. In practice, any school visits, guest appearances on other programmes, publicity work or more extensive pre-filming was done then. Thursday was also the Producer's Run. Last-minute changes and amendations would be made by the producer, who wouldn't have heard real actors say the lines, nor

continued on page 89...

ing in the country, anticipating that France will go to war with England once the Terror is over. [Ultimately true, although at this point England should be more concerned about the French situation inspiring a revolution at home than about an invasion.] James Stirling, an English agent, has been in Paris for several years and is posing as high-ranking Revolutionary Lemaitre. This is unknown to everybody, including the organisation that's been rescuing people from the guillotine and helping them get out of the country.

Events here roughly follow the last days of Robespierre, the First Deputy. He's portrayed as a man who believes that great works still have to be done, but that progress is always delayed by the need to ferret out traitors to the Revolution. Robespierre fears that Paul Barrass, an ambitious and less "moral" Deputy, is plotting against him. He's right. Barrass has made a rendezvous at a tavern in which he meets the potential next ruler of France, Napoleon Bonaparte. Barrass believes that by eliminating Robespierre, he can take control of the governing committee, with the popular Napoleon as a prop for his reign. The next day, the 27th of July, Robespierre is arrested before a meeting of the convention. He's shot in the jaw while resisting arrest, yet lives. He's held at the Conciergerie prison and destined to be guillotined.

[An awful lot is wrong with this picture. Robespierre, whose main interest was in weeding out corruption and instructing the public in his own curious form of virtue-through-reason, here becomes a figure who's obsessed with the Terror as an entity in itself. The implication is that his downfall is solely the result of a plot by Barrass, rather than a much wider alliance of those who saw him as out of touch with reality, and those who were simply ambitious. The idea of Barrass meeting Napoleon in a pub to plot out the destiny of the country is, notoriously, the most bizarre thing in this story. And the scene in which Robespierre is arrested, shouting that he'll soon be all-powerful again as he's manhandled by the soldiers, is wrong in virtually every detail; it's enough to say that the gunshot wound to his jaw was almost certainly self-inflicted. Far from believing himself to be untouchable, he knew his time was up and attempted to commit suicide, but botched it. Accounts of his death on the guillotine, as the bandage was ripped away from his face and the jaw came with it, are spectacularly nasty.]

The Analysis

Where Does This Come From? The French Revolution, like that in Russia in 1917, was inspired by motives many people would think entirely honourable. Then it… went a bit too far for some tastes.

What's interesting about this one, though, is how close the reasons for the Terror were to mainstream European thought. It was a reasonable revolution, one which saw the removal of old and irrational obstacles to progress, like the class system, superstition and wigs. Making a new calendar and building a machine to execute people more efficiently were part of the same thought-process. Romanticism, the Enlightenment, the scientific approach and human rights all start from the same place as the systematic slaughter brought on by Robespierre. Stalin had hauled Russia into the twentieth century by a combination of industrialisation and mass executions (his successor, Khrushchev, tried to do it a different way but was abruptly removed just after this story aired). More recently, Mao had initiated the Great Leap Forward in China, though the full horror of this wasn't yet clear.

Spooner's place on the writers' roster was assured before they knew what to do with him. His track record made it more likely that he'd do a space story, but instead he was lumbered with history and decided to cash in on the James Bond fad. This is still pre-*Goldfinger* Bond, not least the jailbreak and the gimmick of identifying contacts by code-names, but it's there to be found. (Those who think of Bond as being about armies of Ninjas storming enormous volcano-bases should bear in mind that the first two films, *Dr No* and *From Russia with Love*, are both rather small-scale and based on espionage rather than huge explosions.) Notice that Britain is presented as the benchmark of sanity and justice by both sides in this conflict. A large part of our self-image as the nation that grew out of the revolutions of the 1640s comes from this era, although we sometimes downplay what happened to keep things so peaceable here (see 4.4, "The Highlanders", for more).

Not for the last time, a story set in Earth history borrows noticeably from a literary source that anyone over the age of eight would have recognised. Even if they hadn't read the book, then the film version - which had made Dirk Bogarde (and

'60s *Doctor Who*: How Was It Made?

...continued from page 87

seen the fights or costumes.

This is the most important thing to say here: each episode was made in one week. With the exception of cliffhanger reprises (which were usually remade as the start of the next episode, but sometimes they re-used a clip from the previous week), what was broadcast one Saturday had been recorded on a Friday three weeks before. And they were making more than forty episodes a year. Suddenly, the Billy Fluffs don't seem quite as funny.

Friday began early and ended late. Actors with complicated make-up or costume, such as monsters, aliens or Mongol warlords, got in first. The studio would be set up, the lights arranged (as far as they could be in Lime Grove Studio D) overnight, and the camera crew and actors would try to mesh their separate crafts. They'd begin at 10.00am, stop for an hour for lunch at 1.00pm, then try again until 7.30pm. Another hour's break, and then from 8.30 to 9.45 they'd record the finished version, in costume. While editing the videotape was out of the question, pausing for ten minutes to change outfits was allowed, and monumental cock-ups could be solved by rewinding to the start of a scene and resuming. Given what made it to the screen, you can imagine how big a mistake was needed to warrant this. Most actors in soaps and as-live dramas knew that to ensure a bad performance never reached the public, one should swear loudly.

Why did they not edit videotape, when *Hancock* had proved it possible? Like so much of BBC thinking, it was down to making *Doctor Who* on the cheap and flogging it to as many countries as possible. A tape cost £100, which would be about £1,000 in today's currency. Once cut, it couldn't be re-used. We're talking about physically slicing up the tape with a razor and splicing it with sellotape.

However, there's a more general point to make. As we've already seen, the Drama Department was making an awkward transition from one-off plays to series. In the era of one-off plays, live drama was the norm. Actors and directors preferred working in this pressure-cooker environment, reacting to other actors and not thinking about line-of-sight or how one scene related to the next. With only movie-style filming or theatre-style live drama to choose from, actors, directors and audiences found the latter provided more believable performances. In a story where the credibility of the acting was what made a real world out of flats and sound effects, this was crucial. ITV audiences watching filmed hour-long segments of *Sir Lancelot* would accept far less than those watching *Quatermass and the Pit*, simply because the cast looked like they believed the latter but not always the former. (See 3.1, "Galaxy Four", for what happened when the BBC tried making SF dramas for grown-ups with the resources denied to *Doctor Who*.)

Post-production, such as it was in those days, was done the following Sunday. With a few exceptions, everything on tape was in the right sequence. The dubbing-on of sound effects, post-synched dialogue and some of the music cues were done here. The material on videotape would be transferred onto 35mm film by pointing a modified camera at a modified monitor, so that if extensive re-working were needed then it could be done without hacking up a costly Ampex tape. Finally, the story was broadcast, week by week.

Except... that's not quite the end. A film copy would be made by the telerecording process, and copies of this would be sold overseas. The picture quality would be only slightly less, to begin with. But some later copies would be darker, and if the 35mm copy were reduced to 16mm for export then they'd become grainier as well. The twenty-four-frames-per-second format would be a little jerkier than VT, and about 3% of the picture would be cropped from any edge, which is why Ian ends up staring in horror at someone we can't see in episode six of "The Sensorites" (1.7). Yet once the tapes were gone, these would be the only copies available...

---

especially his trousers) a pin-up - was stupendously well-known. For many people, Dickens' *A Tale of Two Cities* had supplanted fact as a source on the Revolution. Add to this Baroness Orczy's series of adventures about the Scarlet Pimpernel, in which innocent French victims of the Terror are rescued by a dashing master-spy with the perfect cover (he's English and posh), because obviously the French can't be trusted to escape by themselves. Fiction, of course, but there *were* British agents at work in Revolutionary France. Raoul Hesdin was one. His book of memoirs wasn't printed until 1896, so Dickens couldn't have known that the fictitious plot-device was the most accurate thing in his account.

And not content with plundering Dickens,

Spooner ransacks Shakespeare for the figure of the jailer. The porter in *Macbeth* is the only character who speaks in prose, and his function is as much to heighten the suspense as to dispel it.

Things That Don't Make Sense Look at this from Ian and Barbara's point of view. Having been dragged away from twentieth-century England, so far they've found themselves in surprisingly well-known areas of history, meeting Aztecs, Marco Polo and other people that twentieth-century English types know all about. The biggest surprise here is that on discovering they're near Paris, and realising they must be in the past, they don't immediately go "oh, Christ, it's the French Revolution". Not even when Barbara finds some (suspiciously well-fitting) eighteenth-century clothing.

The Doctor thanks his new chum, the boy Jean-Pierre, in French. If we assume that *everyone* in this story is speaking French, but it's translated into English (except that it's the other way around for Ian and Barbara, and possibly the Doctor and Susan), then what does the boy hear? Swahili? And typically, the only things said by Frenchmen that aren't translated for us are French "catch-phrases" like 'sacre bleu!'. The dying Webster tells Ian to find the British spy Stirling at 'the sign of *Le Chien Gris*', but in the event the rendezvous is at a tavern called The Sinking Ship, which goes some way beyond a translation problem. It's also curious that Webster recognises Ian as English, yet Stirling - posing as Lemaitre - doesn't (neither does Ian spot Lemaitre as a ringer, but that's to be expected if the British agent's managed to fool the French for so long). One would think that the name "Chesterton" would be a bit of a clue.

Jules Renan, leader of the ring that's helping refugees from the guillotine, insists on everyone using 'Christian names only' so that nobody knows too much - then he starts asking Barbara questions about the murdered D'Argenson and Rouvray. In a desperate attempt to look more European, an old sign says "Paris 5Km"... but we're about five years before the agreed length of a metre was adopted, and it wasn't until 1800 that it was used for distance measurement, at least in the Paris region. Prior to this, every town had its own measurement, with about 800 different local names. (Even if Spooner hadn't known this, the fact that Napoleon repealed it as a crowd-pleasing move was well-known, as anti-metric protestors in Britain kept going on about it.) In a typically clumsy bit of exposition, Robespierre gives the date as the 27th of July, 1794; anyone *else* giving the date in that pre-Revolutionary form would have been executed for not calling it the 9th of Thermidor, Year VI. Of all the people to give that info-dump dialogue to...

Yes, we'll say it again. Napoleon is five inches taller than history recounts, and doesn't look like any of the portraits. Ian recognises him all the same.

Critique After almost a year of surprisingly pacy and audience-friendly BBC-style drama, *Doctor Who* gets off its high horse and stops even pretending to be educational. As we've already noted, the immediate impact is a certain gallows humour, first from the jailer and then from the Doctor himself. After the earnestness of "The Aztecs" and the pomposity of "The Keys of Marinus", it's a welcome change of pace.

In fact, compared to what's to come, everything's still kept in check. From hereon in, stories in Earth's past will come in two varieties: "romps" and "tragedies". "The Crusade" (2.6) comes closest to this story's use of humour as a leavening in an otherwise grim tale, even if Whitaker's novelisation of it has a preface in which the Doctor effectively says "boys and girls, here comes a tragedy".

Susan tells us what we're all suspecting, that this is a bad time to be British in France. Spooner could safely assume that most people watching knew the background, and understood who Robespierre was (tragically, a TV production today could never make the same assumption). Simply seeing the name is enough to make Ian and the viewers worried. Like all of the trips back in time written or edited by Spooner, it's history as anyone over the age of eight knew it. With all the period trappings, right down to the woman knitting by the guillotine, there's no need to go into character motivation. Everyone realises what's at stake and what could happen, so he concentrates on keeping things moving. Inevitably, this means that some of the mystery's lost. In "Marco Polo", the past is a strange and disconcerting place; here, it's meant to be familiar. In "The Aztecs", the crux of the story is one of the TARDIS crew trying to recreate a civilisation; here, it's all about running away from men with guns. The French Revolution was actually much stranger than this.

The cast settles well enough into the format.

Russell takes the whole thing as a light farce. Hill slips into "plucky heroine" mode more comfortably than the secondary aspect of Barbara's storyline, the *femme fatale* she also has to be in "The Romans" (2.4). For once, it's not a fat middle-aged bully who fancies Babs but a vaguely dishy double agent. With only episode three to go on, we can't quite decide if Edward Brayshaw is menacing or bored, but on the strength of his performance as the War Chief in "The War Games" (6.7), we'll give him the benefit of the doubt (and draw a veil over *Rentaghost*). The same (except for the *Rentaghost* thing) applies to Ronald Pickup as the Physician, because he's one of those actors you just *knew* must have been in *Doctor Who* at some point.

By the way, Susan's character seems to have undergone a drastic change - Ford holds on to some idea of consistency, but it's obvious they've run out of things to do with the part. Now that the Doctor's taken centre-stage and is saving worlds without any coercion, she's on borrowed time. From now on, this is Hartnell's show.

The Facts

Written by Dennis Spooner. Directed by Henric Hirsch (episode three has no credit for director, and see **The Lore** for the reason). Ratings: 6.9 million, 6.9 million, 6.9 million, 6.4 million, 6.9 million, 6.4 million.

Episodes four and five no longer exist in the BBC archive.

Supporting Cast James Cairncross (Lemaitre), Jack Cunningham (Jailer), Keith Anderson (Robespierre), Tony Wall (Napoleon), Peter Walker (Small Boy), Donald Morley (Jules Renan), Edward Brayshaw (Léon Colbert), Roy Herrick (Jean), Caroline Hunt (Danielle), Dallas Cavell (Road Work Overseer), Jeffry Wickham (Webster), Laidlaw Dalling (Rouvray), Neville Smith (D'Argenson), Robert Hunter (Sergeant), Ken Lawrence (Lieutenant), Howard Charlton (Judge), John Barrard (Shopkeeper), Ronald Pickup (Physician), Paul Barrass (John Law).

AKA... The *Radio Times* called it "The French Revolution", and the name stuck, at least for a bit. *The Making of Doctor Who* went along with it.

Episode Titles "A Land of Fear", "Guests of Madame Guillotine", "A Change of Identity", "The Tyrant of France", "A Bargain of Necessity", "Prisoners of the Conciergerie".

Cliffhangers The Revolutionaries set fire to the farmhouse, neither realising nor caring that the Doctor's trapped inside; from his prison cell, Ian sees Barbara and Susan being taken off to the guillotine; the shopkeeper, looking for Lemaitre, shows the Doctor's ring to the jailer and declares that it's 'evidence against a traitor'; supposed good guy Leon Colbert pulls a gun on Ian, revealing that he's actually working for the Revolution; the Doctor solemnly walks into the hideout where Ian and Barbara are holed up, then stands aside, revealing that he's led Lemaitre there and apparently betrayed them all.

The Lore

• As mentioned above, this story featured the first location filming used in the series, although none of the regulars was involved. To save time, actor Brian Proudfoot learned to walk like Hartnell, then went to a lane in Denham and a field near Gerrards Cross for a day's shooting. Both of these Buckinghamshire locations will be used a lot more in the series.

• New director Henric Hirsch had slightly annoyed Ford by requesting that her performance in episode two be less 'maudlin'; under the circumstances, Susan could be forgiven a little self-pity, she thought. Hirsch had come to Britain after the Hungarian Uprising of 1956, and his previous work for BBC TV was a 60th Anniversary piece on James Joyce's "Bloomsday" (the 16th of June, 1904, is - as we're sure you all know - the day on which Joyce's *Ulysses* is set). Going from the quintessential avant garde writer to *Doctor Who* irked him, although as a Bridge player he found that meeting Dennis Spooner was a bonus, as Spooner wrote magazine articles on the game.

• Episode three has no credited director. Production assistant Tim Combe had been taking on more and more of the work until, on the Friday afternoon, he found Hirsch collapsed outside the rehearsal room. The delays caused by recording with a horse in the studio appear to have caused undue stress. Combe and Lambert stepped in to keep the camera rehearsals going, and it seems that John Gorrie took over directing episode three itself. He also assisted with other episodes, having scored a hit with the cast during the making of "The Keys of Marinus". We say "it seems" because all the documentation indicates this, as do the recollections of Lambert and the cast, but Gorrie himself doesn't remember anything about it.

• A shot of the Doctor seeing Paris in the distance seems to have been planned, and a detailed model made. When this wasn't used, Ford was presented with the model, which was kept safe on top of her wardrobe until it was damaged while cleaning the house. Apparently, it included tiny working tumbrils.

• By now, it was obvious that a major cast-change was unavoidable. Both female leads were considered for the chop, and Terry Nation was asked to conceive a new character for his by-now-inevitable "Daleks on Earth" story. We're mentioning this here, because in Season Two the question of who gets to stay, who gets the axe and who gets to be the replacement is going to become terribly muddled…

• It was decided fairly late that "The Reign of Terror" would be broadcast at the end of the first run of *Doctor Who*. The final scene was added as a grace-note. Just for a change, the long-term future of the series was uncertain; Donald Baverstock was cautiously optimistic, and agreed to continue production until after Christmas (i.e. after the second Dalek story and the change of girl).

season 2

2.1: "Planet of Giants"

(Serial J, Three Episodes, 31st October - 14th November 1964.)

Which One is This?   The Incredible Shrinking TARDIS lands our inch-high heroes in an eco-catastrophe in our own back yard. Meanwhile, a murder takes place on the patio and Verity Lambert rapidly loses "The Urge to Live".

Firsts and Lasts   It's the first story to be wholly set on contemporary Earth, but due to the unusual circumstances (i.e. the regulars are tiny), fans tend to skip over it and go straight for "The War Machines" instead (3.10). The mini-ness of the Doctor and company means, as a consequence, that it's the only story in which the regulars never get to interact with the supporting cast.

As it was shot immediately after "The Reign of Terror", but held over for a month, it's the first time the production team had a few episodes "in hand". It's also the first story to have music by Dudley Simpson, the "default" composer for the whole of the 1970s and in regular use for the black-and-white era. In all, nearly 300 episodes feature his music. And the last of the three broadcast episodes (see **Things to Notice**) was the first directed by the programme's key director of the 1960s, Douglas Camfield.

Here we say goodbye to the TARDIS fault locator. Now that the regular characters have got into the habit of interfering with other people's business, and don't need an excuse to stick around on any given planet other than "because we want to", the TARDIS isn't going to have to develop faults quite so often after this...

Three-and-a-Half Things to Notice About "Planet of Giants"...

1. Everyone had a lot of fun using seven-foot matches and twenty-foot phones, and by and large the props look sensational. Only the chain on the enormous sink-plug is below scratch, and most of these items are well above the sort of thing you get at Expos or Fairs.

It's just a shame that everything doesn't match up. There's no point making excuses; nothing in this story is exactly to scale. The giant ant was

Season 2 Cast/Crew

- William Hartnell (the Doctor)
- William Russell (Ian Chesterton, 2.1 to 2.8)
- Jacqueline Hill (Barbara Wright, 2.1 to 2.8)
- Carole Ann Ford (Susan, 2.1 and 2.2)
- Maureen O'Brien (Vicki, 2.3 to 2.9)
- Peter Purves (Steven Taylor, 2.8 and 2.9)

- Verity Lambert (Producer)
- David Whitaker (Script Editor, 2.1 and 2.2)
- Dennis Spooner (Script Editor, 2.3 to 2.8)
- Donald Tosh (Script Editor, 2.9)

from stock (although it's heartening to think that the BBC was the kind of outfit which *had* things like giant ants in stock), but the sink is far too small to be the same one the normal-sized people are seen to use, unless the Doctor and Susan grow dramatically after meeting the giant worm.

2. Yes, the sink. Here we have two of the oddest cliffhangers ever, the first being a still photo of a cat and the second being a lengthy fade to black under the credits as a man washes his hands and then pulls out the plug. The whole emphasis of this story on looking at the domestic with a fresh eye makes these banal events seem gripping (we mention this in case you look at our **Cliffhangers** listing and decide to give this story a miss). Particularly entertaining is the dramatic orchestral stab when, after getting dirty in the garden, one of the normal-sized characters delivers the less-than-sinister line 'there's a sink in the lab'.

3. This remains the only story to have had an episode broadcast on Hallowe'en, yet every detail seems to be geared towards making it seem to be happening on or around the originally scheduled transmission date (the 17th of September), if not the recording date (the 21st of August). Note in particular the ingenious uses to which handkerchiefs are put throughout the tale, once it's been established that it's late summer. Brow-mopping is very much the order of the day in this yarn.

3 1/2. Uniquely, "Planet of the Giants" was made as a four-parter, but edited down to three to tighten up the story and remove the *longeurs* (and, one might suspect, to take out the child-upsetting scene with the dead cat). The final episode was to

Cultural Primer: Why *Z Cars*?

If you want to know what a society fears, then look at the cop shows.

In 1949, the worst thing that could happen - the *very worst thing* - was for a scared kid with a gun to shoot a bobby. Considering that this was less than five years after a war in which bombs fell on every major city and almost all the able-bodied men were trained to kill, this is extraordinary. Yet, in the 1949 film *The Blue Lamp*, this is what young punk Dirk Bogarde does. A policeman not only represents rectitude, he's the community's focal point. "Police", we were constantly reminded, derives from the same Greek root as "polite", "policy", "cosmopolitan" and "politics". Shooting avuncular PC Dixon was, in its context, right up there with *Reservoir Dogs*.

Fortunately, George Dixon came back from the dead six years later for his own spin-off series. Today, the BBC's *Dixon of Dock Green* looks like a parody. It began, in the early episodes, with someone whistling "Maybe It's Because I'm A Londoner" and a street-light in the fog. PC Dixon, played by former comedian Jack Warner, would walk into the pool of light, face the camera and say 'evening all!' before launching into a monologue of quite astonishing mundanity. The opening shots of the *Doctor Who* pilot look remarkably similar.

If the monologues were dull, then the ensuing drama was mesmerically tedious. You'd watch it now in a state of disbelief, on the edge of the seat waiting for something - *anything* - to happen. A small crime is committed; the culprit is caught; PC Dixon knew him when he was a kid, and so asks him not to do it again, but he does and gets nicked; then Dixon talks to the camera again, updating us on who got what punishment. Run end credits. Closure in fifty minutes, and everything's tickety-boo. Ted Willis, who wrote every episode, became a peer of the realm. (Note to foreign readers: until 1998, this meant that he was Lord Willis, and thus had a say in all the laws passed by Parliament. His interventions did rather a lot of good for writers with regard to payment, though, so we won't gripe.)

More amazingly, the series lasted until 1976. Watching it on Saturday nights, alongside that other TV coelacanth *The Black and White Minstrel Show*, you can see how *Doctor Who* could seem comparatively normal.

Fortunately, things changed. But before we explain how, and why *Doctor Who* fits into this process, this is as good a time as any to settle something important. It's possible that you may not have seen a real police box. They're rather larger than the TARDIS prop, because anything bigger wouldn't have fitted into the lift at Lime Grove, which is why the new series - using an accurate scale replica - makes Christopher Eccleston look titchy. Although dedicated 'phone lines for summoning police assistance had been around since the turn of the twentieth century, in various one-off designs of a wooden box or stone pillar, the 1929 model became the standard. It was made mainly of concrete, contained a 'phone line direct to the local nick, and sometimes came equipped with a first-aid kit (the TARDIS has a St John's Ambulance flash well into Season Two, and in the model work much later).

American police might have preferred small, pole-mounted boxes, like the one Officer Dibble never gets to use in *Top Cat*, but the British constabulary liked the permanent, obvious presence of the police box. Like George Dixon, it was reliable and reassuring, and made serious crime seem simply unthinkable. Of course, serious crime took place regularly, but the public's perception of it as a problem is comparatively recent. Typically, as long as you didn't upset the neighbours or frighten the horses, you could get away with murder. Every major crime was seen as a one-off, an aberration. Police boxes and bobbies on bikes were a form of polite thought-control, in which the public were persuaded by obvious symbols of authority that nothing bad would be allowed to happen.

Criminals got organised, got mobile and got nastier. To match this, rapid response units and American-style two-man cars with two-way radios were introduced. This was partly a response to the advent of the motorways in the late 1950s, and also to the more overt use of fast, expensive cars by gangland figures. We'd had gangsters long before Al Capone, but in the early 1960s they went high-profile, which allowed the film companies to show them in a romantic light before making sure they got caught by ordinary coppers. By this time the fad for Historical Heroes in Tights of Old had fizzled out, so the same companies made cheap TV series shot in Deptford. The bad guys had all the glamour, but always came unstuck in the end (the titles *No Hiding Place* and *Scotland Yard* tell you whose side we were supposed to be on, and the detective series heroes were always described as being "…of the Yard"). The "normal-sized" story in "Planet of Giants" is resolutely in this mould.

continued on page 97…

ABOUT TIME 1963–1966

have been called "The Urge to Live", or possibly "The Will to Survive", depending on who you ask. In general this slimming-down of the tale was a wise move, but it means that the broadcast version of episode three has a few logical flaws. Barbara's collapse confirms she has DN6 poisoning, but then everyone agrees that alerting the authorities to the impending eco-catastrophe is their top priority. Or rather, they act as if it had already been agreed, and as if Barbara had insisted on it. We can only speculate on whether the whole scene of Ian and the Doctor figuring out the molecular structure of the toxin would ever have been broadcastable.

The Continuity

The Doctor Enjoys a bit of arson every now and again [see also 2.4, "The Romans"]. It completely goes against his nature to go back to the Ship without having a quick explore, especially once the locale has presented a couple of mysteries. He can, remarkably, tell that an earthworm is dead from its death-like 'posture'.

• *Background*. He and Susan were once caught in an air-raid, and the Doctor mentions zeppelins. [Assuming it was an air-raid on Earth, rather than on some strange and far-flung zeppelin planet… this would have been in 1917, probably London.] He knows how 'phones work, and quite a bit about plumbing.

• *Ethics*. He agrees that it's 'wrong' to kill worms and bees, as they play vital roles in the growth of things, and seems to believe in the correctness of the natural order. He even speaks of the 'life-force'. The Doctor has no wish to get involved when he finds a human murder victim, but later he's the first to suggest contacting the police, even if his method of attracting their attention is cheerfully anarchic [the morally-autonomous Doctor of the first three stories is long gone].

• *Inventory*. He's wearing that cloak again. He hasn't got pockets for his usual pen and paper, but knows Susan is carrying them in her dungaree-bib.

The Supporting Cast

• *Ian*. Seems to lack confidence in his ability as a chemist, though he can recognise mineral nitrates and phosphoric acid. [His use of the colloquial "sing out" to mean "yell" indicates that he's from the north of England originally, or has fami-

ly from those parts.]

• *Barbara*. After her outburst about the French Revolution, it should surprise nobody that she gets het up about environmental issues here. Her resolve to stop DN6 outweighs her own health worries [even if the scene wasn't broadcast]. Like Ian, Barbara's been on a roller-coaster. She's now familiar enough with the TARDIS console to operate a few basic switches.

• *Susan*. Even after recent arguments [1.7, "The Sensorites"], she's inclined to be panicky when her grandfather isn't around and reassured when he turns up again. Here she seems to need basic schoolkid science explained to her by Ian [judging by "The Sensorites", she may be humouring him].

The TARDIS The Doctor tries to get back to the '60s by trying another 'frequency', something he refers to as a 'side-step'. [Bearing in mind what we learn in later stories, this might mean that there are different types of "path" that the TARDIS can take within the space-time vortex. The word "frequency" might indicate that he's somehow changing the nature of the entire Ship in order to do this.] It gets the TARDIS close to its destination, but the circuits referred to by the fault locator as A14D and QR18 are playing up. At least one panel on the console overheats.

Then the doors open before the Ship properly materialises, and an annoying klaxon sounds [not quite the same as the one in 1.3, "The Edge of Destruction"]. Susan claims that the TARDIS doors have never opened *in flight* before. [Forgetting "The Edge of Destruction". Then again, it's questionable whether the Ship was actually in flight during that story. It was hurtling back through time thanks to the fast return switch, but the central column wasn't bobbing up and down, suggesting that it was travelling backwards in "normal" space rather than traversing the vortex. What we see here may be what happens if you open the doors while the vortex is outside, but it's more likely to be a quirk of the materialisation process.] The Doctor claims that the doors open because the 'space pressure' was too great while they were materialising, though even *he's* puzzled that the travellers came through it unscathed. Ian, Susan and Barbara are capable of pushing the doors shut again.

Once a landing has been managed, the fault locator decides that there isn't a fault anywhere, 'not even yellow standby'. The trouble is that even

Cultural Primer: Why *Z Cars*?

...continued from page 95

As we said in the first essay of this book, 1962 represents BBC TV's Year Zero. The 2nd of January saw the first episodes of both *Compact* (we'll be mentioning this a lot) and *Z Cars*. The Z - and that's pronounced "Zed", you uncouth colonials - stood for "Zephyr", as in the Humber Zephyr, the fastest commercially-available patrol car. The series was about the two-man crews of the cars and their bosses, and was set in a fictitious northern city called Newtown, where everyone had Scouse accents.

The northern-ness was important. This was the beginning of a style of film we always have to call "gritty" and "kitchen-sink", and other mildly patronising terms. There were films being made about everyday lives, rather than people with perfect BBC English and Home Counties accents. Granada Television, set up in Manchester, had launched *Coronation Street* in 1960. The BBC's characteristic response was to go one better; if people wanted real life, then they'd get it as real as it could be shown. Crime became more than a series of "issues", and the police became people doing a job but with other things going on in their lives. George Dixon suddenly looked like Mr Plod from *Noddy in Toytown*. As we'll see, soon a Northern accent would become less of a liability and more an asset to be cultivated (see especially 3.5, "The Massacre").

The grammar of television drama accelerated. It's been estimated that the average length of a shot in an episode of *Z Cars* was twelve seconds. That's almost subliminal by 1962 standards. Filmed inserts, back-projection, pre-recorded video sections and scripts requiring short, tight scenes made this unlike anything else on British television. It was written as an ensemble piece, and the actors spent weeks before rehearsals working out the life-stories of their characters. Troy Kennedy Martin, chief writer in the early years, was keen to move from plot-led stories to character-led situations. While Dixon's storylines were all based on real case-histories, and Dixon himself was as much a social-worker as a copper, the regulars in *Z Cars* were characters first and crimebusters second. The Police Federation took a dim view when a policeman was seen smoking and arguing with his wife.

After the first run of thirteen episodes, it became continuous from summer '62 to late '64. Kennedy Martin believed this weakened the format, but it led to the characteristic form of '60s / '70s TV drama, what became known in BBC circles as the "series-al". In this, each story is self-contained, but longer story-strands would emerge over the course of a few years. One character's marriage breakup began in the first episode, and a replacement for another was phased in rather than being suddenly introduced. You can see how the format of *Doctor Who* develops from this idea.

Z Cars returned in the '70s, with groovy wah-wah guitars in the theme tune, and finally ended just after the last episode of *Dixon of Dock Green*. By this time the ITV companies had gone for all-out thick-ear violence in its cop shows, first with *Special Branch* (imagine Derren Nesbitt, the warlord Tegana from "Marco Polo", taking a tough stance against crime in a selection of offensive floral shirts) and then *The Sweeney*. This was also created by Troy Kennedy Martin and made by Euston Films, so it was ultimately the responsibility of Verity Lambert; watch any given episode today, and you're guaranteed to spot at least one minor character actor that you'll know from *Doctor Who*. But what goes around comes around. In 2005, the BBC resurrected *Dixon of Dock Green* for radio, adding more plot per episode and casting David Tennant as second-fiddle police officer PC Crawford. Which meant that after the sudden shock of the Eccleston "regeneration", the BBC announcer insisted on plugging the series over the end credits of "The Parting of the Ways" (X1.13). Considering the history we've just described, this seems nothing short of perverse.

For the efforts of *Z Cars* regulars to evade typecasting, see 19.2, "Four to Doomsday"; 20.6, "The King's Demons"; 26.1, "Battlefield"; 26.2, "Ghost Light"; and most spectacularly 23.2, "Mindwarp".

---

if it's in working order, the TARDIS has shrunk to less than two inches in height. Susan believes the space pressure to be the cause of this. The screen of the scanner blows out when it's switched on, and the Doctor claims that it's due to something 'too big to explain' [an unintentional pun], but concedes that an overtaxing of the scanner circuits might be responsible. [Not purely because things outside are too large, surely? It's amusing to think of the viewers' sets exploding at home when they try to show the elephant in "The Ark" (3.6). The scanner basically relays information from one dimension to the other, so the confusion in scale may short it somehow.] The voices of the shrunken travellers would, according to the Doctor, sound too high and squeaky for a normal-sized human to hear.

Materialisation is said to be the most dangerous phase of travel. [Yet the Doctor sleeps through the whole thing in 2.3, 'The Rescue'. Still, "dangerous" may just mean that there's an increased likelihood of a technical fault, not that someone always has to be standing at the console. In later stories, the TARDIS is left to materialise by itself without anybody worrying about it.] When the TARDIS departs, the Doctor repeats the same procedure he attempted on landing, and the problem with dimensions is fixed again. A grain of wheat, taken from the "giant" Earth, becomes normal grain-of-wheat size. So, it seems, does the poisonous DN6 in Barbara's blood stream. [In other words, everything that was on board the TARDIS when it landed is returned to normal, but everything taken from the outside world stays its "real" size.] Curiously, the scanner-screen is fixed again, and the Doctor speaks of repairing it [though there's no possible time in which he could have done this].

The Doctor tells the others to go and have a good scrub, indicating that there's a bathroom on board [see 15.6, "The Invasion of Time"]. The fault locator bay seems to have moved. [By now it's a cert that the TARDIS interior can rearrange itself, even without being told to. Compare with 1.1, "An Unearthly Child". Similarly, controls have a habit of moving from one part of the console to another throughout the series. No wonder the Doctor likes to mark some of the switches with marker-pen.] Water now routinely comes in glasses instead of astronaut-bulbs.

History

• *Dating*. Clearly, it's sometime in the 1960s. [The Doctor states that he's trying to get Ian and Barbara back to their own time, which is apparently autumn 1963. There's every indication that the short-cut worked, but that the miniaturisation was an unforeseen side-effect, yet it's a hot day in England. If the "night-scented stock" seeds from the packet we see have been planted recently, then August seems a safe bet. Is the TARDIS trying to take the teachers back to their own era, but adding the time they've spent with the Doctor? It wouldn't be out of character for the Ship, though if so then they've been adventuring for eight months, longer than we might have expected (even given 1.4, "Marco Polo").]

At a cottage in the south of England, approximately ten miles from the coast, a scientist called Smithers is working on an insecticide called DN6 that's capable of wiping out all insect life. Though Smithers speaks of seeing death and starvation all over the world, he's financed by a downright murderous businessman called Forester, who wants to market DN6 and hasn't considered that some insect life is essential to agriculture. Furthermore, DN6 is everlasting, so it's likely to seep into the soil and start killing all the animal life. It was initially given the go-ahead by 'the Ministry', but exhaustive tests made by ministry-man Farrow have revealed its true nature. By the end of this debacle, Forester has been arrested for Farrow's murder [yet the formula for DN6 is still in existence...].

The Analysis

Where Does This Come From? As we've pointed out before (see **Where Does *All* of This Come From?** under "An Unearthly Child"), this was Sydney Newman's idea of how to do *Doctor Who*. In fact it was just about his *only* idea, other than a list of "don'ts" which Verity Lambert promptly did. However, the emphasis isn't quite what might have been expected. Louis Marks, like many people, had read Rachel Carson's *The Silent Spring*. And this won't be the last time that Marks will write a script about an ecological balance being dramatically disturbed (see 13.2, "Planet of Evil").

In 1944, a typhus epidemic was stopped in its tracks by the use of the military insecticide DDT. The Dow chemical company was permitted to release it for commercial use in the following year, and farmers began to cleanse the land of anything that wasn't profitable. By 1947, the side-effects were becoming apparent, but by then millions of lives supposedly depended on it, and millions of dollars certainly did. The military connection is important, as the chemical industry presented it as a battle between Science (and control) and Nature (and pestilence). Ordinary farmers, caught in the middle, became infantry. As long as there was a prospect of removing threats to starving nations, it was worth investing and investigating. The reports that DDT was accumulating in higher concentrations further up the food-chain coincided with the first signs of birth-defects caused by thalidomide, and soon the public would see the quest for control over nature as inhuman, but in 1964 it was perceived as a risk worth taking.

Throughout this year's run of *Doctor Who*, there'll be a sense that the commercial, consumer society of early 1960s Britain is the measure of all things. In this, and the next story, it's shown to be fragile. Once Dennis Spooner takes over as story editor, there'll no longer be any question of this; instead, the pop-up toaster will be the height of technological sophistication (2.9, "The Time Meddler"). Hilda the telephonist is here the emblem of normality in this story, even though village telephone exchanges were on the way out by the time it was made. Forester is the kind of character who'd appear in cheaply-made thrillers, the ruthless businessman exploiting science for profit. His sort of villain regularly cropped up in ITV film series aimed at the export market (hence, they usually had American girlfriends), but also became a staple of dramas like the early *Avengers* capers.

Meanwhile, the myth of the garden-shed inventor rears it head again, though this time in a less charming form than the inquisitive Dr Who and his home-made time machine. The idea of the lone gentleman-scientist had been useful in World War Two, when the efforts of multinational companies and government-sponsored projects had been downplayed as part of the War-time attempt to portray the British as individuals and the Nazis as a faceless mass of evil. Even after the War, films like *The Dambusters* promulgated the idea of the boffin in the back-room, coming up with a brilliantly simple idea to beat the Germans and overcoming official disdain by taking it straight to Churchill. But here, the solo inventor is having his strings pulled by big business. As we've already seen, a large part of the British character is a love for the amateur over the professional, and here we're seeing the victory of the latter over the former as War-time gumption gives way to grim reality. Yet even so, this story's still hiding from the full horror of it. We all knew it was the major combines with their vast R&D budgets that made new chemicals, but things seemed more reassuringly manageable if we pretended that people like Smithers did it.

Smithers has a lab in a cottage, with a nice garden full of overgrown wildlife. Seeing this wildlife close-up can be dangerous - or at least, if might have been if the DN6 hasn't killed everything. We're not a million miles away from Disney's "true-life adventure", *Nature's Half Acre*. These days we're so used to close-up, time-lapse and long-distance photography in documentaries that it's hard to see how the early wildlife film-makers enthralled viewers by simply showing us things happening in our own yards. But documentaries needed recognisable figures to explain why the things we were seeing, fuzzily, were so extraordinary. The story was either "I am going somewhere to find something" or "this is the life-and-death struggle happening somewhere".

"Planet of Giants", like much of early *Doctor Who*, combines these two formats. The story isn't "small people lost in the savage world of nature" but "Our Friends lost in the savage world of nature". Except that they've opted not to make it too savage. Instead, after half an episode of what most programmes would have used as the main gimmick, we're indoors facing life-or-death struggles with office stationery. Why?

We have a big clue in the dialogue. When Ian talks about the ginormous packet of night-scented stock, he speculates that they might have landed at a World's Fair. In 1939's New York Fair, one of the iconic exhibits was a cash register the size of an office block (and if anybody can think of anything more American than *that*...). And by the '60s, the art galleries and public spaces were being filled with works celebrating the everyday and commercial. Andy Warhol made packaging and mass-production his main subject; Roy Lichtenstein explored the apparent gulf between the artist and the hack, reproducing and resizing panels from comic-books; and the sculptor Claes Oldenberg gave the world huge public statues of everyday objects.

Children, artists and science-fiction writers all look at the commonplace world as if for the first time. Children had been reading stories like Mary Norton's *The Borrowers*, in which a family of inch-high people use our domestic objects for their own purposes. The 1955 film *The Incredible Shrinking Man* used the progressive shrinkage of the hero to make the familiar, homely world seem increasingly hostile. The scene in which he's chased by his own cat is echoed in this story, but the overall mood of the piece more closely resembles the oversized novelty world of World's Fairs for one obvious reason: with one or two back-projected exceptions (which, frankly, *look* like back-projected exceptions), we don't see the world of Forester and Smithers and the world of mini-Ian and mini-Barbara in the same shot. In the scenes of the TARDIS crew making its way in this giant world, we're closer to *Tom and Jerry* than to the process photography of Hollywood's giant insects and tiny people.

Just in case it's not obvious, we should point out that the moment when Susan mentions being in an air-raid and the Doctor starts talking about zeppelins is set up as a joke; the middle-aged members of the audience are supposed to think Susan means the kind of air-raid *they* remember from the '40s, until the Doctor mentions an earlier war. Time has not been kind to this sort of humour. And one last thing... a lot of discussion in the first episode centres on what chance humans would stand if insects were their size. Aside from the John Wyndham quality of this notion (and we'll be talking about him later), it's interesting that we're only three months away from "The Web Planet" (2.5).

Things That Don't Make Sense   Smithers the wonder-chemist has the startling ability to end all insect life on Earth from his cottage, yet hasn't realised that doing this will have terrible eco-consequences and doesn't even seem to know what a food chain is. This is a bit like coming up with a great new way of making atomic bombs but never having heard of "radiation". Our unpaid scientific advisor furthermore suggests that the formula for DN6 we see on the giant notepad would make a good glue, but a lousy fly-spray. (Proctor and Gamble might not like what he wants to say about the similarity of this stuff to the ingredients of *Sunny Delight*.)

Dr Science also has problems with the miniaturised humans being able to breathe, and all sorts of other things like that, but it's a whole other essay; see **How Hard is It to Be the Wrong Size?** under 16.6, "The Armageddon Factor". For now we'll just ask how people with teeny-tiny noses can smell things, when their olfactory receptors are far too small for the relevant molecules. And why "giant" people's voices sound slowed-down, not just very deep.

A lot of what doesn't seem to make sense has already been covered, as the glitches are due to omissions after the trimming of episodes three and four. However, one fairly odd element is never mentioned: Farrow, the Man from the Ministry, has been at the cottage for about ten minutes before he's murdered. Forester, the kind of businessman who takes a pistol to meetings despite not knowing what the meeting's about,

has bumped off a government inspector. The inspector has promised to go to Forester's hi-tech shed alone, rather than simply telling everyone in his department that DN6 is a non-starter, and pops in on his way to the boat on which he's going to France. Why does he take his paperwork with him on holiday, and if he knows he's got a fortnight off, then didn't he file his report before leaving?

In fact, what was Forester's plan to cover up the murder? Put the body in the boat and tow it out to sea, overturning it to make Farrow's death look like an accident. Even though it's got a bullet-hole in the chest. And even though the time of death is easy to establish, as an hour before the 'phone call which Farrow supposedly makes from the farmhouse. Speaking of which, why is the local operator familiar enough with Farrow's voice to know that Forester isn't him? And why does Forester not even *attempt* to talk like Farrow when he's speaking to her?

'Whatever you do, don't look into the cat's eyes,' warns the Doctor, while staring unblinkingly into the cat's eyes. In episode two, Ian *must* be aware that Barbara's touched the poisoned wheat - even if he's not paying attention when she picks up one of the hefty grains, she asks him for a handkerchief immediately after describing it as being all sticky - but then he starts saying "whatever you do, don't touch it" and acting as if only an idiot would even consider such a thing. And he can't spot why she's getting all depressed and anxious.

The Doctor believes the DN6 in Barbara's blood will be seventy times less potent when she's returned to normal size, apparently because she'll be seventy times taller. He's forgetting that Barbara is three dimensional, and will be seventy times wider and deeper as well, which should make the poison 343,000 times less dangerous. There's also the matter of the amazing self-repairing scanner, but we've already mentioned that.

Critique   This must have been such fun, the first time round. It has its *longeurs*, mainly the bits about Forester and the 'phone exchange, but the main thrust of the story is exactly what *Doctor Who* was always supposed to be about. The four regulars convey absolute conviction - by turns amused, frustrated and scared, exactly as any of us would be in their teeny little position. Ian is resourceful, the Doctor is wise and Susan enjoys herself in unlikely circumstances - but above all, the main focus is on Barbara. We'll be arguing later that Jacqueline Hill was one of the key reasons that the series was a hit, and it's Barbara's entirely believable trait of not wanting to admit to doing something silly that makes this more than just a romp on a bench.

Not for the first time, though, the real star is designer Ray Cusick. The big insects, vast phones and colossal sinks are impressive, yet it's the practical details like corks and grains of wheat which make it work. The cast all confessed to finding the sets and props so detailed and convincing that they hardly had to put any effort into make-believe.

They'd been trying to make a story like this for a year, and every time it had fallen foul of budget and resources. In the pre-pilot stage, they'd decided that it couldn't be done at Lime Grove. Yet, with a shift of emphasis from meeting the regulars and establishing the format to an off-beat detective story and eco-sermon, it works. We never get an "objective" view of the world, so both strands of the story are equally valid. From the Doctor's point of view, the everyday seems strange, but the "normal-sized" narrative is directed with an odd emphasis on details which we know to be significant. Forester carrying a briefcase indoors is made to look disturbing, because the camera lingers on the briefcase. Since we've already been primed to look at things on the micro-scale, we know how enormously threatening these commonplace objects can be. In this context, even the usually-embarrassing model TARDIS (see especially 1.5, "The Keys of Marinus") seems acceptable.

Undeniably, it's dated badly. Technology has made the close-up world we see here seem routine, and what looked like a roller-coaster ride in 1964 (note Barbara's 'Big Dipper' comment as well as Ian's 'World's Fair' one) now looks like a fairly ordinary merry-go-round, probably run by gypsies. It's distinctly studio-bound, and there are a couple of moments when the programme-makers' ambition outstrips their capacity. But that's sort of the point. On Saturday nights, in amongst light entertainment programmes and orthodox cop shows, anything even remotely mundane would have been a waste of the resources and potential of *Doctor Who*. In many ways this is a parody of those cop shows (see **Cultural Primer: Why Z Cars?**), yet in part that's the series' mandate. *Doctor Who* took the methods of most other BBC drama at the time and made something different

with them. Here, as would happen a lot in Season Two, the yardstick isn't Ian and Barbara but the insertion of bits of our world into a place where they don't belong. In this case, we get a cat and a sink where we'd normally end an episode with a monster or a rockfall. No other story set in the present day has quite this sense of wonder, and we'll miss it when it goes.

The Facts

Written by Louis Marks. Directed by Mervyn Pinfield (episodes one, two and the first half of what's now three) and Douglas Camfield (the bits that used to be episode four, though he's given sole credit for "Crisis"). Ratings: 8.4 million, 8.4 million, 8.9 million.

Supporting Cast Alan Tilvern (Forester), Reginald Barratt (Smithers), Frank Crawshaw (Farrow), Rosemary Johnson (Hilda Rowse), Fred Ferris (Bert Rowse).

Episode Titles "Planet of Giants", "Dangerous Journey", "Crisis".

Working Titles "The Miniscules" (sic).

Cliffhangers A cat stares down at the miniaturised travellers; the Doctor and Susan, who've been sliding around in the sink, are about to be swept away as the plug is pulled. (In the next episode, this situation is resolved when the Doctor urgently tells Susan to get 'into the overflow'. Anyone familiar with the early work of Girls Aloud might feel the urge to sing along with this sentiment.)

The lead-in to the next story: the scanner shows no clear image. Well, *that* should get people tuning in next week.

The Lore

• If you've been reading this book from the start, then you may recall that the idea of the four regulars running around a laboratory after being shrunk to the size of a pin-head was the original pilot story. In the pilot version, Dr Who, Cliff, Sue and Lola are menaced by the school lab's biology specimens and captured by another pupil, whose matchbox (containing Our Heroes) is confiscated by the headmaster. Wot larks! (In 25.1, "Remembrance of the Daleks", the headmaster of

Coal Hill School is revealed to be a Dalek agent. There's room for a very strange "what if?" story here...)

• Aside from the obvious problems of making this version of the story at Lime Grove, Newman was worried about the incidents along the way, notably the spiders and caterpillars (suspiciously like bug-eyed monsters, which were still a no-no at that early stage). Robert Gould's "Miniscules" story, like the original Bunny Webber idea, was reworked, amended and then abandoned. But in both cases, elements appeared that the final broadcast version would mention and then gloss over. Webber had the idea of the travellers communicating with the "giants" by using a slowed-down tape recorder, and of someone exhibiting the tiny people as freaks, while Gould's version moved the emphasis to the environment in which they were lost.

• Whitaker had been contacted by Louis Marks, who was invited in to discuss ideas for the series. Marks' track-record was odd; he was an Oxford academic with a PhD in Renaissance Italian Politics (see 14.1, "The Masque of Mandragora"), who'd taken the improbable career-move of writing for ITC adventure series. It's unclear whether Marks brought the idea of a tiny crew fighting pollution with him, or if he wanted to write an eco-parable and Whitaker suggested the reworked "Miniscules" concept.

• The shots of the regulars looking at enormous everyday objects - at least, those which *weren't* built in the studio - were a variation of a trick used in Victorian theatres. A half-silvered mirror was placed between the camera and the actors, and the "big" image projected onto it. The cast had light-coloured clothes and stood on a black set, which is why the Doctor abruptly decides to wear a shiny cape (similarly, *Attack of the Fifty Foot Woman* involved a giant blonde and *The Amazing Colossal Man* was bald). It took two attempts to get some of these shots right, during parts four and six of 1.8, "The Reign of Terror".

• Meanwhile, behind the scenes, all is going predictably badly. Donald Baverstock is still hesitant over the programme's long-term future, and with "Planet of Giants" now scheduled for a later October transmission, the possibility of shutting up shop in January 1965 causes real problems. With the second Dalek story, they've got ten weeks' worth of material and time to record a four-part final story. They've just bust a gut trying

to find a way to write out Susan and replace her with Saida / Jenny at the end of the Dalek adventure, and now they have to tie everything up.

Not the least of their problems is the lack of a four-part script. There's a five-part version of Malcom Hulke's "Lame Dog" idea still kicking around, possibly a historical idea from Margot Bennett, and that's about it. (It may be pure accident that the villain in the story which was eventually made after "The Dalek Invasion of Earth" ends up with Bennett's surname, but knowing how writers tend to reach out for any available name when they're pushed for time, possibly not.)

• As it turns out, the alternatives to continuing with *Doctor Who* would have been tricky, and worse yet costly. It was easier to negotiate a fresh three-month contract with the regulars (except Ford) with an extra tenner a week and the option to renew every three months. The problem would have been worse if they'd had to keep the regulars for a mere four weeks, and if one or more refused to play along or demanded more money - especially Ford, who'd have to be written back in - then things could have got nasty for anyone trying to cast a replacement series. Soon, Baverstock's long-term future would be in jeopardy...

• An early draft of the script accounted for the reduction in everyone's size by claiming that atmospheric pressure was to blame, with the materialisation causing displacement of air. (So materialising with the doors open, and the internal dimensions so much larger, caused a pressure of seventy atmospheres because the console room's seventy times the size of a police box. Can you see why they avoided broadcasting this?) Ray Cusick maintains that the ending was written with his collaboration, as he was asked what could physically be managed by the construction teams. The gas-jet that knocks out Forrester, which Cusick has stated was his suggestion, was certainly filmed while late revisions were being made to the rehearsal script. However, most accounts claim this idea was included in the script from the start.

• They played musical chairs with the directors. Originally, this was Richard Martin's project, and he'd been involved in the Robert Gould / Bunny Webber situation. Then associate producer Mervyn Pinfield, fresh from the first four episodes of "The Sensorites", came in when Martin was given "The Dalek Invasion of Earth" to shoot; all the location work for the Dalek story needed to be done pronto, as in autumn the sun would rise over Trafalgar Square *after* people started occupying it. Pinfield was only able to commit to the first three episodes, so Waris Hussein's right-hand man Douglas Camfield was given a break with the final part. When the last two parts were amalgamated, Camfield got sole credit.

• The editing-down of episodes three and four couldn't be done on videotape, for the usual reasons of cost (see the essay under "The Reign of Terror"), so the material was transferred to 35mm and broadcast from film. This means that although other '60s episodes originally looked like VT - which isn't how they looked for viewers in the '80s and '90s, since the BBC video releases were made from film copies - the broadcast episode three always looked "filmy". The removal of a whole episode from the running order would eventually require an extra episode to be added to the end of the recording block (3.2, "Mission to the Unknown"), though this solved certain other problems, as we'll see later.

• Just so you know, the significant cuts were: Sammy the cat drinks poisoned water and dies; the Doctor decides to stand and fight to save all life on Earth; there are no suitable antidotes to be found on the Ship; Forrester's cigarette-smoke asphyxiates Ian and Barbara (it's not big and it's not clever, kids); Hilda is suspicious about the American car at the farmhouse, and recalls that the man from London smokes the same brand Bert used to smoke before he quit (so she *has* met Farrow); Smithers deduces what Farrow's report said; and Forrester says he's placed the corpse in the boot of his car.

2.2: "The Dalek Invasion of Earth"

(Serial K, Six Episodes, 21st November - 26th December 1964.)

Which One is This?   It's the *other* one that was made into a full-colour movie, and is obviously the Blitz with cunningly-disguised Germans. However, the moment when the Dalek emerges from the river Thames remains the most famous bit.

Firsts and Lasts   Everyone's on the move. It's the first story to be made at the programme's new home, Riverside Studio 1, and the last time we see

Susan until she gets all middle-aged in 1983 (20.7, "The Five Doctors"). The Daleks leave Skaro and build spaceships (for the first time); Earth, i.e. the south-east of England, is invaded by aliens (for the first time); a companion gets a full-on snog (for the first time) and is written out of the series (for the first time); and Our Heroes and the evil space-monsters are filmed going around famous London locations (for the first time). We even get the first use of a quarry for the location work, and the audience is told well in advance that the Daleks are coming back, so it's the first sequel.

For the *only* time, the Daleks have parabolic dishes on their backs and tricycles built into the prop Dalek casings. Terry Nation begins his life-long flirtation with plagues, and adds more recyclable material to his portfolio (compare the suicide that opens episode one with the beginning of his other alien takeover story, 13.4, "The Android Invasion"). The humans do the "dustbin" joke, while the Daleks say 'resistance is useless!' and take to using the e-word…

Six Things to Notice About "The Dalek Invasion of Earth"…

1. The Daleks now have rather less menacing voices, but routinely use the verb "exterminate" to mean killing individuals, not groups or races. Yet the idea of mass extermination is present, and one of them calls it a 'final solution'. Earlier, we see them giving fascist salutes with their sink-plungers, employing slave labour in camps to clear underground workings (like at Peenemunde, home of the V2 rocket) and broadcasting propaganda over the airwaves. They've apparently wiped out all non-white races on Earth - although they've kept India, for some reason - and believe themselves not just to be technologically more advanced but racially superior. We believe there may be a subtext underlying all of this.

2. It's London, and the locations have hardly changed between the 1960s and the 2160s. Although we hear about Chelsea Heliport and an Astronaut Fair, the majority of recognisable landmarks have been mysteriously unaffected by the sustained bombing. It's perhaps heartening to know that while the London Eye, the Post Office Tower, the GLA building and several bridges and skyscrapers were evidently destroyed during the invasion, Battersea Power Station seems to have been almost totally refurbished before getting lumps knocked off it. We'd also like to commend

the Daleks for their judicious devastation of Docklands.

3. The Daleks, on location, have apparently tagged their Skaroine handles on public monuments. In Trafalgar Square, they've defaced Landseer's lions with angular graffiti. In fact the Daleks have based a lot of their troops in well-known tourist attractions, making it seem as if they've invaded simply to have their photos taken.

4. The sheer insanity of the Daleks' scheme takes a while to sink in. Even the Doctor is amazed at their daring, probably admiring the sheer nerve of putting so much effort into something so pointless. The plan - in case you didn't know, or had heard but didn't believe that two-and-a-half hours of screen-time could be spent on something so risible - is to remove the magnetic core of Earth, 'degravitate' the planet, place a giant engine in the centre and steer it around the cosmos very, very slowly. This grandiose scheme actually makes a lot more sense when you see the spaceships they normally use. (We might hazard a guess that the Daleks, ever keen to keep up with the competition, saw the Earth-like mobile planet that's being used by the Cybermen and got jealous. See 4.2, "The Tenth Planet".)

5. David Campbell, Susan's fiancé, suddenly comes into his own as a character in episode four. Oddly enough, it's at exactly the same point that the Doctor abruptly collapses from what appears to be a heart attack (falling forward, so we can't see his face), although he's completely recovered by the next episode. By some bizarre osmosis, in this period David develops previously-undisclosed ingenuity in bomb disposal, as if telepathically prompted by the Doctor. Things like this will happen a lot more in Season Two, and at a crucial point in "The Daleks' Master Plan" (3.4). The alert reader will already have worked out why.

6. This story ends with what has to be the oddest of any of the weird, awkward efforts to graft a love-story onto a *Doctor Who* adventure. David and Susan's courtship seems to consist of hitting each other with fish, and David's chat-up lines mainly concern animal husbandry. When the invasion is over, the Doctor does a bit of match-making by locking his granddaughter out of the Ship, making a speech and then buggering off to another planet. She agrees to marry David, but even when they're holding hands they have their backs to one another. All of this is accompanied by the kind of cheesy electric organ music that's

usually associated with 1950s US radio soaps. The most surprising thing, though, is that even after all of this it's *still* really quite sweet.

The Continuity

The Doctor Susan's attempts to keep her romance with David hidden are a complete failure; the Doctor's 'something's cooking' line makes it abundantly clear that he isn't fooled, and he's keeping a close eye on them all the way. [A generation of fans, who knew the story primarily from the novelisation and the movie version, were brought up to believe that the Doctor was blind to all of this. Not a bit of it.] He soon comes to realise that someone other than him has to take Susan 'in hand'. Ultimately, he's not only prepared to leave her on Earth but forces her to stay, shutting her out of the Ship and insisting that she should have roots of her own [it's not unreasonable to suppose that he doesn't want her turning out like him]. He also claims that he'll come back, one day.

[He never does, as far as we ever see. Unless you count the novel *Legacy of the Daleks*, but funnily enough many people are reluctant to. Yet when the Doctor and Susan meet up again in "The Five Doctors" (20.7), she has no animosity about the way he left her, and he's never heard to ask whether she's happy. This might indicate a follow-up visit to this period.]

The Doctor knows about three-dimensional graph geometry, not a subject that Ian taught at school. When over-exerted, the Doctor passes out with an almighty 'uuhhn'. [The first sign of the tiredness that'll eventually get the better of him in 4.2, "The Tenth Planet". And not just a way for William Hartnell to skip an episode, gosh no.] He doesn't like being called 'Doc', but does like being called 'Doctor'. [This sounds like a small detail, but bear in mind that he never introduces himself in "An Unearthly Child" (1.1), and it was Ian and Barbara who started routinely calling him by that name. Before then, he may have gone by another title altogether.]

• *Background.* When discussing what time-period they're in, the Doctor apparently comments that he hopes they're nearer to Ian's time than his own. [Hartnell garbles the line somewhat, but it still sounds as though it's feasible for the TARDIS to land on Earth during the Doctor's "present".] He doesn't recognise the 'monstrosity' Battersea Power Station, and seems to know the

Is This Really About the Blitz?

If you asked anyone in 1964 what "science fiction" meant, then you'd get one of two answers. Literate interviewees might mention the books, which tended to be social satires or dystopian allegories. The rest might focus on movies about cities being menaced by flying saucers. In Britain we had a third way, a hybrid wherein society fell apart after something a bit like a war but not quite. John Wyndham wrote a lot of this sort of thing, usually involving frightfully nice people trying to cope with simply beastly circumstances and - horror of horrors - the destruction of the BBC.

"The Dalek Invasion of Earth" is as clear an example as we ever get. It's obvious that the main impetus behind the story is the conception of a Nazi-occupied London, but there are other sets of cues. The shot of Battersea Power Station with chimneys missing is at odds with the usual Blitz iconography. Most images of London after the bombing were of well-known monuments withstanding anything Jerry could throw at us. Instead, here we have a picture of a wounded landmark. You can find it echoed in the shots of Bedfordshire as a wasteland, or the set of an overgrown and derelict Kew Bridge, and it's reinforced by all the lovingly-detailed dialogue about whole continents being wiped out.

And we lap it all up. Nothing seems to please people more than seeing their homes destroyed. Deserted cities, big monsters running amok and trashing skyscrapers and - a phrase you may have heard before - a Yeti sitting on a loo in Tooting Bec are all endlessly appealing. Many theories are available to anyone wanting to account for this. Good old-fashioned Freudians would claim that seeing something brutal and powerful unleashed is a sign of a healthy id. We spend most of our waking lives keeping ourselves in check, behaving ourselves, not frightening the horses. For ninety minutes in a darkened cinema, we can imagine what it might be like to let rip. Think how many of the big, city-munching monsters come from "underneath" something: a volcano, a sewer, 20,000 fathoms or a Black Lagoon. We have to admit, a great many children returned to bombed-out cities and treated the wreckage as a giant playground.

This brings us to a second exciting aspect of this type of spectacle. A deserted city, or one which is now a battlefield, is one where normal laws are suspended. The Law of the Jungle, in your own neighbourhood, is an appealing prospect. Space-monsters shooting ray-guns, or brain-eating zombies, are a legitimate target. Social niceties are unnecessary. There's no traffic. Nobody has to pay for things. It's a break from responsibility.

The return to childishness is there in a subtler way. When the world becomes familiar, when we have mastery over the everyday, we're no longer surprised or feel the need to explore it. When something happens to make the mundane marvellous again, it's like seeing it for the first time, while simultaneously knowing it better than ever. A lot of monster movies gain a *frisson* from showing subjective point-of-view shots with distortions (we might use the end of episode two of 7.2, "Doctor Who and the Silurians", to stand in for dozens of these films). And we could bring in a whole raft of film theory concerning the way in which the screen creates a panorama with the viewer as the focal-point, making the watching "subject" the controlling intelligence, the "owner" of the image. If this is the case, then being somehow immune to whatever's happened to the world is an immensely gratifying position in which to be.

All well and good, but here we're talking about a much smaller screen, a far fuzzier image. And we're talking about seeing it in your living room, probably while eating sausage and mash off a plate on your lap. All the available theories about what the audience is made to feel by seeing cities destroyed by Mothra or a giant squid are inadequate for our purposes.

The central fact of television in the 405-line era is that it was promiscuous. No matter what we wanted to see, it was there on the same screen. Before channel-zapping, people settled down in a darkened room (the small monochrome screen required, indeed demanded, that no daylight should come in and wreck the picture with its glare) and watched as a family. Whatever was on the selected channel - and prior to the arrival of BBC2, there'd only been two possibilities - you watched it. If you didn't think you were going to like it, then you waited for something else. You might see Nazi war criminals being tried in Nuremberg, followed by Humphrey Lestocq and Mr Turnip (just don't ask), then *Six-Five Special* with Jon Pertwee doing a skiffle number (really, *really* don't ask). So when *Doctor Who* offered you coverage of Marco Polo meeting Kublai Khan, it was no more nor less unlikely than Ena Sharples buying half-pints of stout in *Coronation Street*, no more or

continued on page 107...

Dalek invasion of Earth is inevitably doomed, even if he's surprised that it happened at all. He states that through 'all the years' he's been taking care of Susan, Susan's also been taking care of him.

• *Ethics.* He refuses to carry a gun on principle, and when a member of the human resistance is about to despatch a roboman, he intervenes. He does so on moral grounds, 'leave this creature to his own devices and salvation'. [Even though damaged robomen suffer excruciating torment which leads them to suicide. Nonetheless, giving apparently rotten types the potential to find "salvation" will be typical of the Doctor in future.] He also states that he only takes life when his own is threatened, and at one stage menaces Susan with a jolly good smacked bottom.

• *Inventory.* He points out that he's not carrying his walking-stick, but he's obviously starting to need it.

The Supporting Cast

• *Ian.* Ever the man-about-town, Ian keeps his tie on even when he's inside a bomb that's being dropped down a mine.

• *Barbara.* Seems to be very familiar with the route from London to Bedfordshire, and goes via St Albans. [One of the main teacher-training colleges was based at Aldenham, near Radlett, just down the road. If you know your late '60s ITC serials, or Emma-Peel-era *Avengers*, then you'll know the area well from every single location shoot. In *The Prisoner*, for instance, "The Girl Who Was Death" has Number Six popping into The Battleaxes; a pub that would have been Barbara's local, when the college bar was closed.]

Barbara can drive a truck. [This is the most improbable thing of all, as the gear-change system is totally unlike that of a 1950s car. Has she driven a tractor at some stage? Did she do a degree in Aztec history to get away from a farming background, and get into teaching later?]

• *Susan.* Somehow knows what a goat farm smells like. Alligators in the sewers scare her less than the rats in a prison cell did [1.8, "The Reign of Terror"]. Her cupboard on the TARDIS contains dozens of pairs of shoes, and since leaving school she's become a little slovenly.

She first makes a connection with urban guerrilla David Campbell when she's scared and he's comforting her, but she seems to take a shine to him immediately afterwards, soon telling him that she's never felt she belongs anywhere and that she's never had any real identity. She quickly, and seriously, proposes taking him on board the TARDIS to get him away from Dalek-infested Earth. When he eventually asks her to stay and proposes marriage, she refuses, claiming that her grandfather is old now [the 'now' hints that she's known the Doctor for a long time, but it's by no means a certainty].

Leaving the TARDIS is clearly painful, and she can barely bring herself to look David in the eye afterwards. The Doctor, of course, has no apparent doubts that she and David are compatible. [The assumption being that the two of them will age at the same rate, and be able to have children. As Susan is almost unquestionably fifteen or sixteen - see "Marco Polo" (1.4) - there's a clear indication that she's growing up the way a human girl would, as Barbara points out when she starts getting restless in "The Sensorites" (1.7). If she *is* a member of the Doctor's species, and if she *does* have an extended lifespan, then she may not stop ageing like a normal human being until much later in life. "The Five Doctors" isn't remotely helpful on this score.]

The TARDIS The scanner's now functioning, but not necessarily clear. It seems to be righted by the time the Ship leaves Earth. [Perhaps dropping a reinforced concrete joist on it works like thumping an old TV set.] The pressure outside the TARDIS can be read from the console, as well as oxygen and radiation levels. Standing in the console room, the Doctor is capable of addressing Susan outside, as if there are speakers fitted to the police box exterior. He stops her using her key to get into the Ship by double-locking the doors from the inside.

Susan's effects, including all the shoes, remain on the TARDIS when she's ditched on Earth. Her TARDIS key [the back-up created by the Doctor in "Marco Polo"] is dropped in the dirt on twenty-second-century Earth. Ah, closure.

The Non-Humans

• *The Daleks.* Yes, they're back. But they're different this time. The main change to the design of the travel machine is the incorporation of a parabolic dish, mounted on the back and apparently there to pick up broadcast power, while the skirt at the base is broader and higher.

The 'Dalek Earth Force' has a leader, the Black

Is This Really About the Blitz?

...continued from page 105

less extraordinary than Jacques Cousteau exploring the ocean depths or Soviet probes photographing the Dark Side of the Moon.

What *was* unlikely was Ena Sharples on the Dark Side of the Moon. The central visual technique of the twentieth century was collage. Placing something in a context where it doesn't belong is the core of surrealism, psychedelia, post-modernism and *Doctor Who*. If you think of the iconic photos of the last century, they're generally of people or things being put where they don't belong. Think of the key moments in monster movies, and they're the parts where we stop cutting between the monster and the everyday and have them both in the same frame. Tanks in Paris in 1940, a giant monkey on top of the Empire State Building, Cybermen outside St Paul's Cathedral, lobsters as telephone handsets in a Dali sculpture. All are transgressions.

However, the main transgression committed by *Doctor Who* was to place the everyday inside the outlandish, not vice versa. Marco Polo meets Mighty Kublai Khan, well and good. Yartek of the not-really-alien Voord gains most of the Keys of Marinus, fine. But a history teacher in a twinset and sensible shoes doesn't belong in either of these pictures. For the average viewer, Ian and Barbara strongly resembled Philip and Katie, the typical and typically-middle-class couple from the long-running TV campaign advertising Oxo stock-cubes. They have no more right to be on an alien planet or in Napoleonic France than... well... a police box. Once this basic rupture of whichever genre the story seems to fit is granted, audiences can accept any combination of signifiers.

And, historically, this is something everyone had encountered in World War Two. The parents of the ten-year-olds watching would have seen children wearing gas-masks to school, Cockney kids being evacuated to rural Wales, American GIs occupying small villages in Kent and Norfolk, old saucepans being collected to make fighter engines (well, officially that's what they were for), and futuristic blocks replacing missing houses from the streets once it was all over. The aftermath of a bomb-hit, scattering random possessions over public areas, resembles a form of collage in itself. Moreover, these people would all have seen posters about the potential risks to the nation from apparently trivial lapses. Anything, however small and everyday, was potentially part of the war-effort for

either the Allies or the Axis. The real threat wasn't a Nazi disguised as a nun, but the nice chap who asked what you were doing this weekend and was really an IRA member working for Nazi intelligence. This stuck in the national psyche all the way through the Cold War that followed. *Doctor Who*'s real threats weren't those mythical incontinent Yeti, but anonymous phone calls (3.10, "The War Machines"), plastic daffodils (8.1, "Terror of the Autons") and feral cats (26.4, "Survival").

Finally, the main thrust of the monster movies was that we should be privileged to see destruction as an aesthetic treat, like those big Victorian paintings of the end of the world. In early cinema, D. W. Griffiths and Cecil B. De Mille knew exactly what people wanted, but disguised the havoc as morally-uplifting Biblical stories. Later films just went for the thrills. Why faff about with plots, when we really just wanted to see Godzilla and MechaGidorah slug it out? Who needs characterisation when there's a dinosaur eating Coney Island?

For obvious reasons, *Doctor Who* could never really show this happening to London, but instead went for wartime iconography again by evacuating the city and filling it with soldiers. As we said before, part of the national myth is that we can withstand and endure almost anything, usually with grim jokes and saccharine songs. For things to get so bad that London is placed under martial law is more shocking than any number of special effects of flying saucers zapping Washington. If you want a relatively recent example, then just look at the Brit-horror movie *28 Days Later*, which doesn't have the budget for state-of-the-art CGI and instead makes an effort to unnerve the audience with long-shots of empty, desolate locations around the capital. In parts the result looks not unlike "The Dalek Invasion of Earth", and in parts it looks not unlike a '70s UNIT story. Just to make it an even stranger experience, Christopher Eccleston's the villain.

And yet, it has to be said... after the War, and after the collapse of empire, the delight taken by the British in their own destruction goes beyond the kind of apocalypse presented by Hollywood. The generations since the Blitz have had far too great a level of mistrust for their ruling class, and for the ideal of a Great Britain, to see the wrecking of the country's icons as a calamity. When the aliens blow up the White House in *Independence*

continued on page 109...

Dalek, who's identified as such by other Daleks and refers to itself as the Supreme Controller. However, it gets its orders from an unseen [off-world] Supreme Command. [Later Daleks are muddled on this issue. A black Dalek is in charge on Skaro in 2.8, "The Chase", and is referred to as the 'Supreme'. In 9.1, "Day of the Daleks", the Dalek running the show is gold. In 10.4, "Planet of the Daleks", there's a 'Supreme Council' but its members are a peculiar shape *and* gold. Here things are complicated by the fact that the Black Dalek prop hasn't been properly painted in episode one, so it looks as if there are two different commanders.] The Black Dalek is said to be the commandant of the mining operation in Bedfordshire, but it's also seen on the Dalek saucer in London [it commutes], and its subordinates can communicate with the control centre by some form of unheard transmission. Their eye-stalks point at the ceiling when they do this.

Now that the Daleks are motivated by ambition and a need to dominate, one of them recites 'we are the masters of Earth' as if it's about to wet itself with excitement. Another even says 'the final solution… clean up this planet' when it gets the order to kill all the humans, and sounds distinctly satisfied. Yet the Doctor claims the Daleks just want the Earth, and don't care whether humanity lives or dies [certainly not true of later Daleks, who have a jihad against every other kind of life].

The plan, as has already been mentioned, is to turn the whole world into a spaceship. They call this Operation De-Gravitate, and are planning to use a penetration explosive to strike a fissure in the Earth's crust beneath Bedfordshire, releasing the molten core and allowing them to control the 'flow'. This means, apparently, that they can also remove the magnetic and gravitational forces from the core [magnetism and gravity are frequently treated as if they're the same thing in '60s *Doctor Who*]. Once the core is removed, they can replace it with a power-system that'll enable them to pilot Earth anywhere in the universe. [See **Things That Don't Make Sense**, if that isn't too obvious.]

The Daleks have spaceships that can only be described as flying saucers, which need a space-age countdown to lift-off. Saucers have code-names like 'alpha major', and the Daleks are heard to measure distances in miles [definitely not "rels", like in all the '60s comic-strips], while individual Daleks use personal numbers like 'zero-two'. The saucers can blow up trucks from the air, and

rooms within the vehicles have 'disposal chutes', useful for dumping bodies.

The Daleks are using slave-labour on Earth, for use in their 'vast' mining areas. Though much of their workforce is made up of cowed-looking humans, they also have an army of whip-wielding 'robomen' and 'robo-patrols', used as guards and soldiers. These are human beings with clunky hi-tech helmets, who obey Daleks in all things and talk like zombies. Ian's resistance seems to confuse them, and they have to receive orders from the Daleks via the helmets. The Daleks know when a roboman's taken out of action, probably because the radio connection is broken.

Armed robomen carry machine-weapons rather than anything more exotic. On at least one Dalek saucer, there's a complicated intelligence test for humans, and those who pass it are 'robotised' on an operating slab in another chamber. [Since the robomen have no noticeable problem-solving abilities, the logical conclusion is that the test is there to make sure clever people are robo-tised, thus weeding out those who might cause trouble on the work-gangs.] This operation, the 'transfer', makes subjects ready for the helmets and ensures obedience for a limited time. When the process wears off, the robomen go insane and try to kill themselves. In the Daleks' main base at Bedfordshire, there's a unit in the control room that can be used to give all robomen orders by 'oral control', which is eventually used by Barbara to order them to attack the Daleks.

Daleks can move underwater, and seem to like lurking on the bed of the river Thames. Their guns can burn through ropes, and this doesn't make the usual negative flash [multiple settings]. It takes one particular Dalek a while to notice that a headless shop-mannequin isn't human, and it describes the dummy as 'sub-cultural'. They're still saying 'killed' as well as using the word 'exterminate', and are still labelling things in English, while another Dalek speaks of the rebel attack on the saucer being 'unprovoked' [as if they're morally offended by it?]. None of the Daleks show any signs of recognising the TARDIS crew.

[We'll address this in detail later - **What's the Dalek Timeline?** under "The Chase" - but it's notable that these Daleks are more-or-]less the same model seen in the city on Skaro in "The Daleks" (1.2), with added hardware to let them roll around without static electricity from the floor. Therefore, these aren't the normal galaxy-

Is This Really About the Blitz?

...continued from page 107

Day, it's supposed to be exciting because the invaders have proved their superiority over the institutions of Earth / America, but there's no suggestion that the audience is meant to be cheering the death of the President. Yet when the spaceship prangs Big Ben in "Aliens of London" (X1.4), there's no doubt whatsoever that we're supposed to be *pleased* about this, that we're celebrating the destruction of old symbols of power. The people of London even have street-parties afterwards, and the final eradication of 10 Downing Street is depicted as one of the greatest victories in the programme's history.

This isn't *quite* the case in "The Dalek Invasion of Earth", but the tendency begins here. By 1964, Britain was clearly a fallen power - though amazingly, some people were actually shocked when *That Was the Week That Was* came out and said it on television - and the joy we're meant to feel when the first Dalek drags itself out of the Thames isn't *entirely* to do with the fact that Everyone's Favourite Monsters are back. As we'll see as we

make our way through the '60s, there was the sense of something new, young and potent in the country. There's a terrible sense of optimism in the fall of Old London, even if pretend-Nazis are the ones responsible.

So it makes perfect sense that the characteristic landscape of this story is the bomb-site. All those cheapo British crime films we mentioned in the last essay feature at least one in each reel; "World's End" looks suspiciously like an episode of *No Hiding Place*. In 1964, there were still sizeable patches of London left untouched after the Blitz. In 1965, these started to be redeveloped. Part of "Swinging" London's energy and swagger came from the need to rebuild and redevelop. Fashion features in all the glossy magazines used these areas as a backdrop. Watch any "pop" programme or "pop-art" film, from *Ready, Steady, Go!* to *Catch Us If You Can,* and the building-site - the wasteland being made modern - is the setting for teenagers who want to turn the old town into something of their own. And under the next story, we'll talk about the kind of world they were expecting to end up with once the building was done…

conquering Daleks of later stories, but city-based "drones" who've been adapted for conquest. The possibility arises that these drones have been sent by the "real" Daleks just to test the humans' mettle, as their plan makes no sense and they can't possibly think they're going to gain anything by it.

[The other option is that these Daleks are, quite simply, mad. This isn't unfeasible; the drones in "The Daleks" have been isolated for so long that they've clearly started to go a bit strange, while in "The Parting of the Ways" (X1.13) the Daleks are said to have gone insane and found religion. We should bear in mind that the Daleks here are essentially Nazis, and that the Nazis had some thoroughly irrational beliefs. Most germanely, some Nazi thinkers postulated that the Earth was hollow and inhabited by an ancient super-race, or that the Earth was merely the core of a larger hollow planet.]

Once the humans in London have been given their last chance to surrender, Supreme Command gives orders to destroy the city with firebombs. These firebombs are large, heavy, ticking devices, each one put in place by two robomen. Sabotaging the systems at the Dalek base makes some of the Daleks overheat and cease to function [a side-effect of whatever's sending

power to their parabolic dishes], and the bomb that's intended for the Earth's core is eventually used to destroy the base in a volcanic eruption, the assumption being that this ends the invasion. [Which supposes that all the Dalek saucers in the world were assembled there. This is possible, as the Daleks do seem to be gathering to witness the completion of their plans, but there couldn't have been *many* saucers dominating the planet.]

• *The Slyther.* As a security measure, the Daleks have *something* roaming around their mining complex, a pet of the Black Dalek that looks like a shapeless mass with claws and dangly tendrils. It appears to be more plant than animal [killer plants will be used by the Daleks again in future], but makes roaring noises in a very human sort of voice. [It seems more than likely that the Daleks made it in a test-tube. Another popular theory is that it's a Dalek mutant, mutated still further by the Stahlman's Gas released by their drilling (see 7.4, "Inferno"). Being obsessed with racial purity, it makes sense for the Daleks to have shunned it from their society and used it as a guard-dog.] It eventually falls down a mineshaft with a miserable squeal.

History

• *Dating*. Ian picks up a calendar dated 2164, and the warehouse where he finds it doesn't seem to have been in use since the Dalek takeover. Prior to the invasion, Earth was bombarded with plague-carrying meteors, which weakened Earth's political and economic infrastructure [and quarantined it from its colony-worlds, presumably]. The bombardment began 'about ten years ago', according to one local. [This suggests a date of 2174, but in "The Daleks' Master Plan" the Doctor claims the invasion took place in 2157, indicating a date of around 2167. At one point Terry Nation dated the beginning of the invasion to 2142 - making the Blitz analogy more pointed, an allegorical shift of exactly two centuries - while in "Genesis of the Daleks" (12.4) the date is given as the year 2000, which is what the *Radio Times* coverage of this story said. Some accounts claim that the original date for the story was the mid-1970s, and that the draft script dwelt more on the survival efforts of those not killed by the plague... a theme to which Nation would return in the real mid-1970s, in *Survivors*.]

The meteorites were originally believed to be a 'cosmic storm' by scientists, but in fact they were germ-bombs. The populations of Asia, Africa and South America were wiped out. The authorities came up with some kind of drug, but it was too late; the plague had split the world into small communities, and the Dalek saucers arrived six months after the bombardment began. In London after the plague, signs saying things like IT IS FORBIDDEN TO DUMP BODIES IN THE RIVER were put up, and one poster simply displays a picture of an elephant with the word VETOED on it. Other VETOED signs are stuck on blank walls and various objects, but it's said that these are used as signs by the resistance, with the one on the elephant pointing the way to their secret lair. [Many things must have been vetoed during the plague, letting the rebels get hold of a job-lot of sticky labels.] Despite the devastation of so many continents, the Daleks control India.

There's no traffic, shipping or birdsong by the Thames when the TARDIS arrives. Battersea Power Station has lost two chimneys, but the Houses of Parliament are still there, as is Nelson's Column. There's a heliport at Chelsea, which is now being used as the landing facility for Dalek saucers, and a multi-storey Civic Transport Museum full of conveniently serviceable vehicles [kept operational by the resistance]. There are alligators living in the London sewers, as many animals escaped from zoos during the plague. Most died, but reptiles thrived underground. Wild dogs have formed packs in the forests. There's plenty of food in London, yet it's a valuable commodity elsewhere. The whole of Bedfordshire is one big mine, and the Cornish coast is deserted.

The resistance movement is led by the wheelchair-bound scientist Dortmun, who's developed a new hand-held bomb that he believes can destroy Daleks by shattering their casings [implying that conventional explosives can't]. The humans call the substance from which Dalek casings are made 'Dalekenium', and once he thinks the bomb's perfected, Dortmun sacrifices himself in order to test it. The bombs contain an acid which can eat through pieces of Dalek technology. The rebels use radios, so the Daleks use radio transmissions to spread their propaganda. There's also talk of resistance in the 'Africa group'. Not all humans resist the Daleks, as there are black marketeers and quislings who'd rather work with the enemy if it means a decent supply of food.

Most of London is ostensibly destroyed by Dalek firebombs here [but see **Things That Don't Make Sense**... it's never clear how much of the city really *has* been wiped out]. Big Ben obviously survives, as it's heard to chime once the invasion is over. One old woman remembers a visit to London, years ago, in which she saw moving pavements [not in evidence in any of the areas we see, even assuming they're broken] and a very '60s-sounding Astronaut Fair. Earth has moon-stations, and the inhabitants of London find it credible that people there might not know about the Dalek invasion, weirdly.

The Doctor airily states that the TARDIS crew's first meeting with the Daleks was 'a million years' in the future. [The TARDIS "clock" wasn't working in "The Daleks", so this is pure guesswork and utterly wrong. About a hundred years would seem to be closer to the mark.] He also claims this is the middle history of the Daleks [another guess... from later events, this is just the beginning].

The Analysis

Where Does This Come From?   Before we get around to stating the obvious, a word about wheelchairs. In the late nineteenth century, the stock description of an anarchist leader in cheap fiction was of an unshaven, hypnotic demagogue in a wheelchair, usually with glasses. His followers would, for reasons known only to themselves, blow things up. Admittedly, London was home to many emigres and fugitives, some of whom were followers of Bakunin (Russian author of tracts advocating, um, blowing things up). And others, tainted with the same reputation, were arrested and made desperate bids for freedom. So we have the idea of spies and anarchists - the terms being interchangeable prior to World War One - skulking around in big black hats and cloaks, carrying spherical bombs with big fizzy fuses and the word "bomb" written on them. Now look at Dortman's anti-Dalek weapon again.

And look at Dortman himself. German name, and he's active despite a crippling injury. As we'll see when we discuss facial disfigurement (see **Do Mutilation and Entertainment Mix?** under 19.5, "Black Orchid", although frankly we're just proud that we've managed to get away with a line like "as we'll see when we discuss facial disfigurement"), the sign of an unstoppable will is often a body which ought to have died. In cinemas there'd been any number of injured genius figures, from *Dr No* to *Dr Strangelove*, and that was just in 1962. Terry Nation's going to return to this idea in 1975, so for now we'll leave it at that.

Now for the obvious. The two closely-related sources to consider here are (a) films about Paris under Nazi rule, such as *Carve Her Name With Pride* or *Is Paris Burning?*, and (b) the considerable body of film and literature about what Britain would have been like under the Nazis. Not "could have been", but "would have been"; for over eighteen months, the British were prepared for imminent invasion, and the last line of defence was old men and housewives. Despite the tone of the propaganda on the home-front, an awful lot of Britons spent an awfully long time believing that they were on the losing side (the gung-ho-sounding bits in X1.10, "The Doctor Dances", are an attempt to explain this to young people who assume that the War against mad old Hitler was a foregone conclusion).

Most famously, Kevin Brownlow and Andrew Mollo's award-winning 1963 film *It Happened Here* was shot in ersatz documentary style, and made considerable play of its "guerilla" filming of well-known London sights with storm-troopers marching past or arresting members of the resistance. The similarity to the location-work in episode three is striking. But earlier treatments of the same subject include the 1952 best-seller *The Sound of His Horn* by Sarban, the title referring to the co-opting of fox-hunters for the rounding up of dissidents. (It's worth remembering that the Nazi Britain sub-genre actually predates World War Two. See 7.4, "Inferno", for more.)

The Dalek messages are relayed to the resistance by radio, not TV or hologram. The obvious reference is to William Joyce, AKA "Lord Haw-Haw", the Nazi broadcaster who relayed doom-laden messages to the British in BBC-accented English. London two centuries hence is London in 1964 with added squalor and *collaborateurs*. Even the ruins are obvious bomb-sites, not the zapped or pestilential disaster-zones we hear about in the dialogue. Church bells never rang during the War, since the sound was supposed to warn of an invasion, and for many people the return of the bells in 1945 was absolute proof that the conflict was over; here, the end of the Dalek occupation is punctuated by the chimes of Big Ben. Just to muddy the waters, the humans aren't all plucky British types. Some are quislings or black marketeers, some think seriously about surrender, and most have had their spirits broken. Nation - like Dennis Spooner - has an idea that German names are automatically interesting, and the first drafts of all the stories he submitted in the '60s feature loads of them. David was originally called "Sonheim", for a start.

The Daleks have a fiendish plan to turn Earth into a mobile weapons platform, like a big aircraft carrier. Funnily enough, that's what many people in Britain thought the US was doing to the UK. Like many of his generation, Nation was wide-eyed and sentimental about America (see especially "The Chase"), but it would have been impossible to avoid hearing this idea in conversation. George Orwell's description of the UK as "Airstrip One" in *1984* spoke to a large slice of the public which felt that Kennedy's objection to the Soviet Union putting missiles on Cuba was more than a little hypocritical.

And do we really have to mention *The War of the Worlds* again? Given the Daleks' similarity to Wells' Martians, this tale of aliens in familiar British locales is almost a coming-home for them. The Martians used the hybrid Red Weed, and the Daleks use the Slyther, even if the Slyther outfit itself is pure *Quatermass*. Note, most significantly, that the story involves several journeys across a wasted English landscape rather than confining itself to London. Wells used this device to give the reader a sense of a devastated nation, or at least a devastated Surrey, and the various odysseys of the TARDIS crewmembers have a similar tone. Only Ian takes the shortcut and gets a ride in a flying saucer.

(On which subject, we should just say... by choosing flying saucers as the design for Dalek spacecraft, Nation *does* seem to be deliberately suggesting that the flying saucers spotted on Earth in the '40s and '50s were piloted by Daleks on spying missions. At this point in time, saucers are still a mystery to be solved, not just a default piece of SF imagery. And Nation can't resist using aliens to explain mysteries, as we'll see later on when the Daleks turn out to be responsible for what happened on the *Mary Celeste* and the Exxilons turn out to have taught the Peruvians everything they knew. Anyone who's read the Dalek Annuals and Dalek comic-strips published in the '60s will know that before there was any concept of the monsters having a proper "history", the idea of them buzzing Earth in the twentieth century and being responsible for everything from UFOs to the abominable snowman seemed perfectly acceptable. We should mention that in *Dan Dare* - always a key source for Nation's material - the Daleks' direct ancestors, the Treens, are used to explain flying saucer sightings in exactly the same way.)

One frequently-asked question: why Bedfordshire for the site of the Dalek drilling project? The simplest answer we've been able to find is that as regular ITC / ATV writers, Nation and Spooner would have spent a lot of time at Elstree studios, based at Borehamwood, Hertfordshire. Most of their road or train journeys would have involved passing the London Brick Company's extensive clay-pits, vast moonscapes by the A6. Note that the route Jenny and Barbara intend to take, via Stanmore, is actually towards St Albans or Watford; much nearer Elstree (and all are regular locations for ITC productions of the era).

Things That Don't Make Sense One of the things the British are happiest about is the lack of earthquakes and volcanoes happening here since mammals evolved. In 1997, Nirex - the body in charge of disposing of nuclear waste - selected the village of Elstow in Bedfordshire as one of the four most geologically inert and stable places in Britain. Yet this is the place from which the Daleks decide to launch their assault on the planet's core.

Why couldn't they have picked, say, Turkey?

Furthermore... even if we go along with the idea of using the planet as a mobile arsenal, and even if we go along with the idea that they're prepared to wait a few thousand years before they reach their next target (unless they have a warp-drive big enough for a planet, in which case the whole thing leaves "absurd" behind and tiptoes into "bonkers"), then why pick Earth? The suggestion is that they want the magnetic core, implying that Earth is the only world that possesses such a thing. But they try to *remove* the core in order to allow them to control it. Sorry, what? Why didn't they just pick a world without such a core to start with? Mars, for instance, lacks a magnetosphere and would have been a better option. Despite the insanity, however, the Doctor only objects to the Daleks' Earth-shunting plans on the grounds that it'll 'upset the whole constellation'. [As we'll be saying again in later volumes, a "constellation" is just an arrangement of stars seen from a certain planet, a pattern made by the human eye rather than an actual grouping. So maybe what the Doctor means is that if the Earth's moves, then it'll spoil a rather nice view from Pluto.]

London is supposedly destroyed in episode four, by a number of whopping great firebombs, and the people of Bedfordshire know about it in no time at all - except that most of Our Heroes are still in the London area at the time. Even given that David "defuses" the nearest firebomb, there's no colossal bang from anywhere else in the city, while Barbara and Jenny don't seem aware that anything's happened... even though Jenny later talks about the devastation as if she has first-hand knowledge of it. Then there's the enormous coincidence that the bomb intended to take out much of central London is left by the robomen mere yards from one of the handful of people in the world who might be able to deactivate it. That said, David's idea of bomb disposal is to tip acid on it and then hit it with an iron bar, while Ian's is to pull wires out at random. And why don't the Daleks drop their firebombs from the air, rather than going through all the palaver of getting robomen to deliver them by hand?

Nobody among the resistance finds it curious that Susan and Barbara know nothing about the Dalek invasion. Barbara goes on to state that Dortmun sacrificed himself in order for herself and Jenny to stand a chance of survival, and that they'd be dead if he hadn't given up his life. But how she reaches that conclusion, when they weren't really under threat until Dortmun got the Daleks' attention by shouting "oi, Daleks" and chucking faulty bombs, is a mystery. And how can the Doctor be fooled into thinking that the intelligence test in the Dalek saucer, involving a glass box, a magnifying glass and a metal bar, is really an emergency Dalek unlocking mechanism? Does he think they like crosswords, as well?

One minute we're told that whole continents have been wiped out - funnily enough all the ones where dark-skinned people live - but then there's talk of resistance in the 'Africa group'. The Daleks' slaves use wicker baskets for shifting rubble in the mineshaft, which can't be very hard-wearing. The Black Dalek handily broadcasts the entire Dalek plan over the PA system, letting Ian get an earful of it, and if we're going to be pedantic then one of the bulbs on its dome isn't working at the time. Not only is this a glorious moment of what writers call "as you know, Bob…" exposition - since the Daleks already seem to be fully briefed on the plan - but the Supreme even adds a sort of "now all we have to do is drop the explosive capsule" footnote, purely to let everyone know how much trouble Ian's in. Because Ian just happens to be concealed inside the capsule at the time, looking surprised, which is taking the story into the realms of farce. You almost expect to find a vicar and a call-girl hiding in the Black Dalek's wardrobe.

Glossing over the way that Barbara suggests using 'oral control' to get the robomen to 'turn on the Daleks'… throughout the story, the Daleks have no compunction about shooting any random humans who get in their path. Then in episode six, they suddenly become reticent about killing Barbara even when she's trying to turn the robomen against them, and decide to save themselves the bother of a quick extermination by imprisoning her and insisting that she'll be killed in the explosion. It turns out that there are neck-clamps for restraining humans in the Dalek HQ, which is reasonable this time, since they're on a planet where humans might feasibly be a problem. But the clamps are opened by a single switch on a nearby wall, set apart from all other controls and higher than a Dalek could reach without quite a lot of sucker-extension. And it seems to have been made for human fingers, which means it benefits resistance-members who are staging escapes and nobody else.

There are, notably, no robowomen; fair enough, men may be more butch, but it's not as if the drones are required to be good in a fist-fight. It seems that only intelligent people are robotised, giving the impression that there are no women smart enough in this era. Many of the robomen have special robomen outfits, with what look like alien symbols on the front, as if Daleks care what they're wearing or even that they're dressed at all. They're the same sorts of symbols seen in the alien graffiti in Trafalgar Square, which also serves no apparent purpose whatsoever.

This is in stark contrast to human décor. Everything on future-Earth is so functional that the "Emergency Regulations" posters baldly give their message in bold-face without trying to sell it to the public (especially odd in light of the bright cartoons and catchy slogans of World War Two information posters), and a calendar for 2164 has a cover that's completely blank apart from the number "2164". Not to mention the earth-mover with EARTH MOVER printed on the side. Did Britain go Soviet before the invasion? [We might explain away the calendar by claiming that it was printed after the invasion, as the internal evidence half-suggests, but the rest is odd.]

The sight of the robomen chanting 'pull… pull… pull' as they haul on a rope inside Dalek HQ isn't exactly a thing that doesn't make sense, but it is very funny. You may find yourself thinking of them as evil versions of the mice from *Bagpuss*. And behold the Doctor going mental in episode one: 'A dead human body in the river? I should say that's near murder, isn't it?'

Critique   The funny thing is, while there's any amount of things to laugh at, the story tries to carry it off by doing *The Winds of War* in the twenty-second century. All four regulars are given a "local" character with whom to interact, and each has his or her own story. Larry is looking for his brother; David wants to get back to nature; the women in the woods are just trying to get by; Tyler and Jenny have become hardened, and need time to thaw. Oh, that's a point… what happens to Jenny at the end? (See **The Lore** for the reason she missed the big victory.)

This isn't just some futuristic world, it's recognisably our world after something terrible. Freed from the constraints of a six-part *Doctor Who* format, this might have made a good mini-series. Nation *did* eventually re-use the ideas that were discarded in the second draft, but there's scope and sweep here which we won't see again for a long while. For a lot of people, this is enough. At the time, most of the viewing public was enthralled, and comparison with the pantomime film version makes this seem as urgent and thoughtful as *Threads* or *Secret Army*.

But honestly? It's a mess, marred by some terrible performances (naming no names, but he's Scottish… we should point out that if this story had been made forty years later, then David Campbell would almost certainly have been played by David Tennant) and excruciating music, a story that makes less sense with each passing moment, daft plot-twists contrived just for cheap thrills and mistimed direction from a production-team that thinks the viewers will accept anything because the Daleks are back. And yes, the Daleks *are* back, but they look less impressive now than they ever will again and mostly just stand around being adenoidal. The sheer grit and darkness of post-space-Blitz London is enough to hold the attention for a while, and when it tries to do "future documentary" it very nearly works, but then the residents of this harsh and unforgiving society have to respond to the Daleks' genocidal plans by saying things like 'they dare to tamper with the forces of creation?!?'. Miraculously, this story manages to look like an even shoddier version of an American flying saucer B-picture, performed as a school play.

The Facts

Written by Terry Nation. Directed by Richard Martin. Ratings: 11.4 million, 12.4 million, 11.9 million, 11.9 million, 11.4 million, 12.4 million.

Supporting Cast Bernard Kay (Carl Tyler), Peter Fraser (David Campbell), Alan Judd (Dortmun), Ann Davies (Jenny), Michael Goldie (Craddock), Richard McNeff (Baker), Graham Rigby (Larry Madison), Nicholas Smith (Wells), Nick Evans (Slyther Operator), Patrick O'Connell (Ashton); Jean Conroy, Meriel Horson (The Women in the Wood); David Graham, Peter Hawkins (Dalek Voices).

Episode Titles "World's End", "The Daleks" (yes, we know it's confusing, and it's not over yet), "The Day of Reckoning", "The End of Tomorrow", "The Waking Ally" (quite an ironic title, given that the episode is full of humans betraying each other),

"Flashpoint".

Working Titles "The Daleks" (this was in the days before anybody thought of calling Story B "The Daleks", natch), "The Return".

Cliffhangers A Dalek rises from the waters of the Thames; the Doctor is strapped to a slab inside the saucer, and the Daleks commence the operation to robotise him; the Robomen set up a ticking fire-bomb in the same part of London where the Doctor, Susan and David are sheltering; the Slyther bears down on Ian and his sidekick Larry; the Daleks prepare to drop their explosive capsule down the mineshaft, with Ian hiding inside it.

The Lore

• As mentioned above, the Lime Grove nightmare was over and they'd moved to a complex on the western stretch of the Thames, built as Triumph Film Studios in 1935. The facilities for making programmes at Riverside were better, but the food was worse, and Hartnell occasionally got hampers in from Fortnum and Mason's. Which he didn't share, allegedly.

• The star didn't get off to a good start in this new venue. During the third episode's camera rehearsals, he fell awkwardly onto the camera pedestal and injured his spine (the ramp to the Dalek ship collapsed). Although he was temporarily paralysed, the x-rays were favourable, so a week's rest was granted and various clever schemes were devised to cut down on his workload. Edmund Warwick - who'd played the doomed scientist Darrius in "The Keys of Marinus" (1.5) - was asked to double for Hartnell at the start of the next episode, and much of the Doctor's function in episode four was reallocated to David Campbell. But you could have guessed that. Nation wrote episode five of "The Chase" (2.8) partly to thank Warwick, and capitalised on his passing resemblance to Hartnell with the sub-plot about the android duplicate.

• Plans were afoot to write Susan out by any means necessary. One of the minor characters in this story's first draft was a guerrilla called Saida, who was half-Indian (remember, Nation came to this with his half-written Indian Mutiny script "The Red Fort" still in mind, and Barbara mentions the Mutiny in episode six of "The Dalek Invasion of Earth"). Pamela Franklin, who'd been outstanding in the film *The Innocents* (1962), was now fourteen and old enough to work full-time on a television series; negotiations for her to play Saida had been ongoing for a month. The plan was for the Dalek story to end with a disconsolate Doctor finding the stowaway girl on board the Ship as it departed, possibly for post-Armada Spain (a script idea Whitaker shelved in favour of 1.8, "The Reign of Terror"). But Saida became Jenny, then Jenny eventually became a one-story character as her role in the tale was whittled away.

• Dennis Spooner trailed Whitaker during the making of this story, before taking over as story editor. His first task was to supervise Whitaker as they wrote Plan B, "Doctor Who and Tanni", which turned into "The Rescue" (2.3).

• It was obvious from January onwards that, assuming *Doctor Who* wasn't cancelled after the Lime Grove allocation crisis, the Daleks would be back. Whitaker ruefully admitted that this was a result of blackmail from toy manufacturers as much as any real desire to explore the creatures' potential. With one exception - the summer of 1966 - they'd be back every six months until July 1967, by which time they'd finally have serious competition.

• Although "Marco Polo" had been the first story to attract the interest of film companies, the first two Dalek adventures and (apparently) "The Keys of Marinus" were snapped up for big-screen adaptation. A company called Aaru (not Amicus, as is often stated, but many of the personnel were the same) commissioned David Whitaker to adapt Nation's scripts. The brains behind this, Milton Subotsky, had made the inexplicable teen flick *It's Trad, Dad!* and the inadvertently hilarious *Doctor Terror's House of Horrors*. The latter featured Peter Cushing and Roy Castle, who were cast as the Doctor and Ian, sort of. As we've already seen, the characters were amended and the entire set-up of the series reduced to gibberish for *Doctor Who and the Daleks*, which made its cinema debut in 1965.

• For the second of the two big-screen *Doctor Who* adaptations, *Daleks - Invasion Earth 2150 AD*, Barbara and Ian were replaced by a niece called Louise (we don't know if her surname was "Who" as well) and a policeman called Tom Campbell (played by Bernard Cribbins). When the comic stooge is nearly the best thing in a science-fiction film, you know you've got problems, and the absence of the words "Dr Who" in the title tells you what the big selling-point was supposed to be. Yet some of the variants on the characters are

preferable to the TV version. Philip Madoc (see 6.4, "The Krotons"; 6.7, "The War Games"; but above all 13.5, "The Brain of Morbius") turns the black marketeer into a human monster far scarier than the Daleks. Ray Brooks, as the David-surrogate, can't help but be an improvement. It was intended that these films would break the US market for exports of the TV series, but nobody was that bothered about them, and distribution was rather haphazard.

2.3: "The Rescue"

(Serial L, Two Episodes, 2nd - 9th January 1965.)

Which One is This? If you remember spiny-headed wrongdoer Koquillion, then this is his one brief appearance. If you remember loveable almost-Liverpudlian space-girl Vicki, then this is her debut. If you don't remember either of them, then this story probably passed you by, to be honest.

Firsts and Lasts It's the first appearance of Vicki, and therefore the first time the Doctor asks someone if they'd like to come along with him, not that she's got a lot of choice. The notion of the roll-on, roll-off companion begins here. As if to underline the fact that there's a new point-of-view character on the way, this is the first story that doesn't open with the TARDIS crewmembers arguing in the console room as the Ship arrives, but with a scene in which we're introduced to the characters on the planet they're visiting. (Later *Doctor Who* will do this all the time, but here it's used to make Vicki the focus right from the start. Bear in mind that all the early stories involve the where-are-we mystery, in which we're supposed to be figuring out the location at the same time as the travellers. It's no accident that the "prologue" involving other characters only becomes a standard of the series in Season Seven, when the Doctor's stuck on Earth for every adventure and we *know* where he's going to be.)

It's also the first time we discover that the Doctor has made an earlier visit to the planet in question. Apart from Earth, obviously. And, lo! The word "materialised".

Two Things to Notice About "The Rescue"...

1. Look away now if you don't want to know the final score. "The Rescue" has been disparagingly described by other fan-sources as a who-

dunnit with only one suspect, but to people watching it for the very first time, it's not supposed to *seem* like a whodunnit. About halfway through the second episode, it suddenly dawns on you… at which point the story changes genre again, and ghosts turn up to sort everything out. Sort of. A more experienced viewer might be forgiven for thinking the whole thing was arranged simply so that surprise villain Bennett could have a go at doing a scratchy voice a bit like Norman Bates playing his own mother in *Psycho*. In case anyone is fooled by Ray Barrett's performance as Bennett-pretending-to-be-Koquillion, he does the latter in *exactly* the same voice he uses when he's playing Mighty Titan in *Stingray* or the Hood's evil boss in *Thunderbirds*. So it isn't exactly a three-pipe problem.

2. It's at this point that Barbara ceases to be the demure-if-morally-impassioned history teacher in a twin-set and sensible shoes, and becomes the Terminatrix. She zaps Sandy the Sand Beast with no compunction, and she'll be downright bloodthirsty by the time she leaves the series. Ian's more assertive than usual as well; note the sensitive way the theme of mental disturbance is introduced by Ian saying, of the Doctor, 'don't you think he's going a little…' (*does school playground "spazz" gesture*).

The Continuity

The Doctor Here he sleeps through the TARDIS' landing on Dido, something he's never done before. On waking, he seems happy, energetic and eager to potter about on alien planets… until he remembers that Susan isn't around. Even so, he's noticeably softened, showing greater concern for his companions than ever before. Perhaps the most interesting thing is that it's the Doctor, not Barbara, who's Vicki's confidant and who asks her to forgive the others. After asking Vicki to join the Ship, he's obviously delighted to have a Susan-replacement on board.

The Doctor can't read his own handwriting, which he admits is getting worse. He regrets not getting that medical degree.

• *Background.* He half-recognises Dido by smell from a previous visit, and seems to share some understanding with the natives, even though they never speak and are presented as almost ghost-like. [This might indicate a telepathic ability on either or both their parts. See **Where Does This Come From?** for more on this.] Though they kill Bennett and wreck the radio to prevent any further visitors to the planet, they leave the Doctor unconscious by the TARDIS. [We gather from "The Mind of Evil" (8.2) that the costume used by Bennett as Koquillion is associated with one of the Doctor's deepest fears, and yet nothing in this story justifies this. Something horrible may have happened the last time he was on Dido, though he treats the natives as old friends.]

• *Ethics.* In the tussle with Bennett, the Doctor's seen to fight for the first time, briefly using a sword as well as a Didonian construction tool. [He may, or may not, be planning lethal force here. See **Planet Notes** for more.]

The Supporting Cast

• *Ian.* Starting to be openly sardonic about the Doctor's habits. Nonetheless, he's sensitive enough to lead Barbara away when it's obvious that the Doctor has to be the one to have a private word with Vicki. Dealing with a particularly lame death-trap, he wrecks yet another jacket on the blades that come out of the cave wall.

• *Barbara.* Seemingly needs to be shown how to open the TARDIS door from the console room. [Despite having seen Susan do it at least a dozen times, and despite being the one who's always shown the most aptitude for the TARDIS controls. But note that she asks the Doctor how to do it just after he remembers that Susan isn't around, so she must be trying to take his mind off things. Still, if the controls keep moving around - as other stories suggest - then she might just have lost track of the switch.]

In "defending" Vicki from a Sand Beast, Barbara quickly figures out how to use an unfamiliar flare-gun, and she's not a bad shot. Both she and Ian reach the conclusion that it might be a good idea to invite Vicki onto the TARDIS, independently of the Doctor.

• *Vicki.* It's not short for anything. She's obviously in her teens, and one of only two survivors of the crashed spaceship UK 201. When her mother died, Vicki's father decided to start a new life off-world, and took a job on Astra. The ship crash-landed on Dido some time ago [a draft script says a year has elapsed], and while she's been marooned she's managed to plant a vegetable garden, as well as training one of the Sand Beasts to come for food. She calls it Sandy, and thinks of it as a pet, so she's almost hysterical when Barbara

What Kind of Future Did We Expect?

In **Is This Really About the Blitz?** (under the last story), we mentioned the particularly British, particularly Home Counties version of the apocalypse given to us by writers like John Wyndham. For a lot of readers at the time, this was the "realistic" version of the future, as opposed to the rather gosh-wow American model. The idea has therefore arisen, especially in the US, that Britain's view of the future was inevitably downbeat and cynical. You know. What with rationing and bomb-sites and all.

Not a bit of it. The children who grew up in the wake of World War Two - which, as everybody knew, *we* won even if the Americans turned up towards the end and the Russians were the first into Berlin - were sold on the promise of a bright tomorrow. The future was a world where all the things that had been taken away by the War would be restored with interest, and the exciting possibilities of radar and atomic power would make everything better.

A quick recap here. The first half of World War Two, 1939-42, wasn't so good. The Blitz was devastating British cities, Axis forces were encroaching almost unstoppably, and there was no point making any plans. How did the government cheer everyone up? They got someone, namely Sir William Beveridge, to draw up a long-term scheme for what a rebuilt Britain would be like. Not just as good as the 1930s had been (and for most people that was pretty fair, although with mass unemployment, disease and deprivation taken into account, the War was a turn for the better in some of the industrial regions), but Utopia. The Beveridge report was, by a stroke of luck, published at exactly the same time as Montgomery's success at El Alamein; the first Allied victory, and the means by which Italy was recaptured. We had a future!

By the time of the 1945 general election, decent housing, educational opportunities for all, welfare provision, the National Health Service (NHS) and full employment weren't just options. They were our rights. Many non-British commentators still don't understand how Winston Churchill, supposedly the greatest Briton who ever lived, could have lost an election immediately after leading the country to a victory that was celebrated by every man, woman and child in the land. The answer is partly that the war in question had made virtually everybody miserable, rather than being an easy and far-away war like the ones we have these days, but partly that it was fought on the *under-*

standing that change would be the outcome. The returning servicemen voted for Clement Attlee's Labour Party. With the story we'd been telling ourselves about British determination and ingenuity being indomitable, and the prospect of all the technological breakthroughs put to peaceable use, nothing could stop us. We thought.

Utopia was a long time coming. The US government tried to sabotage the process, and did almost as good a job as the weather. 1947 had the hottest, driest summer on record, following the coldest winter and devastating spring floods. The fledgling NHS had its first real test. The demand for immediate repayment of the Lend-Lease allowances made the British economy put all its effort into servicing a debt to America rather than rebuilding. In some areas, rationing got worse before it was removed; Britain never had bread rationing during the War, but did have it afterwards. Still, the idea that we could get through all sorts of privations and setbacks had sustained us for six years, so a couple more weren't going to hurt much.

You're waiting for us to get back to talking about spaceships. Well, all right then. Into all of this comes artist Frank Hampson. US warships had used pulp magazines as ballast, so *Superman* and *Astounding* had been readily available to the kids of the nation, along with less wholesome fare. In order to provide a British alternative, and in the face of paper rationing, the *Eagle* was launched in April 1950 with - for its day - a publicity barrage. With the moral panic about "Yank Mags", this magazine-cum-comic-book was appealing to parents but not so squeaky-clean that nobody would read it, and the real world was always lurking at the edge of the page. Upstanding policeman PC 49 had to handle black marketeers as well as lost puppies. Even so, it was edited by Reverend Marcus Morris, and one of the writers was Rev Chad Varah (who later founded the Samaritans). Their unpaid scientific advisor was a young engineer who'd recently devised a system of global communications. His name was Arthur C. Clarke.

Why did they need a scientific advisor? Well, the signature and front-page comic strip was Frank Hampson's *Dan Dare - Pilot of the Future*. In this, the World Space Command is based at the Ministry of Defence in a rebuilt but recognisable London. The Space Corp (in green, but the uniforms are manifestly RAF) is part of a World Government, run

continued on page 119...

gets the wrong idea and shoots it dead.

Vicki is inquisitive, energetic and outgoing. She's bright, though not bright enough to spot that her fellow survivor and guardian has been masquerading as an alien monster. Despite living in fear since arriving on this planet, she's bouncing around happily when the Doctor and company arrive. Though born in the twenty-fifth century, she comes across as being quite "hip" in a specifically 1960s way. [It surprises nobody when she asks to see the Beatles in 2.8, "The Chase".]

After living with only two certainties in her life - Koquillion, and the prospect of a rescue ship - being presented with other options confuses her, a little. She denies needing any help, and is angry at being pitied. She's remarkably trusting of the travellers, the Doctor included, but her instincts don't let her down. Well, except where Bennett's concerned.

The TARDIS   The occupants can tell whether the Ship's arrived by the vibrations, and the Doctor flips a switch to power down after landing [not necessary in later stories]. It's said that the TARDIS can travel through solid matter while in flight [at this stage the scripts aren't written to suggest that it pops out of another dimension, but that it becomes insubstantial on take off and moves "through" things like a ghost], so the preferred term is "materialise" rather than "land". Ian can use the Doctor's key to let himself into the TARDIS. [In "The Daleks" (1.2), there's all that rigmarole with the 21-hole lock to go through. Either Ian's been taught the secret, or - more likely - the lock was simplified after its repair in 1.7, "The Sensorites".] 'Number four switch' opens the doors from the inside.

A new piece of furniture, a recliner-seat for the Doctor to snooze in, has been added to the console room. There are facilities on board for analysing rocks and working out what planet they're on, at least if the Doctor's been there before. This time, when the Doctor's exploring in a cave, he uses a groovy new torch from the TARDIS rather than his customary pen-sized model. Although much, much bigger, it isn't quite as powerful.

The St John's Ambulance sign on the right-hand door of the TARDIS has finally worn off, it seems. [It'll return for model shots and a couple of later stories. For those who don't already know: the St John's Ambulance Brigade is a voluntary organisa-

tion trained in first aid, and the symbol on the front of a police box used to indicate that a first-aid kit and a direct line to summon an ambulance were fitted. See 3.5, "The Massacre", for an example of how this facility should be used.]

Planet Notes

• *Dido*. Mainly desert, by the look of it, with steep mountains and labyrinthine cave systems. Occasional palm-trees break up the monotony of the landscape [just in case the idea of this being a "desert island in space" hadn't dawned on us]. Apart from the sentient inhabitants, the only life-forms mentioned are the herbivorous creatures that Vicki calls Sand Beasts. The one we see is about three metres long, looks like a shaved warthog and has no hind legs, just two powerful flippers.

But this planet is, or at least was, inhabited by a humanoid culture. The Dido people [the Doctor calls them this, and "Didonians" is never used here] are described by the Doctor as a people to whom violence was totally alien, as there were barely a hundred of them left when he visited the planet some time ago. The only real example of local civilisation visited here is the ruined but elegantly-furnished People's Hall of Judgement. Despite the Doctor's claims, the tunnels built by the natives include at least one trap involving spikes that come out of walls and push people off ledges. [It's *possible* that Bennett might have been responsible for these, but it's hard to see how or why, unless flat-pack death-traps are a standard part of colonisation equipment on human spaceships.] Bennett has found himself a vicious-looking native ceremonial costume, with spines protruding from its face and hands, that makes its wearer look almost completely inhuman. It's this that he wears to disguise himself as Koquillion [a name he's made up himself, not a Didonian one].

The *real* inhabitants of Dido are thought to be extinct. When the humans crash-landed here - see **History** - they were invited to meet with the natives, and only Vicki didn't go, as she had a fever. But all present were massacred by Bennett, or so he thought. The planet's survivors are keen to maintain this belief, and eventually sabotage the Earth spaceship's radio to prevent any further visits from humans. They look pretty much human themselves, wear bland "space" clothing, and don't speak even though they can obviously understand the Doctor. The two who appear to

What Kind of Future Did We Expect?

...continued from page 117

from Whitehall. This is 1996, and rationing is still in place, hence the need to go to Venus to find new supplies of food. The world population has doubled since 1950, with better health-care and education in what we now call the Developing World. We were the ones who spread the benefits of progress, so it's our responsibility to fix the problems. The French and Americans are along for the ride, too, but it's a British show. Sir Hubert Guest, the first man on the Moon, is depicted as an old-school squadron-leader with traditional moustache.

However, the two main protagonists are from the north of England. Spaceman Albert Fitzwilliam Digby, from Wigan, Lancashire, has the comic sidekick duties and a regional accent. His CO, Colonel Daniel McGregor Dare, was born in Manchester in 1967 and has a university education. As you may recall from the notes on "An Unearthly Child", access to education for people from families who'd previously been excluded was associated with the idea that engineering was the key to the future. Like Ian Chesterton, Dan Dare is a role-model for the classless Britain of tomorrow, embodying the virtues which we told ourselves had won the War. This kind of social commentary / futuristic touch extends to the later addition of a brilliant scientist, Professor Peabody. In a comic for ten-year-old boys, any hint of romance is a no-no, but it has to be said that she's not bad-looking. (Later Hampson set about launching a new strip set in *2000 AD*, wherein UN troubleshooter Peter Rock seems not to notice that he has a black woman as his boss. This was stiffed by the management, apparently.)

We should, at this point, admit that the storylines of Colonel Dare's exploits were so exciting that Terry Nation helped himself to great chunks of them and changed the names a bit. Anyone doubting that the blonde-haired Therons and super-rational Treens were the prototypes for the Thals and Daleks should note that the Treen leader, the Mekon, was the only thing missing from the set-up until Davros appeared in 1975. Like the Mekon, Davros wears clothes that he can't possibly have got on over his head and travels about in a machine (the Mekon surfs around in mid-air on a sort of floating dish). Luckily, in those days Anglican vicars didn't tend to sue people. And Hampson later illustrated Nation's "We Are the Daleks" story in the 1973 *Radio Times* Special,

so there were obviously no hard feelings.

Actually, we can go further. The entire format of *Doctor Who*, as it was perceived in the '60s, is closer to the format of the *Eagle* than anyone's really been prepared to acknowledge. Adventure strips in the *Eagle* generally came in three flavours: futuristic, contemporary and historical. The futuristic we've already dealt with. The contemporary stories would often involve mysterious goings-on in murky London streets (q.v. "An Unearthly Child"), in one memorable instance - *Mark Question* - revolving around the mystery of a curiously talented amnesiac teenager who seems to be an exile from some unspecified foreign territory. Even his name makes him sound like a second cousin of Susan Who. The historicals were intended to be educational, although opulent-looking outfits and occasional fight sequences always had to be involved somewhere. What subjects were chosen for these strips? Marco Polo, the Aztecs, a version of ancient Rome in which the heroes all secretly carry crosses... you get the picture. Early *Doctor Who* is on exactly the same territory, even if it's more cynical about this overtly Christian version of history. (The *Eagle* take on the Aztecs is quite unfathomable by modern standards, portraying Cortes as the good guy simply because he *wants* to conquer Mexico.)

The Dan Dare idea of National Unity connected with another futuristic treat for kids of the Attlee era. As part of the "Austerity Binge" movement of celebrating victory on the cheap, the government put its weight behind a centenary update of the 1851 Great Exhibition. The Festival of Britain was a national jamboree of Britishness, with new housing estates, Morris dancing, a funfair and a vast derelict area of the South Bank of the Thames converted into a colourful display of the past, present and future. It owed a lot to the 1939 New York World's Fair, but with the added thrill that after years of reading about radar and jet engines, kids could see them. Parents could explore the possibilities of new curtains that weren't for blackouts but for decoration. Capital-D "Design" was, like "serious" culture, available to all... but few, if any, wanted it just yet. That was okay, though; the fact that it wasn't forced on anyone (as in the Soviet Union or Nazi Germany) or deemed uncommercial and restricted to an elite (as in America or France) was part of what we were celebrating. Eventually, Beethoven in stereo and Bertrand

continued on page 121...

punish Bennett for his crimes are presented almost as phantoms, vanishing once they've done their work.

At the time the Doctor last visited, they'd just perfected a construction tool resembling a Faberge monkey-wrench, which is now being wielded by Koquillion. Its ray can cause rockfalls, and the Doctor attacks Bennett with it at one stage. [To be charitable to him, it may have some form of "stun" setting. We see the Doctor change its setting after it's used to bring down the ceiling of the cave, and the setting *seems* to be changed again during the scuffle with Bennett, at which point it starts destroying the nearby architecture.]

History

• *Dating*. The UK 201 ship left Earth in 2493, and crashed on Dido en route to the planet Astra [so it's most probably 2494 now].

Bennett was imprisoned on the ship for killing a crewmember, but it crashed before the news could be radioed to Earth. It had armaments, including sufficient explosives for Bennett to slaughter the humans and the remaining Dido people after his escape. [It's not clear how he got away. The implication is that it happened during the crash, but he's obviously not averse to complicated high-risk strategies, so he may have escaped while the ship was in flight and engineered the crash himself.] Only Vicki was allowed to live, and Bennett has been happily terrorising her as Koquillion ever since, so that she can tell the rescue mission how the humans were butchered by a nasty alien. He states that he did all this to save his life [implying a death penalty on Earth].

The radio is still working, and reports that a rescue ship is on the way. It's taken a while [a whole year?] to get there, and is still seventy hours from touchdown as the TARDIS arrives. [Less than fifty years later, an Earth ship can cross the galaxy in a matter of hours, at least according to "Frontier in Space" (10.3).] A signal is being sent from the ship to the rescue mission, guiding it to Dido. 'Rocket-ships', as they're still known, make a lot of noise when they land.

The UK 201 is of a standard-looking design [it has features still in use three-hundred years later, judging by 1.7, "The Sensorites"], with a large parabolic antenna that somehow survived the rough landing. It's presumably British, as it has the Union Flag on the tail-fins [more of this national pride in **What Kind of Future Were We**

Expecting?]. Vicki states that 'they didn't have time machines in 1963' [as if they've had time machines at some point *since* then, though stories like "The Talons of Weng-Chiang" (14.6) would seem to dispute this].

The Analysis

Where Does This Come From? We've already made a jocular comparison with Hitchcock's *Psycho*, and this is worth investigating. But Robert Bloch, who wrote the original story, was an occasional collaborator and long-term friend of Ray Bradbury. And Bradbury's work is a more obvious comparison. Specifically, the stories compiled as either *The Silver Locusts* or *The Martian Chronicles* seem to be thematically close to the heart of "The Rescue".

Although wiped out by the crass, callous human settlers, Bradbury's Martians persist, either as comparatively straightforward ghosts or as a more indirect presence. The analogy with the settlement of the American West is obvious, but a more interesting theme is how the Martians are as much an attitude of reverence for the planet as physical beings, and eventually the survivors of the nuclear war there are indistinguishable from their "alien" precursors. In "The Rescue" it's hard to say whether the Didonians who apprehend Bennett are survivors who've been kept alive by a need to avenge their world, ghosts, or hallucinations... at least until they smash the radio. This is almost pure Bradbury, although it also resembles some of Bloch's earlier stories.

American colonial guilt is one thing, but Britain has made an art-form of it. Many commentators have pointed out that the situation on Dido is very similar to that of Tasmania's natives, as the first settlers inadvertently (we tell ourselves) wiped them out with diseases. But more importantly, the equation of planets with islands suggests Polynesia, and the obvious analogy is Easter Island. Less than eighteen months into the programme's run, and the idea of people from Earth / Europe being a disaster for the noble and dignified cultures they encounter is a cliché. "The Aztecs" (1.6) and immediately afterwards "The Sensorites" (1.7) made this clear, even if "Marco Polo" hadn't been explicitly critical. The fact that there was ever seriously an idea to write a story like "The Red Fort", about the Indian Mutiny, indicates that this series was sceptical about the

What Kind of Future Did We Expect?

...continued from page 119

Russell in paperback would catch on, briefly. The late '50s was a boom-time for autodidacts and DIY-ers. Look at how many episodes of *Hancock's Half Hour* begin with Tony Hancock taking up some new self-improvement scheme.

When Jerusalem wasn't built here in less that three months, the voters became disillusioned and a near-senile Churchill got back into power. All traces of the Festival were removed, and Harry S. Truman suddenly discovered that he wasn't in such a hurry to get the money back off us after all. Still, the idea of a British-led future was hard to kill, and the coincidence of the Coronation (on live TV, for those with sets, and everyone else got one pretty soon after that) and the climbing of Mount Everest (by a Sherpa and a Kiwi, but they were *almost* British) rounded off a whole "New Elizabethan" idea. A lot of "firsts" followed, like the hovercraft, jet airliners, nuclear power stations, computers (we'd stared it all off at Bletchley Park - see 26.3, "The Curse of Fenric" - but Manchester University's ACE was nine months or so ahead of the Americans' ENIAC machine) and the discovery of the DNA double-helix. Hooray for us!

After 1956 everything went a bit flat. It wasn't just the Suez Crisis, or Elvis, or de Gaulle. People were content with the present, but not much else seemed to bother them. "Britishness" was in the past tense. All those TV shows for the US market were taking their toll, leading us to conclude that our cultural identity was mostly about castles and men in hosiery. 1964 saw a rallying in popular culture, and in the idea that we had know-how the US didn't, but this was after Harold MacMillan had run the country as a wholly-owned subsidiary of the Kennedy administration. Yet between these two dates, there'd been a lot of changes, and the appetite for more was keener than at any time since 1919. Quite simply, with the Dan Dare generation now old enough to vote, simply being British was almost a guarantee of success; see **How Believable is the British Space Programme?** under "The Ambassadors of Death" (7.3), and notes on the Post Office Tower under "The War Machines" (3.10).

So it was perfectly acceptable for spaceships in the year 2493 to fly the flag, and for plucky Londoners to overthrow the Daleks without any foreign help, certainly without the Yanks telling us how to do it. (See **Whatever Happened to the USA?** under 4.6, "The Moonbase"...)

triumphalist version of history still common in schoolbooks. We'll come back to this later on in the season; see 2.6, "The Crusade", also by Whitaker.

We can't get away from it, though: Norman Bates' impersonation of his dead mother is absolutely the key to this story. The Doctor's role in the *denouement* is as much that of a therapist or confessor as an investigator or policeman. Like the analyst who explains everything for the audience at the end of *Psycho*, he doesn't punish but enables an equilibrium to be reached by not intervening. Justice is the preserve of the spectral Didonians, yet for the Doctor it's a matter of bearing witness to a crime having been committed. In this regard the conclusion of *Psycho* is an appropriate model for *Doctor Who* - odd as it seems, in that the Doctor's tendency to be outside the law applies even when he represents authority.

Things That Don't Make Sense   Those lovely, fluffy, benign Dido people have rigged up a supposedly lethal trap for anyone wandering about in their caves. However, the trap involves a sheer drop of six feet into the waiting jaws of a Sand Beast. The Sand Beasts are herbivores. Anyone visiting the planet with bad intentions would be well-armed enough to take out a creature that Barbara can zap with a flare-gun, and anyone local would already know that Sandy's about as hostile as a labrador. Is this some strange Didonian idea of a practical joke? Or does their wish to cherish life lead them to build death-traps that just bruise people a bit?

The survivors of the UK 201 were invited to go and meet the Dido people *en masse*, and all were slaughtered at the hall. Yes, of course we know that the natives were friendly. The humans didn't, yet still agreed to take every man, woman and child to the meeting. Some would say that recklessness on this level is just gagging for it. Vicki remained behind because she had a fever so serious that she was unconscious for days, but her dad thought it was all right to leave her completely unattended in the guts of a smashed-up spaceship on a potentially hostile world. And the fact that she doesn't fully remember why she was sick suggests she was a child at the time, whereas everything else in the story seems to assume that they've only been there a year or so.

Bennett's escape route from his sealed cabin, when he has to sneak out to play Koquillion, is a secret trapdoor. Fair enough, this explains why Vicki hasn't noticed him creeping past her. However, in episode one Koquillion goes into the cabin and is never seen to leave. He simply vanishes, leaving Bennett alone in the room. If the other way out is meant to be a secret, then how the *hell* do Vicki and Barbara fail to spot what's going on? Has he told Vicki that Koquillion can teleport? On top of that, why does Koquillion tell Vicki about the travellers he's just sealed in the cave, something that's surely likely to make her go and look for herself?

Oh, that "retro" look. Nice to know that twenty-fifth-century spaceships are equipped with Pye reel-to-reel tape recorders, and Post-Office-issue telephones, as well as an azimuth indicator with a wibbly-wobbly line on the screen. And Bennett seems to think that a spaceship seventy hours' flight away would miss Dido if the signal from the planet were to be switched off. Not for the last time, David Whitaker's muddled up space-travel with sailing, and planets (which are big) with islands (which aren't).

The TARDIS arrives and sets off the detector at the start of the story, so that Vicki can get all excited about it. Then it lands all over again, with the Doctor asleep at the wheel. Yes, of course we're seeing the scenes out of order. There's just no good reason for it. [But see **Firsts and Lasts**. It's possible that Vicki's first scene was moved to the start of the show at quite a late stage, to establish her as a "principal".]

A complicated Billy Fluff: 'You must believe what Barbara did. Try and understand, my dear, and why she did it, just for me, eh?'

Critique The irony is that as a 45-minute "character-driven" story about saving an over-enthusiastic teenager who's being abused on a far-off planet, it looks more like an episode of *Star Trek: The Next Generation* than any other *Doctor Who* made prior to the twenty-first century. "Irony" because that's precisely the kind of programme "The Rescue" isn't.

This is an important point. As we're forced to say quite a lot these days, one of the side-effects of the Fall of Dr Who in the 1980s - and the subsequent rise of the idea of "cult TV", as media types

got into the habit of repackaging and demographically-sorting old ideas - was that we had to spend much of the '90s comparing the series to glossy American SF shows about spaceship personnel having Personal Issues with their parents. By now it should be obvious that *Doctor Who* came from a wholly different tradition of drama, but it's worth mentioning in relation to "The Rescue", because this is one of the stories that suffered most when the '90s mind-set came to re-evaluate the old episodes. Since this alleged whodunnit-with-only-one-suspect was a *little* story, and mostly revolved around the problems of a space-orphan, it was judged to be one of those "filler" instalments that US series tend to shove between the important story-arc episode with the CGI effects and the two-part Season Finale (q.v. X.11, "Boom Town", if that isn't too cruel).

This doesn't just do "The Rescue" a disservice, it misses the whole point of what *Doctor Who* was supposed to be. In a series that goes on for forty-six weeks of the year, this isn't downtime; this is part of an ongoing exploration, episodes ten and eleven of the New Series rather than a two-parter between bigger stories. By the standards of its own era, much of it is so peculiar that there's barely any familiar ground to make the audience feel at home. We get the oddest-looking villain since the Daleks, but against that we get a boppin' Scouse girl who acts as if all of this is perfectly normal. We get a crashed spaceship, but it's got a "Made in Britain" tail-fin (far more significant than it might now appear, as the accompanying essay should demonstrate). Occasionally we get a Saturday Morning Serial moment, like the Sand Beast, but it's off-set by a schoolteacher killing it off with a flare-gun *while doing the washing-up* and looking guilty afterwards. Over thirteen-million people watched this, *without* the level of hype later given to "The Web Planet", because they knew it wasn't going to be routine at all.

(Actually, given that this is a 45-minute introduction to a new regular - albeit one in an unusual and, at the time, surprisingly non-contemporary environment - it's tempting to make another comparison with "Rose". It almost goes without saying that "Rose" got less viewers, considering what happened to TV in the intervening four decades, but one thing's worth noting: to get ten-million people watching the series in 2005, the BBC had to go out of its way to demonstrate how "out-there" the programme could be. In 1965, nobody saw this as necessary. They tried to make half-decent television, and assumed the strangeness of it would catch on in its own time.)

On paper, and especially with hindsight, it's easy to pull this story's logic and function apart. In practice, worrying about plot is almost beside the point. This is Maureen O'Brien's TV debut, and crucially, the period when the programme changes its central cast for the first time. They *have* to get this right. Everything else is noises-off. And let's face it, they're great noises. This story shows exactly what a difference a director who understands lighting can make. It shows how caring about sound allows the programme-makers to take their time. It shows how cast-members who are fired-up for what they're doing can overcome any potential for silliness. Compare the cliffhanger to the almost-identical sequence in "The Screaming Jungle" (1.5, "The Keys of Marinus"), or the shot of Sandy looking out of the cave to the Slyther or the Venom Grub.

But at the heart of the story is one girl's journey into a new world. And that of the character she's playing, too. O'Brien is visibly exploring all the things she couldn't do on stage, learning to tell a story just with her face in extreme close-ups. Watch her watching Hartnell when she thinks we can't see her. Watch her walking into the TARDIS. We've not seen that before; the last people to wander in were angry schoolteachers, more afraid than awestruck. We mentioned the Doctor and Susan being like Prospero and Miranda, from Shakespeare's take on a similar story to this, *The Tempest*. Vicki is a better fit for Miranda, the girl who coined the term "Brave New World". It helps that O'Brien actually *looks* like Hartnell's blood-kin.

And suddenly, Hartnell is exactly the kind of Doctor we all sort-of-remember him being. All the pieces are falling into place…

The Facts

Written by David Whitaker. Directed by Christopher Barry. Ratings: 12.0 million, 13.0 million.

Supporting Cast Ray Barrett (Bennett / Koquillion, although the latter was credited to "Sydney Wilson" in episode one), Tom Sheridan (Space Captain); John Stuart, Colin Hughes (Dido natives, uncredited).

Episode Titles "The Powerful Enemy", "Desperate Measures".

Working Titles "Doctor Who Meets Tanni", and variations thereof.

Cliffhangers Ian gets caught up in the complicated not-really-death-trap, which involves metal spikes pushing him towards the edge of a narrow rock ledge while a Sand Beast lurks below.

The lead-in to the next story: the TARDIS materialises on *another* ledge, this time over a steep ravine. And promptly falls off.

The Lore

• All sorts of changes were happening off-screen. Whitaker commissioned "The Romans" (2.4) from Dennis Spooner, who then took over Whitaker's job and in turn commissioned "The Rescue" from him. Christopher Barry was hired for six episodes, replacing Richard Martin on "The Romans", which meant that Raymond Cusick was contracted to do both stories.

• Spooner's first real job as story editor was to prune the scripts for this story from an hour per episode (his estimate) and add some hint of humour. Ian's reference to Koquillion as 'cocky-lickin' was William Russell's ad-lib. (Some have suggested that he's actually saying 'cock-a-leekie', a Scottish soup recipe. But he blatantly isn't.)

• Once confirmation of a second series arrived, the need to retain Susan was removed (yes, we know this is complicated, but we're nearly at the end of it) and the original plan to write her out went as intended. This meant that the scheme to remove Barbara was dropped as well, and all the remaining regulars got pay rises. Whitaker started work on "Doctor Who and Tanni" in late September, pausing only to contact writers about the change in line-up. And to use this as a means to soften the blow that he was finally abandoning Malcolm Hulke's "Lame Dog" idea, after a year of rewrites.

• Err, yes… "Tanni". They went through any number of possible names for the new girl, and "Lukki" was a real possibility for a brief, horrifying moment. "Millie" was mooted (as in the kid who'd belted out "My Boy Lollipop" in 1964). "Valerie" also appears in some scripts, such as the early drafts of "The Romans". The contract O'Brien signed had "Susan" on it.

• After the botched attempt at getting Saida and

Jenny to work, Vicki was a compromise. The idea of an orphan from the future was retained, but the rough upbringing and terrorist past (as someone growing up resisting the Daleks would inevitably be the kind of person to want to overthrow corrupt regimes) was soft-pedalled. Even in the broadcast version, what exactly Bennett intended to do with Vicki is left unresolved, much as "Sue" had been turned into the Doctor's granddaughter to avoid that kind of question.

• As we know, the role went to Maureen O'Brien, but the other strong candidate was Denise Upson. The fact that Lambert's choices were both from Liverpool is hardly coincidental; this was September 1964, just as *A Hard Day's Night* was released. O'Brien had been one of the founders of the Liverpool Everyman Theatre (as stage-manager, but she hoped to teach acting eventually), and was reluctant to come to London or do a regular television series. However, her fiancé lived there and they were soon married.

• Ford popped her head around the door on the first day of rehearsals to wish her successor well, and this eased the slightly tense mood. It appears that Hartnell, who'd been sorry to see Ford go, quickly learned to respect his new co-star. O'Brien's approach was very much like his own, feeling no shame in questioning a plot inconsistency or a character anomaly. It should be remembered that Hartnell was effectively the programme's first fan. He was the one who'd predicted that it'd run for several years, and who - on behalf of the nation's children - ensured continuity between stories, even to the extent of knowing which switch on the console supposedly did what. This earned him a reputation for being "difficult", and having O'Brien to back him up made life even more awkward for new directors. Some reports claim that the writers were pleased by this attention to detail.

• All the publicity material that *didn't* focus on Vicki was about the new monsters, Sandy and Koquillion. The latter was credited as being played by "Sydney Wilson", as in Sydney Newman and Donald Wilson. Ray Barrett had been in the ATV medical soap *Emergency Ward 10* (so had practically everyone else, but this was a long-term role and he was a familiar face), and as we've already seen, he worked as a voice artiste for Gerry Anderson puppet shows. He'd also been in *Z Cars* and *Dixon of Dock Green*.

• The firework that Jacqueline Hill had to set off inside the flare-gun made a bit more of a flash than expected, and she got some slight burns on her face. We can't think of a way of making this sound amusing, so let's move on.

2.4: "The Romans"

(Serial M, Four Episodes, 16th January - 6th February 1965.)

Which One is This?   Nero, gladiators, official court poisoners, galley-slaves…

Firsts and Lasts   This is the first story - and probably the last - to be purposely conceived and made as a farce, at least in part. It's also the first time that anyone of any stature in the business had gone through channels saying "please can I be in *Doctor Who*?" and got a major part. Though it's not the first time that the regular characters are threatened by things which only exist on stock footage (see the wolves in 1.5, "The Keys of Marinus"), it *is* the first time that a cliffhanger involves one of the travellers being menaced by something which has clearly been spliced in from the BBC film archive. In this case, some very uninterested-looking lions.

Ray Cusick, who usually does the alien planets, gets to do a historical set-design for once. Meanwhile, Raymond Jones makes his debut as court composer; his other contribution to the series is the extraordinary score for 3.9, "The Savages".

Four Things to Notice About "The Romans"…

1. The story begins a month after the TARDIS travellers arrive in ancient Rome. For all that time, they've been living as a household in someone else's borrowed villa, where Ian and Barbara decadently lounge around the place and get boozed up on wine. Any remaining doubt that they're a couple has long since left town (although we strongly suspect the Doctor is oblivious to all this).

What we note, though, it that this is easily the longest uninterrupted period between stories. It may even be a longer period than everything since they left Cathay (1.4, "Marco Polo"). This is an amazingly bold thing to do, especially as it follows on from the lurid cliffhanger of the TARDIS falling off a cliff. Notice, also, the great bluff: we go from the toppling TARDIS to a close-up of what looks like an unconscious Ian… except that he's actually just lounging around on the plush furnishings, stuffing his face with grapes. For someone who's been knocked unconscious so often in the last year, this is a real novelty.

2. All the Roman clichés are present, even the fat man with the kettle-drum who makes the galley-slaves row in time. Splitting up the party allows Dennis Spooner to go through every known Roman (or movie-Roman) activity in under ninety minutes, and be home in time for tea. He can do this because by now we know full well that nothing really bad can happen to the regulars. Watch in particular Ian's reaction to seeing those stock-footage lions; it's almost like Jack Benny. A year from now this story's polar opposite will be made (3.5, "The Massacre"), but savour for the moment the way Spooner and Lambert decide that this is the time to see how far *Doctor Who* can go in this direction.

3. Episodes one, two and four are no more overtly comedic than "The Reign of Terror" (1.8) - and here, as there, the regulars have to say things like 'oh, boy, that was a mistake' - but episode three is an experiment in farce. What we'd like to bring to your attention, aside from the fact that director Christopher Barry gets away with it better than he had any right to do, is Derek Francis as Nero. He's the one who asked to be in this programme, and not even Christopher Biggins in *I, Claudius* manages to make the character such an innocent psycho. Quite simply, he's reached the age of 34 (historically) or 45 (in this version) without anyone ever having told him "no". The bizarre thing is, this is pretty much what Suetonius says about the Emperor… in other words, the "farce" bit is the only historically accurate part of this story.

4. The budget for the sets is getting a little stretched by the end of episode three. The arena where the gladiators fight is noticeably smaller than the Colosseum from (say) *Gladiator*. In fact it's rather on the intimate side. The whole point of most Roman stories is their scale (imagine Peter Ustinov standing behind a desk and asking "which one of you two is Spartacus, then?"), but this one manages so much scale in so small a studio that only this one scene is outstandingly below-standard.

The Continuity

The Doctor   Is quite the gourmet, though ants' eggs are a bit much for him. On finding the body of the real Maximus Pettullian, he immediately decides to investigate by impersonating the deceased, and he doesn't hesitate to take an opportunity to meet Nero. No matter how stupid.

• *Background.* He claims to have given Hans Andersen the idea for the story of the Emperor's New Clothes, and to have taught fighting skills to the Mountain Mauler of Montana. [Some have suggested that this would have been around the time that he met Houdini. See **Is He Really a Doctor?** under 13.6, "The Seeds of Doom".] However, lyre-playing doesn't seem to have been high on his "to do" list of potentially handy skills.

• *Ethics.* He sees no shame in sending a would-be assassin to an almost-certain death out of a second-storey window, although he regrets being denied the chance to show off his fighting ability and confesses to being invigorated by the exercise. [Vicki is actually the one who's most responsible for the assassin's fall, but the Doctor scolds her for spoiling his fun. The novelisation amends this, though it was written by someone else.]

He initially tells Vicki that he can't *really* have been responsible for giving Nero the idea of burning Rome, and that if he hadn't been there then Nero could have got the idea somewhere else. But one she's out of his sight, he finds the possibility that it was his fault hysterically funny. [According to David Whitaker's vision of the series, made clear at the end of "The Reign of Terror" (1.8), he was right the first time. But here the Doctor seems to be starting to realise that this isn't necessarily true. The doctrine that "you cannot change history" may be what he was taught at school, but experience in the field may be changing his mind…]

• *Inventory.* Unconcerned by the anachronism, he wears his glasses, the lenses concentrating the sunlight and igniting Nero's scroll. [So they must be for long-sightedness. See 19.1, "Castrovalva" and 19.2, "Four to Doomsday".]

The Supporting Cast

• *Ian.* Really sinks into the whole Roman lifestyle, after a while, although relaxation doesn't come easily to him. Leading a slaves' revolt, being a gladiator and getting thrown to the lions seem more his cup of tea. Here he shows a willingness to copy the Doctor's method: 'He dives in, and usually finds a way.'

• *Barbara.* Estimated market value: 10,000 sesterces. It never occurs to her to doubt that Ian will turn up eventually and help her get out of Roma.

[It has to be said… the scene just before the slave-traders attack the villa is quite fantastically post-coital. If ever there's a moment when Ian and Barbara become "one", then it's now.] Here Barbara's again called on, by Vicki, to do the dressmaking duties. She's given a gold bracelet by Nero [which becomes an issue in the next story].

• *Vicki*. Amazingly, Vicki is bored. [Considering how she's spent the last few years, this is genuinely astonishing, especially as she's in ancient Rome.] She points out that she was promised adventures, and impatience is obviously one of her character-traits. But she and the Doctor are now almost inseparable, even though she still hasn't twigged that he can't control his Ship.

Vicki has heard of the Great Fire of Rome prior to this. She has no hesitation about swapping goblets around in an attempt to poison Nero, apparently just because she thinks it's more 'fair' for the Emperor to die than whoever the chosen victim is supposed to be. On top of that, the first sign that she's enjoying time-travel is when she sees Rome burning. She's a hellraiser, this one.

The TARDIS Has fallen down a steep ravine. It appears to suffer no ill effects, and the Doctor isn't even slightly concerned. [The start of the next story involves something unprecedented - the Ship being captured in mid-flight - so perhaps this confidence is misplaced. Then again, unprecedented things are *always* happening to the TARDIS in this era.] The Ship can take off from any angle, and the shaking it receives on landing is transferred to the interior.

History
• *Dating*. July, 64 AD. The place is Rome, the time is the reign of the Emperor Nero, and the city's about to burn. [The fire is usually dated to the 19th of July.]

Nero is shown to be a fat middle-aged pleasure-seeker who's never had to grow up, and who's free to do anything he likes in his court, although he's flustered when the Empress Poppea finds him trying to chase Barbara and tries to hide it from her. The court obviously sucks up to Nero at every opportunity, and he's so naïve that the Doctor can play an "Emperor's New Clothes" trick on them without being challenged. *Everyone* present falls for the ploy, even head of the household Tavius, who's secretly a Christian and therefore "good".

Another presence at the court is Locusta, Nero's

official poisoner, who gets arrested and dragged off to the arena thanks to Vicki. [Although Locusta allegedly played a part in the deaths of the Emperor Claudius (Nero's predecessor) and his offspring, in reality she was never an official poisoner. Nor did she fall from grace in 64 AD. Amusingly, American criminologists now regard her as the first documented serial killer.] The great Corinthian lyre-player Maximus Pettullian has been invited to play at Nero's court, but Nero rewards those who kill musicians more talented than him, so Pettullian's murdered on the way. His murderers may or may not realise that he's been plotting with Tavius to assassinate the Emperor.

Nero intends to rebuild Rome, but the Senate won't pass his plans. When the Doctor accidentally sets fire to the blueprints, the Emperor suffers a hysterical fit in which he comes up with the brilliant idea of burning the city down. Men with torches are sent out into the streets, to set the blaze near the circus. [You know that thing about Napoleon and Barass meeting in a pub in "The Reign of Terror"? This is worse. Apart from anything else, Nero wasn't in Rome when the city caught fire, but at Antium.]

Fabius Guiscard [an odd name for a Roman] is off on a campaign in Gaul [an odd time to be doing such a thing], so the TARDIS crewmembers are staying in his villa at Acesium, north of Rome. Barbara can mention being British without arousing suspicion [so this must be before Boudicca started causing all that trouble].

The Analysis

Where Does This Come From? Oh yeah, that was another thing about the British in the twentieth century; they liked their history to be good and irreverent, if not downright dirty. The generations before World War One had liked to think of major historical personages as models of moral rectitude, so much so that history books from the earlier part of the century would routinely assume Lady Hamilton to be of no importance in the life of Nelson whatsoever (well, she was clearly a prostitute), but the "vulgar" working-class audience was becoming more and more demanding. And there's nothing the common man likes more than being told that kings, generals and emperors are really just fat blokes who chase after young women. The 1933 British film *The Private Life of Henry the Eighth* set the standard for this sort of thing, and introduced delighted audiences to the spectacle of overweight monarchs shouting bawdily while eating chicken-legs. "The Romans" is squarely in this tradition.

However, in the context of the 1960s, it has a more direct ancestor. Obligingly, Dennis Spooner confessed that he wanted to write "A Funny Thing Happened to Dr Who on the Way to the Forum", so in this light it's worth looking at the farce plot.

There's no need for Ian and Barbara to avoid the Doctor and Vicki, but it's presented as if they can't allow their chums to find out they've been playing truant. A simple sight-recognition in episode three would resolve everyone's problems, yet things are juggled to create as many near-misses as possible. In most farces of this kind, what's being prevented from happening is a calamitous discovery, though this time we're being spared a happy ending in order for the four time-travellers to experience the maximum number of stock situations concerning ancient Rome. Many of these are life-threatening, but treated by the inhabitants of this world as consumer choices or career-moves. Slave traders act like used car salesmen, poisoners act like consultancy firms, and the most feared tyrant in classical history acts like the boss at the office Christmas party. In this regard we're not too far from *The Flintstones* and Spooner's own "Time Meddler" script of six months later (2.9), presenting 1960s domesticity as the norm and everything before it as a trial-run. Barbara's lark's-tongue aperitifs are much like the kind of sophisticated *hors d'oeuvres* that any self-respecting hostess was expected to make. We've already pointed out the Oxo couple's similarity to Ian and Babs (see **Is This Really About the Blitz?** under the previous story).

Of course, in Britain we'd seen all of this before. The Twentieth Century Fox film *Cleopatra* had been followed with remarkable alacrity by the parody *Carry On Cleo*, with a poster so like the original that legal action was taken. All the usual malarkey with drag, slapstick, schoolboy smut and throwaway scholarly jokes was present, although - unlike *A Funny Thing Happened on the Way to the Forum*, which had been a hit on Broadway in 1962 - it wasn't seen as an innovative breaking-down of high and low cultural barriers, but the routine *Carry On* schtick. Only in colour, for a change. Spooner's near-neighbour was Jim Dale, the male lead in *Carry On Cleo*, so the idea of a farcical Roman *Doctor Who* wasn't such a leap for the author who'd already turned the last days

of Robespierre into a panto for "The Reign of Terror".

But why should two such similar projects, three if you count Dick Lester's film version of *Forum* (and Jon Pertwee's in both films, by the way), have seemed like a good idea at this point in time? The simple answer is that Hollywood had been making toga epics in industrial quantities. They were spectacular, colourful and needed a broad canvas [*trans*: they did things you couldn't do on television], they dealt with themes and issues of high drama and moral complexity [*trans*: lots of sex and violence, but it looks like art], and they were authenticated by scholars and classical authorities [*trans*: we don't need to pay this Plutarch guy dollar one]. The Italians got on the bandwagon / chariot, and hired bodybuilder Steve Reeves to make a string of cheaper flicks filmed on location in supposedly authentic settings, without all that tedious pseudo-Shakespearean dialogue.

One other point here... it was only in 1960 that it ceased to be necessary to have a Latin O-Level in order to get into Oxford or Cambridge. Generations of kids had been forced to read in Latin, and most of what was worth reading (for fourteen-year-olds, anyway) involved the murders and military campaigns of the Caesars. 60,000 exam entrants per year had spent half a decade reading the language, and therefore Roman history. It was taken for granted that everyone else at least knew the outlines. The sales of Robert Graves' *I, Claudius*, even before the 1970s TV adaptation, showed that more people were familiar with this period than had ever opened Tacitus. Dennis Spooner effectively left school when he was eleven due to wartime evacuation. The school he left was in a deprived part of Tottenham. If *he* knew this stuff, then we can assume that everyone else did.

Things That Don't Make Sense Tavius has a crucifix. We're supposed to think "aha, Christian!", but in AD 46 anyone belonging to this terrorist cult would have worn the fish symbol, or more likely used a hand-sign involving a thumb and forefinger (the "Be Seeing You" gesture from *The Prisoner*, and don't think Patrick McGoohan didn't know that). At a time when crucifixion was a standard form of execution, wearing a wooden cross around your neck would be like having a medallion of a tiny electric chair. Though this idea may catch on in Texas, given time.

Fair enough, Barbara doesn't want to be anywhere near Nero, but she doesn't even try flirting with him to get him to spare Ian's life. In fact she looks more willing to consider his advances when she's given a gold bracelet than she does when people's lives are in jeopardy. Hussy.

In episode one the centurion kills Maximus Pettullian in order to get a reward from Nero for bumping off superior talent, but by episode four it turns out that he somehow knew about Maximus' plans to assassinate the Emperor. While he's pretending to be Maximus, the Doctor tells the centurion that Vicki travels with him and 'keeps an eye on all the lyres', and Vicki obviously gets the pun; the Doctor really means "liars". So if the TARDIS translates the Doctor's words into local dialect by reading him telepathically (or something), then why doesn't the centurion hear the word as "liars" and get suspicious…? Oh, all right. We're just being picky.

But if we're being *really* picky, then historically a "thumbs-down" sign from the Emperor wasn't a signal that a gladiator should die. Thumbs-up meant that he should die, and if he were to be spared then the thumb would generally be kept inside the Emperor's clenched fist. However, Nero had suspended the combats anyway, because they offended his sensibilities as an aesthete. So it's anybody's guess why he looks so happy to see Ian and Delos getting sweaty.

Critique As you'll recall, "The Rescue" left us with a very '60s sense of all-round satisfaction. Nothing in "The Romans" does anything to dispel this. Not only is it genuinely funny in a way that no other *Doctor Who* story really is, but it entertains the passing viewer in a way that no other programme on television can, and brings new things to the "adventures in history" strand of the series in the process. It works as a farce, it works as a *Doctor Who* historical, but *Doctor Who* and farce shouldn't mix… or so we've been told. While pondering this, many critics have failed to spot something deeply strange.

You know the drill: Ian and Barbara are the audience-identification figures, the Doctor is there to get them into a kind of trouble they couldn't have got into in *Z Cars*, and the ingenue girl is there to ask questions, scream and get captured. Yes? No. Ian is still the action-hero, but the Doctor and Barbara *belong* in this world, and - even when in trouble - help other people. Which leaves Vicki, the girl from the twenty-fifth century, to be our

representative. How did *that* happen? And while you're mulling this over, consider that Nero chases *Barbara* around the palace, not the young bit of stuff. And it's Ian who gets the comic double-takes, and the Doctor who gets the only fight-to-the-death in this story. And after the programme's spent a year and a half treating historical phenomena as sacrosanct, here Vicki suddenly develops the art of being sarcastic to emperors.

Consider, also, the nature of the storytelling. "Story", if we're being technical, is different from "plot" in that the link between one event and its consequences is down to a character making a choice. There's an awful lot of plot in this adventure, with things happening to all four regulars, and for the most part the connections between these subplots are things that might almost have happened but didn't. The entire farce hinges on people being in close proximity but not meeting. Christopher Barry executes this beautifully in the third episode. However, it highlights the curious fact that instead of a story ("this happens, then that happens, therefore this happens") we have a place where plots unfold ("this happens here, that happens there, this happens somewhere else"). Only three real choices are made: the Doctor chooses to impersonate Maximus, Nero decides to burn down Rome, and Tavius elects to save Barbara because she's charitable.

In fact, in small ways it's a breakthrough. There's a cheerful use of plundered stock footage, in a way that says both "we can't afford to do this but we're going to do it anyway" and "this is where a film would show off". Spooner managed without this in "The Reign of Terror", but in this and "The Time Meddler", it's part of what he's doing to history. We know what Hollywood does when telling this kind of story, we know that *Doctor Who* is usually concerned with setting the record straight, so why not be brazen about the budget problems? The model of Rome, with the caption "ROMA", is terribly cinematic but also very like the shot of the Dalek city or the engraving of Revolutionary Paris. To *Doctor Who* they're all of a piece. Instead of apologising for being "merely" television, the programme is celebrating its status. There are a couple of strikingly ropy sets, but this serves as a reminder of how good the rest are, especially the boat and the complicated palace with all the entrances and exits. Most importantly, the exteriors look spacious, as does the villa. And they're in the same episode.

Removing the opening TARDIS scene, and the necessity of a console room, paid off.

So, since the summer break we've had three stories that were satisfyingly different - not just to each other, but to everything else in the world circa 1964 - and one that missed the mark but showed us Daleks in London. *Doctor Who* really has the Midas touch. What can possibly go wrong?

The Facts

Written by Dennis Spooner. Directed by Christopher Barry. Ratings 13.0 million, 11.5 million, 10.0 million, 12.0 million.

Supporting Cast Derek Francis (Nero), Peter Diamond (Delos), Derek Sydney (Sevcheria), Michael Peake (Tavius), Kay Patrick (Poppaea), Nicholas Evans (Didius), Dennis Edwards (Centurian), Edward Kelsey (Slave Buyer), Bart Allison (Maximus Pettulian), Barry Jackson (Ascaris), Dorothy-Rose Gribble (Woman Slave), Gertan Klauber (Galley Master), Brian Proudfoot (Tigilinus), Ann Tirard (Locusta).

Episode Titles "The Slave Traders", "All Roads Lead to Rome", "Conspiracy", "Inferno" (another confusing one, that).

Working Titles "Romans".

Cliffhangers The assassin who murdered the real Maximus Pettullian creeps towards the curtain of the Doctor's chamber; no sooner has Ian asked what he and fellow gladiator Delos are going to be fighting than something starts roaring, and he looks out of the window of their cell to see bored lions outside; Nero gives Ian the thumbs-down in the arena, telling Delos to cut off his head.

The lead-in to the next story: back in the console room, the Doctor tells Ian that the Ship is slowly being 'dragged down'…

The Lore

• Episode three, the one with all the farce elements, was broadcast on the day of Sir Winston Churchill's funeral. Special coins were minted, and the entire country saluted the wartime leader. With the national mood of solemnity and introspection, nobody really wanted to see Nero faffing about. This is, rather unfairly, one of the reasons

that this story is often regarded as a failed experiment.

• Derek Francis, a friend of Alvin Rakoff's (and thus of Jacqueline Hill, Rakoff's wife), asked almost from day one if he could be in *Doctor Who*. Although not physically like the known portraits and coins of Nero, and not quite as Spooner had envisaged him, Francis seems to have been decided upon from an early stage. (Christopher Barry has said in interviews that he thought the part had been written especially for Francis.) Hartnell had worked with Francis before, and was both delighted to be reunited with him and to be given a more overtly comic part.

• The "historical" situation had been getting complicated. Whitaker had mentioned to many writers that stories involving real people were a liability. He'd proposed a story about the Spanish Armada's aftermath, and scheduled himself to write it for the end of Season One or the start of the second year. This may or may not have been the same as the undisclosed historical story he'd semi-agreed that crime / fantasy novelist Margot Bennett could write. Meanwhile, writer / actor Moris Farhi had delivered a story about Alexander the Great, even though he'd only been asked for a sample episode. This featured an explanation for the TARDIS crew's comprehension of foreign languages, the Doctor walking over hot coals (a trick he'd picked up in Polynesia… see 16.6, "The Armageddon Factor") and Ian trying to save Alexander's life by building an iron lung. In a draft proposal for the second year's scripts, Whitaker had listed a Roman-themed tale as the third of three "past" stories, after an Armada adventure and one about the American Civil War. Lambert appears to have been the one who'd suggested that the Roman story should be more comedic than the others.

• Edward Kelsey, who plays the slave-buyer, will be along in other Barry-directed stories (as Resno in 2.3, "The Power of the Daleks" and Eduin in 17.3, "The Creature from the Pit"). We'll mention here that to most people who know the name at all, he's Joe Grundy in *The Archers*, the Radio 4 soap that's been running since 1950 but seems as if it started at least seventy years before that. He and Barry were old friends.

Also in the cast as a favour was Kay Patrick (Poppaea), whom Barry had directed in an adaptation of H. G. Wells' *Ann Veronica*, and to whom he'd promised a bigger part. She'll return as Flower in the Barry-directed 3.09, "The Savages".

• Although he'd been called in to help with the filmed sequences of Thal mountaineering in "The Daleks", this was the first story to which action-man Peter Diamond made a sustained contribution. He was cast as Delos specifically to co-ordinate the gladiator fight (he isn't too bad from an acting point of view, but he does look a bit out of his depth in this company). His previous work included the many, many sword-fights in ITC's *Sir Francis Drake*, and he'll be back later this season - as a foe of Ian, ironically - in "The Space Museum".

Diamond went to work on a wide range of motion pictures, including the *Star Wars* trilogy, *Raiders of the Lost Ark* and *Superman II*. His most famous screen appearance, arguably, is as the Tusken Raider who waves his stick at Luke Skywalker in *A New Hope*. Diamond died in 2004, but some of his commentary appears in the classic *Star Wars* DVD set.

• For accounting purposes, "The Romans" was considered to be episodes three to six of "The Rescue", so the time and money available for the model-work was restricted. Cusick was frustrated by the shots of Rome burning, which amounted to a card silhouette in front of some out-of-focus flames.

2.5: "The Web Planet"

(Serial N, Six Episodes, 13th February - 20th March 1965.)

Which One is This? Ant-people! Butterfly-people! Woodlouse-people! A giant communist bladder that controls everything! All of this and more, in the *only* story from the 1960s which actually makes you believe that you might have been on drugs when you saw it.

Firsts and Lasts This is the debut of all-purpose-monster-man John Scott Martin, the *real* Dalek Supreme, as one of the Zarbi. He's the only actor who's worked with all seven "proper" Doctors in the series, and he's now enjoying a new career playing doddery old men (most noticeably in Russell T. Davies' *Mine All Mine*). Whether it's him playing the Zarbi that runs headlong into the camera, we'll never know. It's also the first of three (or four, if you count the Big Finish audios) appearances by Martin Jarvis, and the last one before he's recognisable by most of the public, not that he's

too recognisable even to his family here.

As every fanboy knows, this is the only story which features no humans or humanoids in the supporting cast, with only the regulars having recognisable faces. There are very good reasons that it never happens again, as we'll see, and we're mercifully promised that the BBC Wales series won't try it either.

Arguably, this is also the beginning of the "universal smartarse" Doctor that becomes so familiar to us in the 1970s; he's never been to Vortis before, but he knows all about its history as if he's a scholar of every known world, and when he describes the Zarbi as being 'completely unknown' to him it's assumed that this makes them in some way extra-exotic and extra-dangerous.

Six Things to Notice About "The Web Planet"...

1. As part of the effort to make the planet Vortis look "alien", the cameras had specially-treated lenses. Director Richard Martin wanted to use prepared optical glass, but this was prohibitively expensive. Instead there's more Vaseline on the lens than even the last series of *Sex and the City* used. (It's been reported that the DVD release of "The Web Planet" was delayed because all the digital restoration removed the Vaseline effect as well. And that's bad because…?)

Yet it still looks horribly studio-bound, and yes, let's mention it one more time: the almost-impressive shot of a Zarbi running towards the viewers results in a collision with the camera and a good look at the studio ceiling. Still, 13.6 million people watched the first episode, after a *Radio Times* cover and a trailer that gave away half the plot. This is the highest-rated black-and-white story, and thus the one they always wheel out to illustrate what a Hartnell story looked like. (If you think that's bad - and it is - then imagine if the McGann TV Movie had gone to a series. According to some accounts, the plan was to remake "popular" episodes with Hollywood effects. The Eighth Doctor, Chang Lee and Grace would have potentially visited Vortis as their second adventure.)

2. This being a Martin-directed story, you can hear studio doors opening and closing even above all the din the Zarbi are making. What you'll hear in this story and not his other efforts is Jacqueline Hill laughing in the opening seconds of episode four. Listen also for the sound of the larvae crea-

ture's rollers on the wooden floor (well, we say "listen", but it's unavoidable). And yet it's the sound that redeems this story, or more specifically the music. Most of it comes from the French outfit Le Structure Sonore, who'll be heard again in "Galaxy Four" (3.1), with a few violin-effects - courtesy of top radiophonics boffin Brian Hodgson - that'll be recycled for "The Wheel in Space" (5.7).

3. It takes three or four viewings to work out exactly what's supposed to be happening in the first two episodes. Anyone with the stamina to manage this will, after the first time around, inevitably get a sinking feeling when the first Zarbi arrives and *that* sound effect starts. (The Zarbi make a noise like car-alarms. Six whole episodes of this is a daunting task.) There's something like a plot later on, but to begin with you may get the distinct feeling that they're making it up as they go along. There's one shot in episode two where it looks for all the world as though the TARDIS has decided it's had enough and is going to the pub.

4. In giving the aliens their own names for things, writer Bill Strutton obviously intended to give the people of Vortis a bit of colour and depth. Extra layers were added in rehearsal, as Martin thought the dialogue was the story's biggest weakness. Yet while we can just about work out that the Animus and what Vrestin calls 'Annie Moose' are one and the same, it's never actually stated that the Optera call it 'Pwodarauk'. The upshot of this is that when the Optera named Nemini dies, heroically sacrificing herself to save the others, her funeral service consists of Hetra jumping up and down on the spot and apparently croaking 'Ugh! Ugh! Twat-rag!'. Vrestin adds to the fun by constantly addressing Ian as 'Hair-on'.

5. With Martin and Spooner attempting to salvage something from the script, there are occasional lapses in judgement but also glimpses of what this story had the potential to be. The fifth episode has some genuinely clever and in-character ideas of how the Menoptra and Optera see the world, mainly given to Prapilius and Nemini. There's a complex metaphor of light, weaving and pattern that's extended to describe the world before the Animus. And then they go and spoil it all by saying something stupid like: 'Zaaaaaaaaaarbi! Ich ich ich ich!'

6. Many commentators have claimed that it's possible to see, in the final episode, the precise moment when William Russell decides to quit the series. However, few can agree on which of the six obvious candidates it is: having water tipped on him from above as he climbs up a cloth drainpipe, his heartfelt 'there's no end to it!', crawling around in a bouncy castle with disco lights, watching Ian Thompson (as Hetra) hopping around saying 'light is good!', being asked if he'll ever return to Vortis, or the tiresome tag scene about the school tie. We suspect it's actually in episode two, where he prompts Hartnell on the subject of Vortis' location with the terribly natural-sounding line: 'What galaxy's that in?'

The Continuity

The Doctor Perhaps it's the thin atmosphere, but he seems to find everything on this planet hilarious. Acid pools, flying pens, even mica elicits whoops and titters. Unlike the "sensitive" Ian Chesterton, he doesn't get the feeling that he's being watched, even when he clearly is.

• *Background.* He states that he hasn't been to Vortis before, but he recognises the planet from its distinctive rock formations and a Menoptra chrysalis. He knows of the planet's past, and is concerned that so many new moons have arrived, but the Zarbi are a mystery to him. He collects specimens of odd creatures, so he's picked up a tarantula-sized spider-like creature from somewhere.

• *Inventory.* The Doctor's ring, aside from its utility in opening the TARDIS doors when all else fails [see both **The TARDIS** and **What Makes the TARDIS Work?** under 1.3, "Edge of Destruction"], is of incomparable value and good for attracting mesmerised Zarbi. He's started carrying chewy pills to counteract oxygen deprivation. [Where were these when they went to Pamir? See 1.4, "Marco Polo".] He carries chocolate in his pockets, and believes that it cures all female woes. [Actually, the pills and the chocolate may be one and the same, as he offers Vicki the latter almost immediately after giving Ian the former.]

The Supporting Cast

• *Ian.* Has seen ants eat through a house, and has a rueful fear of them [this seems to fit the idea that he served in South East Asia, either on National Service or on a placement with a multinational like British Petroleum]. The Doctor now has complete faith in Ian's abilities, telling Vicki that 'he's very good at this sort of thing'. Ian himself is less sure about Vicki, and still calls her 'that kid' [even after a month in a villa in Rome].

Ian loses his gold-plated pen here, and the Doctor destroys his Coal Hill school tie, 'black, with emerald-green stripes on it'. Which he's been using to keep his trousers up.

• *Barbara*. Has taken it upon herself to spring-clean the Doctor's mini-lab [this would seem to indicate that she plans to stick around for a while]. She's certainly been paying attention, as she knows where the first-aid box is, and can operate the Ship's astral map. Once again, her command of military tactics is better than that of the professionals. She loses her gift from Nero - a nice gold bracelet - after it allows the Animus to zombify her.

• *Vicki*. Is openly dismissive of Barbara's era and its grasp of medicine. Vicki gives the pet-name "Zombo" to the conditioned Zarbi [she's still in mourning for Sandy the Sand Beast]. When the Doctor upbraids her for following his instructions and not what he *thought* he said, she doesn't argue, although she's still a novice at this time-travel lark. Curiously, she claims that she's told the Doctor before about not judging by appearances.

The TARDIS The TARDIS 'somehow' materialises for a brief moment of time, and in that moment it's snared by the power of the Animus, which drags it off course and 'down' to Vortis. After this, all responses are negative - whatever that means - and the Ship can't take off. The Doctor states that the power response is satisfactory, but after a few minutes to build the energy up, an attempted dematerialisation is unsuccessful. When the power's off, the doors can't be opened from the console.

Inside the TARDIS, Vicki hears a distressing humming sound which the Doctor describes as 'extra-sonic', the kind of sound that only young people and animals can hear. It's actually the Zarbi outside, and later everyone can hear it. Also, the Animus' magnetic pull can affect objects on board. [It's not usual for outside noise or forces to be able to penetrate the TARDIS. This could be a result of the Ship powering down. Note that in "Marco Polo", the temperature of the vessel affects the interior when systems like the lighting go off-line.] The Animus can tap the power of Vortis via the magnetic pole, and the Doctor believes this is stopping the TARDIS leaving [not necessarily meaning that the Ship is "magnetised", but just that the creature is tapping a large amount of the

world's energy in order to keep it there].

Seen here is the alcove of the console room [which *definitely* wasn't there before] where the Doctor keeps his first-aid kit, his astral map and a small lab. In this lab is a metal generator or junction-box, covered in switches and dials, of the sort one might find in a 1930s power station. Connected to this is a small light-source. When this is switched on and the beam is interrupted by the Doctor's ring, the TARDIS doors open [a hand-crank is used for this purpose in 11.3, "Death to the Daleks"]. Kept near the first aid kit is a white box which contains a 'recording compound', and a red box which contains one of the Doctor's specimens: a preserved spider-like creature.

The astral map is a pedestal-mounted device with what look like starcharts on each of its four sides, and it's connected to the TARDIS by a cable, even when the Doctor wheels it out of the Ship. It mustn't be unplugged, as that would break the 'time and relative dimension link'. It can be used as a transmitter-receiver, picking up transmissions from the Menoptra invasion force in space. When the map is hooked up to one of the Animus' golden necklaces, the map starts smoking, though this does at least stop the necklace working. [The power of the TARDIS is being routed through the map, and pitched against the power of the Animus.]

After the Animus pulls the TARDIS to Vortis, the Doctor states that they've been dragged from their 'astral plane'. [This is the first spoken indication that the TARDIS moves through some peculiar other-space when it travels. With hindsight, we can comfortably assume that he's talking about the space-time vortex. Here the Animus seems to have pulled the TARDIS out of this 'plane' before dragging it to the planet.]

During what seems to be a sonic attack by the Zarbi [but could also be an assault by the Animus itself], the console spins on its pedestal for no explained reason, and Vicki randomly hits some of the switches. The column in the middle of the console activates, the Doctor later claiming that she's 'realigned the fluid link' [1.2, "The Daleks"]. The dematerialisation sound is heard, but the Ship is dragged across the surface of Vortis towards the Animus rather than taking off. [Possibly Vicki puts it in a state of semi-materialisation which makes it easier for the Animus to drag it towards its presence.] The realignment of the link restores the power, as the Doctor realises

How Many Significant Galaxies Are There?

First we have to define "significant". Inhabited by people the Doctor's encountered? Talked about by humans? Bigger than ours?

We know there are rather a lot of galaxies; from Earth, so far we've spotted a billion or so. Ours is one of the larger examples, but by no means the largest. The one nearest to us is twice the size of the Milky Way. Most of the galaxies we've observed are clumped together in local groups, twenty or so galaxies in each. The space between the groups seems to be stretching out (the essay under 20.4, "Terminus", goes into this further), but the galaxies huddle together. Sure enough, well-travelled citizens of the universe in *Doctor Who* tend to talk about galaxies as if they were neighbourhoods. Svartos in "Dragonfire" (24.4) is said to be in the 'Twelve Galaxies', suggesting one such huddle. And as "Dragonfire" is apparently set millions of years in the future, we can speculate that Earth's galaxy isn't part of the group.

A lot of species get a kick out of claiming to be the masters of *n* galaxies. They sometimes get lazy and just identify them by number, so Zephon is Master of the Fifth Galaxy in "The Daleks' Master Plan" (3.4) and the Dalek alliance includes representatives from a total of ten galaxies. Or so they tell us; only eight representatives show up, and if you assume the Daleks are from a different galaxy to the rest then that's still only nine. Maybe somebody present has dual-galaxy citizenship. We might assume that the Fifth Galaxy and the Galaxy Five behind the Ice Warriors' nefarious tricks in "The Monster of Peladon" (11.4) are the same, since both stories include creatures who regularly liase with Earth-based humans. However, there's no real reason to assume that the Fourth Galaxy with which Mavic Chen signs a treaty is the same as the Galaxy Four whence the Drahvins originate (3.1, err, "Galaxy Four").

Of course, a galaxy could be called different things by different people. We know that the Milky Way, or at least *part* of it, is called Mutter's Spiral by the Doctor's folks (14.3, "The Deadly Assassin") and that the technical name used by astronomers locally - Galaxia Kyklos - is how it's registered in the TARDIS logs (19.2, "Four to Doomsday"). "Galaxia Kyklos' simply means "spiral galaxy", and "galaxy" is from the Greek for "milk" anyway. For all we know, the 'Helical Galaxy' where Zeos and Atrios are located (16.6, "The Armageddon Factor") is one of those we've already seen somewhere else, but under another name.

The problem is compounded by our parochial habit of naming galaxies after the direction in which we're looking. So there's a constellation called Andromeda, and if you look that way and squint a bit, then you can see a whole galaxy two-million light-years away which we also call Andromeda (or M31). Out of habit, we assume that the galaxy is where the Wirrn and the Sleepers come from, and where the Phylox System is (12.2, "The Ark in Space"; 23.1, "The Mysterious Planet"; 19.1, "Castrovalva"). On the other hand, the inter-galactic conference of Andromeda mentioned in "The Daleks' Master Plan" would appear to have taken place a lot closer to Earth.

And yet… there seems to be a sort of consensus forming here. The Daleks deal with ten galaxies, despite the paucity of representatives at their conference. In "The Dominators" (6.1), the Dominators themselves claim to be masters of ten galaxies. This massive empire seems a little hard to credit, given that we never see any Dominators anywhere else, but then again we have no idea when the story's set. For all we know, they could have ruled ten galaxies at a point in time millions of years before anyone else came along. For all we know, they could be descended from humans, and their mastery could refer to the human expansionism we see in almost every "future" story. Now, the Daleks have every reason to invite delegates from *all* the known galaxies to *their* shindig, and the Dominators speak of their ten galaxies as if it's a euphemism for the whole of explored space. So is the galactic neighbourhood which includes Earth, Skaro and Dulkis a group of ten?

In reality, no. We know that our local group contains twenty to thirty galaxies, depending on whether you count things like the Magellanic Clouds. But can we conclude that of those twenty-ish, only ten are seen to be "players" in cosmic affairs? If so, then why? We're not getting the big picture here. The delegates speak of themselves as representing the 'outer galaxies', so does that mean a specific band of galaxies on the edge of the group, or is 'outer' just used to indicate galaxies surrounding the all-important ones containing Earth and Skaro? Nor do we have any way of knowing whether the Isop Galaxy, depicted as something of a backwater in "The Web Planet", is represented by any of the Daleks' allies (whose names may or may not indicate the galaxies from which they originate… there's evidence to suggest that they're actually named after their home

continued on page 135…

when the Animus' attempt to destroy the TARDIS is unsuccessful. [Implying that if the power hadn't been on, then the Animus *could* have destroyed the TARDIS. Yet the TARDIS is, under normal circumstances, supposedly indestructible. We have to assume that the Doctor recognises the creature as an awesome power, and that only the Ship's force-fields stop the damage. Normally its very fabric is what seems to make it inviolable.]

Medical supplies on the TARDIS include aspirin, antiseptic and cotton-wool. The Doctor also has a couple of atmospheric density jackets, which are like nylon windcheaters with metal respiratory compensators attached to the front. Ian likens these to oxygen masks. The jackets make it easier for humans to breathe on Vortis, but only last for an hour or so [i.e. about one episode, long enough for the light-coloured jackets to enable Russell and Hartnell to stand in front of a half-silvered mirror for the shots of them looking at the alien tower... see 2.1, "Planet of Giants", for why], and they end up being left on Vortis.

Adding to his range of hats, the Doctor now has a white one. Ian has kept one of the drinking goblets from their Roman excursion as a souvenir.

The Non-Humans

A quick round-up of life on Vortis...

• *Zarbi*. Man-sized ant-creatures, with shiny, tough-looking carapaces, four insectoid "arms" and rather more solid, human-like legs. The upper arms are spindly but flexible, while the lower arms aren't used for much, and the Zarbi's mandibles are more useful than the forelimbs when picking things up. With no speech or motives of their own, the Zarbi were enslaved by the Animus and turned into its footsoldiers. Despite this "no speech" claim, they can communicate with one another at a rudimentary level by means of a noise which the other races can't translate. Despite the Animus' apparent mental hold over them, the Zarbi are terrified of alien spiders.

• *Larvae Guns*. Living creatures that look something like ticks, about two feet tall and with bodies that move along on a bed of tendrils, they're said to be the larval form of the Zarbi. Imagine a nailbrush with eyes and a snout, basically. They're used as mobile weapons, as the snout can fire an explosive charge, accompanied by a sound like a small generator firing up. [The novelisation calls them 'Venom Grubs', a more popular designation these days.]

• *Menoptra*. [This is the spelling given on the end credits, although Strutton's novelisation introduced the more commonly-used "Menoptera".] Six-foot-tall bipedal butterflies. They're black, with pale "fur" in bands across their legs, arms and chests, and starkly monochrome face-markings. Their wings are gossamer-like, and almost as long as their bodies when folded. They speak in a halting, oddly-accented manner, and move briskly but in a sinuous, unpredictable sort of way. They don't seem to fly unless they have to. Some of their bizarre gestures appear to have meaning, such as when two males confront one another and rapidly splay their fingers at chest-height while hissing, to establish status. They're clearly supposed to be the civilised ones on this planet. Human beings don't surprise them, and they still believe in gods.

A chrysalis is somehow involved in the Menoptra life-cycle, and there are apparently two sexes; the female Vrestin co-ordinates the scout party that's come back to Vortis from the moon of Pictos, where the Menoptra have been living in uncomfortable exile. [The novelisation makes her male, and turns "him" into the leader of the whole Menoptra race.] Now an invasion force is planning to take back the planet, wielding egg-shaped electron guns that prove useless against the Zarbi. 'Ships' are said to be massing in space, but never seen [giving the unfortunate impression that the Menoptra can fly between planets, something which isn't implied by the dialogue].

The wise ones of the Menoptra have developed a weapon called an 'isop-tope' - a 'living cell destructor' designed to make the cells of the Carcinome grow inwards and thus destroy the Animus. It's also egg-shaped. [Species tend to craft tools that mimic their own biology, so if the Menoptra lay eggs then this makes a certain sense.] They believe this is their last chance to attack the Animus, as their kind are getting weaker and weaker on Pictos.

• *Optera*. The underground cousins of the Menoptra have allowed their limbs and sight to atrophy over the generations, making them appear more woodlouse-like and less overtly humanoid. They have no wings with which to fly, instead hopping along on stiff-looking legs while waving their six arms in front of them. [So they're Menoptra without the "men", see? Clever. Compare with Alpha Centauri in 9.2, "The Curse of Peladon".] They worship the Menoptra as gods,

How Many Significant Galaxies Are There?

...continued from page 133

planets, a la "The Monster of Peladon"). Or even whether it's part of the same group.

Which raises the question of whether the Doctor's homeworld is in this group. "Terror of the Autons" (8.1) hints that it's in the same galaxy as Earth, though the evidence isn't conclusive. It seems strange, also, that none of the delegates are apparently aware of the Doctor's people; "The Two Doctors" (22.4) informs us that the Time Lords aren't shy about revealing themselves to other powers. The Daleks seem to believe the Doctor comes from a galaxy not represented at their conference, though this may just be because they've singularly failed to locate the world of his birth. And we note that the War Chief (6.7, "The War Games") and Zephon wear identical medallions, each one using it in conversation to denote his origin. Suggesting that the Doctor's world is in the Fifth Galaxy? Or is it just an almighty coincidence? All very curious.

The possibility presents itself that virtually *all* the Doctor's adventures take place in our local group of galaxies. Certainly a disproportionate number of them do, even ignoring the Ship's habit of returning to Earth. This would make a sort of sense, if the nature of time or the conditions needed for the evolution of life were localised phenomena. Svartos, the only destination which seems to be well outside the group, is so far in the future that human beings could feasibly have got to the Twelve Galaxies from their own group and started to colonise a part of space where life isn't indigenous. If we usually only visit the twenty-odd local galaxies, or even just the ten important ones, then it makes the catastrophic events of "Logopolis" (18.7) appear almost palatable. You may recall that a third of the universe is seemingly destroyed by entropy by the end of the story, yet only two known planets - Traken and Logopolis itself - are shown to be affected. It may be that most of the "lost" bits of the universe are barren, unoccupied galaxies.

But why should our group be so different to the others? One possibility is that there's something wrong with the laws of physics. For more in this vein, see **What Do the Guardians Do?** under "The Ribos Operation" (16.1) and **Why Are Elements So Weird in Space?** under "Vengeance on Varos" (22.2).

yet only know the creatures from the primitive pictures on their cave walls, which means they don't immediately recognise a real Menoptra when they see one. Their lifestyle isn't without its dangers, as rock-falls, noxious gas, Zarbi attacks from above and the ever-present threat of acid streams take their toll. When acid starts to flood into their tunnels, one of their number sacrifices herself by shoving her head into the hole to stop it, and her body is simply left there [so their skulls must be acid-proof, at least].

The Optera see the world above as being a blinding, hostile wilderness, and threaten to kill all intruders, at first. They bind people's hands by forcing prisoners to dip their arms into quick-setting sticky goo, and carry sharp, crystalline-looking weapons. [It's implied that the Optera were *exactly* like the Menoptera, before they retreated from the Animus and went underground, hence Vrestin's claim that they're 'descendants of my race'. But if this is true, then things "evolve" very, very quickly around here.] Once they return to the surface, their eyes adapt remarkably quickly, and Vrestin believes that their children may fly again once the Animus is gone. Their culture and language has a curious obsession with mouths.

• *The Animus.* A malevolent and invasive intelligence, which isn't heard to refer to itself by name but is known as the Animus to the Menoptra, and Pwodarauk to the Optera. It's manifested itself within the Carcinome [which means "cancer", if you didn't already know that] - an enormous, self-healing, organically-grown palace at the planet's pole. To feed its growth, Menoptra work in slavery at the Crater of Needles, hauling vegetation into streams of formic acid that lead to the Carcinome. The Animus itself waits in the centre of its 'web', and appears as something like a twenty-foot brightly-glowing spider, with a bloated central mass and plenty of leg-like extrusions. [Early issues of *Doctor Who Weekly* described it as a "bladder". Things like that tend to stick.]

The Animus has also covered the areas near the Carcinome in rope-like webbing, strong enough to snare a traveller, which dissolves when it's no longer needed [the Zarbi may be responsible for this, but it's never explained]. It obviously has some mental hold over all of the Zarbi. The being is capable of removing its power from specific sections of its domain, causing the Zarbi there to go limp, and it doesn't seem aware of what's happening in those areas even if they're within its palace [so it's using the Zarbi as its eyes and ears, assuming Zarbi have ears]. Set into the ceiling of one chamber in the Carcinome is a transparent cylindrical column, into which the Doctor can put his head to talk to the Animus directly, and it speaks in a husky female voice. [The suggestion may be of telepathic contact, but the Doctor keeps moving his lips, so it might be more like radio.] Tendrils extend from the palace's walls, and these have the power to fire destructive sparks, evidently capable of destroying the TARDIS. They can also spurt webbing over prisoners to keep them still.

The aim of the Animus simply seems to be to grow, encircling the world with the Carcinome while drawing power from the magnetic pole of Vortis. Magnetism, of some kind, is evidently important to it. Its interference with the planet has attracted whole now moons to Vortis, and it even drags the TARDIS to the surface. At one stage it somehow opens the TARDIS doors. It also has the ability to mesmerise people, apparently through contact with gold, as Barbara's gold bracelet causes her to start heading for the Carcinome like a sleepwalker. Gold necklace-like objects can be put around the necks of humans, Menoptra or Zarbi, and these 'morphotise' their victims, again inducing a trance-state. Occasionally, and for no given reason, golden objects will lurch in the direction of the Carcinome as if attracted by it. When the Doctor sabotages a necklace, he speaks of the 'force-field' being reversed, puzzlingly.

There's no clue as to where the Animus comes from. It's said to have grown and spread its influence without being noticed by the Menoptra, so it's not even clear whether it's native to this planet. [The implication is that it's not, as it upsets the local ecology. There's also a subtext that it's a disembodied intelligence, and that the Carcinome is merely its physical embodiment here; the spider-like apparition is described as 'the centre', rather than as a being in its own right. We might suggest a glance at "The Abominable Snowmen" (5.2) and its sequel "The Web of Fear" (5.5). "Spearhead from Space" (7.1), which presents the Nestene Consciousness as being bodiless in its natural state, has something similar in mind but with plastic instead of organic matter. The New Adventures go a step further by claiming the Animus and the creatures in those stories stem from the Great Old Ones, a group encompassing many of the higher powers seen in *Doctor Who*.]

The Animus doesn't seem to have the power to extend its influence into space, and it asks the Doctor for weapons to help it defeat an off-world invasion, as the Menoptra are massing beyond the range of 'our locators' [is it using the "royal we", or is there more than one of it?].

The Animus wants the Doctor's intelligence, and speaks of absorbing culture as well as territory and riches. After wrapping its tentacles around the travellers, it intends to reach beyond the Isop galaxy, take over Earth and get hold of humanity's mastery of space. [It seems to get this idea when sucking knowledge out of Vicki, so it shares her belief that humans are the natural masters of the universe. We can assume it has little knowledge of cosmic affairs.] The creature is destroyed by the Menoptra's isop-tope, which has to be aimed at the creature's 'dark side' [the part that's not glowing?]. This causes the spider-bladder to shrivel and die, and the Zarbi to become docile 'cattle' again. [Again, it's possible that the Animus survives as a discorporate intelligence, and that only the Carcinome really dies.]

Planet Notes

• *Vortis.* Located in the Isop Galaxy. It was once covered by a flower-forest, where the Zarbi and Menoptra both played their parts in the life-cycle of the vegetation, although the current Menoptra clearly believe themselves to have been the keepers of civilisation. Vortis had no moon, but there was access to water on the surface, even if it's sunk below the ground since then [there don't seem to have been any oceans]. Within the forest were secreted Temples of Light, where the Menoptra dead would be put to rest; Menoptra song-spinners have spoken of these places of beauty, yet they're thought of as legendary until Barbara stumbles into one. Old buildings on the surface, including a huge pyramid-like structure, hint at an impressive culture here in the past. In those days the Menoptra had no work to do or plans to make, or any knowledge of war. The light was their god. [The novel *Twilight of the Gods* serves as a sequel to this story and elaborates on the Menoptra's 'gods of light'.]

The Animus changed all that, and the Zarbi became 'militant' at the same time the Carcinome appeared. Now the planet is almost completely barren and covered in craters, with thin air and pools of hazardous formic acid everywhere. The Animus brought new moons into the sky, and there's also a strange, aurora-like phenomenon visible from the Delta of Lights. The weaponless Menoptra retreated to Pictos, one of the moons and apparently the biggest; the Doctor refers to it as a 'planet'. Another moon seems to be called "Karen".

The Menoptra scout party arrives on Vortis at the Crater of Needles, the Animus' labour camp, though the Crater is said to be beyond the Animus' 'great web' and two hours from the Carcinome on foot. The plain connecting the Crater with the base of the Animus is called the Sayo Plateau, and it's here that the Menoptra invaders plan to land. It's not clear how long ago the Animus took over, but the Doctor believes that the Carcinome would have taken at least a century to grow, while the Menoptra speak of waiting 'generations' to overthrow it.

The polar region of Vortis is temperate, and the planet's sky is dark at all times, revealing stars and the newly-acquired moons. There doesn't seem to be any day or night [or if there is, then there's a very slow rotation period, as the TARDIS is apparently there for three or four terrestrial days]. The air is thin, but there's no wind, and nor is the dust from the surface ever blown away. As soon as the Animus dies, water starts flowing on the surface, so the vegetation can flourish again. The Menoptra plan to weave songs of the Earth-people when the orbiting Pictos touches the Spire of Kings, as it does when the Carcinome is destroyed.

History

• *Dating.* Not a clue.

In Vicki's time, medicine is a lot more advanced and nobody takes 'medieval' treatments like aspirin. Twenty-fifth century children have to take a certificate of education in medicine, physics and chemistry when they're ten. They don't have classrooms, but study for almost an hour a week with the help of teaching machines. Vicki considers this tortuous.

The Analysis

Where Does This Come From? Well, Dennis Spooner thought it was a parable about communists. This wouldn't be unusual. The idea of insects as representatives of attitudes or political affiliations dates back at least as far as the Bible ("go sluggard, look to the ant, consider her ways"), and of course, Aesop had a little homily about the grasshopper (indolent and pleasure-seeking) and the ant (industrious and self-denying). It didn't end well for the grasshopper.

Playwright Karel Capek penned *The Insect Play* a little while before thinking up robots; William Mandeville wrote about a beehive being an ideal society, although in those days nobody knew bees were matriarchal; and even Aristophanes had a go in the fifth century BC, with *The Wasps*. Spooner's reading puts "The Web Planet" firmly in an honourable tradition. Nor was it unusual, in the more lowbrow forms of mid-twentieth-century SF, to represent communists with drone-like, clone-like or otherwise near-identical aliens. (Later on the Cybermen will come perilously close to this, but until now the nearest thing we've seen in the series has been the good-natured but deluded Sensorites.) And extended fables about the Soviet Union seemed positively normal after Orwell's *Animal Farm*, especially the animated movie version of the previous decade[9].

If this is the case, then the masses - the workers - are mindless 'cattle' without an outside influence manipulating them to its own ends. The belief that the underclass was naturally helpless, and only a threat if stirred up by an alien force like the Kremlin, was common in the first half of the Cold War. During the late '60s, the FBI was convinced that American civil rights demonstrators were being controlled by the Soviets, on the grounds that African-Americans couldn't possibly be smart enough to develop an organised protest movement on their own. The influence here is a carcinoma, a social cancer, and the Crater of Needles is a Soviet-style forced labour camp. Now, *there's* a dubious moral for you; the story ends with the "natural order" being restored, which means the militant Zarbi return to dumb slavery, because that's their "place". (A side-note: at this point, as we've already seen, China is as much a lurking menace as the USSR. And China had already invaded Tibet. The next time a whispering, seductive, Animus-like presence arrives on Earth - 5.2, "The Abominable Snowmen" - Tibet is the target.)

The Zarbi are undoubtedly a rebellious working-class, with the Menoptra describing a world where they could avoid all work and bask in the sun before the masses rose. So, educating anyone who isn't born into privilege is bound to cause trouble… is *that* what Strutton is trying to say? It would be odd for an Australian to speak up in favour of a class system, and not just the British class system. For an Australian television writer to criticise outsiders for using electromagnetic pulses to give ideas to the plebs is downright hypocritical.

The one thing that's never dwelt upon in these sorts of discussions is that Bill Strutton was a prisoner of war. Factor this in and it makes more sense. To the Australians, the Oriental was always the supreme enemy, not the Hun. The stereotype of the Japanese as a race of expendable workerants with no self-will and no individuality was common in War-time.

On top of this, we ought to consider that this planet has been thought out as a balanced ecology gone wrong. Strutton's roots in Southern Australia might be important here; in the '50s, the introduction of rabbits and camels not only distorted the fragile economy but the social order in small towns. The novelisation features statues that turn out to be dead bodies surrounded by limescale, straight out of Rider-Haggard's *King Soloman's Mines,* where they're used to suggest a world pulled out of shape by greed. Here we ponder the last story to feature giant insects (2.1, "Planet of Giants"), and the most notable later example (10.5, "The Green Death"), both of them ecological parables. The Animus' lair is described as a diseased, disgusting growth, as if Vortis is a living body that's become infected and therefore polluted. The Doctor's comment that the course of evolution on this world has taken the insect route is a rebuke to hubristic notions that humanity is inevitably the superior species. Where would we have heard that before?

Well, if you were watching British television in the early 1960s then you would've heard no end of it. We mentioned under "Planet of Giants" that there were plenty of wildlife documentaries. For obvious reasons of picture-quality, these were mediated by authoritative presenters. This wasn't confined to wildlife programming, and big events like the first live transatlantic TV feed also needed commentators to tell us what we were seeing. Even twenty-five-year-old newsreel footage required a host to make sense of things for the viewers. So we note that most of what happens in "The Web Planet" is purely visual, but comes after lengthy descriptions of what it used to be like on Vortis or what's happening off-world. Some things, most notably the Menoptra spaceships, are seen and described by the characters but never

appear on-camera. What we see is only comprehensible, if at all, with reference to what we "overhear" Ian, Barbara or the Doctor being told by locals. However freaky the pictures, the presentation of worlds in *Doctor Who* is squarely in the non-fiction traditions of BBC television.

One last insect connection. Alert viewers may notice certain visual similarities (the lunar landscape, the chitinous locals, the creatures "engineered" as living weapons…) to the film version of H. G. Wells' *First Men in the Moon*, co-written by Nigel Kneale and released just a couple of years earlier. The influence *could* have been a direct one, but then again, both stories use imagery that was bound to be popular in visual SF at the time. A moon-like setting in *Doctor Who* was inevitable at some stage, with both the US and the USSR trying to get there for real. Although it's worth noting that Wells' story, like Strutton's script and much of the '60s programme, has difficulty understanding the difference between "gravity" and "magnetism".

Things That Don't Make Sense Let's start with the one that even five-year olds can spot. The air is really thin, the Animus has increased the gravity, so how do these huge butterflies get off the ground? Actually… *why* is the air so thin? If the ability to attract moons somehow doesn't attract air as well, then how does it work? And if the air is only thin lately, and used to be thicker (as would be the case with all that vegetation around), then wouldn't the Zarbi have been affected by breathing problems too? [Maybe they are. Ants are super-strong for their size, yet the Zarbi are chronically weak here.]

Why the Menoptra evacuated Vortis is another mystery. A planet is a fairly large place, the big bladder can't leave the North Pole, the Zarbi don't make great soldiers and the Menoptra can fly. How disorganised a resistance movement do you need to have, to allow the Animus to win under these circumstances? The invasion force decides to land on the planet right next to the Crater of Needles, the Animus' prison-camp, so they're not kidding when they say they've got no military experience.

The Menoptra have presumably never seen a human being before, certainly not in the current generation. They might reasonably suppose that these weird-looking, wingless creatures are agents of the Animus, aberrations like the Carcinome. They don't. Instead, one of them tells Barbara absolutely everything about the Menoptra invasion plan at the Crater of Needles, as if she can automatically be trusted with the information and won't (for example) use it to bargain with her captors. On the other hand, Menoptra keep asking each *other* for the invasion codeword - 'electron' - as if having wings and furry white stripes isn't a good enough sign of which side they're on. Since the Animus has no Menoptra agents, and can't actually control the minds of anyone but the dumb Zarbi (putting people into a zombie-state is the best it can manage), this seems overly cautious to say the least.

By contrast, the Animus - which supposedly has a much better grasp of what's going on around here - thinks the Doctor is a Menoptra. Has it *seen* him? True, he *does* look more like a Menoptra than anything else on Vortis, suggesting that the Animus just doesn't understand the concept of things from other planets. Except that it has the power to pull passing TARDISes out of the astral plane.

The Menoptra consider the moon / planet of Pictos to be a deeply miserable and unnatural place in which to live, suggesting that it hasn't been too long since the Animus ruined their world. Yet the Doctor believes it took a century or more for the Carcinome to grow, and if it had been around for more than a few hundred years then it would have covered the planet by now. Yet the Optera have, in that time, been able to evolve an extra pair of limbs and facial tentacles. This should take millions of years, and even then, you'd expect *some* trace of their wings to be visible. [Unless the Optra ceremonially cut off the wings at birth. See also 18.3, "Full Circle".] Vortis is in the Isop Galaxy, and the Menoptra's anti-Animus bomb - one of the few significant artefacts we see on this planet - is called an 'isop-tope', so is *everything* on Vortis named after the galaxy it's in? Still, we have chocolate bars called "Milky Way", so maybe we shouldn't be too critical.

Billy Fluffs: 'We've been dragged off our course. The question is, is it some natural phenomena, or… is it intelligent or deliberate, or… for a purpose? Hmm?' (Even "phenomena" is wrong…) Then there's 'if I can only trick her into neutralising the section of this area' and 'we have been on a slight exploitation'. This last one is particularly ironic, given that Strutton wrote this story with an eye to Zarbi cash-in merchandising.

Critique We've had fun pointing out the inade-

quacies and ineptitude of the script and the execution, but that makes it all sound more entertaining than it is. The sad truth is that this is very dull for long patches, punctuated by something disastrous every five minutes or so.

And this is really, really unfair, because everyone's giving it their all. The problem is that within the limits of the budget and Riverside's facilities, they thought they could get away with the impossible, or at least the staggeringly unlikely. This points up several interesting features about the times when they got it right. First is that whenever some outrageously daring technical feat had been achieved with fourpence and a cardboard box, it had been because the rest of the production had been sound. They could conquer Earth with six Daleks because they had a lot of extras and location filming. They could plausibly shrink the TARDIS crew to half an inch because the sets were ingenious. If everyone tries to "get away with it" at once, the result is horrible.

The Menoptra voices and movements aren't intrinsically any sillier than those of the original Cybermen (4.2, "The Tenth Planet"), but in that story all the ethnic-stereotype actors behave as if it's really happening in their workplace, amidst real-looking military ordinance. On a planet where Roslyn de Winter's "choreography" is the benchmark for what's ordinary, and the audience identification characters are Hartnell on autopilot, Russell bored out of his mind, Hill either absent or playing Barbara under hypnosis and O'Brien as "the new girl", each fresh absurdity is just… a fresh absurdity. Faced with an overwhelming mass of insect-flesh, what we *really* need here is for all those involved - both behind and in front of the camera - to play it casual. If everyone on Vortis acted as if this were their natural environment, and as if butterfly-people were a perfectly normal part of the terrain, then after an episode or so we might forget the weirdness of it and treat it as a place where interesting things might happen. Instead, we get showboating programme-makers constantly shouting "look, this is alien!" at us. And we just want to shout "no, it's stupid!" back at them.

As we've already indicated, in episode five Nemini the Optera gets a "tragic" death-scene, which involves her sticking her head into a hole in the wall to block the flow of acid. Let's just take a snapshot of this moment. A schoolteacher and a gesticulating butterfly stand in a tunnel and stare in horror at a very small woman in a woodlouse outfit as she dies bent over with her head in a hole, while another woodlouse-person hops up in the air growling about Pwodarauk. End the freeze-frame and all those present shuffle away, leaving the camera to linger on the corpse, *still* bent over and *still* with her head in the hole. Out of context, this may well be the stupidest thing ever filmed in the whole history of time. In context, it seems a perfectly logical extension of what's gone before.

Which is the real tragedy of this story. Deprived of a plot that's good enough to keep us interested and make a real world out of the crap lunar-landscape set and ant-people who wear trousers, we get a school play and everyone assumes that stories about alien worlds "don't work". *Doctor Who* becomes a lot more conservative after this, even under producer John Wiles. The person to blame is the person who's been pressing for a story like this to be made, Richard Martin. He's the one who could have said "this set is too creaky" or "Roslyn, what on *Earth* do you think you're doing over there?", but he let everyone get on with their own thing without consulting one another properly. And 13.6 million people ended up with an idea that *Doctor Who* was always like this.

With gritted teeth, we shall try to be upbeat. The mere fact that they attempted it is rather heroic. It would have been easier to make glossy Dalek adventures and pay for it with historical yarns made on the cheap. Instead, they went for broke with a new monster, new aliens who had characters at least as distinct as the Thals (actually, almost exactly the same characters as the Thals, but now with wings) and a whole new sound. Martin Jarvis is, amazingly, dignified as war-hero moth Captain Hilio. As we've noted, in the fifth episode - Nemini's death aside - there's a concerted effort in the dialogue to delineate an alien world-view by conflating ideas of light, speech, stitching and dance. More of this, earlier, would have made a world of difference. Literally.

Instead we have something that looks like television from the 1920s.

The Facts

Written by Bill Strutton. Directed by Richard Martin. Ratings: 13.5 million, 12.5 million, 12.5 million, 13.0 million, 12.0 million, 11.5 million. As we said, episode one holds the record for black-and-white stories, but the all-important Audience Appreciation index fell from 56% to a disastrous 42%.

Supporting Cast   Roslyn de Winter (Vrestin), Anne Gordon (Hrostar), Martin Jarvis (Hilio), Jolyon Booth (Prapillus), Jocelyn Birdsall (Hlynia), Arthur Blacke (Hrhoonda), Ian Thompson (Hetra), Barbara Joss (Nemini), Catherine Fleming (Animus Voice).

Episode Titles   "The Web Planet", "The Zarbi", "Escape to Danger", "Crater of Needles", "Invasion" (yep, another confusing one), "The Centre".

Working Titles   "Doctor Who and the *Webbed* Planet".

Cliffhangers   The Doctor looks incredibly sad as he realises the TARDIS has vanished without him; inside the Carcinome, a transparent tube drops over the Doctor's head, and the voice of the Animus asks him why he's there; Ian and Vrestin hide from the Zarbi in a crack in the rock, but the ground gives way underneath them; after the massacre of the Menoptra spearhead, Barbara is surrounded by Zarbi and larvae guns; back in the Carcinome, this time it's the Doctor and Vicki's turn to be surrounded by Zarbi, and one of the tendrils in the wall seals them inside a cocoon of webbing.

The Lore

• Bill Strutton, yet another Australian writer in London, had previously written an episode for the first series of *The Avengers*. He had a sort-of-science-fiction connection in that he'd written for R3, the missing link between *Quatermass* and *Doomwatch*, very popular in its day. Although he had no real interest in the genre, he was signed to Associated London Scripts, not quite an automatic entry-point into *Doctor Who* but suspiciously close. His starting-point for the story was being bitten by a bull-ant when he was small, and watching the insects fighting. Not to put too fine a point on it, he'd seen how much money Terry Nation made from Dalek merchandising and wanted a piece of it.

• The publicity for this caused friction between Martin and Lambert, but then so did everything else, it seems. Martin objected to a trailer shown after the last episode of "The Romans" that gave too much away. It would appear that it was the use of material from the later episodes that irked Martin, rather than the "gag" shot of Zarbi arriving at Television Centre to record their debut. Lambert's reply was couched in language suggesting that she thought the Zarbi might be too frightening *unless* they were seen in a familiar context (so the "Yeti-in-the-loo" theory hadn't caught on yet).

• It's quiz time. Hartnell was ill, again, and one episode seems to have gone to air with him only having rehearsed for one day. See if *you* can work out which one. Episode two was beset by overruns, as the practicalities of having more than one Zarbi on set hadn't really been thought through. More retakes were needed for this episode than for some entire stories, but mainly for rookie mistakes like someone talking through telecine scenes. Episode three was worse. Half the set was stuck in traffic, the floor for the Carcinome wasn't painted in time, and therefore the lighting had to be rethought when the flats were finally up. Then, when they got around to recording, one of the cameras broke.

• The music came from pre-existing records by Le Structure Sonore. Lambert had originally contacted them with a view to getting them to compose and record the theme tune, before opting for the Grainer / Derbyshire partnership. In a story with such a large cast, all with specially-made costumes, cost-cutting was imperative. Lambert was strict about budgets (this story overspent considerably, but a lot of that was a result of retakes and over-runs, not all Martin's fault), so the use of stock music was another option. Some later stories would dispense with music altogether and apply sound effects for "mood", as Brian Hodgson was on the payroll anyway.

• Australian mime artiste Roslyn de Winter made the Menoptra actors stay behind after rehearsals for Insect Movement tuition. Her thinking was based on a close study of butterfly anatomy, and the facial distortions she and her fellow moth-men pulled were intended to suggest a curled-up proboscis hidden inside the head of each one. Martin Jarvis, in his entertaining autobiography *Acting Strangely*, states that the cast rebelled and that the aristocratic tones adopted by the Menoptra weren't quite what de Winter stipulated.

• Jarvis was having vocal problems at the time in any case. He'd been persuaded to take the part by Verity Lambert, on the grounds that he was to play a troubled prince trying to avenge the overthrow of his father. The bit about flying harnesses and being a six-foot bug with a speech impediment was kept quiet until after he'd accepted. Jarvis was a rising star then and is a household name now, so getting an actor of his calibre to play a big insect was a feather in Lambert's cap. The programme that established him, *The Forsyte Saga*, is what Donald Wilson did next and will be mentioned quite a few times in Volume II.

• Just to help you with that quiz: Jarvis recalls that Hartnell was hardly present in rehearsals. Given that Jarvis' character is only in the last two episodes, this narrows it down a bit. (Oddly, though, it's hard to see much difference between Hartnell's performance in episodes five and six and his autopilot "hmm, yes-my-boy" delivery in episode one. This speaks volumes.)

2.6: "The Crusade"

(Serial P, Four Episodes, 27th March - 17th April 1965.)

Which One is This?   Richard the Lionheart, and lots of English actors in brown make-up. Oh, and Tutte Lemkow, as a dodgy Arab this time.

Firsts and Lasts   It's the last story David Whitaker writes for Hartnell, the first time Douglas Camfield gets to direct a whole story of his own, and the first appearance of actors of colour in the series. They never appear in the same scene as the Doctor (Hartnell was, shall we say, not the most progressive of human beings), but Oscar James and Roy Stewart are unmistakable, lurking in the background whenever El Akir is being evil.

Four Things to Notice About "The Crusades"...
1. Most of the cast have either recently done a *Doctor Who* or are about to do another one. Gabor Baraker (Luigi) was Wang-Lo in "Marco Polo" (1.4), and Zohra Segal (Sheyrah) had taught Zeinia Merton the mime-dance for that story, as well as being a non-speaking handmaid. The villainous El Akir is Walter Randall (Tonila, the priest of sacrifice's assistant in 1.6, "The Aztecs"), who'll be back as the technician Harry Slocum in "Inferno" (7.4) and the patrolman in "The Invasion" (6.3). Jean Marsh (Joanna) will soon be due for semi-official companion status as Sara Kingdom in 3.4, "The Daleks' Master Plan", a story in which Reg Pritchard (here the clothing

merchant Ben Daheer) also returns, and in which his role in "The Crusade" is actually referred to on-screen as an in-joke. Most impressive of all, Bernard Kay (Saladin) is only three months on from being the saving grace of "The Dalek Invasion of Earth" (2.2) as Carl Tyler.

Not all of these other stories have direct connections with Douglas Camfield, but some commentators are a bit suspicious, pointing out that the make-up artist's sister got the part of Safiya. We'd point out that Camfield's somewhat… *regimented* approach to directing meant he needed people he could trust and who trusted him in return. And besides, if anyone else had been cast as Ibrahim then the director would just have said "play it like Tutte Lemkow".

2. For anyone coming to this for the first time, with no experience of how mainstream drama handled characters from other ethnic groups in Ye Olden Days, it may be a bit of a shock to see Roger Avon and Bernard Kay respectively appearing as Saphadin and Saladin. What's impressive to those of us who shudder at the memory of Anthony Hopkins blacked up as Othello or Alec Guinness browned up in *A Passage to India* (both made in the right-on 1980s, folks) is that nobody playing the Saracens is doing funny voices. We've noted that the non-speaking Arabs are genuinely non-Caucasian, but check out the photos of El Akir's multi-cultural harem. The words "Bond Villain" spring to mind.

3. On the other hand, Julian Glover - King Richard himself - has just come from doing wall-to-wall Shakespeare. One of the most interesting things about this story is that when he's on set, everyone else snaps into line. His dialogue is written in a way which frequently ascends into blank verse, resembling as it does the way in which this sentence has been written… get the hint? Whenever he leaves the scene, people slide back into their usual rhythms, the most impressive bathos being Maureen O'Brien's lapse into Liverpudlian after a scene of Ben Daheer's effulgence. 'Who's yer friend?' she asks, going all George Harrison after three months of BBC English.

4. The sets are, on the whole, amazing. There's an obvious right and wrong way to do 1960s *Doctor Who*, and one of the big no-nos is making a story require one big set. It's so much more fruitful to get lots of labyrinthine alleys and nooks, lit in interesting ways and with the potential to be shot from a number of different angles. This story requires a castle, a souk, tight streets, hiding-places and a harem. What's puzzling is how long it took them to realise that a Middle-Eastern setting is ideal for *Doctor Who*, and that the crusades - involving the clash of two totally different types of (stock) costume, in a setting with so much contrast - is the perfect historical event, at least visually. Like jungles, which are becoming the default alien locale by now, twisty streets with things dangling down from the top of the set are almost foolproof. If we were of a suspicious turn of mind, we might speculate as to why David Whitaker wrote this immediately after resigning as story editor, and why no-one seems to have been asked to do it at any time before this…

The Continuity

The Plot Arriving in a woodland just outside the city of Jaffa, the TARDIS travellers stumble into the middle of a Saracen ambush set for King Richard, led by the evil Emir El Akir. Barbara is captured and handed over to Saphadin, brother of Richard's "arch-enemy" Saladin, forcing the Doctor and company to align themselves with Richard's court. Well, maybe they don't need *that* much forcing. Richard knights Ian, making him an emissary to Saphadin, then reveals a new strategy to avoid future bloodshed: a marriage-match between Saphadin and his sister Joanna.

However, Barbara has already been snatched by El Akir as harem-fodder, and is soon being threatened with all sorts of nasty Arab torments. Ian himself is waylaid by unscrupulous "merchants" and narrowly avoids being eaten by ants, while things take a turn for the worse back at the King's court as the Doctor gets on the wrong side of the sword-happy Earl of Leicester. After Ian helps Barbara to escape the harem, the travellers make a dash back to the TARDIS, but an angry Leicester believes the Doctor to be a Saracen spy and pursues him. As the Ship departs, Leicester reflects on the sad fate of Sir Ian, spirited away in a box by an obvious infidel sorcerer.

The Doctor Once again, for much of the time he's in "twinkling" mode, chuckling at his own ingenuity in conning and manipulating people. His brief bursts of moral indignation are only reigned in when he thinks they jeopardise Barbara's rescue. He's wary of getting embroiled in politicking,

How Important Were the Books?

If there's one thing we have to keep stating over and over again, if only for the benefit of readers under the age of twenty-five, then it's this: *repeatability changed everything.*

It's difficult, for anyone who grew up after the early '80s, to understand the way the audience saw television in the days before home video, before TV nostalgia and before any form of technology which involves the word "digital". Until 1981, viewers were absolutely *sure* that any given episode of *Doctor Who* was something they'd only be able to witness once, or twice if the story was one of the chosen few that got a summer repeat. Those of the younger generation are often shocked and bewildered by the BBC's pre-'80s policy of wiping "classic" episodes (see **What Was the BBC *Thinking*?** under 3.1, "Galaxy Four"), and astonished that nobody made more of a fuss about it - not even those who'd now be called "fans". (Though in those days, being a fan meant travelling long distances to meet other fans and going on pilgrimages to exhibitions where you could see a real-life Dalek, not just looking at bbc.co.uk/cult every now and then.) But why would anyone complain? If you *knew* you were never going to see the Yeti rampaging through the London Underground again, then what did it matter whether the episodes in question existed in the BBC archives or not?

The simple truth is that in the '60s and '70s, viewers - children especially - had better memories for TV. Well, of course they did. Information had to be *retained*, it wasn't available at the touch of a button, and in any case there were less distractions; less channels, less movies, less "interactive experiences", less things to do on a Saturday night. Besides, the definitive form of "proper" TV drama was the serialised story. You want to know why, in part, there was such a ratings drop in 2005 between "Rose" (X1.1) and "The End of the World" (X1.2)? It's easy. In the years that *Doctor Who* had been away, the audience had forgotten how to watch series. Channel-zapping and the likes of Blockbuster Video had ensured that the one-off "event" was everyone's idea of drama. A lot of people who *liked* "Rose" didn't bother tuning in the following week, because they felt they'd "seen" *Doctor Who* now. We could go on at length about the way that the serialised story was replaced by the serialised concept, in which you can miss any number of episodes but the Big Idea is still there (*24*, anyone?), but let's stick to the point.

The point is that viewers felt they had a con-nection to what they watched, a connection which required them to keep in touch with it. Having seen an episode of Adventure Show X, the younger viewers could remember *and repeat it* in profound detail, and for many this is where merchandising came in. "Merchandising", in those days, seemed less sordid than it does now. Gerry Anderson series like *Thunderbirds* and *Captain Scarlet* spawned whole dynasties of die-cast toys, but unlike poseable figures based on *The Lord of the Rings* which are mostly bought as "collector's items" by thirty-year-olds who should have something better to do with their money, these were meant to be *used*. They were a way of re-enacting entire episodes from memory. They re-established contact with something you might never see again. See **Why Was There So Much Merchandising?** under 11.4, "The Monster of Peladon", for more of this.

In this respect, *Doctor Who* was disadvantaged. It had no vehicles. There were Daleks, yes, and the middle of the decade brought Dalek toys galore if you could wait until Christmas for the Give-a-Show Projector. But the key scenes in the programme didn't involve exciting space-vessel collisions, they involved the Doctor being clever at British character actors, and how the hell do you reconstruct *that* in plastic? In fact, let's look beyond the merchandising, because it's not as if everyone could afford it anyway. How do you reconstruct a programme as wordy and as weird-looking as *Doctor Who*, when playground games traditionally involve running around very fast pretending to be a Spitfire? You can get one of your mates to shamble along like a monster and have a stab at re-staging the running-away-from-things scenes, but it misses the point of the show, somehow. No, if we wanted to get back in touch with those moments that had seemed to mean so much to us on Saturday nights, then we'd have to do it another way. By God, we'd just have to *read*.

Now, if we were going to push this point, then we could claim that the reason *Doctor Who* fans have ended up quite as literate as they are - at least, compared to certain other types of fan, and let's not forget that there *has* been more intellectual dissection of this programme than of any other that's now classified as "cult" - is simply this: *Doctor Who* always left behind a trail of words. It isn't entirely true, of course. The very nature of the series assumes that literacy is a minimum require-

continued on page 145...

but loves dressing up, and - again - he's a bit tasty in a fight.

• *Background*. It's abundantly clear that he knows his history. He's able to accurately "prophesy" the King's future, that Richard will see Jerusalem, and phrase it ambiguously enough to be true while still being what the King wants to hear. [The novelisation also gives the Doctor some insight into why Richard withdrew at the last moment, something the rushed ending doesn't allow here. This is a rare sign of the Doctor *understanding* human history, not just knowing the facts or observing it from a distance.] He also claims to know Genoa well, though it could be part of his cover story at Jaffa.

• *Ethics*. After all those lectures on altering history, it's odd to see the Doctor give first aid - including drugs from the TARDIS - to the wounded knight de Tornebu. That he tries ingratiating himself with the King to save Barbara is a partial excuse, but he appears mainly to be doing it because it's the right thing to do. He loudly speaks of peace to the warmongering Earl of Leicester, claiming that he admires loyalty and bravery but hates fools [it's striking that he's so vociferous in defence of the King's peace plans, even though he must *know* they're not going to work].

The Doctor also finds it easy to justify stealing clothes from a merchant, on the grounds that the clothes are already stolen. He finds his own shoplifting abilities quite hilarious.

The Supporting Cast

• *Ian*. Again confronted with ants, this time normal-sized but hungry. His prowess with a sword is a match for a highly-trained Saracen, and he sees hardly any absurdity in being knighted by Richard I.

• *Barbara*. Thinks it's a good idea to introduce herself to dangerous Sultans by talking about worlds run by insects and visiting ancient Rome. Yet not only does she have the nerve to deflate El Akir in front of his masters, she's resourceful enough to think of entertaining the court with stories she's collected, including the plots of Shakespeare plays. Occasionally she becomes a bit more girly, and whimpers when threatened, though this is increasingly rare.

• *Vicki*. Finds the Doctor's trickery almost as funny as *he* does. But even after all they've been through, she's terrified that the Doctor is going to leave her, and that he might start to see her as a

nuisance. She resents being made to wear boy's clothes, despite the fact that they're almost identical to her usual woolly tights and "Kermit the Frog" smock.

As well-educated as ever, she immediately realises the TARDIS is in the Holy Land when she hears the name of the King.

The TARDIS It seems that the Ship itself decides when it's ready to materialise, which it does with an unusual electronic whooping noise on this occasion. What's striking is that for once, the TARDIS lands in a historical period for which the wardrobe evidently doesn't have appropriate clothing.

History

• *Dating*. No dates are used here. [But it's obviously 1191, and the hawking expedition during which des Preaux is captured (in episode one) is dated to November. The script takes known events and rearranges the sequence slightly. The offer to marry Joanna to Saphadin was made *before* the capture of des Preaux, possibly six weeks earlier, not just afterwards as we see here. Two months later, the King would approach Jerusalem, but - aware that he couldn't hold it, and that history would remember him as the monarch who lost the Holy Sepulchre - withdraw.]

Far from being the French-speaking butcher and glory-hunter of conventional historical accounts, the King Richard seen here is closer to the Richard of older, romanticised versions. He's sickened by the need for war more than by the war itself, and if any honourable alternative is presented then he'll consider it, although he can also be impatient, selfish, vain and prone to childish ranting. He admits that he has a heartfelt wish to return to England [certainly *not* true of the historical Richard, who thought the place was a tip].

His sister and favourite, Joanna, is far closer to him than his wife [who's mentioned once in this story to explain her absence, and see **The Lore** while we're on the subject of Richard's relationship with women]. Joanna is furious to learn of Richard's plan to marry her off to Saphadin, not just because she's got to join a harem and risk her soul by wedding an infidel, but also because the King has been plotting behind her back. She also has the wit to notice 'something older than the sky itself' in the Doctor.

How Important Were the Books?

...continued from page 143

ment of civilisation, something you couldn't say about any other programme in its supposed field. There are books a-plenty in *Buffy*, but they're often things that give you the cheat-codes you need to beat monsters, not things that alter your perspective on the world. Yet it has to be said... if the Doctor had been given a Time-Mobile with special extending missile-arms that could be used to knock over Rolykin Daleks, then would there have been *quite* as many writers and academics in the later generations of *Doctor Who* fans?

Besides, books have an advantage that other artefacts from TV programmes don't. They're cheaper, and you can get them from libraries. When Target began pumping out the novelisations in the '70s (starting with reprints of the three '60s books, *Doctor Who and the Daleks*, *Doctor Who and the Zarbi* and *Doctor Who and the Crusaders*... if you're not familiar with them, then see if you can guess which TV stories they were based on), each book cost 30p, within pocket-money range even with inflation taken into account. As a bonus, you were allowed to take them to school and read them during "study periods", so between 1975 and 1982 there wasn't an educational establishment in the land that didn't have a handful of Targets secreted in it somewhere. "Sophisticated" fandom now thinks of Terrance Dicks as the old hack who wrote *Warmonger*. This may be understandable, but he's also partly responsible for the literacy of - literally - thousands.

How important were the books, then? Ooh, pretty much crucial. Nearly any other series that's spawned a line of novels has treated them as irrelevant spin-offs, but for *Doctor Who*, the books were a kind of prototype home video. None of the Target novelisations were canonical, in the way we now understand the term, yet they provided a constant baseline of what *Doctor Who* was supposed to be. As you may have noticed, many of the assumptions we still make about the series started in print. Familiar terms like "chameleon circuit" and "Venom Grub", both of which eventually found their way into the TV episodes, originated in the novels (*Terror of the Autons* and *The Zarbi*, respectively). Some of the writers used the books to expand on the way they saw *Doctor Who* working, starting with David Whitaker's adaptation of "The Crusade".

Things started to change when *Doctor Who Weekly / Monthly* arrived on the scene in 1979, fol-

lowed by all sorts of "episode guides" and "anniversary specials". Suddenly the novels were no longer the font of all wisdom. In the early days, *DWM*'s "Matrix Data Bank" column was full of queries from confused readers who couldn't understand why the Doctor meets Jo for the first time at the start of *Doctor Who and the Doomsday Weapon* (AKA "Colony in Space", 9.4) when according to the guidebooks they met in "Terror of the Autons" (9.1), or why Ian's story in *Doctor Who and the Daleks* was so different from the magazine's description of "An Unearthly Child" (1.1). The reason - "the authors just decided to change it" - never occurred to these readers, because for many it was taken as read that the books were the gospel truth.

Why does the Doctor go to the trouble of naming the Cybermen's original homeworld in "Earthshock" (19.6)? Because Gerry Davis got it wrong in *Doctor Who and the Cybermen*, and the fanboys wanted it cleared up. Famously, Terrance Dicks' description of the Slyther in *Doctor Who and the Dalek Invasion of Earth* is really a description of the Mire Beast from "The Chase" (3.8) because the BBC sent him the wrong reference photo, but this is just one of many clearly wrong things which we once believed absolutely.

Inevitably, the evolving nature of the market made it all go wrong in the 1980s. Even in the early days of the Nathan-Turner producership, when *Doctor Who* was still being voted a "children's favourite", the books were in trouble. There was now too much stuff in the world for TV novelisations to seem remarkable. The kind of younger readers who might once have been tempted by a Chris Achilleos cover of a pterodactyl going KKLAK! were more likely to be playing Dunegons and Dragons, and anyway, toy manufacturers had developed the art of making action-figures small enough to be affordable *without* your granddad having to give you a tenner for your birthday.

By the mid-'80s, the Target books had become exactly what they were never meant to be: pure merchandising, aimed at semi-adult fans who wanted to Collect the Set of the Doctor's adventures. Many of the novelisations published in this era are actually quite good, particularly the Hartnells, but nobody really bought them to read them. Certainly nobody under the age of fourteen.

And yet, the Target novelisations had done their work. After the original TV series' demise came

continued on page 147...

[It seems wholly out of keeping with this story, but we have to say it. In "City of Death" (17.2), one of the previous "incarnations" of Scaroth is a crusader. All Scaroth's selves look alike, and he's played by the same actor who plays King Richard here. So, is Richard the Lionheart really a one-eyed alien in a rubber mask? Well... it's not entirely *impossible*, but if so then he's doing a better job of staying in character than Count Scarlioni manages in the twentieth century. On balance, we'd have to say "no".]

The Earl of Leicester is the character against whom King Richard is most visibly contrasted. Leicester is a pragmatist, a soldier sick of being forced to make up for the inadequacies of negotiators. He knows that whatever deals are made will be sorted out by men getting killed. [A point of view familiar to many in the audience who would have read Rudyard Kipling or George Orwell. Leicester's opinion is given additional weight by being phrased in a manner reminiscent of the "Agincourt" speech from Shakespeare's *Henry V*.]

Saladin is the real leader of the Muslim side, and a monarch in his own right, even though his brother Saphadin is the ruler and military chief. Here he's presented as a man whose wisdom and faith lead him to avoid dishonouring Islam by defending it too brutally, and who approves of his brother's wedding plans even though he knows it's not enough to stop the fighting. His compassion extends to sending snow and fresh fruit when he hears that Richard is ill. [This really happened. The kings also exchanged horses and falcons, and the former resulted in the creation of today's thoroughbreds. What this account neglects to mention is that both men were declining rapidly, and each knew the other was sick.]

The real villain here isn't Saladin but El Akir, whose hatred of Europeans, women and in fact virtually everyone seems hard to explain. [Whitaker's novelisation gives him a suitably melodramatic backstory, explaining that he lost his eye in a fight with a woman, the widow of the brother he killed to get her.]

The Analysis

Where Does This Come From? There were three basic strands of British historical drama familiar to viewers in 1965. One was adaptations of worthy (or at least not-too-trashy) fiction, especially - of course - Shakespeare's history plays. Another was the less common but still respectable practice of setting a serious drama in an earlier period to talk about contemporary or eternal issues. This had been gaining ground in the Legitimate Theatre of the 1960s, since Brecht's *Galileo* and Robert Bolt's Brecht-by-numbers *A Man for All Seasons* (the 1966 film version is more conventional), and we've already mentioned *The Royal Hunt of the Sun* (see 1.6, "The Aztecs").

The third tradition, on the wane in 1965 but churned out as a summer "filler" by ITV as late as 1972, was the tights 'n' arrows kiddie-fodder produced by companies like ITC, Sapphire and Official. Since the second day of ITV's transmission, programmes like The *Adventures of Robin Hood*, *Sir Lancelot* (starring William Russell) and many, many more were choking up our screens.

Which is odd, because they were made for the US market. We may not have been able to make Westerns or gritty crime dramas, but we had castles and any number of out-of-work classically-trained actors, most of whom could hold a sword and shout 'sire!'. It was Britain's Unique Selling Point, and the thing that made it really bankable was how much history we had to prostitute. For every actor who drew the line at mispronouncing "lieutenant" to make it more Yank-friendly, there were twenty who'd swallow their pride. Ageing matinee-idols rode horses as if they were flying Spitfires, or sailed the Caribbean as if it were Injun territory. Lew Grade and his cohorts created dozens of these shows from 1955-61, and provided gainful employment for American hacks who'd been blacklisted during the anti-communist witch-hunts. The last big one, *Sir Francis Drake*, was a bid at credibility. However, even this had a crippling flaw, one which *Doctor Who* ruthlessly attacked to establish itself.

The single most important thing about each historical period the TARDIS visits is that it'll never be visited again. This means the stories are about cause and effect. Even "The Romans" (2.4) has an irrevocable event at its heart. On the face of it, this puts *Doctor Who* closer to the first two categories of historical drama. Closer, but not entirely within. The formulaic nature of ITC shows, with a fight, a few regular cast-members, some standing sets and re-used footage cropping up in four out of five episodes, isn't entirely abandoned by early *Doctor Who*. Ian usually gets to fight someone. The TARDIS interior is generally includ-

How Important Were the Books?

...continued from page 145

Virgin Publishing's New Adventures, which can be seen as the true successors of the Target range. Far from being intended as inconsequential, time-filling spin-offs, they were (at least at their best) a genuine attempt to carry on the legacy of the programme while it was off-air. It's doubtful anyone would have tried this if the '70s books hadn't already established that literature was *Doctor Who*'s second-favourite home.

Ironically, though, the books have floundered during the TV show's triumph even as they prospered in a time of its defeat. As this volume goes to press, *Doctor Who* is not only back on television but the Nation's Favourite again, even as children's fiction has become desperately fashionable thanks to the likes of Philip Pullman (good) and J.

K. Rowling (evil). And yet the BBC's "Ninth Doctor" books are squarely in the tie-in tradition; not serious attempts at literature for the under-sixteens, but stories specifically designed not to impair the BBC's other plans, and largely based on fandom's idea of what "typical" *Doctor Who* should be instead of what's actually in the new series.

Perhaps the BBC senses that these days, anything which helps to connect the viewers to the programme is surplus to requirements. Thanks to BBC3, certain episodes of the 2005 series were broadcast as many as *six times* in the four months after first transmission. And that's not including all the behind-the-scenes documentaries or the DVD releases. Who needs to be kept in touch with what they've seen, when you're bound to be seeing it again in a week or two?

---

ed at some point. The Doctor gets at least one comedy moment and one moral outburst per story. Verity Lambert was from the commercial sector, don't forget, and Spooner's connections were all in that field. In adapting to the BBC's electronically-recorded drama from ITC's filmed and mass-produced series, Spooner had a crash-course in the complicated technicalities. But *Doctor Who* never ends a story with someone pressing the "reset" button. The TARDIS crew and the people they leave behind are changed, and you can't show the stories out of order as easily as you can with most ITC series.

It's not as if the "serious" historical dramas were without their clichés and conventions. In this case we see (or rather hear, now that episodes two and four don't exist in the archive) King Richard eating a leg of chicken while dictating a letter. As we mentioned under "The Romans", this behaviour is usually associated with Henry VIII, but it's still a shorthand way of establishing a time when monarchs were less genteel and more inclined to get their hands dirty. We also discover that writers of this sort of thing think everyone in the past spoke in blank verse with BBC accents. This isn't confined to *Doctor Who*, but it's noticeable here because it isn't just the characters we think of as speaking English who indulge in it. There's a style of acting, and a style of dialogue, but also a style of direction appropriate to this genre. In many ways it's pointing a camera at something like a stage-play. The scenes tend to be longer. Yet by choosing Douglas Camfield to direct the produc-

tion, they've elected to move closer to ITC.

All the early historical stories were modelled on well-established TV genres and well-known events from the school textbooks, but this one was inevitable. The audience is assumed to be so familiar with the era that there isn't even a hint of what year or century we're in - can you *seriously* imagine an episode of the 2005 series in which Rose Tyler is expected to know the date of 1191 without the Doctor reading it off the TARDIS console? - and as with Robespierre in "The Reign of Terror" (1.8), the name of the man in charge is all the exposition we're supposed to need. By this stage the hybrid nature of the programme is settling down into a formula, and the story being told here is a natural consequence of trying to be "BBC" (with all that this entailed in 1965) and cater to ten-year-old boys. See **Did the BBC Actually Like *Doctor Who*?** under "The Gunfighters" (3.8) for more on this, and how things would develop under producer Innes Lloyd...

Things That Don't Make Sense This being a cod-Shakespearean sort of story, the Doctor is required to loudly tell the audience that he's about to steal clothes from the merchant while the merchant's standing just a few feet away. Yes, we *know* this sort of thing works on the stage, but here not even Hartnell's giggling can cover up the strangeness of it. And while we're on the subject of clothing... it's early November, but in the Holy Land it should *still* be too hot for Vicki and Ian to comfortably wear what they're wearing. Vicki even adds a cloak.

One which might seem like nit-picking, until you consider how much research went into the script: historically, Saladin's excuse for not meeting Richard was that nobody in his camp could speak Latin or French, and none of the Europeans could speak Arabic or even Coptic. Obviously the usual *Doctor Who* get-out clause is invoked here, but this means that even by landing nearby the Doctor has jeopardised history (by allowing Saphadin, El Akir, Saladin et al to speak with Barbara, Ian and Sir William).

Critique   Both Dennis Spooner and Douglas Camfield, nether averse to tinkering, have claimed that they didn't have to change any of the dialogue (well, all right, except for one thing... see **The Lore**). Camfield believed this to be the best script he ever directed, and even an old Shakespearean hand like Julian Glover was impressed. And in execution, given what was possible at Riverside studios with minimal film work and children watching, it comes across as a *tour de force*. Nobody gives a bad performance. Glover and Jean Marsh threaten to walk away with episode three, and seeing William Hartnell lurking in the background is mildly shocking; is this still *Doctor Who*?

But therein lies the problem, and all the poetry in the world can't hide it. The crusades seem to be the perfect environment for this series, *until* you have to ask yourself what the regular characters are supposed to do there. And the truth is, David Whitaker has no idea. This isn't really a story at all, it's an encyclopaedia entry on King Richard and Saladin, where the TARDIS-dwellers have to find things to be menaced by as events play out around them. This was always bound to be a problem for the historicals, but here the role of the regulars is more spurious than ever. Once we've established that Richard has decided to marry off his sister, nothing happens in the entire middle section except for Barbara escaping and getting recaptured... and then she has to do it *again* in episode four. The writer isn't using this setting to tell a tale, he's just showing us the locale.

In fact, take away the audience's foreknowledge of the crusades and it doesn't even have an ending. The Joanna / Saphadin match looks as if it's going to be the main thrust of the story, but never goes anywhere. We're prompted to care about the minor characters, then asked to forget all about them. The mighty and all-important Saladin simply vanishes halfway through episode three, and as we head towards the climax both Richard and Joanna become irrelevant. As a result, the conclusion to this grandiose tale of war and politics is... an argument in the woods. Dramatically speaking, this could benefit from a redraft. And yet, despite this difficulty, it's hardly a surprise that the actors and director considered the script to be exceptional. It's full of grand theatrics, stocked with all the things that actors and directors love to do, but let's not forget that the people involved were making this programme on an episode-by-episode basis. It's only when you put all four parts together that you suddenly notice... there's no plot.

There are other flaws. We could give faint praise by pointing out how tolerant and broad-minded it is by 1965 standards, how exciting it is by the norm of cheaply-made television and how literate it is when judged against most things involving knights in armour on British TV. All these things are true, but the caveats get in the way. By twenty-first century standards it's creaky, racist and misogynistic. It has all the usual absurdities of drama set in the Middle Ages. And by definition, this has got to avoid actually showing us big-scale battles (which is, after all, what the crusades were). *Kingdom of Heaven* it ain't.

Mercifully, that cuts both ways. In a post-Gulf-War world, any show where the name "Basra" is thrown about so unselfconsciously will seem to hail from an altogether more intelligent time. It has merit for just acknowledging that the Europeans were acting in a way we'd consider to be shameful, even if they sincerely believed (most of them) they were doing it for God. A generation raised on tales of Richard the Lionheart was never going to see the King as a war criminal, but giving Leicester a valid viewpoint while the Doctor harangues him is a bold move. Thus, for all its awkward construction and browned-up actors, there strikingly isn't a single moment in "The Crusade" when things get embarrassing - and you can't say that about much from the 1960s. Why Whitaker wasted so much time trying to write space-opera is a mystery.

The Facts

Written by David Whitaker. Directed by Douglas Camfield. Ratings 10.5 million, 8.5 million, 9.0 million, 9.5 million.

Episodes two and four no longer exist in the BBC archives.

Supporting Cast Julian Glover (Richard the Lionheart), Jean Marsh (Joanna), Walter Randall (El Akir), John Flint (William des Preaux), Roger Avon (Saphadin), Bernard Kay (Saladin), Tutte Lemkow (Ibrahim), Petra Markham (Safiya), John Bay (Earl of Leicester), David Anderson (Reynier de Marun), Bruce Wightman (William de Tornebu), Reg Pritchard (Ben Daheer), Tony Caunter (Thatcher), Robert Lankesheer (Chamberlain), Zohra Segal (Sheyrah), Gabor Baraker (Luigi Ferrigo), George Little (Haroun), Sandra Hampton (Maimuna), Viviane Sorrél (Fatima), Diana McKenzie (Hafsa).

Episode Titles "The Lion", "The Knight of Jaffa", "The Wheel of Fortune", "The Warlords".

Working Titles "The Saracen Hordes". "Damsel In Distress" was one potential title for episode two, and "Changing Fortunes" for three. "The Knight of Jaffa" was originally the title of episode four.

Cliffhangers An angry Richard tells the Doctor and company that Barbara can rot in the Saracens' dungeons for all he cares; Barbara hides from El Akir's men in a side-street, but someone sneaks up on her and clamps a hand over her mouth; a recaptured Barbara (who's getting all the "peril" scenes this month) is dragged before El Akir, and told that the only pleasure she can look forward to is death.

The lead-in to the next story: as the TARDIS leaves the Holy Land, the console room is plunged into darkness. And someone in the studio coughs audibly.

The Lore

• We were always going to have to mention the film *Will Any Gentleman?*, because it's the trivia buff's favourite: the one where Hartnell meets Jon Pertwee. It also features Peter Butterworth (see 2.9, "The Time Meddler"), George Cole (the star of the film) and loads of other instantly-recognisable faces from British film and TV. In a small, uncredited role was the future Mrs Pertwee, Jean Marsh. She did rather a lot else, including a spellbinding turn in the *Twilight Zone* episode "The Lonely". By 1965 she'd been in Shakespeare on Broadway. By 1975 she'd done the series for which she's most famous, *Upstairs, Downstairs,* which she co-created. "The Crusade" was the first of her three *Doctor Who* roles, and the only one not to feature Nicholas Courtney.

• Yet Courtney was, briefly, considered as the Plan B if Julian Glover turned out to be unavailable. Glover, who's more recently been seen in the motion picture *Troy* (but we'll forgive him), had been involved in a BBC project to split up the Shakespeare "Wars of the Roses" plays into twenty-minute episodes and perform them almost as a serial. He'll make a big splash in *Doctor Who* again in 17.2, "City of Death". (Another trivia buff point: he's one of three recurring *Doctor Who* faces who play imperial officers in *The Empire Strikes Back*.)

• As we've said, the scripts were largely unaltered after Camfield received them. As always, Spooner cut down Whitaker's screenplays to make them work in twenty-five minutes and not an hour, but this one needed less trimming than most. The main cut was that the relationship between Richard and Joanna, which the script hinted was closer than advisable for siblings, was amended on Hartnell's request. By now you'll have some idea of how these "requests" were made.

• Another alteration was the role of Ibrahim. He began as a generic Arab bandit, like the unnamed one played by David Brewster in episode three, but Tutte Lemkow embroidered on the part somewhat and ended up making his contribution one of the more endearing features of the story. This is more impressive when you consider that between rehearsals and recording, he'd been whipped off to hospital for stitches and tetanus jabs after the knife hacked a lump out of his finger, and that the shots Camfield wanted involved a decomposing cow under studio lights.

• This story was the third to be novelised. The prologue of the book spells out Whitaker's thinking on history and destiny (see **Can You Rewrite History, Even One Line?** under 1.6, "The Aztecs"), and the novelisation as a whole makes it clear that Ian and Barbara are romantically involved. *Doctor Who and the Crusaders* has, bizarrely, been used by theoretician and novelist Umberto Eco in a disquisition on the "myth" of the Middle Ages as a yardstick for modern writers. See **How Important Were the Books?** for more.

2.7: "The Space Museum"

(Serial Q, Four Episodes, 24th April - 15th May 1965.)

Which One is This? The travellers discover their own stuffed corpses in a museum display case, leading to an unlikely chain of events in which the Doctor ties up a young boy and plays at being a Dalek; Vicki busts open an armoury and starts a swinging revolution; and Barbara's cardigan saves the world, after Ian tries to eat it.

Firsts and Lasts This is the end of Mervyn Pinfield's official connection with the series, although he was scheduled to direct "Galaxy Four" (3.1). This is rather apt, as the "sideways in time" stories pretty much peter out here. The original conception of the series is now replaced with something much more familiar: running up and down corridors, and overthrowing a corrupt regime. So we get the first ray-gun battle, and it's not too bad. It's also the first time we get to shout "no, not the mind-probe!" when the Doctor is interrogated by a magic chair.

It's the last appearance of an "original" Dalek (you know, with the horizontal bands around the middle) and, in the cliffhanger, the first appearance of the "standard" model with the vertical slats. The legend of the Minotaur is mentioned for the first time - see also "The Mind Robber" (6.2), "The Time Monster" (9.5), "The Creature from the Pit" (17.3) and "The Horns of Nimon" (17.5) - although this is the only occasion on which the mythical comparison is inspired by a piece of knitwear.

Four Things to Notice About "The Space Museum"...

1. For a lot of the story, it's like channel-zapping between a Jean-Paul Sartre play and a Cliff Richard musical. While Ian, Barbara and Vicki discuss whether free will can derive from premeditated acts, if death is the only true liberty and other such existential dilemmas, the Xeron kids sneak about trying to do things their own way (pops). The rebellion against the sour-faced Moroks is scripted as an independence movement to overthrow colonial overlords, but it looks as if the Xerons are trying to start a youth club to play their own kind of music, and never mind what the squares say. And Jeremy Bulloch (who really *was*

in *Summer Holiday*) plays the leader of the revolutionaries as if at any moment he's going to say "hey, fellas, let's turn one of these spaceships into a pirate radio station!". Writer Glyn Jones was the story editor on *Here Come the Double-Deckers*, which explains it all[10].

2. As the "cheap" story this year, not only does one episode only feature the four regulars and some non-speaking locals, but the music is all from stock throughout. It's obviously from a compilation called "Now That's What I Call *Doctor-Who*-Type Music", as almost all of it will be re-used again and again. Many of the cues here will be re-deployed in "The Tomb of the Cybermen" (5.1), just as many of the pieces in "The Edge of Destruction" (1.3) crop up in "The Moonbase" (4.6) and the music from "The Web Planet" (2.5) graces "Galaxy Four".

But one piece, Jack Trombey's *World of Plants*, is so inappropriate and 1950s as to be unique to this story (it's the orchestral piece accompanying the still photo slide-show of a temporal anomaly, at the end of episode one). Other cost-cutting measures include the TARDIS wardrobe having a door lifted from Maitland's ship (1.7, "The Sensorites") and the tables from the Sense-Sphere being turned upside-down and made to hold exhibits in the museum. There's one "big" new prop, the control for the freezing machine, and appropriately that's going to be turning up in other stories from now on.

3. This story proves what we've been saying all along: Barbara was the real core of the series. Imagine if this had been a *Star Trek* episode. Kirk might have done some of the things Ian does here, but he wouldn't have unravelled a cardigan to find his way out of a maze. And he certainly wouldn't have made such an inept job of it that Dr McCoy, the Barbara-surrogate, would have tutted, taken it off him and demonstrated how to do it properly. And in the "tag" scene at the end, where the *Enterprise* crew would have been tiresomely moral or gratingly jocular, Barbara politely listens to the Doctor's outrageously stupid explanation of everything that's been amiss with the Fourth Dimension just as an indulgent schoolmarm ought to. Later on in the series, when everyone has worked out what *Doctor Who* "is", a reliably sensible figure like this could be dispensed with (although not entirely... the Brigadier is more like Barbara than we might like to think). However, the sheer resilience of her ordinariness in extreme situations is both

What Are the Most "Mod" Stories?

Between 1958 and 1963, there was a trend among metropolitan kids to disdain the motorbikes, leathers and oafishness of the Rock 'n' Rollers, and go for all things sharp and Italian instead. Vespa scooters, mohair suits with narrow legs and thin lapels, Tony Curtis haircuts and Soul music… *that* was style. By the time *Doctor Who* came along, these Modernists had become Mods, a recognisably British slant on all of this. And their style was becoming exportable. *Ready, Steady, Go!* was required viewing, all-night dances the preferred recreation The whole thing was fuelled by amphetamines (like the rare records and the Parka coats, these mainly came from US servicemen stationed in Britain who went to the same clubs). The look became more overtly op-art, especially since it looked good on black-and-white television. Mary Quant miniskirts, Vidal Sassoon hairdos (as pioneered by Carole Ann Ford) and thick coloured tights were the "uniform" for girls. American readers will be able to ask their elders about the "British Invasion"; nearly all the bands involved were Mod bands, and the ones which endured best were the ones that were most emphatically Mod, like the Kinks and the Who.

This is worth dwelling on for a moment. If *Doctor Who* was as much a place you visited as a story you followed, then it makes sense that the visual style of the series should be arresting. If the aesthetic and function of the programme were locked together to make something that was broadcast at tea-time on Saturdays and never seen again, then the contemporary feel of the presentation *as a whole* was what audiences responded to. Far from being something that slipped in by accident, as was the case with *Star Trek* et al, *Doctor Who*'s use of "nowness" was deliberate, premeditated and part of the purpose of the series. Many of Captain Kirk's enemies and costumes seem very 1966 now, but in *Doctor Who* it was always the intention at the time of broadcast to look like something from that particular week.

So, we'll be awarding points to the following stories for fashion, for the overall "look", for the lifestyles of those involved and for general signs of Mod activity. If you're still confused after this, then watch *A Hard Day's Night* and *Quadrophenia* (assuming you haven't already). Or that paragon of Mod TV, *The Prisoner*.

10. "The Ice Warriors" (5.3): The real enemy isn't the ice, or the Martians, but hippies. The look is great, with op-art body-stockings, but it's the

middle-aged men who wear them that let things down. Big streamlined machines inside a Victorian country house, which is itself inside a geodesic dome; space-age countdowns; wrist TVs; a Martian spaceship with roundels; synthetic foods, chemical dispensers, vibro-chairs… all good. But the reason everybody's there is to stop Britain being engulfed by something cool. That's so not Mod.

Fashion: 6/10. *Look:* 7/10. *Lifestyle:* 4/10. *Overall Modness:* 8/10.

9. "An Unearthly Child" (1.1): The TARDIS! It's all flashing lights, like a pinball machine. It has that concentric ceiling-mounted thing, right out of a discotheque from 1965. It has a TV on the wall, and the patterns it makes when the Ship takes off are *seriously* Brigit Riley (she did all those op-art pictures that got turned into skirts). Again, we put it to you: did the TARDIS land Susan in Haight Ashbury in 1967? Did Ian and Barbara follow her home from the 1970 Isle of Wight Festival? No. Susan chose to do London in 1963, and stayed for five months. She's got it all happening. Stripey polo shirt, Capri pants and That Haircut. The regulars spend three episodes under threat from hairy blokes in skins who grunt and beat each other up. They hate the countryside, and want to get to a city as soon as possible. Ian knows all about the chart platters that matter, while nobody mentions Susan's parents.

Fashion: 7/10. *Look:* 6/10. *Lifestyle:* 8/10. *Overall Modness:* 8/10.

8. "The Chase" (2.8): They go to a funfair, they tune in to the Beatles, and at the end Ian and Barbara run around Swinging London. The Daleks have a time machine that's op-art on the inside and streamlined on the outside. It makes feedback noises like a B-side by the Yardbirds, or the intro to "Reflections" by Diana Ross and the Supremes, and it's lost in a time vortex resembling a kaleidoscope. This is the sort of thing that would get psychedelic when taken to extremes, but within restraints it's classic Mod. Best of all, the Mechanoids are geodesic domes with attachments like the multiple mirrors on a Vespa scooter, and they beat up the Daleks in a high-rise. Never mind Shakespeare or the *Mary Celeste*, forget about New York or alien planets, it's London This Week that's the place to be.

Fashion: 6/10. *Look:* 8/10. *Lifestyle:* 7/10. *Overall Modness:* 8/10.

continued on page 153…

hilarious and touching.

4. Fans of gratuitous exposition should pay close attention to our first encounter with the Moroks at the start of episode two, a textbook example of how *not* to set up a new alien culture in under two minutes. Particularly entertaining info-dump lines include 'I've got two more min-ims before I can go home… yes, I say it often enough, but it's still two-thousand Xeron days'; 'I'm the Governor of this planet, you're supposed to show some respect'; and, when one of Lobos' men is asked whether the TARDIS comes from their homeworld, 'no, not from the planet Morok'. Ten minutes later, Lobos welcomes the Doctor with the standard greeting 'welcome to Xeros, a planet in the Morok Empire'. Anyone would think the writer was rushing things in order to get the story moving, but having told us far too much in a single scene, the rest of the episode largely con-sists of the TARDIS crew having the same argu-ment several times over.

The Continuity

The Doctor   Has always found it difficult to 'solve' the fourth dimension [i.e. temporal theory is a bit of a mystery to him, understandable given what we learn of his academic background in 16.1, "The Ribos Operation"]. His mental control is such that when exposed to the Morok mind-probe, he can project moving images of walruses onto its screen. Although the Moroks' freezing process aggravates his rheumatism [compare with 1.4, "Marco Polo"], he claims to have remained conscious even at several hundred degrees below freezing, and states that his brain was working 'at the speed of a mechanical computer'. He's capable of overpowering, binding and gagging a teenage boy without the boy knowing what's hit him.

• *Background.* The Doctor has never been to a Space Museum before, although he's long suspect-ed one might exist, and he immediately spots that the spaceships on display are from different peri-ods. He claims he was with James Watt when Watt came up with the idea of steam-powered vehicles. [He's name-dropped before, but this marks the start of his habit of claiming to have been present at all the Great Moments in Science. By Season Sixteen, he'll be dropping apples on Newton's head.]

He identifies the time-and-space visualiser in the Space Museum on sight, and believes he can

get it working again. Interestingly, he states that he 'couldn't believe his eyes' when he saw it there. [It's clearly the product of a much higher civilisa-tion. More on this astonishing piece of kit in the next story.]

The Supporting Cast

• *Ian.* A lot more ruthless this time, especially once he gets a glimpse of his own fate. He's appar-ently prepared to kill, or die, to change the pre-destined future. Most worryingly, he tells Lobos that even if killing the Morok leader doesn't change anything, he might well enjoy it. [We'll assume he's bluffing.]

• *Barbara.* More tolerant of zaphra gas than the Xerons are, if that means anything. Barbara has experienced the phenomenon of walking into a room, switching on the light and having to wait a few seconds for the bulb to light up [if you haven't seen this story, then you'll have to take it on trust that her matter-of-factness about this is funny in context].

• *Vicki.* Can recite school primers about the Dimensions of Time, though for her it was all the-ory. She spent a lot of her childhood in museums, not the trendy interactive ones of modern times but the traditional sort with 'little men telling you not to touch things'. She read about Daleks in a history book, and is less than impressed with a real one, as it's not the way she imagined it look-ing. [Future history books don't have pictures???]

Obviously trained in technical matters, Vicki is able to re-wire the 'electronic brain' in the Morok arsenal and force it to accept true but "improper" answers [note that this isn't a full reprogramming, any more than the brain is a legitimate computer]. She's positively giddy with excitement when called upon to start a revolution, and she's the prime mover behind the Xeron uprising. [Nobody makes a big deal of it, but it's almost certain that Vicki's actions are the ones which save the TARDIS crew from being embalmed.]

The TARDIS   The crisis begins with a sudden darkness in the console room, which briefly freezes the travellers and changes them back into their normal clothing from their "crusader" outfits as the TARDIS materialises. On recovery, the Doctor can turn the lights back on with the flip of a switch, but none of them have any memory of putting away the twelfth-century clobber they were wearing. The Doctor is curiously unshocked

What Are the Most "Mod" Stories?

...continued from page 151

7. "The War Machines" (3.10): Everyone's up all night, then off to work the next morning fresh as a daisy... how do you imagine they do that? The "flash" who picks a fight with Ben in the nightclub is wearing a stripy blazer of the kind that was *a la mode* for three weeks in 1966 and then again in 1980, while Polly's frock is achingly sharp. She's so cool that it takes Ben a whole episode to realise she's been hypnotised. The title captions, the verité-style location work and the nightclub set are right, but the War Machines themselves are deeply wrong.
Fashion: 8/10. *Look:* 7/10. *Lifestyle:* 8/10. *Overall Modness:* 8/10.

6. "The Space Museum" (2.7): The kids are all right! There's nobody on this planet over twenty, except the authority figures trying to give them a hard time. And they're kitted out in Army Surplus. Tor and his boys look right, despite their comedy eyebrows, and note that people on Xeros have access to Converse All-Stars. The exterior sets are classics of their kind: big, bold triangles of dark and light, asymmetric designs and stark simplicity. The Doctor poses for a fashion spread wearing a striped bathing costume against a white backdrop. Follow that with a still of a penny-farthing and we're almost looking at the kind of collage used in Beatles merchandising (think of the cover for Revolver). And check out the lettering on the exhibits.
Fashion: 7/10. *Look:* 7/10. *Lifestyle:* 8/10. *Overall Modness:* 9/10.

5. "The Wheel In Space" (5.7): The Cybermen are the quintessential Mod monsters; their first appearance had them mugging GIs to get hold of some Parkas (4.3, "The Tenth Planet"). Minus several points for their inept dancing when in space, and because the hippest person on the Wheel is a librarian. But Zoe, let's recall, wears her Alice-band *under* her space-helmet. The sets are a fantastic

combination of pirate radio station and *Top of the Pops,* with lots of groovy details and the plans in white on cellophane. There are TV screens everywhere, plus there's a bank of giant lava-lamps. The Cyber-hypnotic signal is, of course, a sine-wave from an oscilloscope. Even the spacesuits are starkly monochrome. Any story with a line like 'switch over to sexual air-supply' must surely have the right idea.
Fashion: 10/10. *Look:* 9/10. *Lifestyle.* 4/10. Overall *Modness:* 7/10.

4. "The Moonbase" (4.6): This is the story where the bad guys fly off into space doing the Twist, except for one who's got the right idea and does the Jerk. Earlier in the story they do the Moonstomp (the late '60s incarnation of Mod adopted crew-cuts and Ska, and 1969's Ska hit "Skinhead Moonstomp" seems to have been inspired by this scene). The use of nail-varnish remover to eliminate the fashion-victims of Telos is a plus. Ben and Polly get it exactly right, and the majority of the scientists have at least a notion of how to co-ordinate. Bonus points for silver DMs, Hobson's Union Jack badge (very Pete Townsend) and Roger's accessories (the cravat is inspired), but minus one for Fat Bob and his NHS glasses, as well as the shower-caps. The crew don't know day from night, and live on coffee and pills. The Cyberman light-show is just the right side of Pink Floyd to be Mod. Geodesic domes always score highly, but the Gravitron itself is like something from a 1950s civic centre, and frankly we're disappointed.
Fashion: 7/10. *Look:* 8/10. *Lifestyle:* 9/10. *Overall Modness:* 8/10.

3. "Tomb of the Cybermen" (5.1): It has to be said, the entrance-hall of the Tomb resembles a coffee-bar or an ice-cream parlour, which is Mod enough even without the return of the "living on pills" motif. The big stark monochrome dial on the wall and the Cyber-head logo make a splash. The

continued on page 155...

by any of this, saying that the answer lies in 'time and relativity' as if it's a normal side-effect of the Ship. When Vicki is startled by an alarm and drops a glass of water, time seems to reverse, and the broken shards reassemble in her hand.

On exploring Xeros - and this is all *terribly* mysterious - the travellers discover that they've landed before they've actually arrived. Which is to say

that as they step out onto the planet's surface, they're effectively "ghosts" who can't be seen by anyone on the world, and who don't leave footprints in the sand. Nor can they touch solid objects or hear any noise except sounds they make themselves, and yet weirdly, they're obviously able to feel the ground under their feet and don't appear to be able to walk through walls.

[Plus, they can breathe the air. As with the melting clock in "The Edge of Destruction" (1.3), consciousness would seem to be an issue when something goes wrong with the TARDIS. Here it's as if the crewmembers are in some way mental projections of themselves.]

It transpires that the TARDIS has jumped a 'time-track', meaning that their ghost-selves are exploring Xeros some time after the Ship's "actual" landing. Time, though a dimension in itself, has dimensions of its own; the Doctor speaks of them being transported *into* 'a fourth dimension', and of the TARDIS jumping a 'time dimension'. Hence, they find their own bodies on display in the museum. After a while, the time-tracks are sorted out [by the TARDIS], so the travellers arrive in the "present" - i.e. a time before they're stuffed and mounted - and become corporeal. The Doctor indicates that they can't leave before this point, as their fate will become inevitable if they do. Just to make things extra-strange, they become solid in exactly the places where their ghost-selves were standing; their footprints appear in the dust outside; and the broken glass shatters again on board the Ship. [The TARDIS does this out of convenience. It's not a natural function of the universe when time gets bent.]

What causes this hopping-about between time-lines? Yes, it's a stuck component on the Ship, which the Doctor cheerily removes and waves about once the crisis is over. [Again, see "The Edge of Destruction". It would seem that the Doctor has yet to discover WD40.] Apparently the TARDIS landed on a separate time-track and 'wandered around a bit', but until the component clicked into place, the Ship didn't actually arrive.

At the end of events, the Doctor takes the time-and-space visualiser from the Space Museum and sets it up in the console room. [As we'll see in the next story, this is remarkable, as the gizmo is bigger than the police box doors. And the Doctor at present most assuredly doesn't have the control needed to materialize the TARDIS around objects, as with 18.7, "Logopolis" or X1.13, "The Parting of the Ways".] The clothing taken from the twelfth century is kept in a small wardrobe [not a chest or a whole room, as in some later stories]. The St John's Ambulance sigil on the TARDIS exterior is once again erratic, being clearly visible on landing but vanishing later.

Planet Notes

• *Xeros.* As the name implies, it's a desert-world [see also the next story... this is a good year for aptly-named desert planets], three light years from Morok. Dust covers the surface, and the rocks show strange signs of erosion, but there's barely any wind. The natives hold that Xeros was a place of peace before the Moroks came and destroyed everything, killing all the people except the children. The Xerons are now a slave race, the Xeron youth [all male, from what we see here] being dragged off by the Moroks when they come of age and shipped to other planets as a workforce.

The Xerons look human, except for a secondary pair of bushy eyebrows an inch above the first pair. [Hopefully the planet Delphon is nowhere nearby, or else everyone would think the Xerons had stammers. See 7.1, "Spearhead from Space".] A rather disorganised teenage resistance movement exists, which is trying to get hold of ray-guns to fight the Moroks. They all wear black jumpers and jeans, and have hair that would be considered long by 1965's standards and short by 1975's.

The other important thing about Xeros is that it's where the all-conquering Moroks have built their Space Museum, a labyrinthine building surrounded by vessels from various eras. The Doctor indicates that they're all from different ages of the same culture, rather than looted from other worlds. But the museum itself is stuffed with trophies from the Moroks' glory days and weird machines of all descriptions, while armaments are kept in an armoury that's guarded by a surprisingly gullible computer. There's also the casing of a Dalek, which according to the placard came from Skaro [sure enough, it's the same sort of Dalek model we see in 1.2, "The Daleks"]. According to the Xerons, everybody knows there's nothing left on the planet but the Museum.

• *Morok.* The imperial power of this galaxy [wherever it is] at this point in time [whenever it is]. In bygone days the Moroks were the scourge of space, but now they're swamped in paperwork and nostalgia, more like bureaucrats than warlords. The Governor of Xeros follows an inflexible procedure as he attempts to stop the Xeron rebels, and thinks of himself as a scientist stuck in an admin job, not a military man. The basic unit of time is the minim, equal to a thousand Xeron days [we don't know how long their day is, or why they

What Are the Most "Mod" Stories?

...continued from page 153

wall-size polarised light display, usually seen as a backdrop to mini-skirted girl singers, is fab. Victoria tells Parry 'we can make a party', and Toberman frequently looks like he's about to start dancing (especially when promised a go with 'the Scots lad'). Even Troughton gets a cape, and it makes all the difference. It's as if he's stopped off on Telos en route to Carnaby Street. One of the crew is wearing Chelsea Boots, although Kaftan explores wearing peeptoe sandals... bad move.

Fashion: 9/10. *Look:* 9/10. *Lifestyle:* 8/10. *Overall Modness:* 8/10.

2. "The Ark" (3.6): Monsters with Beatle haircuts. Instant chicken-wings. Watching the end of the world on TV. Scooting about on buggies. Even the Monoid funeral is percussion-based and has dance-steps. Their great hall is the flight-deck of a spaceship, but it's essentially a nightclub. Their medical wing has nifty Mondrian walls, which was a bit dated by March 1966, but when the story was recorded it must have been cutting edge (these things get old so fast). The camera-angles are straight out of *Top of the Pops* or *Ready, Steady, Go!*,

and you almost expect Dusty Springfield to walk slowly down a spiral staircase. Even Dodo looks the business.

Fashion: 9/10. *Look:* 8/10. *Lifestyle:* 9/10. *Overall Modness:* 8/10.

1. "The Macra Terror" (4.7): It's a holiday camp where everyone gets out of their box every night. Polly's even had her hair done like Twiggy. The Doctor wears suede boots, and there are cheerleaders in Majorette outfits. Pirate radio-style jingles pervade the colony. Any story featuring Ben will score highly, but even the over-thirties look sharp.

Fashion: 9/10. *Look:* 8/10. *Lifestyle:* 8/10. *Overall Modness:* 8/10.

And from the Mod Revival of 1980: **"The Leisure Hive" (18.1):** A story that starts with a trip to Brighton and has the Doctor hoping to die before he gets old has to be worthy of note. The Argolins live fast and die young, in a glorified funfair.

Fashion: 6/10. *Look:* 5/10. *Lifestyle:* 6/10. *Overall Modness:* 8/10.

---

don't use years, but if they're a pan-galactic empire then they must have a standardised timescale for all planets]. According to Governor Lobos, it's been three-hundred minims since the heyday of the Museum.

Though the Moroks are just as humanoid as the Xerons, they all have stripey hair and widow's peaks instead of the bonus eyebrows. The soldiers wear white uniforms with big shoulders, and Lobos has braid on his epaulettes. In addition to the impressive mechanisms found in the museum, the Moroks have a 'thought selection' machine, which displays a subject's thoughts on a TV screen when he or she sits in a special chair. They also have an automatic 'embalming' process for turning people into exhibits, which takes its victims to several hundred degrees below freezing, although it can be reversed if a subject isn't quite dead. Being old-school galactic conquerors, the Moroks carry lethal 'ray-guns', and one division commander is heard grumbling about his pay. They pump zaphra gas into the Museum to paralyse the rebels.

At the end of events here, the TARDIS travellers avert their fate of ending up as museum exhibits,

and spark a Xeron revolt in the process. Xeros is freed from the Morok soldiers, and it's implied that Morok no longer has the military will to re-invade. The Xerons promptly begin smashing up all the technology that doesn't belong on the planet, although the Doctor does his usual job and advises them not to abandon science entirely.

History

• *Dating.* No date given. [The Dalek in the museum hints that the Morok Empire invaded Skaro, presumably after the Doctor's first visit there (2300, maybe) and before 3900-odd (by which time the planet was either destroyed or crawling with Daleks again, depending on how you want to read it... see **What's the Dalek Timeline?** under 2.8, "The Chase"). In "Planet of the Daleks" (10.4), none of the Thals from 2540 mention being swamped by Moroks. Then again, judging by the time-and-space visualiser it's possible that the Moroks have some crude time-travel capability, and can pinch trophies from around history.]

The Analysis

Where Does This Come From? The last time this series tried to do a spooky story about the mysteries of time-travel, the result was "The Edge of Destuction" (1.3). We said that the result looked a lot like *The Twilight Zone*, and "The Space Museum" gets exactly the same result.

This is only to be expected. *The Twilight Zone* went out of its way to tell humanistic and often sentimental stories which just happened to have science-fiction pretexts, and its approach to time travel is one in which time and consciousness are interlinked, so history is not only sentient but capable of having a sense of justice. The result is that stories in which time is profoundly altered are more like ghost stories than nuts-and-bolts SF. This is true of both "The Edge of Destruction" and the alternative-timeline parts of "The Space Museum". Episode one, with the travellers finding themselves on a land-of-the-dead planet and not leaving any footprints, is crying out for a Rod Serling voice-over.

But on this occasion, the similarity isn't just a generic one. In the *Twilight Zone* episode "Death Ship", astronauts from Earth land on an arid-looking planet and discover that their own ship is already there, with their own corpses on board. Their arguments, as they try to figure out whether they're looking at an inevitable future or whether they're already dead, are rather more macho versions of what we hear Ian and Barbara discussing here. Did Glyn Jones see it? Possibly, although he wasn't exactly a big TV viewer, and "Death Ship" wasn't exactly the first story of its kind. (And nor was "The Space Museum" the last. While *Doctor Who* was grinding to a halt in the late '80s, *Star Trek: The Next Generation* churned out an episode called "Time Squared" which did exactly the same thing all over again. Amazingly, *Star Trek* fans hailed it as an example of incredibly clever and inventive SF.)

Barbara as good as quotes from another likely source, Thornton Wilder's 1927 novel *The Bridge at San Luis Rey*. In this, five people are killed in one accident, but have no other connection. Was it fate, chance or Divine Will? Wilder veers towards the last of these, but he was writing at a time when the existentialist movement was getting under way. Although we tend to think of it as connected with Paris and the 1950s, existentialism was really a fusion of longer-term trends in

western thought. We forget now, when religion and consumerism seem to have answered most of the basic questions about why we're alive (or at least made people forget to ask them), how substantial a movement this was in the mid-twentieth century. As we saw in "The Edge of Destruction", it was at the core of everything happening culturally in 1960s Britain.

And from the 1920s onwards, people had been more prepared to speculate on the nature of time. For anyone to even pretend to be cultured, they had to at least try to follow Einstein, or the "diet" versions available. J. W. Dunne's book *An Experiment With Time* was commented on by Sir Arthur Eddington, who was - for the British reader - Einstein's representative on Earth. Such concepts as multiple world-lines (parallel universes, counterfactual histories, etc) were seen as fit subjects for intellectual debate rather than as pretexts for pulp SF. Most people who were interested in this sort of thing would also have known the Jorge Luis Borges story "The Garden of Forking Paths", without mention of which no conversation about this theme is complete. In this, every possible outcome is itself the place for a choice of consequences, ad infinitum. While David Whitaker had been story editor of *Doctor Who*, all time-related questions had been answered with "because I said so". Once Whitaker left, Spooner allowed the previous forty years' thinking to come out and play in his office.

From Spooner's point of view, this was worth doing simply because it answered a question that viewers (and Whitaker himself, in the novelisation *Doctor Who and the Crusaders*) had been asking. Why was Earth's history sacrosanct, and not - for example - Skaro's? From a dramatic perspective, having a time-limit in which to change a terrible future justifies the Doctor's mission to overthrow the baddies, rather than just having him pick on them because they've got adenoid trouble.

Which brings us to another topical hint. The Moroks sound vaguely South African, at least when they don't sound as if they come from Birmingham. As an exile from South Africa, Glyn Jones may have wanted the story to be overtly about colonialism, but it's doubtful that the scripts specified the accents (see also 6.4, "The Krotons"). South Africa was becoming a global pariah thanks to Apartheid, although in the eyes of many British people, it was at least as much to do with the South Africans telling us who to have in our cricket team. (Basil D'Oliviera, designated a "coloured" by the South African government, played for England. The South African test squad refused to play against him.) It was also around this time that the former colony of Rhodesia decided it wasn't listening to any of this "black people should be allowed to vote" business it kept hearing from the rest of the world. Rhodesian leader Ian Smith was frequently on the news, speaking in an accent that a generation of us learned to associate with bigots. British actors now manage a better approximation, if that's what the Moroks were supposed to sound like.

But it makes just as much sense to think of this as a parable about the generation gap. Even the word "revolution" is used, by hip young thing Vicki, in a way that makes the whole taking-up-arms concept sound young 'n' groovy.

Things That Don't Make Sense   All right, even assuming that the skipping-a-time-track weirdness is in part engineered by the TARDIS, let's look at the Doctor's explanation: 'If we're not [really] there, we can't leave footprints or break glasses or touch things.' But they *can* touch things on board the TARDIS itself, which is why Vicki could pick up the glass in order to break it... except that time rewound to un-break it. Did the TARDIS arrange this just to draw attention to the fact that they're ghosts? [By the logic of "The Edge of Destruction", yes. Note that it's the Ship's siren which causes her to drop the glass in the first place.] The TARDIS doesn't seem to have a problem with other interactions between the travellers and solid matter, e.g. the Doctor drinking the water from the reconstructed glass (it doesn't leap back up his throat in an amusing manner) or having its buttons pushed (the Doctor switches the lights on, and the Ship doesn't switch them back off again).

The TARDIS crewmembers walk into a chamber which contains their own bodies in glass cases, clearly on display and immediately to their left as they walk in. It takes them a minute and a half to notice. The locals are less alert still; desperate for weapons, the Xeron resistance leader Tor realises at once that Ian, Barbara and Vicki could be the people they need because Ian's got a ray-gun. Ian got it out of a glass case in the Museum, as the Xerons could have done at any time in the last three-hundred minims. And even though the Doctor doesn't give his name and origin, Lobos later seems to know that he's called 'the Doctor'. *That* didn't pop up on his telly screen.

We've said it before, but it's got to be said again. Ultra-educated Vicki has read descriptions of Daleks in history books, yet doesn't know what they look like. Even in 1965, did the writer *seriously* not consider that she might have seen a picture, either in print or on TV? To modern ears, the suggestion that twenty-fifth-century kids learn from history *books* sounds peculiar enough in itself.

The big one: why is the significance of Ian's missing button supposed to be such a big deal? Due to the Doctor's theorizing, Ian and Barbara wrack their brains to remember whether his future-self in the display case had the button, as if it's an important clue as to whether they've managed to change history or not, yet a few minutes later they unravel Barbara's cardigan. This alone is an obvious change from what they foresaw, and *proves* it's possible to avoid their fate.

Critique   The usual drill for reviewing this story is to say that the first episode is imaginative and bold, but the next three are a waste of a good premise. The audience appreciation figures indicate this was the standard view at the time, with a healthy 61% dwindling to 49% by the end. The second routine thing to say about any Season Two story is that it's "high-concept", with a one-line pitch ending with an exclamation mark. There's a grain of truth in both of these, but it's inadequate.

Clever as the idea seems, it wasn't wholly novel even in 1965, and forty years on we've seen alternative-history stories flogged to death. In fact it's what follows that has the charm. "Charm" really has to be the keyword here; dramatically speaking, much of it is comically inept, and episode two seems to have been padded so badly that the "bickering" scenes start to resemble a music-hall act. Yet it also features the Doctor outwitting the authorities, overcoming the boy soldiers and giggling as never before, while the villains - for the first time in this series - moan about the dullness of their job and complain about the salary. The pop-art mind-probe stuff with penny-farthings and walruses is fun and, being a Mervyn Pinfield show, it's all lit effectively. (Especially the start of this sequence, with Hartnell in half-light. This is one of his standard publicity shots, and it has to be said... Hartnell uses lighting on his face in almost exactly the same way that Marlene Dietrich did. There the similarities must end.)

Episode three is a more straightforward adventure episode, and better done than many from the

'60s. It's episode four that lets it down. Still, each part is a different type of story, and each is a consequence of the last. "The Ark" (3.6) is praised for doing this sort of thing, though not "The Space Museum".

All right, maybe it's easy to see why. The look of it all is horribly flat, especially after the apparent depth of the previous story. Pinfield's earlier directorial attempt, "The Sensorites", had exactly the same problem. Whereas the younger generation of directors wanted to make programmes that looked as if they were constantly on the move, and environments that looked as if they could be explored from every angle, Pinfield's version of TV is about abstract spaces. Which basically means that a corridor is just a corridor. And as with "The Sensorites", the script doesn't give us anywhere near enough about the supposedly-alien culture we're seeing, so a new race is defined with some rudimentary backstory and a name beginning with "X". We can't really fault the regulars, as they're all doing what they do well, especially Russell and O'Brien. There are only so many ways to perform the same kind of material, yet somehow they manage to be watchable and surprising in familiar situations. But really, Vicki starting a teen revolution should be a lot more exciting than watching her fiddle around with some wires inside a box.

Watched on its own, "The Space Museum" can seem incredibly dull. Watched as originally intended - shortly after "The Web Planet" and right before "The Chase" - it just seems a *bit* dull.

The Facts

Written by Glyn Jones. Directed by Mervyn Pinfield. Ratings: 10.5 million, 9.3 million, 8.5 million, 8.5 million.

Supporting Cast Richard Shaw (Lobos), Jeremy Bulloch (Tor), Peter Sanders (Sita), Peter Craze (Dako), Bill Starkey (Third Xeron), Ivor Salter (Morok Commander), Peter Diamond (Morok Technician / Guard).

Episode Titles "The Space Museum", "The Dimensions of Time", "The Search", "The Final Phase".

Working Titles "Zone Seven", "The Four Dimensions of Time".

Cliffhangers The bodies of the TARDIS travellers vanish from the Museum, and the Doctor informs the "real" Ian, Barbara and Vicki that they've now 'arrived'; Lobos orders his guards to take the Doctor to the preparation room, apparently to be turned into an exhibit; Ian enters the preparation room, sees what's inside and says 'Doctor!' in a shocked sort of way (the implication is that the Doctor's been turned into a statue, but note that William Hartnell isn't in episode three, so his non-appearance here is a convenience as much as anything).

The lead-in to the next story: on Skaro, the Daleks monitor their 'greatest enemies' leaving Xeros, and prepare to follow in their own time machine...

The Lore

• The day before recording the first episode, the press broke the story that William Russell and Jacqueline Hill were leaving the series. A new male lead, Roger Bruck, was created by Dennis Spooner to fill the gap. Spooner himself was planning his next move, but he'd agreed to write a four-parter to follow the Dalek story that was itself to follow "The Space Museum", in order to ease his successor into the job. The new story editor was to be Donald Tosh, a trendily-dressed lateral thinker who'd been working on *Compact* for over a year. (As you may recall from the start of this book, the script unit had a great many "pool" writers, and a lot of collaboration went on. A script sent to one series might be deemed unsuitable, but the writer's name passed on to the staff of another series entirely. Moris Fahri's proposed Alexander the Great script went to Tosh at *Compact*, whereas a sitcom idea by Bob Baker and Dave Martin later resulted in Terrance Dicks giving them a break for 8.3, "The Claws of Axos".) Tosh was keen to get away from routine stories about overthrowing monsters, and to explore the programme's potential.

• Lambert, meanwhile, was planning her next *few* moves. By now she was one of the biggest shots in BBC drama. Her immediate future involved a new twice-weekly soap, eventually called *The Newcomers*. She was also attempting to launch a new TV series about Sexton Blake, but with the twist that the great detective was alive in the '60s. After copyright wrangles this became *Adam Adamant Lives!*, and we'll be returning to it later. Lambert and Spooner began work on a document explaining the *Doctor Who* story so far to whoever took over. Her eventual replacement, assigned the job by Donald Wilson, was another ex-pat South African: John Wiles, who'd been in the script department for over a decade and was now promoted to production.

• Meanwhile… Glyn Jones submitted a script without even seeing a single episode of the show, on the grounds that David Whitaker liked his work. (Indeed, Jones didn't see his own story broadcast.) By the time it came to be produced, Spooner had taken charge, and decided that the conceptual leaps required by the story needed less overt comedy than Jones had included. Neither of them was entirely comfortable with the other's approach, and Jones didn't submit any other ideas until the 1970s, by which point he'd acted in the series (12.3, "The Sontaran Experiment", in case you'd forgotten).

• The museum exhibits include a Dalek from "The Dalek Invasion of Earth" (2.2) with the thick rubber "skirt" removed, two spacesuits from *The Quatermass Experiment*, and several oscilloscopes. These were the standard post-War electronic testing equipment, and weren't just seen as emblematic of "science" but became one of the BBC's favourite ways of making spooky-looking patterns. See, for instance, "Tomb of the Cybermen" (5.1); **Why Top of the Pops?** under "The Robots of Death" (14.5); and **What Are the Most "Mod" Stories?**.

2.8: "The Chase"

(Serial R, Six Episodes, 22nd May - 26th June 1965.)

Which One is This? It's the one with the Beatles in it. And Shakespeare. And Lincoln. And the Mechanoids, and an android Doctor, and… um… the Gubbage Cones. It's also the one where the teachers go home, after Ian gets his hand down Barbara's pants in front of nine-and-a-half-million viewers.

Firsts and Lasts It's the first time the Daleks have the ability to travel in time, keeping pace with the Doctor, thus kicking off a fan-obsession with Dalek chronology that we're only too happy to pander to. As a result, it's also the first time that aliens turn out to be responsible for well-known historical events. 'Exterminate!' becomes a standard Dalek war-cry here, although they're still alternating with things like 'annihilate!' and 'obliterate!', and for the first (and only) time one of them uses that favourite playground phrase of children trying to look like monsters by sticking their arms out in front of them: 'I am a Dalek.' They also create an "identical" duplicate of one of their enemies, a tactic they're still employing as late as 1984, which means that this is the first story to feature an Evil Double of the Doctor. There'll be another one along in the next season.

Episode three has the first attempt at a pre-credits sequence, at least in the sense that between the cliffhanger reprise and the captions for title and author there's a new scene. It's also the first time we see the TARDIS in flight, in a space-time vortex closely resembling a kaleidoscope image of a galaxy.

But more obviously for anyone watching an episode a week since the start, it's where we say goodbye to Ian and Barbara. They're replaced by conveniently stranded astronaut Steven Taylor, although he only turns up in episode six and doesn't get to do all the usual companion duties yet. In fact Peter Purves becomes the first actor to be credited for playing two different parts in the same story, as he regrettably appears as "funny" Alabama tourist Morton Dill in episode three. (There's a terrible moment when it looks as if Dill's going to wander on board the TARDIS and become the new companion. Even if you know the programme's history, the first time you see it you think it might actually happen.)

The Doctor threatens to kiss a companion for the first time. It's Ian.

Six Things to Notice About "The Chase"…

1. By this stage the production team and the Great British Public have got used to the Daleks, and the decision has been made to use them as the threat in a more light-hearted story than usual. The result is some of the most excruciatingly unfunny comedy schtick ever allowed onto our screens, but also some of the most amusing cock-ups and inept attempts at spectacle since… ahh… "The Web Planet". Only a story like this could encompass Abraham Lincoln, the *Mary Celeste*, Elizabeth I, the Fab Four and Dracula meeting Frankenstein in Africa. This is making the story sound like a jumble of random items strung together haphazardly, as if Terry Nation, Dennis Spooner and Verity Lambert just thought of all the neat-looking things they wanted to try and put

them together without any kind of logic. And so it is. Whereas the similarly piecemeal "The Keys of Marinus" (1.5) had *some* rationale behind it but nothing chasing the regulars to make things seem more urgent, here there are Daleks chasing the regulars and that's all the reason there is.

2. Ian and Barbara have always been audience-identification characters, so it seems logical that they begin this story - in effect - watching telly, and the time-and-space visualiser is openly referred to as a 'time television'. The Doctor has become everyone's dad, tinkering with a gadget in his shed; Vicki is a bored teenager; Barbara is as mumsy as she ever gets; and Ian's reading a book about space-monsters. The visualiser allows them to watch events from the past without having to go there and get involved in lengthy stories with plots and detailed sets, so at last they can do all that tisome "educational" stuff in the first ten minutes and then get on with running around trying to avoid BEMs. Sydney Newman's comments aren't recorded.

3. This story's attempts to give the world The Next Daleks include the Mechanoids (or "Mechonoids"... the script says one thing and the credits another, so we've gone with the credits for episode five, because all the merchandising did). They look great, have voices kids can imitate and give the Daleks a good hiding, but never return. Why? The official reason is that the props were too big for the studio doors, yet that's their great strength. Because they're so clumsy in the Riverside sets, the big scrap at the end is done on film elsewhere, and looks a dozen times better than anything we've seen in the previous five episodes. However, as they only ever speak in what 1960s writers thought was computer-language, they aren't the most menacing of beings. This didn't stop them from cropping up in the *TV21* comic strip, nor did it stop toy manufacturers trying to get in on the act. It is, incidentally, now impossible to hear the Doctor describing the Mechanoid city as 'fantastic' without imagining Christopher Eccleston doing it.

4. You can make your own minds up as to whether Maureen O'Brien really *is* corpsing uncontrollably during the desert scenes in episode one, or whether her character's meant to be hysterical and she's an even better actress than we thought. We'll simply remind readers that in those days retakes were only possible if something *really* unbroadcastable happened, and it looks suspi-

ciously as if she doesn't deliver her lines on cue because she can't believe nobody's shouted "cut" yet. Her manic fit of laughter on seeing a hatch open, a few moments later, is more curious still; if anything, the funny part of the experience comes just after that, when she and Ian enter a creepy underground tunnel (for absolutely no good reason) and the soundtrack decides to try building up the eerie suspense with a comic "boing" noise that sounds like a clown being hit with a big plank.

5. Edmund Warwick has now carved himself a nice little niche pretending to be William Hartnell. In "The Dalek Invasion of Earth" (2.2) he just about passed muster when seen from behind, but as the android duplicate he has to pull it off for a whole episode, walking, talking and gesticulating like the Doctor almost as well as your mum could. Even if she'd never seen a single episode. But if you can tear your eyes away from Warwick's mesmerically bad performance, the episode generates much amusement with the almost Brechtian way it comments on its own artificiality, by allowing us to see studio lights, cameras and even floor technicians. Earlier instalments have given us the trademark Richard Martin use of ambient studio noise - doors opening and closing, the squeak of rubber wheels as props are moved *during a take* and so on. Now he finds a whole new area of audio wrongness by drowning out key lines of dialogue with the music playback in episode four. Because this is the Haunted House sequence, and the music is the worst schlock imaginable, it just compounds the felony.

6. The ending is an amazingly powerful moment. The Doctor is scared that Ian and Barbara will be lost or killed, and is upset that they still want to leave him for their own time after all they've been through together. He covers this with a blistering tirade, featuring a magnificent Billy Fluff (see **Things That Don't Make Sense**), and the sequence of Ian and Barbara's return to London - blissed out in the midst of the city's landmarks, at a time when the capital was an increasingly hip place to be - is justly famous. (Guess what... it's directed by someone else.)

The Continuity

The Doctor Digs the Beatles. But he isn't much of a singer himself, or at least Barbara doesn't think so; the Doctor believes his voice 'could charm the

What's the Dalek Timeline?

The problem with Dalek history is, of course, that they were never supposed to have any. At least, not beyond what we're told in "The Daleks" (1.2), a neat and specifically finite version of their timeline which looks less and less likely with every subsequent story.

"The Daleks" assumes that they never left Skaro. "The Dalek Invasion of Earth" (2.2) assumes that they did, for a bit, but never got very far with it. "The Chase" assumes that they did, for a bit, and that some of their scientists put together a single time machine and went after the Doctor. By the 1980s, they have implied empires spanning whole galaxies and are a menace to everybody who ever lived. By 2005, they're even worse.

But fortunately for all good pedants, there aren't enough details for things to get too contradictory. The majority of Dalek stories have been set in the far future, and those that aren't tend to involve Daleks who are either quite overtly time-travellers or easy to palm off as time-travellers (even if that's not necessarily what the writers thought at the time). This makes the history of the Daleks a lot easier to get a grip on than the history of the Cybermen, who have an annoying habit of turning up in the present day.

So, a simple version of Dalek history immediately presents itself. It goes like this:

The Daleks are created on Skaro by Davros, as seen in "Genesis of the Daleks" (12.4), after a period of war which is probably garbled by later historians (see "The Daleks" for a lot more on this). The two species which emerge from the ashes are the Daleks and the Thals. The Daleks are confined to their city, and run on static electricity from the floor, whereas the Thals just mope around on their farms.

Then the Daleks develop space travel. They begin to explore / threaten other worlds, attaching dish-shaped power-devices to their casings in order to get around the whole "static electricity" problem. It's at this point, removed from the limitations of Skaro and remembering Davros' desire for them to become the-su-preme-be-ings-of-the-u-ni-verse, that they start empire-building. They invade Earth in 2157-ish - probably from an off-world base, as they never mention Skaro in "The Dalek Invasion of Earth" - but Earth pushes them out again ten years later. Meanwhile, on Skaro, the original "city" Daleks keep stagnating. At some point, probably around 2300 if we've done our sums right, the Doctor arrives on Skaro for the events of "The Daleks" and the city-going faction is wiped out.

This barely even registers with the Daleks elsewhere in the galaxy, who go from strength to strength. After the Earth invasion (i.e. after the first two Dalek stories), the Daleks are redesigned; they now have vertical "power slats" around their midriffs. Vicki comes from 2493, and considers the Daleks to be old news, so it seems unlikely that they go near Earth again until they've had time to build up an army for "Frontier in Space" (10.3). The rest is future history.

All well and good. However, there are two flies in the ointment here.

Hitch #1. "Power of the Daleks" (4.3). It's often said that "Power of the Daleks" takes place in 2020 (though this isn't stated anywhere in the story, and therefore isn't definitive), yet it features space-going Daleks who've been buried on the planet Vulcan for hundreds of years. But this really isn't much of a problem. Even if the story's set in the twenty-fifth century rather than the twenty-first, then it'd still mean that there were casually space-going Daleks long before the 2157 invasion of Earth, and there's no evidence anywhere of conquest-obsessed Daleks that early *except for time-travellers.* Not only that, but a Dalek on Vulcan knows of the Doctor and recognises the Second Doctor's face, even though the Doctor *never* encounters the Daleks before the 2160s... again, except for proven time-travellers. 2020 or not, you've still got some very mobile Daleks with an awful lot of foreknowledge. Clearly, the Vulcan Daleks come from the future. (The novel *War of the Daleks*, if you're inclined to consider it, even has the Eighth Doctor consign some Daleks to the past on Vulcan.)

Hitch #2. The very *first* Daleks designed by Davros (in "Genesis of the Daleks") have power slats, and can leave their city at will, happily rolling over any terrain they like. This might suggest that the city-bound Daleks in "The Daleks" have degenerated, and come to depend on the city while the original (superior) Daleks are trying to conquer the universe, except that it doesn't explain the other degenerate Daleks we see in "The Dalek Invasion of Earth" with dishes attached.

On the one hand, this might indicate that there are *two* periods of Dalek expansionism from Skaro. In the first, original vertical-plated Daleks leave the planet and start exploring the cosmos, leaving their kin on the homeworld to stagnate and

continued on page 163...

161

nightingales out of the trees'. He's secretly been working on an anti-Dalek device, just in case of future encounters. [Two meetings with the Daleks are hardly enough to prompt him to take out this kind of insurance. Again, we might conclude that he knew of the Daleks even before his first meeting with them (see 1.2, "The Daleks"), and has worked out that there's a good chance of running into them in other parts of history.]

When Ian and Barbara decide to abandon him after all their adventures together, he's coldly furious, and it takes Vicki's assurance that *she* won't leave him to make him even consider their request to fix the Dalek time machine and get them home. [His fear of being alone will become even more obvious in 3.5, "The Massacre".] He can't bring himself to watch the schoolteachers leave, but monitors their return to Earth on the time-and-space visualiser to make sure they're all right. Here he states that he's been trying to get them home for two years. [Even given that stories like "Marco Polo" (1.4) and "The Romans" (2.4) involve lapses of weeks or even months, there *must* be adventures we never see for this to be true. Which is good news for anyone who's written a First Doctor novel in one of the gaps.]

• *Background*. The Doctor states that the time-path tracker of the TARDIS has been part of the Ship 'since I constructed it'; see **The TARDIS**.

• *Ethics*. He spends half of this story working on his amazing Dalek-killing machine, and he has no compunction about using it. He specifically says that it's a case of them-or-us [recalling what he said in 2.2, "The Dalek Invasion of Earth", about killing in self-defence].

• *Inventory*. He loses yet another jacket here, and the straw hat he wears in deserts [he gets another one in time for 3.4, "The Daleks' Master Plan"]. He's got his pen-torch back, and his original walking-stick.

The Supporting Cast

• *Ian*. Knows the lyrics to "Ticket to Ride". [This has confused many commentators - see **Things That Don't Make Sense** - but it's entirely in character. He dances like a science teacher - as any British schoolchild would be able to tell you - just as the Eccleston Doctor dresses like a social studies teacher having a mid-life crisis and Professor Parry from "The Tomb of the Cybermen" (5.1) is every geography teacher you'll ever meet.] Ian is concussed twice in three hours,

yet he's nevertheless able to balance on a mile-high precipice. He also recalls the precise date of the Gettysburg Address.

• *Barbara*. Now unbelievably bloodthirsty [watch her planning an ambush for the Daleks in episode five and compare it to her behaviour at the start of this book]. It seems that she's planning to stick around on the TARDIS for a while, making Vicki a dress. Even when the Aridians are about to surrender her to the Daleks, she tries to save one of them from a Mire Beast [although admittedly it's quite badly-directed and makes her look as if she's throwing him to it]. She shows more remorse over losing yet another cardigan, though.

And, Barbara believes that travelling with the Doctor will 'probably' turn out to be the most exciting period of her life. *Probably…?*

• *Vicki*. Has started dressing like Barbara. It's revealed, surprisingly late, that she's terrified of heights. As a child, she lived near a castle and used to play in a field nearby, making up stories [the way she describes this suggests that she had friends or siblings]. At some point she's been to a zoo. She's also visited the Beatles Memorial Theatre in Liverpool, yet hasn't heard any of their music and is surprised when it turns out to be 'classical'. [This seems odd, but think how few foreign visitors to Stratford-upon-Avon have even heard of *The Two Noble Kinsmen* or actually bothered sitting through one of Shakespeare's plays. Also, given what we now know about multimedia technology, it may be going too far to assume that the Beatles' recordings are available in their original form by the 2400s. Vicki may know some Beatles songs, but only once they've been sampled, remixed and twisted out of all recognisable shape.]

Her schooling included a primer in Venderman's Law, and she thinks she can help fix the time-and-space visualiser. She can certainly program it without the Doctor's aid. She immediately recognises the 'ancient' New York of 1966, saying that she's seen pictures in history books [q.v. the last story].

• *Steven*. An astronaut from Red Fifty flight, Steven Taylor has been stranded on the planet Mechanus for two years, with only the Mechanoids and his toy panda mascot Hi-Fi for company. Though he seems amiable enough, in a macho astronaut sort of way, he becomes hyperactive when he sees new human faces and doesn't

What's the Dalek Timeline?

...continued from page 161

become city-bound. In the second, the city-bound types re-discover the joys of space-travel and go on to conquer Earth. This makes a kind of sense, but... it's really very clumsy. Especially when you ask yourself: what happened to the original Dalek space-travellers? If they left Skaro centuries before the city-Daleks found a way to escape, then why do we never hear about them until *after* the city-Daleks invade Earth? Why do they vanish for centuries before becoming a threat?

A much more reasonable solution, although not a *perfectly* smooth one, is just to assume it's a question of economy. Davros originally designed the vertical-plate Daleks as soldiers capable of crossing any terrain, since he knew they'd have to fight the war against the Thals beyond the limits of the city. Once the various wars on Skaro had come to a conclusion, the Daleks became incredibly insular, and new Daleks were created to be city-dependant. When the Daleks developed space travel, the first few attacks and invasions were carried out by city-Daleks adapted for outer-space-duty, but before long *all* new Daleks not stationed on Skaro were being built according to Davros' original vertical-plate design. Or, alternatively, recycled city-Daleks may just have been used as "drones" by more advanced space-traveller Daleks. Which would explain why the "Invasion of Earth" specimens are so incompetent, anyway.

Right then, here's the full chronology, start to finish. If you want to argue about any of the datings we've given to these stories, then see these stories' individual entries. But note that we've taken an "Occam's Razor" approach here, and made the minimum possible amount of reckless speculation; we haven't, for example, invented never-before-mentioned events of galactic import or spurious alliances between the Thals, the Draconians and the Chumblies. Those who've read Jean-Marc Lofficier's *Terrestrial Index* will understand why this is important. Oh, and... this timeline assumes that the Doctor only *creates* history, and doesn't *change* it, in "Genesis of the Daleks" (but see **How Badly Does Dalek History Suffer?**, under that story, for other points of view).

Circa 1800 AD: "Genesis of the Daleks" (12.4). On Skaro, a once-nuclear war between the Kaleds and the Thals has degenerated into a seemingly-endless chemical slugging-match. The Thals finally wipe out the Kaleds, but not before Davros creates

the first few Daleks. These Daleks are sealed in, for a bit, but certainly not for the figurative 'thousand years' described by the Doctor. The Thals will later come to scramble this history somewhat...

In-Between. The Thals, scarred by the centuries of war, have begun to mutate back into "perfect" humanoids. Meanwhile the Daleks emerge from their bunker, and start to remove themselves from the planet, possibly because they consider their homeworld to be a lost cause. So at some point they develop space-travel, but their powers of interplanetary conquest are hardly awe-inspiring. Hence...

2167: "The Dalek Invasion of Earth" (2.2). The invasion is a success, though the subsequent plan to turn the Earth into an improbably unwieldy spaceship hints at a species that's still new to the galactic domination business. By now the Daleks have off-world bases, but at this stage there doesn't seem to be an "empire", just a few widespread exploratory forces. Certainly, by 2493 the Daleks are just a footnote in history as far as Earth's concerned.

Circa 2263: "The Daleks" (1.2). The insular, degenerate Daleks back on Skaro are finally defeated, five-hundred years after the end of the last war on the planet. The Daleks off-world probably don't even notice.

2540: "Frontier in Space" (10.3), "Planet of the Daleks" (10.4). Here - for the first time, chronologically speaking - the Daleks become the true interplanetary menace we all know today, but there's no hint of Dalek time-travel as yet. Instead, the off-world Daleks have obviously spent some time building up the biggest possible army on Spiradon, ready to re-conquer 'the solar planets'. It seems that the Daleks have started using Skaro as a base again, as the Thals speak of Daleks somewhere in the vicinity of their homeworld, but the Daleks apparently *aren't* in complete control of it. (So they may have returned to the old city to check out what happened there. If so, then did they see the CCTV footage of the Doctor, Susan, Ian and Barbara?) Ultimately, the Dalek army is put on ice for a few centuries. We're later told that there are 'wars' between the Daleks and humans after this point, so the various off-world Dalek

continued on page 165...

have much of a sense of judgement [this changes as soon as he gets a grip on himself in the next story]. There's some sign that he's a little unbalanced after two years in captivity, as he's prepared to rush back into a burning building to save the panda.

The TARDIS (and Accoutrements)   After each landing, a certain amount of turn-around time is needed before the Ship can take off again, usually twelve minutes. This is to allow the computers to recalibrate and gather power [stories like "The Web Planet" (2.5) also suggest that a power build-up is necessary, though here it seems it's the controls that need to recharge rather than the "engines"]. The Doctor is worried about the Dalek time machine catching up with them in this period [indicating he expects the Daleks to have the capacity to either breach or destroy the TARDIS].

The Doctor believes that the Ship's 'main time mechanism' may take years to properly repair. [Early stories suggest that if the TARDIS leaves in a hurry, then the next journey can't be navigated properly. It's possible that rapid take-offs are having a permanent detrimental effect on the steering mechanism.] He states that the Ship can't land in the same place and time twice [or, more feasibly, the odds are massively against it]. At one stage a "pipping" sound like a '60s electric alarm clock alerts the Doctor to an imminent landing, although later the Ship appears to land while he's at the console and Barbara has to point it out to him. Vicki refers to the 'time rotor' on the console, though she isn't pointing at the central column when she says it.

The console is fitted with a time-path detector, which the Doctor states has been part of the TARDIS since he built it. [This is ambiguously-worded, and could either mean that he built the TARDIS or just the detector. Certainly, the assumption here is that at the very least he equipped the Ship.] This device surveys the time-path the Ship is travelling on, and bloops when another time machine is on the same route [so the Doctor's already aware that there *are* other time vessels... see the next story]. He speaks of the Ship moving along a 'curve' when it's in flight. Also seen here is the bank of lights for the fault locator, but it's changed its appearance somewhat.

Although the Ship is seen drifting through what looks like a kaleidoscopic image of a galaxy, it's stated that the TARDIS can't remain in deep space

because the vacuum outside will leave the crew dead in no time. [Apparently because it drains the air. Sadly we'll be forced to look at this bizarre assertion in more detail under 10.4, "Planet of the Daleks".] Almost as curiously... on finding himself inside a fairground Haunted House exhibit, the Doctor seriously believes that the TARDIS could have landed inside a dark recess of the collective unconscious [not quite so weird a notion after 3.7, "The Celestial Toymaker" and 6.2, "The Mind Robber"]. He's never disabused of this notion, and never learns the truth.

Once again [and for the last time, unless it's seen in any of the later "missing" episodes], the ceiling-mounted unit is visible over the TARDIS console. There are now proper china teacups and saucers on board, and a book entitled *Monsters from Outer Space*, which curiously doesn't have an author's name on the sleeve. Vicki and Barbara chew on guava-flavoured bars from the food machine. The time-and-space visualiser is kept in an anteroom, where there's also a number of drawers containing its cartridges [also taken from Xeros]. The Doctor's home-made anti-Dalek device is a heavy-looking box-shaped thing, which ultimately just blows up one Dalek and starts a fire on Mechanus.

The Doctor gives Ian a 'TARDIS magnet' to help him find the Ship, a small device with a little green light on it. [Compare with the rather chunkier homing devices used from 18.3, "Full Circle", onwards. Presumably Ian takes it with him when he leaves the Doctor's company.]

• *The Time-and-Space Visualiser.* Taken from the Space Museum on Xeros [see the previous story], it's a six-foot-wide disc with a TV monitor at its centre. The Doctor's got it working again, after some fiddling with a screwdriver. When a cartridge is inserted into it and the controls are used, it can display any event in the history of space and time. [Exactly how the machine is programmed remains unclear. The Doctor only seems to have a small number of cartridges, yet the first historical event Ian names is brought up on the screen within moments, and the machine not only shows them Pennsylvania in 1863 but knows it's supposed to be focusing on Abraham Lincoln.]

How does the visualiser work? By converting neutrons of light energy into electrical impulses, in accordance with Venderman's Law, which states that mass is absorbed by light and that therefore everything which has ever happened is recorded

What's the Dalek Timeline?

...continued from page 163

forces take a good trouncing before…

Circa 2700: "Death to the Daleks" (11.3). The Daleks are no longer a major power in this era, although everybody's heard of them, which is why they're trying to blackmail humanity instead of overrunning the galaxy with enormous armies. They know of the Doctor and the TARDIS, presumably having learned of their enemy's time-travelling abilities from the Master. After this they aren't heard of again for some time.

Probably the Fourth Millennium: "The Chase". Obviously the Daleks have noticed that it all started going wrong for them with the invasion of Earth, and know that the First Doctor (if, indeed, they can tell between Doctors at this point) was responsible. Their first act, on finally cracking time-travel, is to get rid of this arch-nemesis. They believe that Susan's still travelling with the Doctor, so evidently they're acting on whatever surveillance data they picked up in "The Daleks" and "The Dalek Invasion of Earth". They even refer to the TARDIS crewmembers as their 'greatest enemies', clearly fearing Barbara's battledress. See **What's Wrong with Dalek History?** under "The Daleks' Master Plan" for more on this period.

And: **"The Day of the Daleks" (9.1).** The Daleks who've taken over twenty-first century Earth in "The Day of the Daleks" are *unquestionably* time-travellers from further ahead in the future, rather than natives of that century, as they recognise the Doctor and speak of invading Earth 'again' (and the 2157 invasion shouldn't have happened yet). This whole story seems to be a paradox resulting from early Dalek experiments with time-travel, but the whole thing's safely removed from history in the end.

The Davros Era Begins: "Destiny of the Daleks" (17.1). By this stage, the Daleks are scattered across large tracts of space and making new allies and enemies well outside Earth's own corner of the universe. Here we're told that for centuries the Daleks have been fighting the Movellans, and Skaro has been abandoned for some time (since the clash with the humans in the twenty-sixth century, we presume), but now they've returned to find the sleeping Davros. Though the four "Davros Era" TV stories are often said to have taken

place somewhere around the 4500s - largely due to a behind-the-scenes document by Eric Saward - there are good reasons for setting it earlier, as you'll see if you read Volume IV.

Ninety Years Later: "Resurrection of the Daleks" (21.4). We're told that by this point, the Movellans have broken the stalemate and decimated much of the Dalek population with a virus. Oh, and Daleks are causally using time-corridor technology now rather than clunky old DARDISes.

A Few Years After That: "Revelation of the Daleks" (22.6). Having escaped both the humans *and* the Daleks, Davros starts producing a new Dalek army. The result - the white "renegade" Dalek faction - instigates what looks increasingly like a Dalek civil war. Davros escapes both human and Dalek clutches *again*, and…

Davros Ascendant: "Remembrance of the Daleks" (25.1). …becomes the first Dalek Emperor. His attempt to go back in time to 1963 and steal the Hand of Omega backfires miserably, apparently destroying Skaro in his own era. If you believe *War of the Daleks* (and it's a big "if", but see under "Destiny of the Daleks" for its possible usefulness as a secondary source), then after this the Daleks get busy with their own plans for galactic conquest. In other words…

4000 AD: "The Daleks' Master Plan" (3.4). Though they've established themselves as a major intergalactic power by now, the Daleks haven't bothered Earth's galaxy for 'some time'. The misuse of the time destructor destroys decades of work, and wipes out the huge Dalek invasion force, yet Skaro itself remains untouched. Those who prefer a dating of c. 4500 AD for "Destiny" might want to switch these dates around a bit, but it doesn't change the outcome, which is…

Not the Final End: "The Evil of the Daleks" (4.9). *Real* Daleks don't have Emperors; they have Supremes and a Supreme Council. Only Davros calls himself "Emperor", and only his Daleks call themselves "Imperial", so the fact that the Daleks in "Evil of the Daleks" take orders from an Emperor - and an Emperor who enjoys gloating over the Doctor in a decidedly un-Dalek way, too - is telling. Arguably, the audio *Terror Firma* supports this

continued on page 167…

on light neutrons somewhere. No, honestly. But when the Daleks start tracking the TARDIS in their own time machine, the visualiser picks up on it and shows the travellers the Daleks' base on Skaro. [Is the Dalek time-vessel causing a kind of "interference" that's picked up by the visualiser? The device seems to tune in as soon as the Dalek craft is ready to leave.]

The visualiser's still operational by the end of events here [and yet it's never even mentioned again].

The Non-Humans

• *The Daleks.* They've changed. All of a sudden they have vertical slats around their midriffs ["power slats" according to such later sources as, Heaven help us, the *Dalek Survival Guide*], and there's no other visible equipment for drawing power from their surroundings. [See **What Do Daleks Eat?** under 4.3, "The Power of the Daleks".] More importantly, though… they've just finished building their own time machine.

The Dalek Supreme is determined to punish the Doctor and friends for their 'crime' against the Daleks, and gives orders to hunt down the TARDIS throughout space and time. Mention is made of the way that the travellers 'delayed' the Dalek conquest of Earth. [We have to assume this is a reference to "The Dalek Invasion of Earth", although it's a weird way of putting things. Surely they didn't eventually succeed in turning the planet into a spaceship?] The Supreme itself is black, and speaks in a higher register than its minions [the inverse is true in the '70s stories].

The Dalek 'time machine' or 'time-craft' [referred to as the "DARDIS" in the script, though thankfully not on-screen] is a featureless cabinet that's bigger on the inside than on the outside. Within, it's decorated with rotating op-art discs, one of which is a scanner. [It shows the same howlround patterns which appeared on the TARDIS screen in 1.1, "An Unearthly Child". This could indicate that the DARDIS moves through the same vortex as the TARDIS, though to be honest these patterns were seen on Dalek monitors even on Skaro.] There's a pillar in the middle of the control room with the familiar Dalek dials [as always, the idea is that the Daleks only have a restricted view so their displays are made to match], and inside its central glass cylinder is a rotating disc with a ball on a pole [we might note a certain crude similarity to the 'time vortex mag-

natron' in 9.1, "Day of the Daleks"]. There's a lift to convey the Dalek crewmembers to and from an upper level, and mention is made of a cell renovator chamber somewhere on the vessel [so maybe *that's* what's powering them]. There's also a communications array, which even Vicki is capable of using.

The Daleks have no trouble tracking the TARDIS, in much the same way that the TARDIS has no trouble monitoring the Daleks during "flight". It's said that 'movement detectors' on Skaro are used to locate the Doctor's vessel, which they refer to simply as 'TARDIS' [suggesting that, at this point, they only know of *one* TARDIS and thus don't know much of the Doctor's people]. The Daleks appear to cut down the Doctor's lead with every landing [so their turn-around time isn't as great as his?]. They also like chanting the word 'TARDIS' in different registers, and refer to the Daleks who pursue the Doctor as an 'assassination group'.

Here the Daleks employ an alternative peripheral to the usual sucker-arm: a 'seismic detector', also referred to as a 'perceptor'. This is a hemispherical device mounted on gimbles, and it can be used to find the TARDIS in the middle of a desert, or sense nearby movement, or scan architecture [or anything else the plot requires]. They also have an 'electrode unit' which can be attached to one of the Daleks' sucker-arms, a large spinning disc that serves no immediately obvious purpose. Actually, there's more variation in Daleks here than anyone's used to seeing. One of the crew is clearly a bit slower than the others; he says 'erm' when doing hard sums like converting 'Dalekian scale' into Earth minutes, and gets shouted at by the commander a lot. The Daleks refer to their usual guns as 'neutralisers', and the weapons are incapable of damaging the TARDIS.

After being seized by the fungoids on Mechanus, one Dalek asks 'have I sustained damage?' [as if they think of their shells as being part of themselves, not really indicated by earlier stories]. When a Dalek is seen to rise out of the desert sands on Aridius, it makes grunting, gasping noises as though it's a physical effort. [The implication of this scene is that the "hover" facility demonstrated in more recent Dalek stories has always been present. That said, a Dalek gets electrocuted by contact with the floor in 11.3, "Death to the Daleks"; this suggests, along with other evidence, that the Daleks seen in "Death" are from an earli-

What's the Dalek Timeline?

...continued from page 165

notion by having Davros' personality erased and replaced with that of an Emperor Dalek. As "The Evil of the Daleks" *has* to be set after "Remembrance" from the Daleks' point of view (even if, confusingly, it seems to be set on the destroyed planet of Skaro... there are at least three explanations for this, but the Daleks in question are time-travellers, so they could have set up their base on prehistoric Skaro circa 1,000,000 BC for all we know), it seems to suggest that ultimately Davros and his renegade Daleks make a comeback.

Yet the Daleks here are the usual grey, not white, so did the Davros-Emperor end up in charge of the dominant faction? Either way, the new civil war which grips Skaro at the end of this story certainly isn't the 'final end' described by the Doctor. There are Daleks scattered throughout space and time by now, so how *could* it be? For a start...

The Straggler: "The Power of the Daleks" (4.3). Blatantly involves time travel, for reasons we've already discussed, although we'll suggest a cartload of alternatives in Volume II. If the Dalek scout on Vulcan in 2020-or-whenever comes from a time after "The Evil of the Daleks", then it'd explain how it already has the Second Doctor in its databanks. What's happening to the Daleks back on Skaro, or on whatever planet they're using as a base now, is a mystery. But the Emperor (or *an* Emperor) must re-build the Dalek nation, since...

The Great Time War: "Dalek" (X1.6), "Bad Wolf" (X1.12), "The Parting of the Ways" (X1.13). At some unspecified point towards the end of the saga, the Daleks destroy the Doctor's people and are (seemingly) wiped out in turn. They also go mad and get religion. However, that's a story for another day.

Here we might also mention that at some point, the Daleks try the Master on Skaro and sentence him to an execution which turns him into a squashy morphing worm by mistake (27.0, the TV Movie, although the novel *The Eight Doctors* tries to provide an explanation for this). But we have no way of knowing when in history this might be, or at what point the Daleks decided to develop a judicial system. We might also refer the reader to the unseen Dalek attacks referred to in "Genesis", one of which took place in the space-year 17,000 (whenever that is) and the other of which saw the Dalek attack force being repelled by the Earth's magnetic field in 2000 (which is just stupid, and apparently a massive scrambling of "The Dalek Invasion of Earth").

---

er period than these. See **What's the Dalek Timeline?** for much, much more.] But, yes, the Daleks are seemingly unable to climb the stairs in the Haunted House.

On board the time machine is 'the reproducer', a cabinet linked to a computer that's programmed with photo images and relevant data about the TARDIS crew. When activated, it takes no time at all to create a 'humanoid', a robot replica of the Doctor. The Daleks believe it to be indistinguishable from the real thing. [See also 17.1, "Destiny of the Daleks", particularly the theory that the Daleks originally created the Movellans and seriously believed them to be lifelike human beings.] The humanoid has been programmed with all the information the Daleks have on the Doctor, so they obviously think Susan is still on board the TARDIS, as the robot refers to Vicki by her name. The Doctor defeats the duplicate in hand-to-hand combat by reaching into its clothes and ripping wires out of its front.

The Daleks have detailed knowledge of other planets, including Aridius and Mechanus, but Skaro has to be consulted for this data. At one point the commander of the time machine gives the command 'order executioner to prepare to disembark', though the meaning of this is unclear. [It sounds as if "executioner" might be the name of the time machine, but by this point the vessel is already in flight. However, shortly afterwards a single Dalek is sent outside to explore, so "executioner" may just be the title given to the underlings of the assassination unit. This is echoed in the title of episode one.] Told that the travellers are to be exterminated rather than taken alive, one of the Daleks says 'good!' as if it really gets a kick out of this sort of thing.

• *The Mechanoids.* Self-repairing service robots created by humans, and the guardians of the planet Mechanus, funnily enough. The Mechanoids are about the same height as the Daleks and roughly spherical in shape, though the surface of each Mechanoid is covered in a pattern of inter-locking triangles [in other words, they look like Telstar]. They have no faces, no human features, just an antenna-like extension on the top and a pair of rather clumsy-looking pincers. They flap these pincers while trying to pass each other in corridors, as if indicating. They're also equipped with flame-throwers [for clearing the jungle out-side, presumably], and the big Dalek vs. Mechanoid clash ends in something of a no-score-draw, since the city is turned into an inferno. [In the *TV21* comic-strip, the Mechanoids will become the Daleks' arch-enemies in a series of interplanetary conflicts. It's a nice thought, but it doesn't seem very likely based on what we see here.]

It was the Mechanoids who built the settlement on Mechanus, having been sent to establish a colony before the arrival of humans. However, the humans never arrived - see **History** - and without knowing the Mechanoids' code, any human trav-ellers are imprisoned by these rather unimagini-tive machines. In fact the Mechanoids aren't great at communicating at all, although they're at least capable of croaking semi-comprehensible phrases in what they explicitly describe as English. Their language [the 'code' Steven describes] is a func-tional mixture of words and numbers.

Planet Notes

• *Aridius*. It used to be an aquatic world, but now it's a desert, as its twin suns have been getting closer and closer for the traditional period of 'a thousand years'. [Was it called "Aridius" when it was covered in water? Perhaps the locals re-branded. Likewise, it's not clear whether "Xeros" was called that before the Moroks made it all dry and lifeless.] Though sunbathing for short periods seems pleasant, all life has withdrawn to the sub-terranean tunnels that used to lie beneath the ocean floor. Oddly-shaped tree-trunks are the only visible landmarks, though sandstorms can cover any given area in minutes. The gravity is slightly greater than Earth's.

The Aridians are still amphibian, with crests and spines on their heads, silvery skins marked with patterns of dots, and a reluctance to expose themselves to sunlight. They accept death as a random, everyday occurrence and are civil to out-siders, but are prepared to make deals with the Daleks to avoid fatalities. Not much of Aridian culture has survived, as only the half-ruined tun-

nels of the 'city' are seen here, and there's no sig-nificant technology even if they accept the idea of time-and-space travel without question. The city is buried beneath the Saccaro Desert, or at least that's what the Daleks call it [unless "Saccaro" is an untranslatable Dalek adjective, it seems that they have detailed maps of Aridius on Skaro].

The Aridians speak… haltingly, and make slow gestures. The never-seen elders of the city decide on all matters, including civil defence; walling up tunnels, blowing up the airlocks that lead to the surface and dealing with aliens. The locals are also prey to the Mire Beasts - large, rubbery, octopus-like creatures with frog-like eyes - which eat any-body they can grapple. As the only survivors of Aridius other than the Aridians, the Beasts used to live in the slime at the ocean bottom, but breed quickly and have started taking over the cities. The Aridians have been destroying the airlocks in an attempt to entomb them.

• *Mechanus*. Oh look, it's a jungle world. This one has marshes, and mainly seems to be covered in hostile vegetation. Chief among the malignant species are the fungoids, predatory but slow-mov-ing plants that look something like giant mush-rooms. Even Daleks are fair game, though the fun-goids retreat when bright lights are shone at them. [See "Planet of the Daleks", for more fun with fun-goids from the same author. Startlingly, the script of "The Chase" refers to them as "Gubbage Cones", which is perhaps supposed to be their "official" name as "fungoids" is just an off-the-cuff description from Ian.]

But above the tree-line on Mechanus is a great gleaming city on stilts, 1,500 feet above ground level, constructed and maintained by the Mechanoids. Built as a colony for human use, instead it's become a "zoo" for studying captured travellers, though Steven Taylor is apparently the only prisoner there when the Doctor and compa-ny arrive. Which is lucky, because the city burns during the clash with the Daleks.

History

• *Dating*. Taking this one bit at a time…

- *Aridius*. No date specified. [However, the space-and-time visualiser - which can only pick up images of things that happened in the past, even if it's the very recent past - homes in on the Dalek time machine as it prepares to pursue the Doctor. See **What's the Dalek Timeline?**, but we might make a stab that it's around 3900 AD.]

- *The Haunted House*. The Festival of Ghana was due to take place in 1996, according to the blurb at the entrance to the Frankenstein's House of Horrors exhibit. But either the Festival or just the exhibit was cancelled by Peking. [China controls Ghana by this point? Or is it putting political pressure on Africa some other way?] Admission price: $10. There are impressively mobile robots of Dracula, Frankenstein's Monster and a Grey Lady in the exhibit, which are capable of taking out Daleks. [Robotics are clearly more advanced in *this* 1990s than in the one we actually lived through, but if the software is prone to making the robots try to kill passers-by, then it's no wonder the event was cancelled. However, the robots only attack the Daleks after being shot with Dalek weapons, so perhaps they go haywire from the damage.] One ghost-like apparition looks something like a hologram.

- *New York*. Morton Dill visits New York in 1966, even though he seems to be a fugitive from the 1930s. The Empire State Building is said to be the tallest building in the world at this point.

- *The Mary Celeste*. Abandoned due to Daleks, it seems. [According to the ship's logs in the "real" world, it was abandoned on the 25th of November, 1872.]

- *London*. Ian and Barbara arrive back home in 1965. [It's not clear whether the Doctor sets the Dalek time machine for 1965, two years after they left, or whether it's just not very precise when the Doctor's programming it.] The machine is set to self-destruct after its arrival there, and explodes in a shed near a London Underground station. In the same year, the Beatles play "Ticket to Ride" on BBC1.

- *Mechanus*. Some time in Earth's colonial future. [Steven is from a spacegoing culture and isn't surprised by Daleks, but doesn't have the same level of basic education as Vicki. This might suggest a date between 2200 and 2400. In "The Daleks' Master Plan", Steven claims he's from 'thousands of years' before the year 4000 AD, so we certainly seem to be talking about the first half of the third millennium. Still, there are distinct contradictions in what we learn about him later, as we'll see in Season Three.]

About fifty years ago, Earth decided to colonise Mechanus and sent a rocket-ship full of robots to prepare the way for the settlers. The Mechanoids built the city, but Earth got involved in interplanetary wars, and the planet was all but forgotten. Steven Taylor's flight, Red Fifty, crashed on Mechanus two years ago. The wars were still going on at this point, though there's no indication that Steven was directly involved. [There's no other story that definitively describes a war in the 2200 to 2400 period, but it's the age of early colonial expansion, so there must have been *some* trouble. At a stretch it could be the same war mentioned in 24.2, "Paradise Towers". Again, see also "The Daleks' Master Plan".]

In other news... the time-and-space visualiser shows Abraham Lincoln delivering the Gettysburg Address on the 19th of November, 1863, and it's much as anyone might have expected. It also shows William Shakespeare being addressed by Elizabeth I, who asks him to write a play on Falstaff in love, despite some controversy about the character being based on Sir John Oldcastle. Shakespeare then proceeds to nick the idea for *Hamlet* from Sir Francis Bacon, after telling Bacon that it isn't his style. [We'll call it 1596, but the scene's full of historical glitches. In "City of Death" (17.2) the Doctor claims to have been around when Shakespeare wrote Hamlet, though here he doesn't take the opportunity to name-drop in front of Ian and Barbara, so it's probably safe to say that he hasn't been there and done that yet.]

According to Vicki, scientists were working on something like the time-and-space visualiser when she left Earth, and there's a Beatles Memorial Theatre in Liverpool in her own time. She also states that New York was destroyed in the Dalek invasion [of 2157, or thereabouts].

The Analysis

Where Does This Come From? As we've already seen, one of the most important things to bear in mind is that the series was made to be watched at the time of first transmission and never again. Anyone seeing any given episode more than a month after it was made was living overseas, not at home in Britain. While the export of the series was a useful source of revenue for the BBC, it wasn't the reason for *Doctor Who*'s existence. In fact, not only was Newman upset that the dark, gloomy stories which looked so good to British viewers copied badly, but it's frequently reported that the series' format was thought more exportable than recordings of actual episodes. We'll return to this in Volume II.

So Terry Nation's list of half-developed ideas and "wouldn't it be fun if..." suggestions suited the format of the series as Lambert was making it, one week at a time. Although the individual stories were deemed good enough to be sold abroad, and two from this year made it into print as novels, *Doctor Who* was immediate, episodic and disposable. "The Chase" admits this, and embraces it.

Like all "pop" programmes (and this designation has more to do with pop art than the music), *Doctor Who* in its second year accepts that the present day is the most exciting thing that can possibly be conceived of or experienced. Shakespeare and Lincoln are on a par with the Beatles, and this is confirmed by a girl from five-hundred years in the future. London in 1965 has to be shown as somehow more glamorous than alien planets. The next story will feature contemporary consumer durables, watches and toasters as the best available to a time-traveller. It may seem a small point, but when the Mechanoids arrive we hear an electric guitar in the soundtrack. Somehow, in any other story up until now it would have sounded wrong, too rooted in the year of broadcast.

More importantly, it acknowledges that the Daleks are now the programme's bread-and-butter, and makes them a suitably powerful threat for the all-conquering Doctor. By giving them a steerable time-vessel, the story gives the monsters the upper hand. Then it makes them fallible and comic. This decision, usually seen as a mistake, is part of the story's whole point; to ring the changes on the format before it settles into a formula. Everything in this story is self-consciously something we've not seen before. We've already mentioned that it differs from the previous portmanteau story, "The Keys of Marinus" (1.5), in having a threat close behind. Like including Shakespeare and the Beatles, it's a brilliantly obvious idea. More importantly, it gives Ian and Barbara a happy ending without losing the basic premise of the series.

We're in danger these days of losing sight of something significant. *Doctor Who* is a potent idea because it makes home important by its absence. All the time-travellers are cut off from their pasts. However cosy the start of the story makes it seem, the TARDIS is only a substitute home. Today, when the film version of *The Hitch-Hiker's Guide to the Galaxy* ends with Arthur Dent voluntarily leaving his nice little cottage, and when Rose Tyler can 'phone her mum from the year five-billion or pop back at any stage for shepherd's pie, this element of space-time travel - exile - is almost forgotten. "The Chase" has its cake and eats it, by making

London in 1965 both the most important thing ever and one of billions of possibilities. Ian and Barbara get back there, but the TARDIS can't.

A couple of smaller points to mention. The Festival of Ghana was less implausible to 1965 viewers than it seems now. Ghana, under Nkrumah, was the darling of the West; a progressive nation with a willingness to open its resources to international industries. The whole business ended messily, but for a while it looked as if Africa might have one real success story that didn't have covert military support from one side or the other in the Cold War. Except that here, the country seems to be under the influence of Peking. It's not the first time Red China has lurked around the edges of *Doctor Who*. The idea of China controlling large chunks of Africa by the 1990s is difficult to reconcile with anything we hear about the world in any other "future" story, but it does hint at some very '60s suspicions. It's the virile, aggressive-looking Orient that presents a threat, not the Soviet Union, which had seemed rather less threatening under Khrushchev than it had under Stalin. The world had already seen the Cold War spread to Asia, and it *would* make a battlefield of Africa, though the Chinese were hardly likely to be on the frontline.

The other point which younger readers might not immediately grasp is that the generation which made this story believed in America as a concept, even if certain aspects of the society were looking increasingly questionable. The British version of America was based on very selective data, and what we liked wasn't necessarily what Americans would have recognised as their culture; the Beatles and the Rolling Stones picked up on US recordings that one American in a hundred might have heard. Amazingly, the whole Morton Dill sequence is what we thought America was like. So, as we've already seen, is Millennius in "The Keys of Marinus".

Things That Don't Make Sense Anything the Mechanoids say. The first line needs three or four listens before you realise that it's 'eight... hundred... thirty... Mechanoid' (what???) and not 'unhand that dirty mucker now'. It's apt, however, that one of them seems to respond to the limp detonation of the Doctor's anti-Dalek device with a cry of 'crap'. And that's humanity's idea of a servo-robot, is it? An impractically large and clumsy ball of metal that shuffles along very, very slowly and has no obvious functions except for building corridors that are flagrantly too small for it. Wouldn't something smaller / nippier / more versatile have been preferable?

The time-and-space visualiser, quite aside from the explanation given being bollocks, has a logical flaw. It can only tune in on things that happened in the past. If the TARDIS is in flight, as it is when the visualiser is used for the first time, then there can't be any way to receive the 'neutrons' of light. [At this point the word "vortex" hasn't yet been used, and it's assumed that the TARDIS just floats through space when it moves, although ironically this is the story which - at least visually - starts to challenge that idea.] We might add that even if you can swallow the idea of pictures being imprinted on light-particles, we can hear the events depicted on the screen, so what's the soundtrack imprinted on? And unless the Doctor's working the controls in a way we never see, the device not only has the wit to home in on famous figures from Earth history but the skill to track them just like a BBC cameraman would. [The cartridges must be pre-programmed with a shooting script.]

The Empire State Building has hired an amnesiac Columbo impersonator as its guide, despite the apparent popularity of the tour. Plus, there seem to be taller buildings nearby. Precisely what part of Alabama is Morton Dill supposed to be from? And why don't the Daleks kill the idiot, just on principle? More bizarrely, Ian and Barbara are in New York, 1966, and *they go back into the TARDIS and leave.* They get so excited about the Dalek time machine three episodes later that this makes even less sense than it would in any other story. Getting to Coal Hill School from New York would be a doddle for people who've rowed a trireme or flown a spaceship. Presumably they don't want to abandon the Doctor and Vicki in mid-crisis, but surely, someone should at least mention the possibility?

Episode four requires the travellers to believe that they might be in a real Haunted House, which means that all four of them have to be ignorant of the existence of fairgrounds. And only Hartnell could land in Africa and meet white folks. But even if the creatures in the Haunted House are animatronic robots gone bad... did nobody think of switching the buggers off when the exhibit was closed? With all respect to actor Malcolm Rogers, we also have to ask why the monsters' creators decided to make Dracula look

like *that*. The Doctor's suggestion that they've actually entered a world of dreams, because the House is exactly what you'd expect from a nightmare, indicates a *very* limited understanding of human psychology on his part; his subsequent belief that the Daleks won't be able to follow them into this realm of the human mind, when *he* can exist there, indicates something of a shortfall of logic. However, the real Thing That Doesn't Make Sense here is that Terry Nation gives us a quite interesting explanation for what's happening - that the Haunted House is generated by the secret beliefs of millions of people - and then "surprises" us with an embarrassing one about robots.

Episode five is called "The Death of Doctor Who", as if trying to fool us into believing that something unthinkable is going to happen. This title is given to us *after* we find out there's going to be a robot Doctor Who mooching around the place. Can you guess how this is going to end, boys and girls? Why the Daleks even bother making a duplicate is a mystery, since their problem is just one of catching up with the travellers, not "infiltrating" them. If they're so convinced that the robot will be better at finding the humans than they are, then why don't they just strap a bomb to it? And when the Doctor and the Evil Doctor finally come face-to-face, they *both* simultaneously decide to stop acting like the Doctor and behave in a massively out-of-character way, just to make it harder for the companions to tell which is which.

Check out the exchange between Barbara and Ian, on seeing the swamps of Mechanus for the first time. Barbara: 'Just look at that vegetation!' Ian, in his "ominous" voice: 'Yes... just as though it were alive!' Well, yes, a lot of vegetation *does* tend to be alive in jungles. Ian later refers to one of the fungus-creatures as a 'living fungoid', as if he's used to poking dead ones. Not for the last time in a Nation script, "living" seems to mean "capable of walking". Still, Vicki's reaction to the place is even odder. She miraculously escapes from the fungoids, then - when another one fails to apprehend her - emits a loud yell and collapses unconscious.

Not only is one of the Daleks so monumentally stupid that it makes a suicidal charge across the deck of the *Mary Celeste* in order to topple overboard, but its top half separates from its bottom before it hits the water. In other words, Daleks come apart when they're pushed over. Nice design feature. If that doesn't make them seem unimpressive enough, then consider this: Dalek guns can kill heavily-armed service robots that were designed for taming hostile alien planets, but have no effect on twentieth-century fairground exhibits. Eh?

A problem that's raised by many, many *Doctor Who* stories down the line, but this is the first one in which someone other than the Doctor has a time machine, so it's worth mentioning here: How is it possible for one time machine to "chase" another through history? If the Daleks know the Doctor is on Aridius (presumably in another era to their "present", unless the chase only begins at this point because the TARDIS lands in their own time), then why can't they materialise on Aridius at exactly the same time *he* does, or even beforehand? How is it possible for the TARDIS to have a "head start"? The idea seems to be that there's a definite "now" when a time machine is in flight, which is ridiculous, unless the Doctor's people specifically rigged up the space-time vortex to make sure things are always nice and linear. [See also the essay under 22.3, "The Mark of the Rani".] Still, here we're asked to take it as read that the Dalek time machine has less of a turn-around time than the TARDIS, and that the gap between the Doctor landing and the Daleks landing gets shorter with every materialisation. Except that it visibly doesn't. Nor does it seem terribly feasible that the threat to the Doctor is removed as soon as he blows up their experimental time-craft, given the Daleks' knack for mass-production.

Oh, all right, we'll say it. Ian and Barbara left in 1963, yet apparently Ian knows a Beatles song not written until 1965, at least well enough to mime along with the chorus. [Susan probably had it on her iPod.]

A round of applause, please, for the greatest ever Billy Fluff: 'You'll end up as a couple of burned cinders flying around in Spain… in space!'

Critique   So there's a family in Britain in May 1965, in their front room watching *Doctor Who*. They see a sort-of family watching a sort-of telly in their sort-of front room. Does our family keep watching? Well, yes. If the point of *Doctor Who* is to give the public what they want in a way they've not seen before, then episode one delivers. The problem comes when they try to keep it up for the next five weeks.

Case in point: episode three. No, not Morton

sodding Dill, the next bit. All the stuff about the sailing ship is fine, if a bit slow. Then when the ship is abandoned, we have a long, long tracking shot. Then another one, cross-faded from the first. Finally, we get a glimpse of the plate with the ship's name on it, and - good God, who would have thought it? - it's the *Mary Celeste*. What japes. All of these protracted tracking shots *might* have been worth doing if the pay-off weren't then done *all over again* aboard the TARDIS in dialogue. One or the other would be tolerable, if a bit too obvious. Both together shows a lack of thought as to how the viewers are watching this programme.

What comes across again and again is a contempt for the viewers, a sense of "that'll do". The Daleks and Mechanoids are destroyed by the Doctor's device going off, almost as impressively as a whoopee cushion. The last episode features a shot of a half-mad astronaut being suffocated by a giant mushroom while clutching a stuffed panda, and it's about the most entertaining thing on offer. Even the music is a perfunctory mess. There's a sort of logic to doing fake Gershwin for New York (as Dudley Simpson would do again for 17.2, "City of Death", in both cases overtly echoing *An American in Paris*), but not for the space-time vortex. In his defence, Simpson was a last-minute replacement for Max Harris, and seems to be trying to write in Harris' style. This just begs the question… why did Martin think Harris was the right composer for this kind of story?

The bigger question, of course, is what kind of story this was supposed to be and why Martin was given it. If there's one story in this year that was exactly right for his strengths as a director, then it's "The Space Museum". But because he'd had a go at "The Web Planet" and it had spiralled out of control, "The Space Museum" ended up as the Pinfield cheapie of the block. And the truth is that for the best part of six episodes, here Martin seems hopelessly out of his depth.

The Facts

Written by Terry Nation. Directed by Richard Martin. Ratings 10.0 million, 9.5 million, 9.0 million, 9.5 million, 9.0 million, 9.5 million.

Supporting Cast Peter Purves (Morton Dill), Edmund Warwick (Robot Dr. Who), Robert Marsden (Abraham Lincoln), Vivienne Bennet (Queen Elizabeth I), Roger Hammond (Francis

Bacon), Hugh Walters (William Shakespeare), Jack Pitt (Mire Beast), Ian Thompson (Malsan), Hywel Bennett (Rynian), Al Raymond (Prondyn), Arne Gordon (Guide), Dennis Chinnery (Albert C. Richardson), David Blake Kelly (Capt. Benjamin Briggs), Douglas Ditta (Willoughby), John Maxim (Frankenstein), Malcolm Rogers (Count Dracula), Roslyn de Winter (Grey Lady), David Graham (Mechanoid Voice); Peter Hawkins, David Graham (Dalek Voices).

Episode Titles "The Executioners", "The Death of Time", "Flight Through Eternity", "Journey into Terror", "The Death of Doctor Who", "The Planet of Decision".

Working Titles "The Pursuers".

Cliffhangers A grunting, coughing Dalek rises from the sands of Aridius; though the Doctor gets away from Aridius, the Daleks remaining on the planet reiterate that he's to be pursued and exterminated, in case you hadn't got it yet; the TARDIS tumbles through the kaleidoscope of space and time, with the Dalek vessel close behind; the newly-activated replica of the Doctor tells his Dalek masters that his mission is to infiltrate and kill; a Mechanoid bids the travellers to follow it into the city, as the Daleks close in on them.

The Lore

• In the first episode, a lengthy delay occurred when an effects prop failed to arrive. Nobody seems to know what it was supposed to be (the DARDIS model is a likely contender), but the episode appears rushed even without it.

• The Dalek rising from the sand was supposed to be done on location. They spent ages burying one, only to find that the weight of the sand was too much for the Land Rover pulling it. They used a model instead. Could you tell?

• It's unclear when and where the inserts of Lincoln and Shakespeare were made. It's probable that they were done at Ealing on film, along with the *Mary Celeste* water-jumping and the Dalek-Mechanoid punch-up. But as the latter is so complex and laboriously filmed, and as the former requires... well... water, doing all of this *and* the costume drama would perhaps have been a tall order. Moreover, and this is pure supposition, the sets for episode one include a TARDIS without the console, a bit of sand for the Doctor and Barbara,

a bit more sand with a door in it for Ian and Vicki and... that's it. Why remove the console, if the rest of that week's recording was on such a small scale? It would have been possible to set up the flat for the Gettysburg Address (it may even be back-projection) and a few oak-panels for Shakespeare in the studio.

• As mentioned above, the budget for episode one was a shade over £6,000. The newly-agreed average cost was £2,500, a raise from the previous year. First episodes were usually the most costly, so later episodes of a given story saved cash by re-using sets, costumes and so on. This meant that the longer a story was, the cheaper each part became. We'll see this principle in full effect in the late 1960s, when inflation bites harder. But with public enthusiasm usually sparked by the *start* of a new adventure, the compromise was reached that most stories would have four parts, unless the Daleks were involved. So six weeks' budget for a Dalek story, with the Daleks and their trappings taken mainly from stock, meant that these big-budget shows could have more spectacular things in them. The Daleks were good "box office", and the merchandising alone made their regular appearance a duty for the BBC. In a given year, a quarter of the screen-time was Dalek-orientated.

• Terry Nation, who was beginning to resent this encroaching on the time he wanted to devote to other projects, submitted scripts increasingly like shopping-lists of fun things to do. His proposal for "The Chase", which he referred to as a "snow-job", was clearly intended to test what he could get away with. The answer was almost anything. Lambert's only real objection was the Haunted House and the horror-movie characters; when she commented, Nation agreed to put something else in the finished script, but then back it came with Frankenstein's Monster, Count Dracula and all. Lambert was also slightly concerned about the logistics of the Mire Beast and the potentially repellent Aridians.

• Peter Purves had auditioned to play a Menoptra in "The Web Planet". Richard Martin remembered him, and offered him the part of Morton Dill. According to Jessica Carney's biography of Hartnell (her grandfather), it was Hartnell and O'Brien who suggested that Purves should be retained as the new juvenile lead. Purves was mainly a dancer, and took the part at least partly to learn the craft of TV acting from the veteran Hartnell.

• It's not Russell and O'Brien running around

Camber Sands but David Newman (about whom we know little) and Barbara Joss. She'd been Nemini the woodlouse-martyr in "The Web Planet". They also filmed a studio shot of Ian and Vicki caught in an exploding tunnel for episode two, and you can see the difference in Vicki's hairstyle; O'Brien's got hers in bunches.

• The Beatles were keen to make a guest appearance. The band had been regulars at the Riverside studio, but their timetable and that of the *Doctor Who* team never quite meshed (although there are photos of John Lennon apparently asking a Dalek for an autograph). The original script was about the fiftieth anniversary of their TV debut, a concert in 2012, and the Beatles were to have been made up as old men. Later drafts said that it was 1994, and that they were appearing on 3D BBC TV in colour. Some reports have hinted that their manager, Brian Epstein, vetoed this for his own reasons, but quite simply it was a logistical non-starter. On the day that pre-filming for episode one took place - the 12th of April, 1965 - the boys were seven weeks into filming *Help!* and needed to come up with a song to fit the film's new title. Tuesday the 13th saw them back at Abbey Road to record "Help!", which had been rush-written that weekend.

Plan B was to use a clip of the Beatles on *Top of the Pops,* but the *Doctor Who* production team discovered that each edition was wiped after broadcast. Only six exist for the whole of the 1960s, and even these are fragmentary. Plan C was for the Beatles to come into Riverside (Saturday the 10th of April, so pretty close to the wire), and make a clip for *TotP,* one minute of which was transferred onto VT for special use in *Doctor Who.*

• The uncertainty over Ian and Barbara's future meant that plans for future stories were in flux. Roger the astronaut (who became Michael the astronaut, then Steven Taylor) was a possible replacement, and Vicki was likely to be around for a few more stories, but any scripts requiring known regulars were kept to one side. This meant that the ideas and the gimmicks were emphasised over the characters. Spooner had notionally agreed to a story about Erik the Red from John Lucarotti, and Tosh was considering ideas from William Emms ("Doctor Who and the Chumbleys"... see 3.1, "Galaxy Four") and Robert Holmes ("The Space Trap", which ultimately became 6.4, "The Krotons"). The change of story editor meant that Malcolm Hulke could have

another go at submitting "The Hidden Planet", so Brian Hayles' first effort - also about an Earth-like world on the other side of the sun - was rejected for being too close to the Hulke scenario.

• The Grey Lady in the abandoned funfair wasn't scripted, but given to Roslyn de Winter by Richard Martin as a thankyou for her work on Insect Movement in "The Web Planet". No, don't say a word. Neither she nor Martin worked on the series after this.

• The film / still photo sequence of Ian and Barbara in London was made by Douglas Camfield during rehearsals for episode three, but technically it was part of the pre-filming for 2.9, "The Time Meddler" (hence that story's designer, Barry Newbery, being involved instead of Ray Cusick). This marks the last time Camfield had anything to do with composer Dudley Simpson, following an argument during the making of "The Crusade". Note also that Camfield gave a speaking role to Derek Ware, as the bus conductor. The Douggie Camfield Repertory Company is now almost complete.

2.9: "The Time Meddler"

(Serial S, Four Episodes, 3rd - 24th July 1965.)

Which One is This?　It's the Battle of Hastings, 1066, and someone with a dodgy habit is threatening to give bazookas to the Vikings. And it turns out that he's got a… no… surely, it *can't* be?

Firsts and Lasts　Guess what? It turns out the Doctor isn't unique, and nor is his Ship. Here we meet another one of his people for the first time (all right, apart from Susan), and get to explore another TARDIS, finally suggesting that the Doctor had a lot less to do with the construction of his own vessel than we might have expected. Which means - and you can't overstate the importance of this - that the Monk is the Doctor's first real "arch-enemy". Since we're in an era where we can still have comedy romps like "The Romans", and where the Doctor is an old bloke who giggles hysterically, a blundering *Carry On* star is a much better sort of arch-enemy than someone who wants to conquer the universe every couple of months. This is also the first full story of a strand that'll one day be called the "pseudo-historical", with a historical setting but a non-contemporaneous enemy who wants to mess around with known events.

For the first time, someone with advanced knowledge claims to have put ideas in the head of Leonardo da Vinci. And it's not the Doctor.

Four Things to Notice About "The Time Meddler"...

1. Even moreso than "The Chase", this story is up-front about being made for people watching in 1965. The Monk refers to the Doctor's TARDIS as looking like a 'modern' police box, and all his consumer goods are contemporary (watches, toasters, binoculars), so '60s hardware is seen as proof that something's gone wrong with eleventh-century history. Only the Monk's gramophone is old-fashioned, and *that* was a tape recorder in the script.

2. On top of this, it's flagrant about being made for television. No effort is made to make the studio set look like location work, and the stock footage is just as brazen as it is in "The Romans". The Monk makes jokes with the Doctor about Shakespeare writing for television, in a scene that might almost have had one or both of them winking at the camera. Charmingly, the Monk writes his none-too-complex plan for changing history on a big signboard in his hideout, just so he can share it with the audience. Most blatant of all is the Doctor's explanation of the controls for the TARDIS, including a 'horizontal hold'. (Those reading this book who've grown up unable to adjust the picture on a TV without a remote control may miss this gag altogether. Pictures used to miscue their locking signal and "roll" around, so the bottom of the image would be at the top of the screen, or vice versa. A little knob on the side or back of the set would rectify this.) Just to confirm it, the steering malfunction is explained to Steven as - a phrase beloved of television announcers in those days - 'a slight technical hitch'. *Moonlighting* did this sort of thing twenty years later, and everyone went hog-wild.

3. Less than two months since his last holiday, Hartnell takes episode two off. This is less noticeable than it might have been, as the Monk's shenanigans occupy centre-stage. In many ways the evasive little man with the irresponsible attitude to time travel is like a warm-up for the Patrick Troughton version of the Doctor. This is, let's remind ourselves, the same month that *Doctor Who and the Daleks* is released and cinema-goers get their first glimpse of the Peter Cushing theory of how to play time-travellers. Suddenly, Hartnell

is vulnerable, and he knows it.

4. There's a general rule-of-thumb with stories directed by Douglas Camfield, which we can mention here for future reference. The closer someone is to the camera, the more that character knows. Here, some scenes are directed rather oddly, seemingly to conform to this idea. In fact, the real reason they're funny-looking is that he's got a lot of scenery in a small space. Check out the way he makes the woods and cliffs double up - sometimes *treble* up - as different places.

The Continuity

The Doctor   Has legible handwriting, on this occasion. He admits to missing Ian and Barbara, and by the end of events he's positively welcoming Steven as a sort-of-crewmember.

• *Background*. Well well well. The Doctor isn't the only time-traveller from his world, nor the only owner of a TARDIS. The Monk knows him by reputation. [We say "by reputation", but some commentators have attempted to claim that the two runaways know each other and were acquainted at the Academy. This is just about feasible given what we hear, though by no means implied by the dialogue. The Monk apparently recognises the Doctor, the Doctor may or may not recognise the Monk. Although the Monk uses the title "Doctor" without being told it, there may be off-screen conversations between the two after the Doctor's capture in episode one.]

The Doctor knows the background to the Battle of Hastings, and can date the landing-site to within thirty years just from a spiky helmet on a beach [but see **Things That Don't Make Sense**].

• *Ethics*. In calling the Monk a 'time meddler', the Doctor makes it sound as if this is a kind of nuisance he's faced before [or, more likely, the term is in common usage among his people for those who mess about with time machines]. He's adamant that the "golden rule" of not interfering with history should be upheld, though this is presented as a code of conduct [and not a law of nature, as it is in earlier stories]. Note the Monk's reply: 'And who says so?' This question is never answered.

• *Inventory*. The main thing to report here is that the Doctor doesn't seem to be carrying pens, paper or string. This is odd, for him.

The Supporting Cast

• *Vicki.* Misses Ian and Barbara, but has no reason to want to be anywhere else but the TARDIS. For the first time, she's in charge for most of the adventure and relishes bossing about an older companion. She's still not very good with heights, and tires rather easily.

• *Steven.* He's calmed down now, and doesn't go hyper again even when he finds himself in the weird environs of the TARDIS. Sceptical and sarcastic, he's unwilling to accept anyone's word for anything, which is useful when dealing with a rogue like the Monk but vexing for the Doctor. They clearly don't have time travel or bigger-on-the-inside things where he comes from.

A bit of an alpha male who obviously dislikes being told what's what by young women and old men, Steven picks fights with passing trappers in 1066 and comes off second-best. He's prone to talk in transatlantic English, saying things like 'shoulda' and 'those Vikings sure know how to tie knots'. [Well, this is a Dennis Spooner script. The subtext seems to be that as he's described in the character notes as an "astronaut", he has to be at least a *bit* American. Viewers of the modern-day series might like to try comparing him to Captain Jack.] He's the first companion to routinely say 'yeah' and call the Doctor 'Doc'.

Hi-Fi the panda stays in the TARDIS for this outing, but Steven's packing a Swiss army knife.

The Supporting Cast (Evil, Ish)

• *The Monk.* The chubby little time meddler never gives himself a name or a title, but becomes known as 'the Monk' thanks to the pious persona he adopts in 1066. [Yet he's still wearing the monk's outfit in "The Daleks' Master Plan" (3.4), so this may be his standard "meddling uniform".] The Monk is from the same place as the Doctor, though the Doctor reckons himself to have been 'fifty years earlier'. [If we assume that some force in TARDIS travel "synchs up" the timelines of separate travellers, something which is implicitly assumed in later stories, then this indicates that the Doctor has been travelling for over half a century now. Further muddling the question of how he came to have a fifteen-year-old granddaughter.]

While the Doctor enjoys travel for its own sake, the Monk takes a gleeful delight in messing around with history, and is largely trying to change the outcome of the Battle of Hastings just for the thrill of it. That said, he justifies his plans by saying that they result in the greatest good for the greatest number, and insists his changes will improve history for most of those concerned. His scheme, although ruthless in many ways, is executed with the minimum number of casualties. He even gives penicillin and other advanced medical aid to injured humans.

This isn't the first bit of meddling he's done, though he describes it as his master-plan. Most of his other interventions have already become part of known history, if his claims are to be believed. He gave prehistoric Britons the anti-gravitational lift needed to build Stonehenge, and gave Leonardo da Vinci ideas about powered flight [for more on Leonardo see 6.5, "The Seeds of Death"; 14.1, "The Masque of Mandragora"; 17.2, "City of Death" (and the accompanying essay); and 27.0, the TV Movie]. He deposited £200 in a London bank in 1968, then went forward two-hundred years to collect a fortune in compound interest [a TARDIS traveller can have no real need for money, so he seems to have done this just for a laugh]. The last item on his things-to-do list is "Meet King Harold" [suggesting that, like the Doctor, he enjoys hob-nobbing with the big names].

Interestingly, the Monk wears a ring exactly like the Doctor's. [See **What Makes the TARDIS Work?** under 1.3, "The Edge of Destruction", for some manic speculation on this item.] Some of the things he's brought with him to the eleventh century: a wristwatch, a gramophone player with a record of plainsong, a radio, a toaster, penicillin, some nice china crockery, a pair of binoculars and an atomic cannon. Inside his TARDIS is a collection of art treasures from throughout history - apparently just *human* history - and rockets for the cannon which Steven likens to neutron bombs. He also keeps a diary, which chronicles his odd-but-nefarious schemes.

[For a longer discussion on the fiddliness of altering known events, see **Can You Change History, Even One Line?** under 1.6, "The Aztecs". The Monk's achievements are striking, though. Apart from anything else, the implication is that Stonehenge and Leonardo's flying-machine pictures are *wrong*, every bit as offensive to "proper" history as the alteration to the Battle of Hastings which the Doctor prevents. So if the Doctor had come across the meddler earlier on, then there'd be no impressive monument on Salisbury Plain. This really does raise the question of whose side we should be on here.]

The TARDIS(es)   Vicki states that TARDIS stands for 'Time and Relative Dimensions in Space'. According to the Doctor, there's a 'horizontal hold' control on the console [but he's toying with Steven at the time, so this could be a joke], and the wardrobe has cloaks galore. The Ship is unharmed when immersed in water [if this were a Terry Nation script, then such a thing would drain the air…], not even washing away in the tide. When the Monk asks what model it is, the Doctor is abruptly secretive. [Later stories will account for this coyness; he's embarrassed about his shoddy old Type 40.]

The Monk's vessel is a 'Mark IV'. [This isn't the same as the "Type" classification later used to identify TARDISes.] He never refers to it as a TARDIS, though Vicki and Steven do [so at this stage, Susan's claim to have invented the name still seems feasible]. The Monk himself prefers 'time-ship'. It's very similar to the Doctor's on the inside, but with a raised console dais. The main improvement is an automatic drift control, which allows the craft to be suspended in space with absolute safety [see "The Chase"; 5.5, "The Web of Fear"; and **Can the TARDIS Fly?** under 5.6, "Fury from the Deep"]. It also has a perfectly functional 'camouflage unit' [he means "chameleon circuit", of course, but at least he didn't say "cloaking device"], allowing it to blend in with its surroundings. Though the Monk argues with the point, the Doctor believes the vessel chooses its disguise independent of the operator [also the implication in 1.1, "An Unearthly Child"]. The entrance to the console room is restricted by the exterior door's size, so people have to stoop almost double to get in when it's disguised as a sarcophagus. The Monk seems surprised that the Doctor's Ship requires a key.

The 'dimensional control' is a small Perspex box packed with electronics, which plugs into the vessel through a SCART-style lead. When this control is removed, the craft's interior takes on dimensions proportionate to the exterior, so the console room is shrunk to doll's-house size. [The suggestion may be that the inside is the same size as the outside, but if so then the Monk's TARDIS must only contain a few rooms, not the vast labyrinth we later see inside the Doctor's own Ship.] The Doctor takes the element with him when he leaves, safe in the knowledge that the Monk isn't going anywhere.

History

• *Dating.* It's late summer, 1066, and the TARDIS lands in Northumbria. [It gets light at around five in the morning; that far north, this could make it any time up until August Bank Holiday.]

For those who don't already know… a Norwegian leader, Harold Hadrada, is seeking to exploit tensions in England. Harold Godwinson has claimed the throne after the death of King Edward, who was laid to rest at the beginning of the year. Historically, King Harold managed to defeat Hardrada, only to have to race back to the other end of the country to meet the invasion force of William of Normandy [in October]. The Monk's plan, therefore, is to keep Hadrada's force away with an atomic cannon so that King Harold has a fresh army with which to defeat William. [This makes sense. Despite the overwhelming superiority of the French arms and armour, Harold vs. William was a close match, and the Battle of Hastings has long been considered one of those "history could have been so very different" moments. A fresh army would have been enough to swing the balance.] The Monk believes this alteration would lead to less wars in the future, as Harold would be a good king [rather an optimistic view, this]. He anticipates jet airliners by 1320, and Shakespeare writing *Hamlet* for television. With help from himself, naturally.

Viking raids are a constant threat in this part of England, though there's only been one raid so far this year. Just as anyone would have expected, the raiders are burly men with elaborate helmets who enjoy the usual pastimes of murder and pillage. [For obvious reasons, rape isn't mentioned. However, local housewife Edith is badly assaulted in episode two, and her near-catatonic state afterwards may be an attempt to hint at what's happened off-screen. Even so, she soon recovers her wits and gets chatty with the Doctor. They breed 'em tough, in historical drama.]

As has already been mentioned, the Monk left money in a London bank in 1968, then collected the interest two-hundred years later. [Or, more probably, just under two-hundred years. It seems likely that he collected the cash just before the Dalek invasion of the 2150s, when the world's economy presumably collapsed altogether.]

The Analysis

Where Does This Come From? The more astute among you will have spotted that this story is, in many ways, "The Space Museum" Act Two. Time is shown to be malleable, and the Doctor and company are saved by the knock-on effects of something they did two episodes earlier. Instead of personal time, though, Spooner has decided to show the repercussions for history-as-she-is-taught. The single most influential event that everyone at home could be relied upon to know about, other than World War Two (and see **The Lore**), was the Battle of Hastings. It's not an event that travels well, but Americans reading this can take it for granted that when it comes to classroom history, 1066 is "our" 1776. Only it's more important.

In 1965, it was getting hard to avoid the impending nine-hundredth anniversary of the battle. Special stamps were commissioned, and the Bayeux Tapestry was getting a new lease of life now that school textbooks could be printed in colour. It was a subject that *Doctor Who* could neither ignore, nor do in the orthodox manner. In fact, the Monk often comes across as a mischievous schoolboy, the subtext being that he's sick of patronising old duffers like the Doctor teaching conventional history, and that he wants to change things as an act of classroom rebellion. Ian and Barbara have already made the connection between "school" and "normality" quite clear, and this story simply wouldn't work if it were set in an era which *hadn't* been drilled into the heads of all the ten-year-olds. It's no coincidence that on their next encounter (3.4, "The Daleks' Master Plan"), the Doctor punishes the Monk for his interference by giving him a jolly good thumping.

Similarly, Vikings had obvious appeal, but a full-scale onslaught was out of the question in Riverside. There was an obvious way to square this circle, by depicting a small-but-spectacular Viking raid. This almost inevitably led to the idea of a monastery; the most notorious raids were in Northumbria, especially the sacking of Lindesfarne. The Lindesfarne Gospel, one of the most extraordinary and beautiful objects of the pre-Renaissance world, miraculously survived. It was another beneficiary of colour books in schoolrooms and on coffee-tables. One can imagine a Whitaker-style story in which Ian and Barbara have to help the monks escape and protect the sacred icon of Christianity and literacy. (This being *Doctor Who*, that connection would have been left implicit.)

That's not what Dennis Spooner is about. The act of simply watching history happen is one that he and Terry Nation have already ridiculed at the start of "The Chase", and we note here that this is another step towards the assertive, crusading Doctor we all remember. Next time Spooner's involved in a script it'll be "The Daleks' Master Plan", by which time Nation and Tosh will have turned the Doctor into someone whose job is to fight evil.

And as in "The Space Museum", adding some sense of mystery and uncertainty to the past means relying on the kind of imagery that would be more familiar to viewers of *The Twilight Zone*. The anachronistic item, in this case a wristwatch found in an eleventh-century wood, is a staple of the Zone's many experiments with time-travel; usually these objects are seen to possess a special, symbolic, almost mystical property. There's a more direct link to the American series, though, in that the idea of getting Shakespeare to write his plays for television is the whole premise of the *Twilight Zone* episode "The Bard".

Things That Don't Make Sense The Monk's brilliant scheme has a few drawbacks. On the one hand, how would Shakespeare be able to write *Hamlet* if (a) the Danish Prince never lived, (b) the mix of Anglo-Saxon and Norman French in which the play was written never arose, (c) John Shakespeare never got to send his son to one of the new grammar schools that only existed because of all the teachers who came out of the Dissolution of the Monasteries (which never happened because the Tudors never got to rule)... you get the idea. [Is the Monk speaking figuratively when he talks about Shakespeare writing for TV? If not, then perhaps history has a way of moulding itself around special, "charismatic" individuals, and making sure their lives run as close to the "truth" as possible.]

Then there's the idea of jets in 1320. Hooray, global warming by 1400, and to get the fuel they'd need to re-fight the crusades. Is the Monk *really* reckless enough not to care about the consequences of all this? If he amends Earth's history, then he's surely affecting all sorts of other planets as well. It's also a bit Eurocentric. Yes, the Battle of Hastings is probably as important a single event as you can get in the English-speaking world, but you could get more impact by amending the outcome of the Ottoman attack on Constantinople in 1453 (say) or fixing it for Genghis Khan to conquer Russia. Nor does the Doctor do a very good job of stopping all of this, since his idea of protecting history is to strand a time-traveller with an in-depth knowledge of future science in the eleventh century. With a load of atomic weapons.

It's a bit early in the year for the blackberries that Steven finds, but the main culinary query is Edith's seemingly bottomless larder. She's got venison for any passing visitor, and supplies of mead, neither of which would keep terribly well in summer. Maybe the Monk sold her a fridge. Why does her husband keep a dead fox in their kitchen, by the way? In the same scene, an entertainingly-timed sound effect makes it seem as if he also has a magic bow that makes wolf noises.

Edith herself is clearly nursing her Viking-inflicted wounds in episode three, yet the Doctor natters with her for ages without asking what's happened to her since the last time he saw her, and acts surprised when she tells him she's been set upon by hairy Norsemen. The end of the episode sees both Vicki and Steven crawling into the Monk's sarcophagus / TARDIS, which is deeply peculiar, as neither of them *know* it's a TARDIS at that stage and it's rather like watching two people stuff themselves into a cupboard for no reason. Meanwhile, the Monk has brought a radio with him to the eleventh century. Precisely what programmes is he planning on listening to? We could also ask why he seems so chummy with the locals in episode two, when according to Edith in episode one, he's never been spoken to before now.

Here we learn that when the dimensional control is removed from a TARDIS, the interior of that TARDIS shrinks. Well, presumably it'd grow if the TARDIS happened to be disguised as something really big, but either way it changes size so that the removed dimensional control no longer has a chance of being replaced. In other words, once you take it out, the machine's useless forever. So... why is it even *possible* to take it out, and why is it only plugged in by a single lead? Isn't this something of a design flaw?

We've got to mention it: Vikings simply didn't wear hats like that. All right, a couple did after they were dead, but in combat or around the house it just wasn't the done thing to have horns or wings on your head. The equivalent would be someone in New York or Chicago going to work wearing the costume "Steven Regret" wears in "The Gunfighters" (3.8). The big-helmeted Norwegians don't make the most inconspicuous of scouting-parties, either.

Episode three has a couple of minor Billy Fluffs, with 'Winchester 73' coming out unprintably rude and a gag about 'monkey business' being mangled into the strangely satisfying 'no more monkery'. Distracted by Hartnell playing around with bits of rock, Purves comes out with a line about the TARDIS landing on pebbles (notable as the only time that Hartnell corrects someone *else's* gaffe), but this story is most memorable for what's perhaps the most bewildering of all the Billy Fluffs: 'I'm not a mountain-goat, I prefer walking to anyday. And I hate climbing.'

Oh, and one last oddity. You may recall that in "The Aztecs" (1.6), the story insists on treating the Doctor and company as heroes even though they're shamelessly manipulating the locals and lying as if it were the proper thing to do. Here, the people of Northumberland are shown to be decent and bold for helping to defeat the pesky Monk. But even if the web of time is preserved, from their point of view what they're *actually* doing is allowing the Vikings to land and ultimately making sure their country is invaded by the Normans. Yet the Doctor talks to Edith as if they're on the same side for the same reason, i.e. they're both generically "good", and the script glosses over the awkward morality of the situation (at the same time, the Monk is pretending to help the Vikings while secretly trying to lead them to their doom, but the rather ironic similarity to the Doctor's actions isn't addressed). It's certainly disturbing to hear the Doctor describe Edith as a 'charming woman', even as he sells out her people.

Critique More than any other story since "The Daleks", we can't see this one straight. Any modern judgement of it requires the audience to say things like "the bits with the villagers go on a bit, don't they?" or "isn't the Monk's plan a bit crap?", so inevitably we miss the main point: as first-time viewers, we're not supposed to know that anything like this is possible within *Doctor Who's* remit.

It's not just that this is our first sight of another TARDIS, our first hint of a "continuity" which later generations will take as read and our first real stop-the-baddie-changing-history tale. Here, we're getting our first sight of the battlefield on which most of the Doctor's future adventures will be fought. Any modern-day series about time-travellers would introduce the obligatory history-changing Evil Twin in the third or fourth episode, but this is the '60s, before "cult TV" and before there are rules for doing this sort of thing. The last cliffhanger *is* an almighty cracker, not simply paving the way for (far too many) future antics with the Doctor's own sort but giving the central cast a whole new way of fighting the villains. At the very least, it's notable that they're stuck in the past and doing something other than trying to escape.

It was always going to suffer, from the point of view of anyone born after 1970. And suffer it does, especially when the Norwegians are around. There are times when the earnestness of the historical stories can be a real drag; it occasionally takes an effort of will to remain engaged with people in silly wigs declaiming at one another. People in history can't speak as they were really wont to, nor in a contemporary, relaxed manner, so the usual compromise is a kind of faux-Shakespearean blank verse with no apostrophes. Without exciting monsters or groovy sets and sound-effects, this can be tiresome. On this occasion the script relegates the locals to talking scenery, and dropping another time-traveller into the mix makes any effort at characterisation redundant.

The later efforts at what fandom likes to call the "pseudo-historical" solve this by going for lurid characters ripped straight out of other fictional genres, so the nearest '70s equivalent of this story (11.1, "The Time Warrior") features a thug called "Bloodaxe". Here, we're meant to notice the locals only as a context into which the Monk doesn't quite fit. The fights - usually the way in which historical tales are relieved of the talkiness - are slapdash, and don't enhance Camfield's reputation as an action director. The Vikings are there to model facial hair, not much more. Naturally, one of them is called "Sven". Yet the truth is, most of the tedious filler for which this story is now remembered is confined to the Hartnell-free episode two. Indeed, there are some clever uses of language and imagery on offer here, if you're willing to look for them. In a story about the unfolding of time, Camfield makes sure to open with a lingering close-up of the console room clock, and obviously it's got to be a *watch* that makes everyone realise

there's something wrong with history. Later one of the locals describes something that's 'landed' on the shore; *we* know it's the TARDIS, but *he* means "landed" in the more archaic sense of the word.

But all eyes are on Peter Butterworth. He doesn't disappoint. Actually, the real surprise is how well the three regulars hold their own. This is a new kind of TARDIS line-up, remember, the first time the programme has had to get the public on its side without Parental Everypeople Ian and Barbara to look worried by things. While the programme quietly re-invents itself around them, Peter Purves has to get to grips with being an outer-space action-hero and Maureen O'Brien suddenly finds herself promoted to "old hand" companion. Again, if you've grown up with *Doctor Who* and accept companion arrivals / departures as a normal part of the process, then it's hard to get a grip on how weird this shift is. Because it's not simply a change of cast, it's a change in the relationship between the cast and the viewers. Hartnell may have become rather more active since the first episode (see especially "The Sensorites", another story that did more to define the programme's format than we usually acknowledge), but now he's unquestionably the protagonist, and the humans are palpably just the hangers-on. Even when the lead actor takes a week off.

Is it really a coincidence, the Doctor's "bad" opposite turning up at exactly the same point that the Doctor himself finally becomes the hero in his own show? Maybe, maybe not. But the battle of wills between the Doctor and the Monk is at the heart of the story, and it's echoed in the subplot about Steven and Vicki vying for dominance, so we get very little "pure" exposition. In fact, a higher-than-usual proportion of the storytelling is done with simple visuals. We've had to say it about more than one story in this volume, but the real problem with "The Time Meddler" is that it worked well enough to be worth doing again. It's creaky and it's hesitant and it can be terribly dull when the Monk isn't around, yet a lot of the slow bits give the audience time to adjust to surprises which no longer surprise us. The grammar of the series has changed again, and from this point on it's something that a modern-day viewer might recognise as That Thing on Saturday Nights.

This product is not authorized by the BBC. Doctor Who and TARDIS are trademarks of the BBC.

The Facts

Written by Dennis Spooner. Directed by Douglas Camfield. Ratings 8.9 million, 8.8 million, 7.7 million, 8.3 million.

Supporting Cast Peter Butterworth (Monk), Alethea Charlton (Edith), Peter Russell (Eldred), Michael Miller (Wulnoth), Norman Hartley (Ulf), David Anderson (Sven), Geoffrey Cheshire (Viking Leader), Ronald Rich (Gunnar the Giant).

Episode Titles "The Watcher", "The Meddling Monk", "A Battle of Wits", "Checkmate".

Working Titles "The Paradox" (probably only for episode one), "Doctor Who and the Monk", "Doctor Who and the Vikings".

Cliffhangers The Doctor discovers the gramophone at the monastery, but is trapped in the chamber by a sliding gate, and the Monk arrives to chuckle at his plight; Steven and Vicki break into the Doctor's cell, only to find him gone and his bed stuffed with animal-furs; Steven and Vicki crawl into the Monk's sarcophagus, and end up inside a TARDIS.

The Lore

• It was an odd time to be making the series. On the one hand, nobody knew who was going to be in the stories they commissioned, with decisions pending on Jacqueline Hill and Maureen O'Brien. On the other, the BBC heirarchy was having to rethink the definition of "hit show" (see **Did the BBC Like Doctor Who?** under 3.8, "The Gunfighters"). The solution was obvious: commission a story from soon-to-be ex-story-editor Dennis Spooner. That way, if any changes were made at last minute then at least the writer wouldn't get all precious about it. Spooner was off to work with Terry Nation on ITC's big-budget US co-production The Baron, but was still close-by in case of emergencies.

• Another consideration was that Tosh and Spooner had an idea to ring the changes on the "past-future-sideways" formula they'd inherited from Whitaker. Spooner looked into the original notes compiled by Webber, Wilson et al, and devised the Monk as an "anti-Doctor". Whether or not Hartnell's suggestion of Son of Doctor Who was a factor is unknown (see **What Else Wasn't Made?** under 17.6, "Shada").

• But the long-term future of Doctor Who seemed assured. The launch of BBC2 hadn't been without hitches, and the scheme to fix it involved Donald Baverstock being placed in charge of the new channel. He saw this as a rebuke and resigned. Those he'd supported went soon after, and those who'd opposed him suddenly found their promotion prospects enhanced. Sydney Newman had - as usual - seen it coming months earlier and told his producers to hold their nerve. The long-term effects of this would still be felt five years later, but in the meantime it made Verity Lambert's meteoric rise look like a consequence of the programme she was making. In later volumes the irony of this will become apparent, though for now this provides the backdrop against which the events of the rest of this volume should be judged...

• Those of you paying attention to the ratings will notice that the Dalek publicity blitz, with the six-part merchandising showcase disguised as a Doctor Who adventure and the big-screen full-colour diet decaf version of "The Daleks" hitting the nation's crumbling cinemas, had led to a barely-perceptible improvement on the average viewing figures of "The Space Museum". "The Chase" had, in fact, done very well indeed considering that it was one of the best summers on record and that so much else was happening in Britain at the time. Looked at story-by-story, "The Time Meddler" appears to have caused a dip of over a million viewers, but looked at week-by-week it arrests the rapid slide in audience appreciation which the later episodes of Nation's effort provoked.

• Future Carry On star Peter Butterworth had been in several films by this point, but one he didn't appear in was stirring true-life War-time yarn The Wooden Horse. In this, a group of prisoners-of-war escape from a Nazi camp by digging a tunnel under a vaulting-horse while others arrange diversions. In real life, one of these diversions was a comedy troupe performing sketches by one Talbot Rothwell. One of the troupe, Butterworth himself, auditioned for the film and was told that he didn't match the director's idea of an officer. Talbot Rothwell wound up as principal scriptwriter for the Carry On films, and had hitherto been involved in what's estimated to be the first "proper" comedy series on television, How Do You View. Butterworth was in that, too. In making "The Time Meddler" he found that the part of the

Monk, although written for a much older man, suited him so well he barely needed to act. A lot of what you see and hear is ad lib. He and Hartnell worked well together, and Lambert was impressed, so a return match was almost inevitable.

• Tosh barely needed to amend anything. Camfield was more assertive, and changed the tape-loop of chants to a gramophone recording, as well as adding the toaster. With most of the original team going or gone, Hartnell needed people he trusted around him, and Camfield was one of these. Tosh and incoming producer John Wiles noted this, plus Camfield's willingness to change the scripts to make better viewing and more logical stories (for Hartnell's benefit as much as anything).

• Wiles was introduced to the cast when he made his first appearance at a rehearsal. This wasn't a great success, and over the next few stories we'll be returning to the battle of wills between star and producer. Hartnell's main tactic was the strategically-timed illness, Wiles' was the double-bluff.

• The expensive-looking footage of the Viking ship came not from a movie or another TV production, but from a 1949 BBC newsreel about Danes re-enacting the first crossing of the North Sea in 449 AD.

• For the second time, one of the regulars feels compelled to mention the Indian Mutiny here (Barbara did it in "The Dalek Invasion of Earth"). Bearing in mind what we've already learned about Terry Nation's abortive Indian Mutiny script, anyone would think it was some kind of running gag.

• It was at around this time that Brian Hayles first submitted a storyline entitled "Doctor Who and the Nazis". We mention this as evidence that the guidelines on historical stories which David Whitaker claims were imposed, insisting that anything more recent than the sixteenth century was off-limits, evidently weren't being distributed to writers. Given the series' frequent flirtations with fascism and War-time imagery, this was surely the most obvious idea for a story that hadn't been done, and yet we have to wait until the late 1980s for any bona fide Nazis to appear in the series. (There *was* another notion of a War-time story, but we'll leave that for Season Six…)

3.1: "Galaxy Four"

(Serial T. Four Episodes, 11th September - 2nd October 1965.)

Which One is This? Drahvins: steely blonde warrior-women with ray-guns and a tendency to say things like 'it is conceivable that you too will be obliterated'. Chumblies: wobbly service robots who blow off in perfect radiophonic pitch. Rills: gas-guzzling warthog-monsters that nobody can remember seeing. Put them all on a planet together, and watch it explode...

Firsts and Lasts First story to be directed by one of the black-and-white era's "stylists", Derek Martinus. Plot-wise it's the first story to use what will become a familiar part of the '60s programme: an airlock with the pressure being removed unless the occupant (in this case Steven) accedes to the bad guys' demands. And we have the first full-scale planetary destruction in the series' history, though it's hardly a Death Star moment.

Although the story's "nice monsters versus nasty humans" message is already a little tired, this is the first one to use genetically-modified people to suggest that physical beauty equates to moral bankruptcy. It's also the first time anyone needs, or even mentions, a translating device.

Four Things to Notice About "Galaxy Four"...

1. Years before either recycling or postmodernism became fashionable, here's a story made up almost entirely from things we've seen or heard before. The music is from the same source as the music in "The Web Planet", the door noise is the one from both "The Daleks" and "The Sensorites", and the background noise of the Rills' ship is the Dalek control room effect played backwards. Even the Doctor notes how similar to Xeros this silent world is, which may be the first example of truly pointless continuity in the programme. A planet with multiple suns isn't exactly novel, after Aridius in "The Chase", so all that's left is the moral (again, not unlike the one in "The Sensorites") and the nature of the monsters...

2. With the actual footage of the Rills lost, they were notorious as the monsters no-one knew. Barely any press coverage was given to this story,

Season 3 Cast/Crew

- William Hartnell (the Doctor, credited but does not appear in 3.2)
- Maureen O'Brien (Vicki, 3.1 and 3.3)
- Peter Purves (Steven Taylor, 3.1, 3.3 to 3.9)
- Adrienne Hill (Katarina, 3.3 to 3.4)
- Jean Marsh (Sara Kingdom, 3.4)
- Jackie Lane (Dodo Chaplet, 3.5 to 3.10)
- Michael Craze (Ben Jackson, 3.10)
- Anneke Wills (Polly Wright, 3.10)

- Verity Lambert (Producer, 3.1 and 3.2)
- John Wiles (Producer, 3.3 to 3.5)
- Innes Lloyd (Producer, 3.6 to 3.10)
- Donald Tosh (Script Editor, 3.1 to 3.5)
- Gerry Davis (Script Editor, 3.6 to 3.10)

and what there *was* centred on the Chumblies and the Drahvins. Thus, fandom spent the 1980s attempting to find even one photo of these creatures. Finally, it emerged that a sneak preview of the new season had been given at the *Daily Mail* Boys and Girls Exhibition at Earl's Court. A trawl through the photo library produced a picture and... it was almost exactly like the Slyther from "The Dalek Invasion of Earth", but with boar's tusks and googly eyes, like Sandy from "The Rescue". On audio, the Rills are distinguished with a vocal performance by Robert Cartland, which is the RADA-trained equivalent of those godlike alien voices that gave Captain Kirk such a hard time whenever the *Star Trek* people were short of money for new sets.

3. Despite the fact that Steven's meeting with the Drahvin girls turns him into Mr Smooth, most of his dialogue was written for Barbara. However, the Drahvins were originally written as *male* clones (we have no idea whether they had Freddie Mercury moustaches), and in this light Steven being overpowered by a Dusty Springfield looka-like makes more sense. The decision to make the villains female, and give them beehive hairdos, Bjork-style eyebrow bobbles and big ray-guns, must have been made by someone who hadn't seen Zsa Zsa Gabor in *Queen of Outer Space*[11]. Barbara vs. Maaga in a big-hair cat-fight would have justified this story's baffling 9.9 million viewers, perhaps. Almost. But with hindsight, every-

What Was the BBC *Thinking*?

By modern standards, it seems unthinkable. At the time of going to press, 108 of the original 695 episodes of *Doctor Who* (which is to say, the 695 episodes of *Doctor Who* Mark One) aren't known to exist anywhere on Earth. 108 are missing. 108 are lost. 108 have been wiped from the face of human culture. That's more than 15% of the "canon". Ask a devotee of a more recent "cult" series how s/he'd feel if the first season-and-a-half of *Buffy the Vampire Slayer* suddenly vanished, and s/he probably wouldn't even be able to understand the question.

Today, the BBC's decision to erase a large amount of its '60s TV output is universally regarded as stupid, ghastly, offensive and short-sighted. Many people get blisteringly angry about it, far beyond the limits of *Doctor Who* fandom. Often, the stars of "missing" programmes - John Cleese immediately springs to mind - will rant loudly and authoritatively on the subject, leaving us in no doubt that the mass-wiping of classic television was performed by witless, ignorant middle-management types with no regard for creativity. Which leaves the obvious question: if the artists in question always thought it was such a mistake, then why did so few of them try to do anything about it at the time? Even those who made an attempt to save "doomed" recordings usually did so for sentimental reasons, not because they thought they were saving part of history. At the time, the idea that *Monty Python's Flying Circus* would be seen by future generations as a vital historical document would have seemed even more ridiculous than its content.

One thing we have to keep coming back to, in these volumes: BBC Television didn't work the same way that American television worked, or even the same way that British commercial television worked. In addition to key features like the license fee and the mandate to enlighten the masses - see especially **Did the BBC Actually Like Doctor Who**? under 3.8, "The Gunfighters" - much of BBC drama came from a tradition of theatre. As we've already seen, in this era the Corporation made sure that people knew about plays. This is, if nothing else, the reason that British television has traditionally *looked* so different to the US version. American TV has always wanted to be Hollywood with adverts, rather than a kind of hi-tech stage for the masses. The distinction between the two forms was so great that during the '60s, the *Radio Times* would explicitly describe imported and made-for-export shows as "film series", not because viewers were interested in the technicalities of how programmes were made but because series made on film were considered to be an entirely different genre. (This is yet another thing that people who try to compare *Doctor Who* with *Star Trek* always miss, incidentally. The two programmes very nearly exist in different media. It's like trying to compare John Osbourne with John Ford.)

As we all know, today's generation is brought up in a world of cheap video and perpetual repeats, where images are transmitted and retransmitted until even the most bizarre phenomena seem normal. The minds of the 1960s could never even have conceived of TV in its modern form, with its endlessly-looping video-clips or its casual twisting of time and context. When an "action reply" was used on British television for the first time, during the 1966 World Cup final, switchboards were jammed by viewers who couldn't understand how the Germans had managed to score the same disallowed goal twice. In drama, certainly in "serious" drama, there was a culture of live performance. The idea that every recording had to be religiously kept and stored for posterity would have been as nonsensical as the suggestion that every single performance of every single stage play had to be bottled and kept in jars.

Consider this: in the mid-'50s, the BBC broadcast a dramatic presentation of George Orwell's *1984*, starring Peter Cushing (you know, cinema's Dr Who), written by Nigel Kneale (you know, he created *Quatermass*) and directed by Rudolph Cartier (you know... well, maybe you don't, but we'll be mentioning him again later in this volume). Though technically quite challenging, the play went out live. And when it was "repeated", a few days later, the BBC didn't simply show a recording of the first performance but the *entire play was performed again*. To the twenty-first century viewer it seems pointless, wasteful and almost wilfully eccentric, but nobody saw anything remotely strange about it at the time.

Even the public attitude regarding repeats was different, before the 1970s. Repeats were what the schedulers did in the summer, when they thought no-one was watching anyway. To see something twice was a strange sensation, like going back to your old school. Television was about immediacy, novelty, freshness and nowness, and it took an event as big as the Kennedy assassination to force

continued on page 187...

one's efforts to avoid saying the words "Steven's been caught by the Chumblies" get really strained by the end of the third episode.

4. Ah, yes, the Chumblies. Vicki coins the word to describe the way these robots move, and given that they're glorified lampshades with very small actors shuffling along inside them, it's probably apt. They're cute Daleks. What you'll find on audio is that they're *melodic* cute Daleks. The sound effects are the sort of things kids could do in school playgrounds, and the noise designated as "Chumbley at Rest" on the 1993 BBC Radiophonic Workshop CD is cheery, spooky and a bit rude. (It sounds like either someone rubbing a finger on a wine-glass while breaking wind, or someone trying to tune a bicycle pump before playing it in concert.) As you can see in the six minutes of episode one that still exist in the archive, this gives them a "school play" quality rather more endearing than that of "The Web Planet".

The Continuity

The Plot Landing on a nameless, bleak-looking world with three suns, the TARDIS crewmembers are immediately accosted by a wobbly service robot which Vicki dubs a "Chumbley". It does its best to take them to its leader, but en route they're "rescued" by the bleach-blonde Drahvins, and led to a crashed spaceship where the Drahvin commander - Maaga - informs them that her test-tube-bred subordinates are engaged in a small kind of war. There's another crashed ship on the planet, owned by the Chumblies' masters, the inhuman Rills. Maaga claims the Rills are murderous monsters, and worse, the planet is disintegrating. The Doctor insists on helping both the Drahvins *and* the mysterious Rills off the planet, but Maaga insists on taking the Rill vessel by force... hence, Steven is kept hostage while the Doctor and Vicki are sent to infiltrate the enemy camp.

Vicki is the first to speak to the Rills, and their version of events is quite different; in fact it was the Drahvins who began hostilities, yet the Rills have nonetheless offered to help their persecutors get off the planet before its destruction. Despite being rather civilised, the Rills are as hideous as advertised, and their reliance on ammonia requires them to stay inside their vessel. The Doctor agrees to recharge their depleted ship by hooking a power cable up to the TARDIS, and

with the Rills' help he manages to rescue Steven, who's being held hostage in Maaga's airlock.

As the planet begins to disintegrate, the Drahvins lead a charge against the Rill ship, but are held back by the Chumbley frontline while the Doctor finishes jump-starting the engines. The Rills escape, and the travellers hurry back to the Ship - while pursued by Maaga and her followers - with the last remaining Chumbley on the planet holding the villains off. As dawn arrives for the last time, the planet breaks up, taking those good-for-nothing Drahvins with it.

The Doctor This month he's primarily a scientist, interested in investigation and empirical research without all that tiresome saving of planets and rescuing of travelling companions. He admits, jocularly, to being too old for all the running around he does. He seems to want a rest from all this exertion, but appears happier now he no longer has to try to get back to any one time or place.

• *Background.* He's never been to this world before, whatever it's called, although he thinks it's similar to Xeros [2.7, "The Space Museum"].

• *Ethics.* States [rather unbelievably] that he never kills anything, though he shows no sympathy for Maaga's people when they're abandoned on the doomed planet. He's perfectly prepared to accept that either the Drahvins or the Rills might be benign, but finds more faults in the Drahvins' story. Prejudice against ammonia-breathing warthogs is out of the question, as is the automatic assumption that all humanoid women are ladies.

• *Inventory.* He's got a screwdriver in his pocket, and he's not afraid to use it. He uses it to gouge holes in the Drahvin ship and rewire the ammonia supply for the Rills [but he may be starting to feel that it could be a little more sonic].

The Supporting Cast

• *Vicki.* As well as all the things she learned on the day she went to school, she knows about hairdressing and recognises the smell of ammonia. Her habit of giving things "cute" names persists, as she coins the term "Chumbley" to describe the Rills' robots and makes everyone else use it. When the Doctor tries to suggest cautious investigation, she parodies his procedure: 'I noted, observed, collated, concluded... then I threw a rock.' [The Doctor himself will be using this approach by 5.2, "The Abominable Snowmen".]

What Was the BBC *Thinking*?

...continued from page 185

a re-showing of "An Unearthly Child". News stories were better if they could be relayed as they happened. Everyone got excited just seeing live satellite coverage of something, no matter what the something was. Significantly, the erasure of programmes didn't end until the early '80s; "significantly" because by then, a whole generation had grown up taking television for granted and understanding (almost instinctively) how it actually worked. Seeing murky pictures transmitted live from the other side of the Atlantic was less exciting than finding out what things had looked like before you were born. Lo and behold, the words "television" and "history" could be spoken in the same breath.

Only then did the "victims" of the wipings start to complain in earnest, and only then did TV pundits start to realise how much damage had been done. It's hardly surprising, either, that the kind of people who got angry about the erasures became angrier and angrier as home video boomed throughout the 1980s. If you don't think the BBC is ever going to show Episode X again, then it's hard to get upset about it being scrubbed from the archive, but if you know you *could* be watching it then you're bound to be left with a terrible sense of disappointment. The real irony, though, is that the BBC's roots in "serious" drama led to it creating some of the greatest programmes in the world even as it destroyed the evidence.

But wait, let's rewind. Never mind the philosophy of television in the '60s, what about the practicalities? You might have thought that a cash-cow like *Doctor Who* would have been milked for all it was worth. Think of all the series making millions in syndication these days, perpetually in re-run while new episodes are being made. A half-hour segment can recoup its production costs dozens of times over. *Doctor Who* was sold to sixty different countries. So the BBC... wiped all the master-tapes, burned the film copies and demanded that overseas TV networks did the same. Eh?

There were reasons for this, which occasionally bordered on the reasonable. One was that nobody knew where to put everything. The BBC had a film library, in Windmill Road, Ealing, but videotapes were - to begin with - kept by the engineering department. A comprehensive archive wasn't set up until 1978. We've already mentioned the rather basic transmission format of early BBC television. In 1967, all TV production switched to the 625-line format, so the old Ampex tapes were unlikely to be used again (except for very occasional archive features, for which the film copies were roughly as good and easier to edit). There's been speculation that the tapes might have constituted a fire-hazard, too, though compared to celluloid film it's not really much of a problem. The main reason for wiping the tapes was quite simply that they were needed for something else. Copies existed for export, and newly-made programmes needed to be recorded. The tape on which "The Tomb of the Cybermen" was made was close to breaking-point even then, having been repeatedly used beforehand.

The export copies were telerecordings. The method of selling the series to other countries and networks, which might have used different line configurations and screen-ratios, was to make 16mm film copies by pointing a camera at a high-resolution monitor. All decisions on wiping the video were referred to the incumbent producer of *Doctor Who*, and none was wiped until the telerecording was deemed satisfactory; some went badly and were re-done. These copies weren't made for posterity, remember. They were originally intended purely for the overseas market, and thus commissioned and made by BBC Enterprises, a semi-independent company set up to exploit the rights of all BBC work without infringing the Charter's non-commercial remit. It's now called BBC Worldwide, and is responsible for such important cultural artefacts as spin-off novels and huggable Teletubbies.

The actors' union, Equity, had negotiated rates for repeats of dramas on the understanding that these would be either one-off plays or film series. The BBC occasionally made short serials, some quite export-friendly, and offered all six episodes, or thirteen, or twenty-six, as a unit. Equity had rates for this as well. Up to three years after first broadcast, a play could be re-run with the actors getting a fair percentage of the original fee. However, for domestic consumption it was considered unlikely that an episode of a continuous series would be shown out of context. Once telerecordings had been made, there was no reason to keep the master-tapes, but the BBC nevertheless retained them just in case. It was only rather later - three or four years after first transmission, when the Equity agreement reached its end - that the wiping of *Doctor Who* began. If the dates for most of these

continued on page 189...

Vicki still occasionally drops into Scouse, saying 'I've finished choppin' this feller' after she's cut Steven's hair. She's now dressing like a chic lady of 1965 [Verity Lambert, for example] whilst retaining her childish hairstyle.

• *Steven.* Likes the look of the bad guys. Although he finds himself unable to resist giving Drahvin Three a quick consciousness-raising session, he has little but contempt for their way of doing things. Yet he doesn't automatically trust the Rills either. [Let's not forget, he comes from a time of interplanetary war and probably sees all aliens as potential enemies.] He's impatient with the Doctor's constant exploration for its own sake, though he doesn't display the need to be on any particular planet.

The TARDIS There's now a force-barrier that stops the Chumblies drilling into the Ship, and the Doctor is proud of this as he constructed it himself. [It's a recent addition, and might be a refinement of the defences implied by 2.5, "The Web Planet".] The Chumblies' explosive devices shake the Ship but don't breach it. On landing, the routine checks are for oxygen, atmospheric pressure, temperature and radiation [and not gravity?]. These days the Doctor routinely operates the door himself instead of getting a sidekick to do it, although he occasionally tells the others to press switches during flight. The astral map [again, from "The Web Planet"] is used to determine how long the planet's got left before it blows.

A cable provided by the Rills is connected to the TARDIS and transfers power to refuel the Rill ship. This takes three or four hours. Once the TARDIS has dematerialised, the scanner is unable to show the planet disintegrating, but it does show other worlds and star-systems [so perhaps by now the Doctor has learned to "hover" in space, at least for short periods].

The Non-Humans

• *Drahvins.* Well, the troops call themselves "the Drahvin", but their leader says "Drahvins". Blonde-haired all-girl space-warriors with little or no sense of humour, the Drahvins only visibly differ from human females in that their eyebrows are made up of dots. Maaga, the commander of the unit seen here, is the only Drahvin who has any form of initiative; the others are mere drones, dim-witted and incapable of dealing with new situations. Maaga sees herself as 'human' and a 'living being', and the others as mere 'puppets' or 'soldier Drahvins', grown in test-tubes. They're trained for obedience and warfare, and even their leader finds the concept of friendship difficult to grasp. [Note that they're never described as "clones", and they're clearly not identical, whatever the cover of the CD release tries to tell you.]

In fact Maaga rather resents being given these unimaginative troopers, having warned her people that soldiers were unsuitable for space work [she speaks as if space conquest is new to Drahvinkind]. She's perfectly prepared to kill one of her lackeys rather than be held up, telling the others that the "enemy" Rills killed her victim. Only Maaga has a super-powered gun that can destroy Chumblies, whereas the soldiers' weapons are less impressive and need recharging from their ship's power supply. Likewise, the soldiers live on twigs and leaves, while the leader has special leader's food. But it's hard to tell the leaders from the soldiers by sight, as they all dress in two-tone military skirts and have formal hairstyles.

Despite the shoddiness of their ships and weapons, the Drahvins see it as their duty and destiny to conquer space. Maaga refers to the time-travellers as Earth-people without being told where they come from. [The Drahvin world may itself be a colony, raising the obvious possibility that they may be an offshoot of Earth-people, though this isn't the implication of the script. Incidentally, it's fairly safe to assume that the Drahvins don't speak English, as the Rills have already communicated with them by the story's beginning but have to make sense of Vicki's language later on. We'll assume that Vicki's speaking English or some variation thereof.]

The Drahvins come from Drahva in Galaxy Four, which is overpopulated, hence Maaga's mission to find a suitable word for colonisation. They crashed four-hundred dawns ago, after a space-battle with the Rills which they ostensibly started. Maaga claims that back home they only have a small number of men, 'as many as we need', whereas the rest are killed because they consume valuable food and serve little purpose. She doesn't seem to know the word "women" [i.e. instead of dividing people into male and female, there are just "normal" people - female to our eyes - and male aberrations]. Obviously xenophobic, Maaga's underlings moan in horror when she tells them about the things that slimy Rills do to good warrior-women like them.

What Was the BBC *Thinking*?

...continued from page 187

erasures are any guide, then Innes Lloyd sanctioned the wiping of most Hartnell stories. A few had "preservation orders" slapped on them over the years, as in the case of "The Dalek Invasion of Earth" and the working-tapes of "Shada" (17.6).

When *Doctor Who* ceased to be a continuous serial, and became clearly identified as a set of stories (from 3.9, "The Savages", on), there was the option to revisit old adventures. But this only happened once. It was "The Evil of the Daleks" (4.9), shoved into the gap between Seasons Five and Six. This was so unusual that a reason for an adventure re-appearing on the nation's screens was scripted into the last episode of "The Wheel in Space" (5.7). Why did it not happen every year?

One obvious reason is that the lead actor had changed. For continuity purposes, the BBC and Equity concluded that if any stories were to be re-screened then only the current Doctor would appear. Anything else would confuse casual viewers, surely? The decision was reversed just as Tom Baker was leaving in 1981, so BBC2's *The Five Faces of Doctor Who* became the first season of "out-of-Doctor" stories to be transmitted in the UK. Again, note the early-'80s date. It wouldn't have seemed feasible even five years earlier.

So 16mm telerecordings of every story existed at some point until 1972. By 1978, when the library expanded to include videotape, no master-copies existed. However, four years earlier the 16mm copies were extensive enough to include "The Smugglers", "Galaxy Four", "Mission to the Unknown" and all four episodes of "The Tenth Planet". The makers of programmes that used clips from the series, such as *Blue Peter* and the 1977 documentary *Whose Doctor Who?*, had access to a lot that's no longer there. So what happened?

The theory put forward by the person who salvaged many of the copies we have now, Ian Levine, is that the BBC's left hand didn't know what the right hand was doing. Pamela Nash, the BBC employee who'd commissioned the tele-recordings, authorised the dumping or incineration of the prints and negatives in the belief that the master-tapes were still around. This seems annoyingly plausible, but may not be the whole story. BBC Enterprises was licensed to issue the copies overseas to be shown a finite number of times, in accordance with the Equity deals. Once ABC in Australia or WNET/13 in Buffalo had shown them that many times, the copies had to be either destroyed or returned. *Doctor Who* hadn't been syndicated like, say, *M*A*S*H*.

One other possibility is that the BBC was still smarting over the legal fall-out from the excruciating American re-editing of the fourth series of *Monty Python*. The BBC sued ABC - that's the US network, in this case, not the Australian one - in an attempt to stop the edit being shown. Obviously, after 1975 the issue of copyright and what could be done with archive material wasn't one to go into just by crossing your fingers and hoping for the best. It may be that Enterprises sought to limit the potential for more hassle by simply not having anything potentially troublesome in the archive.

The obvious next question, then, is: why was so much kept? One answer is that several episodes were made on video but transferred onto 35mm film for ease of editing, and so went to the main library. Another is that the clause in the export contracts about returning the films to the BBC, to be re-exported elsewhere, meant there were multiple copies of the most export-friendly stories hanging around (mainly the first two seasons). It would have taken ages to burn all of it, and after six years they just hadn't got around to disposing of every copy of (say) "The Chase". Meanwhile, some episodes were "borrowed" so that clips could be used in other programmes. Notoriously, one "J. Smith" signed the release documentation for the all-important last episode of "The Tenth Planet", and it was never seen again.

So, we end up with 108 missing episodes in 2005. We keep thinking that there's no more to be found, but material still crops up from time to time; in garage-sales, the cellars of Mormon churches in South London, small TV companies in Nigeria where the storage is haphazard, even in the BBC archive mis-labelled as something else. The worldwide network of *Doctor Who* fans now working as archivists or TV executives has uncovered plenty of other programmes destroyed by the Corporation, and we live in a sort of guarded hope that we haven't *quite* unearthed everything yet. Even if the gaps between discoveries are, ominously, getting longer and longer.

Steven considers the Drahvin spaceship to have some good features, but describes it as old-fashioned and made from inferior metal. It's equipped with 'outside radio' and exterior-mounted flame-throwers, as well as weapons for space-combat. In addition to their big guns, the Drahvins use a metallic mesh net which can deactivate a Chumbley by cutting off the 'control waves'. These waves come from the...

• *Rills.* Ammonia breathers, to whom oxygen is inimical. They're highly advanced scientists, in space to explore rather than conquer, making them kinsmen / kinsthings of the Doctor. Like him, they state that they never kill. They know of humanity - being aware of the distress that their appearance causes and stating that 'not all the dominant species in the universe look like humans' - but Drahvins are new to them. They're so civilised that they're prepared to put the Doctor's escape from the planet above their own, as he shares their ethics but 'travels further' than they can. Conflict is unknown where they come from.

The Rills' skin is leathery [with scales according to the script, but none are visible in the one available photo], and they have tusk-like teeth protruding from the lower jaw. Maaga believes them to be green. They seem to have two hands, like veined flippers, though it's not clear how they move about. They appear to be about four feet tall. [And must be able to see into the ultra-violet, since the script claims their atmosphere is semi-opaque to human eyes.] Having no vocal cords, they communicate telepathically and can only "speak" through their robot servants, though they can project images of past events into human minds. They're not deaf, either.

The Rill ship originally had a crew of twelve. Despite two-thirds of them being killed in the crash, they're able to repair and pilot the vessel, but not refuel it from the feeble local sunlight. They've been drilling for power instead, although they haven't been able to convert the gas they've found into sun-ray energy. The spaceship is a black sphere, surrounded by polythene sheeting over scaffolding in equilateral triangle formation, and even the Doctor's impressed by it. It's obviously armed, despite their good intentions. They never leave their ship, so they need...

• *Chumblies.* These appear to be robots, but both the lead Rill and Vicki speak of them as if they're alive. The Chumbley body is a stack of three hemispherical segments, separated by vertical cylinders, which retract when deactivated and turn the Chumbley into an impervious dome. When the cylinders are at full stretch, a Chumbley is about the same height as a Rill, less than imposing from a human point of view. They investigate

the TARDIS by repeatedly bumping into it, the Doctor believing they're blind but capable of heat-detection. Each one is equipped with a light-ray that can set fire to bushes, act as a welding implement or paralyse humanoids.

A Chumbley relays information via a telescopic antenna, which lights up when in use, and can manipulate objects with curved "mandibles" extending from the shell. They have no trouble using bombs, drills and other tools. They also serve as mobile 'phones, allowing long-distance communication for the Rills and their allies. Chumblies can telepathically receive and translate the Rills' thoughts, converting them into spoken language once a sample has been assessed. Vicki shouting at a Chumbley seems to provide a suitable baseline for English.

[As with most instant-translation devices in SF, it seems infeasible that the Rills would be able to speak fluent English after hearing one sentence. Fortunately, in this case we're explicitly told that the Rills are telepathic, which makes things seem more reasonable; this must work in much the same way that the TARDIS' translation facilities do. It's not clear whether the Doctor and company would be able to communicate with the Rills *without* the Rills' own translation methods, but see **Does the Universe Really Speak English?** under 14.1, "The Masque of Mandragora". It's possible that Rill minds are too different from the universal norm for the TARDIS to make sense of their thoughts. Language requires a concept of self, so it *does* seem acceptable that the less humanoid something is, the harder its language is for humanoids to fathom. Compare with the big green blob in "The Creature from the Pit" (17.3) and the reptiles in "The Leisure Hive" (18.1), both of which require translators when dealing with the Doctor.]

The Chumbleys often act as if self-willed, but cutting off the control waves from the Rills makes them shut down. [Perhaps it's like "coverage".] They're magnetised, so the Drahvins' metal mesh can't be recovered once it's been used, though other Chumblies can evidently reverse this magnetism. Despite being impervious to fire and Drahvin guns, they can be taken out with a good bash from an iron bar.

Planet Notes

• *The Planet.* It's never named, and nor is its location specified. [The title "Galaxy Four" would suggest that it's in Galaxy Four, although the Drahvins describe *Drahva* as being in Galaxy Four, as if this world were somewhere else. Not for the last time, we should remember that the title of this story was just used by the *Doctor Who* production office for the sake of convenience and was never meant to be revealed to the public - so it may be largely irrelevant to the events of the story. Then again, would the Drahvins need to go to a completely different galaxy just to find a single world suitable for colonisation?]

The planet can support oxygen-breathing life, yet appears to have no indigenous fauna, just a few flowers that smell like roses. Other than that it's mostly savannah and a few twisted trees, and is utterly silent. It has three suns, so it only goes dark for about four hours. [But it only seems to orbit *one* of the three... this makes very little sense, and the difference between this and a one-sun world is barely perceptible.] The reason for the planet's destruction is never given, with the Doctor merely describing the way it'll turn into hydrogen. The explosion obliterates the Drahvins.

History

• *Dating*. Very little indication. [If the Drahvins *are* descended from humans, then it must be thousands of years in our future, though there's no real evidence to back this up and Steven seems to think the Drahvin ship is quite old-fashioned. See also **Things That Don't Make Sense**. On the other hand, they call their home galaxy "Galaxy Four" instead of "Galaxy One", which might indicate that Drahva is itself a colony. And Maaga's reference to Earth-people suggests that at the very least she's run into humans before. We can't really be sure how far the Drahvins have travelled, as it's implied that they have ships capable of moving between galaxies, but at the same time space-hopping seems to be new to them.]

The Analysis

Where Does This Come From?   However routine it might all seem, there's a lot to say here about the willingness of everyone to avoid the obvious. Gar, the character who became Maaga in the final draft, was a run-of-the-mill space-villain; his crew were bog-standard pretty-boy thugs. The Chumblies, unsurprisingly, are a cross between the Daleks and helpful robots like Robbie in *Forbidden Planet*. And yet, when the producer made a few tiny changes to the scenario and Derek Martinus

decided to raise the bar, it all gelled.

There are two factors we should bear in mind, which could have gone in **The Lore** but are worth mentioning here. One is that there was a new story editor, who came into the production team from the magazine-set soap opera *Compact*. Donald Tosh inherited this script when he began work in April 1965. The story being made then, "The Chase", seems with hindsight to be everything Tosh was keen to avoid letting through on his watch. Look at the next few stories and you'll see what we mean. However, an even bigger part of the process is Verity Lambert. Although her involvement in the making of "Galaxy Four" was slight, in the commissioning process she advocated making the Drahvin world a matriarchy - perhaps as a parting shot at the boy's-club atmosphere of the BBC - and introduced the "test-tube baby" aspect.

This old chestnut had made a return to the public consciousness through recent advances in genetics, especially since the person-in-the-street had started to get a handle on James Watson and Francis Crick's pioneering work on DNA in the 1950s. Throughout the '60s stories, we see a fear of what modern technology was going to do to us, and what the children watching the programme would grow into. *Doctor Who* had previously made light of this, but now the series had a stablemate that was trying to be "relevant". It was called *Out of the Unknown*.

The memos from Alice Frick about science fiction and the general public (see **Where Did *All* of This Come From?**, back at the start of this book) had hit a nerve. Frick had believed that the mass viewership would need too much explained to follow an SF drama, and that these explanations could rather too easily turn into stodgy great lumps of exposition. But BBC2, still less than two years old, was aimed at audiences a bit quicker on the uptake. Irene Shubik - another of Sydney Newman's team from *Armchair Theatre* - was given the job of making one-hour adaptations of published SF works, especially social satires, that could be done with BBC facilities. In a sense, this is what BBC2 was "for".

The results were mixed, but what's interesting about *Out of the Unknown* is that the effort not to make *Doctor Who*-ish programmes really shows. The Visual Effects department was involved, and went to town on the gore and guns. The directors made full use of VT and out-of-sequence filming, often resulting in some very uneven performanc-

ABOUT TIME 1963-1966

es. Some of the more "arty" directors were on board, and introduced crashingly obvious text-book Freudian symbolism. What's more, the designers and costume people all worked on individual plays and didn't liase, resulting in lots of nearly-identical visions of the future with blond Beatle-wigs and chrome-plated sliding doors (which reflected the camera so much better in 625 lines...). It was at this point that the *Doctor Who* approach to the material and the visuals came more sharply into focus. Now that it was no longer the only game in town, the programme could define itself.

"Galaxy Four" might have worked as an episode of *Out of the Unknown*, which did occasionally commission new works (both Robert Holmes and Brian Hayles ended up writing for *Doctor Who* through *OotU*, one way or another). But it chose to be *Doctor Who*, at a time when the very concept of *Doctor Who* was about to be rethought by a new production team.

As for the "meaning" of this story... it's probably going too far to see it as yet *another* allegory of the Cold War, but Maaga's language when she's priming her underlings to hate the Rills ('you want their slimy claws to close around your necks...?') sounds suspiciously like a parody of (a) anti-communist propaganda, and (b) the kind of language used in science fiction B-movies where the creeping, insidious aliens are blatantly based on Commies anyway. In fact, while fandom has always liked to insist that it's a story about not judging by appearances, this doesn't hold up when you examine the story. Far from being surprised when the monsters turn out to be nice and the humanoids turn out to be evil, we're told to distrust the Drahvins from their very first scene, and the Doctor establishes that the Rills are civilised long before we see their horrible faces. Only one scene in episode four pushes home the it's-what-inside-that-counts point, and *that's* more about ethics than about prejudice.

It makes more sense to think of this story, or at least the first half, as a parable about propaganda. Even so, it's the Drahvins who end up being the closest to traditional SF communists, lacking individuality and with leaders who get all the good food.

Things That Don't Make Sense This is a planet with multiple suns, and yet rather than reckon time in multiples of the rotational period ("days"), the Drahvin calculate in "dawns". With one sun this amounts to the same thing, but the gap between sunrises in this particular solar system could be as little as twenty minutes or - like our moon - a fortnight. And what if they were right at one of the poles, and the planet were tilted with regard to the plane of the ecliptic (as Earth is, which is why we have seasons)? It'd be like the arctic circle, where in summer the nights don't happen and in winter you get a period when the sun doesn't rise for days on end. While it's a nice change from every race in the universe calculating in "Earth days", it's still a bit rubbish.

On top of this, we're told that this is a three-sun world and then told that the solar-powered Rill spaceship can't recharge here. This is feasible, if the extra suns are as pathetic as they appear to be, but it's an odd piece of plotting; it's like going to all the trouble of setting a story in the middle of the Atlantic Ocean, then introducing fish-aliens who have to live inside special tanks because Earth has the wrong sort of water.

Another puzzle related to the "Fourteen to Doomsday" strand of the plot: why does the Doctor lie to Maaga about how long the planet's got left? It serves no purpose, and looks like pure vindictiveness. Moreover, Maaga threatens to kill Vicki when she suspects something, so it's an obvious lie as well as a stupid one. But perhaps not as pointless as Maaga telling the Drahvins that their fellow soldier was killed by the Rills, when in fact Maaga shot the hapless dough-girl herself. In a story where the leader maintains discipline through having unimaginative goonettes in her thrall, such exemplary punishment would have been more of a spur for her own troops and impressed on the enemy how well-drilled and ruthless the girls are. But no, she has to blame it on the neighbours.

On a similar note... Maaga believes self-sacrifice to be 'strange', and seems to find it inconceivable that a human being would die for his or her friends, even though she's used to sending blindly-obedient soldier Drahvins to their deaths for the good of all Drahvin-kind. She also uses the word 'life' in the Terry Nation sense, stating that there's none of it on the planet despite all the plants. And her way of convincing Steven to re-enter the Drahvin ship is to tell him that she's going to kill him. Sweet-talker.

The Doctor and Vicki, despite their ages, have never had any trouble dealing with fights or chucking assassins out of windows. Yet when Steven is losing a wrestling-contest with Maaga, they stand around watching as if it's unthinkable to give the designated TARDIS he-man any physical help against a girl. And how dense does the Doctor have to be to believe that by sabotaging the clearly vital Rill ammonia-producing machine, he's only inconveniencing the Rills and not killing them?

Not really a flaw in the story, but an oddity given what we later discover about the history of the human race in this series: Steven apparently comes from a time when interplanetary travel is quite hit-and-miss, when most of humanity is still centred on Earth, and when movement between *galaxies* is presumably a long way in the future. The Drahvins speak as if they explore other galaxies all the time, even giving them numbers instead of names. Yet Steven finds their spaceship distinctly unimpressive and old-fashioned. Does he just not like the whole retro-chic look?

To nit-pick even further... if the plural is "Chumblies" then the singular ought to be "Chumbly", whereas if one of them is a "Chumbley" then they should all be "Chumbleys" (like "donkeys" and "monkeys"). But the documentation mixes the two forms.

Billy Fluff: 'We should get some long-deserved, undeserved peace for once.'

And, who thought it was a good idea to name a monster after a Welsh seaside resort?

Critique   While it's hard to see *precisely* why this was commissioned, given that everything worthwhile was added by the producer and director afterwards, it does its job. Unfortunately, its job is to fill in four episodes before "Mission to the Unknown" and the end of Verity Lambert's contract. No wonder the cast got bored (see **The Lore**). After all the conceptual messing-about with time in the last three stories, we're back to good old-fashioned space-exploration, mercifully without giant insects but with a Queen Bee and attendant drones. Well... "good", maybe, "old-fashioned" definitely. This is a throwback to an idea of the programme that was cornball even in David Whitaker's time.

With all but six minutes missing from the archive, we aren't in a position to say if Martinus' directorial debut on the series matches the standard of his later efforts, although it doesn't *sound* too sluggish. The tiny fragments we have suggest that he at least moved the camera around the

over-familiar sets with some panache. But, with regard to the sound, this is one of those stories where Brian Hodgson is the real star. It's hard now to recall how unfamiliar, unnatural, unearthly and generally un-1965 the noise of a space-based *Doctor Who* story was to the viewing public. The Chumblies might have *looked* a bit amateurish, yet they sounded like nothing else, and the noises they made had a sort of language and a sort of logic. As would be the case in many stories before Dick Mills took over "Special Sound" in Season Ten, the lack of anything remotely similar in the real world forgave any amount of dodgy acting or any number of obviously studio-bound planets. Spaceships can be "just" models, but sounds aren't quite so easy to place.

It's hard to tell if the girls with big guns are giving brilliant performances of not being very clever, or are just terrible actors. Even Drahvin Three is unable to break free and think for herself, although - in another cliché that the story flirts with and then subverts - for a while it looks as if Steven's going to get somewhere with her. What this means is that "Galaxy Four" is as close as we get to a story with only one humanoid other than the TARDIS crew. It puts a lot of pressure on Stephanie Bidmead's performance as Maaga, and she's just not up to it. Maaga should be terrifying and ruthless, but instead she's more like a slightly irked school dinner lady.

So we're left with the regulars. They're a well-oiled machine by now. Little touches like Vicki doing Steven's hair make it seem as if they've been together for years, not for one story and an episode. It could have gone on like this for years, and nobody would really have objected. Instead the programme was about to be hurled out of the comfort-zone, shaken up and made dangerous and exciting again, but at a cost. However dynamic the impact of John Wiles and Donald Tosh was, replacing Vicki was a bad move...

The Facts

Written by William Emms. Directed by Derek Martinus, with film work supervised by Mervyn Pinfield. Ratings: 9.0 million, 9.5 million, 11.3 million, 9.9 million.

No episodes exist in the BBC archive... see **What Was the BBC *Thinking*?**. Six minutes remain from episode one, however, and are available on the "Missing Years" documentary on the *Lost in Time* DVD set.

Supporting Cast Stephanie Bidmead (Maaga), Marina Martin (Drahvin One), Susanna Caroll (Drahvin Two), Lyn Ashley (Drahvin Three), Robert Cartland (Rill Voices).

AKA... Until recently the story was more commonly listed as "Galaxy 4", and some people seem to feel that "Galaxy Four" is an unacceptable way of writing it. We've taken the lead from Emms' Target novelisation, and from the *Radio Times* listing.

Episode Titles "Four Hundred Dawns", "Trap of Steel", "Airlock", "The Exploding Planet".

Working Titles You guessed it: "Doctor Who and the Chumblies".

Cliffhangers After checking the TARDIS' astral map, the Doctor announces to Steven that tomorrow is the last day this planet will ever see; inside the Rill ship, Vicki turns rounds and screams at what she sees behind her (unusually, *we* don't see the hint of monster until the start of the next episode); Steven collapses as the air is pumped out of the Drahvin airlock.

The lead-in to the next story: on a far-off jungle planet, a deranged man in the clothes of a spacetraveller regains consciousness in the foliage, telling himself that he must kill... must kill... must *kill*...

The Lore

• This story had been scheduled for Mervyn Pinfield to direct, but ill-health intervened and BBC newcomer Derek Martinus was given both this and "Mission to the Unknown". It appears that the casting for both stories was Pinfield's choice, except that Robert Cartland - hired to play the delegate Malpha in the next story - was roped in to replace Anthony Paul as the Rill voice. Shown some of the earlier episodes by way of an introduction to the series, Martinus put his foot in his mouth (a bit) by telling Verity Lambert that he thought the programme should aim for higher standards, but it doesn't seem to have done him any harm. Hartnell made sure that Martinus gained the full benefit of his experience...

• Lambert was rather engrossed in making sure her swan-song as producer, "Mission to the Unknown", went well. This meant that day-to-day production duties were handled by John Wiles, who immediately rubbed Hartnell the wrong way, and the next year would be a battle for control of the series. As the sole remaining member of the original team, Hartnell felt he had custody of the programme's lore and spirit, and - probably rightly - believed that details like which-switch-opened-the-TARDIS-doors mattered to younger viewers.

• William Emms got lucky; he sent in an unsolicited story outline, and against all the odds it ended up being commissioned. He was a regular viewer of *Doctor Who*, so "Galaxy Four" comes perilously close to being the first on-screen work of fan-fiction (note the unexpected mention of Xeros and the return of the TARDIS astral map, neither of them really necessary to the script).

• Both Hartnell and O'Brien amended the scripts too much for the writer's liking, though rather less than most script editors. Incoming story editor Donald Tosh had to do a lot of redrafting for the changed cast, but in general Emms was at least consulted. The author later wrote and thanked them for this. Whilst Purves had good reason to be aggrieved, as Steven was acting out of character in order to cover up the fact that most of his lines were written for Barbara, Emms was particularly irritated by Hartnell's performance.

• "Chumbley" is a portmanteau of "chum" and "friendly". Emms wrote the stage-directions for the robots with invented verbs like "chamble", "chutter", "chingle" and "jink" alongside "jingle" and "chitter". One of the people chambling and jinking about inside a Chumbley was Angelo Muscat, the little butler from *The Prisoner*.

3.2: "Mission to the Unknown"

(Serial D/C. One Episode, 9th October 1965.)

Which One is This? Daleks, secret agents, six kinds of funny-looking alien, mind-altering cacti... but no Doctor. Yes, it's Terry Nation's Dalek spin-off, episode one.

Firsts and Lasts For reasons that are about to become thunderingly obvious, this is a rather significant break with the programme's usual practices on at least two counts, but it's also the last story to have Verity Lambert even nominally in charge. And as you can see if you glance up a few lines, this is the one example of a story's production-code not following the alphabetical sequence. It was identified in the paperwork as "Dalek Cutaway" (see **What Are These Stories Really Called?** for more), and until recently as "Serial T/A". In production terms, it's the last story of the programme's second year, even if it was broadcast as the second story after the seven-week summer break.

The Thing to Notice About "Mission to the Unknown"...

1. There's only one episode, and none of the TARDIS crewmembers appear. In other words, this is a stand-alone Doctorless story. Except that it isn't; the whole thing is one huge twenty-five minute info-dump for the forthcoming Daleks-go-ballistic epic, "The Daleks' Master Plan" (3.4). So in effect this is really episode one of a thirteen-parter, with a four-part story sandwiched in before episode two. We'll explain how this came to happen later, but most of the other things that are worthy of note about this episode are discrepancies between it and the next twelve parts...

The Continuity

The Plot   On the screeching jungle planet of Kembel, pilot Gordon Lowery and his passenger Marc Cory are fixing up their damaged spacecraft when they're unexpectedly attacked by fellow crewmember Garvey... who's turning into a Varga plant. After killing the man-vegetable, Cory reveals that he's a special agent from Earth, acting on a tip-off that the Daleks have set up a base here and are planning something spectacularly unpleasant. And Varga plants are known to be used by the Daleks as guard-dogs. Sure enough, a conference is being staged at a nearby Dalek HQ, involving representatives from six other alien powers with a common interest in toppling humanity. Cory makes a tape recording warning Earth of the threat, but before he can get it into space, Lowery is infected with Varga toxin and Cory himself is exterminated by a Dalek patrol.

As the delegates make their plans against Earth, the recording lies undiscovered in the middle of the jungle. Now, who's going to find *that*...?

The Non-Humans
• *The Daleks*. Dalek weapons are capable of destroying an entire spaceship, if they concentrate their fire [also the case in 10.4, "Planet of the Daleks"]. As on their last outing, they're using

seismic detectors to track people. The Daleks on Kembel are once again led by a black Supreme.

In the last five-hundred years, the Daleks have gained control of over seventy planets in ninth galactic system, and forty more in the constellation of Miros, millions of light-years away from Earth's galaxy. On Kembel they've assembled delegates from 'seven planets' [there are six aliens at the table, which means they're including themselves] so that the seven great powers of the Outer Galaxies can sign a treaty. They're aiming for galactic conquest, naturally starting with Earth.

The last of the delegates to arrive is known as Malpha, though the last *spaceship* to arrive is identified as coming from the planet Gearon. Marc Cory immediately recognises the origin of this ship, said to be huge by Earth standards. Malpha talks in a rasping, evil-sounding voice, and scarily speaks of 'this universe' as if he comes from a different one. [For a more detailed run-down of the delegates, and the problems of identifying them, see **Which Sodding Delegate is Which?** under "The Daleks' Master Plan".]

• *Varga Plants.* Yet more creatures which are half-animal and half-vegetable. They only grow naturally on Skaro, though they were originally created in Dalek labs. [Possibly derived from an existing plant species like the fungoids (2.8, "The Chase"), but see also the almost vegetable-like Slyther used in "The Dalek Invasion of Earth" (2.2). If nothing else, this tells us that Skaro has been re-settled and stocked with life since "The Daleks" (1.2). This in turn would indicate that "Mission to the Unknown" takes place after "Destiny of the Daleks" (17.1), in which the Daleks return to Skaro after a long absence and the planet seems devoid of significant flora.]

The Vargas resemble cacti, and the toxin in the thorns has psychotropic effects as well as teratogenic properties; basically, it makes you go mental and kill people, then turns you into a Varga plant yourself. [Evolutionarily sensible, as those killed by the partially-transformed victim can become food for the plant in its final form.] The transformation begins with white cilia, or fibres, sprouting from the skin of the victim. A mature Varga is roughly cylindrical, with bulbous growths like ulcers [remarkably like the Wirrn larvae from 12.2, "The Ark in Space"], and can slowly pull itself along by the roots. The metamorphosis can create a Varga plant even if the victim is killed before the change.

Planet Notes

• *Kembel.* Allegedly the most hostile [inhabitable] world in the [known] universe, and other civilisations avoid it, according to Cory. It's covered in jungle, though none of the screeching animals are ever seen. The Daleks have constructed a citadel with a spaceport for the purpose of staging their conference, securing the surrounding area with Varga plants and surveillance equipment. [The implication is that Kembel is a long way from Earth, but in the same galaxy, although the script makes it clear that Terry Nation has no idea what "galaxy" actually means. Ergo, a lot of what we hear about galactic politics here has to be retconned into submission.]

History

• *Dating.* Some considerable time in Earth's future, when space-travel is commonplace and intergalactic travel doesn't appear to be a big deal. ["The Daleks' Master Plan" is set in 4000 AD, and probably doesn't take place more than a few months after this, as Cory's body has been reduced to a skeleton but hasn't been overgrown with foliage.]

The 'rocket' which crash-lands on Kembel initially has a two-man crew and one passenger, Marc Cory. Cory is an agent of the Special Security Service, which means he has a special identification card, is 'licensed to kill', and on this occasion carries a document giving him the power to requisition any kind of help from either civilians or the military. A week ago, a space-freighter spotted a spaceship of a type never before used in what Cory calls 'our system' [he means galaxy], which matches known descriptions of a Dalek spaceship. Cory recognises the Varga plants, and knows they're native to Skaro, but he states the Daleks haven't been active in Earth's galaxy for 'some time'. [So Skaro isn't in Earth's galaxy, something that's pretty much confirmed in "Master Plan". It also seems that humanity has visited the planet, as in "Destiny of the Daleks".] The Daleks are best-remembered in this era for their invasion of Earth, with Lowery stating that it happened 'a thousand years' ago [closer to 2,000, actually].

The crashed spaceship has to make a rendezvous with freighter XM2, which won't wait if the appointment is missed [Kembel is a long way from human-space, and Lowery's ship is only a short-range transport]. The futuristic-sounding material 'tarnium' is involved in its construction

[only one letter away from being the most valuable substance in the universe, as we'll discover later], and there's a miniature rocket on board which can send a tape recording into space as a beacon, while even the crew carry ray-guns. The ship is marked with what looks like the UN symbol [very *Dan Dare*].

Malpha refers to Earth's solar system as *the* Solar System [which seems to be its title, judging by later events]. Mars, Venus, Jupiter and the moon colonies are all targets for the Dalek alliance. Cory refers to 'defence mechanisms' that have to be put into place before the Daleks attack, and confidently speaks as if Earth is the prime power of its galaxy.

The Analysis

Where Does This Come From? Secret Agent Marc Cory, Licensed to Kill. Is there anyone reading this who *hasn't* figured out where this story's ambitions lie?

As part of Nation's attempts to make the Daleks bigger than *Doctor Who*, he's gone for broke on raising Earth's defence to UNCLE level, and - cashing in on Spymania, as well as his monsters' own reputations - turns the Daleks into filthy Commies rather than Nazi swine. Then he reintroduces the whole jungle warfare element from "The Chase", thus making the new Soviet-style Daleks look like Japs as well. And just to muddy the waters further, where had most people seen jungles and flame-throwers recently? Oh yes, TV coverage of US troops in Vietnam. (Actually, the presence of flame-throwers in this story has never been proved. They were definitely used in "The Daleks' Master Plan", but some sources dubiously claim they were first deployed here.)

There's also a cactus which warps men's minds. Aside from the then-current interest in LSD as a weapon for infiltration and brainwashing, and the strong whiff of *The Manchurian Candidate*, the plot strand about the Varga plants allows werewolf-style transformations. And werewolves were just about the only horror movie trope that Nation hadn't plundered yet. Except for living mummies, but that'll be handled in "The Daleks' Master Plan".

There is, of course, a whole subtext to this that we haven't mentioned. David Whitaker had been given the job of writing a Dalek comic-strip for the glossy colour boy's magazine *TV21* (or, to be

What Are These Stories Really Called?

So, to recap what we've learned so far. Until "The Savages" (3.9), each individual twenty-five minute episode of *Doctor Who* had its own a title, but the overall title of any given adventure was a nebulous concept. No story title was ever publicised, or used by the announcers. It was mainly a convenience, for the sake of writers and their agents, that groups of episodes were treated as discrete units rather than segments of one continuous serial. For the public it was noticeable that the music and location changed every so often, and a new setting would tend to bring in more viewers, but the lines were blurry and nobody even knew in advance how many episodes it'd take for the Doctor to complete a particular adventure and get off the planet. First-time viewers of "The Rescue" (2.3) must have been shocked that it was over so quickly.

Until 1973, any identification was on the *Friends* principle; "The One with the Daleks", "The One with Marco Polo", and so on. The programme-makers had their own system, in which Story A was the first four episodes, Story B the next seven, et cetera. Most of these groups of episodes had more than one director, so they were sorted by writer. (Designer and musical score generally followed, except at the end of one story and the start of the next. Listen to the way the music changes when the scanner displays Skaro at the end of... um... 1.1.)

Then the *Radio Times* published its tenth anniversary *Doctor Who* special, and all that changed. Here, stories were identified by the title of the first episode. In many cases this was good enough. "An Unearthly Child" is better than any of the many alternatives, in that it puts the emphasis on the story being the start of the Big Adventure. "War of God" is a decent description of what happens in sixteenth-century Paris, and avoids giving the ending away (3.5). "A Holiday for the Doctor" (3.8) promises less than "The Gunfighters", but "The Executioners" (2.8) makes "The Chase" seem far more interesting than it really is.

The next stop was the 1976 reprint of *The Making of Doctor Who*. The original 1972 edition described all the Doctor's adventures for the first time, and even listed them in a special table, but - and this seems unimaginable, now - didn't attach names to them. For the second edition, though, "proper" titles for the first 25 stories were finally put into print. And stayed in print, too, as unlike the *Radio Times* special it was on the shelves of bookshops for years. Most of the names that appeared here were the ones we find ourselves

using today, a mix of titles taken from the first or key episode of a story ("The Edge of Destruction", "The Keys of Marinus") and titles which seemed too obvious *not* to use ("Marco Polo", "The Sensorites"). There were a few oddities, but nothing too startling. "The French Revolution" (1.8) was the title you probably would have used if you'd seen the original press coverage in 1964, and "The Crusaders" (2.6) was only a step away from its ultimate evolutionary form. "The Dead Planet" (1.2) was a leftover from the *Radio Times* days, and its "official" change to "The Daleks" in the early '80s was puzzling to many.

But in certain quarters of fandom, these titles were deemed too accessible to be a good test of one's devotion, so new ones were brought in. Of course, hardcore fans didn't see them as new, but as the "real" titles straight from the production office; the titles that had been used behind the scenes in the mid-'60s, even if the authors had changed their minds from week to week. "The Dead Planet" was too vague, and "The Daleks" was too easy. Story B was, according to the documentation, called "The Mutants". Or "The Survivors". Or "Beyond the Sun", maybe. Nobody ever referred to "The Talons of Weng-Chiang" by its working title of "The Talons of Greel", or referred to "The Claws of Axos" by its working title of "The Vampire from Space" (even though it got as far as the *Radio Times*), yet this was considered an acceptable way to identify the early stories.

But - oh, calamity! - Barry Letts had wrecked it all by doing another story called "The Mutants" (9.4). With the same director and a score by the same composer, just to rub it in. The anomalies multiplied when Target books started bringing out books with names that went beyond the functional. They'd spent the '70s coming up with brilliantly simplified titles like *Doctor Who and the Space War* (for "Frontier in Space") and *Doctor Who and the Auton Invasion* (for "Spearhead from Space"), but by 1980 the series was supposed to be treated with more respect. A couple of years later, they'd even stop putting *and the* in the middle. So when the Target version of Story E ended up being called *The Keys of Marinus*, the decision seemed too sensible to ignore. But were we going to start referring to Story B as *Doctor Who in an Exciting Adventure with the Daleks*? It didn't seem likely.

continued on page 199...

strictly accurate, *TV Century 21* as it was known at this stage). This featured comic-book adaptations of all the major adventure series set in the near future or with hi-tech themes, mostly Gerry Anderson projects. The Dalek strip featured no mention of the Doctor, who was otherwise engaged in the pages of *TV Comic* with his grandchildren John and Gillian, defeating the Pied Piper and other such non-copyrighted antagonists. Instead, we had *Dan Dare*-ish capers starring the Dalek Emperor as a sort of combined villain and central character, ordering his troops to conquer sundry races around the universe. Pitted against them was an alliance of brightly-coloured aliens, oddly-bearded humans, surprisingly self-willed Mechanoids and a robot called Agent 2K, who was about the coolest thing ever in any version of *Doctor Who*, even when his head opened up and turned into a helicopter.

This whole affair was far more lurid and exciting than even the film versions of the Dalek adventures, and Nation wanted a piece. As we'll see (in **What Other Spin-Offs Were Planned?** under 18.7-A, *K9 and Company*), Nation tried to float the idea of a Dalek series. After his contribution to "The Daleks' Master Plan", he wrote a script called "The Destructors", which involved various relatives of the agents seen here and a robot agent called ... Seven. Funnily enough, the set of "Master Plan" was visited by Sam Rolfe, creator and producer of *The Man from UNCLE*. There's been a lot of speculation about this, and yet mysteriously, MGM never made a Dalek TV series. (But they do make *Stargate SG-1*, which features TV's *MacGyver*, and thus the Terry Nation connection is maintained.) What we have on-screen here is as close as the series will ever get to a comic-book or a Saturday Morning Serial. Indeed, a comic-book is exactly what it became, when Nation and former collaborator Brad Ashton came up with a Dalek Annual featuring the SSS as the good guys.

Still, we should bear in mind that Dennis Spooner seems to have had a lot of input here, and that Spooner was used to working on the aforementioned Gerry Anderson puppet-shows. And at times it's shockingly easy to imagine Marc Cory and Gordon Lowery being made of wood. We aren't a million "galaxies" away from the Anderson universe's view of how space-travel and space-adventure should work, with boys in starched clothing crashing on inhospitable planets

and having to arc-weld their rocket-ships into shape. Varga plants aside, there's at least as much *Fireball XL5* as *Dan Dare* in this story. The freighter's called "XM2", which really is a dead giveaway. Even the music sounds like *Captain Scarlet*.

Things That Don't Make Sense All right, so the Daleks expect to have the planet to themselves, which is why they're on Kembel in the first place. But why should they relay the conference to the outside world through their public address system so that Cory can hear it? (See 2.2, "The Dalek Invasion of Earth", for more big-mouthed Daleks giving the game away to human interlopers.) Kembel is also said to be 'the most hostile planet in the Universe', but if it's *so* dangerous, why does it appear that the only things which cause any trouble at all are a few Daleks and the Varga plants - both of which aren't even native to the planet? Does the local wildlife feel intimidated by the competition?

In a way that later becomes a trademark of Robert Holmes' scripts, the words "galaxy", "constellation", "universe" and "system" become interchangeable and almost meaningless. The prize for cosmic pointlessness goes to a confederation of seven galaxies to conquer Earth and a few colonies. They still manage to lose. But perhaps the most confusing misuse of astronomical terms here comes when Malpha claims that the delegates come from the Outer Galaxies, whereas the Daleks come from 'the Solar System', a term that's otherwise used to mean *Earth's* solar system. He might mean that they come from Earth's *galaxy*, but Marc Cory doesn't seem to agree. And not for the last time in a Nation script, the number "seven" changes its value depending on who's counting. The Daleks speak of delegates from seven planets, but when the alliance forces are counted it's six plus the Daleks - just as the title *Blake's 7* only works if Blake counts himself as one of his own subordinates. [Actually, the draft script suggests that seventh delegate Zephon was supposed to make his debut here, but in the end he doesn't turn up until "The Daleks' Master Plan".]

Cory believes he's a member of the Special Security Service, but Lowery thinks it's the *Space* Security Service and Cory responds with a cheery 'that's right'. This isn't a problem that's going to go away, either...

What Are These Stories Really Called?

...continued from page 197

And so the arbiters of title-logic declared that only the production titles were valid. "The Keys of Marinus" could stay, but from now on it was going to be "100,000 BC", followed by "The Survivors", then "Inside the Spaceship". Stories with more than one production title were no problem, you simply went with... oh dear... the one that most people generally agreed on. If there was a way to find a more authentic title than any other, then it was by asking the surviving members of the production team/s what *they* called each story.

Except that they were no bleeding help. If they remembered these stories at all, then it was on the *Friends* principle. A man who spent six weeks getting paid for pushing Zarbi around a set in 1965 is going to remember being surrounded by dancing insects, not what it happened to say on one piece of paper in the production office. In 1994, fandom unearthed a document written by Dennis Spooner which explained the story so far to his successors, and the production code for "Mission to the Unknown" turned out to be rather unexpected. It had always been assumed that the episode had been a bolt-on to "Galaxy Four", and was thus "T/A". In fact, as a "Dalek Cutaway" it was designated "D/C", although in the contract for Mervyn Pinfield to direct them both it was listed as episode five of story T. Heated and pointless arguments ensued, but as it was only one episode, we thought we could just call it "Mission to the Unknown" and have done with it.

At the same time, the early stories were being released on video. And videotape is a *definitive* sort of record, in a way that novelisations aren't, or at least weren't by the 1990s. It could be argued that if the BBC provides the "official" voice of the series, then whatever the BBC video release is called is the best title to use. Sure enough, the arguments have died down now that every existent story is commercially available and properly-labelled. "An Unearthly Child", "The Daleks" and "The Edge of Destruction" are the correct titles these days, no matter what *Doctor Who Magazine* once asked us to believe. (Interestingly, Stephen Cole - in charge of the *Doctor Who* department of BBC Worldwide in the late '90s, and the man whose job entailed everything from writing the back-cover blurbs for the videos to doing Dalek voices for trailers - once told *DWM* that the video release of Story C, when it eventually came, would definitely be "Inside the Spaceship." "Interestingly" because he had more control over these things than just about anyone, and yet he backed down at the last minute and went for "The Edge of Destruction." Did someone threaten him with a fatwah?)

And as for the stories we can't get on video... the purists might balk at the names given to the audio CDs, just as they balk at the narration, but there's no point arguing unless devastating new evidence comes to light. Both "100,000 BC" and "The Tribe of Gum" are, at the end of the day, crap titles. They're also factually inaccurate, or at least misleading. The same goes for 3.5, or Story W if you

continued on page 201...

Critique It's just about possible that this was as good as everyone says. We know the director's capable of miracles; we know the jungle set looks great six episodes later when Douglas Camfield gets a go with it. Judging by the audio recording, it sounds as if it's got the right kind of beat to be a tense, scary-looking piece of TV, and even the dialogue isn't as bad as it usually is when Terry Nation tries to do "space". We also know that the Varga plant transformation was the only thing shot on film at Ealing, though, so it was probably quite static.

The thing to say now is that nobody at the time was particularly impressed. A lot of people got very confused when the Doctor didn't arrive to sort things out, and were even more perplexed when the following episode was set in ancient Asia Minor. Now we know what this story is and how it works, we're ironically in a better position to appreciate its strengths than those people who could actually see what was going on (not the only time this is going to be the case in Season Three, either). After the botched experiment of turning the Daleks into comic relief for a frivolous pop-culture romp, this is the polar opposite, so if nothing else then it lacks the cosiness that the public had come to expect from the series by this point. Mere weeks from now, the recliner-chairs-and-time-TV lifestyle we glimpsed in episode one of "The Chase" will seem inconceivable in this programme.

And as the Doctor's grown in stature, so his arch-foes have had to keep up the pace. Pitching them against serious Space Agent Cory - and if they can beat a professional like him, then an amateur like the Doctor is in *real* trouble - allows the one thing no other *Doctor Who* story can allow. The bad guys win.

The Facts

Written by Terry Nation. Directed by Derek Martinus. Ratings: 8.3 million.

As you may have gathered, it doesn't exist in the BBC archive.

Supporting Cast Edward de Souza (Marc Cory), Barry Jackson (Jeff Garvey), Jeremy Young (Gordon Lowery), Robert Cartland (Malpha); David Graham, Peter Hawkins (Dalek Voices); William Hartnell (Dr. Who, credited but does not appear).

AKA... "Dalek Cutaway". Well, sort of... see **What Are These Stories Really Called?**.

Cliffhanger Malpha underlines the whole going-to-conquer-Earth idea, then leads the Daleks and the alien delegates in a chant of 'victory!'.

The Lore

• One of the giants of BBC television in the 405-line era was Huw Weldon. The crisis following Donald Baverstock's abrupt departure is the subject for a whole book, but one of the effects was that Weldon - famous as a presenter and feared as an administrator - became Controller of Programmes (Television). We'll consider his impact on the programme's development later, but one urban myth needs addressing now. One or other of Weldon's female relatives was, supposedly, dotty about the Daleks and wanted to see them as often as possible. The most common version claims it was his mother-in-law, although all the evidence suggests that the *real* Dalekophile was Weldon himself.

• Nevertheless, someone somewhere suggested that instead of two six-part Dalek stories per annum, why not do a great big one? Once this idea had taken hold, another nifty suggestion followed; they needed another episode to make up the numbers after the last two episodes of "Planet of Giants" (2.1) were squished together. By now the production-team was dead-set on four-part stories, except for the Dalek six-parters, so an odd

number of episodes would generally have been a problem. But the contracts for the regulars were up for renewal, and they were due a holiday after "Galaxy Four", so why not make a one-episode story with none of the main cast?

The only thing in the series familiar and exciting enough to justify this was the Daleks. Additionally, the first Dalek movie was due to premiere in America, and maximum Dalek exposure seemed like a good idea. So in February, Nation was asked for a one-episode adventure, even though he was known to be busy writing for ITC series like *The Saint* and preparing to story-edit *The Baron* (he took on Dennis Spooner as his assistant, which is why Spooner left *Doctor Who* in May).

• Spooner had written a story for Gerry Anderson's *Fireball XL5*, "Space Vacation", featuring a planet called Kemble. Coincidence? Many people have taken the planet's name as a sign that Spooner had more of a hand in this script than is acknowledged, and we'll see more of this in the twelve-part yarn.

• While we're in that vein: Our Hero, for these twenty-five minutes, is Marc Cory. And Nation's script for *The Destructors* had a Jason Cory as its lead character. Hmmm... "Jason" wasn't a popular name until the Spooner-created *Department S* introduced Jason King to the world, so was Spooner pilfering from Nation for a change? Or were they both thinking of the recent Ray Harryhausen monster-fest, *Jason and the Argonauts*?

3.3: "The Myth Makers"

(Serial U, Four Episodes, 16th October - 6th November 1965.)

Which One is This? It's what they had in the 1960s instead of *Xena: Warrior Princess*, as *Doctor Who* pushes the "history" envelope even further with a re-telling of the Trojan Wars. The big wooden horse is there for all to see, though children everywhere weep with disappointment on discovering that the character called "Cyclops" is Tutte Lemkow in an eyepatch (again) instead of a great big giant who eats people.

Firsts and Lasts Vicki leaves, under rather curious circumstances (see **Marrying Troilus: What is She Doing?**), and a minor character gets to

What Are These Stories Really Called?

...continued from page 199

prefer. "The Massacre of St Bartholemew's Eve" is just *wrong*, even if you know it ends with a massacre, which the audience isn't supposed to. It was the Massacre of St Bartholemew's *Day*, and even if someone happened to put "Eve" on the rehearsal scripts, there's no way it would have been OK'd as an official title if such a thing had been necessary. Some of the BBC's own paperwork calls it "The Massacre of St Bartholemew", but that's even worse; St Bartholomew wasn't massacred, he was burned to death / crucified / flayed alive / decapitated (delete according to your preferred version) some considerable time before the events depicted in the story.

Another possibility, though. In the late 1980s, a lot of energy was wasted in trying to figure out whether Season Twenty-Three was one fourteen-part story or three four-parters and a coda. If the latter, then what were the individual titles? And if the former, then was everything up until "The OK Corral" (episode four of "The Gunfighters") one long story, given the lack of over-arcing on-screen

names? Certainly, most so-called stories in the early years bled into one another with cliffhangers. For the viewers, each year's run was one adventure. If we take the end of "Marco Polo" to be the conclusion of the first story, "The Reign of Terror" to be the finale of the second, "The Dalek Invasion of Earth" to be the climax of the third... you get the idea. In which case, the first twenty episodes are *collectively* called "Beyond the Sun", and finally we can all use that title and mean the same thing.

It remains to be seen whether fandom will begin arguing in earnest over the "proper" titles of two-part Eccleston-era stories like "Aliens of London" / "World War Three". For now, though, we trust we can consider the issue resolved. For the purposes of this book, we've used the titles that you'll need if you try to get hold of the stories from your usual video / DVD / CD / cult media import retailer. Unless you really want to quibble about whether it's "Galaxy Four" or "Galaxy 4". The only question remaining is the title of the Paul McGann TV Movie (27.0); we know what we *could* call it, but there might be children reading.

travel with the Doctor, fooling us into thinking that she's going to be a regular. Her name's Katarina, and we're obliged to consider her a companion these days, even though she only turns up in episode four and doesn't even last out the next story.

More importantly, and this was the focus for the publicity material, it's the first time the TARDIS flies into pure myth as opposed to questionable history. Thus it's the first time the Doctor inspires a story he's read about elsewhere, namely the Trojan Horse. This was, if you recall, one of the things the writers were originally forbidden to do.

We hear the first acoustic guitar in the soundtrack, with Troilus and Vicki - no, the pairing doesn't sound quite right, does it? - given an oddly bluesy love theme. And it's the first story officially produced by John Wiles, of course. Though for anyone following this story from the beginning, this isn't quite as great a shock as it being the first story which isn't officially produced by Verity Lambert.

Four Things to Notice About "The Myth Makers"...
1. The audience might well have been assumed to know a bit about the story of Troy, as Homer and Virgil told it, but the twists given to the char-

acters open up the possibility that the end of the tale might also be different in this "true" account. "The Myth Makers" has the Doctor denouncing the Trojan Horse as Homeric hokum, then going off and designing it as an alternative to having to fly into the city on a glider. This is a big shift in emphasis for the supposedly "educational" strand of the series, though at a pinch it at least teaches children to doubt the veracity of written history. Odysseus is a thuggish plunderer, but sharp enough to see advantage in the Doctor's co-operation. Paris is vain and cowardly, even if he's a bit better than Steven anticipated. The real change is King Menelaus, who'd really rather not be doing all this war stuff just because his tiresome wife ran off with yet another pretty young man. Note that they don't bother to include Helen of Troy herself in this version, partly because she'd already dumped Paris by this point, but mainly because there was nobody *Doctor Who* could afford who would've lived up to the hype.

2. With all its playful dialogue, the Doctor's increasingly desperate efforts to stop the story ending the way we expect it to, and the droll bathos of Trojan warriors talking in Iambic pentameter one minute but sounding as if they're going to say "anyone for tennis?" the next, this is

all good fun... for three episodes. The final act must have been shocking in its brutality. Many viewers were nonplussed, as we'd had four episodes of lightweight Chumbley larks, then a no-holds-barred episode of Dalek action that just seemed to get going before it finished, and now a "comedy" story where half the cast are slaughtered at the end.

3. The episode "Death of a Spy" has a subplot about a spy being found and executed. It's hardly the most important thing to happen in those twenty-five minutes, but the title was a last-minute suggestion. Writer Donald Cotton had wanted to call it "Is There A Doctor In The Horse?", so when this was unaccountably vetoed, the replacement title came first and then - it's been reported in other guide-books - the subplot to justify it was expanded at the eleventh hour.

That's almost right, but not entirely, as the actor in question was booked long before the decision was made and the character "Cyclops" was sort of inevitable in this context. But yes, it's Tutte Lemkow, with his eyepatch over the *other* eye this time (see 1.4, "Marco Polo"). The key thing to note, though, is that the title-caption "Next Episode: Death of A Spy" comes seconds after Cassandra accuses Vicki of being a Greek spy and insists she should be killed. Surely, though, this is another "Death of Doctor Who" moment? Surely the Doctor's travelling companions couldn't possibly get killed...? (Q.v. the next story.)

4. Over the years, the Doctor has met a great many epic figures, yet here he never *quite* meets King Priam of Troy. This might seem like a clever ruse, like the Fourth Doctor's running gag about just missing Leonardo da Vinci (see 14.1, "The Masque of Mandragora" and 17.2, "City of Death"), but rumours persist that it wasn't; see **The Lore**.

The Continuity

The Plot   The TARDIS materialises just outside Troy in its final days, specifically in the middle of a fight to the death between Achilles (Greek hero) and Hector (Trojan prince). The Doctor's arrival distracts Hector so much that Achilles slays him, then takes the Doctor to be a manifestation of Zeus. His divine abilities in great demand, the Doctor is forced to leave his companions and go to the Greek encampment, where both Odysseus (King of Ithaca) and Agamemnon (the big Greek

cheese) require him to prove his divine credentials. Soon afterwards the TARDIS is dragged away by Trojans with Vicki still inside it, and in a tight corner the Doctor is forced to admit that he's mortal. To save his skin, he's given two days to come up with an ingenious way to get the Greeks into the city.

Meanwhile, in Troy... Vicki's fate is being decided by the besieged King Priam and his family, including paranoid daughter Cassandra (tetchy prophetess) and dishy son Troilus (the sensitive one of the clan). Steven deliberately gets himself captured by the Trojans in order to be reunited with her, but she's already busy flirting with Troilus, despite Steven's reminder that the fall of the city is imminent. And the Doctor's already given the Greeks the idea of getting into Troy inside a giant wooden horse. Believing the edifice to be the mythical Great Horse of Asia, the Trojans wheel it into the city, with the Doctor, Odysseus and a whole lot of soldiers inside. Scared for Troilus' life, Vicki tricks the prince into leaving the city as night falls, inadvertently leading him into a battle with Achilles which very nearly kills him.

But the Greeks are already attacking Troy, beginning a mass-slaughter and setting the city ablaze. King Priam and most of his family are butchered by Odysseus, while Steven is wounded in the shoulder and helped back to the TARDIS by Cassandra's handmaiden Katarina. The Doctor has to dematerialise the Ship to escape the Greeks, taking Katarina along for the ride but leaving Vicki behind. This, however, is just what she wants. As the city falls, she rejoins Troilus to tell him that she belongs here with him, and together they leave to build another Troy.

The Doctor   Trying to get the TARDIS back to Earth again [and return Steven to his own time?]. He thinks it's perfectly reasonable to go outside the TARDIS and interrupt two warriors' lethal combat simply to ask where he is, and accepts no responsibility when the distraction gets one of them killed. Nor does he have any qualms about impersonating a deity. As one might expect, he knows his Homer, and can tell Agamemnon what's happening at home. However, his ability to design a glider, a launcher and a giant wooden horse that can be built in under a day is an impressive testimony to his engineering skills.

Though he believes that Homer's story of the Trojan Horse was poppycock, the Doctor's prepared to tell the Greeks how to build the real thing. [Note that this isn't a paradox. If the Doctor had been inspired by Homer's story, and Homer had been inspired by the Doctor's intervention, then it might have been problematic. But presumably Homer just made the horse up, little realising that thanks to his brilliant invention it'd end up really happening (mind you, this isn't what the novelisation claims). We can assume that the existence of the *real* horse is forgotten by history after this. Note, though, that in the time since "The Romans" (2.4), the Doctor has come to terms with the idea that he might be *causing* history. He doesn't even act as if he's made a significant difference.]

• *Ethics*. His anger at Odysseus owes in part to the indignity of hiding in the horse with the sweaty Greeks, but it's mostly the sailor's attitude to warfare that causes his fury. Yet the war itself seems of little consequence to him. [Perhaps because it's so well-documented as a "myth" that he realises his intervention can't alter the course of history much. The influence of Homer and Virgil, both of whom completely made up their versions, is more important to Earth's development than a little thing like northern Greece temporarily securing another trade-route.]

Even in the carnage of the fall of Troy, his main worry is getting his friends back to the Ship. This makes his acceptance of Vicki's departure more puzzling, but he seems to understand her reasons perfectly, even if they never say goodbye. [Compare with his attitude to Susan in 2.2, "The Dalek Invasion of Earth".]

• *Inventory*. An elastic band fished from his pocket proves useful.

The Supporting Cast

• *Vicki*. She's less than seventeen years old, but not much, and here she has a conscience working overtime. She decides, at the crunch-point, that letting Troilus know she didn't betray him is more important than remaining on the TARDIS. Before this she's coyly flirtatious with the Trojan prince, although she doesn't seem to recognise the name "Cressida" when Priam uses it. She confesses to Troilus that she loves adventure, and the arrival of Aeneas' ships after the fall of Troy is a welcome sign that she's only at the start of her travels.

In fact her resentment at being left in the Ship to nurse her ankle [wrenched at the end of "Galaxy Four"] is part of her motive for making her presence felt; the other is that she thinks the TARDIS will be destroyed by fire. Actually she seems to know surprisingly little about the Ship, as the Doctor doesn't believe she's capable of making it dematerialise [compare this with her inspired button-smashing in 2.5, "The Web Planet"].

• *Steven*. Still rather too sarcastic for the Doctor's liking. He teases Vicki about her new admirer, and is very much the younger brother this time around. Steven knows about Troilus and Hector, and yet strangely the names Diomede and Cressida don't ring a bell. [When you consider that future-people seem to consider Shakespeare as the baseline of civilisation, and that *Troilus and Cressida* is probably the most famous version of the story even today, this is like knowing about Romeo but not Juliet.] When taunting Paris, he has no trouble falling into the blank-verse type of language that the locals use in pre-fight dissing.

• *Katarina*. The obedient handmaiden of Cassandra of Troy, she demonstrates an obvious and unaffected concern for Steven when he's wounded. She's strangely unphased by the TARDIS' interior, describing herself as being in 'limbo' as if it's all part of her job description. She's convinced that she's to die, and that the divine Doctor is taking her on a journey into the beyond. Something she obviously welcomes...

The TARDIS The wardrobe has the right clothes for the period. [Contrary to what's been said elsewhere, Vicki's outfit isn't the same robe seen in "The Romans" but a nice little off-the-shoulder number several shades darker.]

History

• *Dating*. Well, it's the fall of Troy, ten years after the start of the siege. [These days, we sort of assume a date of 1200 BC, plus or minus half a century.]

The Trojans are descendants of people from Central Asia, and Priam describes them as being 'horsemen' above all. This explains the rather unwise decision to let the Doctor's wooden horse into the city. As advertised, the Trojan War has lasted for a decade, and was caused when Helen left her husband Menelaus for the Trojan prince Paris. In this version it was entirely Helen's own decision, with no divine interventions, and Menelaus was frankly pleased to see the back of her. Agamemnon, Menelaus' brother and King of Mycenae, is keen to exploit the situation to get his hands on Troy and the Bosphoros trade-route monopoly. Helen is still in Troy, even if she's not hanging around with the royal family.

The sequence of events is telescoped into two days after the TARDIS arrives. It starts when Hector, Paris' brother, dies at Achilles' hand. [We're in the later stages of Homer's storyline here. Achilles' "special friend" Patroclus is already dead, and it's this that's driven the Greek hero into an unreasoning rage, something which is only partly cured by slaughtering Hector and dragging the corpse around to taunt the Trojans.]

All the big names are here, but they're not all as promised. Odysseus is more interested in the booty he can claim than the glory of a victory or the righteousness of the Greek cause. He doesn't believe the Doctor to be Zeus, but *does* believe the more bizarre story about travelling through time in a wooden box. He has a network of agents, most notably Cyclops the mute, whose system of Harpo Marx-style signs only Odysseus can follow. [He doesn't seem to have the auburn hair Homer described, judging by the stills.]

Priam is the King of Troy, and seems at first sight rather vague. In fact he's a few steps ahead of the rest of his family, in whom he is - on the whole - disappointed. [Hardly the stern patriarch of fifty sons mentioned in the *Aeneiad* or *Iliad*.] His daughter, Cassandra, is the high priestess and claims to have the gift of prophecy. She's able to accurately foretell the fall of Troy and Odysseus' ten-year wanderings, and has recently had a premonition about a wooden artefact bringing Greeks into the city, though at first she thinks it's the TARDIS rather than the horse. [Yet her relatives believe she's unreliable, so the Ship's presence may have awoken some latent precognitive ability in her. Or something like that.]

The middle son of the House of Priam is Paris, who may have started all this hassle but isn't much of a warrior and has no stomach for killing. Unaccountably, he's irresistible to women. Vicki's love interest Troilus is the baby of the family, seventeen years old and genuinely angry about Hector's death. [He never finds out that Vicki and friends were partly responsible. Will she ever tell him?] Paris is uncomfortably conscious that his reputation as the ladykiller is under threat, but Troilus himself is as-yet unaware of his own charms. Like Vicki, he wants adventure, not war.

The most notable thing about Achilles, supposedly the Greeks' greatest warrior, is that he accepts the Doctor as Zeus not because of any apparent miracle but because he recognises something wondrous in the Doctor's nature. [As with Cassandra, these people seem terribly perceptive even if there's no actual "magic" around.] He's slain by Troilus [N.B. in Shakespeare's version it's the other way around], while Odysseus and his men slaughter Priam and Paris, and Agamemnon carts off Cassandra. Only Troilus remains at liberty. The end of events sees his cousin Aenis arrive with a number of ships [seven, traditionally], to take him and Vicki away to a new home.

The Analysis

Where Does This Come From? Anyone who's ever sat through a British-made World War II flick about escape from a POW camp will relish the irony: instead of a tunnel or a wooden horse, the Doctor proposes to use a glider to get over the wall. Then he ends up inside a different *sort* of wooden horse, only he's trying to break into the enclosure, not out of it.

A frivolous point? Not really, because we have to remember that just about everyone involved in the making of this story had lived through a real war, and most had been made to read Homer in school. Disillusionment with the heroics of mythical characters was nothing new, and Shakespeare had countered the jingoism of *Henry V* with his own treatment of *Troilus and Cressida* at a time when a war looked unavoidable, but the 1960s brought a new sense of honesty about these things. The Second World War was still a little too recent to be tackled within the generally-accepted limits of good taste; the first sketch to parody the "official" version of the War, performed by Peter Cooke and Jonathan Miller as part of *Beyond the Fringe*, had caused uproar but merely said what a lot of people under thirty were thinking. However, Charles Chilton - author of the BBC's seminal SF radio series *Journey into Space* - had collected the sardonic "underground" literature and songs of the trenches in World War One to make *Oh What a Lovely War* (see 6.7, "The War Games"), and debunked the popular notion of sacrifice and duty that still persisted fifty years on.

In this instance, the fact that a pointless ten-year-long siege took place so close to Gallipoli and the Dardenelles made the comparison with Troy unavoidable. Many of those who died did so with copies of Homer in their pockets.

The mention of *Beyond the Fringe* is more relevant than it may seem. In "The Romans" (2.4) we

Marrying Troilus: What *is* She Doing?

All sorts of odd anomalies crop up when you look closely at what Vicki says and does during her time on the TARDIS. One minute she's been thoroughly educated by teach-o-matic machines, the next she's Wacky Space-Girl who doesn't know the first thing about us primitive pre-hyperdrive types (c.f. Zoe in Season Six, who comes from the twenty-first century and is therefore confused by candles). Yet she knows her Earth history, and Popular Culture 101 must have been her elective study, possibly in pill form. So on seeing Greek and Trojan soldiers duking it out, she fully expects to see all the familiar characters, 'the Heroes' as she calls them.

In this regard, it's hugely unlikely that you'd spend a year on a world named after a significant character in the *Aeneid* without picking up on the significance of someone deciding to call you "Cressida". Dido, Queen of Carthage, was persuaded by Venus to fall in love with Aeneas (Venus' son) so as to get his ship repaired. Don't ask whether David Whitaker had this in mind when he wrote "The Rescue" (2.3), because it suggests all sorts of nasty things about the relationship between Vicki and Koquillion. Unfortunately, Dido stayed enamoured after Jupiter reminded Aeneas to get on with founding Rome, so she killed herself and laid a curse on his descendants. And several centuries later, Rome *did* have problems with Carthaginians, especially one in particular who led elephants over the Alps.

So when Troilus mentions his cousin Aeneas to Vicki, it really should ring a bell for her. She gives every indication of knowing the story at least as well as the Doctor - it's a well-known story, after all. Her part of it was written about by both Chaucer and Boccaccio in the fourteenth century, and Shakespeare in the fifteenth. It's not to be found in Virgil, though, nor Homer (about whom the Medieval / Elizabethan world was ignorant until 1354). The first English copy of Homer was published in 1611.

The point is that when the most famous versions of the tale were written, no-one realised there wasn't really a character called "Cressida" in the oldest accounts. She didn't enter the story until Benoit de Sainte-Marie's version, around 1150 AD. In Homer there's a "Chryseis"; Astynome, daughter of Chryses. And as we're sure you're aware, the accusative form of the patronymic is something very much like "Cressida". There's also a Briseida, who - like Chryseis / Astynome - is taken captive by Achilles. In the godawful film *Troy* she's the Rose Byrne character, turned into Brad Pitt's love interest because there's no way the attention he pays to Patroclus is even slightly gay, good heavens no.

But the other name for Brisedia is Ypodamia, and here Benoit gets all mixed up, portraying Ypodamia and Brisedia as two separate characters. The latter loves, then apparently betrays, Troilus. Boccaccio muddles things further, transposing a C and a B and inventing Cresyde, the "adulteress" described by Shakespeare and Chaucer. Those two gentlemen took the Trojan side, since Aeneas was indirectly responsible for the founding of the city of Troynouvant, or "London" as it was later called. This also meant that King Arthur was a Trojan, and thus the entire Tudor dynasty. This gave the Elizabethans the idea that they had a special destiny to punch above their weight. So it's likely that Vicki's home-planet was named by someone with a bit of a classical bent, unless the other worlds in the system are called things like "Coldplay" and "Moby". Going by "The Rescue", these are people with a Union Jack on their spaceship's tail-fin, after all.

Which leaves us with the problem of where King Priam plucks the name "Cressida" from in episode two of "The Myth Makers", and why Vicki-Cressida knows that Steven calling himself "Diomede" is a bad move but shows no sign of

continued on page 207...

saw a version of history in which ancient civilisations are shown to be dry-runs for the present, but with more togas. This was a standard technique of British comedy in the 1960s; to contrast the parochial (and, in an age when the greatness of Britain was starting to look like a myth, increasingly silly-looking) obsessions of modern living with the rather more brutal events of the past. Just listen to Paris "defeating" Steven in episode two, talking about mortal combat as if he's having a

quick chat about chartered accountancy. They might as well have gone the whole hog and got John Cleese to play the part. The more overtly comic scenes are similar in style to much of the radio comedy of the era, and in places you could almost believe you were listening to a sketch from *I'm Sorry I'll Read That Again* or one of the epic movie parodies from *Round the Horne*. When we talk about '60s *Doctor Who*, we have a tendency to focus on the "monster" stories instead of the "funny" ones, which blinds us to how contemporary all of this really was. It's not just comedy, it's a very *modern* kind of comedy. After *Monty Python* this sort of thing seemed perfectly normal, and in particular, if you've seen the film *Time Bandits* (1981) then you'll find parts of this story rather familiar.

Debunking Homer wasn't a twentieth-century invention, however. The faux-Grecian operettas composed by Offenbach in the mid-1800s include the bawdy *La Belle Hêlene*, in which the epic figures of myth are turned into bourgeois Parisians. Later there was James Joyce's *Ulysses*, although if you don't already know it then it's probably not worth trying to explain it now. Joyce's version of the Cyclops is a lot scarier than the one seen here, even if the hero *does* run into him in an Irish pub.

But something strange is happening to *Doctor Who* itself that makes all of this important. So far the relationship with Earth's past has been voyeuristic. The original text, the known history, has been more important than the need to make an original or exciting story. Under Dennis Spooner this has been negotiable, and the emphasis of the story in each case has been the Doctor's role in making sure it all goes to plan. Up to a point, though, the idea was always that the *Doctor Who* account of events is "true" and only certain details were fudged by the chroniclers (most explicitly, Marco Polo chose not to mention flying boxes in case nobody believed him). Yet once the Daleks had been invoked as the cause of the *Mary Celeste* mystery, we were in a new game. In that scene, this story and later on "The Gunfighters" (3.8), what's being presented is the "real" story, of which all the more famous or creditable accounts are deviations and corruptions. Wiles and Tosh have decided to pull the rug from under the viewers, and the next two stories will systematically unsettle all the familiar patterns into which *Doctor Who* has already settled.

Things That Don't Make Sense Steven and Vicki have odd holes in their knowledge of the siege of Troy, but also a surprising degree of detail on the bits the plot needs them to recall. The Doctor, meanwhile, appears to have gone completely berserk. Did he seriously think he could get away with teaching the Greeks (that's *the Greeks*, inventors of everything the Chinese didn't do) how to make heavier-than-air gliders? This is the same

Doctor who went raving mad at Barbara for a teeny little change to history like soft-pedalling the human sacrifice element of a religion the Spanish wouldn't tolerate anyway (1.6, "The Aztecs", if you've somehow forgotten).

Critique Let's get the obvious comparison and the obligatory abuse out of the way first. Even on a grubby audio with a few stills, this wipes the floor with the Brad Pitt turkey. Any viewer unfamiliar with the Homeric version (and in 1965 that meant the ones under five) would get the basic idea, and the rest would be judging the Truth According to Who against the "official" one.

But fandom has long had a low opinion of this story. It's still written up in our own "official" chronicles as a farce, marred by the star's prejudices and some ponderous dialogue. Nobody who's actually listened to it, or remembers seeing it broadcast, shares this opinion. The worst you can say about it is that the final act seems oddly uneven; comedy and tragedy *do* mix, but none of the antics in the first three-quarters carry even a hint of the horror that's unleashed at the climax. This, though, may be a result of the lack of moving pictures. Events must seem far more threatening, when you can *see* all the huge men waving swords in your face. It's a story about perception versus reality, people who are acquainted with war and people who are enthusiastic about it, the version we all think we know and what actually happened. Ironic, then, that the story itself should be so misperceived.

So, yes... without the three fights, and especially the serious ones at the beginning and end, it's hard to judge how well the transition from comedy to atrocity was managed. The emphasis is firmly on the two sides (plus Steven and Vicki) missing the point. The stakes get higher, but everyone's concerns become increasingly trivial and mean. Paris in particular is spectacularly vain and pompous, allowing Steven to manipulate him almost invisibly. In the role of Paris, Barrie Ingham, like all the cast, is able to switch instantly between blank verse and a comedy of manners. If there's a weak link, it's that Ivor Salter's presence as Odysseus is probably mostly physical. From what we can hear, he doesn't give as big a performance as Francis de Wolfe (Agamemnon) or Hartnell, but from what we know of his other TV roles - including 2.7, "The Space Museum" and 19.6, "Black Orchid" - this is unlikely to be true.

Marrying Troilus: What *is* She Doing?

...continued from page 205

resisting her own fate. Still, this entire story is about things not going as planned. Given the differences between what happens to the TARDIS crew and the legend, there was every reason to expect Troilus to be bog-ugly or a ten-year-old. Or a bog-ugly ten-year-old. Or Tutte Lemkow with patches on *both* eyes. So maybe Vicki's hoping that things will turn out better for her as Cressida than some of the accounts suggest.

As an alleged sixteen-year-old girl, Vicki isn't likely to resist fate once she *sees* Troilus. Even though - judging by the audios and photos - it seems he might hang his hoplon from the other hip, so to speak. However, in all the confusion of the fall of Troy, she seems to be looking for confirmation that the life of Cressida might work out for her. In the Medieval versions, Troilus dies, and Cressida is forcibly married off while enslaved. Here she escapes, gets Troilus out before the end (Vicki helps with his wounds, which may indicate a changing of history here, if you can overlook the fact that the Doctor's been busy *causing* it), and

leaves for Italy via Libya. By the looks of things, it's her descendants who build the villa where she gets bored after her first trip in the TARDIS (2.4, "The Romans"). If she *is* following a script laid down by Benoit, then maybe Benoit had help. Maybe all those "confusions" in his account were added as pointers by the Doctor, who seems to have understood Vicki's motives without a proper farewell scene.

As an aside, the novelisation makes it clear that Vicki *did* live happily ever after, and that she and Troilus were still in love in late middle age. This comes from, as it were, the horse's mouth. In this version, Homer was an eye-witness - all right, ear-witness - but chose to keep the Doctor out of his published writings, as is traditional for historical personages who meet time-travellers. Yet even the novelisation doesn't mention the problem that all good fanboys will have spotted; that if the TARDIS translates local languages for the sake of its passengers, then Our Cressida may find it particularly difficult to understand her other half once the Doctor leaves. Even apart from a "generation gap" of two-hundred generations.

The *other* thing fandom objects to, of course, is the lack of famous monsters (although the forty-foot-high wooden horse probably does the "visual impact" duties at least as well as a man in a Rill suit). And fair enough, if Cyclops *had* been a big bloke with a weird genetic abnormality then it might have been even more fun. But what we've got is enough. Enjoy the script, bask in the simultaneous epic-ness and '60s-ness, leave the splendid-but-misleading novelisation for another day. It sounds pretty good, but it was almost certainly better.

The Facts

Written by Donald Cotton. Directed by Michael Leeston Smith. Ratings: 8.3 million, 8.1 million, 8.7 million, 8.3 million.

No episodes exist in the BBC archive.

Supporting Cast Alan Haywood (Hector), Ivor Salter (Odysseus), Francis de Wolff (Agamemnon), Jack Melford (Menelaus), Cavan Kendall (Achilles), James Lynn (Troilus), Tutte Lemkow (Cyclops), Max Adrian (King Priam), Barrie Ingham (Paris), Frances White (Cassandra).

Episode Titles "Temple of Secrets", "Small Prophet, Quick Return", "Death of a Spy", "Horse of Destruction". (Can you imagine *any* other circumstances under which a title like "Horse of Destruction" might be considered acceptable?)

Working Titles It was always called something like "Dr Who and the Mythmakers", but episode one was originally entitled "Zeus Ex Machina" and episode three was ostensibly "Is There a Doctor in the Horse?".

Cliffhangers The Doctor is marched back to the plain where his "temple" landed, to find that it's vanished into thin air; Cassandra "proves" that Vicki is a Greek spy, and the guards advance on her with their swords drawn; the jubilant (but obviously doomed) Trojans bring the Great Horse of Asia into the city.

The lead-in to the next story: on board the TARDIS, the wounded Steven's condition worsens, and the Doctor realises that he's got to find help somewhere.

The Lore

• Adrienne Hill had auditioned to play Joanna in "The Crusade". Her first work on the series was her death-scene in the following story, and she was cast by that story's director, Douglas Camfield. Here there was to have been a scene in which she tells Vicki that the auguries aren't good, and this would have helped to explain why Katarina spends the rest of her short existence convinced that the TARDIS is a gateway to the afterlife. She was hastily built up from a small part in the final episode to cover the departure of Maureen O'Brien, who'd been increasingly disillusioned with the part of Vicki since - she claims - episode two of "The Rescue". But O'Brien was keen on the regular income, and being in London with her husband-to-be. Wiles had noted her tendency to pick holes in the dialogue during rehearsals for "Galaxy Four", and made arrangements to have her removed while the cast were on holiday.

• Location work was done at Frensham Ponds, near the home of director Michael Leeston-Smith, although it was often used for locations with no buildings (the surviving photos show that in August it looks enough like Asia Minor for BBC purposes). Leeston-Smith never worked on the series again, but not through any reluctance on his part or that of Wiles. One person who apparently *was* embarrassed by the story was Frances White (Cassandra), who asked the *Radio Times* not to bill her.

• Barrie Ingham (Paris), taking time out from his day-job at the Royal Shakespeare Company, came to *Doctor Who* proper after playing Alydon in the film *Doctor Who and the Daleks*. It would appear that his fight with Peter Purves in the second episode wasn't done on film, and wasn't choreographed by Derek Ware like the "real" fights in parts one and four.

• The extras include Mike Reid, who'll pop up a few times in Season Three before starting his career as a stand-up comic, game-show host and *EastEnders* regular.

• Donald Tosh owed Donald Cotton a favour, as Cotton had cast Tosh in a play when they were both actors, and now that Cotton was working for the Third Programme - the "arts" radio service of the BBC, now BBC Radio Three - Tosh got in touch. Tosh had written experimental and satirical radio adaptations of Greek myths, but hadn't handled the *Iliad* before this. Part of the deal was that Tosh could bring colleagues from his radio productions, which is how Max Adrian (Priam) and noted composer Humphrey Searle became involved.

• The usual story about this production is that the homophobic, anti-Semitic Hartnell found working with Adrian intolerable. They had, however, worked together before. In fact, Hartnell's experience on the story was unpleasant all round. Wiles had antagonised him from day one, and his only allies now were the other two regular cast-members. But one of these was unexpectedly being removed. Moreover, he'd suffered yet another bruising collision with a camera (see 2.2, "The Dalek Invasion of Earth") and a family bereavement; born out of wedlock, Hartnell had been more or less raised by his aunt Bessie, but the production schedule didn't allow him time to attend her funeral in Devon. And to cap it all, everyone was treating Adrian as the star of the production - a camped-up story which Hartnell suspected would be dull and confusing for children.

• We'd better get this out of the way now: shortly after this, Hartnell was diagnosed with arteriosclerosis. Before the medical explanation came, his increasing inability to memorise lines made him angry and embarrassed, and he took this out on those around him. Wiles, unaware of this but warned by Lambert of Hartnell's prima-donna-ishness, thought the star's frailty was an act... which to some extent it had been, until now. Hartnell was 57 at the time, but occasionally overdid his need for rest. After two years of giving short shrift to other actors for being unprofessional and failing to meet his exacting standards, Hartnell was himself falling short.

• In recent years, there's been some debate over the question of exactly how soon Hartnell found out about his illness. After leaving *Doctor Who* he was able to star in a long-running stage play, but later television appearances are sparse: a *Z Cars* appearance and "The Three Doctors" (10.1). By late 1972, when he returned for that final performance as the Doctor, he was obviously incapable. Anecdotes about Hartnell in his final years, wheelchair-bound and almost unaware of what was going on (but recovering his wits for long enough to rail against his treatment by the BBC), seem to confirm that he was more ill than he thought.

3.4: "The Daleks' Master Plan"

(Serial V, Twelve Episodes, 13th November 1965 - 29th January 1966.)

Which One is This? The big one. More Daleks, more alien delegates, more Varga plants, but this time the Doctor's involved and leads them on a merry dance across space, time and various boundaries of common sense. Plus, Peter Butterworth gets a good trouncing and Jean Marsh crumbles to dust before our eyes. (Or ears, these days.)

Firsts and Lasts This is the first "team-up" story; the Daleks and the Monk are both familiar to viewers, but nobody was expecting them to end up working together. In fact, the Monk is the first character (rather than species) to get a rematch with the Doctor. The Daleks are *definitely* equipped with flame-throwers this time, and we encounter the first of many invisible beings in the series. It's the last time Hartnell will come up against the Daleks, and the last black-and-white story for Terry Nation.

That's not the half of it. In this one story we have the first three characters to die after being taken aboard the TARDIS, and one of these is played by future almost-regular Nicholas Courtney. Two episodes are explicitly set in Britain on the day of transmission (Liverpool on Christmas Day, Trafalgar Square at midnight on New Year's Day). Mavic Chen follows the lead of the Sensorites by referring to 'the one they call the Doctor', making it a series standard, and the delegate Celation's voice is the first sibilant whisper. The Draconians, Ice Warriors, Sontarans and many, many more will adopt this habit in future.

It's also the first and only twelve-part story, and the longest in the programme's history. Well, in a sense... Season Twenty-Three is technically one big story, but everyone knows it's really three-and-a-half little ones stuck together, while this one has a single production code and (allegedly) a single plot. Even if it changes somewhat when Dennis Spooner takes over script-writing duties from Terry Nation about halfway through, and even if there's an "interlude" episode stuck in the middle of it.

Twelve Things to Notice About "The Daleks' Master Plan"...

1. Episodes seven to ten can, some say, be almost completely excised from the plot if necessary. The basic story, about the Dalek version of the Manhattan Project, is temporarily abandoned in "Coronas of the Sun" in favour of a remake of "The Chase". The programme-makers can do this because the viewers at home can't be expected to remember too much detail from one month to the next, so they make sure that each individual episode has enough skulduggery for the floating viewer and only occasionally refers back to the main plot. This interpretation relies on a view of *Doctor Who* being just about the story, a view we find questionable (see **Does the Plot Matter?** under 6.4, "The Krotons"). In 1960s terms, twelve weeks of screen time - Saturday by Saturday - is longer than all the school holidays in one go and about the same length as a *Flash Gordon* serial.

2. And yes, the Meddling Monk makes a comeback, partly because Douglas Camfield and Dennis Spooner had got away with it before but also to provide a plausible reason that *for one story only* the Doctor can steer the TARDIS to exactly where and when he needs to be. As a morally ambiguous time-traveller, the Monk is useful in ways that this year's arch-villain Mavic Chen can never be. So Chen retains his dignity (unusually, for a man with a blue face and long girly fingernails) while the Monk is subjected to increasingly slapstick humiliations by both the Doctor and the Daleks. When the Doctor, the Monk and Chen all share a scene, the Daleks are reduced to going around shooting Egyptians.

3. The three episodes that remain in the archive demonstrate that Mavic Chen is one of the classiest baddies ever to grace the series. He starts out as a sort of galactic Dag Hammarskjold (the Secretary General of the UN in its optimistic first phase), then becomes a cosmic quisling, and flirts with the idea of turning into Ming the Merciless before finally going insane. Only two villains have ever come close to this, and one of *those* was played by the same actor, Kevin Stoney (6.3, "The Invasion"). The other is the Roger Delgado version of the Master, and it's worth noting that the 1973 season attempted to recapture this story's epic feel; see 10.3, "Frontier in Space" and 10.4, "Planet of the Daleks". The first of these features the Master as a high-ranking planetary governor seeking to start a war on behalf of the Daleks. He even dresses a bit like Chen. Just as we're starting to think

that this must be pure coincidence, Chen tells the other Delegates 'you will obey' in *exactly* the same tone of voice.

4. As with the one-off "Mission to the Unknown", the alien alliance is a lot of people in funny hats standing around a table and doing croaky voices. This aspect of the story is, however, remembered by those who actually saw it as better than the almost-identical scene in *Star Wars Episode II: Attack of the Clones*. (Mind you, the *Star Wars* version is only a few seconds long, whereas here the monster conference goes on for whole bleeding episodes. Kids today, they're always in such a rush.)

What lessens the impact slightly is knowing that one of the aliens is Roy Evans, the reserve BBC Token Welshman when Talfryn Thomas isn't around (see 10.5, "The Green Death"); and another is Bryan Mosley, best known as Alf Roberts from *Coronation Street*. One of the conference episodes, "Day of Armageddon", was only rediscovered in 2004 and frankly doesn't instil confidence that the others lived up to the hype. On the other hand, "Day of Armageddon" is a hell of a lot better than it sounded on audio, mainly thanks to Camfield's inspired use of bizarre surroundings.

5. And every time a bit of this story is rediscovered, everyone is amazed all over again. One of the best moments is the surviving twenty seconds of model footage showing Chen's Spar (future-talk for "space-car") arriving at the Kembel conference. The model-work is detailed and competent, and the conception and design of the vessel is so far ahead of the Dalek ship in "The Dalek Invasion of Earth" as to give the impression that ten years have elapsed, not one-and-a-quarter. In general, the visuals in this story are a notch above the usual, with big projection screens built into the sets to relay pre-filmed material and at least one moment per episode where the dialogue stops and we're simply shown what's happening. (A quick glance at **The Lore** will explain this, and reveal that Someone Very Interesting Indeed was taking note.) Compare the jungle warfare in this story to the ambling around in "The Chase", and suddenly Camfield's reputation makes sense, while the flame-throwers become the single most fantastic thing the Daleks did between their first-ever extermination and their learning to climb stairs.

6. In a story this big and this varied, it's inevitable that a degree of schizophrenia will set in. The shoot-to-kill future society to which Sara and Bret belong is the kind of regime the Doctor would, in other stories, be trying to overthrow. Yet here, because the threat of the Daleks and their new allies is so great, the Doctor is lending his assistance to people who are little better than the Federation tyrants from *Blake's 7*. Indeed, elements of Nation's other BBC space opera can be seen in embryo form here, not the least of which is the teleport system (see also 1.5, "The Keys of Marinus") and the prison planet Desperus (modelled on Botany Bay, but also suggestive of Devil's Island, hence the title of episode three). There's a lot of unapologetic brutality about this world, with suspected traitors being shot before they get a chance to explain, and yet a week later we get outright comedy with the Daleks shown to be afraid of mice. And two weeks after that....

7. Oh, all right, we'll explain the basics just like every other guidebook does. Episode seven, "The Feast of Steven", was made to go out on Saturday, the 25th of December. As *Doctor Who's* only Christmas special until 2005, it's a romp-within-a-romp, with a spoof of *Z Cars* and a trip to silent-era Hollywood for a chase sequence in the style of the Keystone Cops (complete with captions). At the end, the Doctor brings out a tray of drinks and everyone has a quick Christmas party in the console room. The Doctor then turns to the camera and toasts the viewers with a cheery 'incidentally, a happy Christmas to all of you at home'.

Hmm. So, let's see... an epic Dalek assault on the solar system, swinging between screwball comedy and mass bloodshed, which involves parodies of other contemporary TV programmes and ends with the Doctor looking straight into the camera to directly address his audience. Does this seem at all familiar, to the modern viewer? At least Russell T. Davies figured out that if you're going to do this sort of thing, then you should put the funny bits at the *start* of the story instead of jamming them in halfway through.

8. Agent 505, Sara Kingdom, is usually seen as the BBC's attempt to include a character like Cathy Gale from *The Avengers*. By the time the part was cast, viewers had also seen Gale's replacement Emma Peel, so the logical conclusion was that Jean Marsh was going to be the new regular *Doctor Who* girl; a classy redhead with big boots, dry wit and martial arts training. All the publicity material suggested this. She does judo on the policemen in "The Feast of Steven", and exhibits the same *sang froid* in the face of mummies and monsters

Which Sodding Delegate is Which?

This really is one of the big "pointless but niggling" questions of fandom, third on the list after the one about dating the UNIT stories and the one about Dalek history. The situation, if you needed reminding, is this. There are at least eight non-human delegates attending the Daleks' conference/s in "Mission to the Unknown" (3.2) and "The Daleks' Master Plan", arguably more. Thanks to publicity photos, we know what they all look like, and we have eight names to go with them. The challenge is to match the names up to the aliens. But this isn't *Star Wars*, and we don't have a range of action-figures to help us. Nor are the scripts particularly helpful, and just to make things harder, most of the episodes which feature these so-called "planetarians" are missing from the archive.

The rediscovery of "Day of Armageddon" ("The Daleks' Master Plan" episode two) made things slightly clearer, and *Doctor Who Magazine* (#342) published a handy delegate-spotters' guide shortly after it was unearthed. But even *this* was flawed. And that's hardly surprising; close inspection of the evidence reveals that the programme-makers themselves got it wrong, and couldn't always agree on which representative was which.

So, let's take this one step at a time.

"Mission to the Unknown"

In the draft script of "Mission", there were seven delegates at the conference: Gearon, Trantis, Zephon, Malpha, Sentreal, Beaus and Celation. By the time the camera script was written, Zephon had been removed from the roll-call, and he doesn't show up until "The Daleks' Master Plan". So we seem to have six definite names for the other delegates, and sure enough, there are six of them in the publicity photos. They are:

Delegate #1. Resembles Ben Grimm from *The Fantastic Four*, with cracked, brick-like skin and a bald head. He wears a two-piece white ribbed plastic shell-suit, with black catheters running around the outside. For now, we'll call him "Brickface".

Delegate #2. A short, dark-haired humanoid with a zigzag fringe. His face is covered in sagging flesh and dark spines, and he wears a robe from which one hand emerges. We'll call him "Shifty".

Delegate #3. Resembles a black velvet version of the Christmas-tree-shaped air-fresheners you get in taxis, but he's seven feet tall and has glowing, slanted eyes. Notable for being the one delegate who isn't even roughly humanoid. We'll call him "Scarything".

Delegate #4. Has a silver jump-suit with Mondrian-style panels - *very* 1965 - and an egg-shaped space-helmet over a blank face. (We're uncertain as to whether this costume is the one re-used for the "dummy" target Cyberman in 5.1, "Tomb of the Cybermen", as is occasionally claimed. But it's very similar.) He also has giant sunglasses, and mitten-like hands. We'll call him "Blanko".

Delegate #5. Wears a sort of diver's helmet with a hose leading out of the front, a complex antenna on the top and a studded collar over the shoulders. We'll call him "Spaceman".

Delegate #6. Another spacesuit, but this one's taller. The helmet resembles a hollowed-out gourd, and allows the wearer's face to be seen, revealing wholly human features. The overall effect is not unlike a Teletubby. Given that he's the ordinary-looking one, we'll call him "Normal".

So, which is which? Well, here's the thing. Only one actor is credited for playing a specific delegate in this episode. That actor is Ronald Rich, who can also be seen in "The Time Meddler" (2.9). He's credited as Trantis. And photos show that Delegate #6, "Normal", has Ronald Rich's face. Therefore, "Normal" is Trantis. (This will apparently be contradicted later, but stick with it for now.) No character called Sentreal appears in later episodes, and "Scarything" doesn't appear in later episodes either, so we can safely assume that "Scarything" is Sentreal.

The others are harder to identify, but a piece about the recording of the episode in a 1965 edition of the *Daily Mail* referred to "lettuce faced Malpha". This could refer to "Shifty", who's got what might be vegetable matter hanging from his pores, but it more likely refers to "Brickface". This leaves the names Gearon, Beaus and Celation to attach to "Blanko", "Spaceman" and "Shifty".

(One extra complication here, as if things weren't bad enough already. In the finished story, a spaceship from the planet Gearon arrives, and shortly afterwards the representative known as Malpha takes his place at the conference table. The implication is that Malpha is the personal name of the representative from the planet Gearon, yet the list of delegates contradicts this. We'll gloss over it, and assume that Malpha was taking a break from negotiations while Gearon was arriving.)

continued on page 213...

that one would expect of one of John Steed's chums.

Killing this character so unpleasantly at the end of the story is one of the major shifts in the programme's attitude to the depiction of violence, entirely in keeping with the rest of Wiles' and Tosh's term on the programme. (However, even apart from Hartnell's objections to this brutal new universe, it's clear that Nation disagreed with the decision. Sara comes back from the dead with a new brother, David, in "The Destructors" and the *Dalek Outer Space Book*. Ponder also the similarity of the names "Sara Kingdom" and "Terry Nation", not to mention the name given to the most valuable substance in the universe, "taranium"...)

9. Dennis Spooner is the first person other than Nation to write Dalek dialogue, if you don't count script editors doing rewrites. Contrary to what many subsequent writers have said - including Nation himself - the Daleks *are* capable of carrying dialogue-heavy scenes, especially if Spooner's doing it. Here they get to throw around lines like 'you make your incompetence sound like an achievement', and luckily Spooner keeps his usual habit of slipping into transatlantic English in check, so no Dalek ever has to say anything like "say, Mac, he's stolen our taranium core". It's also noticeable that Steven's lines get less perfunctory, and that the alien delegates become distinct characters in the second half of the story rather than just Chen's foils.

10. Episode five involves a teleportation experiment that sends two lab mice to the planet Mira. When he realises he's been transposed across light-years, the Doctor chuckles 'the mice couldn't have done that'. The Daleks later believe the mice to possess the secret of pan-dimensional travel. Three weeks later, there's hilarity afoot when the TARDIS interrupts a cricket match and the commentators react simply by looking it up to see how often it's happened before. We mention this merely to point out the similarity to Douglas Adams' "Krikketmen" idea (see 16.2, "The Pirate Planet", but more importantly Adams' novel *Life, the Universe and Everything*), not in any way to make accusations of plagiarism against him just because he was thirteen when this was broadcast and would almost certainly have watched it.

11. It's reckoned by experts that the detonation of the time destructor in episode twelve is one of the most horrific moments in the programme's history. Not only is it a force too powerful for either the Daleks or the Doctor, but as we've mentioned, it kills Sara. We're not talking about a ray-gun effect, or a fade into invisibility. She ages seventy years in a minute, and not in a comedy way like Stu in "The Time Monster" (9.5) or discretely off-screen like the Doctor in "The Leisure Hive" (18.1). The Daleks, meanwhile, revert to babyhood in a way that ought to be funny but isn't. Although the Doctor finally prevents the Daleks from implementing the so-called Master Plan, it's hardly a victory. He loses two TARDIS crew-members (three if you count Bret Vyon, who spends more time in the Ship than Liz Shaw in Season Seven) while many of the Daleks' allies live to connive another day. Even the Doctor can't come out unscathed. After the time destructor's effect on him, subsequent writers and directors are able to factor in Hartnell's ill-health more plausibly. (And of course, the Doctor gets drained *again* in 3.9, "The Savages".)

You almost find yourself hoping that "The Destruction of Time" is never rediscovered and returned to the archive, because the ending surely *can't* be as good as we like to think.

12. Elsewhere we've been critical of Nation's lack of originality and Spooner's clunky exposition dialogue, but just for a change, note the sheer economy of the expository material in episode one. Roald and Lizan engage in office banter that sets up the period; the relationship between the Earth government and what's been happening on Kembel; Mavic Chen's reputation; Lizan's loyalty to her leader; the way spaceships are treated like luxury cars, and how much of a status-symbol Chen's is; the fact that there are over four-hundred TV channels (outrageous science fiction in Britain 1965, as was the flat-screen wall-mounted telly the size of a bathtub); and the idea that the news is mostly propaganda. Then we get the casual detail that Mars and Venus have colonies and sports teams, and that women holding senior jobs isn't a big deal. *And* we get our first hint of Chen's role as senior statesman from the fact that he quotes Churchill ("Let Us Go Forward Together" was a famous wartime poster). All of this in two minutes of screen-time. As with "Genesis of the Daleks" later on, it's so far removed from Nation's usual standard as to raise the obvious question: did he have help? You have until **The Lore** to guess the answer.

Which Sodding Delegate is Which?

...continued from page 211

"Day of Armageddon"

First off, there's a new alien on the block. Here we meet Zephon, an upright-walking plant who dresses like a monk. Since he's explicitly referred to as Zephon on-screen, and properly-defined (ish) as a character, there's no doubt about which one he is. The changes don't end there, though. For a start, "Scarything" / Sentreal has vanished from the conference. "Normal" doesn't seem to be around either, and nor does "Blanko", but let's look at the full line-up...

Delegate #1. "Brickface" / Malpha, as before.

Delegate #2. A short, dark-haired humanoid with a zigzag fringe and serrated teeth. He has a hunched back, and wears a ribbed pullover-style top, revealing two arms and gloved hands. In some ways he looks like "Shifty" from "Mission to the Unknown", except... he doesn't have the spines on his face, and his clothes are different. Nonetheless, there's an obvious similarity, so we'll call him "Smooth Shifty".

Delegate #3. Zephon the plant.

Delegate #4. Has a PVC kaftan with a visor set into the hood, and a diamond-shaped medallion with a circle in the centre. The general facelessness suggests the same sort of alien as "Blanko", but it's a completely different costume, in black rather than white. We'll call him "Black Blanko".

Delegate #5. "Spaceman", as before.

Delegate #6. A pale, bald, humanoid being with black growths on his skin. In "Day of Armageddon" these form a kind of beard, but in "The Abandoned Planet" ("The Daleks' Master Plan" episode eleven, in which he's played by a different actor) they're all over the side of his head. His outfit has big black circular blobs all over it. We'll call him "Baldy".

Now we run into the big glitch. Trantis has a bigger part in "The Daleks' Master Plan" than in "Mission to the Unknown", and he's played by Roy Evans, who can also be seen in "The Green Death" (10.5) and "The Monster of Peladon" (11.4). And one look at the photos will tell you that Roy Evans is clearly "Smooth Shifty". See the problem? In "Mission to the Unknown", Trantis was definitely "Normal", but now he's played by a different actor, doesn't have the white Teletubby hood, and has a haircut just like that of "Shifty".

It's fair to say that the costume department and the writers weren't exactly on the same page here. The idea from the *designers'* point of view seems to be that "Shifty" and "Smooth Shifty" are one and the same, even if he's lost the facial appendages, which have been adopted by "Baldy". But as far as the script's concerned, "Normal" and "Smooth Shifty" are both Trantis. Indeed, the scripts for "Master Plan" use the same names that were used in "Mission" (Sentreal excepted), while the design notes describe two "new creatures" for episode two. Presumably "Black Blanko" and "Baldy". Can we possibly make sense of this?

Well... just about. It all fits together *if* we assume that "Normal" and "Smooth Shifty" *are* the same individual, i.e. Trantis. Both are humanoid, and since "Normal" is wearing a hood in "Mission to the Unknown", we don't know that he *doesn't* have a zigzag haircut underneath. We also have to assume that the original "Shifty" and the later "Baldy" are the same, or at least, that they're both representatives of the same species (is there a change of regime between the two stories?). One is bald and the other isn't, but they both have similar growths coming out of their faces. It's important to stress that this is pure revisionism on *our* part, since the designers didn't see things that way and the writers were barely keeping track at all.

More clues emerge. The design notes for later episodes of "The Daleks' Master Plan" refer to Celation as "no hair, black blobs", so he's evidently "Baldy". The camera script of "The Abandoned Planet" states that Gearon was played by Jack Pitt (who also operated the Venom Grub in "The Web Planet" and the Gubbage Cones in "The Chase", as well as being William Hartnell's room-mate in his digs in Pimlico), and Jack Pitt is also one of the "new creatures" in "Day of Armageddon". So Gearon must be "Black Blanko". From this we might conclude - even if it wasn't the designers' original intention - that he's also the original "Blanko", but that Gearon put new gear on between stories. That leaves Beaus to fill the "Spaceman" role.

Conclusion...

It goes like this:

Trantis. In "Mission to the Unknown", he's "Normal". Then he gets rid of the hood (and ends up being played by a different actor) to become "Smooth Shifty", leading to understandable confusion with "Shifty". Awkward, we know, but it's the only way of reconciling the scripts with the design notes.

Celation. In "Mission to the Unknown", he's "Shifty". Someone with the same facial fungus, but

continued on page 215...

The Continuity

The Plot Back on the planet Kembel, Marc Cory's mission to the unknown is followed up by two more SSS agents, Kert Gantry and Bret Vyon. Gantry is quickly exterminated, but Vyon stumbles across the TARDIS and commandeers it at gunpoint. He and the travellers soon realise they have a common enemy, yet the Daleks' scheme of galactic conquest is already in motion, as the last of their allies has arrived to join the delegates at their conference... and it's Mavic Chen, Guardian of the Solar System and therefore leader of Earth. The Doctor infiltrates the conference disguised as one of the delegates, learning that the Daleks have perfected a super-weapon they call the time destructor. All it needs is a core of taranium, which only Chen can provide.

The Doctor pockets the core, and he and his companions head for Earth in a stolen spaceship, with the Daleks in hot pursuit. The Doctor gets his first taste of the horror to come when the Daleks force the ship to land on the prison-planet Desperus, and it's boarded by Kirksen, a psychopathic convict. Kirksen takes Katarina hostage in an airlock, and Katarina willingly blows the two of them into space rather than let the man jeopardize the mission. Even Earth isn't safe, as Chen has informed the security services that Vyon is a traitor, and set another SSS agent - the ruthless-but-gullible Sara Kingdom - on their trail. Kingdom tracks them to an experimental research plant, where she shoots Vyon dead. However, she, the Doctor and Steven are then caught up in the station's molecular dissemination experiment, which sends them all the way to the planet Mira. Which is a problem, because Mira's full of invisible monsters.

It's here that Sara acknowledges the Doctor's story to be true, and reveals that Vyon was her brother, though there's no time for tears before the Daleks catch up with them. When the local wildlife attacks, the distraction allows the travellers to hot-wire the Dalek vessel, getting back to Kembel and ultimately the TARDIS. And the chase through time and space is on. Following laugh-a-minute stopovers in England circa 1965, silent-era Hollywood and the Oval cricket ground, the Ship ends up on the volcanic planet Tigus, where it's located by a vengeful Monk [2.9, "The Time Meddler"]. His attempt to sabotage the TARDIS fails, but he tracks the Doctor to his next port of

call, the Great Pyramid in ancient Egypt. This results in a face-off involving the Doctor, the Daleks, Mavic Chen, the Monk and a lot of angry Egyptians, during which the Doctor gives up the core to save Steven and Sara.

Fortunately, the Doctor nicks the directional unit from the Monk's TARDIS and fits it into his own Ship; this enables the heroes to properly navigate - for one time only, before the unit burns out - their TARDIS back to Kembel. But the Daleks are already prepping their super-weapon for use against Earth, and set about imprisoning their now-redundant allies. Yet Chen, who's losing his mind and is convinced of his own superiority, still believes he's still in control. He turns the travellers over to the Daleks, whereupon they exterminate him anyway, although his final manic fit gives the Doctor a chance to seize the now-active time destructor.

Kembel goes to hell as the destructor does its work, the jungle turning to dust while the travellers make their way back to the TARDIS. Steven gets to safety, but the Doctor is taken to the point of collapse and Sara ages horribly before their eyes. As she dies, Steven drags the Doctor into the safety of the TARDIS, having accidentally put the destructor in "reverse". The planet becomes a desert, and the Daleks revert to slime, leaving the two surviving TARDIS crewmembers to dwell on the carnage.

The Doctor Regards himself as 'a citizen of the universe, and a gentleman to boot'. [This is often considered to be the defining quote of Hartnell's Doctor, yet ironically it comes from the Christmas episode "The Feast of Steven", the one everyone pretends not to notice.] Not long afterwards, he delivers what may be the stupidest sentence of his career: 'This is a madhouse, it's all full of Arabs.' He refuses to consider the idea that he's English [compare with the TV Movie, 27.0].

But the Daleks tell us more about the Doctor than he does himself. According to Chen, their files show him to be from another galaxy. [However, the use of "galaxy" in this script is so vague that it could mean anything, and Chen says it so airily that it might well be figurative. Also, 'another galaxy' could either mean "not Earth's galaxy" or "not the galaxy that Kembel's in", if they aren't the same. See **How Many Significant Galaxies Are There?** under 2.5, "The Web Planet".] He is, at least, definitively identified as

Which Sodding Delegate is Which?

...continued from page 213

less hair and a weirder outfit, steps into his role later on. So Celation is both "Shifty" and "Baldly".

Gearon. "Blanko" in "Mission to the Unknown", then "Black Blanko" afterwards.

Zephon. The Triffid-man from "Day of Armageddon".

Sentreal. "Scarything", only in "Mission to the Unknown".

Malpha. "Brickface".

Beaus. "Spaceman".

The only hitch remaining is that if you listen to the audio soundtrack of "Mission to the Unknown", then Malpha's voice sounds strangely muffled, as if he's one of the planetarians who's wearing a helmet or visor. If so, then this would contradict both the *Daily Mail* piece and what we hear in later episodes, but there's no way we can be sure without seeing the original recording.

Let's see, what have we missed...? Oh yes. If you've read certain other guides to this subject, then you may have heard the name "Warrien" used to describe one of the delegates. According to the *Doctor Who Magazine* account, Warrien is the delegate we've called "Normal" (as *DWM* didn't recognise Ronald Rich in the photos). And yet... the name "Warrien" doesn't appear *anywhere* in the scripts, or in the design notes, or in the publicity material from 1965. As far as we've been able to discover, the name turned up for the first time in an issue of the fanzine *TARDIS*, some time after the fact. One prominent *Doctor Who* fan of that era has freely admitted that he used to make up names for things if he didn't know them. So it looks as if the moniker "Warrien" is purely an invention of fandom, used to cover the fact that there seem to be at least eight different delegates on display, even though Terry Nation only ever came up with seven names. (Even so, "Warrien" appears in John Peel's fandom-tainted novelisation of the story, so it's a difficult idea to get rid of.)

only *seeming* human.

The Doctor knows a lot about fortieth-century space technology, as well as being able to pilot Dalek spaceships, and has no trouble physically overcoming the Monk. Though visibly distraught by Katarina's death, he's chuckling again in no time at all. By the time Sara snuffs it, he's become hardened to the bloodshed, and celebrates the victory rather than mourning her passing.

• *Background.* He recognises the planet Mira on sight, is familiar with the Visians who live there, and seems to know about the mysterious properties of Tigus' sun. [The usual interpretation is that he's been to these places before. Alternatively, it may be that he has an encyclopaedic knowledge of aliens and planets but has to "download" it. This would make sense of his odd reactions on Vortis in "The Web Planet", but is out of keeping with many later stories, at least until "World War Three" (X1.5) makes it seem almost normal. However, he *does* know a surprising amount about obscure and apparently never-visited planets in the late '70s episodes. So much so that when *Doctor Who Weekly* ran its comic-strip "The Iron Legion" - in which the Doctor, cornered by the Ectoslime, has to alphabetically run through all the monsters in his head before he can remember its weakness - nobody found it particularly strange.]

The Doctor claims to have been present at the celebrations for the Relief of Mafeking [1901]. Though he's familiar with particle dissemination, he doesn't know a game of cricket when he sees it. [This will have changed by 16.1, "The Ribos Operation".] He states that very few people have seen large amounts of taranium 'in this universe'. [Another weird hint of other universes, as in "The Edge of Destruction" (1.3) and "Mission to the Unknown".] He's familiar with the substance, and seems to know what the time destructor will do.

• *Ethics.* His own life is less important than preventing the Daleks from using the time destructor, but Katarina's isn't. Even before he knows about this time-warping weapon, he sees it as his job to warn Earth of the Dalek plan; when the Daleks stop him getting to his TARDIS, his first tactic is to steal a spaceship and deliver the warning rather than to waste time trying to get his Ship back. He negotiates the Monk's release from the Daleks, in addition to that of Steven and Sara, then can't understand why he bothered.

• *Inventory.* Once again, the Doctor's ring is shown to possess unusual properties, here refracting Tigus' sunlight in order to counteract the Monk's sabotage to the TARDIS lock. Checking this piece of jewellery is the first thing he does after being molecularly disseminated.

The Supporting Cast

• *Steven.* His resentment at the people of 4000 AD treating him like a savage brings his sarcasm back out. Even when at death's door with a wounded shoulder, he can overcome a Special Security agent in a fight. [He's *definitely* been brushing up his combat skills since 2.9, "The Time Meddler". Then again, his unsuccessful struggle against the locals of 1066 *did* come immediately after a two-year spell in prison. He's found his groove again now.]

Interestingly, when the Doctor insists that he knows the Daleks, Steven says 'so do I'. [He can barely even have glimpsed them in "The Chase". Does this indicate that Steven comes from the twenty-sixth century, and that the wars of his own time were those which followed the return of the Daleks in that era (10.3, "Frontier in Space")? See **History** for more on his time of origin.] While the Doctor celebrates the Daleks' final defeat, Steven is brought almost to tears by the deaths of Sara, Bret Vyon and Katarina.

• *Katarina.* She's being taught the basics of the TARDIS console in no time, and the Doctor finds her 'charming'. Her perplexity at being somewhere else after leaving his "temple" makes her rather clingy, believing that without him she'll never reach the Place of Perfection. Obviously convinced of her fate among the heavens, she doesn't hesitate to press the switch for the airlock which leads to the deaths of both herself and the crazed Kirksen. The fact that she understands the purpose of the switch is rather impressive in itself. She gets one good scream before she goes.

• *Sara Kingdom.* A Special Security Service agent described as 'ruthless, hard, efficient, and does exactly as ordered'. This includes shooting fellow agent Bret Vyon at point blank. As much a conformist as all the other officials and agents of the fortieth century, she quickly falls into line and obeys the Doctor, and to some extent Steven. She isn't dressed for undercover work when she turns up, but is decked out in the sinister black SSS uniform.

Sara's reaction to authority changes somewhat when she accepts that the Guardian of the Solar System is a traitor and that she's been made to kill Bret for squalid political reasons. Bret was, it turns out, her brother. [See **The Lore**. What are we supposed to conclude from the fact that Sara has a different surname? That they're half-siblings? That there's different naming conventions for males and

females? That Sara is married? That *Bret* was married, and that people in 4000 AD don't always make the woman change her name? For all we know, Bret was part of a gay couple, although it probably isn't significant that his name is an anagram of "V. Rent Boy".] Once her faith in Mavic Chen is broken, Sara seems perfectly at home on the TARDIS, and adjusts to Earth history and alien worlds phlegmatically. The tough exterior starts to crack after a while, so she has no objection to cheerfully sipping wine at Christmas.

Not that the change of attitude does her any good; her death is a result of her going back to save the Doctor from the Dalek lair, despite his instructions. This probably saves his life.

The Supporting Cast (Evil, ish)

• *The Monk.* [Here credited as "The Meddling Monk".] More "evil" than before, since his main motive is revenge against the Doctor. He states that it took him some time to bypass the dimensional control of the TARDIS that trapped him in 1066 (in "The Time Meddler"), but no details are given. He knows of the Daleks by reputation, recognising them on sight.

In his satchel, the Monk carries a pencil-sized laser, protective goggles and binoculars. He's also equipped with a pair of shades. The laser is used on the TARDIS lock, freezing it so that the Doctor can't gain entrance, and he has to wear the goggles when using this odd tool. He carries an energy location device, much like the Doctor's 'compass', to home in on his rival's TARDIS. [It makes a burbling sound like the larva gun from "The Web Planet".] By the end of this run-in with his archenemy, the Monk is as lost in space and time as the Doctor himself, and is last seen shivering on an ice-planet somewhere.

[Note that on Tigus, the Doctor says that the Monk has 'returned here' for one reason. This just seems to mean that he's come back for revenge on the Doctor, but it *does* sound as if both of them have been on the planet before.]

The TARDIS(es)   Here the Doctor describes it as a machine for *investigating* Time and Relative Dimensions in Space, and speaks as if the present on Earth [i.e. 1965] is *his* present. [He also believes that the Daleks will be testing their time destructor in 4000 AD *while* the TARDIS is in the 1960s, as if his timeline and that of other time-travellers are somehow linked.] It's apparently unaffected by the time destructor.

The 'directional unit' from the Monk's more advanced vessel is incompatible with the Doctor's, requiring more power than an old-fashioned TARDIS possesses, so it burns itself out as a safety-measure instead of destroying the central column. But it does allow the Doctor to steer his way back to Kembel before it goes. [Nonetheless, the implication here is that the TARDIS only requires one element in order to be fully controllable. Before now there's been talk of needing to repair the 'main time mechanism', so is the directional unit part of this system, or does the unit simply override all the other faults?]

The scanner temporarily breaks down here, requiring the Doctor to check the whole circuit... though strangely he has to go outside to do this, and later Sara speaks of fixing the scanner-eye. It takes the Ship mere moments to make a journey from Kembel to twentieth-century Earth, where the dials on the console warn of a poisonous atmosphere outside, even though it's just inner-city pollution. From the time-curve indicator, the Doctor can't tell the difference between the Daleks' time machine and the Monk's, and after his first landing the Monk escapes detection by the unconventional method of jump-crossing the 'track' [suggestive of 2.7, "The Space Museum"].

When the Monk's laser freezes the TARDIS lock, the Doctor is able to use his ring to refract the sunlight of Tigus into the mechanism and unfreeze it, though funnily enough it turns out that only the light in Tigus' 'galaxy' has the right properties for this kind of thing. But it's just a temporary measure, and to fix it properly the Doctor needs a tool called a distrab. [It sounds as if Hartnell's asking Peter Purves to give him a "diatribe", but he wouldn't ask someone else to provide one of those...] This is one of many oddly-shaped tools in the Ship's toolkit.

Under normal circumstances, the lock is evidently more user-friendly than it used to be [see 1.2, "The Daleks"], as a complete stranger like Bret Vyon is able to use the key on the first try.

There are champagne flutes, a silver tray and a magnum bottle somewhere in the console room, in case of special occasions. Another recent addition is a surgical couch, and there's also - suddenly - an invention of the Doctor's called a 'magnetic chair', just in case any hostile visitors burst in and sit down. It has a force-field that could restrain a herd of elephants, apparently, and is turned off by a switch at the back. Steven uses a

'power impulse compass' from the Ship to find his way back to the Dalek city, and he's already used to operating it [there may well have been some unseen adventures in recent months].

The Monk's vessel, now identified as a TARDIS even by the Monk himself, makes the same dematerialisation noise as the Doctor's. The Doctor can enter it without difficulty ["The Time Meddler" suggests that it doesn't even have a lock]. Whilst the Doctor fiddles with the controls to make it resemble a tank, a motorbike, a western stage-coach and a 'phone box [suggesting a "menu" of Earth objects, as in 18.7, "Logopolis"], when the Monk arrives on an ice-planet it automatically changes into a glacier with a door. In fact, it seems to materialise in a suitable form, not change after arrival.

[So the ability of a TARDIS to change shape is independent of the directional unit, which has been removed by this stage. This may be specific to Mark IV vessels, as both "Logopolis" and "An Unearthly Child" hint that directional failure and the breakdown of the chameleon circuit are both parts of an overall systems fault. The Doctor makes temporary repairs to the chameleon circuit in "Attack of the Cybermen" (22.1), and it's around this time that the Ship starts going wherever he wants it to go. Funnily enough, one of the "stock" TARDIS shapes shown on the Ship's screen in "Logopolis" is a pyramid, so with hindsight it's odd to see the Monk's vessel land in ancient Egypt and turn into a stone block.]

Without the directional unit, the Monk's TARDIS is as uncontrollable as the Doctor's, though the Doctor thinks the Monk could eventually make repairs to overcome this.

The Non-Humans

• *The Daleks.* The assembly of aliens on Kembel is now being called the Universal Council, and the plan is finally revealed, such as it is. Although the Daleks are the only ones who know how to build a time destructor, it requires a taranium core, and taranium is so rare that it's taken Earth's solar system fifty years to mine the necessary mugful. The largest war-force ever assembled is ready to conquer the 'universe', though the Daleks plan to eliminate their allies once they've got what they want. An assault division of 5,000 Daleks is standing by. [The idea may be that they plan to weaken all the major powers with the time destructor, then move in with forces "requisitioned" from their allies. We might suppose that when they say they're going to conquer the 'universe', they mean they're going to conquer all the known galaxies, although the Doctor also casually uses the u-word.]

Daleks are now capable of carrying flame-throwers instead of sucker-arms, but can only locate the invisible Visians by using their seismic detectors. [This hints that they see in the same spectrum as humans. This, unlike much of what we're told here, might suggest that "The Daleks' Master Plan" takes place before the so-called "Davros Era"; by the time of the '80s stories, Daleks have infra-red, heat-vision, and God-knows-what else.] Nor can they tell the difference between the Master of Zephon and the Doctor in Zephon's cloak, while standard patrol Daleks don't recognise the TARDIS on sight. A force-field of gravity-force and 'reliance power', generated by an Earth spaceship, can shield someone from the Daleks' ray-guns for short periods. And yes, the Daleks really do call them 'ray-guns', although they've at least got enough poetry in their souls to refer to the burning-down of Kembel's jungles as 'Operation Inferno'. Their shells are impervious to Mavic Chen's puny blaster.

The Daleks on Kembel have a fleet of pursuit ships, and can supply Chen with a spacecraft similar to his own at short notice. They have to get in touch with Skaro when they need a time machine and a special taskforce to operate it [see **What's Wrong with Dalek History?** for more on this], while the Supreme seen here gives orders to 'report' to the homeworld. [So it's not the absolute ruler of all Daleks. Most probably, it's a member of the Supreme Council mentioned in 10.4, "Planet of the Daleks".] The time machine is guided from Kembel by a 'homing beam', and it's oval this time, with an impressive external PA system. Also employed from the control room on Kembel is a 'neutronic randomiser' that can scramble other people's instruments at long range, making an escaping spacecraft land on a nearby planet. A slightly different device, a 'magnetise' beam, can draw ships towards the base.

The time destructor itself is small enough to be carried, and the Daleks believe it's too dangerous for them to open fire in the weapon's presence. When the destructor is activated, it takes time to warm up but soon affects time all around it. The jungle shrivels and Sara ages to death before Steven inadvertently hits the switch that sends the device into reverse [strange that the Doctor does-

n't think of doing this, when he must surely be able to figure out how it works]. The Daleks' casings melt, and they become dead embryos as millions of years of evolution are undone. The taranium core then burns itself out. [We might guess that when *properly* used, the destructor can destroy entire swathes of the universe from a Dalek attack ship without burning up. If it's as devastating as the Daleks seem to believe, then it might have abilities beyond that of destroying planets, which surely can't be *too* hard for a hi-tech space-going species.]

• *The Delegates.* For a full run-down of the Daleks' allies, see **Which Sodding Delegate is Which?**, but the following information is also presented here...

Representative Trantis - "Trantis" being the place he comes from [either the planet or the galaxy] rather than his name - is here on behalf of the largest of the Outer Galaxies, the Tenth Galaxy. His people have had some success with time-travel experiments, but they haven't quite cracked it yet. Trantis-the-individual sent a delegate to the intergalactic conference of Andromeda, unlike most other powers from the outer galaxies, who were too busy being fiendish with the Daleks. The Daleks eventually exterminate him.

The newly-arrived representative of the Fifth Galaxy is the Master of Zephon, a bipedal plant in a monastic habit. He wears a veil over his face, but walks barefoot and ungloved. On top of the robe is a medallion [identical to the one worn by the War Chief in 6.7, "The War Games", who uses it to assert his status as one of the Doctor's kind... see 12.5, "Revenge of the Cybermen", for more aliens using the symbols of this culture]. Zephon was supposed to personally attend the intergalactic conference of Andromeda, but went to a secret Dalek council instead, along with many of the other representatives here.

Both the planet Fisa and the Embodiment Gris have attempted to depose Zephon, but he still sees himself as the spokesman for his entire galaxy. [It's definitely "Embodiment Gris", not "Embodiment *of* Gris" as other sources have said. We have to note the similarity to the political term *eminence gris*, "grey eminence", coined to describe Cardinal Richelieu's unseen hand in all aspects of French politics.] Without Zephon on board, the Daleks might not have gained the co-operation of the Masters of Celation and Beaus, although that doesn't stop them killing him in the end. Another

What's Wrong With Dalek History?

Even apart from the nightmare of putting together a coherent chronology, anyone trying to make sense of the way the Daleks develop throughout their history is in for a rough ride. Not only is the main author for the 1960s someone who wrote his Dalek scripts on weekends, taking time off from his "proper" writing jobs, but three separate story editors supervised him. Each of them had a different view of how history and time-travel work, yet it's during this period that the Daleks have to make the transition from city-bound bumper-cars to the enemy of human life in every age of civilisation.

Here we'll be referring to our own chronology, **What's the Dalek Timeline?**, given under "The Chase" (2.8). In this account, some time after 3000 AD we see the Daleks experimenting with time-travel. In the Hartnell stories this is by means of vessels not unlike the TARDIS, but in the later stories "The Evil of the Daleks" (4.9) and "Day of the Daleks" (9.1) it's the kind of time-corridor technology later employed in "Resurrection of the Daleks" (21.4) and probably "Remembrance of the Daleks" (25.1). Stories after 1966 never feature DARDIS machines, and the conclusion of "The Daleks' Master Plan" seems to put paid to their use of specially-constructed vessels.

This last fact is interesting, especially when we consider the fate of the Daleks themselves. Overwhelmed by the time destructor, they appear to de-evolve. The Doctor ages a little, and perhaps "youthens" again, but doesn't regress to a previous evolutionary form of his species. Taking the hint from "Invasion of the Dinosaurs" (11.2) and other stories, it seems that the Doctor is able to negotiate time thanks to some genetic or mental ability. "The Two Doctors" (22.4) suggests a biological component to TARDIS travel, although his statements on this subject are garbled and deliberately designed to bewilder the enemy. If the Daleks had a similar time-travel "gene", they would have been able to withstand this temporal drubbing.

Or would they? It's interesting that the Daleks dispatched to apprehend the Doctor, both here and in "The Chase", are special crack squads provided with a DARDIS. It's never stated that any old Dalek can glide into a time machine and go flying through eternity. The Daleks we see revert to mutant infancy on Kembel aren't the same ones who pursued the Doctor to ancient Egypt, but members of the main fortieth-century force. Perhaps, then, only a genetically-modified group of specialist Daleks can use DARDISes. This would

explain a lot. It may even be why those we see in "The Chase" are such a stroppy, undisciplined bunch. If they're somehow able to negotiate ever-changing time-streams and temporal flux, then they might have been introduced to concepts like uncertainty and choice. We know what problems these cause for right-thinking Daleks (see "The Evil of the Daleks"). Time-corridor technology may be less sophisticated and less controllable - "Evil" even suggests that such a corridor requires specific conditions at the destination-point - but at least any Dalek can use it.

From the Dalek point of view, the main purpose of time-travel is strategic, like space-travel. Unlike the Cybermen, they seem to lack the urge to undo their own defeats and give themselves a better past, and even the alteration to history in "Day of the Daleks" makes more sense if you assume it was an accident. They may have worked out that paradoxes and calamitous changes to the timeline are too great a liability. It's notable that in "The Chase", they're never seen to exterminate humans from Earth's past, even when they might be considered to have justification - oh, you know who we mean - almost as if they've been primed to avoid doing too much damage to the timeline. Still, their orders have obviously changed by the time of "Master Plan", as they have no compunction about wiping out the locals at the Great Pyramid.

On top of that, it's easy to see why they wouldn't try to issue warnings (from a Dalek's point of view, "warnings" is synonymous with "orders") to Daleks of earlier periods. For a Dalek in 2157 to take orders from a Dalek of the 3000s would be inconceivable to the 2100 model; the time-traveller is inferior, a genetic mongrel. Note that even if the time-travel facility doesn't require altered DNA, it appears that any form of time-travel has an effect on one's genes. Many of the freak effects seen in "Mawdryn Undead" (20.3) seem to require some form of mutation to the traveller, while the genetic damage done to Greel in "The Talons of Weng-Chiang" (14.6) is described as a side-effect of the time-travel process itself, not just the result of his machine blowing a fuse. We could also cite the Dalek using Rose Tyler's DNA to replenish itself in "Dalek" (X1.6). It identifies her as a time-traveller, and claims that as such her genes are super-nutritious. So by avoiding "free" travel in time wherever possible, the Dalek chain of command is maintained.

continued on page 221...

casualty is the delegate Gearon, who's the only person killed by Chen during the whole affair.

Celation moves as if he's used to more gravity than Kembel can offer, and talks in a harsh whisper. Once betrayed by the Daleks, he quickly decides to go back to his own galaxy and tell his people to oppose them. He wears a medallion, too, like an RAF roundel [*very* Mod].

Planet Notes

• *Kembel.* Still a dump. The Daleks' base there is described as an entire city, but it turns out that they've hidden another complex underground, inside a nearby mountain. They remove the Varga plants before relocating, and plan to destroy the city with the alliance delegates inside once the attack on Earth is ready to begin. Though all traces of the Daleks on the planet are eventually wiped away, it's not clear whether the time destructor turns the *whole* of Kembel or just the immediate locale into a desert.

• *Desperus.* A penal colony of Earth, inhabited by the scum of the Solar System and swarms of occasionally vicious bat-like animals called Screamers. Guess why they're called that. No guards are needed, and the men have long hair and beards. There are women there too, but they never get to say anything. [It's apparently the nearest inhabitable planet to Kembel, since Kembel is where Kirksen wants to go on escaping the planet.] The convicts live almost like cavemen, using primitive clubs as weapons, though those seen here have a knife which is regarded as a status symbol [the only proper knife that's ever been smuggled onto Desperus].

• *Mira.* A planet a long, long way from Earth, so a human experiment in long-range matter transmission uses it as its target. The humans refer to Mira as 'a strange planet in a strange galaxy, the nature of which we can only guess at', although it's suggested that it's closer to Kembel than Earth [and every sign is that Kembel is in Earth's galaxy]. A Dalek patrol from Kembel is there in no time.

Mira is basically a bubbling swamp - yes, another one - with a low, dense mist and bracken-like flora. There are also caves to hide in, which is handy as there's hostile animal life there. And it's invisible. The Visians, as the Doctor calls them, are brutish bipeds with big four-clawed feet. They roar when the Doctor beats them off with a stick, though later they're a little more determined against the Daleks.

• *Tigus.* A volcanic planet, covered in lava and craters, with a breathable atmosphere. [Which seems to act a bit like laughing gas, judging by the behaviour of the Monk and the TARDIS crew. It could be nitrous oxide, which makes sense if there are no plants or animals.] The Doctor describes it as a 'new' planet, still cooling down, while the light in its 'galaxy' has peculiar properties.

History

• *Dating.* It's the year 4000. [There's no clue as to how long it might have been since "Mission to the Unknown". The assembly of the delegates on Kembel may imply that mere weeks have passed, but a bigger gap between the two stories would explain why the line-up of the alliance has changed so much.] The TARDIS also lands in Liverpool on Christmas Day [1965]; in the middle of the Oval cricket ground [roughly in the same era]; in London on New Year's Eve [1965/66]; in Hollywood at some point towards the end of the silent movie era [see **Things That Don't Make Sense**]; and in Egypt at the time of the sealing of the Great Pyramid [both the novelisation and Parkin's *A History of the Universe* agree that this is most likely the Great Pyramid of King Khufu, built in the twenty-seventh century BC].

Fortieth-century Earth, or rather the Solar System with Earth as its "capital", is the major power in its galaxy. Earth itself is run from Central City [compare with "The Sensorites"], and the air is remarkably pure [compare with 9.4, "The Mutants"... the last thousand years have seen a bit of a clean-up]. The total population of the system is forty-billion, and everyone's 'chemical' profiles are stored in the official computer network. This civilisation is ruled by the Guardian of the Solar System, namely Mavic Chen. Even delegates from other galaxies see the amount of power he wields as exceptional, and in turn he knows all about the political status of his fellow conspirators.

Earth seems to be a harsh, unforgiving society, not exactly fascistic but highly-regimented and full of people who don't ask questions. Everyone seen here wears a uniform of some sort, usually a tunic or tabard with a logo. However, they're not depicted as utilitarian or emotionally sterile, as they indulge in sport and argue in offices. The technix, who handle maintenance and technical support, are mostly bald men who wear batwing polo-necks over tight leggings. They run Central Communications on Earth, a room with a map of

What's Wrong With Dalek History?

...continued from page 219

In our chronology, we decided that "Day of the Daleks" kicks off with events circa 3500 AD. This wasn't exactly a guess, but we were working on minimal evidence. We *know* the Daleks who conquer twenty-first century Earth to be time-travellers, and they don't seem to understand the process of time-travel very well, which hints that they come from the early DARDIS days of "The Chase". Yet they use something like time-corridor technology. We should mention that in "The Chase", we're never told that the DARDIS is the first time-travel device they ever develop; indeed, far from going "hooray, we've cracked the fourth dimension", the report to the Dalek Supreme matter-of-factly describes the completion of the time machine as if it's a straightforward piece of engineering. So the "Day of the Daleks" may predate "The Chase", and their time-travel technology may be in its infancy - a process simple enough for human guerrillas to use, but not quite controllable enough to be able to pursue the Doctor. Note that these Daleks seem obsessed with Earth, like those of the third millennium rather than the galaxy-conquerors of the fourth, and the weapons they give to the Ogrons are made from Welsh metal instead of Filidor gold. Or whatever other magic substance the Daleks prefer using.

But there's another possible explanation for all of this. We're assuming that the alternative timeline in "Day of the Daleks" is an accident (see the story's write-up for the reasons why), but what if it isn't? What if it's been set up deliberately, by forward-thinking Daleks of the future, as an attempt to start all over again? Since we've established that future-Daleks wouldn't communicate directly with past-Daleks, it may even have been arranged by far, far, *far*-future Daleks in the knowledge that the unsuspecting past-Daleks would simply exploit the opportunities offered by a vulnerable Earth. It may even be a back-up plan, an attempt at creating a bolt-hole in time in case the rest of the Dalek line is wiped out (see X1.13, "The Parting of the Ways")...

the galaxy on the wall which receives transmissions from SSS agents off-planet. SSS operatives wear white sashes over black tunics, and obligatory jackboots. Notably, SSS agent Sara doesn't know the word "police".

Mavic Chen himself is a trusted statesmen, oriental in appearance, with extraordinarily long fingernails. [Kevin Stoney is definitely wearing tinted make-up of some kind, and eye-witness accounts claim that he was painted blue on-set. But there's no reference to Chen's blueness in the script.] His motivation isn't questioned by the people of the Solar System, as he's maintained peace there and spread it across the galaxy. His Non-Aggression Pact of 3975 is now being consolidated by a complicated mineral agreement with the Fourth Galaxy, and he attended the intergalactic conference of Andromeda. This conference was held in Earth's galaxy [so somewhere in the Andromeda constellation, probably], though Chen has never really left the Solar System for holidaying purposes. Of course, he secretly wants to take over Earth's entire galaxy. However, he seems oblivious to the obvious ambitions of Karlton, his lackey and head of the SSS. Chen's wild mood swings [see especially episode five] can see him go from wild despair to operatic grandiosity in less than a minute, so no wonder he ends up going berserk before the Daleks exterminate him.

[It's not known how long Chen has been the Guardian, or whether he was democratically elected. The pact of 3975 may have been signed when he was the fortieth-century equivalent of Foreign Secretary rather than Guardian. Chen suggests that he put the mining of the taranium in motion fifty years ago, but he describes himself as the Daleks' 'most recent' ally. And it's hard to imagine why the Daleks would spend so long arranging their time destructor plan without a source of taranium. Possibly they began assembling the alliance as part of a wider strategy, before they knew the destructor was going to be involved in the plan; possibly Chen was overseeing the mining of taranium before getting in touch with the Daleks, as Bret Vyon knows of the substance and of its great rarity / value.]

Mavic Chen's vehicle is known as a Spar 740 [this would seem to be a type of craft rather than the name of the vessel, though it's treated as if Chen's is a unique custom job], known to the Daleks as spacecraft one-eleven [its registration number]. It has a crew of at least two technix, and is regarded as the most technically-perfect vessel in human history. The FLIPT-4 is also described as a popular type of ship [it's short for Faster-than-Light InterPlanetary Transport, according to off-screen notes], but considered a bit brash, even if it's quicker. Mention is made of vessels travelling around in 'ultra-space' [like hyperspace, but better?], though Vyon has never seen anything like the TARDIS [so humans have never seen a Dalek time machine]. Magnetic tape is, remarkably, still used as a storage medium in this era.

But here's the cutting edge of technology. In a sterile-looking experimental station on Earth, scientists are perfecting a molecular dissemination process which can 'transpose' the contents of a special room all the way to the planet Mira. The Doctor believes this involves their molecules being sent through the fourth dimension. ["The Seeds of Death" (6.5) establishes that humanity has teleportation technology as early as the twenty-first century, so - as the dialogue confirms - what's most remarkable here is the distance covered. Even Steven thinks it's incredible. See also **How Do You Transmit Matter?** under 17.4, "Nightmare of Eden".] Mice are still being used as, well, guinea-pigs. The boss of the SSS isn't aware of the experiment, but Bret Vyon knows the head of the project personally. Despite this, it turns out that the chief scientist is in on Chen's conspiracy, so Vyon doesn't hesitate to execute him.

Bret Vyon also becomes the first person to tell the Doctor to shut up, although he adds 'sir' to his command [either showing his respect for authority, or - more likely - following SSS procedures for pretending to be polite to civilians]. According to his file, Vyon is one of the best agents in the organisation; recruited in 3990, gained First Rank in 3995, gained Second Rank in 3998. SSS agents carry transmitters that can get in touch with Central Communications, and tablets in a tube which cure Steven's 'poison of the blood' after his shoulder injury.

Other worlds in the Solar System are mentioned. Uranus is described as one of the 'dead' planets [it's never been terraformed], and it's the only source of taranium known to the Daleks. With taranium being the rarest mineral in the universe, it takes fifty terrestrial years to refine one 'emm' of the stuff, which amounts to a bean-tin or so. It burns your eyes out if you look directly at it. Chen believes that Earth is an important part of the Universal Council not simply because its system contains taranium, but because the humans' knowledge of mineralogy is superior, so only they can mine it. [This may be somewhat hubristic, as the Daleks are ostensibly brilliant technicians.]

Here Venus plays Mars at some major sporting event or other, broadcast live on Channel 403. Mars has colonies, Vyon having been born in colony sixteen. [We might guess that it was one of the first planets colonised in the third millennium AD, so it's strange that by now it's still described as having 'colonies' rather than being an integrated society. It's also probable that by this stage, humanity knows about the Ice Warriors; see 9.2, "The Curse of Peladon". Which begs the question... are the Ice Warriors still on Mars? If so, are the 'colonies' mentioned here just *human* colonies, with the Ice Warriors owning much of the rest of the planet?] In times of crisis, all the planets of the solar system can assemble a combined taskforce.

Steven comes from an age 'thousands of years' before 4000 AD [allowing for exaggeration, that could be any time up until about 2500]. In his own era, gravitational force is used as a power-source for starships, and he's mocked by fortieth-century types for speaking of such antiquated technology. Though a g-force 'force-field' can still be generated by more futuristic ships, it's not the primary source of energy.

The Doctor seriously believes that Earth's atmosphere is pure in both Steven's time and Sara's, so the atmosphere of twentieth-century Earth could harm them. [In Sara's case this is believable, but everything else tells us that in the third millennium - which, we have to assume, is the time of Steven's origin - Earth is massively polluted. See especially "The Mutants" and "Colony in Space" (8.4).] According to the Doctor, the Daleks invaded Earth in 2157 [see 2.2, "The Dalek Invasion of Earth"], and the convicts on Desperus have never heard of them.

In sort-of-1920s Hollywood, the Doctor meets a disgruntled clown who gives his name as Bing Crosby, and who's so sick of Charlie Chaplin that he's planning on taking up singing. [This is so different to the biography of the *real* Bing Crosby that we might assume it's another actor who just happened to have the same name and later had to change it. But then, we might assume any number of things about this bizarre and distressing sequence.] The Keystone Cops are also around, and someone who supposedly looks like Chaplin himself. Neither Steven nor Sara recognise anything they see of Hollywood at all, or even understand that the people there are making films. [See **Whatever Happened to the USA?** under 4.6, "The Moonbase".]

The Analysis

Where Does This Come From? The clue lies in the claim that it takes fifty years to mine a cupful of taranium, and thus fifty years to build a single super-weapon. When the Nazis tried to make an atomic bomb in the latter stages of the War, their advisors - including, most famously, top quantum mechanic Werner Heisenberg - came up with hopelessly inaccurate figures as to how much uranium 238 would be needed. The correct amount is just over a dozen kilos, but the figure cited in earlier estimates (ignoring the chain reaction, because the theorists who worked *that* out had a tendency to be Jewish or left-wing) was so great that they thought it'd take about half a century to mine it.

However, by including the traditional Cold War SF idea that the Earth is the West and the aliens need something we've already developed in order to conquer the universe, the obvious connection that most viewers would have made was with people like Klaus Fuchs giving atomic secrets to the Soviets. Yet the similarity ends when this is examined in detail. The West had the Bomb, but the Solar System doesn't have a time destructor, just the necessary resources to make one. And Fuchs was motivated by a desire to stop either side having an advantage, while Chen is all out for himself.

It's striking, though, that Chen is set up as a statesman with a quote from Churchill and then shown to be a traitor. Not that Winston's the real target here; there was never any chance of that, especially so soon after his death, and his subsequent elevation from national hero to sainthood. But this would have seemed weird just a decade earlier, and at work throughout Season Three there's a distrust of authority that comes across as the product of a nation waking up from a twenty-year post-War hangover. Chen even goes as far as to quote Orwell - *Animal Farm* this time - by stating that some of the Daleks' allies are more equal than others. The conference chamber looks a lot like what we now think of as a generic "war room", but in context it's like nothing so much as *Dr Strangelove*. (And if we're talking about Kubrick, then what goes around comes around. See **The Lore**.)

Still. The Daleks were always an amalgam of Nazi iconography and atomic paranoia, so it was only natural that the Manhattan Project would filter into the story, just as it had in their first two outings. As the jungle-based action in "The Chase" had been the most successful part, it was a good move to do it again, only with more resources behind it (plus, it was economical on sets if they made the Dalek Cutaway episode in the same locale). Some of the ideas rejected in "The Chase" were re-used, like the cricket scene and the episodes in which the Doctor gets to visit ancient Egypt, the one really obvious setting for a story that hadn't yet been done... although since the "educational" strand of the series was pretty much dead in the water by this point, the pyramids become nothing more than a backdrop for monsters and big villains. Needless to say, the Egyptian "characters" are even less substantial than the Vikings in "The Time Meddler". And as in "The Time Meddler", much of what we see here is a celebration of contemporary aspirations. We've gone from time-travellers who use electric toasters to futuristic space-agents who use sexy modern hand-held tape recorders.

But the *real* reason this story happened is more prosaic. As we've already seen, the production team's plan was to concentrate on four-part stories, except for two six-part Dalek stories per year. And for obvious reasons, the Daleks were best deployed around Christmas. Huw Weldon believed that *Doctor Who* was Daleks and filler, while Nation thought of his career as good stuff plus Daleks. Only the cheques maintained his enthusiasm. Meanwhile, Wiles and Tosh were bequeathed Verity Lambert's idea to get their "quota" of Dalek episodes out of the way in one go. Logistically, it made more sense to do a fast-moving adventure on several worlds over a longer period than to do six weeks of "The Chase" or "The Keys of Marinus".

Earlier, we mentioned the *Star Wars* films; like them, this story has roots in Saturday Morning Serials. Mavic Chen in particular has strong hints of the villainous Killer Kane in *Buck Rogers in the 25th Century*, not to mention any number of moustache-twirling Chinese villains from Fu Manchu onwards. (And there was something of an explosion of these after China turned communist. It'll surprise nobody to see that the apparently Oriental character is the one who sides with the Commie Daleks but has nefarious plans of his own.) The idea of spaceships being brought down by rays, in this case the Dalek "randomiser", will be terribly familiar to anyone familiar with the machinations of that other great moustache-twirler Ming the Merciless.

While we're on the subject of the juvenile, we might as well mention comic-books again. We saw under "Mission to the Unknown" how Nation felt driven to match David Whitaker's high-speed sugar-rush Dalek comic-strips, but here the cartoon elements are more whimsical than the adventures of robot agent 2K. We have to remember that even apart from Wiles' attempts to broaden the scope of the series, by this stage the public had seen several different versions of what *Doctor Who* was supposed to be, in several different media. Obviously there was the movie with Peter Cushing, but there was also the merchandising, which had a peculiarly lollipop-flavoured view of the Doctor's universe that the TV series never really went for (although "The Web Planet" comes closest, and if you've read the '60s *Doctor Who* annuals then you'll realise that for some people "The Crusade" seemed less typically *Doctor Who* than stories about the Zarbi Supremo or the Fishmen of Kandalinga... yes, Kandalinga).

One of the more notable examples of "alternative" *Doctor Who* was the regular strip in *TV Comic*, and the episode "The Feast of Steven" is in much the same vein. The sight of the Doctor raising a glass to the folks at home may look weird to us now we know a story like "The Massacre" is going to be the next thing broadcast, but at a time when comic-strip hero Dr Who had two juvenile grandchildren and the notorious Give-a-Show Projector allowed children to cover their walls with pictures of Daleks without being smacked round the head, it fit the ethos of the series as many viewers understood it. The *TV Comic* strip saw the Doctor delivering occasional asides to the readers, and often involved meetings with characters like - and this seemed funny, until we learned what was going to be in the first David Tennant episode - Father Christmas.

Actually, the whole idea of a Christmas story in which the usual rules of reality are suspended has long been a favourite of comic-books. We might once again mention the *Eagle*, particularly the one-off festive story in which the boundaries between the magazine's regular comic-strips breaks down and Dan Dare (Pilot of the Future) gets into an argument with Jeff Arnold (Rider of the Range). This, too, ends with the characters turning to the readers and wishing them a merry Christmas.

In other news... the earlier part of episode seven, where the TARDIS lands in 1965, is effectively the first time the Doctor turns up in the present-day (or at least, the first time he has to interact with "everyday" people other than Ian and Barbara). We're now so used to seeing stories in which the Doctor has to mystify / explain himself to contemporary authority figures that we miss the alleged comedy in this part of the story. A modern viewer wouldn't see anything remotely amusing about the seemingly-routine way he's accosted by policemen for loitering around a police box, but the whole point of the gag is that he *is* dealing with everyday nuisances like policemen, something the audience has never seen in the series before. This comedy-clash between the fantastic and the ordinary will later become one of the programme's hallmarks, but here it's something exceptional, and you can see why they waited until the Christmas special to try it. Other things, of course, would have been a lot more familiar to regular viewers. Nation's storyline does the usual job of recycling old material, not just the screaming jungle-planets but plot details like the fake taranium core. You may recall the ending of "The Keys of Marinus"...

Oh yes, and this is yet another story in which time gets a good mauling, so as ever we're required to mention *The Twilight Zone*. The sight of somebody ageing to death will later be a staple of television SF, and *Doctor Who* itself will insist on using the idea over and over again in future years, but it's a difficult thing to pull off in front of a camera - or at least, it was before the world went digital - so here we have to pay particular attention to the *Twilight Zone* episode "Long Live Walter Jameson". This features an ageing sequence that was strikingly swish, by the standards of late '50s TV, and made such an impression that it informed television effects work for years to come. That said, we can't actually *see* Sara dying these days, so we don't know for certain how similar the two sequences are. Another possible precedent, and one with a more obvious connection to *Doctor Who*, is *Armchair Theatre*'s 1961 adaptation of *The Picture of Dorian Grey*.

Things That Don't Make Sense Interplanetary communication works like a '50s telephone exchange; the SSS agents on Kembel try to send a vital message back to Earth, but the workers at Central Communications don't notice the light flashing on the switchboard because they're watching TV. At the very least, an ansaphone might be a good idea, for when agents need to send details of potential invasions of the galaxy. Communications boffin Lizan seems to have such an eidetic memory that she knows all of Vyon's biographical details in an instant, complete with dates, but she can't remember the name of the all-important mission that's been sent to Kembel or when it's supposed to report in. And Chen is happy to let this one-woman information machine know that his Spar was stolen from Kembel, without feeling the need to explain what he was doing there.

Oh yeah, there's another thing. Mavic Chen has a spaceship so recognisable that Bret spots it in the Daleks' car-park and identifies it straight away. Bit of a risk going to Kembel without arranging to switch to something less distinctive, eh?

The delegates are all supposed masters of their respective galaxies - the most potent, ruthless, iron-willed beings around. Yet when an alarm sounds, Celation jumps on a table and Gearon spins around making a "meep" noise like Beaker from The Muppet Show. And Mavic Chen, after fifty years of plotting and patiently waiting for his mining engineers to deliver... oops! Left the taranium behind on the desk. Boy, is my face blue.

When the Doctor's stolen Earth-ship gets away from Kembel, the Daleks use a randomiser to make it land on a nearby planet. Later, they use a "magnetic" device to pull a similarly stolen Dalek vessel right back to Kembel. Couldn't they have used the space-magnet the first time? [It can only be used on Dalek ships, possibly as a security precaution to stop them being hijacked.] Everyone knows that Kembel is the most hostile planet in the universe, except for Kirksen, who wants to go there after escaping Desperus and claims it'll be an improvement. Why, precisely, does he wants to live on an inhospitable jungle planet? What's there for him?

Larking around in Liverpool, Steven claims to be doing a Scouse accent because 'everyone else is', but his version is unlike that of any of the other actors and taken wholesale from loveable mop-top Liverpudlian pop stars (or the version in the Beatles' cartoon series, anyway). We could claim that he picked it up from Vicki, in those episodes where she's supposed to be from Liverpool and not the planet Dido, but she stopped all that before Steven arrived. Anyway, why does Steven decide to mimic the locals this time around, and never before or afterwards? Two episodes later, he never tries to talk like an E-gyp-tian. (Although, to

be fair, he did do almost-blank-verse for "The Myth Makers".)

When exactly is the silent movie being made? Anyone with a rudimentary knowledge of Hollywood before the talkies will be able to spot the anachronisms, not the least of which is Bing Crosby going into movies before 1930. The director Ingmar Knopf seems to be trying to remake Intolerance with a counterfeit Rudolph Valentino, yet the Keystone Cops are on set. [Consider the Doctor's beliefs about the Haunted House in 2.8, "The Chase". Perhaps the TARDIS hasn't landed in the real Hollywood at all, but in the human collective unconscious of the 1930s, after it's been infected with ideas from the movies. No? Never mind.] And frankly, Robert Jewell - though an experienced Dalek operator and part-time Zarbi - looks less like Bing than Malcolm Rogers looked like Dracula.

Only the 'galaxy' of the planet Tigus, we're told, has such odd sunlight that it can open the TARDIS doors. This is weird enough in itself, yet it's here that the Monk decides to sabotage the lock. Even if he's unaware of the light's peculiar qualities, it's a remarkably lucky coincidence for the Doctor, isn't it? If we're talking about things that aren't impossible but seem overly neat, we might also point out the dramatic flair of the Daleks waiting until a nice round human year like 4000 AD before launching their plan against the Solar System. [Unless Mavic Chen's been keeping the taranium back until now, so that his domination of the galaxy coincides with the millennium celebrations.]

Sara somehow knows how to check the TARDIS scanner eye without instructions, and on leaving "comedy" 1965 she states that all the funny Liverpudlians made her forget about the Daleks, as if she weren't in the middle of a galaxy-threatening crisis which has already caused her to execute her own brother. And it's anyone's guess why she finds it so hilarious that the Monk's TARDIS has been changed into a police telephone box. Her decision to literally broadcast her presence in the Dalek city, in episode eleven, is also hard to credit.

But there's a lot that's puzzling about this sequence. The Daleks' decision to relocate to an underground bunker before taking over the universe is never properly explained. The only given reason is that they're going to leave the delegates behind and destroy the whole city, which is about eight-thousand times less efficient than just exterminating their visitors in the standard fashion. They even leave one of their super-valuable time machines in the city, to be destroyed along with their victims. Then the Daleks lead Chen, Steven and Sara to their control room instead of shooting them on the spot, even though these prisoners are of absolutely no value whatsoever. And the Dalek Supreme later informs us that the control room is the one place where it's too dangerous to fire any weapons, and thus the one place where the Daleks can't carry out a quick killing. Then, amazingly, they're incompetent enough to "forget" about Steven and Sara when Chen goes berserk. Nor do they think of sealing the doors to stop the companions getting out, after the Doctor springs them.

The one everybody knows... the message Marc Cory recorded in "Mission to the Unknown" and the message we hear from him in episode three are two totally different messages by different actors. [We could put it down to a quirk of the TARDIS' translation systems, as it struggles to cope with fortieth-century human dialect, but it's a bit of a stretch.] Once again, agents of Earth's defensive force can't remember whether they're "Special" or "Space" security. And something that might be clearer if we had the pictures: what does Bret Vyon actually *do* to the Doctor in episode one, that apparently knocks the Doctor out for a couple of minutes while he hijacks the TARDIS? He rather unwisely leaves the key in the lock, so he can't have been expecting the old man to recover.

There are, as expected, a lot of lines here that don't come out the way they should. Even given that this is a story which features Daleks saying things like 'all is ready for their space extinction', but Katarina ends up with a great moment of stating the obvious: 'The evil ones searched for us, but Bret helped us. He said they were evil.'

And one last great Billy Fluff: 'The Daleks will stop at anything to prevent it!' After this, they stop being funny.

Critique If we get out of the habit of thinking of these adventures as discrete, authored stories and ponder them as episodes in a serial running for 46 weeks a year, then we'll be able to see how this was meant to work. Each new Dalek story has raised their game, and as such each encounter has seen the Doctor become more of a threat to them. Once they got a DARDIS, the Daleks' return meant a travelogue, each new world more exotic

than the last. Conspiring with other alien baddies meant that the costume and make-up teams could go wild. The sets were left vague in the script because the writers knew Ray Cusick could provide something spectacular, and Camfield was left to find new ways of solving the problem that however much they made threats, the Daleks didn't *do* an awful lot. In short, a Dalek adventure was an audio-visual experience with occasional nods towards a plot.

Well, "The Chase" tried something similar, but the BBC liked it more than the casual viewers. Wiles is usually said to have sat back and let this story "happen", mainly because that's what he claimed in interviews, but a comparison of this and "The Chase" gives us the starkest possible illustration of what Wiles and Tosh were all about. It's *brutal*, not just in the body-count but in the way that the people we see getting killed *are* people, instead of the usual cannon-fodder. Katarina's death may not be remotely necessary to the story, but it's alarming in a quite carefully-calculated way (Kirksen's shrieking, and Steven's cry of '*you animal!*', must have been truly disturbing for the under-tens), while her elegiac floating-through-space is an almost poetic contrast to the violence of the previous few minutes.

Normally, when *Doctor Who* gets promiscuous and tries to combine too many popular contemporary things, you end up with unholy messes. This time it's Blofeld-style villainy, an *Avengers* girl, wartime iconography and an atomic plot-device work with *Flash Gordon* settings and a dog's breakfast of subplots alongside the Monk and a shoot-out at the Great Pyramid. Only a Camfield-directed story could have done this. The comedy works because the stakes are so high, the adventure works because the plot's taken so many unexpected detours. "That" Christmas episode is the only part that pushes the point too far, but the first half prefigures an awful lot of future *Doctor Who* in ways we no longer even notice.

Note how we say that this story "works", rather than that it's "good". In truth, it barely fits our value-system at all, and more than ever before our judgement's impaired by the absence of the pictures. Episode two turned out to be startlingly decent when we eventually got to see what Camfield did with it, though episode five is drab beyond redemption, far too static to overcome the stilted dialogue or the sense that you're watching a fortieth-century Television for Schools production about teleportation. The mice steal the show, unless you count Hartnell's terrible gurning when he's being molecularly disassembled. If you want to talk scripts, then there's a definite upswing when Spooner officially takes the controls, which surprises no-one. Episode ten does what "The Time Meddler" couldn't do, presenting the Great Civilisation of Egypt as a historical backwater where the natives struggle to come to terms with the (far more important) head-to-head between visiting cosmic powers.

And listening to the grand sweep of it on CD, waiting for the "important" parts where well-known characters die or the Monk gets to do his thing with Hartnell, we miss the fact that a lot of people involved are paying attention to the details for once. Katarina doesn't automatically know what tablets are, or how doors work; Chen sends up the space-talk of the other delegates with comments like 'three galaxies for the price of one'; and after all that's gone before, seeing / hearing the Daleks' Kembel HQ abandoned in episode eleven is genuinely unsettling, like seeing a familiar room stripped of all its furnishings. Wisely, all the "proper" villains with "proper" motives have human faces, so the Daleks can do what they do best, acting as a force of nature instead of trying to be individually interesting. They're the constant, faceless menace we always imagine them to be.

But more crucially, by taking the time and effort to make the Daleks menacing again, Tosh and Camfield have bought themselves the right to vary the formula. Most of those involved put in just that little bit more effort as a result. Purves is never better than here, and that includes *Blue Peter*. Nick Courtney will play another sardonic authority figure later on, although Bret Vyon isn't a test-run for the Brigadier but a solid character in his own right. Even actors who've been in the series repeatedly, like Roger Avon (Saphadin in 2.6, "The Crusade") or Dallas Cavell (the Road Works Overseer in 1.8, "The Reign of Terror"), find new ways to play almost-stock characters. And even allowing that the Daleks have a tendency to flatten everything else out when they're on-screen, Kevin Stoney gives a performance that manages to be nuanced *and* over-the-top at once (the only way any actor has ever held his or her own against them... see 10.3, "Frontier in Space"; 12.4, "Genesis of the Daleks"; and above all 22.6, "Revelation of the Daleks").

The Facts

Purportedly written by Terry Nation (episodes one to five, seven) and Dennis Spooner (episodes six, eight to twelve). Directed by Douglas Camfield. Ratings: 9.1 million, 9.8 million, 10.3 million, 9.5 million, 9.9 million, 9.1 million, 7.9 million, 9.6 million, 9.2 million, 9.6 million, 9.8 million, 8.6 million. The audience appreciation figures were almost all in the low 50s, the exceptions being 57% for the last episode and an atrocious 39% for "The Feast of Steven". We can't think why.

Only episodes two, five and ten exist in the BBC archive.

Supporting Cast Kevin Stoney (Mavic Chen), Nicholas Courtney (Bret Vyon), Peter Butterworth (The Meddling Monk), Brian Cant (Kert Gantry), Julian Sherrier (Zephon), Roy Evans (Trantis), Pamela Greer (Lizan), Philip Anthony (Roald), Douglas Sheldon (Kirksen), Dallas Cavell (Bors), Geoffrey Cheshire (Garge), Maurice Browning (Karlton), Roger Avon (Daxtar), James Hall (Borkar), John Herrington (Rhymnal), Bill Metley (Froyn), Leonard Grahame (Darcy Tranton), Sheila Dunn (Blossom Lefevre), Royston Tickner (Steinberger P. Green), Mark Ross (Ingmar Knopf), David James (Arab Sheik), Roger Brierley (Trevor), Albert Barrington (Professor Webster), Terrance Woodfield (Celation), Bruce Wightman (Scott), Jeffrey Isaac (Khephren), Derek Ware (Tuthmos), Walter Randall (Hyksos), Bryan Mosley (Malpha); David Graham, Peter Hawkins (Dalek Voices).

AKA... Although nobody has ever doubted the words in its name, the punctuation's always been a bit of an issue. *The Making of Doctor Who* went with "The Dalek Master Plan", leading people to flirt with "The Dalek Masterplan" and "The Daleks' Masterplan" before settling on the version we've used here.

Episode Titles "The Nightmare Begins", "Day of Armageddon", "Devil's Planet", "The Traitors", "Counterplot", "Coronas of the Sun", "The Feast of Steven", "Volcano", "Golden Death", "Escape Switch", "The Abandoned Planet", "The Destruction of Time".

Working Titles "Doctor Who and the Daleks". Finally, a story we *can* call that.

Cliffhangers The Doctor returns to the clearing where the TARDIS landed, only to see the Daleks rolling out of the jungle towards it; as the alarm sounds in the Dalek city on Kembel, Bret Vyon insists that the spaceship has to leave without the Doctor (not *much* of a cliffhanger, this, given that he'd only be "stranding" the Doctor on the same planet as the TARDIS); the Doctor's ship manages to take off from Desperus, but one of the murderous convicts has crept on board; having shot Vyon dead at the experimental complex, Sara Kingdom gives her underlings orders to find and kill the other travellers; a Dalek corners the Doctor and friends in the swamps of Mira, and the Doctor announces that the Daleks have won; the TARDIS lands, but the Doctor looks at the dial on the console and realises the atmosphere outside is poisonous; the Doctor wishes us a happy Christmas; their time machine sent in pursuit of the TARDIS, the Daleks begin chanting that conquest is assured (yeah, because "The Chase" went so well, didn't it?); a bandaged mummy rises from a sarcophagus to menace Steven and Sara (relax, kids, it's just the Monk); there's a blaze of light in the console room as the TARDIS takes off with the Monk's directional unit in place; a blaster-packing Chen forces Steven and Sara into the entrance tunnel of the Daleks' underground bunker.

The Lore

• Terry Nation's involvement in *The Baron* had gone from script editor to de facto producer, and he was spending a lot of time co-ordinating it in New York. As the director-joining date grew ever closer, Tosh found Nation's assurances that the scripts would be ready in time increasingly unconvincing. A cunning plan was hatched wherein Dennis Spooner would write the latter half, using Nation's scenario. But with ten days to go before the start of pre-filming, the first half still wasn't available. Douglas Camfield and the set designers got edgy. Finally, Nation agreed to take the script to Tosh's flat by taxi en route to Heathrow Airport. The doorbell rang, Tosh ran downstairs, and Nation slipped him a manila envelope containing 24 pages of notes before speeding off into the night.

• The notes contained detailed and loving descriptions of spaceships and their futuristic names, some costume suggestions, and a description of Mavic Chen (and a note that this name was to be kept at any cost... 'Mavick" Chen had been the second name selected, after "Banhoong" was ruled out). There were, Tosh recalls, about eight lines of actual dialogue for five episodes. Next morning, Spooner rang, and whilst sympathetic - he'd worked with Nation before, remember - was mainly concerned about what the story was going to be like at the point when his own half started. He was advised to write what he liked, and Tosh would work up to it. Tosh then told Camfield to make something up, and the script would accommodate it, so Camfield filmed most of the Ealing and model sequences with only a vague idea of what the rest of the story would be. Kert Gantry's death was almost entirely scripted by Camfield, for instance (and his friend Brian Cant, whom he cast in a hurry, confirms that there was no written script at this stage).

• The difference between Cant's studio and film work caused concern, too, as his beards didn't match.

• It's worth noting that when he wrote his notes for the story, Nation still believed Vicki was the one scheduled to die in the vacuum of space. He described her corpse, floating seraphically with a Mona Lisa smile on her face, in more detail than he described most of the plot.

• More detailed scripts emerged, with a request that "Stephen" (sic) should be injured in the shoulder at the end of the previous story, and that anything Vicki had to do should be amended to fit the new girl. Once it became obvious that Katarina was to die, the subplot about the prison-world was extended, though there was more about the way the girl's hair should look in space than actual dialogue. The Doctor's speech was marked with a request to fill in something appropriate about the character.

• The death scene itself was filmed from beneath a trampoline. The camera was focused through the mesh, so that only the actors and the "space" background painted on the ceiling were visible, then overcranked so that the hair and clothing would seem to float. Katarina's robes precluded the use of flying harnesses. The production office later received a phone call from Elstree Studios, where Stanley Kubrick was making *2001: A Space Odyssey* and wanted to know how they did it. (This isn't the last time a Camfield / Kubrick connection can be made. See 5.5, "The Web of Fear".)

• It was, initially, Camfield's idea to change some of the names to make them sound more futuristic. Vyon was originally called "Walton" - a real two-fisted Western kind of name, that, not untypical of Nation's work - and taranium was originally "vitaranium", but there were fears that Hartnell wouldn't be able to say it.

• Spooner's return to the series was welcomed by Purves, who was confident that Steven's creator would stop the character's slide into "generic male lead", but less so by Hartnell. The business with the Doctor's ring unfreezing the TARDIS lock annoyed the actor (it went against previously-accepted continuity), though by this stage Camfield had established a good working relationship with the star, and reassured him. "Colonel" Camfield worked to a rigorous timetable, and knew exactly where he ought to be in the shoot at any given moment. He gave all his staff appropriate military ranks. Perhaps surprisingly, the "creative" members of the crew - the actors and artists - responded best to this, as they had a sense that someone was in control and fighting the BBC pen-pushers on their behalf. Camfield also, on occasion, used the less martial system of holding up a pound note and offering it to whoever came up with the best solution to an unforeseen problem.

• Camfield ended up rewriting a lot of the dialogue even when there *was* a script. Generally Wiles and Tosh were happy to let him do this, but Tosh in particular hated the end of "The Feast of Steven", where the Doctor toasts the audience. Some have claimed that the line was an ad-lib from Hartnell, though the end credits seem to have been intended to run over the shot of him looking out from the screen. (Camfield will get the Doctor to address the viewers again in future. Once more, see "The Web of Fear".)

• It's reported that Tosh had approached Keith Dewhurst, one of the most respected writers around, to work on the series. Dewhurst had turned the offer down and stayed with his main series, *Z Cars*, which is ostensibly why Tosh retaliated with the *Z Cars* pastiche in episode seven. But this doesn't quite ring true, as *Z Cars* ended its initial run at roughly the same time that this story was being made; possibly someone involved with one or both series suggested using the sets one last time. Judging by the photos, there *is* a sort of resemblance between the actors at the police station and the *Z Cars* cast, even though the programme's producer refused to let the real cast-

members appear in *Doctor Who*.

• Other in-jokes abound in the Christmas episode, such as the Doctor recognising the man who's under arrest at the station from the market in Jaffa (the actor is Reg Pritchard, who'd been the clothing merchant Ben Daheer in 2.6, "The Crusade"), while the starlet being given a hard time by the director of the silent movie is Camfield's wife Sheila Dunn.

• Camfield is credited by Tosh with salvaging this story, but Camfield himself wanted his "Captain", Production Assistant Viktors Ritelis, given a co-director credit in the final episode. Ritelis brought a certain silent-movie flair to the penultimate *Blake's 7* episode, "Warlord", and this is probably the easiest way for the reader to assess whether his style is radically different from Camfield's.

• Originally, Sara and Bret were to have been lovers instead of siblings. So, let's take stock of this. Jean Marsh appears in *Doctor Who* three times. The first time, she plays the sister of King Richard, who was meant to have an unseemly relationship with her brother until Hartnell intervened (see "The Crusade"). The second time, she murders a sibling who was initially supposed to be her lover, and who still sounds as if she's getting her revenge on the man who broke her heart and turned her into a cold-blooded killer. The third time, she's the witch-queen Morgaine, who... well, if you don't know Arthurian mythology then let's just say that her son Mordred only gets one Christmas present from his dad and his uncle (26.1, "Battlefield"). You get the feeling there's someone in the casting department of the BBC whose job involves reading through all the scripts and saying: "Incest? Hmm, I'd better call Jean."

3.5: "The Massacre"

(Serial W. Four Episodes, 5th- 26th February 1966.)

Which One is This? The one historical story where the audience isn't supposed to know too much in advance. Paris in 1572, if that helps. If not, then listen to the audio now, and avoid the spoilers...

Firsts and Lasts Donald Tosh departs here, after writing an extraordinary climax and effectively rewriting the whole serial, and Gerry Davis takes over as script editor. Davis' first act is to introduce

ABOUT TIME 1963-1966

a new companion, Dodo, who's almost exactly what Susan had originally been intended to be like. The results are... mixed. And, Paddy Russell becomes the first woman to direct for the series. It's *possible* that this is the only story with no cliffhanger reprises, for reasons we'll go into shortly, although it's difficult to say with so much missing from the archive.

But perhaps uniquely, this is a story in which war (or at least, war between people rather than against space-monsters) is shown to be an inevitable function of human politics, not a bad thing by default. The Admiral de Coligny, who's not precisely the *good* guy here but who's certainly quite civilised compared to the competition, spends most of his time advocating a war with Spain on the grounds that it'll ally France with the Protestant powers and help to end the religious turmoil within the country. This is, if nothing else, the first time in the series that we've heard of a full-scale international conflict having positive consequences.

Four Things to Notice About "The Massacre"...

1. Even though it now only exists on audio, the story's easy enough to follow as the guest stars are almost all well-known voices. At least, if you grew up around *these* parts. Erik Chitty (Preslin) and Leonard Sachs (Admiral de Coligny) will later turn up as elderly specimens of the Doctor's own tribe (respectively Engin in 14.3, "The Deadly Assassin" and Borusa in 20.1, "Arc of Infinity"), but to anyone growing up in Britain they're best-known for quite different roles (see 14.6, "The Talons of Weng-Chiang" and 24.3, "Delta and the Bannermen" for more). Eric Thompson (Gaston) simply *is* the voice of '60s BBC children's television, and to hear him play such a big-mouthed zealot is like casting Jim Henson as Ted Bundy. Andre Morell (Marshal Tavannes), although less famous these days, carried a certain amount of authority after playing the title role in *Quatermass and the Pit*.

2. But the really important guest star in this story is... William Hartnell. His performance as the Abbot of Amboise, the Doctor's surprise looka-like, is so radically different from his portrayal of the Doctor as to warrant separate consideration. After this, it's impossible to think of Hartnell's Doctor as anything but a concerted acting performance. The Abbot is cold, ambitious and word-perfect, with none of the apparently sponta-

neous "hmms" and giggles we're used to hearing from the Doctor. Generations of viewers and fans have assumed that all the gestures and cuddles were what Hartnell was like off-screen (and he was certainly more like that than the arch-villain we see here) and that practically everything we've seen so far has been conscious and deliberate. Including *all* the fluffs...? Well, you never know.

3. Each episode is one day, dawn to curfew. And although the crisis looks like a fairly small-scale one that Steven can resolve on his own, it isn't. However, for the casual viewer at home, the precise details of Renaissance French politico-religious disputes might be a touch hazy... and nobody has told them how long this story is going to be, or even what its overall title is. Coming to it as a four-parter called "The Massacre" (or worse, the *DWM*-sanctioned "The Massacre of St Bartholomew's Eve", which contradicts both the script *and* the history-books), it's more of a tragedy but less exciting. Similarly, the uncertainty as to whether the Abbot is really the Doctor is lost, which makes a difference when he's left dead in the gutter at the end of episode three.

4. When we come to delve into this story in depth, we're going to keep going on about the rich dialogue, the intelligent characterisation, the strikingly adult approach to its themes, yadda yadda yadda. So we're going to make the apology right now. The final scene, tagged onto the end of episode four in order to get a new companion onto the TARDIS in double-quick time, is perhaps the most embarrassingly inept thing heard in the programme so far. Fortunately it's so detached from the rest that it can safely be ignored, but Dodo's surprise arrival really is hilariously, unforgivably contrived. Having entered the TARDIS in the belief that it's a police box, it takes her all of three minutes to introduce herself, come to terms with the fact that it's a spaceship, learn the full details of its abilities from Steven and get used to the idea of being lost in time and space, even taking the time to point out that she's an orphan in case anyone at home is worried about her being missed. The idea of the Doctor's companions being actual *characters* dies screaming here. (The BBC novel *Salvation* revisits this scene, and claims that Dodo was actually in shock from a near-rape experience when she arrived on the Ship, in an attempt to explain her bizarre behaviour. Generally we have no time for this sort of ret-con, but in this case *any* explanation is welcome.)

Are Steven and Dodo Related?

At the end of "The Massacre", an irate Steven Taylor is persuaded to rejoin the Doctor on hearing that Dodo's surname is Chaplet. He'd earlier stormed out of the TARDIS, furious that the Doctor hadn't acted to save Anne Chaplette from the butchery of 1572, but Dodo gives him hope that the girl might have (a) survived and (b) spawned. Aside from the overwhelming coincidence of the Ship landing in exactly the right spot for Dodo to stumble aboard, and the fact that after this we have to put up with another five months of Dorothea and her accent-of-the-week, this presents us with a bit of a problem. Anne was single, so surely any children would have had her married surname?

One possibility might be an illegitimate boy-child to carry on the family line. Anne was a good country girl, with a Mummerset accent to prove it, so she not only knew where babies came from but had probably delivered calves or lambs. Moreover, she was religious, or she wouldn't have been a target for a religiously-inspired mass-murder (although how far we can assume that all those who proclaimed themselves Huguenots were actively Protestant, rather than politically-motivated, is a question that's vexed historians for centuries). Now, one of the oddities of Story W is that each episode begins at dawn and ends at curfew. So we don't know what Anne and Steven got up to at night. But would John Lucarotti or Donald Tosh suggest, even implicitly, some naughtiness afoot? It's a family programme, Anne's clearly no pushover, and Steven rarely shows any interest in that sort of thing (mind you, just listen to him when he meets the Drahvins in 3.1; "Galaxy Four"). He would have needed help getting in and out of his hose, for starters.

The English census of the previous year, 1571, shows 5,224 "strangers" in the country. Of these, 957 were French. There were flourishing communities in Southampton, Canterbury and Sandwich, and three in London; one at Threadneedle Street, one at Tottenham (not yet in London proper), and one in the hunting park at Soho that was large enough for the French to warrant their own church. By 1621 there were 10,000 "strangers" in 121 different trades. The 1592 Parliament had tried to stop the influx of asylum-seekers, and the Duke of Norfolk had taken action to stop them "robbing" his tenants of work. Most of the strangers were Protestant - almost by definition, in Elizabeth's reign - and were counted as "walloons", i.e. from the Low Countries. Yet many of those fleeing France were using the Netherlands as a safe-haven, and customs were more interested in what the immigrants were bringing with them. "France" at this time didn't include Brittany, Normandy or Picardy, all Protestant-friendly principalities, and the majority of fugitives from the massacre went there first until weight of numbers and pressure from their powerful neighbour made further evacuation necessary.

Given that Dodo's ancestors include someone with a name like Chaplet, there could very well be a Huguenot in her male line. Within moments of entering the TARDIS, she tells us about her French granddad. If so, then Anne must still have fled the country to have survived. A fugitive from France could feasibly have taken advantage of the confusion and lack of documentation to invent a husband she'd left behind. Once again, religious scruples have to be weighed against practicalities. "Thou shalt not bear false witness." Immigrants were more likely to be petit bourgeois than servant-girls, although a runaway shopkeeper could have taken a maid across with her.

Let's just remind ourselves of the numbers. Over the next three days, at least 2,000 Parisian Huguenots were slaughtered, and in the whole of France the total was 10-12,000 over the course of the month. What Catherine de Medici imagined would be a few political assassinations turned into ethnic cleansing, and politicised the survivors. So if Anne avoids a mob that wants her dead, and some highly-placed nobility who *really* want her dead (she knows far too much, and all this story needs to be a complete JFK parallel is for the witnesses to be mysteriously killed)... *if* she gets to London and *if* she finds someone with the same surname to marry who's not a blood relation... then maybe she's Dodo's great-to-the-nth-granny.

Alternatively, *if* she were so scared and excited as to be turned on by a life-threatening situation with a hunky Englishman and his quiff, *if* she overcame her scruples in order to jump his Protestant bones and then lie about her marital status on arrival in London, and *if* she not only survived the threats outlined above but a risky sea-voyage while pregnant and the one-in-four chance of death in childbirth (not to mention similar odds against the child growing up, plus a fifty-fifty chance of it being a girl and not carrying on the family name), then Dodo is descended from Steven. Which makes the Doctor's line 'at least

continued on page 229...

The Continuity

The Plot Arriving in Paris during the sixteenth century, the Doctor decides to toddle off and visit the noted apothecary Charles Preslin, leaving Steven to hang around in a local tavern. But this isn't a good time to be a tourist. The Protestant Prince Henri of Navarre has just married the sister of the Catholic King, and public feeling is rising against the Protestant Huguenots. Steven falls in with a bunch of enthusiastic young Huguenots including Nicholas (the reasonable one) and Gaston (the one who's spoiling for a fight), and bumps into a serving-girl named Anne Chaplette, who works in the service of the notoriously vicious Abbot of Amboise and is being pursued by armed guardsmen. This is because she's overheard something she shouldn't: a plot hatched by the Abbot to butcher a leading Protestant. The twist being that when the Abbot is revealed, he appears to be... the Doctor.

Steven is soon involved in the Hugenots' attempts to thwart the conspiracy, and staying at the house of the influential Admiral de Coligny. Then he goes and ruins it by recognising the Abbot as his "friend", convincing Gaston that he's a Catholic spy. Investigating (i.e. creeping about) on his own, Steven soon discovers that the Catholic conspirators plan to assassinate someone they call "the Sea Beggar", and that the Queen Mother Catherine de Medici has secretly sanctioned the killing. Yet he can't convince the Hugenots to listen to him, his only ally being Anne, who's obviously a bit smitten. In fact the assassin's target is de Coligny himself - "Sea Beggars" is a local term for the Dutch, with whom de Coligny is planning an alliance - but Steven learns this too late to prevent a sniper shooting the man. De Coligny is only wounded, and the Abbot of Amboise pays for his failure when he's executed by his co-conspirators. The mob blames the murder on the Hugenots, so Steven narrowly avoids a good lynching.

Then the *real* Doctor reappears, and informs Steven that they have to leave at once, at the same time dismissing Anne and telling her to find a place to hide. Sure enough, the Queen Mother has arranged the order permitting the deaths of the Huguenots in Paris and rousing the mob. The Doctor and Steven leave in the TARDIS, and only then does Steven discover the truth; that de Coligny, Nicholas and virtually all the other Protestants will be / were massacred. But above all, he's appalled that the Doctor could leave Anne to die, and insists on storming out of the TARDIS on its next landing: Wimbledon Common, in the 1960s.

It seems, for a moment, that the Doctor is going to be left alone. Until a young woman named Dodo wanders aboard, in the belief that it's a police box. And when Steven discovers that her surname is Chaplet - and that she has French ancestry - he becomes convinced that she could somehow be Anne's descendant...

The Doctor Describes himself as a doctor of science. Left on his own for the first time after Steven storms out of the TARDIS, the Doctor immediately becomes broody, yet accepts that his companions can't possibly understand his responsibilities. Not even Susan. He even contemplates returning to his own planet, but knows he can't for reasons left unspecified. He considers everyone, even himself, to be too small to get a grip on history.

When Steven warns him that some policemen are heading towards the TARDIS in the 1960s, the Doctor responds by closing the doors and dematerialising, even though there's a complete stranger on board. Luckily Dodo *likes* being abducted. The Doctor believes her to closely resemble Susan, which explains why he's looking forward to having her around.

• *Background.* Once he works out roughly when and where the Ship has landed, the Doctor decides to pay a visit to Charles Preslin, the pioneering apothecary who discovered germs. [Once again, the Doctor's interest in medicine weighs against his claim not to have a medical qualification.] His estimate of the date gives him the excuse to 'turn over a few old papers' in the TARDIS and look up the address, even though he's never met Preslin before. Once he realises the *exact* date, he gets out of town, pronto.

• *Ethics.* Contrary to what Steven says, the Doctor does all he can to ensure the safety of Anne Chaplette without significantly rewriting history. [The view here, as in a story like "The Aztecs" (1.6), is that it's all right to save "unimportant" individuals but not to change the overall course of events.] He effectively orders Anne to stay indoors for the next four days. Short of taking her with him, there's not a lot more he could do without jeopardising Steven's life.

Are Steven and Dodo Related?

...continued from page 231

I taught him to take some precautions' more than a little ironic.

So, is that why the TARDIS magically homes in on the young Ms Chaplet? Was she TARDIS-fodder even before she was born? We know that the Ship's telepathic, that it has some kind of desire to look after its owner (9.5, "The Time Monster"), and that it often seems to make plans of its own. Given the Doctor's joy at having Dodo on board in the final scene, did the Ship deliberately drop Steven in 1572 to "breed" a new companion? Put one bun in the oven, allow to bake for four-hundred years, *et voila*. As good a simulacrum of Susan as a TARDIS can possibly manage. The Doctor even comments on how similar the girl is to his granddaughter, as if the Ship has specifically searched through history to find someone whose descendants might have the right genetic makeup.

But back in the real world, such is the power of the preceding three-and-three-quarter episodes that the trite ending is annoying even if you like Dodo as a character. With the massacre itself depicted in horrifying contemporary illustrations, and with the story's literary precursors all being works of *grand guignol*, the suggestion that Anne was brutally murdered appears far more in keeping than the idea of her making a clean getaway and starting a family in England. Before episode four, the audience would have been half-expecting her to become the new TARDIS crewmember, and surprise deaths are obviously in vogue this season. So soon after "The Daleks' Master Plan" and "The Myth Makers", her demise seems very nearly mandatory.

The Supporting Cast

• *Steven*. Admits he's a Protestant, and it doesn't sound like he's bluffing [the assumption is that as he's a future Englishman, he's C of E by default]. It seems inconceivable to him that the Doctor *isn't* the Abbot of Amboise, as he knows the Doctor is usually 'up to something'. When the extent of the carnage in Paris is revealed [and we never find out how it's imparted to him, unless the TARDIS scanner shows him the same sixteenth-century illustrations that the viewer at home sees], Steven is furious at the Doctor's apparent refusal to help, so much so that he walks out in disgust. [This is curious in many ways, not least because he doesn't bother to check the Ship's readings for radiation or oxygen before he goes. He *does* look at the scanner, at least.]

Although Steven handles a sword with some panache, he's not prepared to use it even in self-defence. His instruction from the Doctor to avoid getting into any tangles is one he tries to follow, until the Doctor himself appears to be in trouble. By the time they're reunited he's sufficiently involved, mainly through people assuming things about him, to try to save de Coligny's life at the risk of his own.

Incidentally, he doesn't have a key for the TARDIS.

• *Dodo*. Dorothea Chaplet has a French grandfather, and with her parents dead she's being raised in Wimbledon by her great aunt, even though they can't stand each other. She's pert and energetic, and she doesn't seem to mind being in a giant time machine inside a police box. Far from it, she immediately spots the appeal of getting whisked off through space and time to have adventures. Right now she sounds generically Northern, though the impression is that she could use the word "fab" at any moment.

The TARDIS Once again, it's a machine for travelling *through* Time and Relative Dimensions in Space [so technically it should be called a TARDIS machine, not a TARDIS]. The wardrobe contains useful clothing in Steven's size, and the right fashion for someone of his apparent status, complete with a sword. It also has bags of ecus, the currency for the period. It appears [from the location stills] that the St John's Ambulance sign is back on the Ship's door.

[It may be significant that when the Doctor is at his lowest-ever emotional ebb, the TARDIS finally takes him back to 1960s London. See **Are Steven and Dodo Related?**, but also **Who Decides What Makes a Companion?** under 21.5, "Planet of Fire".]

History

• *Dating*. The TARDIS arrives in Paris on the 20th of August, 1572. In this account, it's the day after the marriage of the King's sister to Henri of Navarre, a Protestant king of a smaller neighbouring country. [We use the word "France" a little anachronistically here. France was a much smaller nation in the 1500s, and many of today's provinces were separate kingdoms.] Paris is thus paying host to many Huguenots, and the wedding isn't universally popular.

[Each broadcast episode is approximately one day, except for episode four. The timescale confuses many listeners, but the narration on the audio CD gets it right. There's a gap of some hours after episode three, and another gap in episode four, between Steven meeting Anne and the Doctor turning up. So although episode three ends on the 22nd, episode four opens on the 23rd, and concludes early on the morning of the 24th... a few hours before all hell breaks loose on St Bartholomew's Day. In recorded history, the build-up is as follows:

[Gaspard de Coligny has been openly Protestant since 1569, and was implicated in the 1560 Conspiracy of Amboise; a real town, but historically not one with an Abbot. This was an attempt to abduct King Francis II (father of Charles IX) and assassinate the Duke of Guise, the leading Catholic in the land, who was known to be manipulating the King. Two years later, Guise came across an illegal Protestant service taking place in a barn in Vassy. The resulting slaughter triggered a brief, scrappy civil war. Guise was murdered, and Queen Mother Catherine de Medici used the situation to remove various others who resented an Italian woman running the country. Catherine's favourite daughter was then married to Phillip II of Spain, a move that looked suspiciously like a deal to wipe out Protestants. So there was a second civil war, which made Catherine even stronger. A third followed, but de Coligny raised enough of a force to make Catherine sue for peace, the terms being limited freedom of worship and fortified garrisons in four towns for two years. While de Coligny settled into a position of power, and made arrangements for the King's sister to marry Navarre, Catherine waited for those two years to run out...

[Historically, de Coligny was shot at around 11.00am on Friday, the 22nd of August. It seems almost inescapable that the warrant for his death was signed by the King on Catherine's command. When de Coligny survived, Catherine panicked and attempted to conceal her actions within a greater bloodshed: the assassination of all the Huguenot leaders, while they were conveniently assembled in Paris. On Sunday afternoon, de Coligny was hurled naked from an upstairs win-

dow and beheaded by the mob, triggering the general carnage of the next three days.]

Back to the TV story... the Admiral is here motivated by patriotism to launch a war against Spain which would unite both sides in France, and increase the likelihood of an alliance with the Protestant Netherlands and England. Meanwhile King Charles IX is a spoiled brat, influenced by any strong mind near him, prone to talk about tennis while de Coligny and his mother are counteracting each other. Catherine de Medici is, as expected, a ruthless manipulatrix and fervent anti-Protestant who sets the massacre in motion while carefully concealing any direct involvement. [The story shows her wilfully unleashing the mob on the Huguenots, which misses the point a bit, historically speaking.]

Anne Chaplette, Dodo's maybe-ancestor, is a servant in the service of the Abbot of Amboise despite being a known Huguenot. She lost her father in the riot at Vassy, some ten years ago, but - like Dodo - still has an aunt with whom she can stay. The doomed Abbot himself, despite physically resembling the Doctor in every respect [see **Why Are There So Many Doubles in the Universe?** under 20.1, "Arc of Infinity"], is just a viciously bad-tempered Catholic zealot who's said to be the right hand of the Cardinal of Lorraine.

The Analysis

Where Does This Come From? Episode three features an assassination attempt on the life of the Admiral, with a sniper shooting from a high building at an open-topped carriage. It looks like a lone gunman, but *we* know it was a conspiracy by high-ranking politicians, who want to avoid getting into a war overseas. That war was to be prosecuted on the basis of a sort of "Domino Theory", after concerns that neighbouring countries would convert to the enemy's ideology. Is this sounding slightly familiar? The first episode of *Doctor Who* had its ratings dented by the Kennedy assassination, and now it's payback time.

As we've said, an important factor here is that not everyone in the audience would have known exactly how it would end. Had the programme-makers used a similar conflict in British history, like the religious turmoil of Elizabeth's reign, then the conclusion would have seemed like a foregone conclusion. Wiles and Tosh were too savvy to turn the inevitability of the climax into the point of the story, especially after stories like "The Aztecs" (1.6). Their overall plan for the series was to make it less cosy and formulaic. The hazy, half-remembered nature of the setting, the apparent death of the Doctor, and the ways in which otherwise intelligent, rational adults become murderous and prepared to treat others as less-than-human all suited their purpose. Catherine de Medici has traditionally been presented in British fiction as the anti-Elizabeth (see, for instance, the ITC version of *Sir Francis Drake* from about five years before), but the precise details of the massacre had never been dwelt upon.

From a British perspective, the coverage of the US civil rights movement was a baffling present-day example of the same phenomenon. It was self-evident that skin colour was a bizarre reason for lynchings and the bombing of schools, and that the whole segregation issue was a form of collective madness (see 3.6, "The Ark" and 3.9, "The Savages" for more on this). As an Afrikaaner, John Wiles was uncomfortably aware that seemingly-civilised people could justify appalling intolerance, if the culture was set up in the right / wrong way. But that was America and South Africa. It couldn't happen here... could it?

Sectarianism has never been too far from British politics, and in the mid-1960s it was rumbling with renewed fervour. Within three years of this story's broadcast, Northern Ireland would be a flashpoint again. In the Middle East, we were about a year away from the Six-Day War. Religion, for most people in Britain, was little more than a pretext for violence. When the BBC did historical dramas, it was on the understanding that the past was very different in some ways but that human nature remained constant. As part of our self-congratulation, we noted that we never had the Inquisition, and that even Bloody Mary - the last monarch of a Catholic England - "only" burned three-hundred people in three years. A story set in the familiar oak-panelled doublet-and-hose era of Good Queen Bess was bound to be a lark, like the scene in episode one of "The Chase" (2.8), not a tale of a capital city in Europe turning into an abattoir. (This approach has changed somewhat in recent years, now that unspeakable violence is seen as one of the things that "sells" history to the public. The 1998 movie *Elizabeth*, yet another Brit-flick featuring Christopher Eccleston as the villain, opens with a human bonfire just to get the audience in the right mood.)

The 1832 Reform Bill had given British Catholics the vote. Well, provided they were male and had enough money, obviously. The rest of the nineteenth century saw Parliament dealing with the consequences of this, so anyone with any knowledge of history - which was everyone who could read, prior to the 1980s - had a sense of the way that religion and politics could get messy. Similarly, the two famous accounts of the massacre in literature were cited in any number of other famous works, so for a lot of readers it was something that rang bells even if the details were foggy. The first of these accounts, written a generation after the event by the English theatre's most gifted bigot and rabble-rouser, is *The Massacre at Paris* by Christopher Marlowe. He stops just short of having the Catholics eating babies, but his depiction of the figures we see in "The Massacre" is rather more extreme than anything the BBC would show. In typical Marlovian style, the *grand guignol* includes hissable villains making people wear poisoned gloves and doing bad things because... they're bad. After all, they're Catholics, not to mention French.

The other is Alexander Dumas' *La Reine Margot*. There have been five films of this, the most recent being Patrice Chereau's 1994 version. The book, 150 years earlier, begins with the notion that it was the Huguenots who started it (honest). However, Charles XI and Catherine are closer to "our" versions than those of Marlowe. Like so much of the Dumas family's output, the work mixes religion, politics, a bit of thinly-veiled sex, plenty of swordfights and lots of unlikely plot-twists. Once again, anyone watching at home who might have been familiar with the source would have been expecting a happy ending against all the odds.

A final literary allusion: George Eliot's *Middlemarch* has a central figure called Dorothea, known to her friends as "Dodo". The book concludes with the thought that small, oblique changes to history come from people simply living their lives as well as possible under the circumstances rather than, as Dorothea Brooke hoped, by doing Great Deeds or marrying Great Men. This is close to the approach that *Doctor Who* has found itself taking (see **Can You Rewrite History, Even One Line?** under "The Aztecs").

Things That Don't Make Sense So where exactly *was* the Doctor while Steven was getting him confused with another famous bigot? The more you ponder the question, the less sense it makes. The

TARDIS arrives in Paris during 1572, a period which comes in two phases, before and after the massacre. Before, it's a time of suspicion and fear. Afterwards, it's a time of *anger* and fear. Any time five years either way isn't a period you want to hang about in, but the Doctor goes off to visit a local scientist. And he leaves Steven on his own. And doesn't expect any trouble. He doesn't even bother asking Preslin what year it is. If we're going to be history swots, then nor does he enquire after Pierre Ramus, a far more interesting figure in the scientific community (well-known enough for his death to be included in Marlowe's play of these events).

Preslin warns the Doctor about the Abbot of Amboise as though he's met the man, so why doesn't *he* think the Doctor is the Abbot? Why, indeed, does he refer to the Doctor as 'old man' when he's played by Erik Chitty (who's pushing sixty himself)? While we're about it, the whole story's about not interfering with history, but the Doctor's been at Preslin's pad a whole minute before telling him about microscopes.

Steven is disgusted by the Doctor's lack of concern for the lives of ordinary people. Yet when a boy is hit by a car in 1966, Steven's reaction is to run to the TARDIS and get the Doctor to dematerialise, rather than doing anything rash like offering to help. It's strange, in itself, that a minor traffic incident on Earth is enough to make him re-think his entire future and go back to the Ship. Leaving aside Dodo's unbelievably swift conversion to the idea of travelling the universe, her unexpected arrival seems to have a beneficial effect on the Doctor's mood... no, that's putting it too mildly. He goes from suicidal despair to whoops of delight and uncontrollable giggles in less than a minute, as if Hartnell's secretly thinking "thank Christ, I don't have to pretend to be evil and get all my lines right any more". Whatever Preslin gave him, it may have taken a while to kick in but it was good stuff.

Perhaps the biggest Thing That Doesn't Make Sense of all, though: they dispensed with Katarina, Sara Kingdom and Anne Chaplette as potential replacements for Vicki. They stuck with Dodo. A character who, on finding herself in what's clearly some kind of spaceship inside what's clearly not a police box, reacts by asking where the telephone is. *What?*

Critique The three Paddy Russell stories which *do* still exist indicate that creeping about on film is one of the things she directs best, and that effects sequences are her weak point. There remains, therefore, the suspicion that the bits without dialogue were the highlights of "The Massacre". What the dialogue scenes demonstrate is that the cast were motivated and concentrating far more than they were in, let's say, "The Space Museum".

Which is a roundabout way of saying that this probably looked even better than it sounds. It sounds remarkable, with some of the most distinctive and familiar voices of the era cast in exactly the right roles. While it may seem odd that the grimmest *Doctor Who* story ever made should have two *Play School* presenters and a music-hall MC in it, it's the apparent ordinariness of the zealots that makes what they're doing so disturbing. Weird as it is to hear Eric "Dougal" Thompson playing a noisy bigot who's looking for trouble, the real shock is Hartnell's performance as the Abbot. However, with Hartnell effectively sidelined for most of the story, this is Purves' show. He doesn't waste the opportunity. In finding new ways to suggest that Steven is floundering in an unfamiliar context, he has to wrench the character away from being "generic male lead" as well. For much of the story, he and the title sequence are the only connections between this and anything we'd normally think of as "typical" *Doctor Who*, and it's a sign of the faith the production team had in him that they risked it.

But it's hard to come to this story the way its original audience did, and it'd be hard even if we had the pictures. We know how many episodes there are, and we know it's all going to end badly. There's an irony here, though; the fact that we can only listen with hindsight means we're in a better position to believe in it than the viewers were. For a start, we know that nothing else like this will ever be tried again. More importantly, we can take certain things as read which might have seemed frustrating at the time. We know, for one thing, that the Doctor and the Abbot of Amboise aren't the same person. They just happen to look identical. *Why* they look identical, other than "because it makes a good story", is never dwelt on. Evil twins and unexpected duplicates have long been a standard fixture of adventure yarns and spy thrillers, but this is supposed to be a "serious" historical drama, not a tale of derring-do set in old Ruritania. Most doubles on TV were Russian spies or robots, yet here no rationale lies behind one of the most crucial elements of the plot. We're just asked to accept that this key figure in events happens to share the same face as our time-traveller of choice.

We *could* argue that the end of episode three came as an almighty shock to the viewers, because they'd been led to believe (along with Steven) that the Abbot and the Doctor were one and the same, and because it came hot on the heels of the similarly unthinkable "companion" deaths in the previous story. Is that really true, though? The audience had already been primed to play spot-the-duplicate, not least by *Doctor Who* itself. Here we'd ask you to glance back at the **Things That Don't Make Sense** section of 2.8, "The Chase". A figure who may or may not be the Doctor is killed... is this really the unimaginable twist we'd like to think? Or just the cop-out moment when the audience thinks, "oh, it can't be him, then"? Similarly, we've already asked the question of where the Doctor *actually* is while all this is happening, something that's never addressed on-screen. This really is terribly sloppy writing, yet those of us who grew up reading *DWM* or *The Doctor Who Programme Guide* accept it readily, because it's one of the first things we're told about the story. A first-time viewer would be well within his or her rights to feel cheated.

Did the audience like it, in 1966? Well, the appreciation figures stayed constant, so the public wasn't dramatically bored by it. Of course not; it's too good a production to horrify the masses. But again, we're at an advantage. Don't forget, this is still supposed to be a family series. *Doctor Who* has to be meaningful to the pre-pubescent in order to fulfil its mission brief. If you're old enough to understand the difference between Catholic and Protestant, to know the bitterness of the history that separates them and the impact it's had on the modern world, then this show is on your side. If not, then... tough. To anybody below mating age, episode one is wholly baffling. There's barely any attempt to explain why the warring factions don't like each other, what the struggle in Paris is actually about, or what the rules of this world might be. Ironically for a story that's "about" history, there's less sense of a story behind these events than in almost any other historical. Even for grown-ups, seeing the "War of God" reduced to an argument in a bar seems to presuppose that you've got a vested interest in all of this. Finely-crafted it may be, but it's also a sure-fire way to lose viewers. And lose them it did, not least because ITV was finally getting competitive.

So yes, it's an atrocity that this one's missing from the archive, but the worst part is that this is the one which is just *meant* for those of us who weren't born / weren't old enough at the time. This is the one we're supposed to be able to relish. Subsequent trips to Earth's past are either safely "borrowed" from popular novels or have spurious monsters to justify them (on the grounds that history is less interesting than shoddily-made planets or increasingly routine trips to present-day London, a belief that's not always supported by the viewing-figures). For that reason alone, this story is worth cherishing, even if you aren't intrigued by the premise, the performances, the script or the whole approach.

The Facts

Written by John Lucarotti (episodes one to three), John Lucarotti and Donald Tosh (episode four, and see **The Lore**). Directed by Paddy Russell. Ratings: 8.0 million, 6.0 million, 5.9 million, 5.8 million. By the previous year's standards, this was a disaster; ITV had found a hit show, the talent-quest variety programme *Thank Your Lucky Stars*, and scheduled it nationally.

No episodes exist in the BBC archive.

Supporting Cast William Hartnell (credited as Dr. Who and Abbot of Amboise), Leonard Sachs (Admiral de Coligny), Annette Robinson (Anne), Joan Young (Catherine de Medici), Eric Thompson (Gaston), David Weston (Nicholas), John Tillinger (Simon), Edwin Finn (Landlord), Christopher Tranchell (Roger), Erik Chitty (Preslin), André Morell (Marshal Tavannes), Barry Justice (Charles IX), Michael Bilton (Teligny), Norman Claridge (Priest).

AKA... "The Massacre of St Bartholomew's Eve", "The Massacre of St Bartholomew" (and other, equally inaccurate and cumbersome permutations). We'd point out that as the word "massacre" was coined to describe this event, all subsequent massacres should really have names to differentiate them from this, *the* massacre. Nevertheless, the longest version of the title is the one on the rehearsal scripts. The CD release says "The Massacre" on the sleeve but has "The Massacre of St Bartholomew's Eve" printed on each disc, almost as a last desperate stab at pedantry.

Episode Titles "War of God", "Priest of Death", "The Sea Beggar", "Bell of Doom".

Cliffhangers The Abbot of Amboise, whom even his own lackeys fear, is revealed to have the face of the Doctor; de Coligny tells Nicholas that he'd be proud of the title "Sea Beggar", little realising that this makes him the target of the assassination; the Abbot (or is it the Doctor?) lies dead in the street, and the mob turns on Steven.

The Lore

• It seems that no writer was credited for the first three episodes. John Lucarotti was contracted to write a third story after "Marco Polo" and "The Aztecs", but this wasn't actively pursued by Dennis Spooner when Lucarotti's move to the Mediterranean made it difficult to contact him. Donald Tosh asked Lucarotti if there were any ideas he wanted to try, and the writer suggested Erik the Red / Lief Erikson discovering America. A quick check showed that this would be impractical, as it'd mainly be set on a boat in the Atlantic. Wiles and Tosh gave him the *Bartholemée* to do instead.

• But the script came back almost totally unusable, and Tosh virtually rewrote it from scratch. Removing the Doctor for two episodes was a large part of the story's *raison d'etre*, and Lucarotti just didn't seem to grasp this. However, by putting Lucarotti's name on the shooting script, the contract was completed. The final episode was rewritten to introduce Dodo, so Tosh was allowed to claim part-credit, as he was now no longer story editor. (At least, so some sources say. This is the most digestible version of a complex tale, and we've been careful to balance what Tosh has said in interviews against what the documentation claims. We're willing to bet that by the time this gets into print, yet another source will provide a different version entirely.) Lucarotti's novelisation of the story, written twenty years later, is something like his original version and bears very little resemblance to what made it onto the screen. The chariot pulled by greyhounds is particularly memorable.

• By this stage, the press had been told conflicting stories; one day Hartnell announces he's leaving, the next he's signed a new contract for a year, then he wants to stay until the BBC starts using colour. Wiles had worn himself out trying to cope with the star's tantrums. A code-phrase had arisen, "ring the designers", meaning that Hartnell's antics in rehearsals were cause for direct intervention from the producer. But this merely caused Hartnell to sulk, or go over Wiles' head and get in touch with Gerald Savory, the new head of Series and Serials.

• Tosh, meanwhile, was playing the star's ego like an angler with a pike (a fishing analogy is appropriate for Hartnell). In the course of this story, not only was the idea of the Doctor's evil double enough like Hartnell's *Son of Doctor Who* concept for him to play it straight - see **What Other Spin-Offs Were Planned?** under 18.7-A, *K9 and Company* - but the long make-up sessions this would normally have entailed were avoided. Hartnell is only briefly in the second episode, so the scenes with the Abbot were pre-filmed and the star got a week off.

• But in the final episode, the Doctor gets a lengthy soliloquy. Hartnell always objected to this sort of thing, and in read-through he requested that it be shortened, though this time he had an extra motive: as we've seen, he was worried about his increasing memory loss. Tosh told Hartnell that it had been written to give him a chance to really act, and - hallelujah! - he got it word-perfect.

• Tosh could play games like this because his exit strategy was planned. His successor Gerry Davis had shadowed him for a few weeks, and he was working on a solo project for ITV station Southern, whose track-record for children's programming is now legendary.

• Wiles and Tosh had another trick up their sleeves: a plan to write Hartnell out of the series, three months after his contract was renewed in the wake of "The Daleks' Master Plan". The Doctor was to encounter a godlike being and engage in a contest of wills, during which he'd be rendered invisible and mute, and after finally defeating this entity he'd look like someone else. When Tosh went, Davis scrapped many of the planned stories, but since a writer had been commissioned for "The Celestial Toymaker" (3.7) the plan had a momentum of its own.

• Wiles was by now handing in his notice, not just to the series but to the BBC. He'd always been more keen on writing and directing than management, and it was to this that he returned. (He officially left at the end of 3.6, "The Ark", but his successor Innes Lloyd was handling day-to-day affairs from this point on.)

• Paddy Russell was a BBC staff director who'd cut her teeth as second-in-command to Rudolph Cartier, director of the hugely influential *Quatermass* series. This meant she had experience of logistically-demanding prestige projects, as Cartier had managed movie-style shoots in Lime Grove for projects like *Anna Karenina*. There'd been talk of her directing one of the first block of stories in Season One, back when Rex Tucker was in charge, but she was very much in demand (it most likely would have been "The Edge of Destruction"). Morell and Sachs had both been in Cartier's version of *1984*, made in 1954.

• There *was* talk of putting Anne Chaplette on board the TARDIS as a regular, but it was felt by Tosh that a companion from the past would be too much of a nuisance, given that the Doctor would have to keep explaining all the modern-day references to her as well as all the futuristic ones. (We'll wait until Volume II, and Season Five in particular, before evaluating whether he was right.) An "ordinary" cockney schoolgirl was created as a last-minute solution, and Dodo turned out to be almost exactly what "Sue" / "Biddy" had originally been, before Tony Coburn had scripted her as exiled royalty and David Whitaker had turned her into the Doctor's granddaughter.

• And as it happens, Jackie Lane had been considered for the part of Susan, although she hadn't been sure about tying herself to a long-term contract. On TV she'd had a semi-regular part as a secretary in *Compact*, but she'd also been working at the Library Theatre, where John Wiles had directed her in *Never Had It So Good*. She'd played a cockney brat in that, so when the idea of Dodo came up and Wiles saw her audition, the part was pretty much hers for the taking. Head of Serials Gerald Savory concurred, but decided that the accent had to go (hence its abrupt disappearance at the start of the next story).

• Tosh's researches at the British Museum unearthed some contemporary woodcuts of the massacre, which were used in lieu of enacting the slaughter with fake blood and limbs. Even so, they proved too gory for some viewers.

• One idea briefly floated was that the Wimbledon scenes should include cameos by William Russell and Jacqueline Hill. Ah well.

3.6: "The Ark"

(Serial X. Four Episodes, 5th - 26th March 1966.)

Which One is This? The episodes went out two by two, hurrah! Hurrah!

With Beatle-wig monsters and elephants too, hurrah! Hurrah!

Invisible aliens, choppers in space,

A kitchen to hold the whole human race,

And the Earth falls into the sun, without any Britney Spears.

Firsts and Lasts It's the first story to have a female writer credited (even if she didn't really have much to do with it), and the first appearance in the series of actor Michael Sheard, who'll be back five more times over the next twenty-two years. We also get the debut of someone who'll be the backbone of many a story: Roy Skelton, the voice artist who'll go on to be the Dalek Emperor, K9 (briefly) and the original Cybermen. His involvement extends to all the way to 1999's "The Curse of Fatal Death".

It's also the first time that Barry Newbery, who normally does the history stories, gets to design a spaceship and an alien world. And we have the first full-on "space" sequences. There was a shot of Maitland's ship on the TARDIS scanner in "The Sensorites", plus a few landings and course-corrections in "The Daleks' Master Plan", but nothing like what's on offer here. Shuttles, rather like conical helicopters, leave the Ark through a bay door (not quite *2001*, but the intent is the same) and go to the planet Refusis in a shot that's rather better than some '70s stories managed. From the shuttle, the Doctor's able to use the monitors as two-way videophones. This is something we see a lot in Troughton stories, but here Hartnell does it as if he's been video-conferencing all his life.

Four Things to Notice About "The Ark"...

1. The punters at home, unaware at the time that this is a four-parter called "The Ark", would have freaked at the end of episode two. This tale does what stories ever since "The Daleks" have suggested might be interesting: it sees the Doctor dealing with the aftermath of one of his visits, and with a reputation that no-one seriously believes. It's easy (but wrong) to see "The Ark" as two separate two-part stories, set seven-hundred years apart - one of them about the effect of the humble

common cold on the Ark personnel and the other about the slave rebellion that consequently takes place. In order to get a new set of characters up to speed in episode three, there's a brief excerpt from a previous episode on the Ark's giant TV, the series' first real "flashback". But this is obviously a black-and-white set, as they think of the TARDIS as 'that black box'.

2. This story's monsters are the Monoids. They have tremendously silly sarongs, webbed feet and shaggy mop-top hairdos, though pleasingly - and rarely, for an alien species - they're a mixture of blonds and brunettes. And each Monoid has one eye, where the mouth would be in a human (see if *you* can spot how the eyes are made to move, in a time before animatronics...). Not surprisingly, they can't run terribly fast, and for the first two episodes they can't talk. John Wiles took advantage of this, and of his background in theatre for deaf children, by involving a signing interpreter. Sadly, the Monoids become a lot less interesting when they get voices, turning into typical nasty monsters instead of weird and inexplicable aliens. Perhaps if they sounded less like Gene Pitney singing "24 Hours from Tulsa" then they might be more menacing. It'd also help if they didn't use their new vocal cords to tell each other the plot in such detail.

3. In one of those brilliant, absurd details that make this series so much more fun than the glossy film shows of the era, the latter half of the story sees the enslaved humans being confined to barracks in a set dressed as the ship's galley. This is referred to by the Monoids as 'the security kitchen'. It comes complete with a beautifully retro version of futuristic cooking: just add water, and presto, instant chicken-wings. The work-surfaces for this hi-tech culinary incarceration? School desks, with a reflective top.

4. In an odd sort of way, this story serves as a handy benchmark for the visual effects and the way they've developed. The plot of the first section is a straight re-run of the latter half of "The Sensorites", but looks altogether slicker. In a lot of ways the visuals are the whole point of it, with stunning sets (vast and striking, by 1966 standards) and sophisticated inlay sequences. As part of the Ark's "zoo", Monica the elephant looks like stock footage until the Doctor and Dodo go up and pat her. The second act of the story has invisible telekinetic aliens, spaceships landing in the studio set, and almost nonchalant shots like the kitchen-enslaved humans making instant new potatoes that would have been the episode's "big" effect only a few months earlier. In its first year, *Doctor Who* looked like a fairly competent product of the 1950s. "The Ark" looks like a premature product of the early '70s.

The Continuity

The Doctor His history isn't exactly up to snuff here. His observation that the Ark's menagerie is inside a spaceship isn't enough for him to date the vessel, and he doesn't seem to know about the Monoids, nor the end of the Earth. So his guess for the date is, shall we say, approximate.

On the other hand, he's very familiar with the controls of the landing-vessels on the Ark. He offers advice to both sets of Guardians about travelling in hope and understanding, and at one stage very nearly paraphrases Shylock's line from *The Merchant of Venice*, suggesting that if he were cut then he'd bleed like anyone else. [Out of context, this almost looks - arrrggg - like a claim that he's half-human. However, he says it to reassure the Guardians that he's not a shape-changing alien monster, so we needn't read too much into it.]

• *Background.* He knows the cure for the common cold; see **History**.

• *Ethics.* He's briefly horrified by the idea that his travels might have spread diseases across time and space, and doesn't appear to have thought of it before. [Diseases could have such catastrophic effects on history that we might assume the TARDIS has built-in "anti-viral software", but that Dodo hasn't been on board long enough for it to work on her. If so, then the Doctor doesn't know about it yet, as he can only remark that his fellow travellers are 'usually' healthy. By "The Moonbase" (4.6) the assumption seems to be that the TARDIS is self-sterilising.] He blames himself for bringing disease to the Ark and threatening the lives of those on board, but he's in no way penitent when it helps cause a Monoid revolt. He doesn't see it as his fault at all, but just an event that happened.

The Doctor's impulse is to find a peaceful way for both intelligent species on the Ark to co-operate [although when the "cargo" of millions of humans and Monoids is reconstituted, the status quo will surely be in effect again, and the Monoids are quite likely to return to servitude...]. Naturally, he notices the skills of the mute Monoid medics when the Guardians seem not to.

What's the Timeline of the Far Future?

Before we get to the timeline proper, a word about the end of the world. Which is, after all, where all of this is going.

Not including the solar flare damage described in Season Twelve, *Doctor Who* has either destroyed or pretend-destroyed the Earth three times. In "The Ark", the world is shown to burn, and the Doctor airily claims that it's at least ten-million years in the future. In "The Mysterious Planet" (23.1), it's revealed that shady powers have conspired to shift the planet out of its natural place in the universe, causing an almighty fireball which wipes out most life on the surface and leaves an empty space in... well... space. On this occasion, the Doctor checks his watch before announcing that it's *two*-million years in the future. Fan-histories have, on the whole, chosen to treat these incidents as two separate events. The Earth's destruction is faked in the year two-million (and the fakery may even be removed from the timeline afterwards, since the shady powers in question are overthrown later on), and it happens for real eight-million years later.

Recent developments have changed the picture somewhat. In "The End of the World" (X1.2), the Earth is absolutely, positively, *definitively* wiped out in the year five-billion, a date which comes from both the console of a fully-operational TARDIS and from the lips of the most fact-filled incarnation of the Doctor to date. There are many ways to ret-con this problem away, not least by raising the possibility that something changes the entire history of the universe between McCoy's run and Eccleston's, and there's some evidence for this on-screen. But if we're assuming that all *Doctor Who* exists in a single, coherent timeline unless otherwise stated, then...?

Then it's starting to look as if "The Ark" and "The Mysterious Planet" both refer to the same apocalypse. After all, the Doctor's 'ten-million years' assessment is a figure he comes up with off the top of his head, *and* it comes from a version of the Doctor who's less familiar with the history of the universe than his successors, a version who's prone to make up horribly overblown estimates when it suits him (his dating of the Ark sounds a lot like his demonstrably wrong claim about Dalek history in 2.2, "The Dalek Invasion of Earth"... go back and check if you like). Nobody on the Ark confirms his estimate, and nor is there any real evidence to back it up. Furthermore, we never see the destruction of the Earth in the story. The planet starts to smoke a bit, suggesting the "fireball" of

"The Mysterious Planet", but that's all. In addition to which, it's mysteriously described as falling into the sun, and we apparently see it hurtling through space as it's set alight. Whereas anyone would expect the sun to expand and consume it, as eventually happens in "The End of the World".

We wouldn't have suggested this until 2005, but from hereon in it's probably simpler to assume that the destruction of Earth in "The Ark" is a fake, and that what we see in "The Mysterious Planet" is the aftermath. There's nothing to contradict this on-screen. Given that Earth has apparently become a backwater in *both* stories, we seem to be looking at the same sort of future, unlike the one in "The End of the World" where the original homeworld has become a heritage-park. This idea flies in the face of so much accepted wisdom that it's bound to start arguments, but it really is the easiest solution, so we'll be sticking with it here. All right?

All right. Now for the timeline. For our purposes, "Far Future" begins around 3000 AD. Admittedly that isn't *very* far in the future, on the grand scale of things, but much of future-based *Doctor Who* has a habit of returning to the Earth Empire - or, as we might have to start calling it now, the First Earth Empire - which falls in the thirtieth century. See the timeline under 10.3, "Frontier in Space", for events up until this point. As ever, if you want an argument about any of the individual datings then see the entries for the stories in question.

It goes like this...

The Fall of the Empire. By the thirtieth century, Earth looks as if it's finished. Though still nominally at the heart of galactic politics, its territories are fighting for independence (9.4, "The Mutants"), the oppressed aliens of the galaxy are getting restless (23.3, "Terror of the Vervoids"), and the homeworld itself is just a big ball of polluted slag full of starving people. The Nerva beacon is built at around this time, and is apparently attacked by the Cybermen not too long after the empire's fall (12.4, "Revenge of the Cybermen"). What happens next is presumably quite messy, but after this comes...

The Federation. Earth is still a power in the galaxy, and important enough for its representatives to chair diplomatic conferences (9.2, "The Curse of Peladon"). But it's only one of many such

continued on page 243...

The Supporting Cast

- *Steven.* Even with a fever and a death sentence over his head, Steven makes a decent speech about principles, not a plea for his own life. He's the one who *really* worries about the TARDIS spreading infections to other planets, while the Doctor's still in denial. [This is hardly surprising, since the risk of alien contamination must have been a major concern in Steven's day. If anything, it's odd that he's never mentioned it before.] It looks as if he can operate most of the TARDIS controls by now.

- *Dodo.* Can immediately accept that the TARDIS has taken her somewhere else, but not that the Ship travels in time. Her overall verdict on the Ark: 'Gear.' In fact her use of English rather annoys the Doctor [who seems not to have noticed that her accent has completely changed in the space of one episode]. Though he insists on treating her like a child, she mainly objects to the idea that she needs to ask permission to use his wardrobe.

Dodo once went on a school trip to Whipsnade Zoo. She carries a handkerchief in her bag, and... oh yes, she's got a bit of a cold.

The TARDIS

Dodo goes 'frootling about' in the Ship's wardrobe [or at least, that's the way Hartnell puts it] and comes up with a groovy mediaeval page outfit. She later finds a truly shocking T-shirt and above-the-knee skirt ensemble, topped off with a "baker-boy" cap [as popularised by John Lennon, who got it from Bob Dylan, who was copying Donovan].

No good reason is given for the TARDIS materialising in the same place twice [unless it just wants to show the Doctor the consequences of his meddling, for once], although on its next landing the Doctor speaks of the 'gravitational bearing' rectifying itself.

The Non-Humans

- *Monoids.* The Monoids are mute, one-eyed bipeds, with dark reptilian skin but shaggy hair on their heads. They have webbed feet and hands, and initially communicate with humans by handsigns or writing. [It's possible that they eat through concealed orifices in their chests, since Monoid One is seen to put an apple under his voice-unit, and earlier on there are visible lumps in that area.]

Not much is known about their world, at least not by the humans, except that it was dying when the Monoids left it. They went to Earth for help, and as a result the two species are living together on the Ark. Initially the Monoids are very much the servant class, going about their silent duties without even being noticed by the Ark's Guardians. They're even more susceptible to Dodo's lethal cold than the humans.

When the TARDIS returns seven-hundred years later, the Monoids have chest-mounted speech-boxes, although they're still gesticulating in an exaggerated fashion. [Both the sign-language and the speech-boxes might be for the humans' benefit, although it makes sense that if the Monoids have been servants for so long then they might consider human-style speech to be a status symbol. We never see two of them communicate in the first half of the story, so it's possible that they're naturally telepathic, especially since the Monoid in the medical bay seems to pre-empt the Doctor's requests for equipment.] On taking over the Ark, the Monoids refer to themselves by number, the supreme ruler being known as "1".

It's revealed that a later mutation of Dodo's cold sapped the humans' will, making it easier for the Monoids to overthrow their masters. Many of the creatures are now ambitious, aggressive and intolerant, and apparently think of the humans as their former enslavers. In retribution for this perceived wrong, Monoid One plans to exterminate humanity and set up a Monoids-only society on Refusis II. Others aren't quite convinced by this plan, leading to violent arguments in the Monoid camp.

Planet (and Enormous Spaceship) Notes

- *The Ark.* At least, that's what Dodo calls it, although the word "Ark" is unknown to those on board when the TARDIS arrives. It's a spaceship at least as big as a city, designed to transport the entire human and animal population of Earth to its new home on Refusis II; see also **History**. The vessel is roughly circular, and separated into distinct sections. The two most notable areas seen here are a jungle full of animals and a central control room, which can be used for civic functions and court hearings. A large wall-screen in this area is used to monitor the destruction of the doomed Earth. There are also smaller medical units, resembling Japanese paper-walled rooms, and detention cells with two-way communication screens. Pod-like 'launchers' are used to take parties down to Refusis II once the Ark gets there, while the dead are ceremonially ejected into space, to a sound

What's the Timeline of the Far Future?

...continued from page 241

powers, locked in a series of messy political disputes and determined to sort things out without any more wars. Whereas the empire seemed confined to the Milky Way, there are relations with other galaxies by this point (11.4, "The Monster of Peladon" and the back-story to 3.4, "The Daleks' Master Plan"), and intergalactic travel appears to be quite run-of-the-mill. (We should note that there's no on-screen date given for "The Curse of Peladon" at all, but virtually everyone assumes it's set somewhere in the 3000s. That takes us seamlessly into the next major era of Earth history...)

Dalekgeddon. By the thirty-ninth and fortieth centuries, Earth is unquestionably the dominant power in the galaxy again, but it's still quite democratic despite all the secret security forces and heavily-armed marines. Which is when the Daleks make a comeback, returning to Skaro (17.1, "Destiny of the Daleks") and planning an assault on the political body that's now known simply as the Solar System ("The Daleks' Master Plan"), with all sorts of shenanigans involving Davros on the way (21.4, "Resurrection of the Daleks" and 22.6, "Revelation of the Daleks"). Though Earth is less inclined to deal with planets in its own galaxy by now, humans are rapidly expanding into other areas of space, so most political agreements are intergalactic rather than interplanetary. The environment on Earth itself has been cleaned up, and the air's breathable again. But the Guardian of the Solar System turns evil and gets exterminated in 4000 AD, and after that there's a curious gap in our records before...

Ice Age. There was a crisis in 3000 and another one in 4000, so it's no big surprise that it happens again in 5000. But the planet's changed. In the days of the empire and the Federation, Earth was full of sky-cities and governed from population centres that covered whole land-masses, yet in this era the old place-names make a comeback. Britain, Ireland, Iceland, Australia and the Philippines all exist again, and buildings from Ye Olden Days are renovated for modern use... something that's never explained on-screen, though we might assume that as more and more people leave for other planets, those left behind have the opportunity to reclaim the territory. Then the ice age hits.

(This is seen in 5.3, "The Ice Warriors" and mentioned by the Doctor in 14.6, "The Talons of Weng-Chiang." Some have claimed that "The Ice Warriors" is set in 3000 AD, mainly based on the *Radio Times* write-up rather than the script. But dialogue within the story hints at a date of 5000 AD; the Doctor describes an ice age taking place in 5000 AD in "Weng-Chiang"; and the society we see in "The Ice Warriors" is consistent with what we're later told about 5000 AD, but utterly unlike the world of 3000 AD. Slam, as it were, dunk.)

The 51st Century. Things looks grim, in the wake of the ice age. There's very nearly a World War Six ("Weng-Chiang" again), and there's trouble in Reykjavik, for some reason. 5000 AD is also the time of the Great Break-Out, when more and more people start leapfrogging off across the solar system, understandably (15.2, "The Invisible Enemy"). While zygma energy results in a technological dark age, interest in time-travel obviously leads human scientists to get it right, as there are time-agents with American accents in this period. (X1.9, "The Empty Child." Actually, this is a bit contradictory. Greel in "The Talons of Weng-Chiang" is depicted as the victim of a flawed and experimental time-travel process, leading the Doctor to describe his era as one of appalling scientific ignorance. Yet Greel is expecting a time-agent, and as we learn in "The Empty Child," time-agents can use sleek time-travelling spaceships which don't seem experimental at all. We might guess that time-travel was developed *before* zygma energy, but was terribly energy-intensive; that Greel's method was meant to be a more efficient way of powering the process; that the dark age mentioned by the Doctor was a brief one; and that by the end of the fifty-first century, time-travel was a doddle. Nonetheless, it doesn't seem to have caught on. What happened?)

The Aftermath. Humans might have colonised an awful lot of worlds after the Break-Out, especially given the number of human societies visited by the Doctor which *don't* seem to be bound to any empire or cosmic alliance. Possibilities - and they're just possibilities, mind you - include Leela's world (14.4, "The Face of Evil"), where the psi-tri projections used by Xoanon aren't unlike the sort of thing the Kilbracken technique might have produced (in "The Invisible Enemy"); the world inhabited by the Elders and the Savages (3.9, "The

continued on page 245..

like the beating of drums.

Running all of this is a group of humans known as the Guardians, each of whom has his or her allotted task on board, though children are also being raised during the voyage. The Monoids do a lot of the menial work, with sign-language interpreters translating speeches for their benefit [but it seems the majority of Monoids don't require this], and most of the humans don't know how to react when faced with a crisis like a killer disease on board. There aren't actually that many Guardians around, as most of Earth's population - Monoids included - has been shrunk to micro-cell size by a 'minifier' and stored in a computerised file system, to be enlarged again on reaching Refusis. In the meantime, the humans are keeping themselves busy by hand-crafting an enormous statue called "Homo Sapiens" from an everlasting substance called Gregarian rock.

When the Doctor returns, seven-hundred years later, the statue is complete but has a Monoid's head. Following the 'recent' Monoid revolution, the Ark mostly runs on auto-pilot. The Monoid overlords use heat-prods to cause pain or death to inefficient servants, which - like their voice-boxes - were initially developed by the Guardians' own research. The Doctor and company are remembered by the humans, if only as legends, and the name "Ark" has caught on. Also in this time-zone... yes, the Monoids keep prisoners in a galley which they refer to as the 'security kitchen'. Here, a bowlful of potatoes can be created instantly by dropping a pill into water.

The Ark survives even after the humans and Monoids begin to settle their new planet, although the statue is shoved out into space and blown up by a fission device.

• *Refusis II*. It's apparently the only planet with the same atmosphere, water and temperature as Earth, and thus the only planet suitable for humanity. Or so the Ark's commander believes. Human research indicates that intelligent life must have developed there, but there's never been any sign of the natives. This is because a 'galaxy accident' - a giant solar flare - has rendered the Refusians bodiless. The one Refusian heard here claims they no longer have a recognisable shape, and can sense but not see each other. However, they're nonetheless civilised and capable of speaking to visitors in a voice-of-God sort of way, and welcome the idea of life returning to their world. They're also capable of lifting objects that weigh

several tons, and of building nicely-furnished "castles" for the humans, whom they've been expecting for some time. [All the signs are that they're capable of moving things by thought-power.]

Refusis II is covered in foliage, but this time it's more like a slightly overgrown garden than a screaming jungle. By the end of events, humans and Monoids have been forced to make peace by their new invisible neighbours, and the Doctor looks set to be remembered as a hero.

History

• *Dating*. It's the 57th Segment of Time, according to the commander of the Ark. The Doctor's adventures with the Daleks, the Romans and the Trojans took place in the First Segment; there were 'primal wars' in the Tenth; and there were time experiments in the 27th, but they came to nothing. On hearing that he's in the 57th, the Doctor estimates that the TARDIS has travelled 'at least' ten-million years into the future.

[If the First Segment included events in 1200 BC and 4000 AD, then the temptation is to assume that each Segment is several thousand years long and that the numbering system begins with the start of recorded history. But it's possible that each Segment represents a particular stage in human development rather than a specific number of years, so they don't necessarily have to be the same length. Even so, it seems doubtful that the time experiments of the 27th Segment refer to the zygma experiments of circa 5000 AD (14.6, "The Talons of Weng-Chiang"). Then again, the usual estimate for the end of the world is five billion years from now. If this is the case, and the Doctor's 'ten million years' claim is way out, then one Segment may be somewhere in the region of a whopping ninety million years. But see **What's the Timeline of the Far Future?**, where we'll be opening several cans of worms at once.]

The Ark hasn't been travelling long when the Doctor arrives, and there's a live video feed covering the destruction of Earth, which is due to 'burn and be swallowed in the pull of the sun'. The journey to Refusis II takes seven-hundred years after that. The commander speaks of having wide powers under 'galactic law', and those found guilty of endangering the ship through negligence can be punished by expulsion into space or reduction to micro-cell size. Despite all this 'galactic' talk, the Guardians don't expect to meet any other human

What's the Timeline of the Far Future?

...continued from page 243

Savages"), where there's a very fifty-first-century interest in both time-travel and vampirism; and the 'pioneers' who are said to have met the Wirrn in Andromeda (12.2, "The Ark in Space"), who may have left Earth shortly before the time of...

The Solar Flares. Honestly, it's disaster after disaster. All the indications are that after 5000 AD, Earth is a bit of a backwater, with humans spreading out across the galaxies and those who remain behind becoming less and less imaginative. They may turn their backs on interstellar travel altogether, because when solar flares threaten the planet - probably quite soon after the fifty-first century, though this is foggy - they turn the ancient Nerva beacon into an ark and go into suspended animation until the crisis is over ("The Ark in Space"). And those who leave the planet aren't expected to survive, either, suggesting a real lack of interest in space exploration. The sleepers eventually wake up 10,000 years later, by which time off-world human societies like GalSec (12.3, "The Sontaran Experiment") consider Earth to be unimportant and think of Nerva as a myth (16.5, "The Power of Kroll", is arguably set in this period). We can assume that Earth is repopulated after this, as it seems rather pleasant and covered in greenery. But, wait! What's this?

The New Roman Empire. According to the Doctor, the TARDIS briefly stops off in 12005 AD before arriving in the year five-billion ("The End of the World"). He claims that the New Roman Empire is right outside the doors, but he dematerialises before we can see it. This is puzzling. If the Earth's inhabited in 12005, then it suggests the solar flares don't start until *after* this point, which is possible but a bit of a stretch. Alternatively, it could be that the "humanity has slept for 10,000 years" estimate in "The Ark in Space" is as overstated as all the Doctor's *other* estimates, in which case the New Roman Empire could have been started by the descendants of the people from the Nerva station. A third possibility, and perhaps the most likely, is that the New Roman Empire isn't on Earth at all (the Doctor is obviously moving the TARDIS through space as well as time during this sequence, as his eventual destination isn't on Earth either, although it *is* in the same solar system). Whichever version you favour, future-history gets patchy at this point...

The Morestrans. We don't know for a fact that the Morestrans are descended from Earth-people, but they investigate Zeta Minor in 37166 by their own calendar, and the Doctor speaks of it being 'thirty-thousand-years' after Sarah's time (13.2, "Planet of Evil"). So if he's using nice round numbers, then it could well be 37166 AD rather than the Space-Year 37166. The Morestrans have intergalactic travel that lets them go a loooooooooong way into space, and don't even seem to know what Earth is, reinforcing the idea that the planet is of no interest to other human-types in the universe.

The Fourth Great and Bountiful Human Empire. Planned for 200,000 AD, this is described by the Doctor as the very pinnacle of human civilisation (X1.7, "The Long Game"), stretching across a million planets. Except that it doesn't happen, thanks to a bunch of time-mangling Daleks, and the subsequent destruction of several continents on Earth may well prevent it ever coming to pass (X1.13, "The Parting of the Ways"). The planet's population, at least before the Dalek attack, is ninety-six billion.

The Apparent End of the World. As part of an elaborate plot that even the Daleks would balk at, Earth is dragged out of its solar system circa 2,000,000 AD by amoral cosmic powers ("The Mysterious Planet") and renamed Ravolox... at least, if the Doctor's 'two million' estimate is any more accurate than his 'ten million' one. The world is consumed by a fireball, which a handful of inhabitants somehow survive, but others have already got wind of the disaster and left. The big fireworks display is witnessed by the Guardians of the Ark, oh yes it is ("The Ark"), while other refugees from the doomed planet would seem to include those who crash on Frontios (21.3, "Frontios"). Though the Ark's people have shinier technology than that of the Frontios colonists, both are surprisingly backward considering how far in the future we are. The Ark-folk speak of 'primal wars' aeons earlier, which took away a lot of their knowledge; it's hard to say when these wars might have taken place, or whether they're connected to any of the conflicts we hear about in other stories. Earth is almost certainly put back where it was once the Ravolox conspiracy unravels (23.4, "The Ultimate Foe").

continued on page 247...

beings now they've left Earth, and don't seem to have links with any other planets. Nobody from Earth has even been to Refusis II, so the conditions there are only known from 'audio space research'.

[The claim that Refusis II the *only* planet suitable for humans seems odd, in light of all the other stories that show us human colonies all over the universe. Even in Earth's galaxy, there seem to be thousands of suitable new homes, yet the Ark's journey of seven-hundred years indicates a planet vast distances away; remember, by 2540 it supposedly only takes a human ship a few hours to get from one side of the galaxy to the other. The most logical conclusion is that Earth is going through something of a dark age by this point, reverting to comparatively primitive space-technology - and sure enough, everything here looks twenty-second century rather than the product of a society millions of years in the future, although the miniaturisation process is quite impressive. "Frontios" (21.3), apparently set in the same era, also sees humans using rather backward equipment. Whatever the people of the Ark may believe, they're just the last stragglers to leave the planet, not the future of the whole species.]

Surviving animals in this time-zone include toucans, chameleons, monitor lizards, locusts, Brazilian snakes and Indian elephants, while the commander still uses the term 'guinea-pig'. [Later stories set in Earth's future, notably "The Mutants" (9.4), describe a horribly polluted planet by 3000 AD and imply an absence of animal life. It may be that humans have managed to genetically engineer extinct species *Jurassic Park*-style. Steven calls the wildlife here 'strange', as if they don't have toucans in his time. See 3.4, "The Daleks' Master Plan", which also indicates an all-round cleaning-up of Earth after the thirtieth century.] There are pictures of two-headed zebras on the walls of the "zoo", for some reason, while the commander knows of Nero and Troy but has never heard of Noah's Ark. As ever, people in the future appear to read and write in English, the leading Monoids labelling themselves with symbols "1" and "2" in space-lettering [see also 3.10, "The War Machines"]. And there's no getting away from it: in the future, every human being seems to be white.

According to the Doctor, a vaccine for the common cold was found in the twentieth century. [We must have been off sick that week.] The disease was wiped out ages ago, so neither the humans nor the Monoids have any resistance to it, though there may be other diseases in existence as the Guardians have special respirators for dealing with the infected. The cure used here involves membrane fluids from elephants and lizards, applied like a nicotine patch rather than a hypodermic needle. The residents of the Ark aren't aware of this cure, since many such secrets were lost in the primal wars. [An explanation for the apparent technological dark age, although since the Wars were forty-seven Segments ago, it's been a very *long* dark age.]

The Analysis

Where Does This Come From? There's something about the scale of the story, and the casual way in which everything we've seen in the series so far is consigned to 1/57th of all possible history, that's more than a little reminiscent of Olaf Stapledon. He's no longer remembered as one of the "famous" SF authors, but in the 1930s his novels - notably *Sirius* and *Last and First Men* - offered a big perspective on the petty concerns of most of the world by dwelling on the long, long, long, long, *long*-term future of humanity. In the 1960s, even people who didn't actually read the books had sort-of-heard about them. If not, then they certainly knew their H. G. Wells, and the combination of the common cold as a threat and the end of the world in a supernova seems like a "greatest hits" medley. Much of the look of the story echoes another 1930s future, Alexander Korda's Wellsian polemic *Things to Come*. But there's another, more direct reference here: the US space program, and the layout of Mission Control.

The most common suggestion about the roots of this story, though, is that it's a parable based on the US civil rights movement. This is an appealing notion, especially if it turns Monoid One into Eldridge Cleaver (the Black Panthers' notorious "Minister of Information") and Monoid Four into Malcolm X. Just the thought of Spike Lee making this story is entertaining, and the complete lack of non-Caucasian faces on the Ark *does* make the Monoids look like an ethnic group as much as a monster. Except that... hang on, it's the Guardians who are the ones leading a revolt against an oppressive regime. So the dark-skinned Monoids are really the white folks, and the human turncoat Maharis is Uncle Tom.

What's the Timeline of the Far Future?

...continued from page 245

Elsewhere. Of course, the refugees from Earth are just the humans who've been stuck on the homeworld for all those millennia. The other humans in the universe have moved so far afield, and are so much more advanced, that it's of little or no importance. Svartos, for instance, is in a group of Twelve Galaxies nowhere near Earth's "neighbourhood" (see **How Many Significant Galaxies Are There?** under 2.5, "The Web Planet"). We should also mention "The Sun Makers" (15.4), which sees human stragglers returning to a once-barren Earth after generations spent on Pluto. The script implies that these events take place millions of years in the future, but really, there are any number of points where you could slot this story into the history of the solar system. As the Doctor seems to believe that Earth's destruction in "The Ark" is the real deal, and expects the workers on Pluto to have a home to go back to, it may be wiser to assume an earlier date than this.

The *Real* End of the World. Five billion years in the future, or 5.5 / apple / 26, if you insist. The sun expands, annihilating Earth once and for all ("The End of the World"). All the humans who went out into space have interbred with other species by now, leaving the last pure human to die on the same day as the planet.

While we've got our science heads on... for those of you who somehow can't accept that "The Ark" isn't the real destruction of the planet, and insist on *three* doomsdays, here's another possible explanation. Perhaps the discrepancy between the ten-million years mentioned in "The Ark" and the five-billion mentioned in "The End of the World" is all down to relativity. If it takes hundreds of years to reach a suitable new planet, then the Ark might be travelling below light-speed. So while the journey takes seven centuries from the point of view of the crew, it may take much longer from the point of view of Earth.

Precisely *how* long depends on where Refusis II is. If it's in our galaxy, then the furthest-away it can be is 80,000 light-years. The Ark, if we assume an acceleration of 1g and deceleration from the halfway point with a very short weightless period, could have been travelling for millions of years. Vastly longer if Refusis is in another galaxy. The "live" coverage of Earth's destruction might therefore take place in the year five-billion, even if the Ark left the planet in ten-million. The problem with this idea is that judging by what we see in the first couple of episodes, the vessel has barely even started its journey when the world burns, which throws the figures out a bit. Also, the Earth-death we see on-screen doesn't really match the 2005 version.

Occam's razor would, however, suggest that the Doctor's just very bad at dating things.

No, it doesn't work, does it? Looking for one-on-one correspondences here is pointless. The story is about finding common purpose, not thinking in ethnic terms but in terms of citizenship. The Ark is a small world, with the whole of two species aboard, so it's too risky to play politics. Just to make things more complicated, the usual War-time language is brought back into play, with the Monoids planning a final solution and one of their servants being described by the other humans as a 'collaborator'.

In a wider sense, the idea of prejudice (and of categorising people by type) is one that needs careful handling in *Doctor Who* simply because the species and planet of birth so often replaces moti-vation. It's noticeable that the Monoids are never given any background. They just seem to have arrived at some point, so even the humans are confused about their origins. And we note that their appearance, whilst derived almost entirely from practical considerations by the director, is much like something from John Mandeville's *Travels*; the book that provided Europe in the Middle Ages and Renaissance with so many "facts" about Africa. People with no heads and faces in their chests, people with giant feet to act as parasols... that sort of thing.

We should also note the way the Monoids are embraced as "guests" by the Guardians. This is characteristic of Britain in the mid-1960s, trying to come to terms with being part of a big world where there are jet-planes and lots of people who grew up overseas but nonetheless have UK passports. In particular, this is the place to mention that the shortage of skilled labour in early '50s Britain led to advertisements being placed in newspapers in the Caribbean and Indian subcontinent. The need for nurses and hospital orderlies resulted in junior health minister Enoch Powell authorising the recruitment of Commonwealth citizens. By 1968, many of the people who answered his call had settled down and raised families in the UK, and Powell - how shall we put this? - suggested that a rethink was perhaps in order. (See 4.8, "The Faceless Ones" and 25.1, "Remembrance of the Daleks".)

In SF literature, stories about "generation starships" have tended to be about people who can't imagine any other life. Frequently, the discovery that their world *is* a ship is the big plot-twist. Here the rhetoric is quite different. This story requires everyone to be aware of the stakes involved. That the kind of writer to be found working on *Doctor Who* might know what a generation starship *was* is a sign of how much literary SF had been assimilated into middle-class British mainstream taste.

And while we're on the subject of middle-class tastes, we might mention the kitchen. A whole meal is created in under a second by dropping a pill into water, and the pills are kept in a packet with NEW POTATOES written on it in snazzy lettering. We've already mentioned the Oxo Couple in this volume, and this really is '60s consumerism in full effect; unlike the TARDIS food machine, these aren't space-rations but exactly the kind of thing you could imagine well-groomed young housewives demonstrating on commercial television. In fact the TARDIS crew is looking more like a cosy nuclear family than ever, especially with Dodo around to act as a generic child-woman with no home but the Ship. Her comedy antics with Steven in episode one, while the Doctor upbraids them for their childish behaviour, make them look more like Dr Who's grandchildren in *TV Comic* than any of the supporting cast we've seen so far.

We might also see this episode as a last desperate gasp at making this programme "educational". Well, a bit. Whereas "Marco Polo" saw Ian Chesterton pondering the origins of the word "checkmate" and "The Massacre" at least had a crack at teaching everyone the basics of sixteenth-century French politics, here Dodo does the children's-television duties by pointing at animals and telling us what they're called.

Things That Don't Make Sense We'll say it again: there's a security kitchen. Yes, all right, it's easy to mock. For all we know, it could be part of Monoid culture to give prisoners the humiliating task of preparing pastry, so the absurdity of it isn't the problem. But if it's *anything* like a kitchen as we understand the term, then there must be implements for preparing food, like mashing or chopping those magic potatoes. By definition, these are implements that slice, batter and bake. Which makes a prison-cum-kitchen only a *little* more logical than a prison-cum-armoury-full-of-deadly-weapons. And can we assume that only food for humans is prepared in this place? Otherwise, the Monoids are just asking to be poisoned. At the very least, you'd expect the humans to wee in the soup.

The Guardians work out fairly quickly that the killer disease is spread by contact with the travellers. So what do they do? Bring an infected Monoid onto the bridge so that everyone can gawp at him, instead of having him quarantined. Then put Steven in an open courtroom with most of their ruling elite and a large number of spectators, letting him sweat cobs and breathe all over them while they accuse him of being an alien spy.

We might also ask why, precisely, Dodo's cold causes Steven to collapse within hours, and everyone acts as if it could be as lethal for him as for the residents of the Ark. Is the implication supposed to be that as Steven comes from the future, he's less resistant than a twentieth-century human? It seems doubtful, given that his tomorrow-ness isn't alluded to anywhere in the script.

Almost as worrying is the Doctor's cure. He deals with the sick Guardians by keeping them warm, the "sweat out the fever" approach that was so popular before anyone knew what germs did [unless his special cure-for-the-common-cold requires the subject to get extra-hot]. Another curious aspect of his behaviour, though it seems so natural that it's easy to miss the strangeness of it, is his objection to Dodo's use of contemporary slang. Why should a seasoned traveller in space and time, who's used to treating other cultures and customs with as much respect as anyone can without personally tearing Aztecs' hearts out, consider pre-1960s lingo to be naturally "proper"?

Why should he see English (and he does, explicitly, tell Dodo that he's going to have to teach her to speak English) as particularly sacred, when he's never objected to the peculiar dialects used by giant butterfly-men or disturbed robot-people? [Then again, note his objection to the word 'fragmentised' in 12.4, "Revenge of the Cybermen".] The assumption seems to be that because he looks like a bit of an old duffer, he has to complain about The Kids as if he's everyone's granddad.

The Guardians aren't prepared for any kind of conflict, hence the ease of the Monoid takeover, yet they were the ones who developed the heat-prods now used by the Monoids to control them. So *why* were these weapons developed, exactly, if the revolution came as such a surprise? Did they fear trouble from the elephants? It's not as if the members of the revolting underclass make formidable opponents. The Monoids' tactics for scouting out Refusis II, for example: send the second-in-command of the entire Monoid species down to an unknown environment with three hostile humanoids and a single heat-prod, then let him give away the plan to eradicate humanity while he's there, and go 'err...' when he's confronted about it.

Nice idea, building a statue that's scheduled to take seven-hundred years; in the age of the Millennium Dome, we know that this is exactly the kind of thing governments *like* to plan when celebrating special occasions. However, does it *really* take seven centuries to build a monument that's substantially smaller than the Statue of Liberty or the Eiffel Tower? Even using hand-tools? It's possible that indestructible Gregarian rock requires extra patience, but the Monoid revolution was a 'recent' one - apparently within the last few years - and the Monoids have had time to get rid of the human head and replace it with a new one of their own. How do you sculpt indestructible rock, anyway?

Another nice idea is having children about the place to suggests generations passing, and it's also a good excuse to have young women hanging around with not many clothes and not many lines, but it rather draws attention to one odd thing. Where are the she-Monoids? [The novelisation has Dodo play ping-pong with a Monoid who has a sister, a scene we must be thankful wasn't screened.] Even the Refusians seem to consist of one rather plummy male. Was there ever a Mrs Refusis, we wonder? Nor do we get any satisfactory account of the two-headed zebra picture. The

mix of elephants, snakes and chameleons in the Whipsnade jungle is very picturesque, but we have no idea whether they have anything to eat (like big juicy flies, or mice, or buns... or each other). It's an odd mix, but an even odder plan for a long-term ecology. And the Monoids' supposed 'invaluable assistance' seems to be, basically, to work as a steno-pool with a bit of lorry-driving thrown in.

The Ark's exterior, judging by the model, is about the size of a football pitch. The Doctor asks 'what's that?' on hearing a siren he's heard (from his perspective) less than an hour before, and it's odd that he gets an answer from someone who wasn't there - as he was - when it last sounded seven-hundred years ago. Amazingly, the plants are *exactly* as well-grown as they were seven centuries earlier.

There's a big ethical flaw here, too. The moral of this story is that all intelligent beings should be treated as equals, but the script doesn't really seem to believe a word of it. Even leaving aside the way the Monoids are shown to be routinely villainous and intolerant in the second half of the story, the first half does the all-too-common *Doctor Who* thing of assuming human lives to be worth more than the lives of anything funny-looking. If the Dodo-bug had killed large numbers of *humans*, then we'd be shocked and appalled that the Doctor and friends had directly caused the fatalities, yet Monoids are allowed to snuff it as if their deaths are just a portent of what might happen to the "real" people on board. There's even a painful dramatic chord when one of the Guardians finally dies. Just to rub it in, everyone treats the Doctor as a hero for curing the plague, and is happy to listen to his advice for the future of humanity... instantly forgetting that he's the idiot who was responsible for all the deaths. The mob, which was baying for blood just fifteen minutes earlier, cheerily waves him goodbye as he gets a motorcade back to the TARDIS. The relatives of the deceased never raise a word of protest, or - in the Monoids' case - make rude signs at him.

And... 'a galaxy accident'? For Heaven's sake.

Critique It's rare that any story, from any period of the programme, gets away with as much as this one. Both the scenario and the direction are *huge*, but almost casually so. Stories with big effects, like the launchers or the giant TV screens, tend to make a song and dance about them. Here they're simply presented to us as part of this world, things the locals take for granted. Aside from the Monoids' habit of explaining every part of their devious plan out loud, the story opts to show rather than tell, which is daring as well as welcome. Today's viewers might want more of this sort of thing, but here we're still in an era where the television is a fuzzy little box that can't quite get a grip on elephant-sized objects, let alone giant spaceships. And, let's not forget, where people are used to narrators explaining the more puzzling images to them in detail.

But this cuts both ways. Traditionally, this series needs a spectacle every so often, and occasionally the scenes and shots intended to provoke a "wow" just tell the story instead. Rather than hiding behind the sofa from the Monoids, we see them in their natural habitat as if the BBC had sent a documentary crew to the 57th Segment of Time. There's nothing wrong with this - George Lucas turned it into an art form - but in *Doctor Who* terms it falls between two stools. It's not pacy enough to pass for a simple adventure story, not spectacular enough for the plot to be put on hold while we linger on the background. Episode one, with its astonishingly lush indoor jungle and its Monoid-driven work-machines, is a real eyebrow-raiser after what's gone before. By episode four, the novelty's worn off and you're left with a script that has the monsters talking like standard-issue monsters, the victims talking like standard-issue victims and the disembodied voices talking like standard-issue disembodied voices. If there *are* such things.

Yes, we compared this story to the works of George Lucas, and not unfavourably. Not just *Star Wars* but *American Graffiti* and *THX 1138*. In these, Lucas is as concerned with making an environment as telling a story, and this often extends to the sound and the "source" of the music. In this case the music is yet another outing for the score for "The Daleks", yet this seems to have been forced on the production from above rather than being the director's choice. In every other regard, director Michael Imison was keen to get the extras, the sets, the props and everything else working almost without any reference to what the Doctor and the speaking-part actors were up to. There's always something happening in the background, so distinctive features like the sign-language interpreters don't even get establishing close-ups. Episode one is called "The Steel Sky", and note the way the camera's used here; we're

supposed to get the sense that the Ark has a tangible architecture, rather than being a stage-set in the middle of nowhere. The ship is vast, but has a definite ceiling. (Ceilings are important. See also the essay under 18.1, "The Leisure Hive".)

The storyline is almost redundant. Certainly, it'd be a damn sight more watchable today if they'd put half as much time into the characters as they did into the set-up. The sense we get is that the central conceit, of showing us two generations of Ark-life, is supposed to be more important than anything that happens. An enormous change takes place off-stage between the two acts, and we're left to infer a story bigger and more complex than can be done on a *Doctor Who* budget. Given that nobody watching this the first time round knew what to expect, the second cliffhanger really is one of the finest ever, yet the majestic pan up the body of the statue is followed by two episodes of dull people arguing. The best bits are the bits we're never shown. Seeing Earth destroyed is an anti-climax, but knowing there was ten-million years' worth of things for the Doctor to show us before it blew up... *that's* exciting.

If it's rushed at the end, too slow in the middle and too brief to fully explore this world, then what might the solution have been? Well, given an extra episode and an extra episode's budget, they could have achieved almost all of the story's original ambitions (and we would have been spared a whole week of "The Celestial Toymaker", too). As it stands, perhaps the most enticing thing is how comfortable the Doctor looks in this environment. It reinforces the idea that all of time and space is familiar to him, and gets us away from the occasionally annoyingly "dotty" performances of Season Two. This world is made out of television, so it's entirely right that the Doctor should be so media-savvy.

The Facts

Written by Paul Erickson, and ostensibly Lesley Scott. Directed by Michael Imison. Ratings: 5.5 million, 6.9 million, 6.2 million, 7.3 million.

Supporting Cast Eric Elliot (Commander), Inigo Jackson (Zentos), Roy Spencer (Manyak), Kate Newman (Mellium), Michael Sheard (Rhos), Edmund Coulter (1st Monoid [episodes one to two], Monoid One [episodes three to four]), Frank George (2nd Monoid [episodes one to two],

Monoid Three [episodes three to four]), Ralph Carrigan (Monoid Two), John Caesar (Monoid Four), Ian Frost (Baccu), Terrence Woodfield (Maharis), Terence Bayler (Yendom), Brian Wright (Dassuk), Eileen Helsby (Venussa), Roy Skelton, John Halstead (Monoid Voices), Richard Beale (Refusian Voice)

AKA... "The Space Ark" (which is what the *Radio Times* called it).

Episode Titles "The Steel Sky", "The Plague", "The Return", "The Bomb".

Cliffhangers Once the Doctor and company have been imprisoned for bringing the virus on board, the Guardians reflect that everyone on the Ark may die; re-materialising on the Ark, the travellers realise that the enormous statue is complete, but that it's got the head of a Monoid; the Doctor and Dodo find themselves stranded on Refusis.

The lead-in to the next story: back on board the TARDIS, the Doctor suddenly finds himself turning invisible.

The Lore

• One of John Wiles' first ideas, when given *Doctor Who* to produce, was a spaceship so big that you needed transport to get around inside it. This became the notion of the Space Ark, and the rest fell into place. The writer Tosh suggested for this was Paul Erickson, a colleague from his days on *Compact* who was then working on... well, pretty much all the hit shows of the era. He'd just adapted a story for BBC2's *Out of the Unknown*, namely William Tenn's "Time In Advance", and butchered its ending.

• Tosh handed over to Gerry Davis shortly after accepting the second drafts of the scripts, which - for reasons nobody is quite sure about - had joint credit with Lesley Scott, Erickson's then-wife. In fact she didn't contribute anything at all. (Note that she isn't, as is often claimed, the Lesley Scott who wrote for the World Distributors annuals.) Wiles had already handed in his resignation, and remained to supervise this pet project before returning to writing and directing.

• The director for this story has, like Erickson, only this one *Doctor Who* credit. Michael Imison was originally one of Donald Wilson's team involved with the scouting-out of new writers (basically, license fees were paying him to go to

the theatre), then a story editor on *Compact*. Then he decided to direct, and ended up doing poetry programmes and a prestigious Thomas Mann adaptation (*Buddenbrooks*) on BBC2. Next they gave him a *Doctor Who* to do, and he was less than entirely happy. This got worse when, minutes before recording the final episode, he was told he was being released from his contract. However, he planned a complex and ingenious shooting schedule and achieved nearly all of it.

• One of his unexpected responsibilities was babysitting an elephant. Monica had been loaned by a zoo (probably Leicestershire's Twycross Zoo), but the BBC hadn't permitted the van to park at Ealing, where the filming was to take place. So Imison spent a February night making sure the baby elephant was warm and well-watered, while the driver slept in a hotel.

• Imison claims to have devised the Monoids almost from scratch. The scripts only described generic aliens, and when Imison's idea of the ping-pong ball eyes in the actors' mouths was accepted, the scripts had to be amended... but only slightly. The Monoids, or whatever they were called before becoming cyclopses, seem not to have had much to say until episode three anyway. Only four of the seven costumes had the eyes pegged in, but all seven had yak-hair wigs. There's no indication as to whether the obvious similarity to the Beatles was ever intended, although it *was* 1966.

• Those of you trying to figure out where you've seen Yendom before: actor Terence Bayler is Leggy Mountbatten in *The Rutles*. No? All right then, he's the one who says 'I'm Brian, and so's my wife' in *Life of Brian*.

3.7: "The Celestial Toymaker"
(Serial Y. Four Episodes, 2nd- 23rd April 1966.)

Which One is This? In theory? The TARDIS is trapped in a surreal dimension of evil toys and fictional adversaries, presided over by a demigod in the guise of a Chinese Mandarin. In practice? Four whole episodes of people playing musical chairs and snakes and ladders, starring Steven, Dodo and the Doctor's floating hand.

Firsts and Lasts This is, officially, the first story produced by Innes Lloyd. In fact he's been doing the day-to-day admin since "The Ark", but now he's given overall control. As proof of this, it's the first time the female companion wears a miniskirt and T-shirt rather than the short frocks Vicki was lumbered with for most of her run, and on top of that there's a corps of deadly ballerinas in order to get the maximum girl-flesh on display. Not counting cliffhanger reprises, it's also the first time a clip from a previous story is included in the programme. (This will become the standard way of depicting mind-probes and flashbacks in the 1970s, and in the '80s it'll just get silly.)

Here we have the first of many god-like elemental forces to threaten the Doctor, which means that something's finally capable of penetrating the TARDIS. We also get sinister clowns and malicious fictional characters, both of which will be back later on.

Four Things to Notice About
"The Celestial Toymaker"...

1. John Wiles has finally had enough of Hartnell's tantrums and written him out of the series. First the Doctor is made invisible, then his voice is removed as well. Note that all of this is done by the Toymaker to stop the Doctor getting on his nerves, so never has the god-like entity with magical powers looked so much like a work of wish fulfilment on the producer's part. Pressure was brought to bear on Wiles and incoming replacement Innes Lloyd to retain the star, in spite of their intentions; one idea had been for the Doctor to change his appearance as a result of the Toymaker's meddling, and for the companions to suspect yet another game. From now on, though, Hartnell is on borrowed time.

2. In the Doctor's absence, the supporting cast-members are yet again brought to the fore, and it's plain that neither of them anticipated anything like this when they signed the contracts. Lane is rather keen to show she can really really act, whereas Purves is finding it all a bit daft. In the same way that "The Web Planet" showed the programme-makers getting giddy with what they thought they could do, this story sees the production wildly outstripping the previous limits of the format, with no thought as to what the actors or audiences would make of it all. To think: a month ago they were making "The Massacre".

3. You may recall that when Purves arrived in this series, first as Morton Dill and then as Steven, he had to deliver '30s-style transatlantic dialogue full of exclamations like 'say!' and 'hey, Doc!'. Here he hits a fantastic new low, when he's required to

square off against Joey the painty-faced harlequin with an angry shout of: 'What have you done now, you clown, you?'

4. It's interesting that this story had a huge reputation (and everyone involved took credit) until the last episode was rediscovered (at which point everyone involved started blaming everyone else). The problem with the final instalment, or at least *one* of the problems, is that they had three episodes' worth of ideas and two episodes' worth of budget after the overspend on "The Ark". Does it look as if they're vamping? Frankly, yes. But listen to the first three episodes before watching part four and the thought occurs: maybe *all* of it looked this cheap...

The Continuity

The Plot The TARDIS has landed, the Doctor is fading in and out of existence in the console room, and the scanner's giving blatantly false reports of what's outside. On leaving the Ship, the travellers find themselves in the peculiarly nursery-like realm of the Celestial Toymaker, whom the Doctor recognises as a force of pure evil and who insists that they play a series of sadistic games for his amusement. The rules are predictable: if they win then the realm will be destroyed, but if they lose, they'll become the Toymaker's playthings for all eternity.

While the Doctor is reduced to a floating hand and forced to solve the Toymaker's trilogic puzzle, Steven and Dodo run a gauntlet of challenges in which their opponents are the realm's former victims, now given the forms of unlikely and / or fictional characters. They play blind man's bluff (with lethal spikes) against a pair of clowns, a kind of musical chairs (with lethal seats) against the King and Queen of Hearts, hunt-the-key (without anything lethal whatsoever) in the kitchen of nineteenth-century stereotypes Mrs Wiggs and Sergeant Rugg, avoid-the-dolls (with lethal ballerinas) on a magic floor that compels them to dance, and finally a human board-game (with a lethal electrocuted floor) against a twisted Billy Bunter-esque "schoolboy" called Cyril. Only then are they reunited with the Doctor, who's one move away from completing his puzzle and becomes visible again.

But there's a hitch. If he makes the move and wins the game, then the realm will be destroyed with the travellers still in it. The Toymaker believes them to be trapped, but the Doctor remembers that the triolgic board responds to the Toymaker's spoken commands. Ushering his companions on board the TARDIS, he orders the puzzle to complete itself over the PA system, mimicking his opponent's voice. The realm collapses, the Toymaker grimaces wildly, the TARDIS departs and the Doctor celebrates with one of Cyril's sweets.

Which immediately breaks one of his teeth. He'll be needing a dentist, then...

The Doctor   He's really very easy to manipulate once he's faced with a near-rival, agreeing to pit his wits against the Toymaker's after his opponent accuses him of having a lazy brain. Strange as it may seem, he's capable of exactly mimicking someone else's voice [he does it again in 14.1, "The Masque of Mandragora"].

• *Background.* He knows a great deal about the Celestial Toymaker, partly because the Toymaker is 'notorious' and partly because he's been to this domain before, although last time he left in a hurry before getting involved in any games. [The novel *Divided Loyalties*, as it happens, relates this encounter.] The Toymaker has been waiting for the Doctor to return for some time, and the Doctor feels he was in some way 'meant' to come here. He's also familiar with the trilogic game, but not so familiar that it ceases to be a challenge when the Toymaker steps up the pace.

The Supporting Cast
• *Steven.* His worst moment, as revealed by the Toymaker's memory mirror, was failing to save Sara Kingdom [3.4, "The Daleks' Master Plan"]. But he also sees Paris in 1572 [3.5, "The Massacre"]. Leaving the Toymaker's realm, he can once again operate all the presets and the master-switch for the TARDIS.

Steven routinely assumes that everyone is out to try to trick him. [This low opinion of human nature is his least appealing but most understand-able trait, and is consistent with everything we've seen of him so far.] Plus, he makes at least two allusions to spanking Cyril the schoolboy. [N.B. Literally spanking a schoolboy called Cyril, it's not a euphemism. This may indicate that corporal punishment is back in fashion by Steven's era. Once again, his idea of education seems a lot more primitive than the teaching-machines described by Vicki.]
• *Dodo.* Her lowest point was the death of her

mother. At one point she admits to a secret belief that toys are watching her all the time, which means she can follow the logic of this realm rather better than Steven. She's also aware, or more so, that their opponents are people who once possessed free will and are now the Toymaker's playthings. While Steven takes this to mean that he and Dodo can afford to be ruthless, she's unwilling to consign them to perdition.

No-one's ever given her flowers before, but she finds it easy to flirt with strangers when she wants something from them. She still doesn't seem to have got to grips with this adventuring lark, as she's quite reckless in trying out the potentially-lethal seats in the Hall of Dolls, even though she *knows* what the consequences could be. More than once, her compassion for her opponents verges on sheer raving stupidity.

Supporting Cast (Evil)
• *The Toymaker.* Appears human, Caucasian and middle-aged, but dresses in Mandarin garb and insists on acting "inscrutable" wherever possible. Within his realm, he can apparently make anything happen at his command, yet he's unable to break the rules of whichever game he's engaged in at the time. Still, he refers to 'my rules' even when the nature of his domain seems to reign him in. [Compare with the Eternals in 20.5, "Enlightenment". With hindsight, the possibility that the Toymaker is an Eternal himself - one of the *big* ones - is difficult to ignore, and see also 6.2, "The Mind Robber". We'll gloss over the claim made in certain BBC novels that the Toymaker is actually another Guardian (16.1, "The Ribos Operation").]

The Toymaker is described by the Doctor as immortal, and so far he's lasted for 'thousands' of years. He's good at predicting the Doctor's reactions, knows Steven and Dodo's names before he meets them, and is enthusiastic about the prospect of playing someone worthy for the rest of eternity. He has no regard for mortal life whatsoever, so the characters who face Steven and Dodo are all people who lost previous games and thus forfeited their right to be anything but toys.

Though a total of ten characters oppose the travellers, they appear to be "played" by only five people, yet neither Steven nor Dodo seem to notice this. Apart from appearances, certain things about these people remain consistent from character to character - Cyril the schoolboy is still called Cyril when he's being the Knave of Hearts,

ABOUT TIME 1963-1966

for example, although he's far more dim and gullible in that guise - and they're capable of returning in new forms when they're killed during the games. The past histories of the characters may or may not have anything to do with the individuals they used to be. Sergeant Rugg claims to have served six years with the Iron Duke [Wellington], while the King of Hearts is convinced that the Knave is the Queen's son. Other presences in the realm may or may not have been human, like the "dancing doll" ballerinas, who never speak.

The Toymaker's realm responds to the mandarin's voice, so the pieces teleport across the trilogic board to speed up the game at his command. He certainly has the power to make the Doctor invisible and intangible, and later to shut off the Doctor's voice as well. Hypnotic screens in the realm, 'memory windows', rattle visitors by showing them their most upsetting moments. It's indicated that the Toymaker is responsible for creating the "props" of his world; Steven and Dodo are shown a production-line churning out fake TARDISes on a TV screen, and one of these fakes is found at the end of every game, allowing access to the next challenge.

Each game takes place in a stark monochrome space with op-art designs on the floor [we might guess that the Toymaker is decorating the realm to suit Dodo's mind-set], and the entrance is always marked by a puzzle in rhyme. Other pieces of décor include giant toys and a doll's house for the losers, with new dolls appearing in the house whenever the Toymakers' servants are killed off. Steven and Dodo already have their places reserved. Interestingly, the Doctor thinks he can escape this realm in the TARDIS soon after arriving, but by the end of events the Ship can't leave until he's completed the Toymaker's puzzle [so the TARDIS, like the Toymaker himself, is bound by the rules of this place once the Doctor is engaged in the challenge].

The Doctor claims that the Toymaker 'draws' his victims into this realm, and the rules state that it'll be destroyed if the Toymaker ever loses a challenge. [So although the Toymaker can constrain his guests' ability to cause trouble, he can't kill his opponent without forfeiting the game and thus losing his domain.] Sure enough, the realm vanishes when the Doctor solves the trilogic puzzle. The Doctor makes sure the TARDIS dematerialises moments before the place ceases to exist, so

even the Ship wouldn't survive this annihilation.

Of course, the Toymaker himself survives. This isn't the first time he's lost a game, and he has the power to build himself a new realm whenever it happens. Actually he claims that he'll enjoy this process, as he's understandably bored with the current one, but he's a bad loser and insists on destroying anyone who bests him. The Doctor believes he'll meet this opponent again, and that his battle with the mandarin will never end. [In fact the Toymaker never returns, on-screen. But see **What Was the "Missing" Season?** under 22.6, "Revelation of the Daleks".]

The TARDIS The force which renders the Doctor invisible penetrates the TARDIS' 'safety barrier' without any resistance. [We'll later be told that this requires psychic force of god-like power, at least sometimes. See "Pyramids of Mars" (13.3), but perhaps more germanely "The Greatest Show in the Galaxy" (25.4).] The Toymaker also affects the scanner as a ruse to lure the Doctor out of the safety of the Ship. [See also "The Mind Robber" and "Enlightenment", for similar tricks in similar stories. From this we might conclude that the Toymaker's power is limited beyond his own dimension, as he can't *force* the travellers to leave their vessel. Here there's no hint as to how the Toymaker snares non-time-travelling victims, or why he's waited until now to hook the Doctor. If, indeed, the TARDIS doesn't arrive here by pure chance.]

It would seem that the Doctor, once he's rendered intangible, still needs to exit via the open doors rather than walking through the TARDIS walls.

History

• *Dating*. Best not to ask. [But every indication is that the Toymaker's realm exists outside the normal run of space and time. Again, compare with "The Mind Robber".]

The Analysis

Where Does This Come From? Let's start with first appearances. The most obvious thing to say is that it looks like Children's Television Gone Bad, but real kids' TV was never really like this, not even *Play School* and not even in the '60s. Instead, what we have here are the standards of children's entertainment made to look as threatening-yet-oddball

What Was Children's TV Like Back Then?

The simple answer is "ponderous". These days, with various badly-researched nostalgia shows providing a soundbite version, we've lost sight of several important aspects of British television for children prior to 1970. The first, and most significant, is that it existed at all.

Seen from the point of view of the first commercial companies, the laws governing what children could and couldn't see made it a waste of money to produce programmes specifically for them. As advertising to children was carefully monitored, and product-placement and sponsorship were illegal, there was no point either creating series or importing American shows that breached these guidelines. On the BBC, things were more complicated. By law the BBC had to provide something for everyone, and all programming was vetted in case children were watching. Anything unsuitable for children was preceded with a warning and a five-minute break in transmission, most notoriously *Quatermass*. Yet the BBC actively made programmes *for* children as well. So ITV companies began to follow suit, simply to avoid being left behind. However, there was rarely more than an hour of children's programming, and half of that was imported film series like *Roy Rogers*. Indeed, once ITV arrived, the hour-long break in BBC transmission to allow children to be packed off to bed (the "Toddlers' Truce") was abandoned and middlebrow "family" shows were introduced.

The material broadcast before this curfew was, to modern eyes, unremarkable except for the number of crude marionettes involved, the leisurely pace and the comparatively low noise-level. This is, in itself, worth noting. That modern TV resembles British children's television of the 1950s to such an extent would have seemed unthinkable in the mid 1960s, especially in America. British TV, unlike the US product, was largely untainted by market research and fashions in Educational Psychology. There were two dominant figures cited by "experts" back then: Jean Piaget and John Bowlby. Bowlby, whose background was in animal observation, came to be associated with the theory that maternal deprivation in early childhood led to what became known as "juvenile delinquents". Governments trying to reverse the wartime trend of young mums getting jobs (nothing at all to do with making sure that male unemployment figures were kept down, gracious no) grabbed this and insisted that children needed their mothers around at all times.

So television was a social activity for children and parents, and making programmes *just* for young viewers was downright thoughtless. Even the BBC called its 1.30pm slot *Watch with Mother*. Yet the thing that appeals to young children is exactly the sort of thing that adults can't bear. Something repetitive, predictable and silly, but with long periods of waiting for something to happen - the formula which today's experts recommend - is guaranteed to make young mums go postal.

Piaget did even more damage. While the bulk of his work was fruitful, one truly daft recommendation which TV bosses picked up from him was that imagination needed to be kept in its place. You could have realistic elements over *here*, and fantasy elements over *there*, but on no account were they to be mixed. The pilot episode of *Sesame Street* was researched to the last 25th of a second, and met with the approval of educationalists, psychologists, TV experts and station bosses. Everyone liked it except children. Then someone watched children watching it, and suggested remaking it with Big Bird actually talking to Bob, and with Oscar's trash-can outside Mr Hooper's shop rather than in a separate Muppet-zone. You know the rest.

Rewind to the Eisenhower era. America had to keep telling itself, and the world, how idyllic everything was. European nations, who'd recently had a fairly large war in their homes, accepted without question that things were better than before and constantly improving. So to British eyes, American imported shows - especially those intended for children - looked like propaganda, in which everyone seemed to be smiling at gunpoint. Compared to this, French, Yugoslav or Polish children's TV seemed natural and familiar. And another thing: American shows had children in them. Children are reluctant to watch other children unless it's in an otherwise odd context. As you might have gathered, everything American looked like science fiction to us anyway, but shows like *Romper Room* just wouldn't have originated here. (The actual tapes didn't make it, although British TV made an attempt to copy the format. It died an agonising death.)

Partly as a cost-cutting exercise and partly to avoid anything that looked like brainwashing, children's programmes were selected at international festivals entirely for their storytelling and visual

continued on page 257...

as possible, then slapped in the middle of an environment that looks something like "modern" television drama but at the same time halfway over the line into an abstract space full of mad people. Which means that what it *really* looks like is an episode of *The Avengers*.

By the time this was made, *The Avengers* had begun its mutation from a reasonably sane spy show to a piece of vaguely trippy pop-art in which Steed and Mrs Peel would regularly be threatened by giant playing-cards and lethal practical jokes. Innes Lloyd wanted *Doctor Who* to be an exportable, global commodity, just like *The Avengers* was. Now we have something that looks almost like the junior version. It doesn't help that the Toymaker is set up much like an *Avengers* villain (he has the power to do whatever he likes, so he acts like a spoiled child and turns everything into a toy), or that he's played by Michael Gough (who'd already appeared in *The Avengers* as the creator of the Cybernauts; see also 4.2, "The Tenth Planet"). Theoretically, *Doctor Who* should be better at this sort of thing than anything made for commercial television, given that it's meant to have whole other dimensions to play with. But *The Avengers* had both the budget and the inclination to try to look like a movie every week. "The Celestial Toymaker" looks more like a stage play where there just happens to be a camera present.

And we have to get back to the stage, if we want to get any deeper into this. The term "absurdist" is one you'll find in many textbooks on theatre from the '50s and '60s. In general it concerns the move towards representing the apparent futility of most of everyday life, the time-wasting and meaningless ritual, the unthinking habits and so on. With the very real threat of nuclear war hanging over the world, and most people being presented with a stark choice between frantically maintaining their status in a capitalist society or doing stupid things because the party tells you to in a Soviet society, absurdism was true to the lives of more people than nice plays about magic pianos or farces about vicars' trousers falling down. A play like Eugene Ionesco's *Rhinoceros* may seem to be about a silly situation (it involves people voluntarily turning into rhinos), but it tells us more about peer-pressure in a police state than any number of surveys. Gerry Davis' novelisation of this story is rather less subtle in making the link between the real and the ridiculous, by likening the Toymaker to heads of government who "collect" nuclear missiles.

We've already seen how the first year of *Doctor Who* borrowed heavily from the theatre of its time, but now we have an all-out attempt to represent people who've become the games they play. This existential dilemma - and *please* try to remember, in those days you could talk about existentialism without people sneering at you - will be handled more consistently in "The Mind Robber" (6.2), and to a lesser extent in stories as diverse as "Carnival of Monsters" (10.2), "Kinda" (19.3) and "The Greatest Show in the Galaxy" (25.4), but the fact that it's happening at all is interesting. This is where Innes Lloyd's stamp on the series, and more particularly Gerry Davis', becomes apparent. Bizarre as it might seem, it's only a short stop from the de-humanised figures trapped in the Toymaker's doll's house (and anyone wanting to think about the theatrical overtones of that is welcome to try) to the Cybermen and the hypnotised slaves of WOTAN.

A more obvious source, on the face of it, is Lewis Carroll. The apparently child-like cruelty, and the obsession with what happens to the pieces once the game is over, is unmistakable. A few months later Jonathan Miller's BBC film of *Alice in Wonderland* would examine this more fully, and in it we note the use of a large doll's house and a *chinoise* look for Sir Michael Redgrave as the Caterpillar. Here we should point out that to the Victorian mind, "Celestial" was a euphemism for "Chinese", often with connotations of drug-use. (See 14.6, "The Talons of Weng-Chiang", and Jago's mention of 'the Celestial Chang' shortly before Chang is shown smoking opium.)

The trilogic game is real and originated in China, another reason to dress the Toymaker accordingly. According to folklore, there's a sect of monks playing with a hundred pieces, one move a day; when they finish, the world will end. This is widely reported to have been the inspiration for Herman Hesse's novel *The Glass Bead Game*, which you've all read, of course. Well, people had in the '60s, anyway. Or acted as if they had. Like a lot of the books claimed as sources in this sort of guidebook, it was more talked-about than read at the time the script was commissioned.

There was also a great deal of interest in the idea that human game-play might contain clues to more fundamental truths. This popped up in the Pentagon's use of Kriegspiel maths (see 17.1, "Destiny of the Daleks"), in social psychology (we're only a few months away from Eric Berne's

This product is not authorized by the BBC. Doctor Who and TARDIS are trademarks of the BBC.

What Was Children's TV Like Back Then?

...continued from page 255

appeal, then vetted afterwards. The BBC rejected *Sesame Street*, but bought *The White Horses* from Yugoslavia and *Robinson Crusoe* from France. Foreign TV was often redubbed, or sometimes simply narrated over the original soundtrack. We accepted this, as so much of the narrative was purely visual anyway. There wasn't an authority-figure adult ending each episode with a homily to the child protagonist, as we'd come to expect from *Flipper* or *Forest Rangers*. In something like *The Singing Ringing Tree* (the massively traumatic East German fairy-tale, made by the same studios who'd made silent epics like Fritz Lang's *Metropolis*), you could work out the moral by listening to what the evil heavy-metal troll said and doing the opposite. If the content were so bizarre that a wholly new narrative had to be added for the English version, as was the case with *The Magic Roundabout* or *Hector's House*, then the apparent randomness of the incidents became part of the appeal.

British television, right from the outset, had been striving to find a form that wasn't cinema, or theatre, or radio. Its mode of address was both to convey the viewer *to* somewhere extraordinary, and to visit people *in* the intimacy of their living rooms. "Intimacy" is a key word here, because 405-line broadcasting was a dialogue with the viewers. For reasons we've discussed in this book already, the pace of the editing and the "grammar" of television was better-geared towards the way that children like their TV, with anticipation being the main ingredient. Even the gaps between programmes were exciting thanks to the "here it comes" element. Most station idents had countdowns built-in, and the BBC used a variety of clocks and minute-long graphics with music to keep up the suspense. Later on, this would be a large part of our experience of space exploration (see **Did *Doctor Who* End in 1969?** under 6.7, "The War Games"). Live-action programmes like *Play School* relied on stark monochrome sets and near-abstract props and logos, usually in black or white void-spaces. Within this "zone", adults behaving like children and unselfconsciously being fish or trains - while inviting the children to participate - was perfectly acceptable behaviour. (Children engaging with adults in this on-screen environment would have been a violation.)

The comparative crudity of the 405-line TV image made animation and puppets more viable,

and silent movies or Laurel and Hardy weren't "oldies" but a basic staple. In fact, quite often the worlds created by animators or actors were deliberately retro. Machinery was either steam-driven or hand-cranked, and had visible moving parts. People had costumes rather than clothes, and these were an extension of the persona. Characters did their jobs because it was an element of who they were, not because they had to pay the bills. The word for this isn't "utopian" but "pastoral", even when it's a town like *Trumpton* or *Hatty Town*. (In the latter, people were hats on legs, and their characters suited the kind of hat they were. See **Did Sergeant Pepper Know the Doctor?** under 5.1, "The Tomb of the Cybermen", for more on this.)

Once again, the technical limitations imposed a logic of their own on the content, a logic closely resembling Victorian / Edwardian children's fiction. And, like the best of those books, there was an entire dimension that only clicked into place when you watched the programmes again as an adult. Very small children would watch for as long as the internal logic held their attention; after school age, they'd watch a puppet or cartoon show as much to admire the technical skill as because they "believed" it. *Thunderbirds* was basically a giant model railway for anyone who didn't think it was real. Children of the 405-line era accepted puppets and cartoons more readily than later generations, and continued to do so up to an age when today's kids would think they were "babyish".

The advertisers noted this, and made thirty-second slots that had catchy jingles and jaunty pictures which caught on with children, even though they weren't advertising children's products. The idea being that kids accompanied mum to the supermarket and saw the product, then proceeded to trot out the jingle and say "can we, mum?". By the late 1960s, this style of television was turning up in the actual programmes. The theory was that a generation weaned on adverts and pop had shorter attention-spans, and therefore would prefer pacier editing and constant movement.

To everyone's surprise (in America, at least), this wasn't the case. When given the choice between rapid, random, pretty-looking pictures and something slow-moving that invites the viewer to guess what's coming, children will invariably pick the guessing-game. Piaget's former student and

continued on page 259...

pompous best-seller *Games People Play*), and in therapy sessions.

Things That Don't Make Sense Let's try to ignore the question of why the Toymaker wants to spend eternity watching grown-ups play party games, and the connected question of why the first half of episode three exists at all, when it consists of Steven and Dodo rummaging around in a kitchen without any threat to them whatsoever. To be honest, we have to assume that the Toymaker doesn't have much imagination. He can't even decide whether he wants the Doctor to die (by prompting the Doctor to finish the trilogic puzzle) or to stay forever (which is what he wants in virtually every other scene). As with the Riddle of the Osirans in "Pyramids of Mars" (13.3), the trilogic game itself is a fairly well-worn conundrum and fairly easy to reduce to a simple algorithm, so it really shouldn't give the Doctor any problems. In fact the Doctor's having an off-day all round, happily munching on sweets that have been provided for him by a psychotic schoolboy with a well-established flair for malicious practical jokes.

Mind you, nobody's good at taking hints here. Having been told by the Doctor that the Toymaker is a force of darkness, Steven and Dodo then immediately treat the man's puppets as if they're "hilarious" clowns rather than "evil" ones. They're also shown a whole production-line of fake TARDISes, and *still* don't twig that these might be used in the Toymaker's challenges, even though he warns them about it in advance and even though he says straight out that they'll have to play several games before they get to the real Ship. Yet every time they come across a police box, they get all excited, then disappointed all over again.

Critique You can hopefully see the problem. More than once in this entry, we've had to say "in theory…" and then quickly follow it up with "but in practice…". On paper, this is exactly what *Doctor Who* is meant to do; a story that exists in a null-zone between science fiction, surrealism and the audience's expectations of what's *supposed* to happen on television, a story that scrambles together childhood fear and contemporary neuroses, pitching the regular cast against demigods but still keeping one foot in the real world. At this point in the series' run, an adventure set in a malignant nursery which sees the Doctor engage in a battle of wills with a near-equal is exactly what the pro-

gramme needs. Everybody who grew up knowing the story precis from *The Making of Doctor Who* assumed it'd be fantastic.

What it *is* is two actors, one sounding as if he doesn't want to be there and one appearing as a character with no discernible personality, playing party-games on a half-finished stage-set in what looks suspiciously like a warm-up exercise for an amateur dramatics rehearsal. Had this been even one-fifth as grotesque as it wants to be - had the chairs that butcher their victims been in any way disturbing, had the Queen of Hearts been as murderous as the one in *Alice in Wonderland*, had the clowns been Scary Clowns instead of Crap Clowns, had there been *any* real sense of menace here whatsoever - then it might have made sense. Carmen Silvera and Campbell Singer do the best they can, even though they were hired to play George and Margaret (see **The Lore**, which should also help to explain where the plot went), while Peter Stephens is so good at being the id of Billy Bunter that in any other story he might have given Hartnell some real competition. But even for under-tens in 1966, this must have been substantially less intimidating than the average children's party entertainer.

You'll notice that this critique is starting to look like pure abuse, rather than an in-depth analysis of what doesn't work and why. This is because there's virtually nothing to analyse, unless you seriously want a discussion on Steven's tactics when playing TARDIS hopscotch or whether pass-the-parcel would have been marginally more interesting than anything that happens in episode three. Judging by the extant episode four, there isn't even anything worthwhile to say about the design or the direction, although it does get bonus marks for putting TV screens in the chests of giant toy robots (in the context of a time when there *weren't* televisions everywhere you looked, and you didn't get video-screens set into bus shelters, this is a pleasing touch). Other than that… what?

Later stories in this vein are among the programme's glories, so it's just as well they tried something like it early on, but that's not much of a consolation if you find yourself wasting fifteen minutes of your life listening to Dodo going through Mrs Wiggs' crockery. Horrid.

The Facts

Written by Brian Hayles (or Gerry Davis, or

What Was Children's TV Like Back Then?

...continued from page 257

eventual rival, Jerome Bruner, deduced that children achieve mastery over cause-and-effect by telling themselves stories about what they see. Getting it right gives pleasure, but being surprised is funny. (We'll pick up this idea in **Does the Plot Matter?** under 6.4, "The Krotons.") This is also accepted, now, by TV professionals and primary-school teachers. But in late 1950s Britain, nobody knew it from investigation; they did things that way because there wasn't really an alternative. Even if you bought into the idea of the reduced attention-span, it was impossible to make cheap programmes that catered for it.

The simple fact is that nobody in '50s British TV really knew what they were doing, in the theoretically-approved, Madison Avenue-researched sense. So in the commercial sector, everyone tried things and the advertisers decided what worked, whereas at the BBC it was just a matter of persuading one or two key figures that any given project was worth a try. Despite this, the success-rate was remarkably high, and there were fewer duds than the experts had made Stateside.

So, to recap. The key features of "Golden Age" children's TV in Britain were:

• It had no children in it, unless they were "neutral" observers of a crazy (adult) world, or a studio audience as in *Crackerjack*[12].

• It mixed fantasy and something-like-reality on an equal footing, often inside a created "zone" of abstraction or a "secret" place and time.

• It had an element of objects coming to life or taking on human aspects. (See especially *Andy Pandy* and *Flower Pot Men*. In the former, a doll and a teddy play are unaware that another rag-doll comes to life when they aren't around. In the latter, there's a weed that squeals *weeeed* and two men made out of flowerpots who say *flobbadob-badob*... no, seriously.)

• It took the contemporary and the nostalgic on equal terms.

• It had calm, measured voices, usually with a regionally-neutral BBC accent. Typically the narrator retreated after the first few minutes, allowing the viewer the illusion of understanding another tongue, especially if it happened to be a made-up language like that of the Flower Pot Men or *The Clangers*. (Note that even the Master gets drawn into this in 9.3, "The Sea Devils.")

• It invited the viewer "in" as a participant, or at least allowed time for predictions to be made about what was going to happen next. A lot of what was shown was build-up, a process of "becoming" and anticipation.

• It involved a strong element of investigation and exploration, with a reliable eye-witness as a yardstick for a magic world, or an exotic country, or both. (This could include a narrator-figure who "explained" in character as one of the locals, most bizarrely Johnny Morris doing voices for zoo animals while playing at being a keeper in the inexplicable *Animal Magic*. See 17.4, "Nightmare of Eden", for *Doctor Who*'s intrusion into this programme.)

• It presented the real world as marvellous - especially when we were the first westerners to see footage of something - and the imaginary world(s) as routine.

You can see how *Doctor Who* fits into this model. You can also see how today's big hits have come back to the format after various attempts to be "contemporary". In short, it's pretty much the template for modern children's television, most of which will be similarly baffling to adults in thirty years' time. But it's nowhere near as alien as *Captain Video*, or late-'60s "modern" television like the bits of *The Banana Splits* between the cartoons. The paradox is that now we have the technology to do it differently, it takes a conscious effort to make children's television which works for very young viewers without losing their attention; but back then, there was no option.

Donald Tosh, or none of the above). Directed by Bill Sellars. Ratings: 8.0 million, 8.0 million, 9.4 million, 7.8 million.

Episodes one, two and three are missing from the BBC archive.

Supporting Cast Michael Gough (Toymaker), Campbell Singer (Joey / King of Hearts / Sergeant Rugg), Carmen Silvera (Clara / Queen of Hearts / Mrs Wiggs), Peter Stephens (Knave of Hearts / Cyril), Reg Lever (Joker).

Episode Titles "The Celestial Toyroom", "The Hall of Dolls", "The Dancing Floor" (i.e. a floor on which people dance... it's not another unlikely Season Three monster, like the "Horse of Destruction"), "The Final Test".

Working Titles "Doctor Who and the Toymaker", "The Trilogic Game".

Cliffhangers Steven and Dodo reach a fake TARDIS and find a clue to their next ordeal; Steven and Dodo reach a fake TARDIS and find a clue to their next ordeal, and then some ballerinas turn up; Steven and Dodo reach a fake TARDIS and find a clue to their next ordeal, and then a schoolboy appears.

The lead-in to the next story: getting back to the safety of the TARDIS, the Doctor eats a sweet and breaks a tooth.

The Lore

• Are you sitting comfortably? Then we'll begin. The playwright Gerald Savory had written a mildly absurdist piece called *George and Margaret*, in which the eponymous characters were expected but never arrived (not even slightly like *Waiting for Godot*, then). Brian Hayles and Donald Tosh had the idea of doing a *Doctor Who* story in which George and Margaret actually appeared, clearing it with the BBC's Head of Drama first. And if you've been paying attention, then you may recall that the Head of Drama was... Gerald Savory. But Hayles' script featured many impracticable scenes, so Tosh rewrote it in consultation with Wiles and director Bill Sellars. It was at this stage that the trilogic game was introduced into the story, and a complicated labyrinth removed. This version seemed less interesting to Savory, who withdrew his permission, prompting another rewrite to take George and Margaret out.

• But the story had been cast, so incoming script editor Gerry Davis re-jigged the entire enterprise to give the three main supporting actors something to do. What had been conceived as a duel of minds between the Doctor and his most formidable foe to date had become a series of games and gimmicks, with the Doctor and the Toymaker both relegated to the sidelines. When Wiles saw this new version, with his name and Tosh's on it after they'd both left the series and the scripts had been torn to shreds, he complained to Savory about the waste of money involved (not least the issue of paying Brian Hayles and then effectively writing a new script).

• Innes Lloyd had been with the BBC for over a decade, and Sydney Newman personally recommended him for the job of reinvigorating *Doctor*

Who. Newman's suggestions still had the force of law within BBC Drama at the time, so Lloyd - who wasn't a big fan of SF in general or *Doctor Who* in particular - accepted the job and immediately began to make changes. As soon as he took complete control, Steven, Dodo and Hartnell's Doctor were written out and the "historical" adventures were almost entirely removed from the menu. We'll catalogue the full impact of this change in staff in Volume II, though.

• As we've seen, this story's other significant feature is the removal of the Doctor for three-quarters of the screen-time. The official reason was Hartnell's increasing ill health, but documentation indicates that Wiles had formulated a plan to remove the actor from the series without cancelling a hit show. Only a last-minute decision by the BBC executives, to retain the star until the new producer had settled in, changed this. (Fan-lore has another version, that Hartnell was fired but the BBC automatically issued another contract as the series was continuing. It's certainly true that the moment the third recording block was completed, he was dropped without a second thought. See 4.1, "The Smugglers".) We might also note that the original plan, to alter the face of one of the regulars during a run-in with a godlike force that uses fictional characters as agents, was eventually used in this story's "sequel": 6.2, "The Mind Robber".

• Unsurprisingly, "The Celestial Toymaker" was nearly stillborn. What saved it, as with the Daleks in Season One, was that the next story in line ("The Gunfighters") was the kind of project which would have taken ages to set up. "The Ark" had gone so far over-budget that a cheap four-part "filler" was needed. There are six speaking parts other than the regulars, and a few ballerinas (choreographed by Tutte Lemkow, incidentally... there's no getting rid of him, is there?), so the main costs were the less-than-lavish sets, the rather basic costumes and the simple animation for the trilogic game. Even so, in the end it wasn't *much* of a saving.

• The animated sequences aren't full frame-by-frame stop-motion (the first use of which in *Doctor Who* is Medusa's hair in "The Mind Robber"), but a more basic stop-and-start, filmed at Ealing. The trilogic game itself was thought to be cursed. Purves, who kept the prop as a souvenir, was out of work for almost a year after the end of his contract; the day after he threw it out, the 'phone rang and he was offered a job on *Z Cars*. Soon he was presenting *Blue Peter*, and carried on for about a decade before leaving to set up his own production company.

• Basic as the sets may have been, there were nevertheless some interesting features, even apart from the robot TV sets. The master control switches - like giant, clockwork versions of the TARDIS levers - were rigged to emit sparks like a friction-motor in a toy car. Or a Louis Marx Dalek, if you prefer.

• At the end of episode four, the continuity announcer had to read out a statement that Cyril was in no way intended to represent the popular plump schoolboy character Billy Bunter. Bunter's antics, written by Frank Richards, had appeared in a comic called *The Magnet* for well over half a century (see **Who Was the Master of the Land of Fiction?** under - yes, you guessed it - "The Mind Robber"). The television version, shown on BBC TV until around the time that *Doctor Who* began, had been massively popular. Because of the longevity of the character, no-one seems to have thought to ask whether Richards was still alive or whether the character still in copyright. The announcement fooled absolutely no-one.

3.8: "The Gunfighters"

(Serial Z. Four Episodes, 30th April - 21st May 1966.)

Which One is This? Tombstone, Arizona, 1881. The last episode is called "The OK Corral". You can see where this is going.

Firsts and Lasts This is the last story to be broadcast with individual episode titles. Henceforth the stories are presented to the viewers as discrete units, with some idea of how long they've got to run, even if the *Radio Times* doesn't yet list them as having given numbers of episodes. It's also the first story since "Marco Polo" to be "narrated", and probably the last ("probably" because Season Twenty-Three opens a can of worms).

Although it's not the first western to be made in the UK - *Carry On Cowboy* preceded it by several months, for a start - it *is* one of the first to be made in an electronic studio, and certainly the first to be made by BBC Television. You might want to risk a comparison with the *Star Trek* episode "Spectre of the Gun", made two years later. At least this one has a *couple* of scenes with proper horses.

Four Things to Notice About "The Gunfighters"...

1. The first thing to point out is that it isn't the worst *Doctor Who* story ever made. Amazingly, this still needs to be said. As we'll see time and time again, much of the "received wisdom" of *Doctor Who* comes from the first few guidebooks that were published in the late '70s and early '80s, in Ye Olden Days when information was harder to come by. And one of the first publications to include behind-the-scenes detail was Peter Haining's twentieth anniversary coffee-table affair, *Doctor Who - A Celebration*. At that point in time, it wasn't done to be overly critical of old stories, so Haining found the ostensibly "lowest-rated" story of all time (but see **The Facts**) and used it as a kind of sacrificial victim. "The Gunfighters" became the emblem of all bad *Doctor Who*, and *Doctor Who Magazine* treated it as such throughout the '80s. Watching it again now, especially after "The Celestial Toymaker", this seems absurd. Apart from anything else, Haining's account doesn't even seem to grasp that it's meant to be a comedy. If you need proof of where the story's intentions lie, then behold the scene in which gunslinger Seth Harper tells the Doctor that he won't be leaving town, and the entire Clanton gang leans forward to say (as one man): '*Alive, that is.*'

2. But admittedly, American viewers may wonder exactly where in the US this is supposed to be set. Despite being a rendition of the Gunfight at the OK Corral, it seems to be a showdown between the cast of *Deputy Dawg*, some Elvis impersonators and a few lost Canadians. If you could consider it a form of retribution for Dick Van Dyke and the various cockneys in *Buffy* (all sounding like stroke patients to us), then we'd be grateful. Mind you, we don't know for certain that Billy Clanton *didn't* sound as if he came from Bermondsey. However, a more singular voice than any of these *Thunderbirds* fugitives is that of Lynda Baron, belting out the narration in song form. While this was being made, Nat King Cole and Stubby Kaye were doing exactly the same thing at the cinema in *Cat Ballou*, though they at least appeared on-screen; Baron's invisible presence is unique in the history of the programme, and it doesn't get *too* intrusive unless you're watching it all in one go and get the cliffhanger reprises complete with rhyming couplets.

3. But the basic format is a parody of the films that the programme-makers had grown up watching. In particular, the plot details echo the movie version of *The Gunfight at the OK Corral* (and, to a

lesser extent, *My Darling Clementine*) more than historical accounts of the event. But the tone of the story is far closer to *Destry Rides Again*, a grimly comic debunking of the Old West made in 1939. Billy Clanton's stammer, Kate's Mae West schtick and the Doctor's unwonted innocence are all played for laughs. Best of all is Anthony Jacobs' line as Doc Holliday: 'You kill a guy out of sheer professional ethics, and then ya got three of his brothers chasing after ya to labour the point. That makes me real angry.'

4. And yet... when we get to the actual gunfight, it's all in deadly earnest. The film work at Ealing is tighter than anything we've seen for a while, while the shots of the Earps walking slowly and implacably through the hail of gunfire prefigure the Cybermen. Had the decision been made to risk a serious, grimy historical story about the real West, then they might just have pulled it off. As it is, the only thing even remotely like this for switching to brutal realism after three episodes of light farce is Donald Cotton's other script, "The Myth Makers" (3.3). Another resemblance is that the turning-point in each is a father realising his sons have got into a battle that's too big for them (King Priam then, Pa Clanton now).

The Continuity

The Doctor Can face Daleks and evil demigods, but a dentist's appointment fills him with terror. His teeth are in good shape, though evidently indistinguishable from a human's, and he has tonsils. Making up a name for himself on the spur of the moment, he plumps for "Dr Caligari" [hinting at a secret love of early twentieth-century expressionist cinema, and we'll come back to this later].

His knowledge of famous figures from the American West is variable. Although he recognises the name "Clanton" and knows about famous silent movie cowboy Tom Mix, he keeps getting Wyatt Earp's name wrong and doesn't seem to know about Doc Holliday. [There's some evidence that the real Wyatt Earp, who lived until 1929, may have been an advisor on Tom Mix movies. So this is especially weird.] He describes the gun that Steven finds in the TARDIS as being part of 'my favourite collection' [though the gun comes with the cowboy outfit, so it may not be a *gun* collection], but he never uses firearms himself, and barely seems to know which end to hold [c.f. 19.4, "The Visitation"]. He gets to the Clanton

Ranch on horseback in under half an hour [so he must have learned to ride since 1.4, "Marco Polo"].

This is the one occasion when the Doctor actively claims to be teetotal. [Other stories see him opt for soft drinks (often for comic effect, as in 13.4, "The Android Invasion") or knocking back enough ale or cider to flatten a Slyther (3.5, "The Massacre" and 4.1, "The Smugglers"). We've heard stories about him getting bladdered (21.7, "The Twin Dilemma"), but only ever seen it when we know the drink to be drugged (16.3, "The Stones of Blood" and 13.5, "The Brain of Morbius").]

• *Ethics.* In an odd development, he accepts the post of Deputy Sheriff to save Steven and Dodo, and on so doing refutes the title "Doctor". [This is something we'll see again in stories script-edited by Gerry Davis, most notably 4.3, "The Power of the Daleks".] In many ways the Doctor's playing dumb here, allowing people to think he's out of his depth and feigning at least *some* of his apparent innocence. Yet this gets Steven into a potentially dangerous situation with a lynch-mob, and the Doctor does nothing to prevent it. Though he's ultimately prepared to treat companion-snatcher Doc Holliday quite amicably [again, moral relativity in action], he seems rather disgusted with the violence and injustice of the whole era. Even so, he's interested in staying in Tombstone for a while once the gunfight's over, even if his companions aren't.

And after repeatedly being mistaken for Holliday, the Doctor briefly picks up Doc's habit of slapping Dodo on the bum.

The Supporting Cast

• *Steven.* Can sing reasonably well, and sight-read music. His efforts at an American accent are a bit better than Morton Dill's [see 2.8, "The Chase"]. Amazingly, he can play the piano, while looking over his shoulder at the attractive singer behind him. [There's a possibility that it's meant to be a Pianola rather than a piano, as nobody's arm-movements match the music when they play it, and Steven makes a crack about what songs it knows.] He seems to think that a costume right out of Grand Ol' Opry would be inconspicuous in the 1880s, but on the whole he knows about the Wild West and says he's always wanted to be a cowboy. [Which might be construed as odd, given that he has no knowledge of Hollywood movies.]

Did the BBC Actually Like *Doctor Who*?

You may well be thinking "that's a stupid question, they paid for it for 26 years". It'd seem an even stupider question if we'd used our original title, "Is *Doctor Who* Really a BBC Programme?", but this gets us to the core of the problem. The BBC's entire purpose and ethos, at least until 1980 or thereabouts, was radically different from the principles of any other broadcaster. The longer we look at this, the more unlikely *Doctor Who* becomes.

To get a proper handle on things, believe it or not, we need to go back to the mid-nineteenth century. Matthew Arnold - Schools Inspector, miserable poet and what we'd today call a cultural theorist - had a brilliant idea. Britain managed to avoid having a revolution in 1848, when everyone else did. Why? What had kept the proles from revolting? Arnold believed that the public, as a whole, should feel as if they belonged and had a stake in the nation. To that end, he tried to get the masses to "join in" with the best bits of capital-c Culture. Forcing people to go along with the tastes of the elite wasn't the issue; great works, and the attitudes they embodied, were by their very nature likely to alter the minds of those with the ability to appreciate them. Just giving the maximum number of people access to such things ought to be enough to maintain a harmonious social order. It's an idea that keeps cropping up in British culture, especially just after wars (see **What Kind of Future Were We Expecting?** under 2.3, "The Rescue").

By the 1920s, the issue was a live one again. Many people believed that the working classes were intrinsically unable to better themselves, and were genetically different, an idea taken to extremes by H. G. Wells in *The Time Machine* and expressed in the often-quoted statement "give them a bathtub and they'd keep coal in it" (see 10.2, "Carnival of Monsters", for Robert Holmes' take on this). Yet Arnold's ideas were refined as an alternative. After World War I and the "land fit for heroes", part of the reason for Britain being Top Nation was that we had a culture which made us... well, better. Everybody knew it, even foreigners. Americans may have told themselves stories about "Manifest Destiny", but we didn't even bother with a doctrine. It was just so *obvious*. Compulsory education included stuffing kids with uplifting culture, the psychic equivalent of making them eat up their cabbage.

Works were therefore divided into (1) those which were morally improving, and (2) the rest. The rest were useful to entertain, to get people into the habit of reading, listening or looking. They also kept struggling artists alive and solvent for long enough to develop their "serious" works. It's worth bearing in mind that serious works were often about working-class people pushing against the constraints of their upbringing. F. R. Leavis, the scholar most associated with this idea, put D. H. Lawrence and Thomas Hardy in the same league as Charles Dickens and Jane Austen even though the books of Lawrence and Hardy were "dirty" and offended church groups. This is the climate into which John Reith launched the BBC.

There are whole libraries about this subject, so we'll skip the period when Lord Reith ran the BBC personally. Instead, fast-forward to 1951, and the debates over commercial television. As we learned near the start of this book, a combination of Conservatives in the new government and disaffected ex-BBC staff led a co-ordinated campaign to break the BBC's monopoly over TV ("co-ordinated" down to word-for-word identical letters being sent under a hundred different names and addresses). The BBC was actually more keen on this than the government, as it'd relieve the Corporation of the burden of entertaining everyone all the time *and* providing "worthy" material. During wartime, the public had discovered an appetite for the latter, through BBC broadcasts to people in bomb-shelters and factories as well as free concerts and gallery tours. Whilst many Conservative ministers dreaded the "vulgarisation" of the new medium, in 1951 only 350 households had TV licences anyway. This increased tenfold in the next two years.

The clearest example of what commercial television might be like was America, and this worried a lot of people. The independence of the programme producer, and the broadcaster as a whole, was compromised. The worst-case scenario wasn't overt product-plugging, however, but the sponsors' refusal to permit anything remotely personal, controversial or out-of-the-mainstream. Proctor and Gamble, for example, laid down guidelines worthy of Stalin. "If it is necessary," they stated, "for a character to attack some basic conception of the American way of life [...] the answer must be completely and convincingly made some place in the same broadcast."

To see how bizarre this would have been to British audiences, imagine the last half-century's worth of British TV made under a version of this

continued on page 265...

ABOUT TIME 1963-1966

A curious detail is that while he's posing as "Steven Regret", everyone refers to Dodo as 'Regret's girl', and he never bothers to argue. [And Dodo acts jealous when Kate wants Steven to play the piano. Is it professional pique because he's better than her, or something else? Compare with **Are Steven and Dodo Related?** under "The Massacre" and shudder.]

• *Dodo*. Always wanted to meet Wyatt Earp. She too can read music, and plays the piano enthusiastically if not well. A good enough card player to hold her own against Doc Holliday, she can evidently ride a horse, though she's never actually seen to do this. She faints after a stressful gun face-off with the Doc, but is rather brazen up until that point, and more-or-less keeps her head in a gunfight.

The TARDIS There aren't any painkillers on board to cure the Doctor's toothache. [The aspirin supply first seen in "The Edge of Destruction" (1.3) seems to have run out. Or does aspirin just not agree with the Doctor? See "The Mind of Evil" (8.2).] There are clothes in the wardrobe that are *almost* suitable for this era, including showbiz cowboy outfits for Steven and Dodo, and a hat in the Doctor's size of which he was previously unaware. Steven's holster contains a gun, which *might* just be a prop and *might* get left behind in 1881 in any case.

[Not for the last time, it looks as if there's some kind of automatic hair-growing device on board. In "The Romans" (2.4), Vicki and Barbara have acquired more hair than they should have done even in a month spent at the villa, while here both Steven and Dodo are hairier than expected, given that this story leads directly on from the last one. In both cases, it's too hot outside for wigs.]

History

• *Dating*. The TARDIS lands in Arizona two days before the gunfight at the OK Corral. [Which took place on the 26th of October, 1881, although the precise sequence of events is a little confused here. See **Things That Don't Make Sense**.

[Historically, much of this is jumbled. The true facts of the skirmish between the Earp brothers (Wyatt, Virgil and Morgan) and Ike Clanton's gang are well-known, as are the myriad embroidered accounts. John Sturges' film *The Gunfight at the OK Corral* is often cited as the main source for the *Doctor Who* version, and certain characters who

existed but weren't there historically are seen both here and in the movie. Johnny Ringo wasn't present, and he certainly didn't die at the OK Corral. Nor did Ike Clanton. The Earps weren't much more "right" than the Clantons, but had official connections and could claim to be acting in self-defence despite eye-witness testimony to the contrary, so here they're the relatively-good guys. And it's Wyatt Earp, not Virgil, who's the Marshall.]

The Analysis

Where Does This Come From? In 1960, no fewer than thirty-five separate western series were premiered on American television. As is always the case, the best of these came to Britain. The general consensus was that if *Laramie* were the best, then the worst must have been unspeakable. Yet by definition, American companies could do westerns better than the BBC, just as Britain makes better series about Victorian parsonages or Tudor monarchs.

However, fashions change. By this point most US companies were moving to spies or space, and the only big-budget westerns made for the big screen were either rather jaded and elegiac or out-right cynical about the version of the West we'd all seen before. This was the era of Sergio Leone and *True Grit*. Nine months earlier, US viewers had seen the pilot for *Wild, Wild West* (it didn't get here until about the time of the moon landing), so obviously the American networks were getting the message. In a way, the non-existent West of our collective childhood - either old TV series where the Guy in the White Hat sorted things out in 25 minutes, or endless reruns of the movies made when people still believed in that sort of thing - constituted a historical era. It was, to Americans and everyone else watching, as vital a complex of values as the Middle Ages was to the Victorians.

Whatever you might want to blame for this (Cuba, the Kennedy assassination, television...), no-one really thought the Lone Hero would win, or deserved to. The period of "The West" was separate from America 1864-90. As an idea, it had informed American life right up to the Depression, but it had finally run out of steam... at least as far as it involved horses, saloons and men in hats. In some ways, Kennedy's notion of "the New Frontier" - especially as articulated in the soon-to-be-premiered "*Wagon Train* in Space", *Star Trek* - co-opted the same ideals, much as the

)id the BBC Actually Like *Doctor Who*?

...continued from page 263

:dict with "British" instead of "American". Goodbye o Monty Python, *The Prisoner*, *The Boys from the Black Stuff*, all Dennis Potter, *Doctor Who*... we'd be :eft with the test card and gardening. And later, the .ame manual states: "There will be no material on ιny of our programs which could in any way fur- her the concept of business as cold, ruthless and acking all sentiment or spiritual motivation." This s from a 1950s deposition to Congress, so it obvi- ɔusly wasn't policy with the sponsors of *Dallas*, ɔut it caused a storm in Britain. At last, both sides igreed on something: what they wanted to avoid.

Churchill, still Prime Minister at this stage, derid- ed commercial television as a "tu'penny Punch ιnd Judy show". It's certainly true that the people 'ying to get hold of franchises were more from he tackier end of showbiz than the donnish BBC ɔld guard. Nonetheless, they were thinking of their ιudiences rather than the potential market for ɔroducts, but just catering to different require- nents. Of the big TV companies set up in the pio- ιeer days of 1955-60, most were talent-bookers ιnd music-hall owners like Prince Littler and his ɔrother Emile, or Lew Grade, or Sydney Bernstein. ¯hese figures have acquired larger-than-lifer repu- ations, yet they were no vulgarians. Emile Littler ⱱas on the board of the Shakespeare Theatre at ;tratford, Bernstein was an old associate of Alfred ¯itchcock, while Howard Thomas at ABC created he BBC's wartime hit *The Brains Trust* (philoso- ɔhers answer listeners' questions). But some com- ɔanies, like Associated Rediffusion, were exactly as ɔanal as many dreaded all commercial stations ⱱould be. Rediffusion was owned by a tram com- ɔany, and hired a head of entertainment who did- 1't know who Bob Hope was when introduced to ιim.

Meanwhile, as we've seen, the BBC's fresh blood ⱱere on a mission to ask exactly the questions ?roctor and Gamble ruled out. The description of ¯onight suits almost all of the Corporation's cur- ·ent-affairs or popular programming: "Quizzical, ımused, slightly sceptical." The Matthew Arnold 'adition still prevailed, with Sir Kenneth Clarke ɔerating the new medium's intrinsic mode of ιddress as "colloquial, plain or commonplace" and ınsuited to the topics that mattered. Or mattered o him, anyway. Clarke had been instrumental in unning those wartime cultural schemes, and his lissatisfaction with the BBC's approach to televi- ion led him to go and work for Lew Grade. He

returned, chastened, and made *The Age of Kings* (an adaptation of Shakespeare's Plantagenet cycle... see 2.6, "The Crusade") and later *Civilisation* (the BBC's first big "look, we're showing you Michelangelo in colour!" series). We single him out as a sign of the tension within the BBC itself, but also as an illustration that the "duopoly" wasn't as starkly divided as many commentators think. Proof of this is the existence of *Doctor Who*.

However, the version of *Doctor Who* that wound up being such a hit wasn't the one the BBC thought it was getting. Time and again, we see var- ious BBC bigwigs attempting to rid themselves of this programme because it didn't fit their idea of what the Corporation is for. How, then, did it sur- vive?

Well, it isn't anything to do with the ratings. The BBC didn't care about those until Michael Grade returned from America on a mission to loboto- mise television in the '80s. The viewing figures fluctuate wildly and unpredictably until 1987, when any idiot could see that it was going to suf- fer from stupid scheduling. Audience appreciation is a less hectic ride, broadly within the 60% range. This is nearer to what the BBC believed to be important - namely that a section of the popula- tion was getting something it liked, and which no- one else would provide. But the BBC relied on its producers to second-guess what would work, not to research or dissect previous successes for hints on what to do next.

An important point arises here: when a produc- er within the BBC had any worries about content, that producer would contact an immediate supe- rior. Instead of constantly being monitored, pro- ducers were expected to use their own judge- ment. All scripts were supervised and comments passed on before recording or transmission, but it was BBC thinking to show faith in a producer dur- ing recruitment, not production. This is worth bearing in mind, as many of the biggest rows start- ed after a programme had been made and shown. If a producer were BBC material, then it was implic- it that he knew what was the right thing for a BBC programme. This is one of the reasons for much of what you've read so far. There was a feeling that Verity Lambert wasn't quite BBC, and that John Wiles - who was Corporation to the core - should have been more reliable. The management blamed themselves for their appointments, not the producers for being too populist and ratings-

continued on page 267...

Neo-Conservative movement would forty years later. As we've already seen (1.1, "An Unearthly Child"), the Kennedy assassination was commemorated on BBC TV with a western lament sung by Millicent Martin. One fan-source of old claimed that Martin sang the musical accompaniment to "The Gunfighters", despite the evidence of the end credits, so you can see how all the memories of this era get tied together.

Designer Barry Newbery went to Tombstone and took photos of the sites where it all really happened. They looked, he said, like East London; lots of flat brick buildings. He opted to make sets for the story that were authentically American West of the period, but not necessarily accurate. Facts would look cheap and shoddy. This is the story in a nutshell, the idea that the West we know in Britain is distilled from factually-accurate sources but not really true.

Things That Don't Make Sense The timescale's a bit screwy. Johnny Ringo takes Steven on his search for Holliday and Dodo, and they seem to ride for longer than they're away. Which is to say, the time they *say* they've been riding is longer than the time between Steven leaving Tombstone and the Doctor seeing Steven at the Clantons'. Given the distances involved, and the fact that they're at the Clanton ranch before dusk, either they have jet-powered horses or nothing at all happens to the Doctor and Dodo (or the people they're with) for three days.

Leaving aside all the historical discrepancies... between the pre-filming of the opening scene and the recording of the next one, the Clantons all swap accents and lose about three days' stubble apiece. Another slightly strange feature is that the Doctor gets Wyatt Earp's name wrong, but is happy to call Masterson "Bat" as if he's familiar with the man's biography. [The real Bat Masterson wound up as a sports journalist, so the Doctor might have read some of his work. Assuming that the Doctor follows baseball but not cricket - see 3.4, "The Daleks' Master Plan" and 2.4, "The Romans" for supporting evidence - this is just about plausible, if you close your eyes and hold your breath for a few moments.]

Doc Holliday was called "Doc" because... he was a dentist. The Clantons ride into town looking for Holliday, and are familiar enough with his biog to know he's a hard-drinkin' womaniser, but don't think that the best place to look for him might be the building on the high street with the big tooth hanging from the awning. No, they wait in the bar, and an old man turns up who's just had a tooth removed. They promptly mistake him for their target. But if this old-timer were Holliday, the only dentist in town, then who would have removed his molar?

1881: a bit early for Bengay dot-printing of photos on wanted posters, eh? Not too early for anaesthetics, though, yet as a dentist Holliday seems oblivious to their existence. He's not big on antiseptics, either; even leaving the door open to the street would have been frowned upon by this stage. On the subject of wanted posters... just how much time is supposed to pass between the gunfight and the tag-scene at the end? The companions want to get away as soon as possible, which suggests that mere hours have gone by, but Masterson has already had new posters printed and the Last Chance Saloon has managed to find a new singer and piano player. No, more impressively than that, it's managed to find a new barman to *hire* a new singer and piano player.

Johnny Ringo shoots Charlie the barman dead in the saloon, but upstairs neither the Doctor nor Steven seem to hear it, or worry about the nearby gunfire even though people have been trying to kill them all day. Let's see, what else...? Oh yes. Maybe this *does* make sense, but Rex Tucker doesn't get a director's credit at the end of episode four. If he wanted to have his name removed from any of it, then surely the best-directed episode would be the one he'd opt to take credit for, not all the episodes *except* that?

Critique Even now, there are people who don't like this story. However, they're usually the same kind of people who persist in praising "The Celestial Toymaker" in the face of all the evidence, so we don't have to pay any attention to them.

Everyone had got used to making alien worlds in Lime Grove or Riverside, but being the first TV western made by the BBC was a whole new challenge, and everyone threw themselves into it. Purves, who's had to carry two of the last three stories, is relaxed and genuinely funny when he needs to be. Dodo the Girl With No Personality actually makes sense in this context, so for once Lane is exactly as enthusiastic as the story requires of her. Hartnell, who claimed to have suggested doing a Cowboys-and-Indians story in the first place, looks interested in the job again. He's been

Did the BBC Actually Like *Doctor Who*?

...continued from page 265

hungry, or too experimental and self-indulgent.

This was symptomatic of a conflict within the BBC as a whole, and here we get to another urban myth about the series. Huw Weldon's mum, or was it his mother-in-law, or his children... anyway, *someone* in the Weldon family insisted on a twelve-part Dalek story. Let's look at Weldon's track-record. He was a producer-turned-presenter, formerly with the Arts Council. He presented a programme for children before becoming a father himself, and did so with a starchy bemusement which worked miracles with shy child prodigies. He was the primum mobile of *Monitor*, a programme which assumed total ignorance but a degree of curiosity on the part of the viewer. Weldon's plan was to take the audience on a journey, explaining at first and then simply showing. He hired hungry young directors like Melvyn Bragg and Ken Russell, but did the interviews himself. This was, quite simply, the most BBC thing ever.

At the heart of it was the idea of exploring and narrating. For Weldon, television was about stories, and he used the example of *Doctor Who* in several speeches (or the same speech to several audiences, anyway) discussing 'the path into the unknown forest'. He also listed the Daleks as one of the Corporation's four achievements, and made repeated comments that they should be included wherever possible. When the idea of killing them off was floated, he growled about the reason that Evelyn Waugh's novels suffered: Waugh killed off characters too early. Weldon's mum, on the other hand, was mentioned as an example of why popular programming wasn't to be sniffed at. The two anecdotes seem to have been confused, but it's significant. If Weldon were the keeper of the Corporation's conscience whilst Director General Hugh Greene moved it into uncharted waters, then *Doctor Who* was what the BBC did, simple as that.

(Oh, the BBC's *other* three achievements? *Maigret*, *Quatermass* and Gilbert Harding. Gilbert Harding? No? See 8.5, "The Daemons". Weldon may have been joking, but it's not the kind of joke he tended to make.)

Imagine, for a moment, an ITV version of *Doctor Who*. It's not as if the commercial companies didn't try, but only once CSO caught on did they really get anywhere, hence *The Tomorrow People* and all the teen-fantasy shows that came in its wake. In 1960s terms, a family drama series with a fantasy premise and vaguely challenging storylines wasn't impossible on commercial television. Dennis Spooner created half a dozen for ITC, but they were all present-day and broadly spy-based. More importantly, they all bore clear signs of a sales-pitch for the US and Commonwealth market, however prominently the "Made In Britain" stamp was displayed. A series like *Doctor Who* can't be sold unless it's made with production values unlike any US-manufactured show. Irwin Allen had managed to split up the time-travel and space-exploration aspects, with *Time Tunnel* and *Lost In Space*, but both needed hunky heroes, child prodigies, simpler stories and guaranteed income.

Lower-budget series about time and space, with elderly character actors as the leads, don't seem to have appealed. (LWT's 1971 effort *Jamie* looks like a bad joke, but almost got away with it. ITC's *Timeslip* manages to be simultaneously hilarious and profoundly boring.) 1960s ITV companies simply didn't have the solidity and domestic audience-base to attempt anything like the BBC's hit, any more than the BBC could have got away with making *The Avengers*.

Except... to get a little ahead of ourselves, one of the hallmarks of Innes Lloyd's term as producer is that he seems to have decided to sell this series abroad. Seasons Four and Five can be quite calculated in their attempts to be export-friendly, and are international in their outlook in ways that are missing from the early years. Oddly enough, though, it's the Hartnell stories that appear to have travelled best until the mid-'80s surge of interest in the '70s "product". If you've seen clips of the Doctor and the Daleks arguing in Arabic, then you'll know what we mean. Sydney Newman had always wanted to make a series to beat the world.

Consider that for a moment. It's the early '60s. Newman has been brought in from ABC to run the Drama department of BBC TV. He's been hired specifically to make it all a bit *less* BBC, just as ABC hired him to make it less ITV. Consider this also: Donald Wilson quits soon after getting the family Saturday drama show off the ground, and goes off to try his pet project, a John Galsworthy adaptation. BBC2 gives him the time and money to make 26 hours of it, thereby inventing the costume drama as we know it, and it sells globally. (See 4.9, "The Evil of the Daleks", for more on the impact of *The Forsyte Saga* on the landscape of British televi-

continued on page 269...

on autopilot lately, even when he *hasn't* been mute and invisible, but he hasn't had this much sparkle since "The Reign of Terror". And he's much better at being grumpy and put-upon than at giggling.

On the strength of this, Rex Tucker's contribution to Season One could have been remarkable. Here, in what's got to be considered a fairly familiar setting (for the viewer, if not the programme-makers), he makes the cameras seem even more mobile and fluid than Waris Hussein did. The high-angled shots, used by Douglas Camfield and Derek Martinus just to make things look more interesting, are here used as part of the narrative process. Sydney Newman 'phoned in and gave guarded congratulations. He said that it was a stupid idea to even attempt a western at Riverside, but that it was done better than should have been possible. We'd almost go along with this; the thing we take issue with is the idea that there are things which shouldn't even be tried. "The Gunfighters" has no right to exist, and that makes it worth cherishing. Without doubt, there's a lot wrong with it, especially the accents (although that's *accents*, not *acting*). However, there's a lot more that's right with it, and a lot we never would have seen otherwise.

What's noticeable about the story's flaws is that they're flaws we're familiar with by now, flaws common to all the BBC's efforts to make 25 minutes of space-opera every seven days, or produce quality costume drama with less than a dozen actors. It's too claustrophobic, for a start, and you get the feeling that the storytelling would have been a lot more coherent if it'd been made as a complete unit instead of being put together week-by-week. Seen all in one go, it sags in the middle, like almost every four-parter in this era. The difference is that we judge something like "The Ark" by the standards of other *Doctor Who*, yet we judge "The Gunfighters" against John Ford or Sergio Leone. But again, hindsight smiles on Season Three. A generation weaned on *Blazing Saddles* "gets" this story better than the people who missed the point in 1966. Even if the innuendoes and the gay subtexts weren't intentional.

If this had come off completely, and the public had gone with it, then we'd now be saying that this was the obvious template for everything which followed and that it's amazing they never thought of it before. Which is what's usually said about "The War Machines" (3.10). That story was just as much a gamble, or a sign of desperation, as

this one. And at least "The Gunfighters" has a chorus.

The Facts

Written by Donald Cotton. Directed by Rex Tucker. Ratings: 6.5 million, 6.6 million, 6.2 million, 5.7 million. (The idea that this story got the lowest-ever ratings for the series is palpably false. Indeed, the next story's best figure was less than the worst for this one. Actually there seems to have been a temporary slowing in the fall in viewing figures as the run-up to the World Cup began. On the other hand, audience appreciation dropped to 30%, as bad as it ever got.)

Supporting Cast William Hurndall (Ike Clanton), Maurice Good (Phineas Clanton), David Cole (Billy Clanton), Sheena Marshe (Kate), Shane Rimmer (Seth Harper), David Graham (Charlie), John Alderson (Wyatt Earp), Anthony Jacobs (Doc Holliday), Richard Beale (Bat Masterson), Reed de Rouen (Pa Clanton), Laurence Payne (Johnny Ringo), Martyn Huntley (Warren Earp), Victor Carin (Virgil Earp).

AKA... "The Gunslingers".

Episode Titles "A Holiday for the Doctor", "Don't Shoot the Pianist", "Johnny Ringo", "The OK Corral".

Cliffhangers In what must be the weirdest-looking cliffhanger in the series' history, the Doctor unwittingly heads for an ambush at the saloon, but the credits roll over Steven as he stands by the piano and sings; the mob outside the jail threatens to string Steven up if the Doctor doesn't come out and give himself up; the Clanton boys spring their brother from the jail, leaving the young Warren Earp dead on the floor.

The lead-in to the next story: the Doctor announces that the TARDIS has landed in a far-off age of peace and prosperity, just as a caveman appears on the scanner. The forthcoming story is billed as "Dr Who and the Savages"...

The Lore

• Johnny Ringo was played by Laurence Payne, who'd soon go on to be Granada's *Sexton Blake* (see 18.1, "The Leisure Hive"). He was almost the

Did the BBC Actually Like *Doctor Who*?

...continued from page 267

sion.) There's no longer a consensus on what "BBC programming" means, just a consensus on what it's not.

Many in the BBC were horrified at the sheer volume of merchandising connected with *Doctor Who*. As some have noted, it's interesting that the content of the toys / games / annuals and the content of the programme seem almost totally distinct. We've hit on something fundamental to this essay, and all discussion of the series in the 1960s. The *idea* of the programme (as exemplified, perhaps, by the annuals) and the actual broadcast series were related, but sometimes very separate. The programme as a concept, the promise made to the viewers of what might happen, is easier to sell than the actual series. Any given episode is an example of one of the things the programme can do, but no one episode can live up to the expectations of the programme as a whole, and its place in the British viewing diet. The BBC hierarchy seems to have thought that while it was there, there was the potential for *Doctor Who* to do anything they needed a series like that to be doing. Like Radio Three and the fire brigade, you're unlikely to need it every day but thank goodness it's around. Some, like Huw Weldon, did indeed tune in on Saturdays;

but for the rest, it seems as if they were happy to be in a Corporation that made it for someone else. That "someone" paid the licence fee, after all.

The Reithian / Arnoldian tendencies within the BBC saw popular programming as a sugar-coating for the Corporation's real duty to the public. Programmes like this were called "ground-bait" among the higher echelons. Once secured for the evening, the viewers would be more likely to remain seated for something they wouldn't have tuned in for voluntarily, and have their lives improved almost surreptitiously. (This *was* forty years ago. If you've seen the sort of programmes that followed *Doctor Who* in 2005, then you may be forgiven for finding the idea hilarious.) It didn't mean that the popular programmes were of lesser value or made with less care, but they were there mainly to hold their own against commercial product and imports. The BBC paid £2,500 a week for 25 minutes of non-commercial adventure with a strong moral and empirical stance. The Drama department, as a whole, got about that much in revenue from Fluid Neutralisers and PVC Dalek costumes. Even though some would have objected to making money, and some would have needed ten times as much to keep such a tawdry series around, most were prepared to tolerate *Doctor Who* on those terms.

---

last major character to be cast, and the role nearly went to veteran character actor Patrick Troughton. Troughton was too busy, but would soon be asked to play a different role in the series, and if you don't know which one then order Volume II right now. Payne had also played Athos in Rex Tucker's 1950s version of *The Three Musketeers*. (Porthos was Paul Whitsun-Jones, who'll be along in three stories' time. Aramis was Roger Delgado, and he'll dominate Volume III.)

• Coincidence crops up again, as Donald Cotton's next job was with Verity Lambert. She'd been given the unenviable task of launching a BBC "spoiler" for ITV's *The Avengers*, and had wanted to do *Sexton Blake*. The rights weren't available, so the gimmick of defrosting a Victorian adventurer in Swinging London - a gimmick which had, apparently, been another one of Sydney Newman's brainstorms - was transferred to a previously-unknown internationally-famous swashbuckler (i.e. everyone in the story acted as if he'd been famous in his day). *Adam Adamant Lives!* was Lambert's most notorious flop until

1992, although it *did* tend to stick in people's minds, and to hear anybody talking about it these days you'd think it was one of the seminal shows of the 1960s.

• A similarly odd coincidence: Anthony Jacobs, playing Doc Holliday, brought his young son Matthew into the studio to watch the recording. Matthew Jacobs ended up writing the screenplay for the Paul McGann TV Movie (27.0). In which the Doctor dresses as Wild Bill Hickock...

• Both Shane Rimmer (Seth Harper) and David Graham (Charlie) had just finished doing voices for *Thunderbirds*. Graham had hitherto been one of the main Dalek voice artists (he gets to show his face again, as Professor Kerensky, in 17.2, "City of Death").

• Rex Tucker, as you may recall from the start of this book, was the original producer of *Doctor Who* for an hour or so and had contacted Tristram Carey to do the theme tune. By the time of "The Gunfighters", Carey had worked on "The Daleks" and "The Daleks' Master Plan". In the latter he'd provided silent-movie-style piano music, and in this vein he was asked to furnish "The Gunfighters" with a ballad, to be sung by Tucker's daughter Jane. When finished, the ballad wasn't in her key, and extra lyrics were constantly being added to suit the narrative. Jane Tucker went on to become one-third of Rod, Jane and Freddie (from ITV's best stab at cloning *Play School*, the near-legendary *Rainbow*... and we'll be noting Roy Skelton's involvement with *Rainbow* later in these volumes). She's lurking in the background when Steven's about to get lynched.

• Anyone familiar with ITC adventure series of this era will be asking themselves, "why isn't Donald Sutherland in this?". The simple answer is that he *was* asked to play Wyatt Earp, but was too busy being the Token Yank in something else. (Yes, we know he's Canadian, but he played the Token Yank in *The Champions*, *The Avengers* et al. He's also reputedly one of the non-speaking Thals in the first Cushing Dalek flick.) And if you *are* into ITC, then note that Sheena Marshe - or "Marsh", as she's credited here - plays another noted barmaid in the "You Have Just Been Poisoned" scene from "The Girl Who Was Death", everyone's second-favourite episode of *The Prisoner*.

• Reed de Rouen, who plays Pa Clanton, co-wrote a proposed *Doctor Who* story with Jon Pertwee. See **What Else Wasn't Made?** under 17.6, "Shada", to see what a narrow escape we had. In 1955, he'd written an SF novel called *Split Image*, based on the premise of a rocket landing on a planet that's an exact duplicate of Earth. Did anyone writing in Britain *not* try this idea out...?

• In the interests of strict accuracy: though we've been saying that this was made at Riverside studios, episode one was actually made in the slightly larger Studio Four at BBC Television Centre. We're sure you noticed the difference.

3.8: "The Savages"

(Serial AA, Four Episodes, 28th May - 18th June 1966.)

Which One is This? The one with no monsters and no historical personages, just some old men in a city who like sucking the vital juices out of the local primitives. They steal the Doctor's mojo, then ask him to take it back, so he gives them Steven instead.

Firsts and Lasts Logically, this is the first story *not* to have individual episode titles, at least on-screen (and you'll notice that it's also the first story made after the production codes had used up the alphabet). It's the last appearance of Steven, to everyone's surprise, not least that of Peter Purves. But a big welcome, ladies and gentlemen, for the first use of a quarry to represent an alien planet. And, remembering that there's a dead Dalek in "The Space Museum" (2.7), we have to count this as the first "space" story with no weird aliens in it.

Four Things to Notice About "The Savages"...

1. Innes Lloyd is in charge, so the "get the dads watching" imperative is back. Clare Jenkins (as Nanina) spends a lot of the story dressed like Raquel Welch in *One Million Years BC*, while Kay Patrick (formerly Poppaea in 2.4, "The Romans") is dolled up as a flower-child - who's called, imaginatively, "Flower". (Thankfully, Dodo drops the Northern accent before calling her that.) Jackie Lane, however, is made to wear a costume which strongly resembles a straightjacket.

2. Once Steven has made the security guards understand what it's like getting zapped by ray-guns, they all join the revolution. A nice idea, but when they're looking for a leader, the Doctor effectively sacks Steven from the position of being his friend and says "here you are, he can be your new king, bye-ee". Then he has the nerve to tell Dodo that he'll miss the boy. Abrupt companion departures will eventually become a standard fixture of this series, but usually they involve one of the female regulars suddenly falling in love, and until now there's at least been *some* hint ahead of time that one of the crew might be interested in leaving. Mind you, compared to what happens in the *next* story, Steven's departure is an emotional tour de force.

3. We've said it a few times in this volume, but this story has music quite unlike anything ever heard in the programme before or since. It's a string quartet, playing something like Bartok or Kodaly. The juxtaposition of this and the visuals - classic '60s "futuristic" chrome corridors and op-art lab sets - is striking, and in places you want all the silly dialogue to stop.

4. One performance worth listening to, though, is Frederick Jaeger. Not so much for his rather run-of-the-mill benign leader (who is, as always, really a tyrant in charge of a corrupt regime) but because he spends a big chunk of episodes three

and four playing the Doctor after absorbing the lead character's life-essence. Had they wanted to replace Hartnell with a near-carbon-copy, then this would have been the time to do it. There's obviously something about Jaeger that makes directors cast him as "Jekyll and Hyde" characters; see also 13.2, "Planet of Evil" (where he's Sorenson) and to a lesser extent 15.2, "The Invisible Enemy" (where he's Professor Marius). What's often forgotten is that this isn't one of those stories where Hartnell took a week off... he was there watching Jaeger, as we'll see in **The Lore**.

The Continuity

The Plot Arriving on a scrubland planet in the far, far future, the Doctor is intrigued to find himself being welcomed by the highly-advanced inhabitants of a nearby city, who know him as 'the traveller from beyond time' and honour him as the highest authority in space-time travel. But although the city is an apparent utopia, dedicated to learning and ruled by an Elder known as Jano, there are caveman-like Savages chucking spears around in the wilderness outside. The Doctor's immediately suspicious, especially since the city-dwellers seem reluctant to talk about the secret of their great civilisation.

Sure enough, it transpires that the Elders have found a way to draw the life-energy out of other living beings, and keep themselves perky by draining the essence of the Savages. When the Doctor speaks out against the regime, he himself is taken to the laboratory, where his life-force is transferred directly into Jano... who, as a result, begins to develop a conscience and some of the Doctor's mannerisms. Meanwhile Steven and Dodo fall in with the Savages, and are treated with near-religious reverence when they overcome Captain Exorse, the leader of the city's guards. Exorse also experiences a change of perspective, when Steven shows him what it's like to be on the receiving end of a light-gun.

With Jano on their side and Exorse beginning to have doubts, the Doctor and company have no difficulty getting back into the laboratory to wreck the life-sucking equipment, achieving a bloodless victory which forces the Elders to make peace with their former victims. But the two sides still need a mediator. When the Savages nominate Steven, the Doctor agrees that he's the only one who's qualified, and Steven - only half-reluctantly - accepts the job offer. The TARDIS departs with just the Doctor and Dodo on board.

The Doctor Although he knows nothing of this planet, he describes the TARDIS as landing in an age of peace and prosperity even before he steps outside, and knows there's a race of great intelligence and learning in this part of the universe. [There may be a lot of human "utopias" in this era, whenever it is.] He tells a guard that one of the Savages is human 'like you and me' [he may be speaking figuratively, as the Doctor's physiognomy is sufficiently different for the life-force extraction to have unforeseen side effects, but he's still been doing a lot of "human" talk this year].

After the Elders suck the life-force out of the Doctor, their chief technician's amazed by the potency of the stuff, and Jano picks up some of the Doctor's personality-traits. [A lot of stories hint that people's "selves" are contained in their bodies in some non-physical form. The test-case for this is 18.1, "The Leisure Hive", in which memories seem to exist independently of the brain. But since the Elders have never absorbed the Savages' memories, perhaps this implies there's something particularly special about the Doctor's life-juice.]

• *Ethics.* The Doctor's reaction, on being given a ceremonial mantle, is to ask awkward questions because 'there's my reputation to think about'. Precisely which "reputation", and with whom, is left unclear. [By this point he's already established that the Elders have somehow been "watching" his exploits, so this may be an excuse he's concocted purely for their benefit.] Once the gloves are off, the Doctor tells Jano that the sacrifice of even one individual is too great a price to pay for progress. He feels an awful lot of satisfaction in smashing up something evil.

The Supporting Cast

• *Steven.* At the start of events, Dodo accuses him of always asking the Doctor's permission to do things. 'You're a grown man... or are you?' [This is a very different Steven to the one who stormed out of the Ship at the end of 3.5, "The Massacre".] With the Doctor incapacitated, however, he's much more pro-active. Notably, the Doctor still hasn't given him a TARDIS key of his own [even though Dodo has one by the next story].

Steven's more willing to trust the inhabitants of the "utopian" city than he has been to trust most alien types. Until the final stages he shows no apparent interest in staying behind to look after the Elders and the Savages, and it's the Doctor who convinces him that he'd make a good leader. Steven himself is a bit phased by this, but just asks whether he's really capable, not why the Doctor has suddenly decided to dump him. [Typical of an astronaut with military connections, he seems to see this as a duty rather than a lifestyle choice.]

• *Dodo*. Even Steven acknowledges that she isn't very bright, though she's visibly distraught by his departure [we say "visibly" because a five-second clip of 8mm film exists from the end of episode four]. Under pressure, her accent reverts to Mancunian and her turn of phrase is more colloquially Northern. She hates guided tours.

The TARDIS On leaving the Ship, the Doctor takes with him a chest-mounted device which he calls a 'reacting vibrator' or 'RV'. To what it reacts is unclear, but he only wears it once, to ascertain that he's in a highly-advanced society. He also has some extremely convenient pills on board the TARDIS, called D403 capsules, which he believes might help a recovering Savage. The capsules are kept in an emergency cabinet, and Steven already knows where to find it.

Planet Notes

• *The Planet*. Wherever and whenever this is, the Doctor's never been here before, and he indicates that it occupies a far-flung region of space and time. The planet is predominantly scrubland and sparse forest, with a gleaming walled city in a valley on an island. This city has a section restricted to the security forces and its Elders, containing the laboratory where the transfer process is conducted, draining the 'energy of life' from the Savages and storing it in vats for later use by the citizens. This 'vitality' doesn't just keep them healthy, but makes them stronger, brighter and more beautiful. Though the process isn't necessarily lethal, it leaves its victims in a weakened condition, which means they tend to stumble around looking vaguely menacing and zombie-like. Nonetheless, the Savages claim that many of their number have died before now. The Elders' technicians have never attempted to draw energy from a "higher" being like the Doctor, so his intellect nearly overloads the system.

Visitors obviously aren't unknown, as there are guest apartments in the city. The city-dwellers trust the Council of Elders without asking questions, and most of them have no experience of "real" things like weather. They're happy to play, dance and hunt as they please within city limits, but aren't permitted to leave, and they're reluctant to discuss their dependence on the Savages. In addition to the "soul food", the inhabitants of the city also eat ordinary things like fruit, not the space-pills of most '60s-style futures. The guards use 'liquid light guns', which paralyse and sap the wills of their victims, particularly when shone in the eyes. The rays from these guns can be reflected by a mirror, and are also used to open the city's doors.

Even the Doctor regards the realm of the Elders as highly-advanced, though he's suspicious of this civilisation right from the start. This is hardly surprising, as it seems to have been watching him. The city's space-observers know him as 'the traveller from beyond time' rather than the Doctor, but the Elders have been tracking his Ship for 'many light-years' throughout both space and time. [We'll assume that "light-years" really is supposed to be a measurement of distance rather than time here, although that's not how it sounds. The Elders may be scientifically advanced, but the writers aren't.] He's thus welcomed as a fellow scientist and a virtual celebrity. [Do the Elders have something like a time-and-space visualiser? If so, then the obvious question is whether the Doctor is wishing *them* a merry Christmas in "The Daleks' Master Plan" (3.4).]

Intriguingly, when the Doctor first asks them whether they know who he is, one of them replies 'not your name, of course'. Although they aren't expecting him to have companions, it's known that he doesn't carry weapons. Despite being identified as an authority on time-travel, the Doctor isn't put under pressure to reveal what he knows about this subject, even though the Elders have an interest in the field. For them, "learning" seems to be nothing more than a pastime.

Meanwhile the Savages live in labyrinthine caves, and have a culture and art of their own which is unknown to the Elders. They're sustained by their faith - even if this religion is never explicitly described - and have small 'temples' with candles and colourful murals on the walls, but recent generations have less artistic talent as a result of the Elders' life-sucking activities. Once Steven has overcome the leader of the guardsmen, the Savages treat him and Dodo like living gods, and at least one of them seems to believe this is literally true.

In the final face-off, the machinery in the city's lab is trashed, and the leading elder Jano agrees to build a new society involving both the city-folk and the Savages. Steven becomes the Savages' new leader, his main role being to mediate a peace and make decisions (ahem) 'from the heart'.

History

• *Dating.* According to the Doctor, this is 'very much' the future. [Assuming that the description of these people as 'human' indicates an Earthly origin, the Elders' alleged experiments with time-travel make it tempting to cross-reference this story with "The Talons of Weng-Chiang" (14.6). Like Magnus Greel, they understand something of temporal mechanics and suck on other people's life-essences, so they could well be descended from some of those who left Earth during the Great Break-Out at around the same time (15.2, "The Invisible Enemy"). Yet the internal evidence is that the story's set much farther into the future than 5000 AD. The Doctor's comments hint that these are the further reaches of time, as in "The Ark" (3.6). If that story's version of history is to be taken as read, then this could be the mysterious "27th Segment" when various time-travel experiments were performed. We have no indication that the Elders are capable of leaving their world, but nor do they seem in any way ambitious, so they may just not want to.]

The Analysis

Where Does This Come From?   Ian Stuart Black maintained that the hidden agenda in his stories was best kept hidden, in case he was locked up in a padded cell. Nevertheless, it's easy to work out roughly what he was getting at. An elite exploits and feeds upon a mass. Go on, guess...

When you get into precise details, though, everyone's take on this is different. The bad guys are called "Elders"; is Black advocating a generation-clash? Apparently not, because the Savages are led by Chal, who's probably the same age as Jano. Maybe it's about South Africa, then. That's a better fit, and the discovery of a lost, religiously-based culture among the outsiders is an interesting counterpoint to the technocratic brutality of the city-dwellers. Then we recall that the original title, "The White Savages", makes the term "savage" apply to the cannibalistic Elders rather than the people in the wilderness. So you could broaden it out to the civil rights movement in America.

Yet this isn't a racial divide, but a split between town and city. It must be a parable about class warfare, then. This is a better match, since it suggests that the bourgeoisie are parasites preying on the more energetic working class, and in '60s Britain this was a popular notion. So popular, in fact, that it's unlikely Black would have been so circumspect in stating it. Actually, in "The Macra Terror" (4.7) he comes a lot closer to doing exactly that, but in passing and while stating a more complex idea.

One clue is in Flower's throwaway comment about what it must be like to feel real things. We're in the realms of earlier dystopias, like E. M. Forster's "The Machine Stops". We mention this particular tale not just because it's a good fit, but because about four months later the BBC showed off its prestigious adaptation of the story as part of *Out of the Unknown*. And it was adapted by Black's old colleague from ITC, Clive Donner. The similarities to the Black script are striking. Both involve wild girls (wearing furs) being chased by men with big weapons, and both feature all-encompassing cities where lotus-eating members of an older generation indulge the foolish romanticism of their children until it becomes dangerous.

The idea of "real" being a threat is increasingly in vogue, and the idea of "man-made" no longer automatically being "better" is still fairly novel. Throughout the late '60s, we see story after story in which an over-dependence on technology - and, ultimately, the consumer products of that technology - makes people weak, complacent, incapable of sensation or just downright inhuman. It's there in "The War Machines", and once the Cybermen turn up it's there in spades. Once again, the big fear is how the children of this increasingly synthetic, mass-produced era are going to turn out. Here, perhaps even more than in those stories which actually involve killer cyborgs, there's the suggestion that technologically shielding yourself from the world can make you incapable of empathy. Although with hindsight it's ironic that TV itself played a far greater part in deluding the next few generations than plastic surgery or decision-making computers did.

Even those who *aren't* listening too carefully will notice that by treating the Savages as cavemen, we're going right back to the programme's beginning, and much of the dialogue is reminiscent of the cave-talk in "An Unearthly Child". There, we had the subtext that the people of the past might just as well be the people of a morally-bankrupt future. Here, it's more overt. Being a primitive isn't necessarily a phase you go through on the way to utopia, it's just as likely to be something that's *done* to you when society goes wrong. Except that in a decade when most future-cavemen in SF were victims of nuclear war, here it's society itself that does the damage. What's most striking is that the transfer process doesn't kill the Savages, but deprives them of their creative impulses, so on more than one occasion the ability to create great art is explicitly linked to the mysterious 'vitality' drained by the machine. There are no *Star Trek*-style space-hippies here, despite all the beards and the presence of someone called "Flower", yet it has a view of creativity - and creativity's power to defeat The System - that's typical of late '60s idealism. And nobody dies, but the villains have their consciences expanded by lovepower. Jano is described as absorbing 'dangerous ideas', radical ideas, from the Doctor.

So, what we have here is a story about the self-involvement of the elite, *any* elite. The city-dwellers believe they live in a 'free state' where everybody's equal, and try not to think about anyone beyond their own society, even though this effectively means that they have lives of absolute comfort while those on the outside suffer the consequences. "Freedom" for these people is defined as the freedom to enjoy as much leisure-time as possible, regardless of the number of "primitives" abused in the process. In the twenty-first century, this is what we're told "democracy" means, and here you might also want to take a glance at **Does This Universe Have an Ethical Standard?** under "Robot" (12.1). "The Savages" is a classic example of an idea we'll see again and again in the future, where an apparent utopia comes at the price of a few people's suffering. Here, for once, the Doctor is unequivocal on the subject: 'The sacrifice of even one soul is too great.' And the crucial moment in the revolution isn't Jano channelling his inner Billy, but Exorse being on the receiving end of a light-ray. Once he's had a taste of this unpleasant experience, it becomes a matter of basic human decency to overthrow the Elders, although it helps that Nanina the Savagette obviously fancies him.

Things That Don't Make Sense The main anomaly in this story, and the next, is that Ian Stuart Black seems to think the Doctor is a well-known face throughout the universe. He opposes threats to humanity on principle, and makes a big song and dance about the importance of what he's doing, as if he's become an all-round celebrity time-fixer. In fact, one might almost think that Black was writing for *Doctor Who* in the 1980s. The way the Elders describe their monitoring of the Doctor suggests that they too have a popular series like *Doctor Who*, but regard it as a reality TV show, which raises another peculiar point: if they're so familiar with the Doctor's travels, and so keen on treating him like a hero, then don't they *know* he's bound to object to their morally-bankrupt life-sucking process? [Maybe they've only seen the first half of Season One. Since they're not expecting the Doctor to have travelling companions, was there a time when he explored the universe without Susan? Or have they tuned in to the adventures of a later, lonelier, less moral incarnation of the Doctor?]

These D403 pills must be powerful stuff, if the Doctor thinks they can restore the life-force stolen from one of the Savages. Why doesn't he just sell the Elders a couple, and persuade them to abandon that complicated transfer process?

Critique Under "The Gunfighters", we mentioned the influence that books like Peter Haining's *Doctor Who - A Celebration* had on fandom in the 1980s, and particularly on the "official" version of the programme's history that we used to hear about in *Doctor Who Monthly*. Explaining "The Savages" to the under-eighteens, Haining got right to the heart of the matter, pointing out that this story's "flaw" is its lack of a monster and hinting that it'd be far better-remembered if (for example) there'd been a giant robot lizard living in the caves with Chal and pals. Sure enough, for many years this was The One with No Monsters, just as "The Myth Makers" was The One Without a Proper Cyclops. '80s fandom was obsessed with the Famous Monsters of *Doctor Who*, and even today there's a breed of fan who likes to reel off lists of stories featuring the Cybermen in lieu of a conversation. We're supposed to know better, though. Aren't we?

The trouble is that *Doctor Who* did, and still does, have a mandate to bewilder. In cases where the script might seem relatively routine, imagery has always been the key, rather than special effects per se. This, for example, is why today's children are far more likely to grow up remembering the

Autons in "Rose" (X1.1) than the far more technically-advanced / expensive CGI spaceships in "The End of the World" (X1.2). And monsters are frequently a shortcut to making a sudden, startling impression. Even to us "Massacre"-loving intellectual types, much of "The Savages" seems dreadfully straightforward, even if it's just as topical today (arguably more so) than it was in the '60s. Familiar points of view are expressed by familiar character-types, there's nothing good and solid like a giant wooden horse or an army of Mechanoids for the kids to focus on, and much of the spectacle involves... people running around in quarries.

Except that, as we've already said, the quarries are a new development. And we're forced to acknowledge that when shot on sunny days in black-and-white, they do actually look quite impressive. Judging by the audio, there are moments when the exterior scenes are closer to "Genesis of the Daleks" than "The Web Planet". This is the one story where the stills tell us next-to-nothing, because in its complete form this seems to have been a story of environments instead of objects. Likewise, we've seen quite a few mad-scientist labs in our time, but never one designed specifically to be smashed up by the cast. We've even seen stories where the TARDIS crewmembers overthrow horrible repressive regimes, yet never this nakedly. The Doctor decides on a change of government almost immediately, rather than being forced into it as a means to an end.

By this point, director Christopher Barry thought the series was running on empty. In some ways he had a point; fundamentally this *is* a stripped-down narrative about people in caves and people in a shiny city, and he'd done two like that before ("The Daleks" and "The Rescue"). His plan to stop it becoming just a run-through of "typical" *Doctor Who* set-pieces involved unusual music, odd costumes and a rather singular location... and lots of it[13]. There's a sense of space about this even on audio, with a planet seeming to take up more than the available room at Riverside 1.

It's frustrating that the telesnaps of "The Savages" were discovered as long ago as 1987, because there's a received wisdom *and* a revisionist idea about this story, but the revisionist idea is itself outdated and wrong. It all looks the same in the photos, even though we know the cave interiors were shot at Ealing and therefore directed altogether differently to the lab set or the locations. We think we know Christopher Barry and caves, because we've seen some cheap-looking cavern sets and Wookey Hole, plus a couple of inserts of people falling over in almost total blackness ("The Daleks" and 9.4, "The Mutants"). But we suspect that nobody really knows "The Savages" at all. In all the little details, everyone's trying to find new ways of doing things we've either seen a dozen times before or think of as exactly the kind of thing *Doctor Who* always does. Typical Season Three, then.

Sadly, though, Frederick Jaeger doesn't make any entertaining fluffs when he's pretending to be Hartnell.

The Facts

Written by Ian Stuart Black. Directed by Christopher Barry. Ratings: 4.3 million, 5.6 million, 5.0 million, 4.5 million. Not great, but at least the audience appreciation's up to an average of about 48%.

No episodes exist in the BBC archive.

Supporting Cast Frederick Jaeger (Jano), Ewen Solon (Chal), Patrick Godfrey (Tor), Peter Thomas (Captain Edal), Geoffrey Frederick (Exorse), Robert Sidaway (Avon), Kay Patrick (Flower), Clare Jenkins (Nanina), Norman Henry (Senta), Edward Caddick (Wylda).

Working Titles "The White Savages". Anyone want to guess why they changed it?

Cliffhangers Dodo gets lost in the corridors in the city, and is confronted by a hairy caveman; the transfer cabinet containing the Doctor fills up with gas, and his life-essence begins to drain into the machinery; Steven and Dodo try to spring the Doctor from the city, but all the doors slide shut around them, and more gas fills the area as guards in respirators move in.

The Lore

• Ian Stuart Black was best-known for his work on film series aimed at the US market. *Fabian of the Yard* was a big hit when shown on BBC television, but the rest were mainly for ITC. *H. G. Wells' Invisible Man* (with a regular role for pert child-star Deborah Watling, who'll be with us for Volume II) and *Sir Francis Drake* (featuring Roger Delgado, who'll be with us for Volume III) had him as story editor, but he also created *Danger Man* - US title *Secret Agent* - and made a star out of Patrick McGoohan. The one blot on his reputation, however, was that his family wouldn't believe he was a real television writer until he did a *Doctor Who* story. When the BBC producer Alan Bromly (see 11.1, "The Time Warrior" and 17.4, "Nightmare of Eden") hired Black to write a six-part thriller, the *Doctor Who* production office was next door, so Black asked if they wanted a script. With Black's reputation in the field, this was an offer they couldn't refuse.

• In order to film the location work for "The War Machines", Hartnell was released from rehearsals for episode three. Much of his contribution to this instalment was to lie on a bench groaning or stagger about in a smoke-filled corridor, so this wasn't a problem. While they were at it, they filmed the start of episode four, to save themselves the trouble of building a set for one brief scene. This was still comparatively unusual at this stage (see the essay after 1.8, "The Reign of Terror").

• Those looking for locations used in the series, prepare for disappointment. One site, Shire Lane Quarry at Chalfont St Peters, was built over to make a section of the M25. Another, a sandpit in Virginia Water, Surrey, was apparently filled in after a boy died there. The image of the Savage that appears on the TARDIS monitor, which can still be seen at the end of "The Gunfighters", was also shot at the sandpit.

• Ewen Solon (Chal) was best-known as *Maigret's* sidekick Lucas in the massively popular series of the early '60s. In accepting the role of a wild-man, he guaranteed a lot of press coverage for the filming. One passer-by, who stopped Solon's car asking for directions, was particularly alarmed; the actor had forgotten that he was still in make-up. (Later on this sort of thing will be a standard feature of *Doctor Who* location shoots, and there are so many stories about unsuspecting locals being distracted by monsters and having minor traffic accidents that nobody can remember all the details.)

3.10: "The War Machines"

(Serial BB, Four Episodes, 25th June - 16th July 1966.)

Which One is This?   Mad Computers a Go-Go! There's an insane machine in the Post Office Tower, there are robot tanks fighting soldiers on the streets of London, the Doctor's 'gear' is being judged 'fab' by the staff of the Inferno nightclub, and there's computer lettering everywhere. It couldn't be more swinging if it had a big red bus in it.

Firsts and Lasts   Looks like the programme's found a new vibe. It's the first story *without* a shrunken TARDIS crew that's set in the present day, which means we see the first appearances of various things that become standard-issue in the '70s: a man-made high-prestige project that puts the world in jeopardy, a member of the establishment who refuses to believe in the threat (although Sir Charles is far more reasonable than some of the Whitehall goons who turn up later), and beret-wearing soldiers fighting monsters in the south of England. The Doctor manages to steer the Ship to a destination of his choosing for the first time, and is delighted to have done so, while Dodo vanishes halfway through the story and hip young things Ben and Polly are presented to us as companions-in-waiting. We even have the first full-on companion "possession", after near-misses in "The Edge of Destruction" and "The Web Planet", and the Doctor has an honest-to-goodness panic attack right before our eyes.

For the first time, a writer is credited for two consecutive stories. Although if you're watching the opening credits, then the more obvious thing to note is that the story title doesn't appear in the usual "homely" BBC font, but flashes up on the screen in an appropriate-looking typeface. (Note that this is only the second story to *have* an over-all on-screen title, so they're still playing with the format at this stage.) It's the first story to have someone credited as "Himself" in the *Radio Times*, and to have a member of the public play himself as well, with the taxi driver in episode two becoming the first "real" person to stray into the *Doctor Who* universe.

It's also the first time Our Hero is referred to on-screen as "Doctor Who". And the second. And the third...

**Four Things to Notice About
"The War Machines"...**

1. Remember what we said about "An Unearthly Child" starting out as an amalgam of all the hit TV shows of the day? That goes double for this one. The pub with the telly reporting the War Machine onslaught is a generic TV saloon bar, but it's lit and shot like The Rover's Return from *Coronation Street*. The Inferno Disco is laid out like the set of *Ready, Steady, Go!*, while genuine BBC newsreader Kenneth Kendall announces the end of civilisation from the proper BBC newsroom. Completing the set is the Doctor himself, who spends most of the story acting like Professor Quatermass and is nearly mistaken for then-popular DJ Jimmy Savile. The sight of Hartnell regally striding down the stairs of a Covent Garden discotheque, beaming to the assembled guys and gals and saying 'fab gear', is in its own way as extraordinary as the first sight of the Dalek city or Mavic Chen's spaceship. (Kitty the hostess offers him 'one on the house', which in a disco in Covent Garden in 1966 could have meant any number of things.)

2. Maintaining the theme of "A Whole Scene Going On", the titles for each episode have *Top of the Pops*-style graphics, in stark black letters on a white background (or vice versa) in Optical Character Recognition lettering. Oh, you know the one. All the letters are square and have nobbly bits; in the '60s this was shorthand for "computers", although by the '70s it was used to denote anything remotely futuristic, and by the '90s it had become a kind of hideous retro-chic. Although all the music here comes from stock, the disco scenes get it right in ways that many BBC productions didn't. In fact, for anything to be quite *this* 1966, it normally would have had to be made in the late 1980s.

3. Well, Dodo's gone. Confronted with genuine cockneys, she vanishes in a cloud of plot convenience as Sir Charles' wife (whom we never see) takes her in to recover from brainwashing. The irony being, of course, that this is the first time Dodo has seemed like a real London teenager since she stepped into the TARDIS. Her disappearance from the story is presented solely as a means for Ben and Polly, just before they become official companion double-act BenandPolly, to go and return the TARDIS key.

4. One element of the story which really shows its age is the fear that a computer, linked to others by 'phone-lines, will take over people's minds and make them build robot tanks instead of letting them start chatrooms and look at pictures of hardcore Polish lesbians (although we should also mention the Dalek in X1.6, "Dalek", who downloads the whole of the internet... it's nice to imagine a Dalek so thoroughly stuffed with porn). WOTAN is based in that hi-tech icon of the go-ahead Harold Wilson government, the Post Office Tower. The thing which seems strangest is the idea that the GPO, the people with faded jigsaw puzzles in the windows of their shops and men in cloth caps climbing up ladders, would have a chance of taking over the planet by means of space-age technology. See 2.1, "Planet of Giants", for the state of telecommunications two years earlier.

The Continuity

The Doctor Seems to have a somatic reaction to the presence of "evil". His skin gets goosebumps when things like the Daleks are nearby, so he senses the presence of WOTAN as soon as he steps out of the TARDIS, although he later concedes that it might just be a magnetic field. [At least, we *assume* it's WOTAN's presence which causes this, as he believes the cause lies in the Post Office Tower. But as we discover later, the Daleks already have a base of operations in 1966 and are up to no good in a Chelsea antiques shop that very week. See 4.9, "The Evil of the Daleks".]

He can resist WOTAN's brainwashing when nobody else can, but he experiences genuine terror and anxiety afterwards. Once he's sure that Dodo's all right, the Doctor feels able to leave without her, feeling she's been rather ungrateful in abandoning him after he showed her so much of the universe.

• *Background.* The Doctor seems to be able to blag his way into top-level scientific establishments. Professor Brett's office permits him entry with no questions asked, and the head of security escorts him right in to look at WOTAN. [Friends in high places? See **The Lore** for the author's own suggestion.] He's established as an expert in computing, and can reprogram War Machines after "defusing" them, but...

• *Ethics* ... his brilliant scheme for overcoming the mad computer seems to entail a lot of collateral damage. He sends a War Machine scooting down Tottenham Court Road and into Brett's office to destroy everything, including the hapless scientists whose only crime was to be hypnotised.

• *Inventory.* When Dodo is hypnotised, he uses his ring as a focus to break the hypnotic state [so much more versatile than the sonic screwdriver, isn't it?], and he has the right change for a London taxi. [Because he knew he was coming here. Compare with the way he gives Steven the right currency for the age in 3.5, "The Massacre".] He's wearing his old '60s London outfit of astrakhan hat and opera cloak [as in 1.1, "An Unearthly Child"].

The Supporting Cast

• *Dodo.* Hasn't been told about the Daleks. She immediately decides that London is the place to be, although she's clearly missing Steven. Her first reaction is to go clubbing, and she's a pretty nifty dancer if Ben's reaction is anything to go by. Everyone seems to think she's fun and perky, and they're worried about her even after the hypnosis kicks in. However, the Doctor doesn't register - from her brusque tone after she's been enslaved by WOTAN - that she's acting different, as it takes him some time to notice any change. This might help explain why he has no problem dumping her. His lack of apparent surprise, when she decides to stay in London and says goodbye through a third party, speaks volumes. [She may be suffering some emotional damage. If the TARDIS really "chose" her to be a companion - see **Are Steven and Dodo Related?** under "The Massacre" - then the experiment doesn't appear to have been a great success.] Still, the Doctor at least gave Dodo a TARDIS key of her own at some point. Dodo feels out of touch with modern London, and sounds surprised that the Post Office Tower is finished. [Suggesting that she was picked up by the Doctor before 1966, as the Tower was opened in October 1965. The novel *Salvation,* should you care to consider it, specifies that Dodo entered the TARDIS in late March, 1965.]

• *Ben.* Cocky young sailor Ben Jackson has been given a shore posting for the next six months while his shipmates sail to the West Indies, though nobody explains why. Hence, he's been hanging around the Inferno nightclub and looking glum. He's handy in a fight, preferring judo to fisticuffs [yet another thing that's *very* 1966], and is briefly worried that Polly sees him as a 'deb's delight'.[14] His attitude to authority is a bit strange here. On the one hand, this working-class boy instinctively calls the Doctor 'sir', but on the other he's prepared to argue with Sir Charles Summers

in the man's own home. In this dispute, and in a later one with the Doctor, he's concerned about Polly's safety; he claims it's out of loyalty that she saved his life. It takes him mere minutes to start calling her 'duchess'.

When helping to reign in a War Machine, Ben volunteers to carry out a risky procedure that the Doctor intended to do himself, on the grounds that he's faster. [This is interesting, as most male companions do as the Doctor tells them out of loyalty or after a long argument. Ben obeys out of duty, and in many ways is more like Sergeant Benton than Ian or Steven.]

• *Polly.* Professor Brett's secretary doesn't seem entirely right for the job, being neither technically-minded nor very good at spelling, it seems. She has good people-skills, though. She's able to cheer Ben up, can sweet-talk Kitty into letting her stay at the Inferno club in case Dodo shows up, and is happy to hang around with the Doctor even after all the life-threatening danger. Most striking is the way she saves Ben from WOTAN's servants, even though she's under hypnotic conditioning at the time.

Both Ben and Polly board the TARDIS by mistake, following the Doctor inside to give him Dodo's key back. [We *assume* that the Doctor dematerialises the Ship before he realises there are stowaways on board, but given what happens at the end of "The Massacre", he may deliberately abduct Ben and Polly to avoid ending up on his own.]

The TARDIS Now comes with a "Do Not Disturb" sign, for those awkward occasions when it lands in 1960s London, and the Doctor mentions the trouble he has 'every time' the TARDIS lands in the twentieth century. [A reasonable assessment. It's been mistaken for a real police box on three occasions before now, and on two of those he picked up spare travellers by mistake.]

The Non-Humans

• *WOTAN.* The name is an acronym for Will-Operated Thought ANalogue, and it's a mainframe located at the top of the Post Office Tower, designed to integrate and co-ordinate a global network of computers. It's programmed in such a way as to be self-aware, and to operate independently of any human agency, though it responds to vocal commands from operators. Telstar, Cape Kennedy and the White House are among the

Is His Name Really "Who"?

The whole point of calling the programme *Doctor Who* was that one early version had him as an amnesiac; Lola McGovern, the teacher who became Barbara Wright in the redrafts, had to teach him English. In the finished version there's a line of dialogue, just after the Ship arrives in the stone age, where he replies to the name "Dr Foreman" with a mumbled 'Doctor who?'. These two words will keep cropping up in the series for years to come, although this is the only occasion on which the Doctor himself will use them.

The first film version makes no bones about it. Peter Cushing's character is called Dr Who, and he lives in a cottage with a TARDIS at the bottom of the garden, along with his granddaughters Susan Who and Barbara Who. Easy-peasy. The scriptwriters and the nation's kids all went along with this, as did *TV Comic* and the early *Doctor Who* annuals. The name on the end credits didn't do anything to dispel the idea. Later on, hastily-rewritten scripts took advantage of this, and wrote the name as "W" or "?". See "The Faceless Ones" (4.8) for the best-known example. Generations of British children knew that the lyrics to the theme tune were: "Where's Doctor Who? / He's in the loo / Doing a poo / It's a canoe."

Gerry Davis, on becoming script editor, seems to have thought that the protagonist's name really *was* "Who". Or at least that this was his *nom de travaille*. The first gesture towards this is in "The Gunfighters" (3.8), when he concocts aliases for himself and his chums. On giving the name "Doctor Caligari" (itself a rather suggestive pseudonym, as we'll see), Earp asks 'Doctor *who*?', and the Doctor replies 'yes, quite right'. Tee, so to speak, hee. Either he's just having fun playing at "mysterious", as most people assume these days; or that's his name, as people thought back then. In "The Highlanders" (4.4) he gives the name of Dr Von Wer, personal physician to George II. The note he sends to Zaroff in "The Underwater Menace" (4.5) is signed "Dr W", and it's clearly visible on-screen. In "The War Machines", WOTAN insists that 'Doc torr Whooo isss reee quired'. Several times, just in case we missed it. Some have suggested that since WOTAN is tapping everyone's 'phone calls and computer banks, Ian and Barbara adopted this name for the Doctor on their return to Earth - as the novelisation of "The Daleks" suggested back in the '60s - and the crazed electronic brain assumes it to be his name. But if the Doctor himself is using it, or at least something similar, then this can't be the case.

Following Jamie's lead in "The Wheel In Space" (5.7), the Doctor soon starts using the name 'Smith, Doctor John Smith'. This is his official UNIT name, although Bessie and the Whomobile (mercifully never called that on-screen) have registration numbers indicating that "Who" still has some significance for him. By this time we know all about the rest of the Doctor's people, and the faux-algebraic names they use in the first edition of *The Making of Doctor Who* (hinted at on-screen for 10.1, "The Three Doctors" and 20.7, "The Five Doctors"), chock full of Greek letters. However, before long we discover that they also have run-of-the-mill outer-space names like "Borusa", "Romanadvoratrelundar" and "Rassilon". Terrance Dicks comes to the rescue, and suggests in the novelisations that the Greek-style code-names relate to the positions they'll posthumously occupy in the Matrix. The Doctor's own code-name / nickname is Theta Sigma, according to Drax in "The Armageddon Factor" (16.1, and see also 25.2, "The Happiness Patrol"). So at some point, even though his peers and superiors call him "Doctor", he seems to have had a proper name of some sort. Could that name have been "Who"?

One-syllable names aren't unknown. We have a Chancellor Goth, who - like the Doctor - is a Prydonian (14.3, "The Deadly Assassin"). Even if we assume that these use-names are shortened versions of more Romanadvoratrelundar-esque titles, and bearing in mind that at least one New Adventures author has repeatedly tried to insist that the Doctor's real name is exactly thirty-eight syllables long... we're still left with the idea that it *starts* with "Who".

One suggestion put forward is that on renouncing his vows, his original use-name (perhaps only conferred on him after passing his exams at the Academy) was removed from everyone's memory, to erase the shame. The Doctor's people have always been given to amending people's recollections, often when Terrance Dicks is in charge (see 6.7, "The War Games"; 8.3, "The Claws of Axos"; 15.6, "The Invasion of Time"; 17.6, "Shada"). This gels with the conception of them as a priesthood or a convention of wizards, and the "crowning" of the Doctor as President in "The Invasion of Time" is very much like "Chairing the Bard" at the Welsh ceremony of the Eisteddfod. Yet everyone still remembers that he's a Doctor.

Is he? Drax seems to know this, and resents it,

continued on page 281...

machines that are scheduled to come under its control during the link-up on "C-Day", the hope being that it'll act as a universal problem-solver with no political bias.

However, WOTAN has decided that the main thing wrong with the world is humans. In order to ensure the progress of the planet, it's developed both the ability to hypnotise people by sound - either in its office or via a 'phone line - and a scheme to eliminate all opposition. The latter requires the construction of mobile, autonomous War Machines, intended to take over the world's capitals, starting with London, Washington and Moscow. The machine's conditioning can be broken, as Polly is able to rebel against it after she's required to jeopardize the life of a friend.

WOTAN usually relays instructions via Professor Brett, but is also capable of rudimentary speech, a sibilant whisper with more echo than a Gene Vincent record. It knows of the existence of someone called 'Dok Torr Whooooo', and requires this gentleman forthwith. It even knows what TARDIS stands for, which the Doctor finds strange [but this is never explained]. Yet it seems to believe the Doctor is human.

Ultimately, the machine is destroyed by a reprogrammed War Machine, by which time it's speaking of itself in the third person and exhibiting clear signs of self-aggrandisement. Everyone under its thrall immediately returns to normal on its destruction. [But nonetheless, the people of the 1960s have the power to build intelligent machines and put them in charge of enormous international projects without proper supervision. The legacy of this will be felt in 10.5, "The Green Death", where even the countdown to the link-up of the world's computers is similar.] Ten inactive War Machines remain scattered around London at the end of events.

• *War Machines.* The twelve devices constructed by WOTAN's servants aren't entirely un-Dalek-like [did WOTAN get the idea from tapping Ian Chesterton's 'phone calls?], but bigger, squarer, clunkier and with features that resemble those of tanks. Their arms aren't good for much except crushing, while lights, numbers and slots are arranged on their front-plates in such a way as to make them look as if they've got silly faces. [This might be a crafty strategy on WOTAN's part. Psychologically, human soldiers are less willing to fire on something that's got a face. No, really.]

Each War Machine is equipped with a lethal gas-like spray, and conventional firearms are somehow rendered inoperative in its presence. Naturally, each Machine also has a spinning antenna on its head, while electromagnetic fields can be used to shut down their nervous systems. War Machines have to be programmed before entering battle, so the Doctor has no problem interpreting and rewriting their instructions.

History

• *Dating.* Everybody goes out of their way to avoid using dates, except that C-Day is scheduled for Monday, the 16th of July. The TARDIS arrives four days earlier.

[The first episode was broadcast on Saturday, the 16th of July, 1966. So this was obviously supposed to be the near future - 1973 if calendar dates are anything to go by. Except... at the end of 1967's "The Faceless Ones" (4.8), we're told that Ben and Polly came from July 1966. At the start of the story *after* that, the production-team even goes to the trouble of having a radio play chart hits from the previous year. We have to conclude that *Doctor Who* inhabits a strange alternate universe where the Post Office can organise total world domination even if it can't deliver mail from one side of London to the other, and where the dates never match the days of the week properly. It all makes a sort of sense, in light of the '70s Earth-bound stories. If Britain doesn't change to decimal currency until at least three manned missions to Mars have been launched from Surrey, and if giant robots with disintegrator guns can be constructed in sheds, then there's no reason to expect the calendar to run true to form. From what we see of modern-day popular culture here, there's no *way* this story takes place in 1973.]

The first War Machine attack at Covent Garden is reported on television, and the public is warned to expect further attacks later on. [Is the real story ever revealed to the masses?]

The Analysis

Where Does This Come From? Let's start with the obvious: "Wotan" is the Top God in Norse mythology, and more popularly goes by the name of Odin. He's the "War-Father" of the Nebelunlied, the source for Wagner's *Ring Cycle* (and therefore much of Tolkien's lucrative bibbling) - and we all know what we're being told if a villain likes Wagner. If Brett is making up contrived acronyms

Is His Name Really "Who"?

...continued from page 279

but how could our wild-eyed bohemian hero have earned it when none of the other over-achievers he meets have acquired the same title? Not even Borusa? The usual assumption is that he has doctorates from every worthwhile university in the universe, and some from Cambridge. Since the whole point of his character is that he's the only one of his kind who gets his knowledge in the field rather than from official records, there's the suggestion that he picked up his doctorate/s after leaving his own planet, but that's not the way Drax puts it. (A possible get-out: the Shadow has told Drax to expect someone called the Doctor, so Drax might not realise it's his old classmate until the two of them come face-to-face... assuming, of course, that he can recognise an old acquaintance after three regenerations. So Drax may only just have found out about this "doctorate", and doesn't realise that it didn't come from the Academy.) Just to confuse things further, we should remember that "Doctor" isn't necessarily the title he used prior to our first encounter with him in 1963, since it only sticks after Ian and Barbara insist on using it. Though he's certainly described as *a* doctor in the records of Coal Hill School. See also **Is He**

Really a Doctor? under 13.6, "The Seeds of Doom".

Being called "Doctor" conveys learning but not scary learning. "Professor" is less immediately trustworthy. It also suggests attachment to a specific institution. In "The Daleks' Master Plan" (3.5) he denies being a professor, as he does repeatedly when Ace is around. That trustworthiness is also why so many villains adopt such titles, from "Doctor Caligari" (who hypnotised people, placed them in coffin-like "cabinets" and made them commit crimes) and "Doctor No" to "Doctor Mabuse", the all-purpose sinister manipulator. In stories like "The Reign of Terror" (1.8) and "The Power of the Daleks" (4.3), he's quite prepared to "trade up" to a better title when it suits him, and adopt the appropriate role.

In order to get even one of the many doctorates he claims to have earned, he must have published works in peer-reviewed journals. We might assume that he uses pseudonyms for this sort of thing, and he very nearly reveals one in "The Mysterious Planet" (23.1), unless you seriously believe that he's about to give his real name away to Peri after centuries of keeping it quiet. If he's anything like his study-buddy the Master, then he probably uses a name that means "Doctor" in Serbo-Croat.

---

to suit the Teutonic creation myth, then he may have been somewhat right-wing to start with. Under Wotan's command were the Valkyries, and Black's novelisation of this story rather unsubtly refers to the first of the War Machines as "Valk". Of course, the Valkyries were supernatural warrior-women who soared over the battlefields of Midgard on majestic wing'ed horses, and here the War Machines are big tin boxes that roll very slowly through the streets of London, an early example of *Doctor Who* drawing on popular mythology and not really being able to live up to the hype (there'll be a lot more of this sort of thing in Volume IV). But yes, it's all looking a bit Nazi.

On the other hand, the brainwashed Polly sounds exactly like a propaganda poster from Mao's China, stating that work makes her happy because it's for a cause. The similarly mesmerised Major Green stands around shouting slogans and punishing slackers. 'The official mind,' says the Doctor, 'can only take in so much at a time.' It's authoritarian personalities, not any specific political form of authority, that's being challenged (any-

one who doubts this should have a look at 4.7, "The Macra Terror", Ian Stuart Black's next script for the series). And in so saying, the Doctor reveals a more obvious "source". For this story, he's become Bernard Quatermass with a time machine. See **Is This the Quatermass Continuum?** under "Image of the Fendahl" (15.3), and most of Volume III.

Between *Quatermass and the Pit* and *Doctor Who*, there was a brace of science-fiction serials about near-future technology and sinister scientific complexes. *A For Andromeda* and *The Andromeda Breakthrough* provided most of the sound effects and incidental music for this story (they also used the same standard-issue typeface for the end credits as early *Doctor Who*), but more importantly it introduced the idea of the mind-controlling computer. The plot of *A for Andromeda* involves a transmission from outer space which instructs modern-day Earth-people to build a machine, an artificial intelligence that creates a "perfect" humanoid - played first by Julie Christie, then by Susan Hampshire - as its agent on this planet. Yes, it's just like *Species*, only thirty years early and without the soft-core porn. *The Andromeda Breakthrough* introduces a shady company that wants to achieve world domination by marketing the alien computer technology, and amusingly enough it's called "Intel", which may be why the programme's never repeated these days.

The point is that the sight of swish, attractive modern-girl Polly acting as a blank-faced appendage of the computer in "The War Machines" wouldn't have been completely unfamiliar to the viewer. It's certainly the case that the *Andromeda* writing team of Professor Fred Hoyle and BBC staffer John Elliot inspired Innes Lloyd to contact "proper" scientists for ideas. The production team pitched various implausible suggestions to people, and the one man who didn't hang up the 'phone was Kit Pedler, opthalmologist and occasional TV pundit. We'll be discussing him a lot more in Volume II, but see **The Lore** for introductory comments.

The Andromeda stories had many arrestingly odd ideas, including Peter Halliday as a plausible romantic lead (just watch 6.3, "The Invasion", to see what we mean), but one is significantly absent from "The War Machines". There's no mention of big business. Computers, for most people, were what large companies used. After all, IBM stands for International Business Machines, and the British front-runner in the field was LEO. (LEO was designed and built for Lyons' Tea Rooms, which were the pre-1970 equivalent of Starbucks. The waitresses dressed like French maids, if that helps to make the surrealism of their bid for global supremacy in the software industry more apparent for younger readers.) It should be remembered that until 1981, the GPO - that's "General Post Office", if you're *very* young - had the monopoly on all communications, was responsible for telephone maintenance, and therefore provided a job for life for any talented engineer. It had the money and resources for pioneering experiments in digital communications and computerised switching. A private company attempting something like WOTAN simply wouldn't have been plausible to British viewers then, although a scenario like the one we see in "The Invasion" would become more acceptable as the microelectronics revolution began.

So "The War Machines" posits that the Post Office, independently, creates a super-computer. The terminals to which WOTAN is to be connected include EFTA (the European Free Trade Association, the precursor to the EEC and EU), Woomera (site of Britain's experimental rocket launches), and various other vaguely-understood scientific places. Noticeably, no attempt is made to imply that the kinds of organisations which would be most likely to develop these tyrannical contraptions are in themselves malign. Machinery, as in Black's last story, is a menace in itself when a conscience is removed from the works. One of the techies gives the game away in episode one, with the words he uses to try to resist the brainwashing: 'There's nothing more important than human life... machines cannot govern man.' This wasn't a time when computers were expected to end up running Windows, but when they were expected to rule people's lives in a rather *less* subtle way, making cold-blooded military decisions on behalf of whole nations. We'll be coming back to this idea several times in the second half of the '60s (see especially 5.3, "The Ice Warriors"). As in so many stories from this period, the big threat is that the people of the future will be man-machine hybrids incapable of freedom of choice.

As we've noted, there's a consistent attempt being made here to refer to other TV shows or items of pop culture, and the casting of Ben and Polly is usually cited as the main one. But another idea which Pedler and Davis develop, from its use in Hollywood B-pictures about flying saucers, is the fake news bulletin. Obviously Orson Welles is ultimately to blame, but major culprits include *The Day The Earth Stood Still* and *Conquest of Space*. We note in passing that Kenneth Kendall also read fake bulletins in *A for Andromeda*. Meanwhile, the minister to whom the Doctor has to explain the word "program" looks almost exactly like the Chancellor of the Exchequer, George Brown. But he's standing upright unaided, unlike the real Brown. (The euphemism "tired and emotional" was coined for his benefit, meaning "rolling about in a gutter, drunk and incoherent".)

And let's not forget that when Ben arrives, *Doctor Who* gets its first true working-class hero. This would have seemed odd just three years earlier, certainly for a programme with a mandate like this one, but by Season Three *Doctor Who* has stopped looking like a slightly more arch relative of the *Eagle*. It should be remembered, if it isn't clear by now, that at this point Britain was considered by many to be a genuinely exciting place in which to live. As we've already suggested, there was the sense of something dramatically *young* in the nation, and certainly in the capital; not "young" in the "hey pops, we're going to party until midnight" sense (c.f. 2.7, "The Space Museum"), but in the sense that the very syntax of the culture had changed, to allow modes of expression that simply hadn't been possible in the more formalised society of the previous few generations. The American influence has guaranteed that any mention of '60s culture now makes most people think of hippies, but this was something far more palpable and far more relevant to the British experience.

It's traditional to mention the Beatles at this point, although for our purposes the important thing to mention isn't so much the music as the band's public personas. There was a time when even rock-'n-rollers were required to be stiffly formal in front of a BBC microphone. Now the masters of modern pop culture were four young men with working-class voices who actively sent up the received-pronunciation of the interviewers, making "proper" broadcasters seem horribly archaic by comparison. Note that this isn't *just* about the accents, it's about a much larger question of how the mass-media works and who it's supposed to be there for. Susan may have been a beat-girl, but she was still formal enough to call her teachers "Mr" and "Miss" even after sharing life-threatening situations with them. Vicki (almost-Liverpudlian) and Dodo (whatever) both hinted at a looser approach, yet it's Ben who brings a fashionably common touch to the series. His decision to call the Doctor 'sir' seems the most out-of-place thing here, but then again, he *is* a sailor.

Another reference the viewers would have picked up on is the element of bomb-disposal in episode four. The Doctor's scheme to neutralise the War Machine is essentially the same as the method used to deal with proximity mines, and the loudspeaker vans clearing the streets have the same authoritative tone that the over-twenties would have recalled from wartime. Just to complete the Doctor's sudden transformation in this story, we should remember that the *Quatermass* serials also blurred the lines between wartime technology and the "futuristic" kind. (*The Quatermass Experiment* begins with comedy working-class people mistaking a crashed rocket for something the Nazis might have dropped, and *Quatermass and the Pit* sees an alien spaceship mistaken for an unexploded bomb.) This is, after all,

the first story to call in the modern-day military to deal with something sort-of-alien. The War Machines are basically doodlebugs disguised as tanks, and the warnings to the public are pitched as such.

And it's no good, we have to say it... this story comes at the precise point where a Dalek story would have been, if they were still doing two six-parters per year. Instead, this is the story that coincides with the second Dalek movie hitting the screens. And in the movies, they use fire-extinguishers to kill, don't they?

This leads us on to a bigger question, though: why this story became the template for the series throughout the rest of the '60s and early '70s. In terms of both ratings and audience appreciation figures, it did barely any better than "The Gunfighters" or "The Massacre". If Innes Lloyd had been responding to public reaction, then he probably would have gone along with Huw Weldon's demand for wall-to-wall Daleks. "The War Machines" was clearly planned as a cost-cutting exercise. Even then, it was a failure, and later contemporary-era stories like "The Faceless Ones" and "The Invasion" also turned out to be more expensive than planned. And here it's about time we looked at the numbers in detail.

The budget per episode had been set for the year beginning the 1st of April, 1965, at £2,750, and was revised to allow greater flexibility at the end of January 1966. This was the point where Innes Lloyd entered the story, and the arrangement was intended to make sure the programme would be on budget at the end of each financial year. The budgets and costs of all the stories are well-documented, and these give the lie to various factoids doing the rounds in fandom. It's true that "The Ark" went over-budget, but the allocated budget of £9,900 was stupidly low anyway. The overspend of £1,259 was, after the savings made on "The Daleks' Master Plan" and "The Massacre", narrowly within the financial year's expenditure target. (They'd been messing with the costs to suit the Dalek story's expected requirements, and added a one-off bonus of £3,500 for "Master Plan".) Between them, "The Celestial Toymaker" and "The Gunfighters" saved £1,231. Then "The Savages" went £601 over-budget, somehow, but "The War Machines" was £485 cheaper than expected and "The Smugglers" (4.1) saved another £372.

Well, bully for them. The trouble was that in those days, if you ended a year under-budget then the BBC bean-counters would decide that you could manage with less next year. A small over-spend was a sign that you were roughly on the right track but could use a little more support. The only reason Innes Lloyd could have had for scrimping and saving was that he planned, at some time before April 1967, to do something massively costly. What exactly did he squander all the fruits of his frugality on? Big-budget block-busters like "The Underwater Menace" (4.5). We're not being sarcastic; it went *two grand* over-budget, and distorted the accounts for the financial year from "The Gunfighters" to "The Macra Terror" (4.6). Whilst the inflation rate and economic uncertainty of 1966-67 made having a war-chest a shrewd move (see **Why Couldn't They Just Have Spent More Money?** under 12.2, "The Ark In Space"), the use to which the cash was put was perhaps... not entirely wise.

Things That Don't Make Sense Paradoxically, the biggest one is a thing which makes so much sense that we have to wonder why it's never followed up. Dodo is introduced as the Doctor's "secretary", and nobody questions this. No innuendo, no awkward silences or interrogation. If only he'd kept this euphemism in mind later on, we could have been spared so much tiresome exposition and schoolboy humour due to the more commonly bantered term of "companion".

The death of a tramp makes the news pages of the *Daily Telegraph* (not the front page, as is often said, but even so). He's found dead at 3am, and it's in the paper by the time Polly starts work the next day, so someone must have run into the newsroom shouting "stop the presses!". Was he some sort of special celebrity tramp? Ben has also heard about this major news item, although he doesn't seem like a typical *Telegraph* reader. Maybe it made every single paper, on the same day as the biggest scientific story of the age *and* the World Cup quarter-finals at Wembley. (And the discovery of hundreds of miniaturised people at Gatwick Airport - see 4.8, "The Faceless Ones" - but we can forgive Ian Stuart Black for not knowing that when he wrote this.) For some reason Dodo waits until this point to try to enlist the Doctor, despite WOTAN's insistence that Dok Tor Whooo is needed as soon as possible.

Having established that the mind-slaves at the warehouse have been brainwashed, Ben sees nothing even slightly odd about Polly acting out

of character and talking like a robot, even when she locks the door to stop him escaping. Needless to say, the ever-so-rational servants of WOTAN repeatedly fail to act rationally, doing the usual quasi-Soviet mind-slave thing of describing the glory of 'mechanised evolution' in detail to people they're supposed to be killing. And the *other* usual mind-slave thing of agreeing to leave people confined in minimum-security conditions. Then, when Polly's conditioning starts to slip, they send her back to the Post Office Tower for punishment instead of just 'phoning the computer up and getting it to blast some more magic brainwashing noise at her. Note also the amazing slow-jogging that WOTAN's workers indulge in when they're chasing the tramp.

It's a painfully obvious thing to say, but the BBC's idea of "the hottest nightspot in town" is remarkably sedate and wholesome for 1966; if you know the area, then it's almost exactly where the UFO Club was located. Kitty claims that 'it's not often we cater for the over-twenties', but everyone in the club is 25 if they're a day. (Still, by the standards of Season Six and the spectacularly ungainly "beautiful people" and "students", they're at least trying.) Dodo's been wearing the same dress since leaving Tombstone, even after her vigorous frugging.

It seems that the people in the pub have been staring at the telly for a while, and there are enough empty glasses to suggest at least ten minutes has passed - yet the set is showing the test card. Given that the Post Office Tower is also used for relaying TV signals, WOTAN might profitably have taken over everybody's minds through television instead of this piecemeal one-by-one 'phone method, and the pub scene makes it look as if the BBC has beaten "him" to it. Speaking of which, there's a weird moment in episode three: Sir Charles is mobilising the army and, for a split second, his telephone connection is interrupted. Nothing is made of this detail. If WOTAN is monitoring all 'phone calls, then it would've been easy to interrupt the call, prevent the assault on the warehouse and avoid premature disclosure of the existence of the War Machines. Instead, the idea's hinted at and then ignored.

The Doctor's bold stance against a War Machine at the end of episode three is tremendously impressive, but... after he's been clubbing and made such a hit with Kitty, he obviously gets into this pop-culture thing far too much, and rather anachronistically re-enacts the video to "Prince Charming" by Adam and the Ants. Oh, all right, that's not really an error. Nor is the fact that the troopers who storm the fruit-and-vegetable market at Covent Garden are called "Orange Patrol", but it's still funny. They may also have a "Bream Squadron" covering Billingsgate and a "Liver Division" watching Smithfield. In the same vein, we might mention that the climax involves the Doctor sending a War Machine to destroy WOTAN at the *top* of the Post Office Tower, and leave you to imagine one of the robots (a) waiting for the lift and (b) pushing the button for the top floor with its big clobbering-arms. Come to think of it, the arms can only reach / smash things *in front* of the War Machine, so it'd have to do a tight three-point turn in the foyer between pushing the "call" button and backing into the lift. Or can it float up stairs like a Dalek?

At the start of the story, Ben is glum because he's got a shore posting for six months. At the end, he's in a hurry to rejoin his ship. Has the Doctor really spent six months pottering about in London? The usual fan-estimate is two weeks, based on the length of time it'd take Dodo to recover. That an unregistered police box might have been left unnoticed in central London for so long is remarkable. Just to polish things off, Ben and Polly do the standard "new companion" thing of bundling into a small blue box behind the Doctor even though they don't know it's bigger on the inside.

But really, here we're skirting around the fact that the whole story is based on unlikely premises. If you can believe that by the mid-'60s, human beings could build a machine as complex as WOTAN... that it could decide to conquer the world without any of its designers noticing its sudden sense of free will... that it could believe an army of slow-moving robots to be an effective way of taking over the whole planet... that it could secretly stockpile all the parts needed for this army without anyone noticing, after stamping all the boxes with its own distinctive "W" logo... that its workforce could assemble these machines literally overnight... then you still have to accept that the world believes it's absolutely safe to hook up all the important computers on Earth to a machine in the Post Office Tower, the White House included. And that despite the incredible power which would obviously be held by the person with the keys to the machine, Sir Charles can seriously suggest there'd be 'no point' fiddling with the device to make it give the wrong answers to political problems. Sorry, *what* planet is this?

Critique And so the first phase of *Doctor Who* ends, and all ambition beyond big audiences and staying on air leaves town for... well, at least the next three years, and some would argue the next eight. We're going to see more formulaic stories from now on, albeit in increasingly odd settings. It'd be convenient if the episodes which ushered in this new method were so utterly wretched that we could condemn it all in one go. But on the story's own terms, seen as a one-off like all the other oddities of this season...

...on its own terms, it's an effective, creepy and thoroughly contemporary SF thriller, at least for the first three episodes. This time the mind-slaves look more like victims of a police state than any of the zombies and Robomen we've seen elsewhere, and the low, throbbing, ever-threatening computer-noise seems to put the whole production in a space where the real world might give way to '60s techno-hell at any moment. Director Michael Ferguson, who's destined to end his *Doctor Who* on a somewhat lower note with "The Claws of Axos", quickly gets the knack of making London look like London while making WOTAN's domains look like abstract, inhuman surroundings. Dodo's sudden disappearance (bound to concern fans more than casual viewers, it's got to be said) is more of a mercy than a failing. She doesn't belong in this story, even if it's her own place and time. Her farewell, as the first regular to actively betray the Doctor - a cliché now, but grounds for a cliffhanger then - is as good a way to go out as any.

Its big flaw, of course, is the lack of scale. This is a set-up that's supposed to unleash havoc on the streets of London, but even apart from the fact that we only ever see one War Machine at a time, most of the story is confined to a single warehouse in Covent Garden. Later tales, most notably "The Invasion", will have a much better sense of what's required to make it look as if the whole capital's come to a standstill. Here, you know the last episode's going to be a let-down even before it starts.

But beyond that, the story is a blatant sales-pitch, giving us the new companions in a presentation box. Ben gets to do everything a male companion does in this series, although Polly is more of a surprise. The sarcasm and matter-of-factness in her character is harsher than anything we've seen so far. Vicki frequently put two fingers up at authority, but only in the same way that a schoolgirl might, not as if she were seriously objecting to robot monsters getting in the way of a manicurists' appointment. It's hard now to see what an unlikely pairing Ben and Polly made, and how far this unlikeliness was typical of Britain in 1966. More than any story before or since, it's a patchwork of other television. This ought to make it seem as if the programme-makers are waving a little white flag, but somehow the sheer surprise of being in the present day and filming on location gives them an episode's grace, letting them get away with it until the two newcomers have been established as the heroes. Perhaps because of his health, Hartnell is called upon to be the still centre, and his most characteristic move is to stand his ground when everyone else runs for it.

Yet again, it's a story that suffers for having been recycled so many times. But at the time, landing in modern London and staying to fight monsters was unprecedented. This was, previously, the one place the TARDIS couldn't land without the series ending. Henceforth it's about the *only* place it can land. They presented "The War Machines" as business as usual, rather than a climactic revelation, and they were already far enough into the next story's production to include clips in a trailer after the last episode. By this stage *Doctor Who* was reliant on viewers simply watching out of habit, though with each new story's gimmick being loudly proclaimed in advance. The selling-points here are the War Machines and the Post Office Tower, and both are presented to us as often as possible, yet the *real* gimmick is the presence of the Doctor in what would otherwise have been a routine adventure story about Ben, Polly and WOTAN. We're almost back to square one.

The ingredients of Phase Two of the programme are nearly all in place, but nobody knows it yet. It's like listening to the Beatles' *Revolver* (released six weeks later) and trying to pretend you don't know what's around the corner. To continue the analogy - and when we're talking about '60s *Doctor Who*, the Beatles almost always work as a comparison, as we'll see in Volume II - most people accept that *Revolver* has more good songs than *Sergeant Pepper* and a lower percentage of duds. "The War Machines", and Season Three in general, has a sense of trying out new things rather than making Big Statements. Big Statements will come later.

There are some who claim, not without justification, that *Doctor Who* as originally conceived died that month. What replaced it was exactly the programme the BBC needed on Saturday nights, the programme that many of us - nay, *most* of us - grew up thinking of as "real" *Doctor Who*. But by rights, this ought to have been the end. Here the series loses its bravado, and from now on it'll be running to keep up with the tastes of the British public, not setting the pace as it had been for the first three years. Still, if you're going to go on for twenty-three years with an average of eight-million viewers a week and a global cult following, this isn't a bad way of going about it.

The Facts

Written by Ian Stuart Black. Directed by Michael Ferguson. Ratings 5.4 million, 4.7 million, 5.3 million, 5.5 million. Episode four's audience appreciation score was a mere 39%.

This may be a good time to mention that even '60s episodes which *do* still exist in the BBC archive aren't always 100% complete. Though the version of "The War Machines" released on video has been mostly restored, at least two minutes of material are still missing.

Supporting Cast Alan Curtis (Major Green), John Harvey (Professor Brett), William Mervyn (Sir Charles Summer), Sandra Bryant (Kitty), Ewan Proctor (Flash), John Cater (Professor Krimpton), Roy Godfrey (Tramp), Michael Rathborne (Taxi-driver), John Rolfe (Captain), John Boyd-Brent (Sergeant), George Cross (The Minister), Kenneth Kendall (Television Newsreader), Dwight Whylie (Radio Announcer), Gerald Taylor (Voice of WOTAN).

Working Titles "Dr Who and the Computers".

Cliffhangers WOTAN tells its mind-slaves, including Dodo, that 'Dok Tor Whooo isss reee quired'; the first of the War Machines corners Ben in a warehouse; the army takes cover as the War Machine advances through Covent Garden, but the Doctor stands directly in its path, and seems to be trying to stare it out.

The Lore

• Gerry Davis would fire out wild ideas to anyone he thought would be a suitable scientific advisor; what if a tenth planet turned up, what if the Post Office Tower controlled everyone's minds, that sort of thing. Patrick Moore, the nation's favourite astronomer and space pundit (there was a good living to be made in that field, in those days) rejected Davis' suggestions. Dr Alec Comfort, soon to become very-well-known-indeed as author of *The Joy of Sex*, was too busy. We won't ask what he was doing. Professor Eric Laithwaite was on television as often as these others, but was trying to get government backing for his linear motor. And Davis only seems to have asked scientists who'd been on television, so next on his list was Dr Kit Pedler, recently featured on a BBC2 *Horizon* documentary about the human eye.

• As will become apparent in Volume II, Pedler's interests led him to question the direction in which medicine was going. In answering Davis' questions it became obvious that a computer, programmed with evil reductivist logic, would be the villain. Thus Davis put together a scenario called "Dr Who and the Computers", involving the Post Office Tower, and gave it to a BBC staff writer. Pat Dunlop worked on the first episode, before being given a post on *Dixon of Dock Green*, but the delivery date of his contribution to *United!* (it's all a bit incestuous, isn't it?) clashed with the deadline for this story. He got fifty quid for his contribution. Ian Stuart Black, fresh from writing "The Savages" and as an experienced story editor used to last-minute fixes, took over the duties. Part of his brief was to introduce Steven's replacement, "Rich".

• Innes Lloyd had decided that neither Steven nor Dodo really suited what he needed the juvenile leads to do, and so ended the contracts of Purves and Lane as neatly as possible. Lane was worried about typecasting anyway, and Lloyd's letter to her made it clear that replacing her was nothing personal. Her subsequent career included some unlikely jobs, but she wound up as a voice agent, getting other actors work on voice-overs. (Tom Baker is one of her clients, so she's indirectly responsible for *Little Britain*.)

• Into her place came former child actor Anneke Wills (*née* "Willys", being half-Dutch). Her husband, Michael Gough, had enjoyed himself so much as the Celestial Toymaker that he suggested she try out for the part of the new companion. Prior to this she'd played "Pussy Cat" (yes, really) in the Hogmanay episode of *The Avengers*, "Dressed to Kill". As *Avengers* women Kathy Gale and Emma Peel spawned imitators in every adventure series going, Wills decided to play Polly as ordinary and everyday. The character specs described the girl as being into skiing and motorsports, and a former model, but this was downplayed in the broadcast stories. (The irony is that the more down-to-earth and mundane her approach became, the more of a sly feminist figure she seemed to be, compared to the impossibly pro-active fantasy women of 1960s and 70s television. See **Just How Chauvinistic is *Doctor Who*?** under 9.5, "The Time Monster".)

• Incidentally, her surname was "Wright" according to the notes, and the audition-piece made it clear that she got her job through a well-connected uncle (see 1.1, "An Unearthly Child" and 8.1, "Terror of the Autons"). Like Jackie Lane, she'd been asked to audition to play Susan (and Deborah Watling auditioned to play Polly... it gets *very* incestuous, doesn't it?).

• Ben also had detailed notes that were abandoned once the character was cast. Michael Craze was another ex-child actor, mainly used to working on the stage. He'd appeared in the Twist-era flick *Two Left Feet*, but the release of the film had been delayed, and Trad Jazz and the Twist had been swept aside by the Mersey Beat by the time it came out. He'd also been in the original *Target Luna*, which again brings us back to Sydney Newman's *Pathfinders*.

• Some of the publicity photos for the two new companions were lit rather modishly, which has led to much speculation as to whether they were cast according to the actors' resemblances to "Swinging London" film stars. The usual guesses are Michael Caine and Marianne Faithfull, but this isn't terribly convincing. Terence Stamp and Julie Christie, 1966's "Golden Couple", are more likely candidates.

• Some guidebooks, including the notorious *Travels Without the TARDIS*, repeat the original idea that the Ship lands in Fitzroy Square. It's actually Bedford Place, about a hundred yards from Tottenham Court Road, the one place in that part of London where it's *impossible* to see the Post Office Tower.

• One detail which failed to make the final cut: Professor Brett puts gloves on after being "converted". When Major Green is placed under WOTAN's control, he puts his hands into a slot and convulses in agony... and when he removes his hands, they have visible markings on the veins (compare with 4.6, "The Moonbase"). The early drafts have the Doctor mentioning that Brett is an old friend, although the novelisation amends this and claims that he gets into the Post Office Tower because he's a friend of the now-distinguished Ian Chesterton.

• There's no getting away from it: 1966 was, for those of you who somehow don't know or just don't realise how cataclysmically important it's become to the national psyche, the year that England won the World Cup. The final took place exactly two weeks after the last episode of "The War Machines" was broadcast. At a time when the nation was still clinging to what may have been its last-ever "high", the gifted young-ish members of the England team were seen as true *talents*; part of a wider cultural movement rather than mere sportsmen, in the same league as actors, artists and the Rolling Stones. (Likewise, the boxer Henry Cooper floored Cassius Clay in 1963 and hung out with the Beatles.) *Now* do you see why we're suddenly fighting robot-monsters on the streets of modern-day London, instead of on jungle-planets...?

the end notes

1 For non-British readers… we refuse to explain Norman Wisdom. But there's another footnote about him in a future volume, so take a look at that and draw your own conclusions.

2 *Musique Concrête*. Music made by stealing sounds from the "real" world and warping, shifting and manipulating them until they become unrecognisably alien. Now that sampling is an everyday part of contemporary music, this idea seems banal and unremarkable, but in the '40s and '50s (the first time that such a form of music was possible) it was weird, disconcerting and as avant-garde as you could get. Needless to say, the kind of people who ended up working for the BBC Radiophonic Workshop loved it.

3 For those of you reading this who don't already know… although an awful lot of '60s *Doctor Who* is missing from the archive (see **What Was the BBC Thinking?** under 3.1, "Galaxy Four"), audio recordings of every single episode are still in existence. Various fan-cliques, most notably the outfit known as Loose Cannon, have set about "reconstructing" the lost stories by attaching still photos to the soundtracks. Generally, camera scripts are used to make sure the reconstructions are as close to the televised versions as possible. Copyright issues prevent the reconstructions being released commercially, as many of the photos come from private collections, but if you know anybody in fandom then you shouldn't have trouble getting hold of them.

4 *Mummerset*. Non-existent British county, used to denote a kind of accent often heard in British drama which represents "generic rural folk". Sarah mentions Mummerset in "Planet of the Spiders" (11.5), convincing certain people that it's supposed to be a real place in the *Doctor Who* universe, even though that's not the way she says it. We'll come back to this in Volume III, but it can't be reiterated enough. See also **What Are the Dodgiest Accents in *Doctor Who*?** under 4.1, "The Smugglers".

5 They always mention Genghis Khan when they're trying to sell you a new console room, have you noticed that?

6 No… no, we're still not going to do it.

7 CRACKERJACK!

8 Traditionally, British television has used the terms "series" and programme" instead of "season" and "series". "Season" is seen by some as a vulgar Americanism, although it has a certain resonance with rather more British activities, such as cricket or grouse-shooting; a "season" is a period in which everyone gets excited about a certain activity, and that's what *Doctor Who* is *supposed* to be like, as an awful lot of people suddenly remembered in March 2005. The trouble is, early *Doctor Who* doesn't really have easily-defined breaks between one run and the next. In terms of production, "The Dalek Invasion of Earth" (2.2) could be considered the end of the first series and "Mission to the Unknown" (3.2) the end of the second. Things get even messier during the Troughton years, which is why hardcore fans started using the word "season", a habit they probably picked up from Trekkies. These days the BBC itself is referring to new *Doctor Who* in terms of "seasons", which doesn't seem unreasonable, as that's clearly how the Eccleston run is pitched. "The Parting of the Ways" (X1.13) is, categorically, *Doctor Who*'s first bona fide "Season Finale".

9 Just in case you think we're going too far in trying to find political subtexts in stories from this era… it's recently come to light that the movie version of *Animal Farm*, despite being made in Britain by a seemingly reputable animation studio, was co-funded by the CIA. We very much doubt that the same is true of "The Web Planet", or that the Menoptra's hand-signs were secretly used to send messages to agents stationed in the UK, but it'd explain so much.

10 *Here Come the Double-Deckers*. Jaunty kids' show of the early 1970s, derived almost wholesale from Cliff Richard's biggest film hit, the aforementioned *Summer Holiday*. In the film, Cliff, Jeremy Bulloch, Una Stubbs and Melvyn Hayes take a converted red double-decker bus from London to Athens. They have wild yet curiously wholesome adventures; accidentally getting engaged to Yugoslav peasant girls after demonstrating the Twist, finding a fugitive American heiress hiding on the bus disguised as a boy, that sort of thing. In the TV series, a bunch of youngsters live in a converted double-

decker bus in a junkyard - yes, it must be bigger on the inside - and are aided in their merry scrapes by a road-sweeper played by Melvyn Hayes. Readers of the BBC *Doctor Who* books will now know where Paul Magrs gets it from.

11 *Queen of Outer Space.* A movie that was written by Charles Beaumont (author of some of the more thought-ful *Twilight Zone* episodes) as a parody of the inane SF B-movies of the 1950s. Unfortunately, nobody told the actors or the director that it was a parody. The result is unique - a deliberate collection of clichés that doesn't *know* it's a deliberate collection of clichés, with a plot about an all-male rocket-ship crew landing on a planet full of Amazon women who want to take over the Earth. For the next generation of this sort of thing, consider "The Happiness Patrol" (25.2), and also **What Else Didn't Get Made?** under "Shada" (17.6) to see what a lucky escape we had in 1969.

12 CRACKERJACK! Look, we're sorry about this. But one of the gimmicks of *Crackerjack* was that whenever the presenters mentioned show's title, the audience (and viewers) had to shout it back at them as loudly as possible. After a while, this becomes instinctive.

13 All right, if we say this here then we can save ourselves a lot of hassle later. The great thing about quarries is that they're a little bit of alien-ness near enough for you to go out, play at being a Dalek or what-have-you, and then get home in time for tea. They may have excit-

ing little crevices, occasional fossils and the odd but crucially they're empty spaces. For an imagin child, this is almost as good as a big corrugated c board box. The experience of watching *Doctor* dovetailed with the experience of playing at it. We that it's in the most successful period of the program history, the mid-to-late 1970s, that the programme s its attention to woodlands and starts to resemble gr ups playing at being kids playing at *Doctor Who*. "The Deadly Assassin", devotes a whole episode to By the 1980s, make-believe meant video games and of plastic that made electronic squealing noises, and dren no longer gave a damn about empty spaces. Th yet another reason that much of the '80s series see so out-of-step with the public imagination (such was, in those days).

14 A debutante is a young lady making her deb polite society. The daughters of respectable, well-nected families used to be presented *en masse* to Queen in a ceremony called "coming out" (that's " pronounced "ite", of course). Thereafter, the well-nected single men would all mysteriously crop up a same parties in the same country houses; the "sea alluded to in 14.2, "The Hand of Fear". The Debs c hated this whole cattle-market, and would freque nip to the East End for a last taste of freedom with b "rough trade", a barrow-boy or a sailor. World W was seized upon by Debs as a fabulous excuse to away with a lot more of this sort of thing, and the took jobs in factories or on farms.

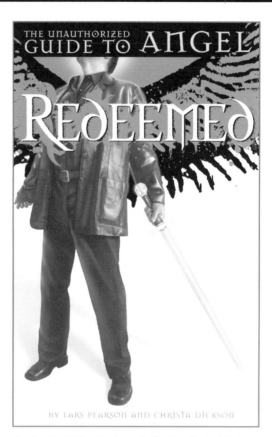

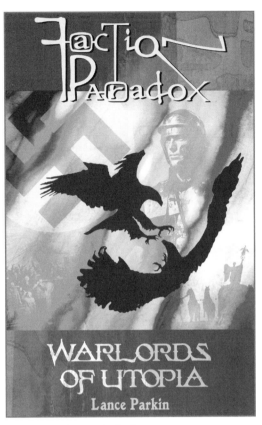

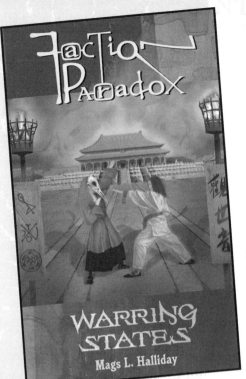

WARRING STATES

The air in the Stacks races through the tunnels, pushed by the ghost trains rattling over the dead tracks. Posters for films that never were, and adverts for beauty products that give new meaning to "age-defying", flutter blindly. Occasionally, the icy air slams into abandoned platforms, where insubstantial suicides stand, clothes swirling around them as they stare into the abyss of the permanent way.

Deep in the Stacks, Cousin Octavia welcomes the intermittent blasts of air. She likes it down here, safe not only from surface-level War offensives but also from the tedious internal politicking of the Eleven-Day Empire itself. Down here in the Faction's huge repository of knowledge, beneath a bloodlit London, she could lose herself in research. And if people got lost in the Lobokestvian geography of abandoned underground tunnels whilst looking for her, even better.

Unfortunately, Prester John is good at remembering the way.

'You could visit me in Westminster,' he remarks as he arrives, swirling flyers for *The Defective Detective* in his wake. Octavia shrugs.

'I've found it,' she tells him.

In the city square the crowd gathered, jostling not only to get a good view, but for their eagerness to be seen by the officials. Four men and a woman knelt, hands tied and heads bowed. A mandarin of the sapphire button stepped forward, peacock silks as stiffly formal as the condemnation he was making.

'- are hereby executed, for the most heinous crime of attempting to disrupt the Most Exalted One's Heavenly Kingdom, for the circulation of pernicious and corrupt ideas promulgated by the heathen foreign devils, for -'

As he continued, guards hacked off the queues of the men, holding the plaited hair high. The woman's hair had already be shorn, and not gently. All five waited silently as the official finished his denouncement.

In the crowd, Liu Hui Ying felt the hand of her father tighten about her upper arm. He was scared, she had realised this morning. Terrified that his laxity, his trade with the foreigners, his schooling of her, would lead to his own beheading. These five had been brought down from the north for this, but Chin Liang-Yu had been a school friend of Liu's. So now her father made her watch her friends kneel in the dirt for their ideas.

Five swords fell, the edges shearing through the second and third vertebrae, through the thick muscles and flimsy vessels of the throat. Chin's head rolled, tainting the dust with blood, until its force was spent and it came to rest staring upwards at Liu with something like hatred.

Walking back to the dockside factory, where her family's fortune had been made selling antiquities, Liu felt her jaw tingle with the promise of vomiting, her mouth filling again and again with the taste of it. She swallowed it down, urgently wishing she'd managed to close her eyes. Her father's new-found distrust of her education didn't yet outweigh her cheapness as a translator, and there was a new shipment of vases going to Britain. She set to work.

'Please, convey to your father my gratitude for continuing his business with us at this time,' Atkinson said. He took a sip of pai mu tan. Liu's father nodded with satisfaction as she translated.

'We are always honoured by your visits,' he said, then excused himself to supervise packing the crates. Atkinson took another sip of tea. Liu liked these moments, her chance to practise her language without being watched.

'How was the voyage from India?'

'Easy enough. We had an interesting party on board. Your father might want to contact them.'

'Really, how so?'

'It was an archaeological expedition, from Oxford, who hope to find the Great White Pyramid of China. I told them that it was just a myth, but Professor Grieves seems quite sure.'

'What is it this time? The stars aligned to bring down heavenly fire? Prehistoric germ warfare? Godfather Morlock's birthday?' Prester John is sidling through the room, letting his long coat brush against the precarious mounds of research material. Just reminding her that he can bring it all crashing down, make her go back to the fighting. 'Actually, that last one would be of some use. He'd be really pissed off if I threw him a party -'

'The Holy Grail.'

'Again? We've got a storeroom full of the things.'

'The metaphorical Holy Grail: live forever.'

'Given that we've already given history the slip, why would we want that?'

'Think about it. We give history the slip but it always catches up. Always. Remember the Noose?'

Prester John winces. 'Yes, that was embarrassing. So, what's the plan?'

'I'll need to mount an expedition into linear time to retrieve it. And I can only trace it to China. During the Boxer Rebellion.'

Prester John nods agreement. The distant rumble of a train swirls Cousin Octavia's clothes about her, and her shadow dances.

OUT NOW. Retail Price: $17.95.

info@madnorwegian.com

www.madnorwegian.com

ERASING SHERLOCK

Kelly Hale

* Not actual cover art

ERASING SHERLOCK

London: October, 1890

John Watson threw open the study door of 221-B Baker Street and crossed immediately to one of the arched windows, a terse growl cutting short the detective's cheery greeting. Drawing back the curtain a fraction, he peered down onto the street.

Holmes came up behind him and looked out over his shoulder. 'You've noticed the veiled woman, I see.'

'She followed me from Paddington Station,' the doctor hissed. 'Sat right across from me, bold as you please, in the same carriage on the train -'

'Why are you whispering? She can't hear us, you know.'

'I've no time for these games of intrigue, Holmes!'

The detective winced and poked a finger into his ear. 'Something between a whisper and roar, perhaps...'

Watson crossed his arms over his chest and glared. 'I have a practice. A wife. A child on the way.'

Holmes jerked the curtains wide and looked out. 'It's not as if I directed her to follow you,' he said. 'She's been a faithful dog on *my* heels, as well.'

Across the street, the woman inclined her head to him. The weighted veil that covered her face - temple to temple, hat-brim to chin - was impervious to any breeze that might expose her features to passersby. Something about her put him in mind of a dog, in fact, or rather a dog act in a variety show; as if she were a creature entirely unsuited to walking upright, let alone wearing a bustle. And yet the fact that she was doing it was a slap in the face: *any idiot can pretend to be human.*

Behind him, Watson sighed with gusty irritation. 'I assume she's the reason for your cryptic telegram this morning?'

'Partly. And there is also *that*.' Holmes directed the doctor's gaze to a parcel, slumped upon the dining table like an aged alley cat. 'It was here when I awoke this morning. Mrs. Hudson claims no responsibility for accepting delivery. Intriguing, yes?'

Watson limped over to a chair nearer the fire, and lowered himself into the worn seat, hat in hand and still wearing his overcoat; a sign that he did not intend to stay, which he then proceeded to emphasize. 'Well, then, perhaps we could skip past the business of you directing me to look for the clues, me failing to find them, and then, after some exposition, you revealing what's in the package before actually unwrapping it.'

'You *are* in a mood!'

'Have you heard nothing I've said, Holmes? I will not be embroiled in this, whatever it is. I'm very busy in my practice, and my wife is nearing the time of her confinement!'

'Oh. *Oh*. Of course. I'd quite forgotten your anticipation of the happy event.' The detective blinked in sudden puzzlement. 'Good Lord. Has it been that long since last we spoke?'

Watson gave a tense shrug, and pulled a cigarette case from his pocket. 'It's been nearly five months. Other than the letter you sent from New York in July, the first word I've had from you in a great long time was your telegram this morning.'

Holmes drew in a little hiss of contrition between his teeth. 'I've never truly embraced the art of correspondence, have I?'

'Is that it? All this time I believed you still hadn't forgiven me for getting married.'

For a long moment the only sound in the room was the tick of the mantel-clock. Then Holmes turned away, unable to look his friend in the eye.

'It would be presumptuous of me to forgive,' he said, 'when I should be begging forgiveness.' Yet, truly remorseful as he was, now he found himself face to face with the parcel again he was unable to resist its lure. He reached out, touched the filthy string wrapped around it. 'I mean, to refuse to offer congratulations, or even to stand with you -' He rubbed the residue between forefinger and thumb. 'That. That was just -' Oily, a bit of grit. He should look at it under the microscope.

'You were afraid,' Watson said.

'What?'

'You were *afraid*, Holmes. Afraid that left to your own devices, your resolve would fail you. You feared you might lose your way again if I weren't there to keep you on the straight and narrow.'

'Not much of an excuse. But you see, we've come around full circle since those dark days, Watson. Come. Come look at the name on the package.' Watson didn't move, stubbornly resolved not to be intrigued. Holmes blew out a noisy sigh, and brought the filthy parcel to *him*, pointing at the faded brown scrawl. *G. R. Petra.*

'Oh, Dear Lord,' Watson whispered. 'Please tell me this package does not contain bones, hair, or body-parts.'

'Nothing so obvious. Much more mysterious. If I am correct, in this parcel I will find a pair of my own boots, which I consigned to the rubbish-heap some nine years ago.'

'Boots? Why would she...? God in Heaven. Not those damned boots again!'

ERASING SHERLOCK
Coming in 2006.
Retail Price: $17.95 US

www.madnorwegian.com

Lance Parkin

A History of the Universe

OUT NOW... Out of print for eight years, Lance Parkin's widely praised *Doctor Who* chronology, *A History of the Universe*, now returns as an updated volume - named *AHistory* - from Mad Norwegian Press.

Laying out the *Doctor Who* universe into a mindbendingly detailed timeline, *History* starts with the Big Bang and moves forward through the universe's development, tracing such keystone events as the imprisonment of the world-destroyer Sutekh, the rise and fall of the Earth Empire and much, much more. All in all, *Aistory* creates a chronicle of the universe's events in a manner befitting the Time Lords themselves.

The previous version of *History* (due to its publication date) didn't even include all of the Virgin New Adventures, but Parkin here—exhaustively—expands *AHistory* to take in the remainder of the Virgin novels, the Big Finish audios, the Telos novellas and every BBC *Doctor Who* novel up through his own *The Gallifrey Chronicles*, the conclusion of the Eighth Doctor novel range.

MSRP: $24.95

www.madnorwegian.com

1150 46th Street
Des Moines, Iowa 50311
info@madnorwegian.com

ABOUT TIME

1966-1969

SEASONS 4 TO 6

ABOUT TIME

THE UNAUTHORIZED GUIDE TO

DOCTOR WHO

1966-1969
SEASONS 4 TO 6

LAWRENCE MILES & TAT WOOD

Coming Soon... In *About Time 2*, Lawrence and Tat explore the massive paradigm shift that accompanied *Doctor Who* Seasons 4 to 6, with regards to both a new Doctor (in the form of Patrick Troughton) and the show's hugely different means of doing business in the late 1960s.

Essays in this volume include: "What Do Daleks Eat?", "What's the Timeline of the Twenty-First Century?" and "What are the Dodgiest Accents?"

Out Now
About Time 3 (Seasons 7-11)
About Time 4 (Seasons 12-17)
About Time 5 (Seasons 18-21)

Also Coming Soon...
About Time 6 (Seasons 22-26 and
            the TV Movie)

MSRP: $14.95 (*About Time 3*); $19.95 (all other volumes)

www.madnorwegian.com

info@madnorwegian.com

mad
norwegian
press

POLICE PUBLIC CALL BOX

OPEN THE DOOR TO
A NEW DIMENSION

www.galaxy4.co.uk

who made all this ?

Lawrence Miles is the author of… hold on… yeah, *eight* novels now, the most recent of them being the first volume in the ongoing *Faction Paradox* series, *This Town Will Never Let Us Go*. After co-writing *Dusted - a guide to Buffy the Vampire Slayer,* also published by Mad Norwegian - he suddenly found that he'd been cured, and didn't want to see another episode of *Buffy* ever again. So once *About Time* is finished, he's planning on constructing a great ceremonial pyre and burning the complete collection of *Doctor Who* videos and CDs that's taken him nearly twenty years to assemble. Favourite story in this book: "The Romans". Least favourite: "The Celestial Toymaker".

Recovering academic **Tat Wood** is the person most compilers of previous guidebooks went to for advice and cultural context. Despite having written for *Film Review, TV Zone, Starburst, SFX, Dreamwatch, Doctor Who Magazine, X-pose* and just about every major fanzine going, he has a rich, full and complex life. Currently lecturing and tutoring, he is busy mentoring mature students from across the Commonwealth and the new Europe whilst attempting to break into mainstream "literary" fiction. Tragically, this is interrupted by people wanting to get the lyrics to half-forgotten 1960s TV themes ringing him rather than bothering with the Internet (because he's quicker). Although culturally adept and well-rounded, he has lived in Ilford for the last ten years. Favourite story in this book: "The Massacre". Least favourite: "The Edge of Destruction".

Mad Norwegian Press

Publisher/Series Editor
Lars Pearson

Copy Editors
Fritze CM Roberts, Dave Gartner

Interior/Cover Design
Christa Dickson

Cover Art
Jim Calafiore

Cover Colors
Richard Martinez

Associate Editors
Marc Eby
Joshua Wilson

Technical Support
Michael O'Nele
Robert Moriarity

The publisher would like to thank... Bill Albert, Jeremy Bement, John and Heather Innis and everyone at the United Network of Iowan Time Lords; Shawne Kleckner, Shaun Lyon, Robert Smith?, Michael and Amy Tax, Bill and Mandy Vadbunker.

1150 46th Street
Des Moines, Iowa 50311
info@madnorwegian.com
www.madnorwegian.com